Emma Blair Omnibus

AN APPLE
FROM EDEN

THIS SIDE
OF HEAVEN

Emma Blair Omnibus

AN APPLE
FROM EDEN

THIS SIDE
OF HEAVEN

EMMA BLAIR

timewarner
paperbacks

A *Time Warner* Paperback

This omnibus edition first published in Great Britain
by Time Warner Paperbacks in 2003
Emma Blair Omnibus Copyright © Emma Blair 2003

Previously published separately:
An Apple From Eden first published in
Great Britain in 1998 by Little, Brown and Company
Published by Warner Books in 1999
Reprinted 2001
Copyright © Emma Blair 1998

This Side of Heaven first published in Great Britain
in 1985 by Arrow Books Limited
Published by Warner Books in 1997
Copyright © Emma Blair 1985

A CIP catalogue record for this book is
available from the British Library.

ISBN 0 7515 3510 9

Typeset by
Printed and bound in Great Britain by
Clays Ltd, St Ives plc

Time Warner Paperbacks
An imprint of
Time Warner Books UK
Brettenham House
Lancaster Place
London WC2E 7EN

www.TimeWarnerBooks.co.uk

AN APPLE
FROM EDEN

Chapter 1

'*L'amour.*'

Bridie Flynn sighed, then repeated the word. '*L'amour.*'

'You what?' queried Teresa Kelly in astonishment.

'It's French for love,' Bridie informed her. 'I go prickly all over every time I say it.'

Teresa shook her head. 'I suppose you learned that from one of those daft books you're always reading.'

'They're not daft at all!' Bridie retorted. 'Amongst other things they're very informative. Why, I'd be lost without my books. Thank Heavens for the library. The best thing I ever did was joining.'

Bridie glanced about her. The rest of the family were out – a rare enough event as there was usually someone else around in the evenings. Her mother, father and sister Alison had gone to visit Granny Flynn who was suffering from lumbago. As for her brother Sean, who knew where he was? He could be anywhere. Probably with one or some of his many pals.

'You know what I'd really like to have been in life,' Bridie suddenly stated.

'What?'

'A schoolteacher.'

Teresa gave a derisory laugh. 'You, a schoolteacher! My my, we have got ideas above our station, haven't we? Our kind don't become schoolteachers. That's for posh folk.'

Bridie pulled a face. 'I know. But a lassie can have dreams, can't she? If things had been different, if I hadn't been born into an ordinary working-class family, then that's what I'd like to have been. A spell at university, then training college followed by teaching.' Her eyes took on a faraway look. 'Oh but that would have been grand. The bee's knees.'

'Well, it's the lemonade factory for you, my girl, and thankful you should be that you have a job at all. There's many don't, as you well know.'

Bridie thought with distaste of the lemonade factory, her place of employment, as it was Teresa's, since leaving school.

'I don't know about *l'amour*, but if it's boys you're talking about, well, I'm certainly not against them. Quite the contrary.' Teresa giggled. 'I wonder what it's like?'

'What's what like?'

Teresa gave her friend a conspiratorial wink. '*That. L'amour.*'

Bridie reddened slightly. 'I'm not just talking about *that*, though of course it is part and parcel of love. No, I mean the act of being in love, of existing for someone else and they for you. On counting the hours, minutes and seconds till you see them again. The sheer elation of being in their company. The thrill when they touch you, the bliss of their lips on yours. The time spent together when the rest of the world ceases to exist.'

Teresa snorted. 'Well, there sure isn't much of that around here. Could you imagine my ma and da gazing adoringly into each other's eyes? The only thing my da stares adoringly at is food when it's put in front of him. Especially after a hard day's graft. Then he gazes adoringly enough. Particularly if it's his favourite mince, and potatoes. I swear he'd murder for a heaped plate of that.'

Bridie lean't further back into the rather ancient fireside chair which had belonged to Pat and Kathleen Flynn since early on in their marriage, one of the first items of furniture they'd acquired, and even then it had been second hand from Crown Showrooms in the town.

'You can mock all you like, Teresa Kelly, there's a Prince Charming out there for each and every one of us. Or if there isn't there should be. And one fine day I'm going to meet mine. I just know it.'

'You're away with the fairies, you are. Always have been in my recollection, and God knows I've known you long enough.' Teresa stared hard at her friend. 'Those silly books you've forever got your nose stuck in have a lot to answer for, and that's a fact. They've made you expect too much out of life. You'll settle for some nice lad just like all the rest of us, someone plain and ordinary and a far cry from a blinking Prince Charming. There'll be the wedding followed by weans and years of toil as is the case with all the women round here. There'll be precious little time for gazing adoringly into eyes when you'll be spending most of your time down the steamie boiling dirty nappies or else at home slaving over a hot stove and trying to make ends meet.'

Despair filled Bridie. What Teresa said was true enough, though she was reluctant in the extreme to accept it.

'Life's real, and hard,' Teresa went on. 'What you read in those books of yours are only stories. Sort of . . . well, things to get you out of yourself. A pretence if you wish.'

Bridie closed her eyes and pictured a handsome, dashing young man with flaxen hair and piercing blue eyes. '*L'amour*,' she breathed again. 'A meeting of souls.'

Teresa barked out a laugh. 'Your arse in parsley, hen. A meeting of souls indeed. Utter tosh.'

'It is not!' Bridie retorted fiercely.

'It is sought. Och, I admit when you find the right chap there should be a lot of lovey-dovey stuff during your courting. But that, from what I understand, is soon over once the wedding ring is on your finger. Then it's down to reality and getting on with it.'

Bridie came to her feet and leant against the mantelpiece. She suddenly wished her friend would leave so she could get back to her current book. There was still a while before bedtime, time enough for a couple of chapters at least.

Bridie started when she heard the front door open.

'Cooeee, we're home!' Kathleen Flynn called out. 'Get the kettle on.'

And so ended the conversation about *l'amour* and Prince Charming.

'Come in,' Willie Seaton responded to the knock on his study door. As he'd expected it was Ian, his only son.

'You wanted a word with me, Pa.'

Willie indicated an adjacent chair. 'Sit yourself down. And aye, I do wish a chat.'

Willie rubbed his eyes which were painful from long hours poring over ledgers. He was going to have to give in and see an optician, he told himself, something he'd been fighting against these past few years. But although he still considered himself a relatively young man at forty-four, time was beginning to take its toll.

'Would you care for a dram, son? I know I'm ready for one.'

Ian immediately rose although he'd only just sat. 'Yes, I will join you, Pa. I'll do it.'

Willie produced cigarettes and lit up, not offering the packet to Ian who didn't smoke.

'Hard day, Pa?'

Willie nodded. 'What about yourself? What have you been up to?'

'Did a bit of rabbit shooting earlier. Knocked over half a dozen of the buggers. Mrs Kilbride was pleased to get them.' Mrs Kilbride was their cook.

'So it'll be rabbit stew or pie tomorrow,' Willie mused, which pleased him. He enjoyed rabbit, hare even more.

'There you are,' declared Ian, placing Willie's drink in front of him, before returning to his chair.

'*Slainte!*' Willie toasted.

'*Slainte*, Pa.'

Willie tasted his drink, smiled in appreciation, then steadily regarded his son. 'It's a fortnight now since you returned home from your studies. I wanted to give you time to settle back in before speaking to you.'

Ian nodded, knowing what was coming next. 'What do you have in mind?'

'You've always been aware you'll be taking over from me some day. Though not for a while I hope. I have no wish to depart this world just yet.'

Ian laughed softly. He and his father got on extremely well, and always had done. With one exception that is, but that subject had long been accepted by Ian, the animosity forgotten.

'So when do I start?'

Willie nodded his approval. 'Keen, eh? That's the stuff, lad. I like keenness in a person. Apart from anything else it shows character. And I hope the son and heir of Willie Seaton would have that.'

Willie squirmed himself into a more comfortable position while Ian waited patiently for him to go on.

'I want you to learn as I did and my father before me, which means starting at the bottom. When you're finished there won't be a job on this estate, including mine, which you won't be able to do if necessary. Understand?'

'The hard way in other words,' Ian commented ruefully.

'Exactly.'

It was what Ian had expected. Thanks to his studies he was well versed in the theory. Now came the practical side of things. He had to admit he was looking forward to it.

'You start next Monday under Jock Gibson. Jock is getting on in years and it won't be too long until his retirement. When that happens you'll be the next estate manager.'

Ian thought of Jock Gibson, a dour Scot, though kindly underneath, if ever there was. He'd known Jock all his life.

'While you're working for Jock he's the boss and you do as he says. I don't want you trying to pull rank on him. Is that clear?'

'Quite clear, Pa.'

'It would be rude if nothing else and I can't abide rudeness. Never have.'

Ian recalled the several cuffs he'd received when a youngster for cheeking his father, incidents he still vividly remembered. There had been nothing token about those cuffs, they'd hurt like billy-o. Willie wasn't joking when he said he couldn't abide rudeness.

'And make sure you dress properly. You're going to get more than your hands dirty.' He added sarcastically, 'It wouldn't do to ruin one of those smart suits of yours now, would it?'

Ian laughed. The idea of him turning up for work under Jock wearing a suit appealed to him. He was almost tempted to do so just for a lark. Dear old Jock would have a fit.

'Indeed, Pa,' he replied in mock seriousness.

Willie took a deep breath. He'd been looking forward to this ever since Ian had been born. How proud Mary would have been, just as proud as he himself was. Darling, lovely, departed Mary.

'Any queries?'

Ian considered that. 'I don't think so, Pa. Except for remuneration of course.' That was said slightly tongue in cheek.

'Your allowance will continue as before. And consider yourself lucky, it's far more than the estate workers get.' Willie decided to tease his son. 'Though on second thoughts perhaps I should pay you what they earn. That way you'd really learn the value of money. That a ha'penny is hard come by.'

Alarm flared in Ian. Surely his father wasn't serious? 'Pa?' he queried anxiously.

Willie's eyes twinkled. 'Just a wee josh, son. You'll continue on with your allowance as I said.'

He finished his whisky, stared at the empty glass for a moment, then looked again at Ian and smiled. 'I believe I'll have another. It's not every day you welcome your son into the firm.'

Ian again did the honours.

'Your father tells me you're starting work on the estate this

7

Monday,' Georgina Seaton, Willie's second wife, said to Ian across the dinner table.

'That's right, Georgina.'

'Good.'

Willie indicated to a hovering maid to refill the wine glasses. Georgina covered the top of her glass with a hand, having had her quota. Ever mindful of her figure she took great care with what she ate and drank.

'I must say it's all very exciting,' she declared.

Rose Seaton made a small harumphing sound.

Ian raised an eyebrow. 'You wish to make an utterance, sister dear?'

Rose shook her head.

'Oh! I thought you might have.'

'Only that it was so quiet and peaceful when you were away,' she stated sweetly.

'I thought you missed me.' That dripping sarcasm.

'Dreadfully. It was so dull without you charging about the house. That and the general hubbub you always seem to cause when you're around.'

'Rose!' Willie admonished sharply.

'Yes, Pa?' she smiled, innocence itself.

'I'll have no such banter at the dinner table. It's most unseemly.'

Georgina secretly enjoyed 'such banter' as Willie called it. It livened things up. She glanced at Willie and not for the first time wondered what her life would have been like if Harry had lived. Harry who'd gone to war and never come back. Harry whom she'd simply adored. He'd been another lively one, just like Ian.

'Georgina?'

She roused herself from what had been only a few moments' reverie. 'Yes, Willie?'

'You had the strangest expression on your face. Are you all right?'

'Perfectly, thank you very much.'

'Not a tinge of indigestion, I trust?'

She laughed throatily. 'Not at all. I was simply reflecting on how delicious this lamb is. Mrs Kilbride has quite excelled herself. I must remember to compliment her.'

Rose, with a tendency to plumpness, agreed with Georgina about the lamb and considered whether or not to have a second helping. She envied Georgina her figure and Georgina's discipline regarding it.

'I thought we might play whist after dinner,' Willie announced. 'Or canasta perhaps.'

Ian and Rose both inwardly groaned.

'I was thinking we might play the gramophone,' Ian said.

Georgina would have much preferred the gramophone to whist or canasta. And several dances with Ian who was a marvellous dancer, unlike Willie who was terrible. Many a time Willie had succeeded in trampling on her feet.

'I think the gramophone is a splendid idea,' Georgina declared.

That didn't suit Willie at all. He'd had his mind set on a game of cards. 'How about we have some whist then the gramophone?' he suggested hopefully.

Georgina decided to humour him. 'Better still. That way honour's satisfied all round.'

Willie beamed at her, Georgina's heart sinking when she recognised a particular gleam in his eyes.

It was going to be one of *those* nights.

Kathleen Flynn glanced over at the mantelpiece clock. As was usual on a Friday Pat was late home from work. She knew where he was – the same place he went every Friday evening after being paid – the pub.

Kathleen sighed. How much, or little, would he bring back with him this time? And how drunk would he be? Mind you, she was lucky, a lot luckier than many in their street. Pat rarely hit her, while others she knew got a right battering each and every Friday night.

She didn't begrudge him his drink, it was the culmination of a hard week's graft after all. A man had to have something to look forward to. If only he wouldn't get carried away and spend so much.

Kathleen briefly closed her eyes. How she hated the eternal scrimping and scraping, half the time robbing Peter to pay Paul. How many Thursdays and Fridays had they been reduced to eating bread and dripping? Times without number.

Another half-hour she calculated. For Pat never left until after last orders.

Would he eat something or go straight to bed? You never knew with Pat. It never bothered him that when he did insist on going straight to bed without a wash he made a terrible mess of the sheets. He was a coalman after all. As far as he was concerned that was something for her to worry about.

'Why don't you put the kettle on?' Kathleen suggested to Bridie sitting opposite, her face in one of the books she constantly devoured.

Bridie blinked and looked up. 'Did you say something, Ma?'

'Why don't you put the kettle on?'

'Not for me, Ma, I don't fancy a cup right at the moment. Shall I put the kettle on for you though?'

Kathleen considered that. It seemed a waste to make a pot just for herself, tea being so expensive nowadays. Why, only the previous week it had gone up again, that and many other things. It was scandalous. How was a body supposed to get by on those prices! If only wages would go up as well, but there was little likelihood of that.

'No, I'll leave it for the now,' she replied.

Bridie nodded and returned to her book. *The Maid of Avalon* was a humdinger in her opinion.

Willie rolled off Georgina. 'That was wonderful, darling. Thank you.'

'It *was* wonderful, thank *you*,' she lied in the darkness.

As was his custom, after every session of lovemaking, he took her into his arms and held her close, savouring the perfumed smell of her.

'Happy?' he queried softly.

'Completely.'

'That's fine then.'

'And you?'

'You know I am. Just being with you makes me so.'

'It's the same with me.'

He released her. 'Goodnight then.'

'Goodnight.'

Georgina waited for him to turn on to his side, facing away from her, as he always did. She smiled cynically when that happened.

How predictable he was in bed, she thought. How utterly, awfully predictable. Sometimes she felt like screaming at just how predictable he was.

She drew in a slow, deep breath, trying to calm herself. Willie was the only man she'd ever slept with. Was all lovemaking like theirs? she wondered. She couldn't believe that to be so. Surely there had to be some satisfaction in it for the woman.

She'd asked him in the past to try and take longer which he'd genuinely tried to do. To no avail. Willie's clock was a fast one, hers slow. His alarm bell always went off long before hers was ready to ring.

She didn't love Willie, never had. Perhaps that had something to do with it; she didn't know. If only she had someone to talk to, to discuss the matter with. But that sort of thing was never spoken about in polite society, of which she was most definitely a member.

Willie began to snore gently, informing her he'd dropped off. Quickly, as again was *always* the case. Other nights he might toss and turn, but never after they'd made love.

She thought of Harry. What would it have been like with him? The same as with Willie, or different? That was something she'd never find out.

Willie had asked her if she was happy and she'd lied by saying yes. Truth was, she wasn't *un*happy. Dissatisfied perhaps. Frustrated was the word that came to mind. Frustrated that when they joined it didn't give her anything like the pleasure it gave him. It was as if she was forever trying to climb a mountain but never getting to the top, always being stopped halfway. Sometimes not even halfway.

She moved restlessly, knowing it would be some while before sleep claimed her. She was all on edge, a-jangle.

Should she or shouldn't she? She'd feel guilty after, a little soiled somehow. Guilty and ashamed.

It was only the previous year she'd discovered she could do such a thing. The idea had simply never entered her head until one particularly bad night after Willie she'd found herself doing it without thinking. And then . . . oh the glorious release, release that had made her gasp and shake all over.

How fearful she'd been afterwards that Willie might have realised, but he'd been asleep and known nothing.

Her hand crept downwards to find herself. She would, she decided.

Sean Flynn let himself into the house, pausing to listen just inside the door. As he'd expected the rest of the family were in the land of Nod.

He closed the door and then tiptoed through to his bedroom. He groaned as he began to undress. Christ, but he hurt. At least, as far as he could tell, none of his ribs was broken, but he'd be black and blue come morning.

He suddenly grinned, thinking of the other two. What a pasting he'd given them. He'd be sore tomorrow but not nearly as sore as that Proddy pair. Hell mend the bastards.

It had been a good night he decided, though he could have done without the rammy. And trust him to be on his own, for once caught without his pals around to help and back him up.

He hadn't meant to jostle the Prod, it had been an accident. But that hadn't stopped them waiting outside the boozer and jumping him.

'Effing Prods,' he muttered. 'Effing bloody Prods.'

He hated them.

Jock Gibson watched Ian stride towards him and smiled inwardly. He had a little treat planned for Ian's first day.

'Hello, Jock,' Ian greeted the estate manager.

'During working hours I think it had better be Mr Gibson,' Jock stated.

Ian swallowed. Jock had always been Jock for as long as

he could remember. Even as a wee boy it had been Jock. 'I understand.'

'That would be best in the circumstances, don't you agree?'

Ian nodded. 'Whatever you say Jo—, Mr Gibson.'

'Fine then.'

Ian rubbed his hands together. 'So where do I begin?'

'I thought with the pigs. You'll be helping mucking out. A filthy job I admit. But one that has to be done.'

'Of course.'

'The lads there are expecting you, so off you go. I'll drop by later to see how you're getting on.'

Pigs! Ian thought ruefully as he walked away. He'd never liked pigs. Nasty, unpredictable creatures.

His nose wrinkled in disgust as he approached the first pen and he got a whiff of what lay ahead.

Bridie came hurrying up to Teresa and the pair of them fell into step together.

'Another Monday morning and another week at the lemonade factory,' Bridie groaned. 'The thought makes me sick.'

Teresa grinned at her friend. 'Oh come on, it's not that bad.'

'Bad enough. It's the boredom that gets me down more than anything. Repetition, repetition, repetition. Bottles into boxes, bottles into boxes, bottles into boxes.'

'Well, if you're that cheesed off you could always ask the gaffer to shift you to another part of the factory. That would make a change if nothing else.'

'Fat chance of that. Do you not remember Sheena McLaughlan tried that last year and got told to get on with what she was doing in no uncertain terms?'

Teresa pulled a face. 'Oh aye, I'd forgot.'

'Packing is where I started and where I'll no doubt finish, whenever that might be.'

'When you find your Prince Charming you mean?' Teresa teased.

'I suppose so.'

They walked a little way in silence. 'Are you going to the dance next Saturday?' Teresa queried. 'Who knows, you might meet Prince Charming there.'

Bridie thought of the dance in question, a local affair held once a month. She had about as much chance of meeting Prince Charming there as she had of flying to the moon. Still, you never knew.

'I haven't decided yet.'

'There was a lad at the last one took my eye. But he never asked me up.'

'You never mentioned.'

Teresa shrugged.

'Nice, was he?'

'I've no idea as we never spoke. But he looked nice enough. The shy type I'd say.'

'Not too many of those round here,' Bridie commented. 'They're a forward lot by and large.'

'True enough.'

Bridie recalled the last dance they'd attended, the one Teresa was referring to. She'd been asked up far more times than Teresa, as was usually the case. Teresa was verging on being plain while she . . . well, she was hardly a ravishing beauty but folk did say she had 'looks'.

'It'd be a laugh,' Teresa went on.

'Hardly that,' Bridie commented wryly.

'Well, where else do you want to go? There's always the flicks, though you won't meet any fellas there. You don't get a lumber at the pictures.' Lumber meant meeting someone and being escorted home.

'I don't really fancy the flicks either.'

'You're becoming a right stick in the mud, so you are. I suppose you'd rather stay indoors on a Saturday night with one of your books.'

Bridie didn't reply to that.

A few minutes later her heart sank when the lemonade factory came into view.

'Here we go again,' Bridie muttered.

'Here we go,' Teresa agreed.

Chapter 2

'Well, I'll be damned!' Willie exclaimed. He was at the breakfast table sorting through the morning post.

Georgina glanced up from her kipper. 'Bad news, darling?'

Willie beamed at her. 'Quite the contrary. It's from an old chum of mine who served alongside me in the First Essex. He's going to pay us a visit.'

'That's nice.'

Rose was the only other person at the table, Ian having long since gone to work.

Willie re-read the letter then laid it aside. 'It'll be wonderful seeing Andrew again. He's a terrific chap.'

'You certainly sound enthusiastic,' Georgina commented.

'How old is he?' Rose queried.

Willie considered that. 'About the same age as me I suppose.' He suddenly chuckled. 'Far too old for you, my poppet.'

Rose coloured slightly. 'That wasn't why I asked at all.'

Willie regarded his daughter thoughtfully. He sometimes

regretted not having sent her off to school as he had Ian. Not that the various tutors hadn't done a first-rate job, they had. It was simply that she lacked a wider experience than might have been otherwise.

'Is this Andrew married?' Georgina enquired.

'Doesn't say. Certainly wasn't when in the army. I recall he was engaged at one point, to an Irish lass . . .' He broke off and shook his head. 'Sad business.'

'What happened?' a curious Rose asked.

Willie's expression became grim. 'She was killed and let's just leave it at that. Andrew was deeply hurt. Took it very badly indeed.'

This sounded intriguing, Georgina thought, wondering how the fiancée had been killed. 'So when's he coming?'

'Beginning of next month. He's not certain about the actual date yet but will write again when he is. In the meantime I shall write to him saying we shall be delighted to have him as a guest for as long as he wishes to stay.'

Willie paused, then said, 'Andrew is Drummond of Drummond whisky. We must get some of that for when he's here. Can't offer him another brand now, can we?'

'I'll speak to Mrs Coltart and see it's ordered,' Georgina declared. Mrs Coltart was the housekeeper who did all the ordering and buying for the household.

Willie leant back in his chair, breakfast temporarily forgotten. 'It's six years since I last saw him, I wonder if the old bugger's changed much.'

'Willie!' Georgina admonished, nodding in Rose's direction.

'Wouldn't it be fun if he'd gone bald or something,' Willie chuckled. 'That would upset him. He was always rather vain about his good looks. Bald and a paunch,' Willie chuckled further.

'You're being evil,' Georgina chided.

'Quite the ladies' man I remember. Had an easy way with them that I always envied. Myself and quite a few others.'

Pity he was so old, Rose reflected. This Andrew Drummond sounded fun.

'I'll write later today,' Willie announced.

'A gang of our own?' Noddy Gallagher repeated.

Sean nodded. 'Why not? There are enough of us, to get started anyway.'

'All Catholics of course,' Sammy Renton said.

Sean gave him a withering look. 'Of course, you eejit. That would be the whole point.'

Sammy grunted.

'I like the idea,' Mo Binchy declared thoughtfully. 'We could hardly rival the Billy Boys or the Norman Conks yet. But who knows, one day.'

Sean's eyes gleamed. 'I've even got a name for us.'

'Oh aye?' prompted Noddy.

Sean glanced from face to face. There were ten of them present, huddled over cups of coffee in an Italian café they frequented. All eyes were glued on him, something he was enjoying.

'The Samurai,' he stated proudly.

The response was blank stares.

'The what?' Bobby O'Toole queried.

'The Samurai,' Sean repeated.

'And what the hell's that when it's at home?'

Sean's expression became one of superiority. 'You're a bunch of ignorant sods, so you are. Samurai are Japanese warriors.'

'Is that a fact,' breathed Jim Gallagher, Noddy's brother.

'How come you know that?' Mo queried of Sean.

'I saw a picture all about them last year at the Poxy Roxy. They have funny haircuts and carry bloody big swords which they use to cut their enemies' heads off with. It was a rare film. I took Maeve Dunphy, you know her with the really big ones, and she got all upset with me.' Sean laughed. 'Said I was more interested in the film than I was in her.' He laughed a second time. 'And she was right too.'

'Will we have to carry bloody big swords?' Dan Smith queried, shivering at the prospect. This was frightening and exciting at the same time.

'Not to start with anyway,' Sean replied slowly. 'I mean to say, Japanese swords aren't exactly thick on the ground around Glasgow. Perhaps we can eventually lay our hands on a few though.'

'The Samurai,' Sammy Renton mused. 'It certainly has a ring about it.'

A murmur of agreement ran round the group.

'If we're going to be a proper gang then we'll need someplace to meet. If we gets lots of members then this café will hardly do,' Sammy went on.

Sean nodded. 'I've already thought of that too. You know that old condemned building at the end of Thistle Street. The one they've been going to pull down for years but never got round to it. Well, how about there?'

'Would it no be dangerous, I mean, it's condemned after all?' Mo Binchy queried.

Sean shot him a contemptuous look. 'Are you feart? Is that it?'

Mo went quite red. 'Don't call me feart. I'm nothing of the sort.'

'Well, I had a shufty round the other day and it's all shored up inside. There's nothing to worry about.'

'That settles that then,' Don McGuire stated emphatically.

Noddy Gallagher cleared his throat. 'If we're going to be a proper gang and all that we're going to need a leader. A heid bummer so to speak.'

Sean sat back in his chair and waited, not wanting to put himself forward, confident someone else would.

'That has to be Sean then,' Jim Gallagher duly obliged. 'If he agrees that is.'

'What do you say, Sean?' Bobby O'Toole queried.

'Is that what you all want?'

Another murmur of agreement ran round the group.

Elation swelled in Sean. The leader of his own gang, oh that was dandy indeed.

'So be it,' he declared.

'Would you care for a brandy, son?' Willie enquired of Ian, sitting slumped on a sofa.

'You appear done in,' Georgina smiled.

Ian nodded. 'I am. It's all this hard physical work that I'm not used to. It really takes it out of you.'

'You'll soon toughen up,' Willie commented, smiling also. 'Georgina dear, something for you?'

She shook her head.

'And what about you, Rose?'

'A sherry would be lovely, Pa. Thank you.'

Ian closed his eyes. He ached all over despite the hot bath he'd wallowed in for over half an hour. Toughen up, his pa had said. The sooner the better.

'I'm thinking of planning a trip to Edinburgh, darling,' Georgina informed Willie. 'I desperately need some new clothes.'

Desperately, Willie thought wryly. Why, she had wardrobes full of clothes.

'Can I come, Georgina?' Rose asked hopefully. Sometimes Georgina took her on these trips but on other occasions her stepmother preferred to go on her own.

'Of course you can, Rose. We'll stay for several days at least. How does that sound?'

'Exciting,' Rose beamed.

'And it'll be new clothes for you too.'

'Spiffing!'

Willie groaned inwardly. More expense! Honestly, those two thought money grew on trees. Still, if he was honest with himself he didn't really mind. He enjoyed indulging the pair of them. What was money for after all? As the saying went, you couldn't take it with you.

When he came to hand Ian his drink he found he'd fallen fast asleep.

'He's going to ask you up,' Teresa whispered excitedly. She and Bridie were at the local dance, sitting side by side on two of the chairs that lined the wall.

'Who?'

'Him coming over. The chap in the blue suit and swanky tie.'

Bridie quickly picked out the young man in question. He had a serious, determined expression on his face as he carved his way in their direction.

'How do you know it's me he's going to ask?'

'He's been watching you for some time now. I'm surprised you haven't noticed.'

Watching her indeed. She had another look at the chap whom she'd never seen before. There were lots of people present who were friends and acquaintances or whom she recognised as regulars to these dances. This was a new face.

The chap came to stand in front of them. 'Hello,' he

said, almost defiantly, to Bridie on whom he was focusing his entire attention. For some reason she found that a little disconcerting.

'Are you for up?'

The usual charming proposal, Bridie thought wryly. She slowly rose. 'That would be nice.'

'Right then.'

They took a position on the floor, the band struck up and he swept her into his arms. 'I'm Bob,' he stated.

'And I'm Bridie.'

He wasn't a bad dancer, she thought. Not brilliant but not bad either.

'Do you live round here?' he queried.

'Near by. And you?'

'Not that far away. Walkable, you understand?'

She nodded. 'I haven't seen you here before?'

'That's right. I usually go into town to the Locarno. It was a pal suggested we come tonight and I thought, why not for a change?'

'Good band,' she commented.

'Aye, fair enough. Not a patch on the ones at the Locarno, mind. They're something else. Ever been there?'

'You mean the Locarno? No, I'm afraid I haven't.'

'Maybe I'll take you some time.'

Bridie laughed. 'You are quick off the mark. What makes you think I'll stay up for a second dance far less go to the Locarno with you?'

'Because of my devastating charm and wit,' he flashed back in reply.

Bridie laughed again. 'I can tell you're the modest type.'

'Modesty never got you anywhere, that's my belief.' He suddenly gave her a huge smile. 'You're lovely, so you are.

A real cracker. But then you must have been told that hundreds of times before.'

'Are you taking the mickey?'

He detached a hand from her waist and waved it over his chest. 'Cross my heart and hope to die if I'm doing that. I mean it, you're a cracker all right. The best-looking lassie here tonight in my opinion.'

'Flattery will get you everywhere,' she replied somewhat coyly.

'That's what I'm hoping, Bridie. That's what I'm hoping.'

When he asked her to remain on for the next dance she, fascinated, agreed.

'Well, goodnight then the pair of you,' Teresa said to Bridie and Bob, Bridie having insisted that Teresa accompany them while Bob walked her home.

'Goodnight,' Bridie and Bob answered in unison.

Teresa giggled before turning and hurrying into her close – the entranceway into her Glasgow tenement.

Bridie and Bob, hand in hand, continued on their way.

'At last I've got you to myself,' Bob said.

What a character, Bridie thought. Despite his bumptiousness she rather liked him. And would go out with him if asked.

A few minutes later they reached Bridie's close which was lit with soft yellow gaslight.

'This is it,' she declared.

Bob glanced into the close then back at her, giving her another of his broad, disarming smiles. 'We can't stand here, shall we go inside?'

She'd already decided about that as well. 'All right.'

'We'll go through to the back close,' he said. 'There's more privacy there.'

Bridie wasn't so sure about that. The back close, an area out of sight of the rest of the close, was for serious snogging while a quick kiss was what she had in mind.

'I've only just met you,' she whispered.

'So what! I feel like I've known you all my life.'

And with that he tugged her in the direction of the back close.

'So how did it go?' Teresa demanded as Bridie joined her. It was Monday morning again and the pair of them were on their way to the lemonade factory.

Bridie's face hardened. 'If you're referring to that Bob, I stupidly went into the back close with him which turned out to be a terrible mistake. The man is an animal.'

They fell into step, hurrying on their way.

'What happened?'

'Before I knew it he had me pinned against the wall with his tongue so far down my throat I honestly thought I was going to choke. His hands were everywhere, and I mean everywhere. It was horrible.'

Teresa's eyes were wide as saucers. 'How awful.'

'It was, believe me. At one point I thought he was going to rip the front of my dress. Completely ruin it.'

'So what did you do?' Teresa couldn't wait to hear.

'He was far too strong for me to push off so when he finally got his tongue out of my mouth I told him if he didn't stop I'd scream the place down and then he'd have my father and brother to deal with. And that they were both real hard nuts.'

'So *did* he stop?'

'Sort of. He was full of apologies, saying he didn't know

what had come over him and all that guff. But even as he was telling me that he was still touching me. He even tried to get his hand up my skirt.'

'An animal right enough,' Teresa agreed with a nod.

'I'd only just met him, for God's sake. What did he take me for?'

'Some blokes,' Teresa sympathised, shaking her head.

'It was so unromantic, Teresa,' Bridie complained bitterly. 'There was no tenderness or affection. Nothing like that at all. Just sheer lust. He was like a maniac.'

'Well, that's the end of him.'

'You're darned tooting.'

'He seemed such a nice chap too.'

'It only goes to show how you can misjudge people.'

'Aye,' Teresa agreed. 'Aye indeed.'

Georgina glanced out of the tea-room window at the castle dominating the Edinburgh skyline. She and Rose were having a break during their first day's shopping.

'My feet hurt,' Rose stated, emphasising that by pulling a face.

Georgina brought her attention back to her step-daughter. 'Badly?'

'Oh, I'll survive.'

'I hope so. We've a lot more to do today.' She paused, then said, 'If they really are that bad you can go back to the hotel and we'll meet up again later.'

'Oh no!' Rose exclaimed in sudden alarm. 'Being here is such a treat I don't want to miss out on a moment of it.'

Or miss getting something, Georgina thought. Something she entirely understood.

Rose reached out and picked a cream cake from the

stand in the centre of the table. 'These are so yummy,' she declared.

Georgina frowned at her. 'Do you really think you should? It is your third after all.'

Rose averted her gaze. 'I said coming to Edinburgh was such a treat and this is part of it.'

'Hmmh,' Georgina mused, studying her stepdaughter. 'I do believe you're putting on more weight.'

'I'm doing nothing of the sort,' Rose protested.

'Oh yes you are, and you know it. You really should learn to curb your appetite, young lady. You'd have an extremely good figure if only you'd learn to look after it.'

Rose placed the cake on her plate and studied it. Should she or shouldn't she? It was such a temptation.

'You want to be popular with the young men, don't you?'

Rose nodded.

'Well, stuffing yourself full of cakes isn't the way to accomplish that.'

It was true, Rose reflected miserably. Trouble was she had such a sweet tooth, and a liking for food in general. If she ate the way Georgina did, like a bird, she'd end up starving all the time. Where was the pleasure in that?

'Of course some men do prefer plumper ladies, it can't be denied. But in my experience they're in the minority.'

That made Rose feel even more wretched. With a sigh she pushed her plate away. 'There,' she declared.

Georgina nodded her approval.

On the dot of eleven o'clock everything came to a halt for the morning break. Bridie reached for her flask. A cup of tea would be a welcome relief.

Teresa came hurrying over. 'Have you heard?'

Bridie frowned. 'Heard what?'

'The whisper has been going round since early on. A number of staff have been given the push. Nobody seems to know exactly how many yet.'

Bridie was shocked. 'The push?'

Teresa nodded vigorously.

Sally Dunn and Vicky Grieve, co-workers, joined them. 'What's that you're saying, Teresa? We couldn't help but overhear.'

Teresa repeated herself.

Sally and Vicky were as visibly shocked as Bridie. 'But why?' Vicky demanded.

'It seems sales have been falling away over the past few months and as a result it's been decided to have a cut-back on staff.'

Bridie's flask and tea were forgotten. This was terrible news. The worst. For what happened if sales fell even further? More staff for the chop was the inevitable conclusion.

'Do we know who these people are?' Sally asked.

Teresa shook her head. 'Though I imagine we'll find out at dinner-time.'

Bridie loathed her job at the lemonade factory, but it was a job and a wage coming into the house. Who knows how long it would take her to find another job should she lose this one. They were hard to come by.

'It makes you think, doesn't it,' Teresa said.

'Aye,' Vicky breathed. It would hit her particularly hard to be laid off as she lived alone with a crippled mother.

They continued speculating amongst themselves until it was time to resume work.

'Co-al! Co-al!'

Pat Flynn scanned the surrounding tenements for the

cards issued by his firm which, when placed in a window, told him that coal was needed. He reined in Jasper, his horse, when he spotted one.

With a sigh Pat tied off then jumped to the ground. This particular customer, a Mrs Buchanan, was a new one, she and her husband having moved into the area only a few months previously.

He manoeuvred a bag on to the side of the cart then heaved it on to his back, a back protected by a thick leather pad.

Into the close he went and up four flights where he found Mrs Buchanan waiting for him with the door open.

'Just put it in the bin,' she instructed.

There was the usual swirl of dust as the coal thudded into the almost empty wooden bin situated inside the kitchen.

Pat shook out the bag. 'One or two?' he queried.

'Just the one. I'll go and get my purse.'

Pat's reply was a grunt.

Mrs Buchanan made to move away then stopped as though she'd suddenly remembered something. Turning again to Pat she smiled. 'I'm sorry to be in my dressing-gown. It's quite lazy of me at this time of the morning.'

Pat shrugged. 'Nothing new to me, missus. You see all sorts in this job. You'd be surprised.'

'I suppose you do.' She clutched the dressing-gown more tightly about her. 'I'll find that purse.'

Good-looking woman, Pat reflected when she'd disappeared from view. Lovely pins, from what he'd been able to see of them. An unusual face too, brown eyes and blond hair. You didn't come across that combination very often. How old? Early thirties, he judged. Strange there wasn't any sign of children. There was invariably some evidence knocking about. Maybe the Buchanans couldn't have any.

Mrs Buchanan returned with a ten-shilling note. 'I'm afraid this is all I have. Have you got change?'

'Oh aye, plenty of that.'

He delved into the leather bag that dangled from his waist and was soon giving her what she was due.

He noted the peculiar expression on her face and wondered about it. She seemed quite mesmerised.

'There we are then,' he declared when the transaction was complete.

'Thank you, Mr . . . ?'

'Flynn.'

'An Irish name.'

'Aye, we are that. Second generation in both my case and my wife's.'

'You're married then.'

'With three children. The oldest is nineteen.'

'Quite grown up.' She smiled.

'He is that.'

'And the others?'

She was chatty, he thought. 'Two lassies. Bridie and Alison.'

Mrs Buchanan nodded, while her eyes strayed briefly to his wrists. Something he didn't fail to notice.

'I'd better get on my way then,' he stated.

'Of course. I'm holding you back.'

'Not at all.'

And with that he headed for the front door.

'Bye!' Mrs Buchanan called out as she was closing the door.

'Bye!'

Odd woman, he thought as he remounted his cart.

Though exactly why he couldn't have said. Perhaps it was that peculiar expression he'd noted. And why glance at his wrists the way she had?

They were perfectly ordinary wrists as far as he was concerned!

Pat sat studying Kathleen who was busy darning socks. She hadn't aged all that well, he thought. Her hair was shot through with grey and pulled back in a tight bun from her lined face. She'd also put on considerable weight since their marriage. Her bosoms were far larger than they'd been then and sagging now where before they'd been tight and firm.

Well, what did you expect after having, and nursing, three weans? Of course that took its toll. Stood to reason after all.

He wasn't exactly a spring chicken himself any more. Far from it. And as for a lined face, years out in all weathers had left their mark. His hair was still jet black though, he reminded himself proudly. And lots of it. There was no thinning or receding he was glad to say.

'Penny for them?' Kathleen queried, glancing across at him.

'Eh?'

'Penny for them.'

He pursed his mouth and shook his head. 'Only day-dreaming, that's all.'

'About?'

'Nothing in particular. Just day-dreaming.'

And with that he picked up the evening paper from his lap and again immersed himself in it.

*   *   *

'Andrew!'

Andrew shut the car door and strode to meet his friend. The pair of them warmly shook hands.

'Welcome to The Haven,' Willie declared.

Andrew glanced over Willie's shoulder at the pile called The Haven and thought it even more magnificent than Drummond House. In fact in some ways it reminded him of . . . He swiftly put that memory from his mind.

'So how are you, old bean?' Willie queried.

'In the pink. And all the better for seeing you.'

Willie chuckled. 'Come on in and meet everyone. With the exception of my son Ian, that is. You'll meet him later.'

'Jolly good.'

Willie's arm went round Andrew's shoulders and they mounted the long line of stone steps that led them to the massive oak door.

Chapter 3

'I know it's early but how about a drink?' Willie queried, rubbing his hands together. 'It's not every day a chum I haven't seen for years turns up.'

The four of them were assembled in the drawing room, Willie having already made the introductions.

'Not for me, Willie. But a little soda water would be nice,' Georgina replied.

Rose thought of the conversation she'd had with her stepmother in the Edinburgh tea room. 'Same for me, Pa, thank you.'

'And what about you, Andrew?'

'Whisky if you have it.'

'I not only have it, I have Drummond.'

Andrew laughed. 'That would be excellent.'

Willie busied himself with the drinks. He'd also have whisky.

'Can I ask what brings you to this part of the country?' Georgina queried of Andrew.

'Business. I'm en route to visit a few people. I'm a great believer in the personal touch, can work wonders in my opinion.'

'I understand. Willie tells me this is your first time at The Haven.'

'That's right. I should have been before but . . .' He shrugged. 'Something always got in the way.'

'I hope this business of yours isn't too pressing,' Willie said. 'We're hoping you'll stay a few days.'

Andrew hadn't planned on that. The night yes, but not a few days.

'Oh please do,' Georgina urged.

Andrew considered. 'Do you have the telephone here?'

'We do indeed,' Georgina replied.

'Then I shall make several calls later today and give you my answer afterwards.'

'Splendid.'

What a handsome, dashing man, Rose was thinking. He certainly didn't look as old as her father, but considerably younger.

There was something dangerous about Andrew Drummond, Rose decided. That was apparent even on this short acquaintance. He wasn't a man to be trifled with.

Willie handed Georgina and Rose their soda waters then returned for the whiskies.

'Are you married now, Andrew?' Willie enquired. 'You never mentioned in your letters.'

A lopsided, slightly cynical smile twisted Andrew's mouth. 'No I'm not. That's just never happened.'

Willie regarded Andrew thoughtfully. 'Pity.'

Andrew, still smiling, shrugged.

Willie changed the subject. 'So what have you been

doing, apart from running your distillery that is? And which I'm sure you're being most successful at.'

Andrew accepted the glass Willie gave him. 'Not a lot, to tell the truth. The distillery takes up most of my time.'

'But you must do something else?' Georgina queried with a frown.

'A bit of this, bit of that. I shoot on occasion, and have even been known to use a fly rod.'

'And socially?'

'I used to receive quite a few invitations, but rarely nowadays. I simply never took them up.'

'You have changed,' Willie mused, sitting down beside his wife.

'I suppose so.'

'Willie says you were quite the ladies' man at one time.'

Willie shot his wife a warning look which she chose to ignore.

'I suppose I was,' Andrew confessed. 'But that was in my salad days.'

'Surely you'll have to get married sometime,' Georgina went on. 'You'll need a son and heir to pass the distillery on to.'

'There is that,' Andrew acknowledged. 'It is a matter I have given some thought. But until the right woman comes along . . .' He trailed off and had a sip of whisky.

'You were engaged once I understand. But your fiancée died.'

This time the look Willie gave Georgina was withering. 'That's correct.'

Georgina waited for Andrew to continue, but he didn't.

'I say, how are those sisters of yours?' Willie asked, again changing the subject. He was furious with Georgina for trying to probe.

'Fine,' Andrew replied. 'Charlotte married the local minister and they now have two children. They're very happy. Nell is also married with a brood of her own.'

'Good for them,' Willie enthused.

'Charlotte keeps an eye on the distillery for me when I go off on these occasional trips of mine. She ran it by herself for a while after Pa died and I was still in Ireland.'

'By herself!' Rose exclaimed. 'She must be an extraordinary woman.'

'She is. A very determined and resourceful lady. I have every admiration for her.'

'I thought I might give you a tour of the estate after lunch,' Willie proposed.

'I'd like that.'

'Not all of it of course. You'd have to stay a week for that. It is rather large.'

'And thriving I trust?'

'Oh, very much so.'

'He works ever so hard,' Georgina stated. 'Too hard at times in my opinion.'

'I'm afraid it has to be done. However, I'll soon have Ian to help and that'll take something of the burden off my shoulders.'

'Did you enjoy Ireland, Mr Drummond?' Rose asked.

'Andrew, please.'

Rose blushed. 'Andrew then.'

'Yes, I did. In retrospect that is. At the time I wasn't so sure.'

'I loved it,' Willie declared. 'Dublin is such an exciting city. It positively throbs.' He smiled at Andrew. 'We have a great deal of reminiscing to do.'

'Indeed.'

'Do you remember . . .'

'He's a very sad and lonely man,' Georgina said to Willie that night after they'd retired.

'That's the impression I got.'

'Fun though. I enjoyed his company.'

'I thought you did.'

Georgina paused in her undressing. 'What did happen to his fiancée, Willie?'

Willie glanced away. 'That's something I think Andrew should tell you himself. Which I doubt he will. You could see how touchy he is on the subject.'

'I'm intrigued, darling. Positively intrigued.'

'Then you'll just have to stay that way. I'm not willing to discuss the matter. Let's just say it was all bound up in The Troubles over there.'

'The Troubles?' she repeated, her tone innocence itself. She was probing again.

But Willie wasn't taken in. He knew his wife only too well. 'And that's an end to it,' he stated firmly.

Her curiosity was killing her. But when Willie spoke like that nothing would budge him.

He could be such an obstinate man.

Rose crawled beneath the sheets and lay back to think about Andrew Drummond. What a pity he was so old. Ten years younger and . . . Well, who knew.

Closing her eyes she conjured up a picture of him. Recalling the way he smiled, the habit he had of flicking back a lock of hair when it dropped over his forehead. The delicate hands that had a somewhat feminine quality about them. The only thing that was feminine about him.

With a sigh she opened her eyes again, knowing she was going to have trouble sleeping. Andrew Drummond had disturbed her in a way no other man, of whatever age, had ever done before.

'Andrew!'

He turned to find Rose tripping towards him. 'Hello.'

'Hello as well,' she said on reaching his side. 'Do you mind if I join you?'

'Not at all. I was just admiring those roses.'

She glanced at the roses in question. 'They are rather splendid, aren't they. Do you like gardens?'

He gazed about him. 'Very much so. I find them, especially when the flowers are in bloom, extremely relaxing.'

'Do you have one at your house?'

'A number actually. I take great delight in strolling amongst them whenever I can.'

Strolling alone, she thought. 'I should like to see them one day.' Now that could be construed as being forward, she chided herself.

'And so you shall. It was already in my mind to invite the family to Drummond House. To repay your hospitality for having me here.'

Andrew bent and smelt a rose. 'Beautiful,' he murmured.

As he was, she thought.

'I have a friend in Dalneil, that's the village where I live, who sits for hours in his garden when the weather's clement. It's his favourite place. Only a small garden, mind you, as he lives in a cottage, but he says it inspires him.'

'Inspires?'

Andrew smiled. 'Jack is a writer. And pretty successful too. He's had several plays on in the West End of London, one also in New York.'

'I say. How thrilling!'

'Jack almost went to see the New York production, but in the end didn't.' Andrew paused. 'Did I say see? I meant listen to, for Jack's blind.'

'How awful for him,' Rose sympathised. 'Has he been blind from birth?'

'No, it happened during the war on the Western Front. Your father and I were lucky in being posted to Ireland for the duration. Jack and my elder brother Peter were the unlucky ones. Peter was killed and Jack not only blinded but horribly scarred on the face.'

'Your elder brother. Does that mean he would have inherited the distillery?'

Andrew nodded. 'It was always his by right. I had a career in the army planned, but of course all that changed when Peter bought it. His death literally broke my father's heart. He dropped down dead when he received the official telegram.'

Rose covered her mouth. 'That's ghastly.'

'Peter was Father's favourite, between the pair of us I mean. I believe Pa always considered me the black sheep of the family.'

'Surely not?'

Memories came flooding back. 'Oh yes, I'm afraid so. And he was quite right. I was a bit of a bounder when younger. More than a bit when I come to think of it.'

That only added to his charm she decided. 'But you're a changed man now?'

Was he? Perhaps. Perhaps not. It was said that leopards never change their spots after all.

'That's for others to judge. Not me.'

Rose stared at his finely chiselled features, then glanced away as an emotion she'd never experienced before trembled inside her.

'Was Peter much older than you?' She was being crafty here. At least so she hoped.

'Two years.'

'And how old would he have been now?'

'Why, eh . . . Forty I suppose.'

Which told her what she wanted to know. Andrew was thirty-eight, twenty years older than herself. An insurmountable barrier? Not really in her opinion, though many would have thought so. Father had been wrong about Andrew's age, Willie being forty-four.

'Do you miss him?'

Andrew considered that. 'Yes I do. We were never very close, but he was my brother when all's said and done. Yes I miss him. Though I have to say Jack Riach has been far more of a brother to me than Peter ever was.'

'You're very fond of this Jack, aren't you?'

'Extremely. He and his wife Hettie have been good to me. I can drop by there any time and be welcome for a meal or whatever. Jack and I try to go once a week to the local pub together. We invariably have a good laugh.'

'I've never met a writer,' Rose stated. 'But then what do you expect being born and brought up on the estate. It's very limiting, you know.'

'You shall meet Jack and Hettie when you come to Drummond House, that's a promise.'

'Thank you,' she smiled.

'Hettie used to work for Jack when he farmed. A farm

he sold after he lost his sight and couldn't personally run it any more. He adored that place and yet he sold it. I can understand why.'

'And what did Hettie do for him?'

Andrew gave a small laugh. 'She was a dairy maid. A real down-to-earth country lass if ever there was. The pair of them are a strange combination, but it works. They idolise one another.'

'Would you care to walk for a while?' Rose asked.

Andrew frowned. 'I really should be getting back to the house. Your father will be wondering where I've got to.'

She tried not to show her disappointment. 'A short walk then? Just enough to stretch the legs.'

He conceded. 'A short walk it is. And during it you can tell me all about yourself.'

She laughed. 'I've already explained, there's very little to tell.'

Pretty girl, he thought. If a trifle overweight. Nice personality too.

They walked for longer than Andrew had intended.

'Now don't forget,' Andrew said to William. 'You'll come to Drummond House.'

'In the winter when things are quieter round here. You have my word.'

The two men shook hands.

'I really have enjoyed myself. Thank you all.'

'It was a pleasure having you, Andrew,' Georgina declared. They'd come out to see Andrew off, with the exception of Ian who was working.

Did he know her well enough? Andrew decided he did. Going to Georgina, he pecked her on the cheek. 'You've been most kind.'

'Not at all. As I said, it was our pleasure.'

He turned to Rose who was finding his departure a terrible wrench. Andrew Drummond had made a big impression on her. A very big impression indeed. She'd have given anything for him to be staying longer and couldn't wait for the proposed visit to Drummond House.

'Goodbye, Rose.'

'Goodbye, Andrew.'

Disappointment flooded her when he started towards the car. 'Don't I get a kiss as well?'

'I say!' Willie exclaimed. 'Where's your modesty, girl?'

Rose blushed deeply. 'I'm sorry. I didn't mean to offend.'

'You didn't offend at all,' Andrew declared gallantly. 'I'm the one at fault.' And with that he returned to Rose and kissed her as he'd kissed Georgina.

'Thank you, lovely miss,' he smiled, amused by her continuing blushes.

'Have a safe journey,' Willie said.

'I'm sure I shall.'

Andrew climbed into the Rolls and wound down his window. 'Here we go then.'

He started the car which purred sweetly into life. 'Toodeloo!' He waved.

It was with a heavy heart that Rose turned towards the house. It might have been a short acquaintance but she'd miss Andrew dreadfully.

Once inside she headed for her room, wanting to be alone.

Sean Flynn gazed about him, taking in the flickering candles illuminating the room of the condemned house they'd taken over as their own. There were ancient curtains on the window, closed to ensure their privacy, while a number of broken-down sofas and chairs provided seating. It was hardly the Ritz but suitable for their purposes.

'Home from home,' he breathed, which raised a laugh from the others present.

'Some home,' Don McGuire commented, raising another laugh.

Mo Binchy gingerly sat on one of the sofas, liberated from a dump, in case it collapsed under his weight. 'What now?' he queried.

Sean focused on him. 'How do you mean?'

'I mean, what now? Where do we go from here, O leader?'

'Less of your bloody sarcasm. Don't you know it's the lowest form of wit.'

'That's me,' Mo riposted. 'Real low life.'

Sean produced a cut-throat razor which he'd stropped before coming out. 'I think we should have a gang insignia. Our own mark so to speak.'

Sammy Renton frowned. 'What sort of mark?'

'I'll show you.'

Sean took off his jacket and dropped it to the floor. He then partially rolled up the left sleeve of his shirt. 'A cross right here,' he declared, indicating a patch just above his wrist.

Sammy swallowed hard.

'Done with that razor?' Noddy Gallagher queried.

Sean nodded.

That was greeted with a deathly silence.

'I'll go first,' Sean proposed. 'Once marked you're in the gang for life. And no one can be a gang member without it.'

'Christ,' Jim Gallagher whispered.

Sean did it quickly. One deep stripe was instantly followed by a second. Blood spurted from the cuts and ran down his hand.

Sean stared triumphantly at them. 'Who's next?'

There were no takers.

'Come on, you bunch of jessies. Who's next?'

Don McGuire came forward. 'See's that razor, Sean.'

When they left the house a little later all bore the mark of the Samurai on their left arm.

'Have you heard the latest?' a clearly worried Vicky Grieve queried of Bridie and Teresa as they arrived in the cloakroom where they hung their coats, exchanging them for the large white aprons they wore while working.

'What's that?' Bridie asked.

'The rumour is there's to be more sackings.'

Teresa swore. 'Are you sure?'

'It's only a rumour, mind. That's all I know.'

Bridie bit her lip.

'What'll I do if I lose my job?' Vicky choked. 'God help me if I do, what with my ma and that.'

This was a worry, Bridie thought. A real worry. 'Sales must have dropped again.'

'If the rumour's true,' Teresa added. 'It might just be a right load of rubbish. Someone said something that was overheard wrongly and passed on the same way. That could be all it is.'

'Aye,' Bridie agreed.

'Whatever,' Teresa went on. 'We'd better get moving. I for one don't want to be late on the floor with the rumour of possible sackings flying about. I don't want to give them any excuses to pick on me.'

The three of them quickly changed and hurried from the cloakroom.

Ellen should be along any minute now, Andrew thought, staring up at the ceiling. He was eager for her presence, and body.

It was Jack Riach who'd given him the idea one night when they were talking in the pub. Jack had been worried about his 'wellbeing', as Jack had called it.

Andrew had been amused when Jack had come out with the suggestion, further amused by Jack's embarrassment.

'What made you think of that?' he'd asked.

'I heard of someone else who'd come to the same arrangement,' Jack had lied in reply, not wanting Andrew to know that the arrangement had been between him and Hettie when she'd been his dairy maid.

'One of the servant lassies?' Andrew had repeated.

'Perfect, if you fancy one that is and she'll comply. You'd have to be careful in picking the right one. One who'll keep her mouth shut whether she agrees or not.'

Andrew had considered that a wise piece of advice.

He brought himself out of his reverie and yawned. What was keeping the damned girl? He wanted her and he wanted her now.

Andrew smiled in the darkness. Ellen Temple had been the only one he'd approached and a good choice it had been. He'd read her character correctly. Underneath that prim exterior lay a natural tart. And so it had proved.

A deal had been struck. An agreed sum paid once a month and the assurance that she'd be well taken care of should she fall pregnant.

How long had it been now? Just over a year, Andrew reflected. A year of having access to her body whenever he wished it. And a fine body it was too, a body she was enthusiastic in using. Just as she'd been enthusiastic about learning all the little tricks and refinements he'd taught her.

Andrew's ruminations were disturbed when his bedroom door opened and a shadowy figure slipped inside. The door was closed as silently as it had been opened.

The shadowy figure flitted to the side of his bed where Ellen dropped her dressing-gown to the floor. Still wearing her nightdress, which would soon be removed, she got in beside Andrew and snuggled up.

'I was beginning to think you'd gone off me. You've been back a whole week without giving me the nod until tonight.'

His hand sought out a breast. 'I haven't been in the mood, that's all.'

'Are you certain about that?' she queried anxiously.

'Absolutely.'

She sighed with relief. The last thing she wanted was to lose this added income. An added income that would one day release her from the life of service she so loathed.

Strictly business, Andrew thought, that was the nice thing about their arrangement. He didn't have to pretend to be romantic in any way.

'If you weren't in the mood before you certainly are now,' she whispered as his hardness pressed into her.

'Let's get you out of this,' he whispered in reply, always preferring her to be naked when in bed with him.

The nightdress was removed and tossed aside.

Kathleen Flynn shook Bridie's shoulder. 'Time to be up, lass.'

Bridie groaned as she came awake. She never liked

getting up in the morning. Especially when she had work to go to.

'I'm dead beat,' she declared. 'Alison has kept me awake most of the night.'

Bridie and her younger sister Alison shared a cavity bed in the kitchen. This was a peculiar Glasgow device, a bed set in a wall recess looking rather like a cave.

'Why's that?'

'She's got another cold. Hour after hour she was sniffing and snorting. And talk about being restless!'

'I'm sorry,' Alison wailed from underneath the covers. 'I couldn't help it.' She popped her head into view. Her eyes were puffed and streaming, her nose quite red.

Kathleen placed her hands on her hips and studied her youngest child. 'I don't know how you manage it, young lady. If it's not one thing that's wrong with you it's another.'

Alison clutched the bedclothes to her chin. 'It's not my fault, Ma. I don't ask to get ill all the time.'

'You manage it nonetheless,' Bridie retorted caustically.

Kathleen leant across Bridie and felt Alison's forehead. 'Aye, you've got a temperature right enough.'

'I'm sorry,' Alison repeated.

Bridie lay back and closed her eyes. She was so tired that for two pins she'd have taken the day off work. But that was something she daren't do. Fourteen people had now had the sack at the factory and she didn't want to be amongst the next batch if there was one. And if what she heard was true, that sales were still dropping, there could well be.

'You'd better get a move on, Bridie, before your father and Sean come through.'

Uttering another groan Bridie swung her feet out of bed.

It was the same every morning, Kathleen was up first, then Bridie so that she'd be dressed before her father and brother came through to shave and have their breakfast, which was invariably a cup of tea and thick slice of bread.

Bridie padded to the sink where she splashed cold water on her face. A quick dry and then back to her clothes which she began to put on.

'I feel like death warmed up,' she complained.

Alison was about to say, 'And you look it', then thought perhaps not in the circumstances. 'Can I have a hanky please, Ma?' she asked instead. 'I had to make do with my sleeve during the night.'

'Of course, lassie. Of course.'

'I just hope you haven't given me your rotten cold,' Bridie admonished her sister. That would be disastrous.

Chapter 4

M rs Buchanan was waiting for Pat by her door. 'Good morning to you, Mr Flynn,' she smiled.

Pat's reply, weighed down as he was with a bag of coal, was a grunt.

'Come away in,' she said, leaving the door open as she followed him into the kitchen.

What a glamour puss, Pat was thinking as he filled the bin. She was all done up like a dish of fish.

'Just the one again?' he queried, shaking out the bag.

'That's right.' The smile so far hadn't left her face. 'Are you in a hurry, Mr Flynn?'

He frowned. 'Why do you ask?'

'I wondered if you had time for a bottle of beer. My husband left some behind when he went away and I never touch it. I will have a wee whisky on occasion, but never beer. Filthy stuff in my opinion.' She laughed, a tinkling sound.

Pat had never refused a free alcoholic anything in his life. 'That would be nice,' he replied, also smiling.

'Right then.'

She delved into a cupboard and produced a screwtop. 'I'll just get a glass to go with it,' she declared, handing him the bottle.

Pat wasn't fussed whether he had a glass or not. He watched her as she opened another cupboard. Classy piece right enough, he thought. She didn't half look smart in her warpaint.

'Dougal, that's my husband, is in the Royal Navy. When he goes to sea it can be for months on end.'

Pat accepted the glass from her. 'That wouldn't suit me at all,' he said, making conversation.

'Dougal loves it. Joined when he was only fifteen. He was at the Battle of Jutland you know.'

'Really.'

'Lost quite a few of his mates there. But he was fortunate to come through all right. That was the only action he ever saw. What about yourself, Mr Flynn, were you in the war?'

'Wasn't nearly everyone,' Pat replied softly.

'Did you see action?'

Awful memories crowded his mind. Vividly recalling that particular day when he'd come within a whisker of . . . 'Oh aye, I saw a bit.'

'Which regiment were you in?'

'The HLI. Highland Light Infantry. And a better bunch of blokes you'll go a long way to find.'

Pat had a long pull of beer. 'That's grand stuff,' he declared, wiping froth from his mouth. 'It sure hits the spot.'

Mrs Buchanan stared in fascination at the wrist of the hand he'd used, where thick tufts of hair jutted from under his cuff. Her mouth went dry thinking what the rest of him would be like. Should be like.

'Mrs Buchanan?'

She started. 'Sorry, I was lost in thought there for a moment.' The smile returned. 'Something I've got to do later,' she lied.

Pat topped up his glass, the smell of the heavy perfume she was wearing strong in his nostrils. It was a pleasant smell, very feminine. He couldn't remember the last time Kathleen had worn scent or perfume. He found himself comparing Kathleen and Mrs Buchanan. There was no contest, Mrs Buchanan won hands down.

'I'm Geraldine by the way.'

'Oh aye.'

She raised a well-plucked eyebrow in anticipation.

'Pat,' he said slowly. 'Short for Patrick of course.'

'Of course.'

He couldn't resist himself. 'My wife's called Kathleen. As Irish as Pat and Flynn.'

Geraldine's smile became slightly razored. She didn't reply to that.

Pat saw off what remained in his glass and then emptied the bottle into it. 'This is certainly going down well. I had quite a thirst on me. It's the coal you see, it gets in your throat.'

Offer him another? she wondered. And decided not to. She mustn't be too pushy. That might scare him off. 'How are the children?' she enquired.

'Och, the wee lass's got a bad cold. There's always something wrong with that one.'

'I'm sorry to hear so. Alison, isn't it?'

He nodded. 'That's right.'

She swallowed hard when a tuft of hair suddenly popped up from underneath his collar. Now she knew for certain. God, how she adored hairy men, the hairier the better. Hair covering their chests, their backs, their bottoms. Hair . . .

'Well, that's that,' Pat declared, laying the empty glass to one side. 'Thank you very much, Geraldine. It was most appreciated.'

'I'm sure you deserve a little treat.' The treat she had in mind wasn't beer.

'I'll see you next time then.'

When he'd gone she closed the door and leant back against it. In her mind's eye she was picturing Pat stark naked, hairy from neck to toe.

'Oh God,' she whispered, wishing not for the first time that Dougal wasn't a sailor and came home every night like most normal men.

But a sailor he was and she had to put up with it.

With certain exceptions that is.

Andrew laid the tray he'd been carrying on the table then placed Jack Riach's pint and whisky in front of him. It was one of their Friday nights out at the local.

'I've been meaning to ask for a while, how's your little arrangement going?'

Andrew stared at his friend whose eyeless sockets were covered with dark glasses. Although Jack knew an arrangement had been made, he didn't know the name of the lassie it was with. 'Fine.'

'That's good then. No problems?'

'None at all.'

Jack nodded. 'A man shouldn't be alone all the time, Andrew. It isn't good.'

'I'm not alone, Jack. I'm at the distillery every working day.'

'You know what I mean. I worry about you, old pal, rattling around in that big house all by yourself.'

'I'm hardly that. There are the servants.'

'Not quite the same though, is it. You need a proper companion, Andrew. In other words, a wife.'

Andrew sighed. 'Not that again.'

'Your Alice was years ago. In the past. We're in the present which has to be lived.'

Andrew conjured up a picture of Alice in his mind. Dear sweet Alice whom he'd started out wooing because of her wealth and then fallen in love with. Even now, after all this while, just thinking about her brought a lump to his throat.

'Apart from anything else, Andrew, you need a son and heir to pass the distillery on to.'

Andrew gave a low laugh. 'Someone else said that recently.'

'Oh?'

'Willie Seaton's wife. The chap I served alongside in Ireland.'

'Well, she's right. And so am I.'

'All in due course, Jack. All in due course. I'm sure the right person will come along in time. And I'm hardly decrepit yet.' He thought of his last session with Ellen. 'Hardly,' he repeated with a chuckle. Ellen could certainly testify to that.

'You want to get out and about more.'

'To where? Besides, when I get home most nights all I'm good for is having a meal, a few drams and then bed.'

'I don't believe that.' Jack held up a hand. 'I know you work hard, but the rest is a state of mind. You don't really want to do anything so you don't.'

'Nonsense.'

Jack picked up his pint. 'Is it?'

Andrew found himself thinking of Georgina Seaton. Now there was a woman he could be interested in. Pity she was already married.

Jack cleared his throat. 'Changing the subject. Can I ask your advice?'

'Naturally. What is it?'

'First of all, promise you won't laugh.'

'I swear. As if I'd laugh at a friend.' That was said tongue in cheek, as Jack was only too well aware.

'I'm serious about this.'

'Oh go on, Jack, you're blethering on like an old biddy.'

Jack took a deep breath. 'I've only spoken about this to Hettie, no one else, apart from you tonight that is. Nor will I.'

Andrew waited patiently.

'Do you think I'm up to writing a novel?'

Andrew had no compulsion whatever to laugh. If anything he was taken aback. 'What sort of novel?'

Jack cleared his throat. 'A love story actually.'

'I see,' Andrew murmured, and tasted his dram.

'Well. Do you think I'm being daft? Overreaching myself?'

'I don't think that at all. It would be a big departure for you, as I'm sure you appreciate. There must be a huge amount of work in a novel compared to a play.'

'I know,' Jack replied softly, and nibbled a thumbnail. 'I must confess, the whole idea rather frightens me. It's a tremendous challenge, but that in itself is exciting.'

'I do believe you've already made up your mind to have a go.' Andrew smiled.

'I have nothing of the sort!' Jack protested.

'No?'

Jack shook his head. 'I swear.'

He had really, Andrew thought. Jack just didn't know it yet. 'Well, I hope you go ahead. And, having a great deal of faith in you, I'm certain if you do you'll carry it off. So there.'

Jack groped for his whisky, wishing he had the same faith. '*Slainte!*' he toasted.

'*Slainte*,' Andrew responded.

Rose reined in her horse Trixie and, after a few moments, dismounted. She needed a breather after a good gallop.

'Come on, Trix, let's have a little walk,' she said, patting the mare's nose.

Trixie whinnied in reply.

As they walked Rose thought of Andrew Drummond, wondering what he was doing at that very moment. Work probably, it being a Wednesday morning. He was bound to be at the distillery. Unless he was off on another of his business trips, that is.

When they went to Drummond House she must ask Andrew to take her round the distillery and show her everything. Just the two of them if possible, she didn't want her father or Georgina playing gooseberry.

Was she being silly? she asked herself. Andrew hadn't shown any particular interest in her, not that sort of interest anyway. He'd been polite of course, and attentive, when they were together. But that was only manners.

She recalled the kiss on the cheek he'd given her as he was leaving and reaching up caressed the spot where his lips had touched her. She flushed slightly remembering her embarrassment at asking for the kiss. Shameless hussy, she thought, which made her smile.

'Andrew,' she said. How she enjoyed saying his name. 'Andrew.' A tremor ran through her as she said it a second time.

Winter seemed an eternity away, years not months. She knew it to be her imagination but the days were positively dragging by. Each so long it made her want to scream from frustration.

Oh to be in his arms, to have his lips on hers and not her cheek. For them to . . .

Rose shook her head. Enough of that, girl, she chided

herself. She shouldn't be having such thoughts. Not about Andrew or anyone else.

Remounting Trixie she continued on her way, trying unsuccessfully to get Andrew out of her mind.

God, but they were tedious, Georgina reflected. She loved her parents dearly but her yearly week with them was hell. No wonder her father was called Boring Bob behind his back. A nickname he'd had for as long as she could remember.

She gazed in distaste around the somewhat shabby room, shabby as was the rest of the house. A house that, in its entirety, could have fitted into the drawing room of The Haven.

Well, maybe not in its entirety, there were two floors to it after all, but it seemed that way.

'More tea, darling?' Margaret Galbraith queried.

'No thank you, Mum.'

'Bob?'

'A spot more wouldn't go amiss.'

Georgina stared at her father. A small, balding, waspish man, he looked exactly what he'd been in life, a clerk. He blinked back at her through wire-framed spectacles.

'Yes, Georgina. You wish to say something?'

'No, Father. I was just thinking.'

Bob knew Georgina disliked her visits there, which he could well understand. She'd become used to far grander things after all. Far grander things and people. But it was her duty to come, to visit her mother if nothing else.

Margaret took Bob's cup and refilled it. 'What do you intend doing tomorrow, dear?' she asked Georgina.

'I thought I might go shopping.'

That scandalised Margaret. 'But you've already been shopping twice, Georgina. You'll have bought up the whole of Perth before you're finished.'

Georgina laughed. 'Hardly!'

'Why don't you take your mother with you this time,' Bob suggested.

Georgina sighed inwardly. That was the last thing she wanted. If her mother went along all she'd get was a constant lecture on how expensive everything was and how much she was spending. Her spending horrified Margaret.

'Mum?'

'I'll stay at home if you don't mind, dear. I'd planned a spot of baking.' She beamed. 'Your father so enjoys my baking, isn't that correct, Bob?'

He nodded.

What a relief, Georgina thought. What a blessed relief.

'Georgina, this is incredible. How are you?'

Georgina, just stepping out of a cab, turned to stare at Andrew Drummond in surprise. 'Why, hello!'

'Here, let me,' he said, and paid off the driver. 'What are you doing in Perth?' he queried as the cab drove off.

'My parents live here. I visit them once a year. And you?'

'A little bit of business.'

'I see.' She smiled.

'So where are you off to?'

'Just the shops.'

'Looking for something in particular?'

She shook her head. 'Passing time, that's all. My parents are lovely, but not in long stretches. They tend to be rather . . . claustrophobic, shall I say.'

Andrew laughed. 'I understand.' He glanced about him. 'As we've bumped into one another, why don't we take coffee? It's about that time of morning.'

Something jumped inside her. 'That would be splendid.'

'There's a coffee shop not far from here that I sometimes frequent. We could go there.'

'What's it called?'

'Darling's.'

Georgina smiled. 'I know it well. An excellent choice.'

'Pity I sent away that cab,' he commented, looking to see if he could spot another.

'We can walk,' she protested. 'It's only a few minutes' stroll.'

Offer his arm or not? Not, he decided. 'Then shall we?'

Andrew's eyes lit up when the cake stand was placed on their table. 'French cakes,' he enthused. 'I adore those. Have ever since I was a nipper. Especially the chocolate-covered ones. Yummy.'

Georgina laughed. 'Do you have a sweet tooth?'

'Not really. But French cakes are an exception. I'd murder for one.' For a brief instant a strange glint came into his eyes.

'Coffee for two please,' he instructed the waitress who'd reappeared to take their order.

'Certainly, sir.'

'So, where are you staying?' Georgina enquired.

'I'm not. I motored down early and will motor back later on this afternoon when my business is concluded.'

'In that gorgeous Rolls-Royce.'

'Yes,' he murmured.

'You will have to give me a spin in it when we come to Drummond House.'

'I'd be delighted.'

He really was such a handsome man, she thought. Quite dishy as the younger folk would say. Far better-looking than Willie. Not that Willie was unattractive, far from it. But he wasn't in the same league as Andrew Drummond.

58

'How are things at The Haven?' he enquired politely.

'More or less the same. Nothing changes there very much. It can be quite humdrum actually which is why it's always such a pleasure getting to a city.'

'Even Perth,' he grinned. Perth might be lovely but it was hardly the most exciting of places.

'Even Perth,' she agreed. 'For the shops.'

'So tell me, I never did find out. How did you and Willie meet?'

She vividly remembered the occasion, a night that had completely altered the course of her life. 'At a small gathering held by mutual friends.'

'Here in Perth?'

She nodded. 'Willie and I struck it off right away. Well, one thing led to another and eventually to marriage.' She paused, then added reflectively, 'So many women of my generation never got a first chance, far less a second.'

Andrew frowned. 'Second chance?'

She hesitated, then went on. 'There was a chap before the war, his name was Harry. We were very much in love and intended marrying. Then the war happened and . . .' She sucked in a breath. 'Harry was killed in France.'

'I'm sorry,' Andrew sympathised.

'I thought I was left on the shelf, there being so few men to go round after the war. That's why there are so many spinsters of my generation.'

'And then Willie popped up and that was that,' Andrew smiled. 'He whisked you off the shelf and the pair of you lived happily ever after.'

'That's right.' It was too, she reflected. For she was happy, though only to an extent. She'd never loved Willie, not when she married him, or now. Fond of him, yes. Very fond. But that was as far as it went. Her feelings for him were nothing like those she'd had for Harry. Now that had been true love.

If only Willie could satisfy her in bed it might make a difference, but he didn't, and never would. She'd become reconciled to that. Even if he had she still wouldn't have loved him, but she might have felt more towards him.

What a catch Willie had been, a catch she'd grabbed with both hands when given the opportunity. Never in her wildest dreams had she imagined she'd end up mistress of a grand house like The Haven, or with a husband so wealthy. Harry, bless him, had worked in a bank as a teller. A good job, he'd often assured her. And he'd had aspirations. He'd be a manager one day he'd repeatedly said, it was only a matter of time and passing the appropriate exams.

Harry, whom she still achingly missed. Her biggest regret was that they'd never made love. Even when he was off to fight she'd still refused him, wanting to be a virgin on their wedding night. Well, she had been on her wedding night, only it had been Willie she'd given herself to and not Harry.

'He's a wonderful man,' Andrew declared, referring to Willie.

'Yes,' she agreed. 'Wonderful.'

Andrew wondered why the mood between them had suddenly changed. Before it had been light and jocular but within the last few moments it had become sombre.

'So now I know how you and Willie met.'

She was lucky, she reminded herself, damned lucky to have had that second chance.

Even if love was absent.

'Pooh!' Rose exclaimed. 'You don't half pong.'

Ian Seaton glared at his sister. 'Well, what do you expect

after a day like I've put in. It wasn't only hard graft but nasty smelly work, I can tell you.'

'You don't have to tell me, the smelly part is obvious.' Rose wrinkled her nose in disgust. 'Pooh!' she repeated.

Sometimes his sister irritated Ian beyond belief. 'Anyway, I'm off for a bath now,' he declared.

'And don't you need one.' Rose's derisory laugh followed him up the stairs.

'Well, well, well,' Sean muttered, and gave a small belch. He and the rest of the Samurai were out for a Saturday night booze-up.

'What is it?' Noddy Gallagher queried, noting Sean's expression.

Sean nodded across the horseshoe-shaped bar. 'Remember I mentioned those Proddy bastards who jumped me a while back.'

'Aye.'

'That's them over there.'

Noddy peered in the direction Sean had indicated. 'Which ones?'

Sean described the two in question.

'What's up?' Jim Gallagher asked on joining them.

Sean explained the situation.

'I don't think they're regulars here,' Jim mused. 'I've certainly never seen them before.'

Sean recalled with grim satisfaction that he'd beaten the Prods, though at no small cost to himself. He'd been sore for days afterwards. His hand went to the hard metal object he was carrying in his inside jacket pocket.

'It's time we started making a name for ourselves,' he declared softly.

'You mean as Samurai?' Jim queried.

Sean nodded. 'Exactly.'

'What do you have in mind?'

'Get the lads over here. This is a night those bastards are going to remember for the rest of their lives.'

Noddy swallowed hard, shivering at the look on Sean's face. It was frightening.

'Right,' Jim said, and moved off.

Sean's eyes strayed to the clock above the gantry. They'd wait till nearly closing time and then leave. In the meantime he'd ensure he wasn't spotted by the Prods.

One moment the Prods were laughing and joking between themselves, the next they'd been set upon and bundled into an alleyway.

'Give them a right doing,' Sean instructed, landing a heavy punch.

The Prods didn't have a chance, they were simply overwhelmed by numbers. When they were both on the ground the boot went in.

'Keep them conscious,' Sean yelled, his own boot flashing.

A Prod screamed in agony as the boot found its mark between his legs.

Sean stepped back and reached into his inside pocket. The cutthroat razor he produced had an ebony handle.

'Now hold the fuckers there,' he hissed.

The Samurai swiftly obeyed.

Sean straddled his first victim to smile evilly down at him. 'Remember me?'

The Prod didn't answer.

'Remember me, you bastard?'

'Fenian cunt.'

Sean laughed and made small circles in the air with the

now fully opened razor. 'Well, you're certainly right about me being a Fenian, and proud of it I am too.'

The pinioned Prod spat at Sean. 'That's what I think of you and your like.'

Cold fury erupted in Sean as spittle ran down the front of his shirt. 'You're going to regret that.'

'Stop it, Tom. Don't antagonise them any further,' the other Prod counselled.

'Is that your name then, son? Tom.'

'Up yours.'

'Tom what?'

'Tom Thumb.'

Sean laughed again. 'Quite the comedian, aren't you?'

Mo Binchy glanced anxiously at the entrance to the alleyway. 'Hurry up, there are always lots of polis around on a Saturday night. We don't want to get caught.'

'We won't get caught,' Sean replied.

He bent over Tom. 'We're the Samurai. Don't forget, pal.'

There was no reply.

Tom shrieked when Sean scored a deep cut down one side of his face. He continued shrieking as another furrow was added on the same cheek.

Two furrows on each cheek, then Sean sliced off a thumb.

'There's your thumb, Tom.' Sean leered malevolently, placing it on the lad's chest.

Tom didn't reply. He was out cold.

Then it was the second Prod's turn. Two furrows on each cheek, only he got to keep his thumbs.

Chapter 5

Willie found Ian standing by a window staring out over the autumnal landscape, his son clearly lost in thought.

'Am I intruding?'

Ian started and turned to face Willie. 'No, I was just . . . thinking I suppose.'

'Oh?'

Ian watched his father light a cigarette. 'About how much I love this place.'

Willie smiled.

'Always have done. I wouldn't want to live anywhere else. Not in a million years.'

'I know what you mean. It's the same with me, I wouldn't trade The Haven for any other place on earth.'

Ian nodded.

'How's the work coming along?'

'Fine.'

'Enjoying it?'

'Some of the experiences I could do without,' Ian replied ruefully. 'But on the whole it's . . . well, you could call it good fun.'

'Jock Gibson treating you all right?'

'He's a hard taskmaster right enough. But fair, you have to give him that. He's well respected and admired by all those under him. As I hope I'll be when in time I take over his job.'

There was a change in Ian of late, Willie thought. A resolve about him that hadn't been there before. And certainly a new maturity. 'So what's it tomorrow?' he enquired.

'I'm not sure. Mr Gibson hasn't said.'

Willie smiled inwardly at the use of the title Mister.

'There are some trees needing felling so it might be that.' Ian shrugged. 'On the other hand it could be any of a dozen things. I won't know until I'm given my instructions.'

'Would you say you've learnt a lot?'

'Oh certainly. But more importantly I've learnt how much more I've still got to learn.'

Willie chuckled, pleased by his son's progress. When he passed on, the estate would be left in good hands. Of that he now had no doubt.

'Was there . . . anyone special when you were away studying?' Willie asked casually.

'You mean a girl?'

'That's right.'

Ian shook his head. 'I met a few nice lassies I have to admit, but no one you would call special. Why?'

'You'll get married one day and I just wondered . . . Well, you understand.'

'When I meet someone like that you'll be the first to know. All right?'

'All right,' Willie agreed.

He moved to stand beside Ian. 'Talking of loving this

place, your mother certainly did. She said to me once that every day she spent here was a sheer joy.'

Ian smiled to hear that. 'I still miss her.'

'As do I, son. As do I. She was a wonderful woman with an enormous heart.'

Willie's face clouded with memory recalling Mary's death from influenza. Her last words, as he'd held her in his arms, were that she loved him. What a terrible loss that had been. He'd thought the anguish of her passing would kill him as well.

'I'm glad you've long since made up your differences with Georgina,' he said softly. 'As I explained a dozen times in the past, she was never trying to take your mother's place.'

'I understand that now,' Ian replied. 'It was stupid of me, and selfish, to expect you to go through the rest of your life alone.'

'You were young, lad, and deeply hurt. You saw Georgina as an intrusion on your mother's memory. But, as they say, life goes on. Even I had to accept that after a while. And you can't deny Georgina's been good for me, not to mention yourself and Rose.'

Ian thought he couldn't deny it. Georgina made Willie happy and that was what counted. 'Tell you what, Pa, why don't we go for a walk? Just the pair of us, together.'

Willie nodded. 'I'd like that. A lot.'

'We could go down to the churchyard and pay our respects?'

'We could do, Ian. We could indeed.'

A beautiful warmth pervaded Willie as they left the room. Moments like these were so precious.

Kathleen glanced round in surprise as a long-faced Bridie entered the kitchen. 'What are you doing home at this hour?

Why aren't you at work?'

'I got laid off, Ma.'

'Laid . . . Oh my God! Your father will be furious.'

'It wasn't my fault, Ma. Do you think I wanted to be shown the door? Hardly.' Bridie slumped into a chair. 'There were three of us got the push this time. And I was one.'

Kathleen, who'd been washing dishes, dried her hands on a towel. This was awful.

'Could I have a cup of tea? I need one.'

'Aye, me as well.' Kathleen busied herself with the kettle, her mind whirling.

'Pa can't blame me, Ma. It would be completely unfair if he did.'

Kathleen knew that to be true enough. But you could never be sure with Pat, all he would see was a wage not coming into the house. It would be just like him to fly off the handle.

'Teresa's still there. Though worried sick she'll be next.' Bridie shook her head. 'I simply can't understand why there's been such a slump in sales. Glasgow folk have aye been heavy lemonade drinkers.'

Bridie was still in a state of shock from her sacking. She'd guessed the moment she'd been summoned to the manager's office what lay in store for her. And her guess had been only too right.

'Well, you'll just have to get something else,' Kathleen declared. 'First thing the morn's morn you're out doing the rounds. And tonight we'll look in your da's paper to see if there's anything there.'

Bridie nodded her agreement.

'And I'll ask around when I'm out and about. There's always the possibility that someone will have heard of a job going.' A possibility, but not much of one, Kathleen thought.

*   *   *

Hettie Riach's eyes were filled with tears when Jack finally stopped talking. 'So what do you think?' he asked after a few seconds' hiatus.

'It's a smashing idea for a book, Jack. I . . .' She broke off, then smiled. 'It's about us, isn't it?'

'More or less. Though changed somewhat. I want a happy ending. The hero doesn't come back blinded and scarred in my story.'

She went over and knelt in front of him. Reaching up she gently stroked his cheek. 'You'll always be my hero. For ever and for ever.'

A lump came into his throat. 'It's funny how things work out, isn't it? If it hadn't been for the war and my wounds we'd probably never have got together.' He paused, then added, 'And what a loss that would have been.'

'For both of us, Jack. For both of us.'

'Are you certain? You don't regret anything?'

'No,' she whispered. 'I swear.'

He recalled the cocky gallant of yesteryear, the dashing figure who'd used Hettie as no better than a common whore. Paying her for their weekly rendezvous where he'd have his way with her. What a different man he was now from that person.

He grasped Hettie by the hand. 'You're the best thing that's ever happened to me, Hettie. God does indeed move in mysterious ways.'

'Your husband must have left quite a bit of this stuff behind,' Pat commented drily to Geraldine Buchanan. This was the fourth time he'd been invited to stay on and have a beer.

Geraldine dropped her gaze. 'To be truthful, Pat, I've bought the last couple in.'

He raised a bushy eyebrow.

'I enjoy the company you see. It gets so lonely being on your own.'

'I can imagine.'

'And being new here I haven't any friends in the area. Oh, the neighbours are polite enough, but that's as far as it's gone so far.'

'Where did you move from?' he asked.

'Paisley.'

He waited for her to go on, and when she didn't asked, 'Why was that?'

She had no intention of giving Pat the real reason behind their move. Dougal had found out about Charlie, the last man she'd been entertaining while Dougal was away. What a ruction that had been, Dougal storming round to Charlie's house and punching him. That evening Dougal had informed her they were moving, he didn't care where as long as it was out of Paisley. She never had discovered who it was had told Dougal or how that person had known about Charlie.

'It was to be closer to Dougal's parents,' she lied. 'Now it's far easier to pop over and see them than it was while we were in Paisley.'

Pat nodded that he understood.

'It's the evenings that are the worst,' Geraldine said. 'They just seem to go on and on when you're alone.'

Pat had another swallow of beer and didn't reply.

'I was wondering . . .' She trailed off and dropped her gaze again.

'Wondering what?' he prompted softly, pretty certain he knew what was coming next.

'Don't get the wrong idea but I was wondering if you'd care to drop by some night. We get on so well that we could have a right old laugh together. I'd lay in some beer of course, and whisky.'

Beer *and* whisky, both compliments of Geraldine. What a temptation. And the rest too, he thought. Get the wrong idea indeed! She must think him daft.

'I'd be ever so appreciative,' she said.

I'll bet you would, he thought, regarding her over the rim of his glass. In all his years as a coalman this was the first time he'd ever had an offer like this.

'Well, Pat?'

He decided not to commit himself right away. He had to think this through.

'How about I give you an answer next time I come up with your coal?'

She gave him an alluring smile. 'I doubt your wife would be pleased if you told her.'

'Pleased! She'd have a fit. No, Geraldine, if I do decide to come Kathleen won't be knowing anything about it. I can assure you of that.'

'It gets so lonely,' she repeated wistfully.

Randy cow, he thought.

'Any luck?' Kathleen queried as Bridie walked through the door.

Bridie shook her head.

'Where did you try?'

'Templeton's, the carpet people. They suggested I go back in a month when they might have something. Then I tried a big bread bakery in the Cowcaddens. There was nothing there either.'

Kathleen bit back her disappointment. She'd come to rely on what Bridie gave her at the end of the week, just as she relied on Sean. Little enough though it was in both cases. Damn Pat for being such a boozer.

Bridie sighed. 'I'll go out again tomorrow. Who knows?'

Who indeed, Kathleen thought.

'You on a committee!' Kathleen exclaimed in astonishment.

'Aye, me.'

Kathleen stared at Pat in wonderment. 'Would you credit it.'

'I was right proud I can tell you. It's quite an honour for the Union to ask you to serve on a committee.'

'What's the committee about?' Sean queried from where he was sitting.

'The taking care of widows and orphans,' Pat replied glibly.

Sean shook his head. 'Don't take offence, Pa, there's none intended. But it's hard to see you on a committee. You're not the type.'

Pat winked at his son. 'Hidden qualities, Sean.'

'What's a committee?' Alison piped up.

'A group of people who talk about things and then decide on them,' Pat informed her.

'Is it important to be on a committee?'

'Very, lassie. Indeed it is.'

'And what nights will this committee be held?' Kathleen enquired.

He played his trump card. 'Fridays.'

Kathleen's eyes lit up. That meant Pat wouldn't be going to the pub. What a blessing, not to mention saving of money. This was terrific news.

'It might vary of course,' Pat went on. 'But as far as I understand it will mainly be Friday nights.'

Kathleen couldn't have been more delighted.

'Well, are you proud of me, girl?'

Kathleen went to him and pecked him on the cheek. 'I am, Pat. I never thought a husband of mine would be on a committee. That's quite something.'

He laughed. 'You'll see me in a new light now, eh?'

'I will that,' she replied, pride swelling within her. Her man on a committee! He'd be running for Parliament next. On the Labour ticket of course.

Hook, line and sinker, Pat congratulated himself. The committee thing had been inspirational, so it had.

Inspirational.

Despite three large drams in the pub round the corner Pat was still nervous as hell. He'd never done anything like this before. He was quite unnerved.

Think of the beer and whisky, he reminded himself. Aye, think of those and get cracking. It's not as if she was ugly or anything, quite the opposite. And his for the taking.

He timidly knocked on the door and waited.

What a fool he'd been, Pat reflected ruefully. What a bloody idiot. They'd sat there drinking for hours and he hadn't made a move. Not a single one, not even to kiss her.

He closed his eyes, remembering the vision that had been Geraldine Buchanan. And a vision she'd been too. Dressed up to the nines, smelling like . . . well, no woman he'd ever smelt before.

When he'd left her disappointment had been obvious, though she hadn't said anything. It had been simply, with a big smile, I hope you'll come again soon, Pat.

Would he? He didn't know.

Imagine him being scared! It was a joke when you thought about it. Him, Pat Flynn, scared of a woman. Scared to get to grips with her. And yet he had been. He groaned.

'Pat?'

He opened his eyes to stare at Kathleen who was gazing at him in concern.

'Are you all right, Pat?'

'A wee bit of indigestion that's all. They had some sandwiches there that couldn't have agreed with me.'

'I must say you looked real smart when you went out to your committee. Collar and tie and everything.'

'Aye, well you have to.'

'And it all went well?'

'Didn't I say it did.'

'And you spoke?'

'Once or twice.'

He glanced over at Bridie whose head, as so often, was buried in a book. He couldn't imagine where she got her bookishness from. Certainly not him, or Kathleen. During their entire married life together he'd never known either of them open a book to read.

He yawned. 'I suppose I'd better get on through. Being on a committee makes you tired.'

'Especially after a hard day's work,' Kathleen added sympathetically.

'Aye, it does that.'

Bloody idiot, he thought, heaving himself out of his chair. But at least the beer and whisky had been good, and lots of it.

Ian, sitting on a fallen tree, opened the packet of sandwiches that had been made up for his lunch. He was starving, but then who wouldn't be, grafting the way he had that morning.

'What have you got the day?' Jimmy Carruthers asked in a friendly way. He was one of the four of them working together.

Ian peered inside the sandwich he'd taken from the packet. 'This one's egg.'

'I like egg,' Jimmy commented affably. 'I often have it myself.'

'What's yours?'

'Spread.'

Ian loathed spread, no matter what sort. Unscrewing his flask he poured himself some coffee.

As he hungrily munched, Ian reflected on the plans for the estate that had recently been forming in his mind, plans he wouldn't mention to Willie until he was manager.

The estate was well run, there was no denying that. But times change and Willie hadn't really moved with them. Ian didn't blame his father, that's the way Willie was. Someone straight out of the old school.

Ian continued eating and ruminating, finding the former satisfying, the latter exciting in the extreme.

'Let me get this straight,' Andrew said. It was another of his and Jack's nights at the local. 'The plot is about a domestic servant who's secretly in love with her employer, a young wealthy landowner. Right?'

'Right,' Jack nodded.

Andrew couldn't help but smile. 'And this landowner doesn't know until he gets back from the war?'

'That's correct.'

Andrew sat back in his chair and gazed at his friend. 'Why do I think this has a somewhat familiar ring about it?'

Jack feigned innocence. 'Do you?'

'It wouldn't be about you and Hettie by any chance?'

Jack had the grace to blush. 'Certainly not.'

'Are you sure? Your plays have been autobiographical after all, about your experiences in the trenches. So why not your book?'

Jack cleared his throat. 'Hettie was never a domestic servant.'

'She was your housekeeper when you first moved in to the cottage. And you employed her before that.'

'True.'

Andrew laughed. 'You never were a good liar, old cock.'

Jack had a drink of beer while he thought. Damn Andrew for seeing through his story. He'd wanted that to remain strictly between Hettie and himself.

Suddenly it dawned on Andrew where Jack had got the idea for the arrangement between him and Ellen. It wasn't something Jack had heard about at all; a similar arrangement had existed between Jack and Hettie. Of course! It made sense.

'I think it a good plot, as far as it goes,' Andrew said slowly.

'Do you?'

'But a bit thin so far, wouldn't you say.'

Jack shrugged. 'I've got to work out the details, flesh the whole thing out so to speak.'

'Can I make a comment?'

'Of course.'

'Your protagonist comes back safe and sound I take it. All in one piece?'

'Uh-huh.'

'It might be more poignant if he returned disabled to find out the servant still loves him despite that.'

Jack tensed. 'What sort of disablement?'

'How about an amputee? God knows, there are enough of those came home from France. A chap who'd lost both legs for instance.'

'I want a happy ending, Andrew.'

'To my way of thinking that is a happy ending. The chap reappears thinking his life is more or less finished. Only it isn't. I do believe you could do a lot with that.'

'Hmmh,' Jack murmured.

Andrew snapped his fingers. 'Of course!'

'Of course what?'

'What if . . . I'm no writer, mind. This is only a suggestion. Instead of the domestic simply being secretly in love with him, what if they'd had an affair before the war?'

Alarm flared in Jack. Had Andrew guessed about him and Hettie?

'He'd have to be a cad naturally, a real bounder who was just using her for his own pleasure, completely oblivious to the fact of her true feelings.'

Jack winced inwardly. For hadn't it truly been something like that?

Andrew went on. 'When he comes back, minus his legs, he's a totally changed man. No longer the cad and bounder. She helps him come to terms with his injuries and during this period he genuinely falls for her. Eventually they marry and Bob's your uncle!'

Andrew beamed across the table. 'That sounds pretty good to me.'

Jack sipped his whisky and didn't reply.

'Well, old cock?'

'It has potential,' Jack murmured.

'More than potential I'd say.'

'Maybe you should be writing this book and not me,' Jack commented drily.

'Hardly. Haven't got that sort of imagination.'

'Well, you were doing all right there for a few minutes.'

Andrew laughed. 'I was too, wasn't I? But no, writing is your province, Jack. Not mine.'

A cad and a bounder, Jack thought. That hurt.

'Anyway, I'll leave it with you,' Andrew declared. 'Only trying to help after all. That's what friends are for.'

Andrew threw his whisky down his throat. 'Drink up and I'll get a couple more drams in.'

'It's my round,' Jack said, reaching for his wallet.

Andrew stood. 'By the way, have you got a title yet for this epic?'

'I'm considering *An Apple From Eden*.'

'*An Apple From Eden*,' Andrew mused. 'I like it.'

'He suggested what!' an aghast Hettie exclaimed.

Jack repeated himself.

Hettie sat. 'Does he know about us? Have you ever mentioned that you used to pay me, Jack Riach?'

'I swear, Hettie, not a word.'

'It would be so embarrassing if he did know. Imagine if it got out that I'd taken money from you before the war. My reputation would be in tatters. Our reputation. Oh Jack!' she suddenly wailed.

'There's no question of that,' Jack assured her. 'Andrew never mentioned cash when we were talking. Only that the couple had had an affair and that the chap in question was a bounder who returns from the war completely changed as a person.'

That calmed Hettie a little. 'You swear you've never told him?'

'I just have sworn. Only two people know about you and me, and that's you and I.'

Hettie swallowed hard. 'I got the wind up there for a moment.'

'There's nothing to worry about, I promise.'

'I sincerely hope so.' But there was a niggle of doubt in Hettie's mind.

Sean strolled over to the lassie who'd caught his eye, a pretty piece with dark hair and dark eyes. She was wearing a long blue dress with a cream lace collar and turned-back cuffs that he thought rather becoming. Her shoes were black of the button-bar variety.

'Are you for up?' he queried.

She rose and smiled tremulously at him. 'Aye, fine.'

'Right then.'

He grasped her by the arm and steered her on to the floor. As the dance had been organised by the chapel he knew she must be Catholic.

'What's your name?' he asked as the band struck up.

'Muriel. And you're Sean Flynn.'

He glanced sharply at her. 'How did you know that?'

A combination of fear and awe came into her eyes. 'You're the leader of this new gang, I hear.'

'Aye, that's so. The Samurai.'

'Is it true you gave two Prods a real doing, marked them and cut off one's thumb?'

His chest expanded with pride. 'True as you're here the night.'

Muriel shivered, unable to believe that such a worthy had asked her to dance. 'You must be right hard,' she said.

He gave her a condescending smile.

So, people were talking about him and the Samurai. Word was getting round. It made him feel ten feet tall.

At the end of the final number he said – didn't ask but said – he'd take her home. Muriel was thrilled.

He acknowledged a conspiratorial wink from Noddy Gallagher as he swaggered, with Muriel on his arm, from the hall.

Chapter 6

'Come away in. I'd almost given you up.' Geraldine greeted a nervous Pat.

'Sorry I'm late. It was just one thing after another.'

'It doesn't matter. You're here now, that's all that counts.'

Geraldine closed the door again, her eyes gleaming. She was determined this wasn't going to be a repetition of the last visit which had been so dreadfully disappointing.

She ushered him through to the sitting room where she instructed him to take a seat.

'You look smashing,' he declared. Her dress was cream, the hem about six inches above her ankles. It was tied loosely at her waist by a strip of matching material.

'Why, thank you.'

That perfume, he thought. Erotic wasn't in Pat's vocabulary, but if it had been it's the word he would have used to describe the perfume and the effect it had on him.

'Dram?'

'Please.'

She moved sinuously across to a sideboard and opened it. He couldn't take his eyes off her buttocks when she bent over. They mesmerised him.

'Soda as last time?' she queried.

'Aye, that's right.'

She poured a small one for herself, a large one for Pat, adding soda to both. She then bent again to retrieve a bottle of beer from the same sideboard cupboard.

'There you are,' she smiled, handing Pat the bottle and his dram.

'Better service than the pub,' he joked.

Geraldine sat facing him and they proceeded to make small talk, she periodically getting up and refilling his glass.

Pat sighed, that well-known warm glow spreading through him. Oh, but this was grand. The very dab.

'I couldn't help but notice, and I hope you don't think me being rude, that you're a hairy man, Pat,' Geraldine said in what was almost a croon. 'Dougal's the same way. Hairy all over.'

'I'm certainly that,' Pat retorted.

Something twisted inside Geraldine's stomach. It was taking all her self-control not to throw herself at him and rip his clothes off.

'I adore hairy men,' Geraldine went on. 'I find them so . . . attractive.'

'Oh?'

'So attractive,' she repeated, a husk coming into her throat.

'I, eh . . . I don't ever really think about it. That's how I've been for most of my life. Ever since I sort of grew up like.'

Geraldine had another sip of whisky. 'Why don't you come and sit beside me on this sofa,' she suggested, patting the cushion next to her.

'Can I have another drink first?'

'Certainly, help yourself.'

Geraldine was ready to home in for the kill.

Bridie felt wretched. She'd been so close, so very close. Now she was home all she wanted to do was burst into tears.

'Well?' Kathleen demanded anxiously when she entered the kitchen.

'I had it, Ma. I know I did. And then he asked me what school I went to and that was that.'

Kathleen swore under her breath.

'The moment I mentioned St Xavier's his whole attitude changed. He went on with the interview as though my being Catholic didn't matter, but it did.'

'The dirty Protestant dog,' Kathleen muttered. The old Glasgow story, what school did you go to? Not are you Catholic or Protestant, but which school did you go to? How many Catholics had missed out because of that question. Catholics without number.

Bridie ran a hand over her face. 'It was a great job too. Good money. And then . . .' She broke off and sobbed.

'There there, lass,' Kathleen said, hurrying to her daughter and enveloping Bridie in her arms. 'It isn't the end of the world.'

'It's so unfair, Ma. Why should me being Catholic make any difference? It's whether or not I can do the job well that should count.'

'I know, Bridie. The world's a harsh place at times. And as you say unfair. But there we are. That's how it is and we just have to live with it.'

Bridie sobbed again.

'Shall I put the kettle on?'

'That would be nice, Ma.'

'And I have a wee packet of chocolate biscuits in. We'll have a couple of those each. But don't mention them to Alison or that greedy madam will scoff what's left given half the chance.'

Kathleen, heart heavy with Bridie's disappointment and the reason for it, held her daughter for another minute before releasing her.

'I thought I might write to Andrew Drummond and propose we visit next month. What do you think, Georgina?'

'That's fine by me, Willie, as long as you feel you can get away.'

Rose's face had lit up. At long last she was to get to see Andrew again. 'How wonderful!' she exclaimed, and clapped her hands together.

Georgina glanced over at Rose in surprise. Now why should her stepdaughter be so excited about going to see Andrew Drummond?

'I'll stay behind if you don't mind, Pa,' Ian declared. 'I don't want to disrupt my work here.'

Willie nodded his approval.

Disrupting his work had nothing to do with Ian's decision not to accompany the rest of the family. The real reason was that he didn't like Andrew Drummond very much. There was something disturbing about the man that bothered him. Something he didn't trust.

Rose was positively bubbling inside. How she'd been looking forward to this.

'You seem very keen, Rose,' Georgina commented quietly.

'And why not,' Rose prevaricated. 'It'll be lovely to go somewhere different, to get off the estate for a while.' Then, ingenuously, 'Surely there's nothing wrong with that?'

'Nothing,' Georgina agreed, still wondering.

Ian roused himself from his chair. 'If you don't mind I'm off to my bed. Today was a killer.'

'Not too much for you, brother?' Rose remarked sweetly.

He glared at her. 'Not in the least. It was tiring, that's all.'

Willie sighed. Did those two never let up? What annoyed him most was that it was all so unnecessary. Why couldn't they just get on?

'Goodnight, lad,' he said, forcing a smile on to his face.

'Goodnight, Pa, Georgina.' Ian drew in a deep breath. 'Goodnight, Rose.'

'Goodnight, brother dear.'

Rose went back to thinking about Andrew Drummond.

Willie glanced up from his paperwork when there was a knock on the door. 'Come in,' he called out. He was dreading this, it was so distasteful.

An ashen-faced Lizzie McTaggart appeared followed by Mrs Coltart, the housekeeper. Mrs Coltart's expression was grim in the extreme.

Willie leant back in his chair to stare at Lizzie through eyes that had gone quite cold. 'Well, Lizzie, what do you have to say for yourself?' he demanded.

'Oh please, sir, let me have another chance. I'll never do it again, I promise,' she blurted out.

'But it wasn't the first time though, was it, Lizzie? According to Mrs Coltart you've stolen quite a number of things.'

'Some of which were found in her room,' Mrs Coltart commented quietly.

Lizzie hung her head in shame.

'All small articles, knick-knacks and the like,' Mrs Coltart went on. 'Which she no doubt thought wouldn't be missed. But I knew they'd gone all right. It was only a case of finding the thief.'

There was a few seconds' silence, then Willie asked softly, 'Why, Lizzie? Why?'

Lizzie shrugged.

'That's hardly an answer.'

'I thought to sell them to make a wee bit extra,' Lizzie finally choked.

'Indeed.'

Lizzie swallowed hard. 'I know it was wrong. I'm sorry. Honest I am. Please don't sack me, I like it here. Everyone's so friendly.'

Mrs Coltart snorted. 'If you want my opinion, Mr Seaton, should you find a rotten apple in the barrel then throw it out. There's nothing else for it.'

'I could prosecute, you know, Lizzie. That might mean going to prison.'

A thoroughly frightened Lizzie reeled where she stood. 'Oh, Mr Seaton, you wouldn't do that. The shame.'

'Aye,' Willie murmured. 'Shame indeed.'

'My ma and da would be mortified. They'd disown me so they would. I couldn't bear that.'

Willie knew the McTaggarts, a fine upstanding, church-going family. Mortified they'd certainly be. As for disowning their daughter, that was a distinct possibility.

'Mrs Coltart, any further comments?'

'No, sir. I've stated my feelings.'

Mrs Coltart was right, he told himself. A rotten apple had to be discarded. Though, because of the parents, it pained him to do so. Lizzie had to be punished, there was nothing else for it.

'I won't prosecute,' he declared, which brought a gasp of relief from Lizzie. 'But I'm afraid I will have to let you go.'

'Oh please, sir,' she pleaded.

Willie shook his head. 'Nor will I give you a reference. That's out of the question.'

'But . . . but . . .' Lizzie stuttered.

'I simply can't, Lizzie. What if you should succumb to temptation again? That would reflect on me.'

'I think you're getting off lightly, my girl,' Mrs Coltart said to her.

'You have half an hour to pack your things and leave. Mrs Coltart, stay with her the entire time if you don't mind and escort her from the premises. When you've done that come back and see me here. We'll have to discuss a replacement.'

'Yes, sir.'

Thoroughly distasteful, Willie thought as he rocked forward and continued with his paperwork.

'Pat, is there something wrong?'

Pat tensed in the darkness. He and Kathleen were in bed. 'How do you mean?'

'It's been weeks now since . . . Well, it's just so unlike you.'

She meant lovemaking of course. The fact was he'd gone right off Kathleen since sampling Geraldine's delights.

'Are you ill in some way?' Kathleen further probed.

'No,' came the gruff reply.

'Well then?'

'I just haven't felt like it, nothing more.'

Kathleen considered that. It had certainly never happened before. During their entire married life Pat had been regular as clockwork where that was concerned.

'Now wheesht, woman, and go to sleep.'

He'd have to make an effort soon, he thought. Otherwise Kathleen might get suspicious.

He imagined Geraldine, picturing the pair of them together, and smiled. He still couldn't get over what it was like to be with her. Utterly fantastic. That body *and* free booze too.

Sheer bloody paradise.

'Hey, Sean, haud on a bit.'

Sean turned to see Bill O'Connell hurrying towards him. The pair of them were in a long stream of men leaving Barry's Iron Foundry after the day's shift.

Bill fell into step beside Sean. 'How's it going?' Sean asked.

'Real dandy. And you?'

'Couldn't be better. So what can I do for you?'

'I was wondering, Sean, you and me have known each other a long time now. Right?'

Sean nodded that was so.

'I've been hearing about this gang of yours. The Samurai, isn't it?'

'Correct. It's Japanese you know. That's what their warriors were called.'

'Is that a fact?'

'It is. I chose the name myself.'

'Real class, Sean. Real class.'

Sean smiled in appreciation.

'The thing is, I rather fancy joining. If you'd have me that is.'

Sean considered the request, and couldn't see any objection. 'The others have a say, mind. It's not just up to me.'

'But you could put in a good word like. Would you do that for me? I'd be hellishly obliged.'

'Of course I will.'

'Thanks.'

Sean thought with satisfaction this would be the fourth new member since the Samurai was formed. He had no doubt the others would be only too pleased to welcome Bill into the fold. Apart from anything else Bill was a right hard nut. He'd be a real asset.

'Tell you what,' Sean said. 'We're having a meeting the morrow night. You wait for me outside my close at half seven and I'll personally take you along. How's that?'

Bill beamed. 'I'll be there. You can count on it.'

'On the dot, mind. I'm not hanging about.'

'On the dot,' Bill promised.

'There just isn't anyone available locally, Mr Seaton. I've asked everywhere,' Mrs Coltart announced.

'Hmmh,' Willie mused. If his housekeeper said that was so, then it was.

Mrs Coltart waited patiently for a reply.

'I suppose we'll just have to advertise,' Willie said eventually. 'We have done so before as you know. Though I have to say I prefer local lassies.'

'Shall I leave that to you then, sir?'

'Yes, I'll deal with it, Mrs Coltart. Thank you for what you've done.'

She left him to it.

Ellen squealed. 'That hurt!'

Andrew grinned to himself. Of course it had hurt, he'd intended it to. 'Are you complaining?' he queried, a hard edge to his voice.

'No, not at all,' Ellen replied hastily, thinking of the money.

'Now keep quiet. I don't want anyone to hear.'

Ellen gritted her teeth as Andrew continued with what he'd been doing.

'Can we get Mrs Black to call? I've lost weight and my clothes need taking in,' Rose requested of Georgina. Mrs Black was the wife of one of the estate workers and a first-class seamstress, her occupation before marrying.

Georgina studied her stepdaughter. Rose was quite right, she had lost weight.

Rose ran a finger along the inside of the waistband of the skirt she was wearing. 'See what I mean.'

Georgina nodded her approval. 'Well done you, Rose. I've noticed you haven't been having puddings of late.'

And she'd been doing without other things too, Rose thought with satisfaction. The effort had been worth it. And she intended losing more weight before their visit to Drummond House. She wanted to be sleek and svelte when she next met Andrew.

'I've taken a leaf out of your book.' Rose smiled at Georgina.

Georgina had a thought. 'I do believe it's time we went to Edinburgh again. Instead of having your current wardrobe redone we can replace it.'

'A whole new wardrobe!' Rose gasped. Pa wouldn't like that. She could almost hear his objections.

'Well, maybe not an entire new wardrobe,' Georgina replied, thinking that had been something of a rash proposal. 'But certainly quite a few items. It is your birthday coming up after all. I shall persuade Willie that what we get will be his and my present to you.'

Georgina smiled inwardly. She knew exactly how to get Willie to agree to this. She'd entice him in the bedroom, then, when he was all worked up, put it to him. It was a ploy she'd used countless times before and one which never failed.

And while in Edinburgh she'd also buy for herself. She wanted to look her very best when they went to Drummond House. Andrew Drummond rather fascinated her.

Shopping, it was the best tonic in the world and something she absolutely adored.

Sean was passing a junk shop when he caught sight of an article in the window that brought him up short. Moments later the door bell was pinging as he went inside.

The shopkeeper was old and fat with thinning hair, a long lock of which he had plastered across the top of his forehead.

'Yes, sir, can I be of assistance?'

Sean jerked a thumb in the direction of the window. 'There's a sword in there I'd like to look at.'

'You mean the Japanese sword, sir?'

'Aye, that's the one.'

Sean watched the shopkeeper move away. A Japanese sword in Glasgow! What a stroke of luck. He might have searched high and low for years before coming across one for sale. It was his lucky day.

'There we are, sir.' The shopkeeper smiled, laying the sword in front of Sean.

Sean wrinkled his nose. 'It's a bit rusty, isn't it?'

'Some rust, I grant you that, sir. But it will polish up beautifully.'

'That's as might be.'

Sean lifted the sword and pulled it slowly from its black enamelled scabbard. The rust was mainly confined to the hilt, with only a few spots on the blade.

'What's the asking price?' he queried.

'Thirty shillings, sir.'

Sean pretended to be shocked. 'You must be joking! What are you, a comedian or something?'

The shopkeeper inclined his head slightly. He was used to haggling. 'These are extremely rare,' he countered.

'So what? It's only an old sword when all's said and done. It's probably been lying in that window of yours for years.' Sean ran a hand over the scabbard. 'See what I mean!' he exclaimed when his palm came away covered in dust.

The shopkeeper grinned ruefully. 'It has been with me for a while, I admit. But that doesn't take away from its value.'

'I'll tell you what,' Sean said, sounding reluctant. 'I'll give you ten bob and I reckon I'm still being done.'

The haggling continued until at last a triumphant Sean left the premises having bought the sword for a pound. A pound he could ill afford but nonetheless a pound he considered well spent.

'Here, look at this, Bridie,' Kathleen said, tapping the newspaper she'd been reading.

'What is it, Ma?'

'A position as a maid on a big estate.'

Bridie rose from her chair and hurried across the room to stare over her mother's shoulder at the ad Kathleen was indicating. 'I don't know,' she demurred. 'Look where it is. It would mean leaving home.'

'Aye, that's so,' Kathleen agreed.

'What are the wages?' Pat asked.

'That's not mentioned,' Kathleen informed him.

He sniffed. 'A domestic servant. A bit of a comedown for a Flynn. Plenty of Irish folk have been domestics, but never us Flynns. We've always considered ourselves above that.'

'Beggars can't be choosers,' Kathleen commented quietly.

'Unemployment the way it is there are bound to be lots of applicants,' Bridie said.

'True enough,' Kathleen agreed. 'But it wouldn't do any harm to write. No harm at all.'

'And it is in the country,' Bridie mused, straightening up, thinking how wonderful it must be to live there. Trees, grass, animals no doubt. The prospect sent a little thrill racing through her. What a difference it would be to the life she'd known so far. The dirty grimy Glasgow streets, the filth, the squalor. Air that could make you choke when you breathed it in.

Suddenly she was filled with excitement, wanting this job badly. 'I'll write straight away and catch the morning post. There's nothing to lose after all except a sheet of paper, an envelope and a stamp.'

The country, Bridie thought again, eyes shining. Oh but wouldn't that be lovely.

'What's that you're carrying?' Sammy Renton queried when Sean strolled into the room of the condemned house where the others were already gathered and awaiting his arrival.

Sean held up the long brown paper-wrapped object. 'You'll never guess. It's a wee present from me to us all.'

'Is it a piece of fancy plumbing,' Mo Binchy joked, and guffawed.

'Or a year-old turd?' Dan Smith said, which raised a laugh all round.

'Very funny,' Sean retorted, and began unwrapping the object.

'Wow!' Bobby O'Toole exclaimed when the sword was

revealed. A sword that sparkled and was completely free of rust, Sean having attended to these matters in the privacy of his bedroom.

'Holy Mother of God,' an awed Noddy Gallagher whispered.

'It's the genuine Japanese article,' Sean proclaimed, brandishing the weapon.

'Is it sharp?' Bill O'Connell queried.

'As my razor. It would cut your head off quick as wink.'

'No thanks, Sean,' Bill hastily replied, fingering his throat. 'I'll go without that if you don't mind.'

That raised another laugh.

'Would anyone else like a demonstration of head cutting?' Sean teased.

The response was a chorus of refusals.

Sean waved the sword in front of him. 'Not bad, eh?'

'Where did you get it?' Jim Gallagher asked.

'A junk shop I happened to be passing. Cost me a quid.'

'She's a beauty,' Noddy Gallagher commented.

'It is indeed,' Sean agreed.

'Can I hold it?' Mo requested.

'Aye, sure.' Sean handed it over, Mo holding the sword gingerly while he admired it.

'I thought we'd put it in pride of place on the mantelpiece. What do you say?'

Sammy Renton nodded at Sean. 'That's a grand idea.'

'Will you take it outside anytime?' Mo Binchy enquired.

Sean's eyes gleamed. 'Who knows, Mo. Who knows?' He grinned wolfishly. 'Maybe.'

'So, what's the big mystery?' Bridie demanded of Teresa, the latter having arrived at her house to urgently request they go for a walk together.

'I couldn't talk with your parents and sister about. What I have to say is confidential like.'

Bridie noted how twitchy her friend was. 'Well?'

'You know I've been going out with that chap Tony from work.'

Bridie smiled. 'And what a surprise it was when he asked you. You were quite taken aback from what you said.'

'I was. He'd never shown any interest before, and then suddenly, out the blue, would I like to go out? Darned tooting I would. I jumped at the chance.'

'So what's the problem?'

Teresa swallowed hard. 'Remember that dance we went to when the bloke mauled you in the back close.'

Bridie remembered only too well. 'Horrible it was. He was a right animal.' She stopped abruptly. 'Has Tony done the same to you?'

Teresa coloured. 'In a way, only in my case it wasn't a mauling, more of his being insistent.'

'Insistent?'

'Aye, you know.'

'You didn't let him touch you . . . *there*, did you?'

Teresa was now bright red. 'I did.'

'Oh Teresa, how could you!'

'It was easy enough at the time, Bridie. He's not a bad looker, and his kissing! I just melted. I didn't know whether I was coming or going, only that I liked it.'

Bridie shook her head. 'I'm ashamed of you, Teresa Kelly, I really am.'

Teresa almost changed her mind then about telling Bridie the rest. But she had to confide in someone, unburden herself. 'I'm afraid it went further than touching,' she stated in a quiet, cracked voice.

Bridie was aghast. 'You mean . . . ?'

Teresa nodded.

'All the way?'

'All the way,' Teresa repeated.

Bridie couldn't believe she was hearing this. It was awful. Apart from anything else, what if Tony opened his mouth and word got round?

'That's not the worst thing though,' Teresa went on, tears beginning to overflow.

Bridie knew with sudden certainty what was coming next.

'I've missed my monthly.'

Chapter 7

Andrew bustled into the drawing room where the Seatons were grouped together talking. 'Sorry I wasn't here to meet you but I got caught up at the distillery. A minor crisis that I had to sort.'

He was slightly dishevelled, a lock of hair having escaped over his forehead, which Georgina thought charming. Catching his eye she smiled.

'I see you've already been given a drink, good.' Andrew nodded his approval to Ellen who was also in the room.

'One for you, sir?' Ellen enquired.

'Please. A Drummond.'

'Well,' said Andrew, briskly rubbing his hands together. 'How was the journey?'

'Thoroughly enjoyable,' Willie replied. 'I must say your Perthshire scenery is quite beautiful.'

'Why, thank you. I've always considered it to be so.'

The long-awaited moment had finally arrived, Rose thought gleefully. She was in Andrew's company again.

And how wonderful that felt. A small flush of excitement crept on to her cheeks which she hoped no one noticed.

'Here you are, sir,' Ellen said, offering a silver tray to Andrew.

'Thank you, Ellen.' So prim and demure while on duty, he smiled inwardly. Well, he knew what the real Ellen was like, a different creature entirely.

Andrew held his glass aloft in a toast. '*Slainte*. And welcome to Drummond House.'

'To Drummond House and you, Andrew,' Willie responded.

Sean was alone in the condemned tenement, sitting gently caressing the sword on his lap.

What now for the Samurai? he wondered. Were they just a gang, a bunch of hooligans? Or could they be something else? Only what?

The other city gangs did nothing, at least not that he was aware of, except fight and create holy terror wherever they went. Surely there could be more to it than that.

And then he had the glimmerings of an idea. Profit. Was that it?

Not just a gang but some sort of business that made them money.

'Money,' he murmured aloud. 'Money.'

He continued caressing the sword, deep in thought.

'This saddle of lamb is really superb,' Charlotte, Andrew's sister, pronounced. 'Mrs Clark has excelled herself.' Mrs Clark was Andrew's cook who'd been with the family for years.

'I'll pass on your compliments,' Andrew replied.

'No need, I'll tell her myself later. I'll also ask her what

96

she's done to make it different to any saddle of lamb I've ever tasted before.'

Andrew laughed. 'Oh come on, sis, you know Mrs Clark won't divulge any of her secrets.'

'She will to me,' Charlotte stated firmly. 'You see if she doesn't.'

How contented his sister looked, Andrew observed. Being a minister's wife and a mother suited her. He couldn't have been more pleased for her, she thoroughly deserved her happiness.

Charlotte was doing a splendid job of hiding the unease she always felt on returning to Drummond House. On the one hand it held so many wonderful memories of her childhood and growing up. On the other, it was in this house that her first husband Geoffrey had hanged himself.

Poor Geoffrey, what a changed man he'd been on returning from the war. So changed she'd hardly recognised him as the same person. She'd put it down to the war, of course, and tried to cope. And then the dreadful truth had finally emerged.

Geoffrey had lost his manhood to a German grenade. The torment he'd gone through because he was unable to be a proper husband, as he put it, to her. Torment and despair that had ultimately driven him to taking his own life.

She closed her eyes, recalling how it had once been between her and Geoffrey. Those golden, carefree days before the conflict, in stark contrast to the time afterwards. There were still occasions, usually late at night when John was fast asleep but she lay awake, when the nightmare vision of Geoffrey hanging there came back to haunt her.

She knew she couldn't blame herself for his suicide. She'd done everything in her power to assure him what had happened didn't matter. Except it had, very much so, to Geoffrey, God rest his soul.

Andrew was thinking how gorgeous Georgina was looking that evening. She was wearing a low-waisted dress in silk georgette. The bodice was cut straight and beaded in a swirly pattern. Thin straps with matching beading snaked across her shoulders. The skirt had soft gathers that fell into points at the hem.

Was it the stunning dress or something else that had brought such a twinkle to her eyes? he wondered. Again, he thought it a pity she was married. And to a friend at that. Forbidden territory. Beyond the Pale.

'I've never met a writer before.' Rose smiled across the table to Jack Riach.

'Me neither,' added Georgina.

Hettie gazed in admiration at Jack, sitting beside him as she always did, helping him with the meal.

'There's one thing I've been wondering about,' Rose said hesitantly.

'Which is?'

She cleared her throat. 'I hope you don't think this rude or insensitive of me, I don't wish to offend.'

Jack guessed the question. 'How does a blind man write? Is that it?'

'Yes,' Rose nodded.

'I'm also curious about that,' Georgina said.

Jack laughed. 'It's simple really. I dictate to Hettie who puts it down on paper. She then reads the dictation back to me and does any changes I wish to make. As I said, simple really.'

'Oh!' Rose exclaimed. Now why hadn't she thought of that. 'You must be a very clever man to write,' Rose went on. 'I envy you the ability.'

'He is clever,' Hettie agreed.

'I wouldn't say that,' Jack demurred.

'Come on, Jack, you're just being modest. You're a hero hereabouts. And I'm not referring to the war either. Getting not just one but *two* plays on the West End stage takes some doing,' John McLean stated.

'I was lucky,' Jack, becoming embarrassed, replied.

'Luck be damned,' Andrew declared. Then, to the rest of the table, 'Jack is about to start his first novel, aren't you, Jack?'

Hettie tensed.

'A novel!' Georgina exclaimed. 'I say. What's it all about?'

'I really don't want to talk about it,' Jack answered. 'Anyway, to be truthful, I'm not quite certain what it's all about myself yet.'

Fibber, Andrew thought. Jack knew well enough. He gestured to Heather, one of the maids, to refill their glasses.

Willie was thoroughly enjoying himself. The meal was splendid as was the company. He couldn't have asked for a better evening. And later, perhaps, he and Andrew could do some more reminiscing. Which might also be the chance to put the proposal he had in mind to Andrew – the reaction to which was uncertain.

'Do you keep horses, Andrew?' Rose queried.

'Of course.'

'Would it be possible to go out for a ride tomorrow morning?'

Andrew recalled another young lady who had also enjoyed riding. That was how he'd met her when her horse had bolted and he'd gone to the rescue. The start of what had become a love affair.

'That's fine, Rose. Tell the groom to give you Sophie. She's probably the best horse for you.'

'Thank you.'

When the main course was cleared away, dessert was offered. Both Rose and Georgina declined.

'Another?' Andrew queried. He and Willie were alone, the McLeans and Riachs having left long since while Georgina and Rose had excused themselves and gone up to bed pleading that it had been a long day.

'Please.'

Andrew fetched the decanter and crossed to Willie, recharging first Willie's glass then his own. They were reminiscing about their time in Ireland.

Willie hesitated, then said, 'It's been on my mind for a while now to go back there, you know. Take Georgina and Rose, make a holiday of it.'

Andrew sat. 'Really.'

'Not for too long, of course, a fortnight seems about right to me. The thing is, I'd love to see old Dublin town again and show Georgina and Rose the sights.'

'When shall you go?'

'In the New Year, certainly before spring when it all starts to get hectic again on the estate.'

Andrew pondered that. 'You might have a rough crossing at that time of year.'

'Possibly.' Willie laughed. 'At least we won't have to worry about damned U-boats and being torpedoed.'

'True,' Andrew mused.

Willie had a sip of whisky. 'Have you ever thought about returning?'

That startled Andrew. 'No, I can't say I have. When I left I . . .' He broke off. 'I certainly never envisaged a return.'

Willie swirled the amber liquid round his glass. 'May I speak openly, Andrew? As one friend to another?'

'Go ahead.' He leant back in his chair and waited.

'It worries me that you've never married. None of my business, of course, but it worries me nonetheless. I can't help thinking you may still be carrying a torch for Alice.'

Andrew continued watching Willie, and didn't reply.

'It seems to me that going back there might help. Lay the ghost so to speak.' Willie took a deep breath. 'If you wish me to shut up just say so.'

Andrew had a swallow of whisky. 'That's all right, old boy,' he said in a voice that was just above a whisper.

'Would I be correct about Alice?'

Andrew gave a self-mocking laugh. 'If anyone had told me before I met her that one day I'd carry a torch for a dead woman, any woman come to that, I would have roared in their face. And yet, that's precisely what's happened. I have met women over the past few years, but no one I could really get interested in. Not that way anyhow.'

Willie nodded that he understood.

'How did you manage it, Willie, after you lost your wife?'

'I don't know,' Willie replied slowly. 'I too thought I'd never be interested again, then I met Georgina and all that changed. I do believe Mary would have given her blessing to the union. In fact I'm convinced of it.'

'Perhaps there's a Georgina somewhere for me,' Andrew mused. 'Though I haven't come across her yet.'

Willie lit a cigarette. 'And Ireland,' he queried through a cloud of smoke. 'Why don't you come with us? We could travel as a foursome, myself, Georgina, Rose and you.'

Would it help? Andrew wondered. He simply didn't know.

'Can you leave the distillery for a couple of weeks?'

'That would depend entirely on Charlotte. She would have to take my place while I was away. But yes, given enough time to arrange things I'm sure I could.'

'Then you'll think about it?'

A number of seconds ticked by before Andrew finally answered. 'I'll think about it,' he promised.

Bridie was hovering by the front door when she heard the postman mount the stairs and then go on past. She turned away in disappointment.

'There should have been a reply by now,' she said to Kathleen on re-entering the kitchen.

'It might still come.'

Bridie shook her head. 'The people on the estate might at least have had the courtesy to answer my letter, even if it was to say I wasn't suitable or the position had already been filled.'

'That's the toffs for you. No manners whatsoever,' Kathleen declared angrily.

Bridie just didn't know where to try next for a job. Despair, which was never far away these days, filled her yet again.

Andrew, Willie and Georgina were emerging from the distillery when Rose appeared riding towards them.

'There she is now,' Willie said. He was cross with his daughter for not turning up when she should.

Rose reined in and slid to the ground. 'Is it over?' she queried.

'Yes it is,' Willie retorted. 'We waited and waited then finally went ahead with the tour when you failed to show. What happened?'

Georgina gave Rose a hard, disapproving look which Rose ignored.

'I'm afraid I got lost.' To Andrew she said, 'Sophie's a beautiful horse. We had a fantastic time together.'

'I'm pleased.' He smiled.

Rose hadn't got lost at all. For the past half-hour she'd been observing the distillery waiting for them to come out again. It was part of a plan she'd hatched the previous night after the arrangement to tour the distillery had been made.

Rose patted Sophie on the nose. 'Who's a lovely girl then. You are, Sophie.'

'You might at least apologise to Andrew,' Willie declared.

'I am sorry, Andrew. Truly I am. I was so looking forward to the tour and now . . .' She pulled a face. 'I've missed it.'

'Hardly your fault you got lost. Easy to do in strange surroundings. Another time perhaps.'

'Unless . . .' She trailed off. 'Probably not. I don't deserve it. I've caused you enough trouble as it is.'

'Hardly trouble, Rose. Unless what?'

'Do you think you could bear to take me round now? I'd be ever so grateful.'

'Rose!' Willie admonished. 'You can't ask that.'

Andrew laughed at her crestfallen expression. 'Of course I can, Rose. I'd be delighted to do so.'

Her heart leapt. The plan had worked. She'd get him to herself after all, just as she'd hoped.

'Could you take Sophie back for me, Pa. Please?'

'I suppose I'll have to,' Willie grumbled, grasping the reins.

'See you both later,' Rose called out as she and Andrew went inside.

*   *   *

'And this is the inner sanctum,' Andrew declared, throwing open the door.

It smelt of him, she thought. A most pleasant odour as far as she was concerned. She glanced around. 'Very workmanlike.'

'I'll take that as a compliment.'

'It was meant as one.'

'So tell me, Rose, what do you think of my distillery? You've seen it all now.'

'Wash stills, pot stills, wort and all sorts of other funny names. It all seems very complicated to me.'

He laughed. 'Not that complicated, I assure you. But it does take some learning which I had to do more or less from scratch when I returned from Ireland. My brother Peter was the one trained to take over, I had no experience of the distillery whatsoever. I soon learnt though, I was a willing pupil.'

He rubbed his hands together. 'Can I offer you a dram? I'm going to have one myself.'

That shocked her. 'Whisky! Women don't drink whisky.'

'My sisters do. They were brought up to it as are all the women in my family. It's a tradition with us.'

'How extraordinary,' she commented.

'How about a weak one with lots of water. Nor will I take offence if you don't like it, whisky is something of an acquired taste.'

'And *strong*,' she pointed out.

'That too.'

She decided to tease him. 'I hope you're not thinking of getting me tipsy in order to take advantage.' She fluttered her eyelashes. 'Are you?'

'Most certainly not,' he protested.

She turned slightly away. 'Who knows? I might even enjoy succumbing.'

The little minx was flirting with him, he thought. Well, well, well.

'You might,' he replied slowly, seeing Rose in quite a different light. She'd lost weight, he now noticed. It suited her. Made her more mature somehow.

And how fetching she looked in her riding gear. Underneath the hacking jacket was a plain white, broadcloth shirt undone at the neck, that tucked into fawn jodphurs which in turn were tucked into black leather riding boots. He wondered what sort of underwear she had on.

Rose felt herself flushing under his direct gaze. Damn! She could have done without that.

Andrew smiled inwardly on seeing the flush. 'I'll get those drams,' he stated, and strode past her.

Rose swallowed hard. What on earth had possessed her to say 'succumb'. God alone knew what he'd made of that.

'Here you are,' Andrew declared. 'Well watered down as promised.'

He held his own glass up in a toast. '*Slainte!*'

'*Slainte*,' she responded, and nervously had a sip. It took all her self-control not to screw her face up in a grimace. Whisky was foul! She'd never tasted anything so awful.

'The verdict?' he queried with a smile.

'Very nice,' she lied.

'I'm impressed.'

'Are you indeed?'

'Oh yes.'

She had another sip, thinking it as foul as the first. If his sisters could drink this stuff then so too could she, she told herself.

When they finally left the distillery her head was swimming.

Georgina, standing at their bedroom window, saw Andrew and Rose coming towards the house. To her surprise she found herself feeling jealous. She wished it was her out there with him.

'What are you staring at?' Willie asked.

'Andrew and Rose on their way back here. They must have enjoyed themselves, they're both laughing.' That fact increased her jealousy. Again she found herself thinking of Andrew in a way she shouldn't.

Georgina turned to Willie. 'Are you all right, my dear?'

It was now his turn to be surprised. 'Yes, fine. Why do you ask?'

She went to him and stroked his head. 'No reason.'

Women baffled him at times, Willie thought. They were creatures that quite defied understanding.

Teresa hurriedly left the breakfast table and rushed to the sink where she was violently sick. Her mother, Father having already left for work, stared on in astonishment.

'Teresa?'

Mrs Kelly went to her daughter and put a consoling arm round her shoulders. 'What caused that, girl?'

Teresa shook her head. 'I haven't been feeling well, Ma.' Which was true enough, she hadn't. There had been recurring bouts of nausea over the past few days.

Mrs Kelly placed a hand on Teresa's forehead. 'You don't have a temperature.'

Teresa picked up a cup and pumped cold water into it. She swilled out her mouth and then spat into the sink. 'That's better.'

'Perhaps you should stay home today.'

'No fears, Ma. I don't want to be given the push like Bridie. I'm going to the factory if I have to crawl on my hands and knees.'

Mrs Kelly could well understand the lass's predicament. There had been two more sackings since Bridie. 'Well, sit down for a moment or two while I clear out this sink.'

'I'm sorry, Ma. I couldn't help it.'

'There's no need to be sorry. If you're ill you're ill. Nothing more has to be said.'

Teresa staggered back to her chair and plonked herself down. She now knew without any shadow of a doubt she was pregnant. She might have missed only one period but all the dreaded signs were there. Up the duff. In the pudding club! If Ma found out, if Da . . . All hell would break loose.

And it had happened just the once, that was what was so unfair. It wasn't as if she'd been doing it with Tony for months on end. There had only been that single occasion in the back close. He'd tried since of course but she'd always managed to stop him.

'You are looking pale now I come to think about it,' Mrs Kelly commented from the sink.

Teresa didn't reply. She couldn't go on being sick in the morning. Her ma wasn't daft, she would soon realise what the situation was. She groaned inwardly. What to do? She'd speak to Bridie that evening, she decided.

'She really is the most beautiful car, Andrew. I think I shall try and persuade Willie to buy one,' Georgina said as the Rolls purred through the Perthshire countryside. Andrew was keeping the promise he'd made when in Perth and giving her a spin.

Andrew drew into the side of the road and switched off the engine. Rolling down the window he inhaled deeply.

'Shall we get out and stretch our legs?' she suggested.

'If you like.'

She waited for him to open her door.

'The Pass of Killiecrankie,' he declared when they were both standing together.

'Wasn't there a famous battle fought here?'

'Oh indeed. A lot of good men died that day.'

She gazed about her. 'There is a melancholic feel about the place. It sort of lowers, if you know what I mean.'

Andrew thought of that long-ago battle and tried to imagine what it must have been like to take part. For some reason an image of his brother Peter came into his mind.

'Can I ask you something, Andrew?'

He roused himself from his reverie. 'Of course.'

'It's personal.'

'Go on,' he said softly.

'I asked Willie what happened to your fiancée, but he wouldn't tell me. Said it would have to come from you.'

'I see,' Andrew murmured.

'Will you tell me?'

He closed his eyes for a moment, memories flooding back. Dreadful memories that didn't only include Alice.

'The Fenians murdered her, torched her house. She and her mother and father were burnt to death.'

Georgina covered her mouth. 'How ghastly!'

McGinty, Andrew thought grimly. At least the Fenian bastard had paid, him and his. An eye for an eye, a tooth for a tooth. He hoped the bastard was roasting in hell.

'And you've never got over it?'

Andrew ran a hand across his face, remembering . . . remembering . . .

'Andrew?'

He shook himself, returning to the present. 'Sorry. I was miles away.'

'With *her*?'

'Yes,' he said. 'I was thinking of Alice and what might have been.' He paused, then added quietly. 'A single night and it was all over. My future, hers, all gone.'

'A single night?'

'The one she died.'

Compassion filled Georgina. He'd obviously been very much in love. Suddenly the day wasn't so glorious any more.

Andrew sighed. 'But that's in the past. Gone for ever. Now is what's important, and tomorrow.'

She wanted to take him in her arms, hold him, comfort him. 'Yes,' she agreed.

He turned to face her, a crooked smile lighting up his face. 'And you?'

'Something similar. The war.'

'I see,' he murmured.

'Why . . . Why does it all have to be so difficult. So painful?'

He shook his head. 'I don't know. Perhaps that's what life is really all about. Pain. Pain and the way it affects you. The way you cope.' He shook his head again. 'I don't know.'

Georgina stared up over the Pass of Killiecrankie, imagining the clash of swords, the screams of wounded and dying men, the total carnage of battle. It was horrible.

The Pass of Killiecrankie was a spot Georgina would never forget after that day.

Two wounded souls had touched.

Silence descended between them.

'Willie has asked me to go to Ireland with you,' Andrew eventually said.

'Really?'

'He said it might help lay the ghost.'

'Of your Alice?'

'Yes.'

'I wasn't aware we were going to Ireland. I knew Willie was thinking about it, but not that we were actually going.'

'Well, it seems you are.'

'And shall you come?'

'Until now I wasn't sure, hadn't decided. But now I have. I will.' Again he thought of McGinty and McGinty's family. Revenge was fine, but in retrospect . . . It took away part of yourself, your soul. In the afterlife he'd pay for what he'd done. Of that he was absolutely certain.

Georgina shivered. 'It's cold.'

'We'd best be getting back.'

She laid a gloved hand on his arm. 'I'm sorry for what happened, Andrew. Truly I am.'

'So am I,' he replied softly. 'So am I.'

Chapter 8

Bridie and Teresa were having another walk together so they could speak freely. 'You're absolutely certain?' Bridie queried.

'I couldn't be more so. I was sick again this morning, that's the third time this week. Ma's beginning to look at me very strangely indeed, though so far she hasn't said anything. Besides the sickness and missing period I just feel different. It's hard to explain, a sort of . . . contented wellbeing that wasn't there before.'

'You'll have to face Tony about this, Teresa,' Bridie counselled. 'Tell him he must do the proper thing and stand by you.'

But would he? Teresa worried. There was no saying.

'When are you seeing him again?'

'This Friday. We're supposed to be going to the flicks.'

'Then speak to him on the way home. Explain the situation.'

The street was hardly the place to give a chap such news,

Teresa thought. It would have to be the back close where the deed had taken place.

'From what I know of Tony he's a decent lad. He won't let you down.' Bridie hoped she was right.

'What's wrong with you?' Ian Seaton demanded of Rose sitting in front of the drawing-room fireplace. 'You look miserable as sin.'

Rose snapped herself out of her reverie. 'Do I?'

'Worse.'

She'd been thinking of Andrew and her stay at Drummond House. It had all gone well enough but, to her disappointment, Andrew hadn't taken any special notice of her. Not in the way she'd wanted anyway. Now she wouldn't see him again before the proposed visit to Ireland some time in the new year.

'Well?' Ian queried.

'I suppose I'm just down in the dumps.'

'Oh. Any special reason?'

'No,' she lied.

'I know how you feel, I get that way myself occasionally. Though not too often I have to admit.'

That afternoon Rose had come within an inch of confessing her feelings about Andrew to Georgina, then at the last moment had decided not to. Some instinct had warned her that would be the wrong thing to do.

If only she could talk to someone though. Certainly not her brother, she wasn't going to hand him that kind of ammunition.

'Is there anything I can do to help buck you up?' Ian asked kindly.

'No, I don't think so.'

'How about a joke. Or some funny faces?' And with

that he contorted his features and squinted both eyes inwards.

'Idiot.' She smiled.

'See! It's working already.'

If only a few funny faces could sort out her troubles, she thought.

'Perhaps a board game then? I could dig out one of those we used to play as children.'

'No thanks, Ian. I'm not in the mood.'

'Oh well,' he sighed. 'Don't say I didn't try.'

'It's sweet of you and I appreciate it. But I'd really rather be left alone.'

'If you wish.'

'Thank you, Ian.'

At the door he paused and glanced back at his sister who'd gone into herself again. He closed the door quietly behind him.

Bridie was outraged. 'He said what!'

'Wanted to know if I was certain the child was his.' Tears welled in Teresa's eyes to go running down her cheeks.

'I hope you smacked him for that.'

Teresa shook her head. 'I was too taken aback, too hurt. I mean, how could he possibly think I might have been with someone else? What does he take me for!'

'And what about getting married?'

'He wouldn't entertain the idea, Bridie. Said he was too young and didn't earn enough money. He also said it was best we didn't see one another again.'

'He just . . . walked away?'

'More or less.'

Fury filled Bridie that her best friend had been treated in

such a manner. If Tony had been present *she* would have slapped him.

'Oh Bridie,' Teresa whispered. 'What am I to do?'

'Tell your folks I suppose. What else?'

Terror lit up Teresa's face. 'Pa will thrash me with his belt, and it'll be the thrashing of a lifetime. As for Ma . . . I daren't even think what she'll say. She'll be beside herself and go on about our good name being dragged in the dirt.'

'Surely your father won't thrash you, being pregnant.'

'Oh aye, he will. And I wouldn't put it past him to do it on my bare backside either. My pa's got a terrible temper.'

They walked a little way in silence, Teresa snuffling into a handkerchief.

'There is of course another way,' Bridie said eventually.

'How do you mean?'

'There are women who I've heard can get rid of it for you. I don't know any myself, but they are around.'

Teresa went white. 'That's a mortal sin, Bridie.'

'Aye,' Bridie agreed.

'I could never do such a thing, murder my own baby.'

'It is a grisly prospect right enough. But consider the alternative. I don't mean the thrashing or your ma having fits. Who'd marry a lassie with a bastard in tow? Not many round here. If any at all.'

'They'll call me tart and whore,' Teresa whispered, wishing with all her heart she'd never gone out with Tony, or let him . . . She shuddered.

'At least Tony's kept his mouth shut so far, that's to his credit, if little else is. And I can't see him bragging that he's got you in the family way. Not when he's abandoned you like he has. That would hardly put him in a good light.'

Murder her baby, Teresa thought, and shuddered again. A mortal sin if ever there was. If only she could wake up and find this was all a nightmare. What she wouldn't have given for that. Only she wouldn't be waking up, for although it was a nightmare it was real enough.

They arrived back at Bridie's close. 'Do you want to come up with me?' Bridie asked.

Teresa shook her head. 'No, I'll go on home.'

'And face the music?'

Teresa considered that. 'Not yet. Who knows? A miracle might happen. I could still lose it naturally.'

'Aye, there is that possibility.' Though unlikely, Bridie thought. Teresa was as healthy a young woman as you'd find. Still, as Teresa said, a miracle could happen.

'Oh Teresa,' Bridie murmured, and touched her friend gently on the cheek.

Teresa attempted a smile which was pathetic to see. 'At least things can't get any worse. There's at least that.'

'Aye, there's at least that.'

Bridie was humming as she washed up the breakfast dishes. Kathleen had gone to the communal toilet their family shared with the other two families on the landing.

Kathleen re-entered the kitchen. 'You'll never guess what.'

Bridie turned to her mother. 'What?'

Kathleen held up a letter. 'They've finally decided to answer your application.'

Elation filled Bridie for a brief moment, then died. 'Throw it on the table, Ma. I'll read it later.'

'It might not be bad news.'

Bridie shrugged. 'Some hope after all this while.'

'You never know. Come on, open it. If you don't I will.'

She picked up the tea towel and dried her hands. 'All right, give it here. May as well get it over and done with.'

It was from the estate right enough, Bridie saw from the postmark. Anyway, who else would it be from? She never received any mail.

Bridie unfolded the single sheet of paper and quickly scanned its contents. Colour mounted her cheeks.

'So?' Kathleen demanded.

'They . . .' She couldn't contain her excitement. 'They want me to go for an interview next Monday and they'll reimburse my expenses getting there and back.'

Kathleen laughed and clapped her hands. 'There you are. It wasn't bad news after all.'

Bridie simply couldn't believe it. She'd become convinced there wasn't going to be a reply to her application. Now she not only had a reply but an interview too.

'I wonder how many they'll be seeing or have already seen?' she mused.

'Aye, there is that,' Kathleen nodded.

'I'll have to get the money for the rail ticket and things, Ma. That's going to be a problem.'

'You leave that to me, lass. I'll see to it.'

She mustn't get too excited, Bridie told herself. It was only an interview after all, not a job offer. It could still all come to nothing.

Hettie answered the door to find Andrew standing there. 'Andrew! What a lovely surprise. Come away in.'

'I'm not intruding I hope?'

'When did you ever do that. You're welcome as always.'

Not for the first time he thought what a wonderful atmosphere the inside of the Riach cottage had. Warm, cosy and . . . full of love. It enveloped one like a blanket.

They went through to the sitting room. 'Where's Jack?' he queried, seeing the room empty.

'Upstairs putting wee Tommy to sleep. Telling him a story no doubt. Something horrible about pixies and goblins probably, Tommy adores those. The more bloodcurdling the better.'

'Is the lad well?'

'Never better. Now how about a cup of tea, or perhaps something stronger?'

'Whisky would be fine.'

'Then whisky it is.'

Andrew settled himself into a comfortable chair. 'I came to ask Jack's advice.'

'Oh?'

'You remember the Seatons who came to stay?'

'Of course. Nice people. It was a grand night.'

'Willie is planning a holiday in Ireland and wants me to go with him. Or them actually. I said yes, but now I'm having second thoughts.'

She handed him a glass. 'And why's that?'

'You know my fiancée was killed by the Fenians, Hettie. Ireland has bad memories and associations for me.'

'I see.' She sat facing him.

Hettie didn't know about McGinty and neither did Jack. Only he did. It was a secret he'd never divulged to anyone.

'Are you scared?'

That startled him. 'Scared? I wouldn't put it exactly like that.'

'Then how would you put it?'

He considered that. 'I'm not sure. There's certainly nothing to be scared of.'

'Except what's in yourself,' she said softly.

He smiled at her. 'How very perceptive of you, dear Hettie. Jack fell on his feet when he married you.'

'And so did I, Andrew. Most certainly so.'

'I envy the pair of you. In the nicest way of course. You're so very happy together.'

'I certainly can't deny that,' she agreed.

Hettie studied Andrew, seeing the loneliness that was in him. A loneliness he so often succeeded in disguising.

'Will you go?' she queried.

He closed his eyes for a second, then opened them again. 'It would mean going to the graveyard. I couldn't be in Dublin and not.'

'You're saying that would be opening an old wound.'

'Definitely, Hettie. Definitely.'

She sighed. 'Well, I don't know what to advise, Andrew. It seems to me only you can make up your mind whether or not you go. But . . .' She trailed off.

'But what, Hettie?'

'If I was in your shoes I would.'

He nodded.

'By the way, speaking of the Seatons. Jack says that lassie Rose is sweet on you.'

Andrew stared at her in amazement. 'Jack says?'

'Heard it in her voice. Don't forget that being blind Jack's other senses are heightened. He hears things, nuances if you like, that we sighted people often miss.'

Andrew recalled the day in his office when Rose had flirted with him. He thought it just a female lark. But perhaps there was more to it than that.

'I'm old enough to be her father,' he protested.

Hettie raised an eyebrow. 'She's pretty.'

'And *young*.'

Hettie didn't reply to that.

'Hmmh,' Andrew mused.

'Would the age difference worry you all that much?' Hettie queried softly.

'If it didn't me it certainly would her father.'

They both laughed.

'Willie would turn cartwheels if he thought I was interested in Rose. No no, the whole thing's preposterous.
Completely out of the question.'

'I liked her,' Hettie stated. 'I liked them all, but particularly her. You could do worse, Andrew Drummond.'

'She's far too young,' Andrew repeated. 'Only a child.'

'You've a lot to learn about women I fear, Andrew. Oh, I
know you may have had plenty of experience with them in
the past, but you still have a lot to learn.'

It suddenly dawned on Andrew that Ellen Temple was
only a few years older than Rose. But that was different.
Quite different. And Ellen wasn't the daughter of a friend
and ex-colleague.

'Oh come along, son, you've always got a few quid stuffed
away somewhere. Lend it to me, it's only for a few days.'

Sean Flynn shook his head. 'Honestly, Ma, I'm skint. If
I had it I'd give it to you.'

Kathleen wasn't sure whether to believe Sean or not. 'Are
you certain? This is important.'

'I swear to you, Ma, on any saint you care to name, I'm
totally and utterly broke.'

When Kathleen had gone Sean sat on his bed, angry with
himself for not being able to help his ma whom he held in
high esteem. Money, why did so many things always boil
down to that? If only he was rich, able to afford whatever
he fancied. My God, wouldn't that be something.

He thought of what it must be like being a toff. No hard
graft for them, but a life of luxury. A big house, car, fancy
women. Never having to worry where the next penny was
coming from.

It could be worse, he consoled himself. He was in work, things would be ten times harder if he wasn't. Look at Bridie, she never went out nowadays unless it was searching for a job. Poor bitch. He pitied her.

He swore, then lay back on his bed. A big house, car and fancy women. The stuff of dreams.

Or more than that?

Kathleen stopped outside the pop shop, a place she loathed going into. It was so degrading and she always felt soiled after being in there.

'Why hello, Mrs Flynn.' The pawnbroker smiled at her when she was inside.

'Hello, Mr Gordon.'

'Your dad's watch again, is it?'

She hated when he said that, which he always did. For years now she'd wanted to slap Mr Gordon across the face. 'I'm afraid so.'

'A little financial difficulty I take it.'

How he got under her skin. 'I wouldn't be here if there wasn't.'

'Aahhh!' he sighed.

He loved the plight of the poor unfortunates who had to use him, she thought. Positively revelled in it. The man was an utter swine through and through.

Kathleen laid her father's watch on the counter. How often had it been here? she wondered. Times without number. 'The same amount,' she said.

Gordon considered beating her down a little, add a bit of zest to the day. Then decided to be magnanimous. 'Naturally.'

It would be enough, Kathleen thought. Bridie would have her train ticket.

'I'll be back to reclaim it next week,' she stated when the money had been counted out and safely deposited in her handbag.

'Of course,' Mr Gordon replied.

She had to force herself not to slam the door behind her. If anyone could make you feel small it was Mr bloody Gordon.

'That's wonderful!' Teresa exclaimed, having called in on Bridie and been told the news about the interview.

'I'm thrilled to pieces.'

Teresa's face fell. 'Except it means that if you get it you'll be away from here. What will I do for a pal?'

'I'm sorry, Teresa, there's nothing I can do about that. Besides, it's only an interview. There's no saying I'll get the job.'

That brightened Teresa somewhat. It wasn't that she didn't wish Bridie every success with the interview, she did. But on the other hand it would be awful to lose her.

'Monday morning you say.'

'Aye, that's right. I've already been to the station and bought my ticket. I'm raring to go.'

Pat came into the room. 'I'm off out then, hen,' he declared to Kathleen.

'He's on a very important committee,' Kathleen informed Teresa. 'What about that!'

'A committee,' Teresa repeated. 'I'm impressed.'

'Oh aye,' Kathleen went on proudly. 'My Pat's becoming somebody nowadays so he is.'

'What sort of committee?' Teresa enquired.

'To do with the Union,' Pat lied. 'Right then, that's me.'

'Wait and I'll walk you out,' Kathleen said. 'It's time I fetched Alison.' Alison was at a neighbour's playing with their daughter who was in her class at school.

'Aye, sure. But come on then, I don't want to be late. Looks bad.'

Kathleen hurried from the kitchen to get her coat, with Pat following her.

'So tell me,' Bridie said to Teresa when the outside door had clicked shut. 'Have you spoken to your folks yet?'

Teresa shook her head. 'I've been too feart. Anyway, the morning sickness seems to have stopped. At least for now. Which gives me some breathing space.'

'You're going to have to speak to them sooner or later.'

'I know. It's just . . . Well I keep hoping for that miracle to happen. I pray every night that it will.'

'And if it doesn't?'

Teresa thought of her father and his belt. And that would only be for starters. She hung her head.

Bridie took her friend in her arms and held her close.

'Jesus, you're good, Patrick Flynn,' Geraldine Buchanan murmured to him later that night.

He visibly swelled.

'It's like being rogered by a steel piston.'

Pat had never heard the word roger used in that context before but understood what it meant. 'Aye, well, there you are!'

She ran a hand over the forest of hair covering his chest. Dougal was good in bed but couldn't compare to Pat. What a find he was.

'Will you get me a drink?' he asked.

'Of course.'

'Whisky and beer. I'm thirsty as hell.'

She laughed. 'I'm not surprised after that performance. You were terrific.'

Kathleen never said that to him he reflected. She took it all as a matter of course. Nor was she as responsive as Geraldine who, on occasion, could make so much noise he thought the neighbours must surely hear.

Geraldine slipped from the bed and into her negligée, an exotic delight Dougal had brought her back from the Far East. It was made of pure silk and patterned with fiercesome dragons and brightly hued birds.

Pat watched her as she tied the belt round her waist. What a figure, he thought, smiling at the memory of what he'd just been doing to it.

'I'll just be a minute, lover,' Geraldine said, and left the room.

Lover! Pat sighed with satisfaction.

Bridie stared in awe through the window of the car that had been sent to meet her as The Haven came into view. It was like something out of one of those romantic novels she read.

And the grounds surrounding it, they defied description. She might have died and gone to paradise.

Bridie closed her eyes. Dear God, Holy Father, please let me get this job. Now I've seen this place I've never wanted anything so much in my life. I'll work ever so hard, I promise. They'll never find fault with me. Not in a thousand years.

She opened her eyes again to continue staring at The Haven. How many rooms did it have? She couldn't even begin to imagine. Oodles and oodles.

Bridie glanced down at her clothes in dismay, her church Sunday best. The black three-quarter-length coat suddenly looked old and shabby while the shepherd-checked tailored suit she had on underneath was hopelessly out of date and fashion.

She was only going for a position as maid she reminded

herself. They wouldn't expect her to turn up looking a glam puss or wearing the very latest style. No, no, she was adequately dressed and neat and tidy with it.

What would this Mr Seaton be like, she wondered, for it was he who'd written to her? Formidable no doubt. And posh as all get out. She must mind her P's and Q's right enough.

Excitement throbbed within her.

Mrs Coltart popped her head round the door. 'Can I have a word with you, sir?'

'Of course, Mrs Coltart.'

She came to stand before him.

'Now what can I do for you?'

'I've just interviewed the last girl for the maid's post, sir, and wish to talk to you about her as she's the one I'd like.'

Willie leant back in his chair. 'So what's the problem?'

'It's her religion. She's a Roman Catholic.'

'Aahhh!' Willie breathed.

'We've never had a Catholic here before, sir, and I don't know your feelings on the matter.'

'She's definitely the one you want, Mrs Coltart?'

'Definitely, sir. There were only four applications as you're aware and as far as I'm concerned she's the most suitable.'

'And why's that?'

'Her enthusiasm, sir. She was bubbling with it.' Mrs Coltart smiled. 'She'd never been outside Glasgow before and thinks the countryside is absolutely wonderful. She was full of it.'

Willie made a pyramid with his hands and frowned in concentration. A Catholic working at The Haven? He wasn't at all sure about that. It might lead to trouble. 'It *was* a poor response to my advertisement,' he murmured, still thinking.

'Very, sir.'

'I expected far more applications.'

'In truth, sir, so did I. But there were only the four.'

'What about the rest of the staff, would she fit in?'

'I believe so, sir.'

'Not only as a person but with the religious difference?'

'I still believe so, sir. If I'm wrong, and there was conflict, then the matter would have to be sorted.'

He nodded. 'Did you explain there isn't a Roman Catholic church hereabouts?'

'Yes, sir. She was disappointed but said she'd just have to put up with that.'

'Hmmh. What's her name?'

'Brigit Flynn, sir. They call her Bridie.'

Willie gave a soft laugh. 'You can't get a more Catholic name than that. Irish I presume.'

'Descent, sir.'

Willie took a deep breath. 'Leave this with me, Mrs Coltart. I wish to mull it over for a while.'

'Certainly, sir.'

Mrs Coltart left him to it.

Kathleen's eyes were fixed on Bridie as she eagerly tore open the letter that had just arrived. Seconds later Bridie squealed with delight.

'I've got the job, Ma. I've got it! I start the beginning of next month.'

Kathleen breathed a sigh of relief. 'Well done, lass. Well done.'

Her prayers had been answered, Bridie thought in exaltation. Thank you, God. Thank you.

Chapter 9

'We must be feeding this lassie too much,' Mr Kelly commented affably across the tea table.

Teresa went very still, a piece of sausage halfway to her mouth.

'Oh?' Mrs Kelly smiled at her husband.

'Look at her, she's putting on weight like billy-o.'

Mrs Kelly glanced at Teresa. 'I do believe you're right. I hadn't noticed.'

Teresa returned the piece of sausage to her plate and swallowed hard. She *had* started putting on weight though she'd been pretending to herself that she wasn't.

Mr Kelly chuckled. 'It's your good cooking, Ma. And her healthy appetite.'

Mrs Kelly was frowning. 'She hasn't been eating more than usual. So why should she suddenly start putting on weight?'

'It must be the cakes,' Teresa muttered.

'Cakes?' Mrs Kelly queried.

Teresa's mind was whizzing. 'Aye, a few of the lassies at

work take it in turn to bring some in. Cream cakes and the like. It's just a wee treat amongst ourselves,' she lied.

'She's always had a sweet tooth, Ma. You know that.'

Mrs Kelly nodded her agreement. That was true enough. She had a sweet tooth herself, simply adoring chocolate whenever she could get her hands on some.

Should she speak up now? Teresa wondered, quailing at the prospect. No, she couldn't, not after that cock and bull story about cakes. She couldn't see her father's belt from where she was sitting, but pictured it in her mind. The belt would be pulled free and . . . She shuddered inwardly.

Her da might appear the genial sort, always laughing and joking. But you crossed him at your peril as many, including herself, had found out. As though a switch had been flicked he'd turn from a nice, pleasant man into a raging monster. She'd seen it happen many times.

'Well, you'd better watch it, girl. We don't want you becoming a two-ton Tessie now, do we?'

'No, Da.'

'Go easy on those cakes.'

'I will, Da. I promise.'

'A funny thing happened at work today,' Mr Kelly declared, changing the subject, and the others listened attentively while he recounted the story.

She was running out of time, Teresa thought desperately. Who would've imagined she'd have already begun to show!

'What's a Samurai?' Alison Flynn piped up from the floor where she was playing with her golly.

'No idea, lass,' Pat replied from behind his newspaper.

'You know, don't you, Sean? You're the leader of that gang.'

Sean could have wrung his little sister's neck. 'Leader of a gang?'

Pat's newspaper slowly descended to his lap. 'What's all this then?'

'She's blethering, Da. Forget it.'

'I am not blethering,' Alison snapped hotly. 'Molly Molloy's parents were talking about it the other day when I was round there. They didn't know what a Samurai was either.'

'Son?' Kathleen queried softly.

'*Are* you in a gang, you stupid bugger? Do you want to get yourself marked or something? I thought you had more sense.'

Sean glared at his father. 'So what if I am. What's it to you? And don't call me a stupid bugger ever again.'

'Or what?'

'Stop it you two,' Kathleen said sternly. She then rounded on Sean. 'Are you?'

'Yes I am.'

'And its leader?'

He nodded.

'Holy fuck!' Pat swore, and dashed his newspaper to the floor. 'I can't believe I'm hearing this.'

'The Samurai were ancient Japanese warriors,' Sean explained to Alison.

Bridie, who'd been out to the toilet, breezed in, then came up short. 'What's going on?' she queried, looking from face to face. Something clearly was up. You could have cut the atmosphere with a knife.

'Your brother is the leader of a gang,' Kathleen informed her.

Bridie was incredulous. 'You must be joking. Our Sean?'

'Aye, our Sean,' Kathleen responded.

'Well, not for long,' Pat declared. 'I forbid you to belong to any gang, Sean, far less be its leader.' He leant forward. 'Do you hear me?'

'I'll do what I bloody well like. I'm not having you lay down the rules to me any more.'

Pat was immediately out of his chair. 'How dare you speak to me like that? I'm your father.'

'So what?' Sean replied insolently.

Kathleen also came to her feet ready to divert any trouble. 'Will you two give over. I'm not having any trouble in my house.'

'He started it,' Sean declared.

A frightened Alison had gone to Bridie and taken her hand. Bridie squeezed it reassuringly.

'It doesn't matter who started it. Enough is enough.'

Pat was staring daggers at Sean. 'You're going to finish with this gang. I want your word on that. Heaven's sake, do you know what the gangs get up to? You could end up dead or scarred for life.'

'That's right, son,' Kathleen agreed.

Should he lie, make a promise he had no intention of keeping? He didn't see the point. If he lied they'd only find out eventually.

'I'm old enough to make my own decisions. And I'm staying in the gang and I'm staying its leader.'

'Like hell you are!' Pat roared and, pushing his way past Kathleen, advanced on Sean who instantly leapt up.

'Don't hit him, Pat, don't hit him!' Kathleen pleaded, clutching at Pat's shirt.

He tore himself free and continued on towards Sean.

'Hit me and you'll regret it,' Sean spat.

Pat's fist flashed, smacking Sean on the shoulder. 'I won't be defied,' he shouted. 'I won't be defied!'

The blow was only a glancing one but enough to make Sean lose his temper. 'Right, you old fart, you've been asking for this for years!'

Kathleen screamed as the two men fell upon one another. 'Holy Mary mother of God,' a wide-eyed Bridie whispered. This was awful.

Alison whimpered and fled behind Bridie's skirt from where she peeped out.

A kitchen chair went crashing. Pat roared again when Sean's fist found its mark. Blood spattered from his nose.

Neither of them was pulling their punches, this was in deadly earnest. Another kitchen chair went clattering away.

Sean grunted, that had hurt. He lashed out in retaliation.

'Stop it! Stop it!' Kathleen shrieked, hitting them both.

Some mantelpiece ornaments, including a plaster madonna, went tumbling to the floor where they all broke.

Pat succeeded in getting Sean in a bearlike grip, the pair of them swaying to and fro.

Suddenly it was all over. Somehow Sean's head smashed into his father's chin knocking him unconscious. Pat's arms dropped away and when Sean released him he fell to lie sprawling.

Sean stood over Pat, sucking in deep breaths. 'You old fart,' he repeated.

'You've killed him!' an hysterical Kathleen gasped. Next moment she was on her knees beside the fallen Pat. Bridie, with a now crying Alison still clinging to her skirt, hurried over.

'Pat, Pat, speak to me,' Kathleen urged, slapping him lightly on the cheek. Pat's reply was a groan.

'He's not dead,' Sean stated.

'No thanks to you!' Kathleen retorted.

Bridie knelt beside her mother. 'He's just knocked out, Ma. He'll soon come round.'

'I'm off,' Sean declared and, wheeling about, strode from the room.

Pat opened one eye, then the other. 'What happened?'

Kathleen explained.

'Where is he now?'

'Gone out.'

Pat was secretly pleased. He didn't fancy another tangle with Sean. The lad had surprised him.

'Let's get you back into your chair,' Bridie suggested.

'Oh, Dada. Dada,' Alison wailed.

'I've been thinking,' Georgina said.

Willie looked over. 'Usually when you say that it costs me money.'

She laughed. 'How right you are. As it could in this instance.'

Willie sighed. 'Well?'

'Why don't we have a party on Hogmanay? Invite about a dozen folk or so. Maybe more.'

'What a smashing idea,' Rose chipped in.

'Who would we ask?'

'The McLarens I thought. Their daughter Moira isn't long back from Switzerland. It would be interesting to hear how it went over there for her.' Moira McLaren had been to a Swiss finishing school.

Ian grunted. He remembered Moira as a horrible little so and so. They'd never got on.

'Hmmh,' Willie mused. He rather liked the idea of a party. It was ages since they'd entertained properly. 'Ian?'

'Sounds all right.'

'We could also invite Andrew Drummond.' Rose smiled innocently.

That startled Georgina, inviting Andrew being the whole reason for her suggesting the party. Now Rose had saved her the trouble of mentioning him.

'He must be lonely in that house all by himself,' Rose

went on. 'Though no doubt he usually goes to his sister's on Hogmanay, or to his friend Jack Riach's. Coming here would be a change for him.'

Georgina eyed Rose shrewdly. Not for the first time she wondered about Rose's interest in Andrew. There again, Andrew *was* excellent company.

'I quite agree,' Willie said. 'It would be a change for him. And while here he and I could discuss plans for Ireland.'

'Settled then?' Georgina asked.

Willie nodded. 'You go ahead and do what has to be done. A Hogmanay party it is.'

Georgina smiled inwardly with satisfaction while Rose was trying hard not to show her excitement.

'That's brilliant,' Teresa said. 'I couldn't be more happy for you.' Bridie had just told her the news about her job.

'We're all delighted,' Kathleen declared. With the exception of Pat that was, for he was still scornful of a Flynn being a domestic.

'I start the beginning of next month,' Bridie beamed.

'I'll miss you.'

Bridie's face fell. 'I am sorry, Teresa. But you do understand.'

'Oh aye.'

'I'm going to love it there. You should see the house and grounds, they're fantastic.'

Teresa nodded. Catching Bridie's eye she glanced meaningfully towards the door.

Bridie was puzzled only for a moment, then got the message. 'Anyway,' she declared. 'I've been home all day and could use a breath of air. Do you fancy a walk, Teresa?'

'I do indeed.'

'I really am pleased for you,' Teresa said as they left the close.

'Thank you. Now what's all this about? Has that miracle happened?'

Teresa gave a hollow laugh. 'If only it had. No, I need your help, Bridie. The help of a pal.'

'Of course. Just say.'

'I've, eh . . .' Teresa broke off, she still couldn't believe she was going to be doing this. But in the end, what choice did she have? 'I've decided to use one of those women we spoke of and want you to come with me for support.'

Bridie frowned. 'What women?'

'The ones who . . .' She gulped. 'Give you an abortion.'

Bridie halted and stared at Teresa in consternation. 'Are you serious?'

'I'm afraid so. I couldn't face bringing up a bastard, Bridie. And as you pointed out, what man would marry me with one of those in tow? I'd be a spinster for the rest of my life.'

'But you were so against it.'

'I know. I know. Only I've changed my mind.'

'A mortal sin, Teresa. Don't forget that.'

Tears welled in her eyes. 'I'm not forgetting. But maybe God will be merciful. Understand my reasons and forgive me.'

They resumed walking, Bridie full of sympathy for her friend. It was a terrible decision to have to make. 'I thought you didn't know any of these women?'

'I didn't. And then, quite by chance, a name came up in conversation at the factory. She's called Mrs Quinlan and she's agreed to do it this Friday.'

'You've been to see her?'

'Well, I had to. You can't just turn up at her door and ask for it to be done there and then.'

Bridie was curious. 'What's she like?'

'I wasn't sure what to expect, some old crone perhaps. But Mrs Quinlan is as normal as can be. She's not even old. Late thirties I'd judge, maybe early forties.'

'What about money?'

'I've been saving up for a while now. Nothing much, just a wee bit put by every week for a rainy day.' She laughed again. 'Well if this isn't a rainy day I don't know what is.'

'How much?'

'Five quid. Paid up front on the night.'

'I see,' Bridie murmured. The last thing she wanted was to be party to this sort of thing, but she could hardly let Teresa down. Teresa certainly wouldn't have let her down if the positions had been reversed, not that they ever would have been.

'What time Friday night?' she queried.

Sean, Noddy, Jim Gallagher and Mo Binchy strolled into the ice-cream shop which was empty apart from the owner behind the counter.

'Hello, Mr Rizzio,' Sean said casually.

'Hello, lads. What can I do for you? Some nice cornets with raspberry sauce on top perhaps?'

'It's more what we can do for you.'

Rizzio's face became anxious. There was something wrong here. He could tell. 'Like what?'

'You get trouble from time to time, don't you?'

'Not really.'

'Well you could do. I'm certain of it.'

Mo Binchy pretended to slip, knocking over a large glass

bowl of wafers in the process. The bowl smashed on the floor sending wafers flying everywhere.

'Oh, sorry, Mr Rizzio,' Mo said. 'How clumsy of me.'

'Hey, you do that intentionally.'

Mo was all innocence. 'What a nasty thing to say.'

'You did. I no wrong.'

'An accident,' Sean smiled thinly. 'Amazing how they happen when you least expect it.'

Rizzio was becoming extremely uneasy. 'What this all about?'

Sean glanced around. 'Lovely place you've got here. It would cost a lot of money to do up again.'

'Do up . . .' Rizzio spluttered.

'You know how violent this area is. Fights break out all the time. If a big one happened in here it could wreck the shop. I can just see it, broken tables and chairs, ripped wallpaper, even your ice-cream machine there might get broken.'

Rizzio was appalled. That sort of damage could put him out of business.

'Mind you, it wouldn't if you were protected,' Sean said slowly.

'Protected?'

'Aye, by the Samurai. Have you not heard of us?'

Rizzio shook his head.

Sean produced his cut-throat razor, flicked it open and laid it on the counter in front of the now terrified Italian. Rizzio stared at the razor as though it was a deadly snake about to strike.

'We're the gang round here,' Sean stated. 'There are lots of us in it.'

'A gang,' Rizzio said, and swallowed hard.

'Some of the others are outside making sure we're not disturbed like. Understand?'

Rizzio nodded.

'Now for a small sum per week we'd make sure nothing happened here. We'd put the word out that if it did whoever was responsible would have us to deal with. And that wouldn't be healthy for the person or persons. Get my meaning?'

'Oh yes,' Rizzio breathed.

'So what do you say?'

'It's daylight robbery.'

'Not at all,' Sean replied smoothly. 'It's insurance, that's all. And that's how you should think of it.'

Mo Binchy put his heel on a piece of broken glass and scrunched it underfoot. Rizzio winced at the noise it made.

'Why me?' Rizzio queried.

'Why not? As I said, you've a good business here, it would be a crying shame to see it . . .' He broke off and shrugged. 'Well you know.'

'And what this . . . insurance cost me?'

The agreed sum had been two pounds a week. Sean now changed his mind thinking, what the hell! The man was almost shitting himself.

'A fiver.'

'A fiver,' Rizzio gasped. 'That no possible.'

'Oh yes it is,' Sean said, voice loaded with menace. 'Oh yes it is.'

'And what if I tell police?'

'That would be a terrible mistake on your part.' He picked up the razor. 'One you'd regret the rest of your life I assure you.'

Rizzio knew he was beaten. Sean's threats were no idle ones. You didn't make idle threats in Glasgow.

Rizzio nodded. 'I take your insurance.'

'Payment starts right now and someone will be round once a week to collect from now on. Clear?'

'Clear,' Rizzio mumbled, going to his till.

Number one, Sean thought triumphantly. The first of many.

Ian Seaton was in a bad mood. The weather that day had been terrible, little outside work had been done on the estate and those who had been outside had soon been soaked through. He still felt chill, despite the roaring fire and bath he'd had, and wondered if he had a cold coming on. He listened to the rain. Had it stopped at all since early morning? It was hammering against the window panes.

'Ian?'

He glanced over at Georgina. The pair of them were alone in the drawing room. 'Yes?'

'Can I speak frankly?'

He raised an eyebrow. 'If you wish.'

'You worry me sometimes.'

'Do I indeed. Why, Georgina?'

'You never seem to show any interest in women. It doesn't seem natural to me.'

He laughed, amused. 'Do you think I might be a nancy boy or something?'

Georgina coloured. 'Such things are known.'

'Well, you can put your mind at rest. I have no interest in that direction, nor have I ever dabbled as some chaps do at school. I'm quite normal.'

'I'm pleased to hear it.'

He leant forward. 'You didn't really think I was queer, did you?'

'No, but . . . well it does happen, even in the best of families.'

'I like girls well enough, Georgina, but you can't say they're exactly thick on the ground round here now, can you?'

This time she laughed. 'True enough.'

'I meant suitable ones of course. There are always the maids, mind you, but I hardly think either you or Father would be best pleased if I cast an eye in that direction.'

'No,' she agreed.

'Besides, I'm too busy at the moment learning about the management of the estate to worry about girls. I doubt I'd have the time to go gallivanting even if I wanted to.'

'I hardly meant gallivanting.'

'Call it what you will. Come the evening I'm far too tired to think of anything other than food and bed.'

'Fine then.'

Ian lapsed back into his own thoughts which brought an end to that conversation.

'This is it,' Teresa said, stopping outside a close. 'Mrs Quinlan is two flights up.'

'How do you feel?'

Teresa gave Bridie a pained smile. 'How do you think? I'm scared out of my brain.'

'Aye,' Bridie sympathised. 'I can well understand that.'

Teresa stared into the close which had cream tiles to halfway up its walls. Her stomach was knotted, her heart beating wildly. She'd have given anything not to have had to go in there.

'You can still change your mind,' Bridie said softly.

Teresa laughed hollowly. 'Can I? I don't think so.'

Bridie took her friend's arm. 'I'm with you. Just remember that.'

'And I'm grateful. Far more than you probably realise. I doubt I could do this on my own.'

'It's almost eight, Teresa. We should go on up.'

Teresa sucked in a deep breath. 'I just hope it doesn't hurt too much, that's all.'

Bridie failed to see how it couldn't.

For the umpteenth time Bridie glanced at the clock on the mantelpiece. It was over an hour now. What was keeping them?

She started when she heard a muted scream. Dear God! She suddenly began to sweat profusely, her armpits quickly awash, sweat coursing down her back.

And still the clock continued to tick.

'All done.' Mrs Quinlan beamed, ushering Teresa into the sitting room where Bridie was waiting.

Bridie caught her breath at the sight of Teresa, whose face was milk-white and strained in the extreme.

'Everything go all right?'

'Perfectly,' Mrs Quinlan replied, still beaming. 'Now I recommend you take her home and put her to bed where she should stay for the weekend if she's any sense. Come Monday morning she'll be right as rain.'

Teresa staggered over to Bridie and clutched her. 'Let's get out of here,' she mumbled.

'I'll see you both to the door,' Mrs Quinlan declared, still beaming.

'How was it?' Bridie queried as they slowly made their way down the stairs, Teresa holding tightly on to her.

'Don't ask. And don't ask how she did it. The answer to that would give you nightmares.'

Teresa began to cry and they stopped while Bridie searched for a handkerchief.

Teresa woke from what had been a deep sleep. Not fully awake, but a sort of peaceful state in between.

Her ma had been full of concern when Bridie had explained that she'd come over ill which was why Bridie had brought her home. Mrs Kelly had thanked Bridie profusely and then proceeded to take her through to bed which, at that moment, had been the most welcome sight she'd ever seen.

The pain had gone, she realised. That terrible griping pain that had been gnawing at her insides ever since . . .

'Dear God, forgive me please. And understand,' she muttered. 'I'll be a good girl from now on. It'll never happen again. I swear to you on all that's holy.'

Sleep was beckoning her again, blissful, blessed sleep. Sleep she desperately craved.

Was it her imagination or could she really hear a voice saying she was forgiven? Imagination surely. And yet it seemed so real somehow.

Forgiven.

She drifted off with a smile on her face.

Mrs Kelly answered Bridie's knock. It was Saturday morning. 'Hello, Mrs Kelly. I thought I'd call by and see how Teresa is. Maybe cheer her up a little.'

Mrs Kelly's face crumpled. She tried to speak, but couldn't. She tried again, and this time succeeded. 'Oh lass, oh lassie,' she croaked.

A sudden chill ran through Bridie, goosebumps breaking out all over her. 'What is it? What's happened?'

The crumpled face collapsed even further while tears sprang into what Bridie now saw were red-rimmed and puffy eyes.

'It's Teresa. She had a haemorrhage in the middle of the night and . . . and . . .' Mrs Kelly swallowed hard. 'And died.'

Chapter 10

'Turn round, girl,' Mrs Coltart instructed.

Bridie, wearing the black and white uniform she'd been issued with, did as she was bid.

Mrs Coltart nodded her approval. 'It'll do. Though when you have the chance you might take the hem up an inch. Can you do that, Bridie?'

'Yes, ma'am.'

'Well turn round again then.'

Mrs Coltart studied Bridie who'd arrived earlier that afternoon. 'The girl you're replacing was dismissed for theft and not given a character. I trust we'll have no such problems with you.'

'You won't, Mrs Coltart.'

'Right then. Now go and find Jeannie Swanson whom you're sharing a room with, she should be on the second floor, and she'll show you what to do. Stay with Jeannie till the end of the week by which time you should have learnt the ropes. At least as far as your current duties will be. Do you understand?'

'Yes, ma'am.'

'Then off you go.'

'Thank you, Mrs Coltart.'

Bridie went in search of Jeannie Swanson whom she found easily enough.

Bridie's eyes were popping at the amount of food that had been laid out for their supper. The table was positively groaning.

She accepted a tureen from the girl next to her and helped herself to thick pea soup.

The atmosphere in the servants' hall was warm, literally, and friendly. Everyone seemed most relaxed.

Mrs Kilbride, the cook, reigned at one end of the table, Mrs Coltart at the other. They kept their own counsel, but others were chatting amongst themselves. It was Mrs Coltart who'd said grace.

When the meal was finally over Bridie felt as though she must surely burst. Whatever else you could say about being a domestic, lack of food wasn't something you apparently had to worry about.

Not at The Haven anyway.

Bridie collapsed on to her bed, an iron affair that was surprisingly comfortable, having just completed her first full day, and groaned. 'My feet are killing me. As for my legs, they ache like billy-o.'

Jeannie Swanson, a thin stick of a girl with large, protuberant eyes, grinned at her. 'You'll soon get used to it, I promise you.'

'And getting up when we do. That's something else. I rose early in my last job, but that was a long lie compared to this.'

Jeannie started to remove her uniform. 'Apart from the moans do you think you'll like it here?'

'Oh yes. The rest of the staff are ever so nice and helpful.'

'Aye, they're a good bunch right enough. We all get on well so I hope you fit in.'

'I'll certainly do my best.'

Jeannie paused, then glanced curiously across at Bridie. 'Is it true what I hear? That you're a Catholic?'

Bridie nodded.

'We've never had one of those here before.'

'Is it likely to cause a problem, Jeannie?'

Jeannie considered that. 'I don't think so. We're all fairly tolerant, at least to the best of my knowledge we are.'

Bridie lay back on the bed, quite exhausted. 'Tell me about Mrs Coltart,' she requested.

Jeannie poured water from their jug into the bowl it had been sitting on. 'She's very fair. True she can be a Tartar at times, but only with those who've asked for it. Strict, mind, oh she is that. But as I said, fair with it.'

Jeannie washed her face which she then dried with the towel provided. There were two towels, one for each of them. The water in the bowl she slopped into a bucket.

'The only trouble with being here is that it's so isolated. When you get your day off there's absolutely nothing to do or anywhere to go.' They were given one day off a month.

'That won't bother me,' Bridie replied. 'I shall walk which will give me enormous pleasure. The countryside around here is so beautiful it quite takes my breath away.'

'Aye, it is that,' Jeannie agreed.

'Walk and read. If I can lay my hands on any books that is. I love reading.'

'The master has a library downstairs,' Jeannie informed her.

Bridie sat up. 'Really?'

'He must have thousands of books in it, at least it seems like thousands. All of them leather bound.'

'What sort of books?'

Jeannie shrugged. 'I don't know. I've never really bothered to look.'

A sudden gust from under the door caused their single candle to flicker wildly sending all kinds of weird and wonderful shapes dancing round the room's walls and ceiling.

'It's cold up here as it always is in wintertime,' Jeannie said, shivering. 'The sooner I'm in bed the better.'

Me too, Bridie thought and, getting up, also began undressing.

Jeannie slipped a flannel nightdress over her head and once that was on removed her underthings.

'Last one into bed puts out the candle,' Jeannie declared, diving under her covers.

A library, Bridie marvelled. She couldn't wait to see it.

'Goodnight,' she said slightly later, snuffing out the candle.

'Goodnight, Bridie. Sweet dreams.'

'And you.'

Pat reined in Jasper. The card was in Geraldine's window which meant she wanted a bag of coal. It also meant he'd be having a bottle of beer.

She was waiting for him on the landing, a nervous smile on her face. 'Hello, Mr Flynn. How are you today?'

Mr Flynn?

'Please come in, Mr Flynn. You know where the bin is.'

There it was again, Mr Flynn. And why was she acting so strangely?

'Dougal,' she whispered as he went past her.

No wonder she was nervous, her husband was back from

sea. There would be no bottle of beer today, or Friday night visits for a while. He inwardly cursed.

'I'll get your money,' Geraldine declared as he was emptying the coal into the bin, and hurried away.

Pat was shaking out the bag when he heard a man's voice, though he couldn't make out what the man was saying.

Geraldine reappeared. 'There you are, Mr Flynn,' she said, handing him the correct money.

'Thank you, Mrs Buchanan.'

Pat was leaving the kitchen when Dougal came into view. He was very tall and very powerfully built with hands the size of shovels. Not someone he would wish to tangle with, Pat thought. No indeed.

'Nice day for this time of year,' Dougal commented affably to Pat.

'It is that.'

Pat was consumed with jealousy as he left the Buchanans. All he could think about was what Dougal would be enjoying that night.

Something he'd come to regard as his.

'The committee work is finished for a while,' Pat announced to Kathleen later on.

'Oh?'

'We've done what had to be done. For the present anyway.'

'I see.'

He glanced across at Sean sitting morosely in a chair. He was wary of the lad ever since the fight, uncomfortable in Sean's presence. He was only too horribly aware that the balance of power in the house had changed, and that he was no longer top dog. In truth, his son now frightened him.

'But we'll be meeting again soon enough. Though I don't

know exactly when.' How long before Dougal returned to sea? he wondered. He had no way of knowing.

Pat shrank back a little as Sean suddenly came to his feet. 'I'm off out,' Sean declared to his mother.

'Will you be late?'

'No idea, Ma. I'll be back when I get here.'

Pat felt himself relax as the outside door clicked shut.

Rose stared at herself in her vanity table mirror. She touched both cheeks, thinking how good her skin was looking. She could now see bones where she hadn't before. Losing weight certainly suited her.

She smoothed down the sides of the envelope chemise she was wearing, the chemise of silk crêpe de Chine and the step-in style. It was neatly trimmed in front with rows of lace insertions, top and bottom edged with lace to match. Set off with rosettes, the chemise had silk ribbon shoulder straps.

Only two more weeks till Andrew arrives, she thought, a thrill of expectation running through her. He was coming for four whole days! Four days in which to try and get him to notice her the way she wanted him to.

'Andrew,' she whispered, and sighed. How she craved seeing him again. With all her heart and soul.

She coloured at the sudden thought of him standing there staring at her, his gaze feasting on her near nakedness. How vulnerable that made her feel. And excited.

In her mind's eye he was now bending down kissing first one bare shoulder, then the other.

'My darling,' he murmured.

A hand crept round to enfold a breast which he began to lightly caress. Her eyelids drooped at the sensations which tingled inside her. Sensations to die for.

Rose brought herself out of her reverie with a laugh. She

was being daft letting her imagination run riot like that. Quite silly really.

There again, who knew? The time might come when fantasy became reality. Beautiful, wonderful reality.

And it would, if she had anything to do with it. She was determined about that.

Oh yes.

'Jack?'

'Yes, Hettie?'

'Why are you looking so odd?'

He chuckled. 'Am I?'

'Your expression is very odd indeed.'

It was night and Hettie had just returned from putting Tommy to bed, which had taken quite a while as he hadn't wanted to go to sleep. And when Tommy wanted he could keep himself awake for ages, fighting sleep all the way.

'I was thinking about the book,' Jack stated.

'And?'

'I'm considering changing the ending. Not a happy one as I intended, but something tragic.'

'But you were so adamant . . .' She trailed off.

'Of course I haven't decided yet. I'm still toying with the idea.' Jack rose from his chair. 'I'm going out into the garden for a breath of fresh air.'

'But it's freezing out there. You'll catch your death.'

'Not if I put my coat on.' He hesitated. 'Tell me, Hettie, are the stars out tonight?'

'Yes.'

'A clear moonlit night with lots of stars?'

She smiled. 'Yes.'

'Aah!' he sighed. 'I love starry nights. Thousands of sparkling pin pricks shining down from heaven. It's a

147

sight I've always found so uplifting. It makes you sing inside.'

Hettie laughed. Sing indeed! What a funny way Jack had with words at times. But he was a writer after all.

'Except during the war,' Jack said softly. 'Starry moonlit nights could be the most dangerous of all. It's the visibility you see. For both sides. An awful lot of good men went west on nights like that.'

Hettie could well imagine. 'Don't forget the coat,' she said.

'I won't. I promise.'

Once outside he lifted his face to the heavens. He might be blind but he could still see the stars.

Andrew was standing at his bedroom window gazing out, waiting for Ellen to arrive.

He was in a troubled mood. The proposed Irish trip still worried him. How was he going to react when there?

Well or badly? That was the question.

Alice, how he missed her. Dear sweet Alice whom he'd come to adore with every fibre of his being.

He closed his eyes. Remembering . . . remembering . . .

'Just our luck to be stranded in bloody Ireland when there's a war on,' Second Lieutenant Roberts complained to Andrew, as the pair of them were out riding.

Andrew was a far more experienced rider than Billy who'd only taken it up eighteen months previously. He glanced sideways at his friend not at all sure he agreed with those sentiments.

'Think of the promotions that will be going,' Billy went on. 'There are bound to be stacks.'

Only because of casualties, Andrew thought grimly. He

gazed about him. It was beautiful countryside, lush in the extreme. But he wasn't too keen on the climate; it rained even more than in Scotland.

'That Captain Kennington's a right bastard,' Billy said. 'I can't tell you how much I dislike him.'

Andrew smiled. He got on with Kennington well enough, it was simply a case of how you handled the man. Toadying, some people might have called it, but it worked and, as far as he was concerned, that was all that mattered.

'You rub him up the wrong way,' Andrew commented quietly.

'It's his attitude that gets me, supercilious swine.'

Andrew reined in on spotting another horse, the rider a woman obviously in distress.

'I say, look at that,' Billy exclaimed. 'The beast appears to have bolted.'

'She needs help,' Andrew declared, kicking his horse forward. Billy immediately followed.

Andrew urged his horse, a powerful gelding, into a gallop. Slowly he began to narrow the gap between him and the woman.

The young woman heard their approach and turned her head to stare at Andrew and Billy. 'Help!' she cried.

'Just hold on,' Andrew shouted back, thinking she could easily be killed or badly hurt if she came off at that speed. He was well ahead of Billy whose horse wasn't nearly as fast as his.

Yard by yard, aided by some clever manoeuvring on his part, Andrew gained on them till at last his horse and hers were neck and neck. Leaning across he managed to grab the bridle.

For a few moments it was a fierce clash of wills between them, then the horse began to ease back and gradually slow.

When the horse finally came to a halt Andrew leapt to the ground and grabbed hold of its reins. He then assisted the young woman down.

'Thank you,' she panted. 'That was truly frightening.'

'What happened?'

She gave a wry grin. 'I was stupid and arrogant enough to think I could control Midnight, which clearly I can't.'

Midnight was an apt name, Andrew thought. The animal was velvet black from nose to tail.

'Just let me catch my breath a minute,' the young woman said, placing a hand on her chest.

Billy came charging up, reined in and also dismounted. 'Everything all right?'

'I think so,' Andrew replied.

Midnight whinnied and threw his head, but Andrew had him firmly under control.

'Dashed large beast for a girl,' Billy commented.

'He's my father's horse,' the young woman explained. 'My own is unwell and I wanted a ride. A mistake with Midnight as you witnessed.'

Andrew stroked a neck that was flaked with foam. 'There there, boy. There there,' he crooned.

'I'm Alice Fortescue by the way,' the young woman said.

'Andrew Drummond, Second Lieutenant in the First Essex based at Dublin Castle. This is my chum Billy Roberts, also a Second Lieutenant with the same regiment.'

'Delighted to meet you, Miss Fortescue,' Billy declared, giving her a small bow.

'And I the pair of you. Who knows what the outcome might have been if you hadn't been on hand.'

'How far away do you live?' Andrew enquired.

'Several miles in that direction,' Alice replied, pointing off to their left.

'Well I think it best we walk the horses for a bit,' Andrew said. 'They all need a breather after that.'

Pretty girl, Andrew was thinking. He placed her in her late teens, possibly early twenties. She was dressed in a black hunting jacket below which flowed an ankle-length grey skirt.

'I lost my hat somewhere along the line,' she explained. 'It just blew off.' She shuddered. 'I don't mind admitting that gave me quite a scare. Father will be furious if he finds out.'

'Well, we won't let on, will we, Billy?'

Billy grinned. 'Find out what?'

Alice smiled. 'You're both very kind and gallant.' She pronounced the latter in the French fashion.

'As every army officer should be,' Andrew retorted.

The three of them laughed at that.

Andrew could see she'd got her breath back. 'Shall we get started then?' he suggested. 'I'll lead my own horse and Midnight.'

'Fortescue isn't an Irish name,' Billy commented as they got underway.

'The family is originally English. We came over here in the seventeenth century when we were granted lands for services to the Crown. Lands that succeeding generations have managed to enlarge considerably.'

'I see,' Billy nodded.

'We don't think of ourselves as English any more, but Irish through and through, albeit we're Protestants.'

That was interesting, Andrew thought. 'And what does your father do? If you'll pardon my inquisitiveness.'

'He runs our estate, which is quite a task I can assure you. He'll be out now, doing whatever.'

Damn it, Andrew thought, when it started to rain. A light

smir as the Scots call it which nonetheless soon had them soaking. Alice seemed oblivious to it.

They made small chat as they proceeded in the direction of Alice's house till eventually Andrew decided they could remount. Alice was instructed to take Billy's horse, the smallest of the three, while Andrew took Midnight.

'Is this your land we're on now?' Andrew enquired as they proceeded onwards, keeping the horses to a walking pace.

'Oh yes. Everything round here is ours.'

Andrew wondered just how rich the Fortescues were. Considerably, he reckoned. Though owning land didn't always equate with having money in the bank.

Andrew reined in Midnight when the Fortescue house came into view. Dear God, he thought, it made Drummond House look like a cottage! It was vast.

'Greystones,' Alice smiled to Andrew.

'Very imposing I must say.'

'Far too big of course, costs an absolute fortune to maintain. We only live in the central part, both wings have been shut off for years.'

'You're not a large family then?'

'No, only my parents and myself. They'd hoped for more children but weren't blessed.'

'I have a brother and two sisters myself,' Andrew informed her. 'While Billy here is one of five brothers of whom he's the youngest. That right, old thing?'

'That's right,' Billy confirmed.

'I'd have loved to have brothers and sisters,' Alice said wistfully. 'But it wasn't to be.'

'They're a dashed nuisance at times I can tell you,' Billy grumbled.

'True enough,' Andrew nodded.

'But you wouldn't be without them, surely?'

Andrew considered that. 'I suppose not. Billy?'

'I suppose not either. Though in the past, when I was growing up, they could make one's life a misery.'

'Well I'd still love to have someone,' Alice said.

They came on to a long drive that wound its way towards Greystones, the drive intermittently flanked by conifer trees. Then they were on to the driveway itself which, it seemed to Andrew, could have taken an entire regiment of cavalry.

They dismounted in front of terraced steps leading to a massive wooden door.

'Would you care to come in and dry out a bit?' Alice asked.

Andrew was about to accept when Billy produced his watch. 'I'm afraid that's impossible, Miss Alice. We really must be getting back.'

Andrew sighed. 'Duty calls I'm sad to say.' If Billy said it was time to get back then it was.

Alice's face creased with disappointment. She'd taken a shine to these two young, personable men. 'I can't thank you enough for what you did,' she said to Andrew.

'My pleasure, miss. In every cloud, what? It gave us a chance to make your acquaintance.'

A smile replaced the look of disappointment. 'You're most kind. Perhaps you'll call another day.'

'Perhaps,' Andrew replied.

He formally shook her hand after which Billy did the same. Then he and Billy remounted.

'Goodbye, Miss Alice,' Billy said.

'For now,' Andrew added.

They waved as they rode off.

Andrew brought himself back to the present with a shake

of the head. How clear it all was in his memory, that first day he'd met Alice. That day and many others. So very very clear.

He started when a hand was placed on his arm. 'Oh, Ellen, it's you. I never heard you come in.'

'Sorry, did I startle you?'

'No. Not really.'

Suddenly the last thing he wanted was Ellen in his bed. Not after what he'd just been remembering.

'I've changed my mind about tonight,' he said softly.

'I see.'

'Nothing to do with you, so don't worry. It's simply that I've decided to stay up and think about some things. Business matters.'

'In the dark?'

'I do my best thinking in the dark. Helps concentrate the mind.'

She hesitated. 'You're certain it's not me?'

'Absolutely, Ellen. Now toddle off.'

She gave him a quick peck on the cheek then quietly left the room.

The *last* thing he now wanted, he thought, taking off his heavy winter dressing-gown and climbing into bed.

He wondered what had become of Billy Roberts, they'd never kept in touch. He must ask Willie if he knew when he was at The Haven.

'Oh I'm sorry, sir,' Bridie said hastily and returned the book she'd been glancing through to its place.

Ian regarded her with amusement. 'Do you like books?'

'Oh yes, sir. I've always adored them.'

'And what was that one?'

'Dickens, sir.'

He raised an eyebrow. 'Have you ever read him?'

'Oh yes, sir. But I prefer Sir Walter Scott myself.'

Ian was amazed. A maid who read Dickens and Sir Walter Scott. How fascinating.

'It's a wonderful library, don't you think?' he smiled, making a gesture that took in the entire room.

'Oh yes, sir. That smell, it's unmistakable. Books, books and more books. It's a smell you only get in libraries and bookshops.'

'I see you're supposed to be dusting.'

'Yes, sir. I only stopped for a few moments. I swear.'

'The temptation was too much I take it.'

She coloured slightly. 'Yes, sir. I apologise, sir.'

'There's no need for that. We're not slave drivers after all. At least I hope we're not.'

'No, sir.'

He studied her, thinking how attractive she was. For a servant girl that is. 'You're from Glasgow I believe.'

'That's correct, sir.'

'It must be quite a change for you coming here.'

'It is, sir. A change for the better. The countryside is lovely. I plan long walks in it on my days off.'

'Indeed. And what about reading?'

Her face fell. 'That's the only problem, sir. I don't now get much time for that as you'll appreciate. And even if I had it's impossible for me to lay my hands on books. All mine came from the public library.'

'Which aren't exactly thick on the ground round here,' he commented wryly.

She grinned. 'Not exactly.'

'What's your name?'

'Bridie, sir.'

'It suits you. Sometimes people's names don't but yours most definitely does.'

He crossed to a large imposing desk, extracted a folder from one of its drawers, the reason he'd entered the library in the first place, and headed for the door.

'Goodbye for now, Bridie.'

'Goodbye, sir.'

She hurriedly resumed her dusting.

Chapter 11

'You remember Moira McLaren, don't you, Ian?' Rose smiled. It was the Hogmanay party and the drawing room was humming with conversation. In the end thirty invitations had been sent out, all of them taken up.

Ian's jaw nearly dropped open. My God! he thought. What a stunner. Where was the horrible little so and so he'd once known and thoroughly disliked? In Moira's case the ugly duckling truly had turned into a swan.

'Of course. How are you, Moira?' he said, extending a hand. The hand that briefly touched his was cool and elegant.

'I'm very well. And you?'

'Learning the estate business at the sharp end. Hard work, but enjoyable and rewarding.'

He took in her dress which was made of dainty all-over embroidered net, the skirt displaying graceful godet flare inserts of harmonising silk georgette crêpe that had also been used for a cascade scarf. A nosegay situated on the shoulder added a pretty touch.

Moira was thinking that he'd matured considerably. She warmed to him in a way she never had previously.

'I understand you're not long home from Switzerland,' he said.

'That's right.'

'And how was it there?'

She pulled a face. 'Boring beyond belief. But it did have its moments I suppose.'

'Wasn't it a finishing school?'

'The boredom nearly finished me off.'

Ian laughed.

'But now I'm back and that's all that matters.' She glanced around. 'Quite a do you've laid on. I've no doubt we're all going to have a wonderful time.'

'That was the idea. There'll be dancing later. Scottish dancing to an accordion. I do hope you'll have one, if not several, with me.'

'That would be jolly.'

'It's settled then.' He signalled to a maid carrying a tray of drinks.

'A little refreshment?' he proposed.

Rose smiled to herself. It was as though she wasn't there, Ian and Moira were so intently focused on one another.

Muttering an excuse she left them to it.

Georgina had managed to manoeuvre Andrew into a corner of the room where, temporarily at least, she had him to herself. The scent of the cologne he was wearing filled her nostrils. 'Well, Andrew, any young lady on the horizon yet?'

He found that somewhat direct, and wondered at the strange glint in her eyes. 'I'm afraid not, Georgina.'

'Maybe I shall do something about that.'

He regarded her quizzically. 'Who exactly do you have in mind?'

Myself, she thought. Though would never have dared say so. 'That's my secret, Andrew.'

'Secret, eh?'

She was teasing him now. 'I don't want any resistance on your part. I know what men can be like when they think something, or someone in this instance, is being pushed at them.'

'Hmmh,' he murmured, and had a sip of champagne.

Rose was watching them enviously, wishing it was she who was with Andrew. The two of them alone together.

'I say, Rose?'

She turned her attention to Alastair Dundee, a drippy lad who'd been mad on her for years. 'Yes, Alastair?'

It was a good five minutes before she could get away.

Bridie was helping lay out the buffet supper that Mrs Kilbride and the kitchen staff had been slaving over for days. There was enough to feed the entire British army, she thought as she placed a platter of smoked ham on one of the special trestle tables that had been brought in for the occasion.

Ham, venison, hare, rabbit, pork, beef, those were the meats. Then there were salads of all varieties, potatoes, bread, pickles and chutneys. The *pièce de résistance* was an enormous bowl of trifle dominating the centre of the buffet. Her mouth watered just looking at it all.

'Some feast, eh?' Jeannie Swanson commented, placing yet another platter alongside the one Bridie had just put down.

'I'll say.'

'I hate to think what all this must have cost.'

'A king's ransom,' Bridie said.

'Aye, no doubt.'

'Still, you have to admit, it does look gorgeous.'

'Oh, to be a toff,' Jeannie sighed.

'Rather than be a toff you'll be unemployed if you don't stop chattering and get on with it,' a well-known voice rebuked them.

Both girls swung round to find the housekeeper there.

'Sorry, Miss Coltart,' Jeannie gulped.

'I should think so. Now hurry up, there's still plenty more to be done.'

Bridie and Jeannie scurried away.

'Enjoying yourself?' Willie asked Andrew a while later.

'Very much so.'

'Get enough to eat?'

'Plenty, and more.'

Willie nodded his approval. 'Good.'

'Some interesting people here tonight. I had a marvellous chat with a chap called Ogilvie.'

'Oh yes,' Willie said. 'Richard Ogilvie. Bit of an explorer in his time. Did he mention?'

'Yes. I found his tales of Africa quite fascinating.'

Willie glanced around. 'Can't see Georgina anywhere. Seems to have vanished.'

Andrew couldn't spot her either. 'Probably a call of nature, old boy. Or caught up elsewhere.'

'Probably.'

Willie took out his pocket watch and snapped it open. 'About an hour to go.'

'The new year, 1925,' Andrew mused. 'I wonder what that will bring.'

'I wonder,' Willie repeated.

*   *   *

'Ladies and gentlemen, can I have your attention please!' Willie called out.

Gradually silence descended.

'Five minutes to midnight. Can you all please ensure that your glasses are charged.'

Bridie was one of those whose duty it was to see that this was the case.

Rose joined Andrew. 'It's hot in here, isn't it.'

'Bound to be with so many people present. Not to mention several fires blazing.'

There was a sheen of sweat on Andrew's neck which Rose found fascinating. She blushed at the sudden thought of licking it off.

'You all right?'

'As I said, it's hot.'

'You're not going to faint or anything, are you?'

She smiled. 'Of course not, silly. I'm fine, simply hot that's all.' In truth, if she was being honest, it wasn't only the heat of the room that was making her that way, but also the proximity of Andrew.

'Miss Rose, a top up?' Bridie queried, brandishing a bottle of champagne.

'Please.'

'And you, sir?' she asked as she filled Rose's glass.

'Thank you.'

When she'd done that Bridie moved swiftly on.

'That's a nice cologne you're wearing,' Rose remarked. 'I noticed it earlier.'

'I'm glad you like it.'

'More men should wear cologne I always think.'

'Yes, I quite agree. But it is a personal thing. Many men consider it effeminate.'

Something Andrew could never be accused of, Rose

thought. He was one hundred per cent male. His maleness positively oozed out of him.

'A minute to go!' Willie called out.

Rose knew what she was going to do, and thrilled inside at the prospect.

It was almost as if everyone in the room was holding his or her breath, Andrew thought, staring out over the assembly. There again, this was the biggest moment in the Scottish calendar. The English could have their Christmas, for the Scots it was Hogmanay. Seeing out the old year and ushering in the new.

'Ten . . . nine . . . eight . . .' Willie counted down.

Willie raised his glass aloft. 'A happy new year to ane an' a!'

The room erupted, well wishing, back slapping, handshaking and toasting going on everywhere.

'A happy new year, Andrew,' Rose said, gazing deeply into his eyes.

'And a happy new year to you, Rose.'

He bent to kiss her on the cheek, but at the very last instant she moved her face so that his lips landed on hers.

That startled Andrew, who only now remembered what Jack Riach had said about Rose.

Rose wished Andrew would put his free arm round her, but naturally that was out of the question. But it would have been lovely.

'Well,' Andrew murmured when their lips parted.

Suddenly embarrassed, Rose glanced away. She didn't regret having done that, not in the least. She only wished she could do it again.

The accordionist appeared and immediately struck up. It was now time for the dancing.

An Apple From Eden

People moved away from the centre of the room to line the walls. The furniture had been rearranged the previous day so that there was now a large area where the dancing could take place.

Willie took Georgina's hand and led her on to the floor, quickly joined there by others.

The accordionist stopped, announced an eightsome reel, and then struck up again.

Ian was already up with Moira McLaren.

'Rose?'

Her heart leapt. 'If you're asking me to dance I'd love to, Andrew.'

'Then shall we?'

'Here you are, Bridie,' Miss Coltart said, handing her a schooner of sherry.

'Thank you, miss.'

'It's the only time of the year I condone drinking amongst the staff. But it is Hogmanay after all.'

'Yes, miss. Happy new year.'

Miss Coltart's face softened. 'And you, Bridie.'

There was still masses to do, the celebrations would go on for hours yet, so Bridie didn't linger over her drink.

At last, Georgina thought some time later, when she saw Andrew approach. She'd been waiting for him to ask her up, which he was now surely going to do.

'The whisky is all Drummond you'll be pleased to hear.' Willie beamed at Andrew.

'I should hope so.'

'Champagne is fine, but it gets tedious after a bit. Not like good old Scottish whisky, eh?'

'Never that.' Willie had quite a load on board, Andrew noted. Unlike himself who'd been taking it easy.

'I was wondering if you care to dance, Georgina?' he asked.

'I'd be delighted to.' She handed her glass to Willie. 'Take care of that for me, darling, will you? Andrew and I are about to trip the light fantastic.'

Andrew laughed. 'Hardly that.'

'We'll see.'

It was a rare event for Willie to get drunk, but he certainly was now. He sat heavily on their bed and ran a hand over his perspiring forehead.

'Went excellently I thought,' he slurred.

'Yes it did.'

He struggled out of his jacket and threw it aside. 'Wine and whisky, shouldn't mix them.'

'No you shouldn't.'

He beckoned to her. 'Come here.'

Georgina crossed to Willie who pulled her on to his knee. 'You were the belle of the ball tonight. Know that?'

'Was I?'

'Without a doubt. By far the best-looking woman there. I couldn't have been more proud.'

She hoped he wasn't going to kiss her, which he promptly did. His lips were sloppily wet which she found disgusting.

'How about a little . . . ?' He broke off and winked slyly at her.

Georgina laughed. 'You're in no fit state for that sort of thing, Willie Seaton. You wouldn't be able to manage it.'

'How do we know unless I try?'

'I know all right. Now the best thing for you is to crawl

into that bed and get some sleep. You're going to have a dreadful hangover in the morning.'

'Never!'

'Oh yes you will.'

She slipped from his lap. 'Here, let me help you with those trousers.

'Don't need any help,' he further slurred.

She stood watching in amusement as he struggled with his braces, eventually managing to pull them over his arms. 'You're right, it is difficult,' he confessed.

'Let me.'

She removed his shoes and socks, then assisted him out of his trousers. 'I'll hang this lot up,' she declared.

Willie wormed his way up the bed until his head was resting on the pillows. He closed one eye in order to try and focus, something he was suddenly having a problem with. 'Best-looking woman there,' he repeated.

Moments later he began to snore.

Bridie's last thoughts before she dropped off were about Teresa. As always she'd remembered Teresa in her prayers and asked God to forgive her.

She recalled the funeral and how awful that had been. As had the wake afterwards. During the latter Mrs Kelly had drawn her aside.

She'd denied knowledge of knowing anything. As far as she was concerned Teresa had died of a sudden haemorrhage, presumably the result of internal bleeding, and that was that.

Mrs Kelly hadn't believed her, but was willing to accept she'd keep her mouth shut about the real reason for Teresa's death. It was an unspoken pact between them to save Teresa's reputation and the Kelly family's good name.

Goodnight, Teresa, she said in her mind.
Then she was asleep.

Georgina sat staring at herself in her vanity mirror. Dare she? Dare she actually do it?

She pulled the duck-egg blue negligée she was wearing tighter about herself. She knew such things went on, were commonplace even in certain circles. It was wrong of course, terribly wrong. But oh so very tempting.

Willie snorted and turned over. Georgina glanced at him and thought of their lovemaking two days previously. Another failure as far as she was concerned. He'd left her so high up in the air it had taken ages for her to come down again. Nor, because of the circumstances, had she been able to give herself satisfaction.

Georgina drew in a deep breath, then slowly exhaled. She was tipsy, but not to the point where her thinking was muddled, not fully appreciating what she was contemplating. There would be no excuses come morning.

She smiled inwardly. Hardly come morning for it was already that. But it would be hours before anyone stirred in the house, apart from a few of the staff. The party had finished so late it would be noon before most were up and about.

Dare she? That was the question. She could make an awful fool of herself which would be terrible. There again, as the saying went, nothing ventured nothing gained.

And she was so curious. So very very curious.

Andrew came groggily awake, dimly aware that Ellen was sitting on his bed. Now why was that, he hadn't asked her to come? Then he remembered he wasn't home but at The Haven. His eyes snapped open.

'Sshhh!' Georgina whispered, placing a finger over her lips.

'Georg . . . what's wrong?'

'Nothing's wrong.'

'Then why the hell are you here?'

'I just wanted to . . . be with you.'

'Jesus Christ!' Andrew swore, pulling himself upright. 'Where's Willie?'

'Sound asleep, drunk as can be. It'll be hours and hours before he comes to.'

Andrew's mind was whirling. This was bloody dangerous. 'You'd better get back to him at once. On you go and we'll forget all about this madness.'

'Please don't be cross with me,' she pleaded.

'I'm not cross.'

'Yes you are.'

He studied her in the darkness. 'What do you mean *be* with me?'

'I should think that was obvious.'

'But you . . . you're Willie's wife and he's my good friend.'

'I know,' she replied softly, reaching out for his hand which he quickly snatched away.

'I thought you found me attractive,' she said. 'I've seen it in your eyes.'

'I do, Georgina.'

'As I do you.'

'That doesn't alter matters. I can't take advantage of a friend's wife. Only a bounder would do that.'

Georgina hung her head. 'It wasn't easy for me to come here. I knew I risked making a fool of myself.'

He softened towards her. 'You haven't done that.'

'No?'

'You've simply made a mistake, that's all.'

'I see.'

'Now you'd better leave.'

Georgina shivered. 'It's cold in here. Our room is far warmer.'

'Then you'd better get back there.'

'I don't want you to think I make a habit of this kind of thing. The truth is, I've only ever been with one man in my life, and that's Willie.'

Andrew wasn't sure whether to believe that or not. 'Why me then?'

'Because you fascinate me. I keep wondering what it would be like being made love to by you. I wonder all the time and have done ever since meeting you.'

Andrew swallowed hard. Dear God, he'd never realised. Forbidden fruit, he reminded himself. Beyond the Pale. 'I'm flattered, Georgina, honestly I am. If things had been different I wouldn't hesitate. If you were even someone else's wife, not a friend's. But I just couldn't.'

'I understand.'

Damn it, he thought. He was becoming aroused. If only she didn't smell so damned gorgeous. She moved slightly so that one of her breasts was silhouetted against the curtained window.

He swore again when she began to cry softly.

'You mustn't do that. You musn't,' he pleaded.

'I'm sorry.'

And then Georgina played her trump card. The one she'd hoped she wouldn't have to play. But having gone this far, why not?

Standing, she slowly undid the belt of her negligée, and held the garment open. 'I want you to see what you're missing before I go.'

It was too much. What a sight. What a glorious sight. His resistance crumbled.

Andrew banished Willie from his mind as, with a groan, he reached for her.

Georgina lay staring at the ceiling, not having slept a wink. Alongside her Willie continued to snore.

She couldn't believe what it had been like. The sensations she'd felt, the things Andrew had done to her. Again and again he'd brought her to fruition until she'd thought she must surely die from the sheer pleasure of it all.

She ran her hands over her breasts, they still throbbing, over her stomach and along her thighs. Thighs Andrew had so recently been between.

What an experience. One simply out of this world. And to think she'd been missing that all these years. Compared to Andrew, Willie was . . . well, pathetic. There was no other word for it. Pathetic.

That wasn't fair, she chided herself. She was being cruel. But it was true nonetheless.

Andrew. She wanted to shout his name aloud. A few short hours and she'd come to worship the man.

She shivered in recollection of how it had been between them.

Andrew was pacing his bedroom as he'd been doing since shortly after Georgina had left. How could he have been so stupid. So bloody weak willed! What he'd done was appalling.

One thing was certain, it must never happen again. If Willie ever found out it would destroy the poor bugger, and that was something he never wanted to have on his conscience.

He'd been all right until she'd opened her negligée. Then he'd been lost. Quite overcome at the sight of that voluptuousness.

Andrew stopped and ran fingers through his hair. Go home straight away? That's what he wanted to do. But what would he say to Willie, what possible excuse could he make? None he could think of.

Willie would be upset to say the least, wishing to know why he was going. What was wrong. Had he been insulted. What?

No, he had to stay and brazen it out. That was all he could do. And pray Georgina didn't pay him any more visits.

He glanced at the door which he'd already checked earlier. It didn't have a lock, worst luck. He'd have felt a great deal safer if it had.

Andrew threw himself into a chair. What he wouldn't have given for a glass of whisky right then. Several glasses. And now he was going to have to get dressed and go downstairs. How long before he had to face Willie? Not long he shouldn't think.

He must keep the guilt out of his face. He must.

Andrew swore viciously, bitterly regretting what he'd done. At least part of him did.

If only she'd been someone else's bloody wife!

He met Georgina first, bumping into her in the corridor. She was positively glowing.

'Hello, Andrew,' she beamed.

'Hello, Georgina.'

'There's some late buffet luncheon set out to tide us over to dinner. I've already had a plateful myself.'

'How's Willie?'

She chuckled. 'Like a bear with a sore head, which is

precisely what he has. An extremely sore head according to him.'

'Is he up and about?'

'Well, he is up, but I'm not sure whether he's about yet.' She dropped her voice. 'Andrew . . .'

'No,' he interjected quickly. 'It never happened, understand? It just never happened.'

'Oh, but it did,' she replied, eyes sparking.

He stared at her in dismay. 'Well, it won't ever again. I assure you.'

She touched him lightly on the arm. 'I thought you enjoyed it.'

'I did. But that's irrelevant.'

Now that she'd tasted the delights he had to offer she wasn't about to give them up. Oh no. Somehow, some way, Andrew would be hers. She'd decided that while dressing.

'I'd better get along,' Andrew said.

'Goodbye for now . . . lover.'

Andrew blanched, and moved on his way.

'You look very sombre.'

Andew turned to find Rose standing beside him. 'Do I?'

'Sombre to the point of being grim. Have you also got a hangover?'

Andrew shook his head. 'I feel right as rain.'

'Poor Father. He swears he'll never mix wine and whisky ever again.'

'I haven't seen him yet. Is he that bad?'

'Terrible. His eyes are all sunken and he cut himself shaving. He's feeling very sorry for himself.'

'He'll survive.' Andrew laughed. 'I should know. I've suffered a few hangovers in my time.'

'Were you very wild when younger?'

That surprised him. 'Why do you ask?'

'You have that air about you. I think you must have been very wild.'

'A bit,' he acknowledged.

'I think young men should be. It shows spirit. And every worthwhile man should have that.'

'I see. I take it you're an expert on these matters,' he teased.

'Perhaps I am.'

He didn't want to pursue this any further. 'I've been standing here looking out this window contemplating, strange as it may seem, having a drink. Would you care to join me?'

'There's nothing I'd like better, Andrew.'

'Then let's find one.'

Chapter 12

It was his first day back at work after the new year which didn't please Pat Flynn one little bit. He'd much rather have been home in front of a nice cosy fire than out here in the snow. He glanced up at a leaden grey sky from which millions of swirling snowflakes were falling. No signs of a let-up there he thought.

He reined in Jasper when he spotted one of their cards in a window. Another sale, one of many in an exceptionally busy morning. He'd have to return to the depot shortly and reload. At least that meant he'd get a cup of tea.

He was about to jump down from the cart when a couple appeared round a corner heading in his direction. It was Geraldine and Dougal, the pair arm in arm.

Dougal said something which caused Geraldine to laugh and pull herself even more tightly to him. She looked happy as Larry.

Pat turned his face away, not wanting them to see his expression. Jesus, but he was jealous.

'Why, hello, Mr Flynn,' Geraldine said as they came alongside.

'Hello, Mrs Buchanan. And you, Mr Buchanan.'

'Not the best of days for your job,' Dougal commented with a smile.

Pat shrugged. 'That's how it goes.'

Then they'd gone past, continuing on their way.

Pat glared after them. How long to go before Dougal went back to sea?

He wished to hell he knew.

'You what!' Jack Riach exclaimed. It was a Friday night and he and Andrew were in the local.

'You heard me.'

Jack sat back in his chair. 'I'm disappointed in you, Andrew.'

'I'm disappointed in myself. I feel rotten about it.'

'I should think so.'

Andrew had a swallow of whisky. 'You should have seen her though, Jack. She's got a magnificent body.'

'Which you simply couldn't resist,' Jack replied sarcastically.

'She was standing there naked, flaunting herself in front of me. I'm not made of stone, Jack. I'm only flesh and blood after all.'

'She's that good looking?'

'Believe me, she is.'

'And she just turned up in your bedroom out of the blue?'

'Out of the blue, Jack, I swear.'

'Had you been leading her on in any way? You know, flirting and that sort of thing?'

'No I hadn't. I did dance with her at the party of course,

174

well that was obligatory. She was my hostess after all. Manners dictated that I did. Not that it was a chore, quite the contrary.'

'How extraordinary,' Jack commented, feeling for his pint.

'I kept as much out of Willie's way for the rest of my stay there as I could. Out of his way and Georgina's. I ended up spending quite a lot of time with Rose.' Andrew hesitated, then said, 'You were right about Rose.'

'You didn't . . . not Rose as well?'

'Of course not!'

'I'm glad to hear it,' Jack replied drily.

'She is very pleasant to be with. In fact she rather reminds me of . . .' He broke off.

'Who, Andrew?'

'Nobody.'

Jack smiled. 'I can hear it in your voice, old boy. It's Alice, am I right?'

'Only a little. The occasional gesture, the odd inflection. What she does do is ride like Alice, there were times when, if I hadn't known better, I would have sworn I was back in Ireland and it was Alice I was watching.'

'Interesting,' Jack mused. 'Speaking of Ireland, how does all this affect your plans?'

'I did consider cancelling, but Willie would be terribly put out if I did.'

'So you'll still go.'

'Yes.'

'And what if Mrs Seaton takes it upon herself to visit you again?'

'She won't, I'm convinced of that. Hotels are too public, Jack. Besides, hotel bedrooms have locks on their doors. So I'll be quite safe.'

Jack chuckled. 'It's funny hearing you talk about being safe from a woman. Usually it's the other way round, or it used to be in the past anyway. They had to worry about being safe from you.'

'Aye, true,' Andrew said with a smile. 'But that was a long while ago. Before Alice.'

'Before Alice,' Jack repeated, and nodded his understanding. He couldn't imagine what it would be like to lose Hettie. The end of the world as far as he'd be concerned. Hettie had become everything to him. Hettie and wee Tommy.

Andrew had a swallow of whisky, emptying his glass. Following that with a pull from his pint. 'Anyway, I really want to go to Ireland now. I was in two minds for quite some time, not sure at all how I'll react. And I'm still not sure. But I've come to the conclusion that it'll be a good thing for me to go back. No matter what happens.'

'Well, it couldn't be going better,' Sean Flynn declared to the rest of the Samurai. They were gathered together in the condemned tenement.

He indicated the pile of money in front of him. 'Look at that, eh?'

'It's like taking sweeties from a baby,' Sammy Renton chuckled. 'A few words from you, Sean, a bit of a threat like, and they're falling over themselves to give us cash.'

Sean nodded, that was true enough. After Rizzio it had just got easier and easier as word got round. The shopkeepers not already on their list were almost reaching for their tills the moment he and some of the others walked through the door.

'So what are we going to do with it?' Bobby O'Toole queried, gesturing at the money.

'A divvy?' Dan Smith suggested hopefully. 'Then we could all go straight down the boozer and have a whale of a time.'

'That's a possibility,' Sean acknowledged.

'Do you have something in mind?' Jim Gallagher asked, guessing that he did.

'I have.' Sean paused for effect. He was getting the hang of this leader thing, he thought. 'I propose we use it to rent ourselves a proper place which we can fill with decent furniture.'

'A proper place?' Jim frowned.

'Aye, look about you. This house stinks and it's got rats in it. I hate rats.'

'We could get a cat,' Bill O'Connell joked.

'Bugger a cat,' Sean snapped in reply. 'A decent house with decent furniture. Now what do you say?'

'I still fancy a divvy,' Dan Smith grumbled.

'Shall we take a vote on it then?'

Dan Smith was the only one to vote against the house and furniture idea.

Ian was shown into a room where Moira and her mother were sitting. It was a Sunday afternoon. His eyes immediately sought out Moira's.

'Why, Ian, how nice of you to call,' Delphine McLaren declared.

'I hope I'm not intruding.'

'Not at all. We were just about to take coffee. Will you join us?'

'That would be lovely.'

'If you'd ring that bell pull for us then.'

Ian crossed to the indicated bell pull and tugged it. He then returned to the ladies and sat close to Moira. He'd have liked to sit beside her on the sofa but thought that a bit forward.

She'd expected this to happen, Delphine thought with satisfaction. She hadn't failed to notice how well Ian and Moira had got on during Hogmanay. Well, it certainly suited her purposes, the Seatons were an excellent family to marry into, should it come to that. Which she fervently hoped it would.

The three of them began making small talk.

'Is something wrong or worrying you, darling?' Willie enquired.

Georgina, at her vanity table brushing out her hair, glanced at him in the mirror. 'No, why do you ask?'

He shrugged. 'You haven't been quite yourself of late. In fact since the party.'

'I can't say I've noticed.'

'Distant somehow, detached.'

She carefully laid her brush on the table and turned to face him. Oh dear, she thought. Had she been distant and detached? She certainly hadn't meant to be.

'It's probably the time of year,' she smiled. 'I've never enjoyed winter as you well know.'

He gave an inward sigh of relief. It would appear he hadn't offended her in any way, which he'd thought might be the case. 'I wondered if it was me getting drunk on Hogmanay? I did apologise as you will remember.'

'No, silly. I wasn't put out by that. Most of the male guests were one over the eight when they left anyway, why should you be any different? Hogmanay is Hogmanay after all.'

She must be more careful in future she told herself. Truth was since new year's morning she hadn't been able to get

Andrew out of her mind, awake and asleep. Andrew, and their lovemaking. How she desperately craved for another bout of that. Craved so much there were times it made her teeth ache.

As for Willie, she hadn't exactly gone off him. No, that would be taking it too far. He was still the kind, generous man he'd always been, and still a most unsatisfactory lover. Perhaps she had been somewhat detached as Willie put it. Yes, she must be more careful.

'Anyway, Ireland is coming up shortly,' Willie went on. 'I'm sure a break away from here will do you the world of good. Buck you up, what?'

'I'm sure,' she replied, returning to her brushing.

She couldn't have been more sure about anything. For Ireland meant Andrew.

She didn't know how. But she'd engineer another bout of lovemaking between the pair of them.

She trembled at the thought.

'Come in, Mr Flynn,' Geraldine Buchanan said.

Mr Flynn, that meant Dougal was still there. Pat swore inwardly.

'You know where the bin is. I'll just go and fetch some money.'

Pat upended the coal bag into the bin. How much longer before that sod Dougal went back to sea? How much bloody longer!

Geraldine reappeared. 'And how have you been, Mr Flynn?'

'Fine, thank you.'

'All this snow gets you down, don't you think?'

He nodded, accepting a ten-shilling note from her. He delved in his bag for change.

'Thank you,' she said, accepting it.

'Goodbye for now then.'

She let him get to the door. 'Oh, before you go.'

He hesitated. 'Yes?'

Her face broke into a huge smile. 'Would you care for a bottle of beer, Pat?'

'Bottle of . . .' He broke off, had the cow been teasing him? 'Where's Dougal?'

'Gone away again. Two days ago. And it'll be a long voyage. He doesn't know where but he does know it'll be a long one.'

'You . . .'

Geraldine tinkled a laugh. 'I couldn't resist it, Pat. I simply couldn't. Your face when I offered you the beer was a picture.'

'This Friday?' he croaked.

'I'll be waiting.'

She bent to open a cupboard, provocatively sticking her bottom in the air.

If Pat hadn't been so filthy he'd have had her there and then.

'Hey, you, come here!'

The pimply-faced lad turned to face Sean and Mo Binchy. 'Aye, what is it?'

'You've been nicking off Harris's the newsagent's. Haven't you?'

'Fuck off.'

He made to move away but Sean grabbed him and spun him round. 'I'm talking to you, son. Where's your manners?'

'Who the hell are you?'

'We're the Samurai and we give Mr Harris protection. Do you understand?'

For a moment fear flickered in the youth's eyes. He'd heard of the Samurai. 'Protection?'

Sean produced his razor. 'That's right.'

Pimple face stared at the razor, then up again at Sean. His mouth had gone dry. 'I didn't know that,' he replied, still trying to give an outward show of bravado.

'Well, now you do. I'm giving you a warning. If it happens again we'll come after you, and when we find you . . .' Sean flicked his razor several times. 'Mince.'

There was no reply to that.

'Have I made myself clear?'

The youth, his assumed bravado ebbing away, nodded. He knew what the result of a razoring was like.

'Now hop it. Bugger off.'

The youth didn't exactly leave at a run, but it wasn't far off it.

Pat swaggered into the kitchen. 'Well, that's me off to my committee meeting,' he announced.

'You look very smart, Pa,' Alison said.

He beamed at her. 'Why, thank you, lass.'

'You do indeed,' Kathleen declared. 'I'm right proud to see you like that.'

If only you knew, he thought. If only you knew.

Bridie brushed snow off a fallen tree, making a space for herself, and sat. How stupid this was, how incredibly bloody stupid. She banged her gloved hands together trying to restore some warmth to them. She was frozen through.

A glance at the sky told her it wouldn't be long before it got dark. What then? She daren't even think of that.

She mustn't panic she told herself. That would be fatal. Once she'd caught her breath she must trudge on.

'Hello.'

Bridie started and swivelled round to find Ian Seaton staring at her, his expression one of puzzlement. She gasped with relief. 'Thank God!'

'What are you doing out here all by yourself?'

She rose from the tree. 'It's my day off and I went for a walk. Only somehow I got lost.'

'I see.'

'I've absolutely no idea where I am.'

He smiled. 'City girls shouldn't go wandering around the countryside alone. Especially not in weather like this. What if I hadn't happened along?'

She hung her head. 'I know. I've just been telling myself how stupid I've been.'

'How long have you been out here?'

She shook her head. 'Ages. And a lot of that time has been spent trying to find my way back again.' Bridie suddenly sobbed. 'I've been so scared.'

Ian went to her and took her into his arms. 'There there. It's all right now. You're safe.'

'You must think me a fool.'

'Not a fool exactly. Silly perhaps, but not a fool. As I said, city girls shouldn't go wandering around the countryside alone. Especially . . .'

'Not in weather like this,' she finished for him.

They both laughed, which brightened her considerably.

'Let's make a move then,' he said. 'Are you up to it?'

'I'll have to be. I'm certainly not staying here.'

She fell into step beside him. 'Where have you been?' she asked.

'There's a stretch of fence been blown down and I was sent out to see precisely what the damage was.'

'Lucky for me you were.' Bridie glanced about her.

'These trees are spooky.' They were passing through a large wood.

'Only if you're not used to this sort of thing. I find them rather comforting myself.'

'Comforting?' She found that hard to believe.

He nodded. 'Yes. But don't forget I was brought up on the estate and know it in all its moods and seasons.'

'It's very large, isn't it? The estate I mean.'

'Very.'

Somewhere an owl hooted, a melancholy sound.

'The trouble started when I left the path I was on,' Bridie explained. 'I wanted to explore. Except I explored too far and couldn't find the path, or any other path, again.'

'Next time I suggest you don't leave the path, or go beyond sight of the house.'

'Don't worry, I won't. I'll be extremely careful from now on.' Bridie shivered. 'I've probably caught my death of cold.'

'Have a bath when you get back.'

'I can't. We're only allowed one a week and I'm not due mine till next Tuesday.'

Ian had forgotten about those particular staff arrangements. 'Tell you what, I'll have a word with Mrs Coltart. I'm sure she'll make an exception in this case.'

'That's very kind of you.'

'It's the least I can do.' He smiled.

What a lovely smile, she thought, really noticing it for the first time. 'I shall always think of you as my knight in shining armour,' she declared.

That amused him. 'Why so?'

'Well, I was a damsel in dire distress and you came to my rescue. My knight in shining armour.'

He laughed, liking the idea.

'Perhaps I shouldn't have said that, me being a maid and you the son of the house. I didn't mean to be impertinent.'

'I know that, Bridie.'

'Thank you.'

He'd forgotten she read a lot, no doubt where her fanciful ideas came from.

They emerged from the wood into a field bounded on three sides by high hedges. 'The house is about half a mile from here. It shouldn't take us too long.'

Bridie was glad about that, she was exhausted.

'Have you ever read the story of Robin Hood?' he asked.

'Oh yes. It was terrific, though sad at the end when he died.'

'Then you know of Maid Marian.'

'Of course.'

He was teasing her now. 'That's how I shall think of *you* in future. If I'm the knight in shining armour you shall be Maid Bridie. As you said, you are a maid after all.'

'But not that sort.'

'No?'

If she hadn't been so cold she'd have blushed on realising to what he was referring. 'Well, yes I am.'

'So Maid Bridie you shall be.'

She wasn't going to let him get entirely away with that. 'And you will be Sir Ian of Seaton.'

'Done.'

Sir Ian of Seaton, that further amused him.

Kathleen was on her way home from 'the steamie' as the communal wash house was known. She was struggling under the weight of the weekly laundry.

It never seemed to let up, she thought. From morning to

night it was all go. Cooking, cleaning, ironing, on and on it went in a never-ending circle.

Sometimes she wished . . . But what was the point in wishing for something that would never happen? Her lot was housewife and mother with the drudgery that accompanied those roles. Drudgery that made you old before your time. Lined your face, ruined your figure, reddened and chapped your hands.

She sighed. A nice cup of tea when she got in. And a biscuit she'd put by. Then it was down to ironing before Alison arrived home from school.

At least it wasn't all bad, she reflected. Bridie was working for toffs and her man was on a very important committee.

Aye, it wasn't all bad.

Hettie had watched Jack get more and more fidgety with every passing day. From past experience she knew what that was leading to.

'Monday morning,' Jack suddenly said. 'We'll make a start then.'

'All right.'

He shook his head. 'I'm still not certain I can manage a novel though.'

'Well, you won't know until you try, will you?'

'That's true enough,' he grudgingly admitted, and gnawed a thumbnail.

'There's something I've been meaning to speak to you about, Jack. Do you think you could buy me a typewriter?'

'A typewriter,' he mused. 'I can do that without any bother. But don't you have to go on some kind of course to learn how to use one?'

'That's the proper way of doing it, but I can hardly go on a course in Dalneil.'

They both laughed, their village being a small one.

'So I thought I'd try and teach myself. It can't be that difficult. I shall simply persevere until I've mastered it.'

And master it she would, he thought. That was his Hettie for you.

'It would make it all so much easier, Jack. And more professional too.'

He nodded. 'A typewriter you shall have.'

Too late for this book, Hettie reflected. But if Jack did manage a full manuscript there might be others.

'Monday morning,' he repeated, and went back to gnawing his thumbnail.

Bridie snuffled into one of several hankies she'd had to borrow, feeling wretched beyond belief.

The bedroom door swung open, and moments later Jeannie Swanson breezed in carrying a tray. 'Your luncheon, madam,' Jeannie announced in an affected posh voice.

Bridie struggled to sit up in bed where she'd been sent by Mrs Coltart when the heavy cold had manifested itself. Mrs Coltart had said she was to stay there until better.

'What is it?'

'Chicken broth and freshly baked bread. Mrs Kilbride told me she doesn't want to see anything left when the tray is returned.' Jeannie set the tray in front of Bridie. 'And a book from Master Ian.'

Bridie's eyes lit up. Sure enough, there was also a book on the tray.

'How kind of him,' she breathed.

'Gave it to me personally. Said it should help keep boredom at bay.'

Bridie picked up the book and glanced at the title, delighted it wasn't one she'd already read. '*Fame*,' she murmured. 'By Micheline Keating.' A quick glance at the back informed her it was the story of a great actress who rose from the gutter, and of her daughter who eclipsed her triumphs. 'I say, it couldn't be better. Sounds like a cracking tale.' She frowned. 'I wonder where Master Ian got it from?' Not leather bound, it clearly wasn't part of the library downstairs.

'He explained that. Said his sister Rose bought it last time she was in Edinburgh. He also mentioned that Miss Rose reads a bit herself and will be happy to lend you more books in future.'

'How wonderful. When you next see the pair of them will you thank them for me?'

'I'll do that,' Jeannie replied. 'Now you get on with that soup before it gets cold.'

Bridie laid the book to one side and hurriedly attacked her meal. She couldn't wait to get started on *Fame*.

Jeannie laughed as she left the bedroom. She'd never seen Bridie so excited. The book would do her the world of good.

Willie lit a cigarette and sucked the smoke deep into his lungs, thinking how enjoyable a cigarette was directly after a meal.

'You've been seeing Moira McLaren, I understand.' Georgina smiled at Ian.

He glanced over at his stepmother. 'That's right.'

'Is it serious?'

Rose sniggered, which earned her a disapproving look from Georgina.

Ian shrugged, trying to be nonchalant. 'I've no idea. It's early days yet.'

'But you do like her?'

'I'd hardly be seeing Moira if I didn't,' he replied sarcastically.

'Pretty lass,' Willie commented.

'Good figure,' Rose added, and sniggered again.

'Rose!' Georgina admonished.

Ian glared at his sister. Trust Georgina to bring up the subject of Moira when Rose was present.

'When are you seeing her again?' Georgina queried.

Ian sighed. 'With all due respect, isn't that my business?'

'I'm only showing an interest.'

Being nosy more like, Ian thought.

'Have you kissed her yet?'

'That's enough, Rose,' Willie said quietly.

'Well, I too was only showing an interest, Pa.' She rounded again on Ian. 'So?'

'That's for me to know and you to wonder about.'

And having said that Ian got up and left the room.

Bloody prying women, he thought angrily.

Chapter 13

Andrew stood on deck staring out over the choppy sea.
There it was, just discernible, the coast of Ireland.
He closed his eyes. Remembering . . . remembering . . .

'I don't believe it,' Billy Roberts exclaimed softly. 'I just
don't believe it.' He and Andrew were sitting by themselves
in the mess having a drink, and Billy had just glanced at the
front page of that evening's newspaper.

'Don't believe what, old boy?' Andrew smiled.

'Wait a moment, let me read this through.'

Andrew sipped his whisky, wondering what had per-
turbed his friend.

Billy looked at Andrew, his expression grim. 'It's the
Fortescues,' he said, voice tight.

'What about them?'

'They're dead!'

It was a joke, Andrew thought. Billy was pulling his leg.
'Oh yes? All three I suppose.'

'All three,' Billy nodded. 'Here, read for yourself.' And with that he passed the newspaper to Andrew.

The headline hit Andrew like a hammer blow. Greystones, their home, had been gutted by fire. He went white as he read through the report.

'I am sorry,' Billy murmured when Andrew finally stared up from the paper.

Andrew was in shock, his mind reeling. This couldn't be true. It had to be a lie. It had to be. Alice, *his* Alice dead!

'Let me get you a refill,' Billy said, and picking up Andrew's glass he hurried to the bar.

Andrew started re-reading the article. The tragedy had occurred the previous night according to it, the entire family and some servants perishing in the blaze. Other servants had escaped to raise the alarm, to no avail. Arson was suspected.

Alice! Dear sweet Alice whom he loved and was engaged to. Alice dead.

Billy was still at the bar as Andrew rose and stumbled from the mess. All he wanted was to be alone.

Alice dead.

It was impossible. Impossible.

He managed to hold back the tears until his room door was shut and locked behind him.

'Andrew?'

Andrew blinked, then turned to find Willie standing a few feet away. 'Oh, hello.'

Willie stared at him in concern. 'I say, are you all right?'

Andrew pulled out a hanky and pretended to blow his nose, but was actually wiping tears from his eyes. 'Perfectly.'

'You do look rather rough, old boy. Here, have a swig from this.'

Willie produced a hip flask which he handed to Andrew.

'Thank you, I don't mind if I do. It's damned chilly out here. Doesn't take long to get through to the bones.'

Andrew unscrewed the flask's top and took a deep swallow. He sighed. 'That's better.'

'I think I'll join you.'

Willie also had a swallow and then stowed the flask away again, into the depths of the heavy Crombie coat he was wearing.

'How's Georgina?' Georgina had succumbed to seasickness shortly after they'd got underway and had remained in her cabin ever since.

'No change there I'm afraid. She's convinced she's going to die.'

'Still that ghastly colour you mentioned?'

Willie nodded.

'And Rose?'

'Continuing to play nursemaid. Thank God she was with us. I doubt I'd have managed by myself. The female side of things, you understand.'

Andrew took a deep breath. 'Tell Georgina she won't have to suffer for much longer. I've just sighted Ireland. It shouldn't be too long before we dock.'

He pointed into the distance. 'There she is. The Emerald Isle.'

Willie guessed then why Andrew was looking so awful. Memories. Not pleasant ones either.

Willie snapped open his cigarette case and proceeded to light up. The smoke he exhaled was immediately snatched away by the wind.

'It'll be strange going back, don't you think?' Willie said, making conversation.

'Very.'

'I wonder if it's changed all that much?'

'I shouldn't imagine so.'

'I hope it hasn't. It would be nice if it's just as it was.'

Andrew wished Willie would stop prattling on and go away. He wanted to be alone with his thoughts.

'Does it bother you, me speaking like this?'

'Not in the least,' Andrew lied.

'Good. That's a healthy sign.'

They stood in silence for a few minutes while Willie continued to smoke. When Willie had finished his cigarette he threw the butt overboard.

'I'd better get below again and give Georgina the good news.'

'I'll stay on up here.'

'We'll meet up at disembarkation then.'

'Right.'

When Willie had gone Andrew returned to watching as the coast of Ireland loomed closer and closer.

The first thing Andrew did on reaching his hotel bedroom was unpack the two bottles of Drummond he'd brought with him and pour himself a stiff one.

Glass in hand he crossed to the window and gazed out over St Stephen's Green. A park he and Alice had strolled in on several occasions.

He thought of the following morning and what he intended doing. It brought a lump to his throat.

Andrew rose as Willie and Rose approached the table he'd secured for them. 'No Georgina?'

''Fraid not,' Willie replied. 'She went straight to bed and intends remaining there until tomorrow.'

Willie assisted Rose to a seat and then sat himself.

A wine waiter came over and they placed their order. Then they fell to studying their menus.

'I'm so excited,' Rose declared, finally laying her menu aside. 'It's the first time I've ever been abroad.'

'It'll widen your horizons.' Willie smiled at her.

She lowered her voice. 'Their accents are very odd. I can hardly understand what they're saying.'

Andrew laughed. 'You'll soon get used to it. I know I did.'

Willie glanced about him. He'd dined here many times in the past, always with fellow officers. It was Dublin's finest hotel with an excellent reputation. It had never crossed his mind for them to stay anywhere else.

Rose, still with a lowered voice, said, 'Doesn't it all smell so different to home. So very foreign.'

Andrew chuckled. 'That's because it is.'

She pouted. 'No need to be sarcastic, Andrew Drummond.'

'Who me?' he replied, pretending mock innocence. 'As if I'd do such a thing. Particularly to a beautiful young lady like yourself.'

Rose blushed. 'Thank you. If you're being serious that is.'

'Never more so, Rose, I assure you.'

At which point their conversation was interrupted by the arrival of a waiter to take their food orders.

'Can we go sightseeing after dinner?' Rose asked halfway through the main course.

Willie picked up a crisp white linen napkin and wiped his lips. 'I'm afraid not, darling. I can hardly leave Georgina.'

She'd known that's what he'd say. Her face appeared to

fill with disappointment. 'Sorry, I should have thought. Yes, of course you must. And I can't go out by myself.'

Andrew smiled, realising what her game was. 'How would it be if I took you?' he suggested.

The disappointment instantly vanished. She'd achieved what she'd been after. 'Would you, Andrew!'

'My pleasure to do so.'

'None of those dives and haunts you used to favour, Andrew,' Willie said with a frown.

'Dives and haunts,' Rose repeated, eyes wide. That sounded wonderful.

'Don't worry, Willie. I wouldn't dream of it. She's your daughter after all.'

'Precisely.'

Andrew thought of a little club he'd frequented in Baggot Street. Friendly, discreet and, in his opinion, perfect for Rose. He only hoped it was still there.

'Now don't drink too much of that champagne. Your father would be furious if I took you back tipsy.'

'I won't,' Rose promised.

Andrew turned his attention to the singer, an Irish woman with flowing black hair and piercing blue eyes, thinking she was very good. Not to mention attractive.

'Any idea what she's singing about?' Rose asked.

Andrew shook his head. 'I don't speak a word of the language. Though from the sound of it, it might be a love song of some sort.'

A love song, Rose thought. How romantic. 'You said to Pa you wouldn't be accompanying us tomorrow morning. Would it be rude to ask what you're doing instead?'

He took his time in replying. 'I'm going to visit an old friend. Someone very special.'

'That sounds mysterious. Is it a woman?'

He nodded.

Jealousy filled Rose. 'I see.'

Oh no you don't, he thought. You don't at all.

'A woman you obviously knew from before, I take it?'

'That's right, Rose.'

'And haven't seen since?'

'You are inquisitive, aren't you?'

'I'm sorry,' she apologised. 'I didn't mean to be . . .'

'Nosy?' he interjected.

She dropped her gaze. 'You're telling me to shut up.'

'Not at all. But shall we change the subject.'

'If you wish.'

'I most definitely wish.'

The singer finished her song and the audience broke into rapturous applause.

'Thank you for a fabulous evening,' Rose said to Andrew as they waited for the hotel lift to descend.

'You're welcome.'

She looked into his eyes and wondered at what she saw there. Something she couldn't fathom. Something that sent a shiver through her.

Once upstairs he walked her to her room. 'Well, goodnight, Rose.'

'Goodnight, Andrew. I hope you enjoy tomorrow.'

Enjoy? It would be far from enjoyable. He made to turn away.

'Don't I get a kiss?' Her heart fluttered at being so forward. She could hardly believe she'd just said that.

He turned back to her in surprise. 'Rose, I . . .'

He had to break off when her lips landed squarely

on his. Instinctively his arms started to go round her, then realising what he was doing he pulled them away again.

'Thank you,' she whispered when the kiss was over.

When he returned to his room he locked the door securely behind him.

The grave was well tended, which pleased him. As was her parents' one alongside. He'd wanted to bring some flowers but there had been none to be had anywhere. It was simply the wrong time of year.

'Hello, Alice,' he said softly. 'I've come to visit you. It's been a long time.'

And then he couldn't speak any more, his throat too choked for words.

He began remembering . . .

It was a combined funeral for Sir Henry, Lady Fortescue and Alice and the church was packed. Andrew was present with Billy Roberts there for support.

The hymn finished and they all sat. 'Now we will pray,' the minister announced.

Andrew didn't hear a word of the prayer. All he could think of was Alice and how much he desperately missed her. He still couldn't really take on board that he'd never see her again, that she was gone.

At the end of the prayer he looked up and the first person he saw was Seamus McGinty.

Was that the hint of a smile on McGinty's face? Surely not. It couldn't be. And yet . . . and yet . . .

Then Andrew recalled the conversation with Sir Henry when he had mentioned the two Protestant houses in West Cork being torched by Fenians. And the row Sir Henry had

had with McGinty and the fact McGinty had threatened him, a threat Sir Henry had dismissed.

Suddenly, and with absolute certainty, Andrew knew it was McGinty who'd torched Greystones. Or if he hadn't done so personally had been behind it.

Arson had been suspected but so far the police hadn't made an arrest. Their investigations hadn't come up with anything.

But Andrew knew who the culprit was.

Sitting there in church, consumed by grief and hatred, Andrew swore an oath to himself.

McGinty, the bastard, would pay.

An eye for an eye.

So it would be.

Willie had knocked on Andrew's door and, on not receiving a reply, gone looking in the hotel bar where he now found him. He hesitated on seeing Andrew's face.

'Can I join you or would you prefer being left alone?'

Andrew pointed to a chair. 'Sit down.'

Willie did and beckoned a waiter over. 'Refill?'

'Please. Just ask for Scotch, they don't stock Drummond.'

Andrew took a deep breath. 'So how was the day out?'

'Grand. I showed them Dublin Castle where we used to be billeted, which they thought quite impressive. And a few other places. We had the most splendid lunch in a fish restaurant we came across. The prawns were magnificent, every bit as good as I remembered them.'

Willie gave their order, then turned again to Andrew. 'How about you?'

'I went to Alice's grave.'

'Oh.' That explained Andrew's expression when he'd come into the bar. 'How was it?'

'Pretty awful to tell the truth.'

'That's understandable.'

Andrew locked his fingers together and twisted them. 'I was pleased I went though. Painful as it was.'

'Will you go again?'

'Oh yes. At least once before we leave. I'll also go to Greystones at some point.'

Willie nodded. 'Did visiting the grave . . . help in any way?'

Andrew considered that. 'It's too soon to say really. But I think so.' He paused, then added, 'Yes, I do believe it did.'

'Good.'

'I never went back after the funeral, you know. Couldn't bear to. Several times I almost did, but changed my mind at the last moment. If it was painful today God knows what it would have been like then.'

Willie was thinking of his dead wife Mary. He still went to her grave at least once a month, staying for ten or fifteen minutes on each occasion. It had become a ritual with him over the years. He never asked Georgina to accompany him, the visits were strictly private affairs.

Their drinks arrived and Willie signed for them.

'I intend getting drunk as a lord tonight,' Andrew declared.

'I see.'

'The other thing is I shall be having dinner in my room. It's all right talking to you here like this but I won't really be fit company for the ladies.'

'I shall make your apologies and say you're not feeling all that well.'

'Thank you, Willie.'

When Andrew went to pick up his glass he noted his hand was shaking.

Willie noted it too but didn't comment.

Andrew stared grimly at the burnt-out shell of what had been the McGinty farmhouse. It hadn't been rebuilt and he wondered if Greystones had.

So long ago and yet it was as though it was only yesterday. An eye for an eye he'd sworn. And so it had been. McGinty, the bastard, had paid in full for Alice and her parents.

Andrew slowly closed his eyes, remembering . . .

He'd bided his time, now the score would be settled. He was standing in front of the McGinty farmhouse in the early hours of the morning, three full jerrycans of petrol at his feet.

The house was dark, the McGintys, he presumed, fast asleep. It was an overcast night with no stars or moon showing. Perfect for his purpose.

He thought again of Alice, dead and lost to him, all because of the Fenian bastard inside.

He picked up two of the jerrycans and walked softly towards the house. Stopping at the door he opened both cans. Then, using a knee to assist, he began pouring petrol through the letter box.

When the two cans were empty he took them back to the third with which he returned to the door and letter box. When that can was empty he took a deep breath, struck a match, dropped it through the letter box, picked up the can and ran like mad.

There was an enormous *whoof!* behind him which brought a smile of grim satisfaction to his face. He placed the can beside the others and turned to watch.

It didn't take long. Seconds later he could see flames licking behind the front downstairs windows and then wisps of smoke began to appear.

Would the smoke get them or the fire? Andrew wondered. If neither he had an alternative.

There was the sound of a small explosion. Now what was that? Could have been any of a dozen things.

Then he heard a female scream. Mrs McGinty or the daughter? He couldn't tell. Whoever, someone was now awake.

A young woman appeared at an upstairs window and threw it open, staring out in blind terror. She clearly considered jumping, then changed her mind and vanished from view.

Andrew took out his service revolver just in case it was needed. Using his thumb he slipped off the safety catch.

He wondered if they'd try the rear door. Well, if they did they wouldn't have any luck there, he'd jammed it. If they did come out it would have to be at the front.

The daughter's name was Roisin and she was twenty-two years old. Andrew knew that from discreet inquiries he'd made. She was the McGintys' only child, just as Alice had been the Fortescues'. Roisin opened the front door and rushed out, her long hair ablaze.

Andrew took careful aim and shot her through the head. She tumbled to the ground, hair still ablaze, where she lay still.

The entire house was now an inferno. Through the open door Andrew could see banks of flames leaping and dancing.

Mrs McGinty was the next to emerge, coughing and spluttering, her nightdress burning at the hem.

'For Lady Sybil, you bitch,' Andrew muttered as he pulled the trigger a second time.

And then McGinty was there, stark naked, which Andrew considered, for some reason or other, an added bonus. McGinty stopped to stare at the bodies of his wife and daughter.

Andrew pulled the trigger a third time, only there was to

be no quick bullet in the brain for McGinty. Andrew shot him in the stomach.

McGinty grunted and slumped to the ground beside his wife where he writhed in agony, blood dribbling from his mouth.

Andrew went and stood over him, smiling at the knowledge of how excruciatingly painful that particular death could be. McGinty stared up at him through bulging eyes.

'It's for my Alice and her parents the Fortescues,' Andrew explained, wanting McGinty to know why he'd done all this.

'Protestant cunt,' McGinty croaked through a froth of pink-tinged bubbles.

'You're going straight to hell, and that's exactly where you belong. You're going to roast,' Andrew crooned in reply.

McGinty continued to writhe, all the while clutching where he'd been shot.

Then Andrew had an idea. He put his revolver away and grasped McGinty by the shoulders. McGinty, too weak to resist, groaned as Andrew dragged him towards the doorway.

The heat was almost too much for Andrew but he was determined to do what he intended. Sweat rolled down his face as he hoisted McGinty to his feet and pointed him at the door.

'No . . . no!' McGinty choked.

'And the roasting starts here,' Andrew declared, pitching McGinty inside.

McGinty screamed and continued to scream until it was all over.

Andrew collected the three jerrycans and tossed them through the door as well, then beat a hasty retreat.

He walked away, not looking back. Alice had been avenged.

And sweet revenge it was.

Chapter 14

Kathleen frowned. She was putting the weekly wash together and it seemed to her she'd caught a whiff of scent. Picking up the shirt Pat had worn to the last committee meeting she brought it to her nose.

She hadn't imagined it, there *was* a definite smell of scent. And a rather nice one too, she thought.

But how could Pat get scent on his shirt? There wouldn't have been any women at the meeting for him to accidentally rub up against. So where had it come from?

Kathleen stared at the shirt in consternation, unable to think of an explanation for this. How on earth had scent got on Pat's shirt!

She shook out the shirt and examined its front. Nothing untowards there. Neither on the collar nor body of the shirt. Turning it round she began examining the back.

Kathleen caught her breath when she saw the faint red smudge close to the left armpit. She smelt that too to confirm it was what it appeared, lipstick.

She went very cold all over. Scent on his shirt and a smudge of lipstick could only mean one thing. Pat, her Pat, her husband, was seeing another woman.

Tears welled into her eyes. Surely not, Pat and someone else. And yet there was the proof.

Still clutching the shirt she staggered to a chair and slumped into it. It seemed obvious there were no such things as the committee meetings, they were just an excuse for Pat to meet up with whoever the bitch was. What a fool she'd been. What a complete and utter fool.

Why? That was the question, why? Hadn't she been a good wife to Pat? As far as she was concerned she had. She hadn't been remiss in any way.

All right, their marriage was fairly humdrum. But they had been married for years and people like them didn't have exciting lives anyway. It was a constant day-to-day struggle just trying to make ends meet.

Another woman, it seemed . . . well, just impossible. It had never once entered her mind that Pat might stray. Men like him didn't, at least she wouldn't have thought so.

Kathleen sniffed, and wiped the tears from her eyes. What a hammer blow this had been. And so completely out of the blue. She was stunned to say the least.

What to do? Confront him with it later on? She wasn't sure about that at all. Apart from anything else it would be embarrassing and humiliating.

She stared again at the shirt. Then, on a sudden impulse, grasped hold of it with both hands and tried to rip it. But the material was too strong for her and refused to be ripped.

Not to be beaten Kathleen got out of the chair and crossed to the drawer where she kept a large pair of scissors. She didn't cut the material, but stuck the point of the scissors through it and ripped it that way. Not just once but several times. When she was finished she felt a whole deal better.

'Damn you Pat Flynn,' she muttered. 'Damn you to hell for a cheating bastard.'

'Is something wrong, Kathleen?' Pat enquired on returning home from work that evening. The atmosphere was icy cold.

'No,' came the terse reply.

'Ma's in a bad mood,' Alison declared.

'I am nothing of the sort.'

'Oh yes you are, Ma. You've been ever so grumpy since I got back from school.'

'Can I get you anything?' Pat asked.

She glared at him, wanting to smack him across the face. 'Just sit down and be quiet while I get on with tea.'

'What is it tonight?' he queried.

'Potted hough.'

Alison pulled a face. 'I don't like potted hough,' she complained.

'That's too bad, young lady. It's what I'm serving up. If you don't want any you can go without.'

Pat glanced at Alison and raised his eyebrows. Heaven knew what this was all about. It was obvious Kathleen was in a right old paddy.

'Get off me!' Kathleen hissed and pushed Pat away. They had just come to bed. The thought of him touching her made her want to vomit.

'Will you please tell me what's wrong? You've been in a hellish mood ever since I arrived home.' He didn't really want to make love to her but had thought it might ease the situation, whatever that situation was.

Kathleen didn't reply.

'Is it me? Have I done something? Or have I forgotten to do something?'

Kathleen turned her back on him. Let him get that from his fancy piece. He'd get no more of it from her.

'Kathleen?'

Again there was no reply.

'Buggeration!' he swore angrily.

'Another cup?'

Ian Seaton shook his head. He'd had more than enough.

'Me neither,' Moira McLaren smiled. The two of them were alone, on a Sunday afternoon with Ian paying what had become a regular weekend visit.

Moira glanced at the window, purposefully showing off her profile of which she was justifiably proud. 'I do hate winter,' she declared.

Ian shrugged. 'It's not that bad.'

'I much prefer summer. We'll go for picnics when that arrives. I know the most beautiful shady spot beside the river. It will be quite heavenly.'

Ian smiled, totally charmed by her. 'I'm looking forward to the first one already.'

Moira brought her attention back to Ian. 'Tell me about your week,' she requested. 'Was it terribly hard?'

'Oh, very.'

She didn't really wish to hear about his week on the estate which would undoubtedly be boring in the extreme, but she knew men enjoyed talking about their work, and themselves, which was why she'd made the request. She forced herself to sit and listen attentively, apparently hanging on his every word, as Ian prattled on.

*   *   *

Bridie sighed as she closed *Fame*, which she'd just finished. It had been absolutely smashing.

She glanced over at the sleeping Jeannie Swanson, smiling when Jeannie gave a soft snort. She then laid the book carefully aside and blew out the candle situated by her bedside.

When Miss Rose returned from Ireland she'd give her back the book and ask if she could please borrow another.

That night she dreamed of being a great actress.

'Hello, Bridie, how are you today?'

'Fine, thank you.'

He decided to tease Bridie. 'What, no title. I thought it was to be Sir Ian of Seaton?'

Bridie flushed slightly.

'And I was going to call you Maid Bridie.'

She was aware of being teased. 'So you were, Sir Ian.'

'Sir Ian,' he mused. 'You know I really do like the sound of that. A title in the family at last. Pa will be delighted.'

Bridie was suddenly anxious. 'Oh you won't tell him, please? It was only our little joke between the pair of us.'

She was a pretty little thing, Ian thought. Couldn't compare with Moira of course, but pretty enough. She'd make some lucky chap a dashed fine wife.

He chucked her under the chin. 'Don't you worry, Bridie. I shan't tell Pa or anyone else. As you say, it's our little joke between the pair of us.'

'Thank you.'

'Sir Ian?'

She smiled. 'Thank you, Sir Ian.'

'Bye, Maid Bridie.'

'Goodbye, Sir Ian.'

Laughing softly, Ian continued on down the corridor.

*   *   *

Sean gazed with satisfaction round the sitting room of the three-bedroom tenement house that they'd rented. Between them they'd painted it then decent second-hand furniture had been bought and installed.

'It's quite a wee palace,' he declared.

'Aye, it is that,' Bobby O'Toole agreed from the sofa where he was lounging.

'There's just one thing still to be done,' Noddy Gallagher said. 'And by you, Sean.'

'What's that?'

Jim Gallagher produced the Samurai sword from behind a chair. 'The nails are already in the wall, Sean. All that's left is for you to do the honours.'

Sean accepted the sword from Jim and crossed to the fireplace. Standing on the hearth he hooked the sword on to the nails.

'Looks even better here than in that other dump,' he declared to mutterings of agreement.

Sean rounded on the gang. 'I've been thinking. As time passes our numbers will continue to grow, no doubt about it. That being so we can't allow everyone in here, it wouldn't be long before we'd be packed like sardines.'

That got a laugh from several of the others.

'So from now on only present gang members are allowed to use this place. Me as leader, and you lot as lieutenants. Anyone who joins after today is just an ordinary gang member who defers to us, right?'

'Right!' came the delighted chorus of replies.

Lieutenant, Mo Binchy thought. Oh, that made him proud right enough. It really made him someone.

'Now I've got some other plans,' Sean announced.

He sat while the others prepared to listen.

*   *   *

Georgina placed her cup back on its saucer. She, Willie, Rose and Andrew were in a coffee shop where they'd stopped for a rest and refreshment. 'If you'll excuse me for a few minutes I want to drop by a chemist shop I noticed on the way in.'

'Chemist shop?' Willie repeated with a frown. 'Is something wrong, my dear?'

She patted him reassuringly on the hand. 'Nothing at all, Willie. I merely need a few articles.'

'Shall I come with you?'

'No, you stay here. I'm quite capable of going into a chemist shop by myself after all.'

'Of course you are.'

Willie hurriedly helped her with her chair as she got up. 'A few minutes only,' she repeated, and swept away.

'I'll come to your room around midnight tonight,' Georgina said quietly to a startled Andrew shortly afterwards. She and Andrew were walking a little behind Willie and Rose.

'Are you mad! What about Willie?'

'Don't you worry about Willie. I'll take care of him. He'll know nothing about it. I promise you.'

'You can't, Georgina. It's far too dangerous. What if you're seen, for God's sake!'

'I won't be. And even if I am who's to know I'm keeping an assignation.'

Andrew swallowed hard. 'No, Georgina. I want nothing to do with this.'

She thought of the desperate craving inside her, a craving only Andrew could properly satisfy. She had to go to bed with him. She just had to. Her whole body ached for it.

'Scared?' she teased.

'Damn right I am. I've told you, Willie's my friend.'

'And I'm your lover. Don't forget that.'

'You're nothing of the sort. Not in the real sense anyway. It was once and once only.'

Her eyes glittered with determination. Since marrying Willie she was used to getting what she wanted. 'Around midnight,' she repeated.

At half-past eleven Andrew switched off his bedside light, and lay back to wait. Damn and blast the woman, he thought. Damn and blast her to hell.

He closed his eyes, recalling the night of passion they'd had together. The voluptuous body that had so eagerly moulded itself against his. The sweetness of her mouth. The firmness of her breasts. The hot wetness that had . . .

He snapped his eyes open again. He mustn't give in. All right, so he desired her, but that wasn't the point. He had no intention of continuing their relationship. If Willie was ever to find out it would be the end of the man.

What he couldn't understand was how she would get away from Willie. Surely she wasn't just going to wait until he fell asleep and then take a chance he wouldn't wake to find her gone. That would be sheer insanity.

'Willie?'

There was no reply.

'Willie?' Said a little louder.

Again no reply.

Turning to him she grasped his shoulder and gently shook him. 'Willie?'

Still no reply or reaction.

Georgina smiled to herself. The draught the chemist had sold her had done its stuff. Willie was out for the count and would stay that way until morning. Three drops for a good night's sleep the chemist had advised. She'd put six into the cocoa she'd had room service bring, and insisted he finish before they went to bed.

She slipped from under the covers.

Andrew heard a small sound as the doorhandle was turned. Christ! she'd come after all. He'd almost persuaded himself she wouldn't.

There was a pause, followed by the soft rattling of the doorhandle being repeatedly turned, to no avail. The door was securely locked.

'Andrew?' Her voice was quietly urgent. 'Andrew?'

How long would she stay there? he wondered. Seconds only if she had any sense. He couldn't believe he was keeping a beautiful, and available, woman from his room. The callous Andrew of old would have had no compunction about letting her in, friend's wife or not.

'Andrew, I know you're in there. Open up.'

He took a deep breath, then ran a hand over his face. He was surprised to find his forehead damp with sweat.

'Andrew!'

Go away, he silently commanded. Go away, Georgina!

A furious and very frustrated Georgina did just that.

If looks could kill, the one Georgina shot Andrew next morning across the breakfast table would have sent him tumbling stone-cold dead to the floor.

Willie yawned. 'Sorry,' he hastily apologised. 'I'm still frightfully tired for some reason. Most unlike me after a full night's sleep.'

'You were very restless,' Georgina lied. 'That's probably the reason.'

'I slept like a log myself,' Rose informed them.

Andrew was feeling most uncomfortable, having already decided to beg off accompanying the Seatons that day. Instead he'd go to Greystones, his last port of call. And later, perhaps Alice's grave again.

'How about you, Andrew?' Georgina smiled thinly. 'Did you sleep well?'

'I did, thank you.'

'Good.'

Willie yawned again. 'Dear, oh dear, what's wrong with me?'

'Old age, Pa?' Rose teased.

He smiled benignly at her. 'Wait till it catches up with you, my girl, you won't be so flippant then.'

'You're not old, Willie,' Georgina snapped. 'You're in your prime.'

'Aaahh!' he sighed. 'If only t'were true.'

How cross she was, Andrew thought. But then that was perfectly understandable. Cross, and gorgeous with it. He addressed himself once more to his bacon and eggs.

Andrew stood at the ship's rail watching the Irish coastline recede into the distance. He knew, beyond the shadow of a doubt, he'd never return there.

'Andrew.'

He turned to find Georgina standing beside him. This was the first time they'd been alone since the night she'd come to his hotel bedroom.

'Hello, Georgina. Taking a turn on deck?'

'Something like that. Willie's having a nap so I came up for some fresh air.'

He sniffed. 'And fresh it certainly is. I've always liked

sea air, it's so bracing I find.' He was nervous about this, wondering what she was going to say.

'I've never been so embarrassed and humiliated in my life,' she stated.

'I told you not to come,' he replied softly.

'I felt so . . . cheap . . . so dirty.'

'I'm sorry about that.'

'You were inside, weren't you?'

'Yes,' he admitted.

'I knew you were. You could have at least let me in.'

'And then what?' He shook his head. 'No, what I did was for the best, believe me.'

Tears misted Georgina's eyes. 'You don't understand, Andrew. You don't at all.'

'No?'

'I don't wish to sound disloyal to Willie, which I suppose is laughable in the circumstances. I told you he was the only other man I've ever been to bed with, and that's true. The thing is, he just doesn't satisfy me. Not in the least. I never knew what it could really be like, what I've been missing all these years, until you.'

Andrew gazed out over the sea.

'I had more pleasure with you that night, Andrew, in that one night, than all the times put together that I've been with Willie.'

'He can't be that bad, surely,' Andrew said softly.

'It's the difference between day and night where you and he are concerned.' She coloured slightly. 'He doesn't have anything like the stamina you have, or the experience. You did things to me, made me feel sensations, I'd never dreamed of.'

She paused, then said meaningfully, 'Can you blame me for wanting more of the same?'

He couldn't, but wasn't going to admit to the fact. If only she wasn't Willie's damn wife!

'You must think me a shameless hussy talking like this.'

'Not at all, Georgina.'

'But I wanted you to understand, fully understand. And now you do.'

'I'm so sorry,' he said.

'Not nearly as much as me, I can assure you.'

He shouldn't say this, he really knew he shouldn't. But he'd taken pity on her. 'There are other men you know.'

She stared grimly at him. 'Other than you, you mean.'

'Yes.'

'Men I could . . . have an affair with.'

He was hating this. 'It seems a possible solution. Don't you think?'

Georgina bit her lip. 'I suppose so. Except I wouldn't know where to start. You just sort of wandered into our life and it went from there. My curiosity got the better of me.'

'In what way?'

'If there was a difference between men, or if they were all like Willie. The answer stunned me somewhat.' She hesitated, then went on. 'I don't regret anything, Andrew.'

He did, but didn't say so.

'If I do have a regret, and I surely do, it's that there can't be more of the same. More nights like the one we had.'

He could suddenly smell her, a smell he found terribly exciting. Closing his eyes for a brief second he pictured her as she'd been when she'd opened her negligée to him. A twitch, and then a stronger twitch. He was becoming aroused.

'I'd better get back.' Georgina smiled sadly.

'Before you go, what did you do to Willie before you came to my hotel bedroom?'

The sad smile became an amused one. 'A sleeping draught I got from the chemist. Willie went out like a light.'

He nodded. 'I thought it must be something like that.'

She fixed him with her gaze. 'There's still plenty left, Andrew. Any time I wish to use it.'

And with that she turned and left him.

Andrew stared after her. Get behind me, Satan, he thought. Get behind me.

Andrew pulled up in front of Drummond House and switched off the car's engine. He sat there for a few moments thinking how good it was to be home again.

As it was a Sunday Charlotte wouldn't be at the distillery so he'd drop by the Manse later to see how she'd got on. Not that he had any worries in that respect, Charlotte had run the business before he had after all.

He thought of Ellen; he'd summon her to his room that night. It might only be a fortnight but it felt as though he'd been away for months.

He needed a woman and he needed one badly.

Very badly.

Andrew sighed and rolled off Ellen. That had been quick by his standards. But was only an hors d'oeuvre as far as he was concerned. The main course would follow shortly.

'Are you all right?' he asked.

'I'm just trying to catch my breath, that's all.'

He laughed softly.

Ellen wasn't sure what Andrew's reaction was going to be to this, but it had to be said. She just hoped he wasn't going to be angry.

'Andrew.'

'What?'

'I'm getting married.'

He came on to one elbow. 'Who to?'

'George Forsyth. You know him.'

'Of course I know him. How long has this been going on?'

'A wee while. He proposed last week.'

'Well, congratulations, I suppose.'

'You're not cross, are you?' she queried anxiously.

He laughed again. 'Why should I be? It's only an arrangement between you and me after all.'

'It's a big chance for me. He came into that small farm when his father died. He needs a wife and I consider myself lucky that he's asked me.'

Andrew thought of George Forsyth. A personable young man if a bit of a clod. 'Do you love him?'

'He loves me. At least he swears he does.'

'That doesn't answer my question, Ellen.'

'No,' she whispered in the darkness. 'But I'll come to, given time. And I'll make him a fine wife. He wouldn't get better.'

'I presume this means you're going to leave?'

'That's right.'

'Well, I can only wish you all the very best, and I mean that. I'm happy for you.'

'Thank you.'

He was going to miss her, he thought, but was already wondering if there was anyone else in the household he could approach to strike the same arrangement. He couldn't think of anyone offhand.

He ran a hand over her naked thigh. 'It's none of my business, but have you and George . . . ?'

She turned her face away from him. 'Yes.'

Sharing a woman with George Forsyth he found quite

repugnant. He wouldn't have Ellen in his bed again. 'I think we'd better stop this after tonight, don't you agree?'

'If you wish.'

'I believe it best. So when's the wedding?'

'June.'

That was only a couple of months off. 'I'll give you a damned good present. How's that?'

'You're very kind,' she replied appreciatively.

He wouldn't have her to bed again, he reflected, but in the meantime she was lying here beside him. George Forsyth or not, it would be stupid to lose the opportunity. Who knew when he'd get another.

Ellen had well earned her money when she finally left Andrew's bedroom.

Willie laid down the last of the ledgers he'd been studying. 'You've done well in my absence, Ian. By which I mean you haven't mucked anything up. At least not as far as I can make out.'

'Thanks, Pa.'

Willie regarded his son. 'And how's Moira?'

'Fine. Tip top. I was there again on Sunday.'

Willie nodded his approval. He had high hopes of this relationship. 'We must have her and her parents over to dinner shortly. I'll speak to Georgina about it.'

'Sounds grand.'

'Right, you toddle off and get on with your other duties. The old man's back in charge.'

'Who in the hell can that be?' Pat grumbled when there was a knock on the outside door. He was tired after his day and, having had tea, had thought to settle down for a snooze.

'I'll get it,' Kathleen said, and hurried from the room. She knew precisely who it was.

'We've a visitor,' she announced on returning to the kitchen. 'Father O'Banion.'

'God bless all here.' O'Banion smiled.

Pat struggled to his feet. 'This is a surprise, Father.'

'And sure, isn't the world full of them,' O'Banion replied in his thick Irish brogue.

'Alison, you come with me. We're going out for a while,' Kathleen declared.

That further surprised Pat. 'You're not going out with the good Father here?' he protested.

'Ah, but you're the one I've come to see, Pat.'

'Me?'

'You indeed.'

Kathleen bundled Alison from the room, closing the kitchen door behind her.

Pat was mystified. Then he thought he had it. 'I know, it's because I haven't been to confession lately.'

'Not for some time I understand.'

Pat shrugged. 'You know how it is, Father. You miss once which becomes twice, and so on.'

'I'm sure God will understand when you explain that to him one fine day,' O'Banion replied, still smiling.

Pat blanched.

'Now may I have a seat?'

'Of course, Father. How rude of me. Please . . .' He indicated a chair. 'And how about a cup of tea? I'm afraid I've nothing stronger in the house.'

'No tea for me, Pat. But thank you all the same.'

Pat sat facing the priest. 'Now what's this all about, Father?'

*　　*　　*

The house was empty when Kathleen returned. A quick examination of her now empty purse, which she'd inadvertently left behind, told her where Pat had gone.

Pat, who'd been to a pub he didn't normally frequent, one that sold neither beer nor spirits but poured glasses of cheap red wine and strong cider, a lethal combination when drunk in tandem, as was the custom there, was roaring drunk when he arrived home.

'Don't wake the wean!' Kathleen pleaded when, wild eyed, he came bursting into the kitchen.

Pat grabbed Kathleen and pushed her out of the room and into their bedroom. 'How did you find out?' he demanded.

She explained about the scent and smudge of lipstick.

'And you went to the priest, you fucking bitch!'

'I . . .'

Kathleen got no further. Pat's balled fist flashed to crack against her cheek.

And that was only the start.

'What the hell happened to you, Ma?' Sean demanded next morning on seeing his mother's battered face.

A horrendously hungover Pat tensed. He'd returned the previous night before Sean had come home so his son knew nothing, nor had heard anything, of what had happened.

Kathleen dropped her gaze for an instant. 'It was my own fault, I was going to the toilet when I tripped on the stairs and fell the length of them. You can see the result.'

'It looks right sore.'

'It is, Sean. It is.' Not only on her face but all over her body, Pat had given her a humdinger of a leathering.

Pat turned away, filled with relief. If Kathleen had told the truth, who knew what the outcome might have been.

Chapter 15

Who knows how these things happen? Or why? The only thing certain is that they do.

Ian was going upstairs, deep in thought, when he met Bridie coming down. Their eyes met, locked, and in that instant they each saw the other quite differently. In that instant they fell in love.

Ian stopped in his tracks, flustered, while Bridie reddened. Their eyes remained locked.

'I, eh . . . I, eh . . .' Ian stuttered.

Bridie broke their gaze to study the carpet beneath her feet. She could feel her heart going nineteen to the dozen. She was as stunned as Ian.

'How are you today, Bridie?' Ian eventually managed to get out.

'Fine, thank you, sir,' she replied in a small voice.

'And a beautiful day it is too.'

'Yes, sir.'

His mind had gone from being suddenly numb to

whirling. He couldn't believe what he was feeling. He had a mad impulse to wrap her in his arms and hold her tight. Hold her tight then kiss her deeply.

Bridie swallowed hard. What she'd seen in that moment was the prince of her dreams come to life. This was for real, she told herself, not a story book imagining or a bit of banter between the pair of them. She'd called him her prince that day in the wood, and now . . . Now he actually was.

'I'd better get on,' Ian said, and brushed past her.

Bridie went around for the rest of that day in a daze.

'What's wrong with you?' Jeannie Swanson demanded as they were getting ready for bed.

'Nothing, why?'

'You look very strange.'

'Do I?'

'Very. Are you ill?'

Not ill, Bridie thought. But in love. Desperately so. So much she ached from it. She shook her head.

Jeannie shrugged. 'I see you've got another book to read.'

'Yes, I borrowed it from Miss Rose.'

'You wouldn't get me wasting precious sleep time on a book. We get little enough as it is.'

'I enjoy it,' Bridie replied simply.

'You'd have to, and that's a fact.'

Bridie smiled thinly and continued undressing.

A few minutes later she was snuggled up in bed with the candle flickering by her bedside. She opened her new book and attempted to start it, but all she could see was a jumble of words overlaid with an image of Ian.

Ian meanwhile was sitting on the edge of his bed trying to make sense of what had occurred, and utterly failing to do so.

It was ridiculous, he told himself. Preposterous! How

could he fall in love with a housemaid. The whole thing
was laughable.

Except, if it was that, why wasn't he laughing?

'How's the book coming along?'

Jack Riach sighed. 'I wish I knew.'

'Oh?'

'The more I get into it the more lost I seem to be.'

Andrew frowned. 'Lost? I don't understand.'

'Neither do I really. You know the expression about being
unable to see the wood for the trees, well that about sums it
up. I'm in there somewhere, but just can't for the life of me
get an overall picture.'

Andrew wasn't sure what to make of that. 'What does
Hettie say?'

'That it's all right.'

'There you are then.'

Jack had a sip of whisky. How he looked forward to these
Friday nights out with Andrew, always pleased when they
came around again. 'It's just as difficult as I imagined it
would be,' he declared softly. 'The scope is so much bigger
than a play.'

'You'll cope.'

'I only hope so.'

'And how's Hettie getting on with her typing?'

Jack smiled. 'I love sitting there listening to her trying to
learn the infernal machine as she now calls it. Tap tap tap
tap tap, it's very soothing.'

Andrew smiled, not for the first time wishing he was in
a relationship as good and strong as Jack's. How he envied
him, in the nicest way possible.

'Have you heard from the Seatons?' Jack enquired casually,
already knowing what Georgina had tried to do in Ireland.

Andrew shook his head. 'No.'

'Maybe just as well if you ask me.'

'I'm not.'

Jack laughed. 'I see.'

'No, you don't. The girl I had an arrangement with at Drummond House is leaving to get married.'

'Ah!'

'Damn and blast.'

'That would be Ellen Temple then.'

'You've heard of the impending marriage I take it.'

'Something of the sort. George Forsyth, I understand.' Jack chuckled. 'He'll keep her busy. A lusty lad is George by all accounts.'

It depressed Andrew to think of Ellen. She had been so . . . well, convenient. And not bad in bed either, once he'd taught her a few tricks. Tricks that had been taught him years ago.

'So what are you going to do now?' Jack queried.

'I'm not certain. I'll have to think about it.'

'There must be someone else in your employ who'd like the same arrangement.'

'Possibly. As I said, I have to think about it.'

'And in the meantime you're thinking about Georgina Seaton?'

Andrew gazed into his pint. 'To be truthful, Jack, the answer's yes. I haven't slept with Ellen since she told me her news. And frankly . . . you know how it is.'

'You always were a libidinous swine.'

'That's me,' Andrew agreed.

'And how about the young one, Rose?'

'I said before, I'm not interested.'

'Then why is it I don't believe you?'

Andrew sighed. 'Honestly, Jack, there are times when I think you can see into my very soul.'

Jack laughed. 'Being blind does have its compensations. Your voice gives so much away, Andrew. It's most express-ive.'

'If she was older, then perhaps. But it's the age, Jack. That and . . . her being Willie's daughter.'

'Hmmh,' Jack mused.

'Despite the age difference we do get on rather well. We spent a considerable amount of time in each other's company when in Ireland.'

'You said. While you were keeping out of stepmama's way.'

Andrew saw off what remained in his whisky glass. 'Will you have another round?'

'I'd be delighted to, old boy. And several after that.'

Both men laughed.

Pat strolled into the kitchen. 'Well, that's it then. I'm off to my committee meeting.'

A tight-lipped Kathleen refused to look at him.

'Kathleen?'

'If you must,' she forced herself to say.

'Oh but I do. I most certainly do.' He knew he was being cruel, but couldn't stop himself. She should never have set that damned priest on him. That was going too far.

'I'll be home around the usual time,' he said.

Kathleen didn't reply.

'Bye, Pa,' Alison beamed.

'Bye, angel.'

He sauntered from the room and moments later the outside door snicked shut.

Kathleen swore inwardly. How could he do this, how could he? It was beyond her.

At least she'd stuck to the promise she'd made herself. Pat

wasn't getting any at home. Nor would he ever again. Let him go to his fancy piece. Hell mend the pair of them.

It was nearly midnight when a far from sober Pat left Geraldine Buchanan's. Hands deep in pockets he set off down the street.

It hadn't been as good as usual, and he didn't know why. Oh, there had been drink a-plenty with Geraldine looking just as desirable as always. And yet, if he was honest with himself, he hadn't enjoyed it, or her, nearly as much as he normally did.

Conscience? he wondered. Probably. It had been different somehow when Kathleen didn't know about him and Geraldine. Different and more exciting.

Pat shook his head. What was he complaining about? All the free bevvy he could get down his throat and a woman like that to boot. There was certainly nothing to complain about.

He stopped and closed his eyes for a few moments, feeling giddy. He hoped he wasn't going to be sick, waste of good alcohol that.

He opened his eyes again to stare up at a sky filled with stars, stars that all seemed to be staring directly down at him.

He suddenly shuddered and was filled with dread. God was watching, and judging him. He knew that. Just as he knew he was in the wrong. It frightened him.

Pat stumbled on his way.

'Are you working or having a wee day-dream to yourself?'

Ian started, then smiled somewhat foolishly at Jock Gibson whose approach he hadn't heard. 'I'm sorry. You're quite right. I was day-dreaming.'

'Oh aye?'

'A personal matter.'

'A personal matter is it!' Jock replied sarcastically. 'Could you not day-dream about that on your own time?'

'I said I'm sorry, Mr Gibson.'

Jock regarded him shrewdly. 'There's been something wrong with you these past few days. I've noticed it.'

Ian didn't respond.

'Anything you want to talk about?'

Ian shook his head.

'Well, if it's that personal and bothering you so much maybe you want to speak to your father.'

'No, I'll work it out myself.'

Jock nodded. 'Well, I want you to do a bit of logging later on so for Pete's sake keep your mind on the job when you've got an axe in your hand. I don't want you doing yourself damage.'

'I will and I won't, I promise.'

Jock grunted. 'See that you do.'

Ian watched Jock walk away. It had been Bridie he'd been thinking of, wondering about. He'd spoken to her again that morning in passing, nothing much, the usual sort of thing. Was it his imagination or had she seemed as ill at ease as himself? It had certainly appeared so. Ill at ease and most uncomfortable.

Again he'd had the mad desire to wrap his arms around her and then kiss her deeply.

'Silly bugger,' he muttered to himself, and got on with the task in hand.

How handsome he was, Bridie thought, standing at a window observing Ian trudge home from work. He paused for a second, and seemed to stare directly at her which caused her to blush. Hurriedly she turned away.

225

She mustn't think of this in a romantic sense, she told herself. She could no more have Ian Seaton than fly to the moon. He was of the landed gentry, way beyond her, she a working-class Glasgow lassie.

And yet . . . oh, but it was lovely to dream. If only things had been different. If it had been at all possible.

But it wasn't, she must always remember that. Ian would marry this fine Moira McLaren he was courting, or winching to use the Glasgow word. And what a beauty she was. A right looker and no mistake.

Bridie sighed. How had this happened to her? Falling in love with the master's son. It was daft when you thought about it. She had no hope there, none at all.

'Ian.' She said the word aloud. Tasting it, savouring it. A common enough name in Scotland, perhaps the most common, but now it had taken on a whole new meaning for her.

'Ian.'

She shivered.

Imagine being married to him. Sharing the days with him, and the nights. Her throat was suddenly dry at the thought of the latter. She and Ian in bed together. He . . .

It could never be. Would never be.

But wouldn't it have been wonderful.

'Are you taking the piss, son?'

Sean stared at Bob Mather, owner of The Sheugh pub. 'Not in the least.'

'Let me get this straight. I'm supposed to pay you protection money, is that it?'

'Insurance is a better word.'

Bob laughed. 'Away to fuck, you wee nyaff. Don't try to put the frighteners on me. I could eat you and this poxy lot with you for breakfast.' Bob stuck out a barrel chest. 'Do you know who in the hell I am?'

'Of course.'

Bob brought his face to within inches of Sean's. 'I don't think you do, son. I used to be the middle-weight champion of Scotland. One punch from me and you'd be flat on your arse and staying there.' He gestured at Mo, Noddy, Jim and Bill O'Connell. 'Same with these cunts. A single punch each and that would be that.'

'Are you all right, Mr Mather?'

The speaker was a barman wearing the traditional white jacket. 'Oh aye, fine, Tam.'

Another barman appeared from out back. 'Come over here, Alex,' Bob called out.

Bob turned again to Sean. 'This is Tam, he fought in the war. That right, Tam?'

Tam nodded.

'How many Jerries did you kill?'

'I don't know how many in all, but a definite six in hand to hand.'

Bob smiled at Sean. 'And you, Alex, how many did you kill?' he said over his shoulder.

'Like Tam, I can't say how many in all. But five in hand to hand.'

'Five,' Bob repeated, eyes glittering. 'And how did you do the last bastard?'

'I strangled the fucker.' Alex paused, then added softly, 'Very slowly.'

A tremor of fear ran up Sean's spine. This was a different proposition entirely to scaring an ice-cream shop owner and the like.

'And let me tell you this, sonny boy,' Bob went on, his tone chilling. 'These lads, and others like them, are always here. So you try any funny business and you'll find you've bitten off more than you can chew. Understand?'

Sean didn't answer.

Bob grabbed him by the lapels of his jacket. 'Do you understand?'

Sean swallowed. 'Yes.'

'Good.'

Bob released Sean. 'Now get your miserable arses out of my pub before I have them kicked out.'

'That was humiliating so it was,' Mo declared when they were outside, and spat on the pavement.

Sean glared at him.

'Well, it bloody well was.'

'Are we going back mob-handed?' Bill O'Connell asked.

Sean didn't fancy the idea of going up against the likes of Tam and Alex. He didn't fancy it one little bit. Not even with the advantage of a razor.

'Let it be for now, all right?'

Bill gave a sigh of relief. Nor was he the only one.

When they got to 'the place', as they now referred to it, Sean took himself off to a bedroom where he closed the door before lying down. A bed a number of lassies associated with gang members had already had experience of.

Sean knew one thing was certain. He wasn't going to be beaten. He was damned if he was.

But what to do? Aye, what to do?

'Sammy, I've a wee job for you.'

Sammy Renton glanced up at Sean. 'And what's that?'

'You've heard what happened at The Sheugh?'

Sammy nodded.

'Well, leave it a few days and then get yourself round

there. You must be casual like, I don't want you to arouse any suspicions, but try and find out if Mather has a family, and if he does what it consists of.'

'That should be easy enough,' Sammy replied.

'And I mean it when I say casual like. Even if it takes going back a couple of times. We'll pay for the drink.'

'Hey, why him?' Mo queried.

Sean gave Mo a withering look. 'Because they know you now. You'd be spotted the moment you walked through the door.'

'Oh!'

'Got it?'

'Aye, Sean,' Mo said sheepishly.

'Have you got a plan?' Jim Gallagher enquired.

'Maybe,' Sean replied thoughtfully.

She'd been pointed out to Sean by a classmate. He now went over to the lassie who was just leaving school with several of her pals.

'Are you Annie Mather?' he smiled.

The girl, whom he knew to be eight years old, stared suspiciously at him. 'What of it, mister?'

'I wonder if you'd do me a favour, Annie.' He produced an envelope from his pocket. 'Would you give this letter to your da.'

She gazed at the envelope, then up at him. 'Why don't you do it yourself?'

'The letter's urgent and I have to get off to work. I do shifts you see,' he lied, handing her the envelope which she reluctantly accepted.

'You're a good lass. Thank you very much.'

And with that Sean strode swiftly away.

*   *   *

'A letter?' Bob Mather frowned. This was strange indeed. 'From a man at the school gate?'

'That's right, Da. He said it was urgent.'

He took the envelope. 'You'd better get off and have your tea.'

'Can I go out to play afterwards?'

'Ask your ma. That's her department.'

Bob opened the envelope, pulled out the single sheet of paper it contained, and started to read. He went white.

The message was simple:

SHE'S A PRETTY LASS. IT WOULD BE A TRAGEDY IF SHE WAS TO BE RAZOR-SCARRED FOR LIFE.

'Is Mr Mather about, Alex?'

Alex glared at Sean and the others with him. 'Aye, I'll get him for you.'

Sean glanced up the length of the bar where Tam and another barman were staring at them. The look on Tam's face spoke of a desire for more hand-to-hand combat.

Bob Mather appeared. 'What do you want?'

'Twenty pounds a week. First payment now.'

Bob could hardly contain himself. 'Call yourself a man, threatening a wee lassie.'

'Your pride and joy I shouldn't wonder, being an only child.'

Bob's lips thinned until they almost disappeared. He didn't doubt for one moment that the threat in the letter was real.

He reached for his wallet.

They went straight from The Sheugh to an off-licence

where they bought whisky and screwtops of beer. Then it was back to 'the place' to celebrate.

Sean couldn't have been more chuffed.

'I enjoy walking so much,' Moira McLaren declared.

'So do I,' Ian smiled. That was true enough, he did enjoy walking. But he wouldn't have elected to go for one by himself on a Sunday afternoon, because he got enough of it during the week while working on the estate.

Moira slipped an arm through his. 'Mind?'

'Not at all.'

There was a feline look about her that day, he thought. She might have been a cat who'd just consumed a large bowl of cream and was now lying in front of a roaring fire.

He glanced about, ensuring they weren't being observed. Then stopped. 'I want to kiss you,' he stated.

Her answer was to close her eyes and pucker.

Her mouth was sweet, her scent strong in his nostrils. He could feel her breasts pressing against him.

'That was lovely,' she breathed when the kiss was over.

Lovely? It certainly hadn't been distasteful in any way. And yet there had been a certain nothingness about it. No fire, no real passion. At least none that he'd experienced. He wondered what it would be like to kiss Bridie.

Moira reached up and stroked his cheek with a gloved hand. 'A penny for them?'

'Nothing. I wasn't thinking anything at all,' he lied.

'You appeared to be.'

They resumed walking. 'My father and stepmother are very keen on us, you know.'

'So are my parents.'

'They all . . . seem to see us having a future together.'

'Do you, Ian?'

There was a few moments' silence before he replied. 'It is early days, Moira. Don't you agree?'

That disappointed her. 'I suppose so.'

'We don't want to make a mistake after all. Do we?'

'No,' she reluctantly agreed, for she was set on having Ian for her own.

He thought again of Bridie. How could he be talking like this, even if it was half-heartedly, about having a future with Moira when he was in love with another woman. It was absurd.

Moira shivered.

'Are you cold?'

'I am a bit.'

'We'd better start back then.'

They turned around and began retracing their steps.

'There will be toasted crumpets when we get in,' Moira stated.

'Yummy.'

'And coffee.'

'Just the ticket.'

Would he always love Bridie? he wondered. Or would that pass as quickly as it had happened? He had no idea whatsoever.

Moira, arm again through Ian's, pulled herself closer to him.

'Flynn!'

Sean stopped work. 'Aye, what is it?' The speaker was his foreman Neil Donaldson.

'I've been meaning to speak to you.'

'Well, now's your chance.'

Donaldson didn't like Sean, the bugger was too cocky

by half. Cocky and cheeky with it. 'It's about all these days off,' he said.

'What about them?'

'This can't go on, Flynn. It seems you're only here half the time.'

Which was true enough, Sean thought. He'd been busy with Samurai business.

'I've been ill. I can't help that,' Sean declared defiantly.

'That's as may be . . .'

'Are you calling me a liar?' Sean interjected aggressively.

Donaldson took a step backwards. 'Nothing of the sort.'

'You'd better not. Or else . . .' He left the threat unsaid.

'It's just . . . well I've got my boss to account to. And he's mentioned you on several occasions.'

'Has he indeed,' Sean smirked. 'I didn't know he was even aware I existed.'

'He does, believe me. The thing is, you've got to buck up, Flynn, or it's the sack I'm afraid.'

'The sack,' Sean mused.

'Aye, the sack.'

Sean made a sudden decision. He didn't need this poxy job anyway. His income from the Samurai was more than enough to live on.

'Tell you what,' he smiled. 'Why don't you take your job and stick it up your arse.'

Sean laughed as he strode away. He was finished with hard graft for ever. From here on it was the life of Riley for him.

'Up your arse!' he shouted back over his shoulder.

Chapter 16

Kathleen's eyes flew to the clock then back again to Sean when he strolled into the kitchen. 'Why aren't you at work?' she demanded anxiously, remembering the last time a member of the family had returned home unexpectedly.

'Because I've left. Told them what to do with their job in no uncertain terms.'

Kathleen's hand went to her mouth. 'You what!'

'You heard me, Ma.'

He crossed to a chair and threw himself into it. 'What a relief to leave that bloody hell hole. I've always hated it there.'

'But . . .' She was suddenly angry. 'What do you think you're playing at, Sean? You know how hard jobs are to come by these days. God knows when you'll get another.'

'I won't be getting another, Ma. I'm finished with all that.' He fixed her with his gaze. 'And don't you go worrying about the money I give you every week. You'll get that as usual.'

'But how can I when you're not working?'

He tapped his nose. 'That's for me to know.'

She guessed this was to do with the Samurai of which she'd been hearing dreadful tales of late. It was a subject never discussed in the house.

What was it all coming to? she wondered in despair. A husband who was seeing another woman, a son who was a gang member and now, it seemed, living off that. She shook her head and turned away.

'It'll be all right, Ma, I promise.'

Would it? She doubted that.

Sean clasped his hands behind his head and closed his eyes, thinking of those he'd left behind at Barry's Iron Foundry. A bunch of wankers, he thought. That's what they were, a bunch of wankers. Not like him. He was the clever one.

'Any chance of a cup of tea, Ma?'

'What time is this to put in an appearance?' Kathleen queried next morning when Sean entered the kitchen. 'It's gone ten o'clock.'

'No need to get up early any more, is there.'

Kathleen sighed. 'I suppose you'll be wanting your breakfast.'

'Aye, that's right, Ma.' He placed a ten-shilling note on the table. 'I fancy something a bit special this morning, to sort of celebrate like. Why don't you go down the shops and get some bacon and eggs. For the pair of us.'

'Bacon and eggs during the week!' she exclaimed, scandalised.

'A wee treat, eh.'

Kathleen eyed the ten-shilling note. 'Is that part of your lodging money?'

'No, it's extra. I can afford it.'

Kathleen reluctantly picked up the note, her mouth watering at the prospect of bacon and eggs. 'I only hope you can,' she said, crumpling the note in her hand.

Sean laughed as he crossed to the sink to get washed. The life of Riley he'd told himself, and that's precisely what it was going to be from here on.

'What is it? What's wrong?' Hettie demanded, having found Jack sitting alone with the most terrible expression on his face. She immediately went and squatted beside him.

He reached out and found her hand. If he'd been capable of crying he would have, but his tear ducts had gone along with his eyes. 'Oh Hettie,' he croaked.

He brought her hand to his mouth and kissed it, taking great comfort from that. 'I was thinking about the war,' he said softly.

'Oh.'

'There was one young chap, I don't even know his name but he couldn't have been more than seventeen or eighteen, who fell off a duckboard one day. Within seconds he was up to his waist in mud.'

Jack paused, and swallowed hard. 'I can still hear his screams as he continued to sink. We did all that we could but the mud had too strong a hold on him. If only we'd had a rope we might have saved him, but we didn't and there wasn't time to fetch one.'

'Oh, Jack,' Hettie murmured, and rubbed his hand against her cheek.

'When the mud reached his neck I couldn't look any longer and turned away. I stayed turned away until those awful screams were finally silenced. When I looked again there was nothing to show where he'd gone down. Nothing at all. He'd completely vanished.'

Jack shuddered. 'I think we feared the mud most of all. If we had to go we all prayed it would be quick and clean. A bullet through the brain, blown to bits in an explosion, that sort of thing. But the mud . . . that evil foul-smelling mud. God alone knows how many men it claimed.'

Hettie couldn't even begin to imagine what it must have been like. Horrendous beyond belief.

'It's a scene I'm going to put in the book,' Jack said. 'It'll help the reader understand why my hero changed so much between going off to the Front and coming back. That scene and others which haunt me.'

That night Jack dreamed it was he in the mud and not the young lad he'd told Hettie about. He woke with a great gasp, sitting bolt upright, to find himself covered in hot, sticky sweat.

When he explained to Hettie, who'd also woken, she took him into her arms and rocked him as she would a baby.

'Thank you, darling,' Willie said, and stroked Georgina's bare shoulder.

Another failure, she thought bitterly. All right for him, but for her? That was a laugh. She'd have to remedy matters later when he was asleep.

Willie sighed. 'We should have a child you know. One of our own.'

That startled Georgina somewhat. 'A child?' she repeated.

'Wouldn't it be nice?'

Yes, she thought, it would be. She'd always wanted a child. Ian and Rose were hardly the same thing. 'We haven't been blessed so far,' she replied. 'There's nothing I can do about that.'

'I appreciate the fact, Georgina. I merely mentioned that it would be nice if we ever were.'

She tried to imagine what a child of theirs would look like. Would he or she favour Willie or herself? Or would he or she be an amalgamation of both?

'I'd wish for another boy,' Willie mused. 'Not that I'd mind a lass, but if I had my preference it would definitely be a boy.'

'Why?'

'I've no idea. It would simply be my preference.'

A boy, she thought. Her son. Their son. 'What would we call him?' she queried.

Willie considered that. 'How about Willie after me? The name Ian was Mary's choice, that of her father.'

A little Willie she thought, and laughed inwardly.

'What do you say?'

'It would be fine, and appropriate.' She was pleased it was dark and Willie couldn't see her expression. 'And what about a girl?'

'You suggest.'

A girl, she wondered. What would she call a daughter? 'I don't know,' she said eventually.

'You must have some idea.'

'I've always rather liked Rebecca.'

'Rebecca,' he murmured. Biblical. 'Yes, I approve of that.'

Willie was in a chatty mood and it was ages before he finally dropped off leaving Georgina to do what her body was craving for.

During it she thought of Andrew Drummond.

*   *   *

'Can I come in?'

Andrew glanced up and there was his sister Charlotte who'd popped her head round the office door. 'Of course. It's lovely to see you.'

'As it's almost coffee time I've taken the liberty of asking for a cup.'

'Saves me the effort.'

Charlotte perched on the edge of his desk. 'So how are you?'

'In the pink.'

'Hmmh,' she mused.

'You sound unconvinced.'

'That's because I am. There's been something wrong with you lately. I've no idea what, but definitely something. It's been worrying me.'

Andrew shook his head. 'There's nothing wrong, Charlotte, I swear.'

'You've been very edgy, irritable. Snappy almost. John's noticed it as well.'

He knew the reason for that. After such a long time without he'd got used to having access to Ellen Temple. Now she was denied him he damned well was irritable. He hadn't realized it showed so much.

'Maybe it's just the time of year,' he lied. 'The changing of season, that sort of thing.'

'Could be.'

He leant back in his chair and ran a hand through his hair. 'I'm looking forward to summer. Let's hope it's a good one.'

Charlotte's gaze went to the second desk in the office, the one that had originally been her brother Peter's. She could see him sitting there, and her father Murdo where Andrew now was.

'Do you ever wonder what it would have been like if the war had never happened?' she asked softly.

'Occasionally.'

'Father might still be alive. Peter certainly.'

'And I'd no doubt have remained in the army. Probably off in India or whatever. At least a Captain by now, possibly even a Major.'

'And very grand you'd be too,' she laughed, teasing him. 'I can just imagine it.'

'Grand maybe, but not pompous I hope. You get a lot of that amongst the senior ranks.'

Charlotte suddenly glanced away, her mood completely changing. 'And I'd still be married to Geoffrey. He'd never have . . .' She trailed off, hanged himself being what she hadn't said. Poor, demented Geoffrey, unable to live with himself because he couldn't be a proper man any more.

'How different things would have been,' a sombre Andrew murmured.

At which point their conversation was interrupted by the arrival of coffee and biscuits.

'Do try and buck up,' Charlotte said as she was leaving.

'I will, sis.'

He kissed her on the cheek, and then she was gone.

Andrew returned to his desk, not feeling in the least like work any more. He thought of Georgina Seaton, something he'd been doing a great deal of recently. How tantalising that prospect was. Tantalising, and forbidden because of Willie.

He had a business trip coming up during which he'd have to pass relatively close to The Haven. He could arrange it so that he'd be there on the Friday coming back which meant he could spend the weekend with them.

He closed his eyes for a brief second, recalling Georgina in all her naked splendour.

'Christ,' he groaned.

He hadn't approached any other of the female members of staff at Drummond House due to the fact, on reflection, that he simply didn't fancy any of them. There was only one and she was a mere fourteen. He just couldn't bring himself to proposition a fourteen-year-old. He did have some scruples after all.

Or did he?

He decided he did. But did they still include Georgina?

Willie signalled to Bridie who was tending table. 'Can you pour some more wine please.' He smiled.

Ian was feeling acutely uncomfortable with Bridie and Moira in the same room, the McLarens having come for dinner. Moira was seated beside him wearing the most exquisite dark blue voile dress. It boasted clusters of fine tucks, hemstitching and narrow ruffles trimming the square collar. The front of the waist was set off with pretty pearl buttons, harmonising in shade with the colour of the dress. Moira looked quite stunning in it.

The evening was agony for Bridie who'd done everything she could to try and get out of serving at table. She positively hated Moira for being so beautiful. While she . . . well, was downright plain by comparison.

'More wine, Miss McLaren?' she queried on reaching Moira.

Moira covered her glass with an elegant hand. 'No thank you.'

Bridie, who'd been desperately trying to keep the daggers out of her eyes, moved to Ian.

'You, sir?'

'Please.'

'What do you say, Ian?'

Ian glanced at his father. 'I'm sorry, I missed that.'

As Bridie left Ian's side her uniform brushed against him sending a tingle through him. Again he wondered what it would be like to kiss her. Would there be a different reaction to that he'd had when kissing Moira?

Georgina was bored. She'd thought the evening would be rather exciting but it was turning out to the contrary. Probably her mood, she reflected.

The big news, and Georgina's stomach contracted at the thought of it, was that Andrew was coming in a fortnight's time to stay the weekend. Mind you, that was something of a mixed blessing. He'd be with them, but unavailable to her.

Damn! she inwardly swore. Those few nights were going to be absolute hell. Sleeping with Willie and Andrew so close. Lifting her glass she drank almost half its contents at one go.

Rose wasn't thinking of Andrew, but had been earlier. She thrilled at the prospect of seeing him again. Perhaps they could go riding, she'd enjoy that. Especially if it was just the two of them.

Delphine McLaren was pleased to see Ian and Moira getting on so well together. What a handsome couple they made, she thought not for the first time. And he such a catch! Things couldn't have been rosier as far as she was concerned.

Bridie finished her wine round and replaced the bottle on an antique silver and cork coaster. For an insane moment she imagined how glorious it would be to have an accident and pour some of the wine over Moira's dress which she envied dreadfully. Idiot, she berated herself. She'd probably get the sack for such an 'accident'. Or at least a severe ticking off.

*   *   *

Bridie glanced up in surprise as Ian entered the room. She was clearing away after dinner.

'Hello,' he smiled.

She nodded, thinking not for the first time that night how dashing he looked.

'Moira's lost a pearl button and thinks it might be in here,' he explained.

She set down the dishes she was holding. 'I'll help you search for it if you like.'

'That's kind of you.'

She felt a blush tinge her cheeks. 'If it fell off it's probably round where Miss McLaren was sitting.'

'Probably, if it's here at all.'

Their gaze held for several seconds. Then, embarrassed, she glanced away.

'I must say Miss McLaren looked awfully pretty tonight,' she heard herself declaring.

'Yes. I agree.'

For some reason she could have slapped him for that, wondering why he was staring at her in such a quizzical fashion. Her blush deepened.

'Is something wrong, Bridie?'

She shook her head. 'Nothing at all, sir.'

'Sir? What happened to Sir Ian of Seaton?'

She knew he was teasing her and wished he wouldn't. It was totally inappropriate in the circumstances. 'Not indoors, sir.'

'But we're alone, Maid Bridie.'

Those words sent a thrill through her. A thrill that seemed to tickle her insides. She tried to reply but maddeningly the words stuck in her throat. She thought of all the men she'd known in Glasgow, none of whom even began to compare with Ian Seaton.

'Let's search then, shall we?' he proposed.

They both crossed to Moira's chair and started looking, Ian going down on his hands and knees to peer under the table.

'It doesn't appear to be here,' he frowned.

What a lovely bottom, she reflected. All taut and hard and . . . This time her blush was what they call in Glasgow a real 'reddie'. She was beetroot.

'I hope it isn't lost,' Ian murmured. 'It might be difficult to match a replacement.'

'If it's in the house I'm sure we'll find it. It's bound to turn up in time.'

'No doubt,' Ian agreed, scanning the area around them.

Then Bridie spied the button glinting underneath the drawn curtains. God alone knew how it had got there.

She swiftly crossed and picked it up. 'Here we are,' she stated.

Ian beamed at her. 'Clever lass. Moira will be pleased.'

Bridie didn't give a fig whether Moira McLaren was pleased or not. But Ian was, and that mattered a great deal.

She went to Ian and handed it to him. For a brief moment their hands touched which Bridie found quite unnerving.

'I'd better get on,' she stammered. 'Miss Coltart will be wondering what's keeping me.'

'Just tell her what happened and she'll understand. I'd hate to get you into trouble.'

His concern touched her.

'Thank you, Bridie.'

'It was nothing.'

He smiled once more, his eyes fastened on her face. 'And don't go walking in the woods by yourself again.'

'I won't. I've learnt my lesson.'

He would have liked to stay and chat with her but that was impossible, the company was waiting. 'Goodbye for now then.'

'Goodbye.'

He left the room, shutting the door behind him.

Bridie briefly closed her eyes, thinking of Moira McLaren and Ian. She had to admit they made a handsome couple together and seemed well suited. She could only wish them well.

When she came to pick up the dishes she'd set down she found her hands to be trembling.

Andrew, who'd already been to bed and then got up again, paced the drawing room with a large glass of whisky in his hand. There was a fever in him which had nothing to do with any illness.

It was cold in the room, the fires having gone out, but he didn't notice it. All he could think of was Ellen Temple upstairs.

He swallowed his whisky and crossed to the sideboard where he poured himself another hefty one.

It was ridiculous, he thought, that he, a grown man, should be acting like this. It wasn't as though he cared for Ellen, he didn't. It was what she had to offer that was disturbing him.

He wouldn't go to her, he told himself. He damned well wouldn't. Surely he had more self-control than that.

Andrew slumped into a chair and ran a hand over his forehead. If he was honest with himself it wasn't really Ellen who was bothering him, but Georgina. She was who he really wanted. Ellen would only have been a substitute, had she been available.

A fortnight until he visited the Seatons, and then what?

Would he play Judas? He feared he would. In fact it was almost inevitable.

He swore, then swore again.

Moments later he was back at the whisky bottle.

'Is it me?' Geraldine Buchanan asked softly.

'Is what you?'

'That's wrong.'

'There's nothing wrong,' Pat replied just a little too hastily, and unconvincingly.

'Oh yes there is. It's as though you're with me and not with me at the same time.'

Pat shook his head. 'That's not so.'

She regarded him quizzically. 'Has something happened? Is that it?'

'Nothing's happened, Geraldine. I swear.'

'Then why the coolness?'

He didn't reply to that.

'Come on, Pat,' she urged.

He sighed, deciding it might be best to unburden himself. Though he was loath to do so. 'It's Kathleen, she's found out about us.'

'Ahh!' Geraldine breathed. That explained it. 'How?'

He told her about the scent and smudge of lipstick.

'Careless of me,' Geraldine replied.

'It doesn't really make any difference,' Pat went on.

But Geraldine knew it did. 'Is she aware you're here tonight?'

Pat nodded.

Poor bitch, Geraldine thought. 'Will she leave you?'

Pat barked out a laugh. 'Not a chance. Where would she go, and how would she keep herself? People like us don't leave one another. Only death separates us. Once wed we're bound together for the rest of our lives. That's just the way it is.'

There were those whom it didn't bother to commit adultery, Geraldine reflected, and she was one of them. She was able to completely divorce what she did with Pat from her relationship with Dougal. But clearly it wasn't the same with Pat.

'So what happens now?' she queried.

'We go on as we have, I suppose. I don't intend changing anything. No fears.'

Geraldine was curious. 'And what about Kathleen? Do you love her?'

Pat stared blankly back. 'What the hell has love got to do with it? She's my wife, and that's that.'

Typical Glasgow male, Geraldine thought. She'd often wondered what Dougal got up to when away. Those foreign ports he visited where women were always available. Did he indulge? She suspected he did. Nor did she feel jealous about that.

Geraldine ran a hand through the forest covering Pat's chest. How she adored hairy men, the hairier the better. And Pat was hairy. She didn't want to lose him. He was perfect for her when Dougal was away.

'Why don't you pour us both a drink,' Geraldine suggested. She needed one. That had been quite a session. Pat might be disturbed about his wife knowing but it hadn't physically affected his performance in any way.

Pat handed her a glass then studied her from beneath thick bushy eyebrows. 'You're class so you are, Geraldine. Real class.'

She smiled. 'Thank you.'

'I never thought I'd ever get to go with a woman like you. You're sheer bloody magic.'

'Am I indeed?'

'Oh aye. A real lady.'

'Hardly that, Pat. But I appreciate the compliment.' And she did. She found it touching.

'You're not to worry about this, Geraldine. If I have been . . . well, not quite myself it'll soon pass. I promise you.'

Sean strolled out of The Thirty Shilling Tailor wearing the new suit he'd had made and which he was extremely pleased with. Wasn't he the dandy, he thought with great satisfaction.

Now what to do with the rest of the day? There wasn't any Samurai business to attend to. The boozer of course. A few pints and a natter with whoever might be there.

What a lark this was. No more Barry's Iron Foundry, but him swanning about as if he was Lord Muck.

Another three pubs were paying them protection since The Sheugh, and more would follow. The story of Mather's wee lassie had got round which had put the fear of God into the other publicans. Not to mention shopkeepers and the like.

Who knew where this might lead?

'Rose, how are you?' Andrew smiled. 'It's lovely seeing you again.'

Not as much as seeing you, she thought. 'I'm fine, Andrew. And yourself?'

'Enjoying life, Rose. Enjoying life.'

Now what did that mean? Had he found someone? Jealousy stabbed through her to think he had. Jealousy and extreme disappointment.

Andrew was nervous and had almost decided not to come at the last minute. He'd actually parked the Rolls far down the drive, wondering whether or not to go on. But in the end lust, for it was no more than that, had got the better of him.

'You've lost weight,' Rose commented.

'Have I?'

'I think you have.'

She had too, he observed. What had once been a plump pigeon was turning into a right cracker. Her bust was fuller too, he noted. Or was that merely his imagination? He didn't think it was.

'How was your journey?' she queried.

'Nothing untoward.'

'I thought we might go riding later. Or perhaps tomorrow?' She'd been determined to get that suggestion in as soon as possible.

'Tomorrow sounds fine. I'd like that.'

Her eyes sparkled. 'Then it's agreed.'

'It's agreed,' he laughed.

'Well, if you'll excuse me I think I'll have an early night,' Ian Seaton declared, stifling a yawn that he'd faked. Truth was, he just didn't like Andrew Drummond's company. There was something about the man, something he couldn't put his finger on, that disturbed him.

'Goodnight then, son,' Willie said.

Ian rose, went to Georgina and pecked her on the cheek. 'Toodooloo!' he called out as he left the room.

Andrew had been trying to have a private word with Georgina since his arrival, and so far had failed. There had always been someone else around.

Willie glanced at the clock, then got up. 'I have to make a phone call. Shan't be long.' And with that he also left the room.

Andrew focused on Rose. If only she too would go. 'What time shall we start out tomorrow?' he asked her.

'I thought directly after breakfast.'

'That's fine by me.'

'What's all this?' Georgina queried.

'We're going riding,' Andrew informed her.

Rose held her breath, hoping her stepmother wouldn't ask to come. But Georgina didn't really like riding and was unlikely to want to accompany them.

Andrew saw off what remained in his glass, having already noted the decanter was empty.

'Would you care for another?' Georgina asked.

'Please.'

'Would you do the honours, Rose dear.'

Rose went to the decanter to discover it empty. 'I'd better ring for more,' she said.

Damn! Andrew inwardly swore.

Andrew began undressing. He'd begun to think he'd never get Georgina alone and then suddenly the opportunity had presented itself. A surprised Georgina had quickly agreed to visit him later. All he had to do now was wait.

Georgina was in a lather of excitement and desperately trying not to show it. Andrew wanted her, she could hardly believe it. She couldn't imagine what had made him change his mind. Not that she really cared. All that mattered was he had.

She joined Willie in their bedroom carrying two balloons of brandy. 'I thought we might have a nightcap.' She smiled.

He stared at her in amazement. This was most unlike Georgina. 'A nightcap?'

'I just felt like one. I hope you'll join me.'

Willie shook his head. 'I've had a bit of indigestion come on. I'd better not. But you go ahead.'

Her excitement evaporated. She hadn't banked on this. 'How about if I send down for some hot milk. Would that help?'

'I don't think so,' Willie replied, rubbing his stomach. A gleam came into his eyes. 'But I know what might.'

Georgina felt like screaming. Not tonight of all nights! Oh please God, no.

'I must say, you're looking particularly attractive, and seductive. Not that you don't normally, but even more so at the moment.'

Geraldine had a large swallow from the balloon without the drops in it. She could cheerfully have murdered Willie.

'Come on, join me,' she urged. 'Brandy is good for the stomach.'

He again shook his head. 'Not tonight. I'll give it a miss if you don't mind. Now why don't you come over here.'

How long was she going to be? a drowsy Andrew wondered. It was getting so late he was rapidly going off the idea. A good dinner plus lashings of wine and whisky were taking their toll. He felt his eyes drooping.

At long last Willie was asleep. But what use was that without the drops inside him? It was just too risky, just too damned risky to go to Andrew under the circumstances.

As usual she'd been left high and dry, her body aching for release. And Andrew who could more than effect that release was only a few doors down the corridor.

She'd take the chance, she decided. To hell with it. As

gently as she could she started to pull back her side of the covers.

'Georgina, darling, cuddle me.'

There it was. That was it. She was stuck for the night.

'Of course, Willie.'

'Aahh!' he sighed as her arms encircled him.

Chapter 17

'R ace you,' Rose challenged.
    'You're on!'

Rose quickly kicked her horse into a gallop and sped off with Andrew hotly in pursuit.

She laughed, thoroughly enjoying this. That and the fact that for once she had Andrew to herself. She urged Trixie to go even faster.

Rose could certainly ride a horse, Andrew thought in admiration. Again he was reminded that she sat a horse just like Alice had done.

They raced for all of five minutes before Rose reined in, unaware that Andrew had let her win.

'There!' she gasped as he came up beside her.

Andrew took in her blazing eyes and flushed cheeks, thinking how gorgeous she looked. Delicious in the extreme.

'Well done,' he congratulated her.

'Thank you, kind sir.' Rose slid to the ground. 'I think we'd better walk them for a bit. Don't you agree?'

He also slid down. 'Quite.'

They began walking the steaming horses, both of them on the inside. 'I'm so pleased you've come to visit,' she declared.

'Oh?'

'Don't be coy with me, Andrew Drummond. It doesn't suit you.'

'Well, I'm pleased to be here.'

'Pity it's only for the weekend.'

He shrugged. 'That's all I can manage, I'm afraid.'

'The trouble with weekends, those you enjoy anyway, is that they tend to fly by. At least that's my experience.'

'Mine too.'

Rose clapped Trixie on the neck, Trixie whinnying in response.

'I did a lot of riding in Ireland,' Andrew said slowly.

'Really?'

'The Irish are mad on horses. And damned fine breeders to boot. But you probably already know that.'

She glanced sideways at him, wishing he'd stop and take her in his arms. She shivered at the thought.

'Something wrong?'

'No.'

'Certain?'

'Absolutely, Andrew.'

They walked on a few paces. 'I dreamed of you last night,' she suddenly stated.

That surprised him. 'I'm flattered.' He'd done a bit of dreaming himself, but it hadn't involved Rose.

'It was ever so lovely.'

He wasn't quite sure what to reply to that.

'Don't you want to know what happened?'

'In your dream?'

'Of course, silly.'

'Then what happened?'

A strange look came over her face. 'I couldn't really tell you. I'd be too embarrassed.'

'*Now* who's being coy?'

She laughed. 'I suppose I deserved that.'

'So what did happen?'

'I said I can't tell you.'

'But it was *lovely*,' he repeated drily.

'Very much so.'

'If you're not going to tell me then why bring it up in the first place?'

'Because I wanted you to know.'

'You're a teasing minx, Rose Seaton.'

She laughed again. 'Perhaps I am.'

'Who should have her bottom spanked.'

She came to an abrupt halt and stared at him. 'What an awful thing to say.'

'Well, it's true.'

She turned away. 'Perhaps I wouldn't mind that. If it was you doing the spanking.'

He wagged an admonishing finger at her. 'Rose, you should be ashamed of yourself.'

'I've heard that some people do it all the time. To each other that is. It gives them pleasure.'

'And where did you hear such a thing?'

She shrugged. 'I can't remember.'

'Fibber.'

'I am not!' she replied hotly.

'Oh yes you are.' His gaze dropped to her rear, thinking . . . He hastily put that thought from his mind.

'Fiona Bell,' Rose declared.

'And who's Fiona Bell?'

'A friend. She also told me all sorts of other interesting things.'

'Like what?'

Rose didn't reply for a few moments. 'About the birds and the bees I suppose.'

Andrew couldn't help smiling. 'I see.'

'I tried to get Georgina to explain to me some years ago but she wouldn't. And of course I couldn't ask Father. He'd probably expire on the spot if I did.'

'But come on, Rose, you're a country lass. You must have seen animals.'

'Oh yes. But that's just basics. I wished to know . . . well, more than that.'

'Very enterprising of you,' Andrew commented drolly.

'Well, it is difficult. You must agree. I mean . . . well, there's the wedding night to consider. I want to be aware of what I should be doing.'

'Maybe you should leave that up to the chap?'

'And what if he knows nothing either? That would be awful. And quite unsatisfactory I should imagine.'

Andrew had a sudden thought. 'And was that what you were dreaming about last night?'

Rose went scarlet.

'Well?'

'Sort of,' she mumbled.

'You and me that is.'

Oh Christ, she thought. Her and her big mouth. Why hadn't she kept it shut. This must sound dreadful. 'You know I like you,' she said.

'And I like you.'

She took a deep breath. 'More than like, Andrew. Or like in a different way if you prefer.'

'Were we in bed together?' He was teasing her now.

'In a way.'

'What do you mean in a way? We either were or weren't.'

She turned to him, but wouldn't look him in the eyes. She was still bright red. 'You think I'm too young for you, don't you?'

'Yes.' That came out baldly, matter of factly.

'Well I'm not, Andrew Drummond. And it's high time you married. I've heard Pa say so on a number of occasions.'

'Have you indeed.'

'He worries about you.'

Andrew glanced up at the sky, a picture of Alice in his mind. 'I worry about myself sometimes. As for marriage, I've nothing against that where I'm concerned. In due course, I imagine, when the right woman comes along.'

'Which I'm not?' she queried in a small voice.

'Most decidedly not. You're the daughter of my friend, for God's sake.'

'So?'

'The age difference, Rose. Remember that.'

'I have thought about it, and it doesn't matter. You're not exactly decrepit, Andrew. And a lot younger than Pa. He may be your friend but I fail to see how that matters. If anything it's a bonus.'

'How do you make that out?'

'Wouldn't it be nice to marry the daughter of a friend? No remarks now, but it's almost like keeping it in the family.'

Good grief, the girl was actually proposing. Or suggesting he do. That stunned him. 'I think we'd better terminate this conversation,' he said.

'Why?'

'Because . . . it's inappropriate, that's why.'

'Is there someone else, Andrew?'

He shook his head. 'No.'

'I wasn't quite sure. There have been occasions when it seems to me there might have been.'

'Well, there isn't, I assure you.'

Forward? She didn't give a damn any more. This was far too important. 'Kiss me, Andrew.'

He stared blankly at her. 'I beg your pardon?'

'You heard. Kiss me.'

'I, eh . . . This isn't a party now, Rose.'

'I'm well aware of the fact.'

He studied her grimly. 'You really are the most precocious child.'

'I am not a child!' she retorted. 'I'm a grown-up woman. Now kiss me, damnit.'

What else could he do? 'All right.'

She moved into his embrace. 'And kiss me properly.'

'You mean passionately?' he teased.

'Precisely.'

When it was over her eyes remained closed.

'Rose?'

'Now do it again.'

He laughed. 'You are a glutton for punishment.'

'There was no punishment about that,' she sighed. 'None whatsoever. Now do it again.'

Georgina stood at her bedroom window watching Andrew and Rose cantering back from their ride out. She was still furious about the previous night, and deeply frustrated. There was only one night remaining during which she could get to Andrew's room. Somehow she had to, she simply *had* to.

What had made things worse was Willie wanting to make love to her. Of all nights for him to pick it had to be that one. What an acting performance it had been on her part. If awards were given for such things she would certainly have been honoured.

She sighed and moved away from the window, not wishing Andrew to see her.

How to get some of those drops down Willie's throat that evening? How!

And then she had another idea. One that sent prickles up her spine.

Andrew had bathed after his ride and was dressing when his bedroom door opened and Georgina entered. He stared at her in amazement.

'What is this?' he demanded. 'Are you out of your mind?'

She went straight to him. 'Maybe I am.'

'The servants, anyone could have seen you.'

'That was a risk I was prepared to take.'

'Well, I'm not,' he exploded. 'You'll have to leave at once.'

'No please, please. Don't send me away just yet.'

'Where's Willie?'

'Busy with estate business. He'll be tied up for quite a while. Hours probably.'

Andrew glanced at the door, nervous as could be. He certainly hadn't bargained for this.

Georgina wrapped herself around him. 'I'm sorry about last night, truly I am.' She went on to explain what had happened.

There was a wildness about her, Andrew observed. That and an abandonment which he found very erotic.

'I must have you, Andrew, I must,' she breathed huskily. 'You've no idea what I've been going through.'

He liked the idea that she was begging, that too was erotic. Despite himself he found he was becoming aroused.

He suddenly pushed her away. 'Not now, not like this, Georgina. It's out of the question.'

'Willie's away from the house, Andrew. He won't find out.'

Christ but she was tempting. A ripe peach just waiting to be devoured. His hand went to a breast which he gently squeezed. Georgina moaned in appreciation.

What a to-do, he thought. First the daughter proposing to him, and now the stepmother begging him to have her. His ego swelled.

'But the servants, some might come in,' he protested.

'They won't. Your room has been done while you were out riding, there won't be anyone till early evening when it's time to light your fire. We're quite safe.'

He was still in two minds about this. But he had to admit, it was exciting. 'We'd have to be quick,' he said.

She groaned. 'Not that, Andrew. That's the last thing I want.'

He swore inwardly, thinking it lucky the door had a lock on it. 'Wait here,' he said.

Georgina hurriedly began to strip.

Jesus, he thought later, Georgina asleep and cradled in his arms. That had been unbelievable. There had been nothing tender and loving about it, quite the contrary.

Georgina's eyes flickered open. 'Thank you, my love,' she whispered.

Her body was at peace, completely satiated. That had been even better than their first time together. She stretched languorously, every fibre of her being relaxed.

'Georgina, I don't wish to seem ungentlemanly, but you really must go. Willie . . .' He trailed off.

She marvelled again at what she'd been missing in life.

There was simply no comparison between Andrew and Willie. Any comparison would have been a joke.

'I'll try and come again tonight,' she whispered.

He wanted her to, that was the trouble, where common sense told him he should forbid it. They'd already taken a big enough risk as it was.

'If you do you must be very careful,' he warned.

'I will be. I swear.'

'If we get caught out there'll be all hell let loose. Not to mention the end of your marriage I should think.'

For the moment Georgina didn't care about any of that. All she could think of was Andrew and what it was like being with him. If only he was her husband instead of Willie. Oh, but that would be Heaven on earth.

'Now come on, you'd better leave,' he declared, disentangling himself and swinging out of bed.

Her expression was as though she was about to purr. 'Do I really have to?'

'You know you do.'

She sighed. 'I suppose you're right.'

'I am. Tempus fugit.'

Georgina sighed again. The last thing she wanted to do was get up. She could have stayed in his bed for ever. 'Andrew?'

'What?'

'Come here.'

He raised an eyebrow. 'Why?'

'I want to touch you while you're still naked.'

She squirmed on to an elbow exposing her breasts, breasts still flushed from their recent activities. Her eyes had narrowed almost to slits.

Andrew, against his better judgement, went to her and sat alongside. 'This won't do, Georgina. Not at all.'

She ran a hand over his groin, thinking, remembering, what pleasure that had given her. Exquisite pleasure. 'You're a lovely man, Andrew Drummond. I wish I'd met you years ago.'

'Do you?'

'Oh yes,' she crooned.

For someone who'd only slept with two men in her life she'd certainly learnt quickly, Andrew reflected. Not only quickly but had been the most eager of pupils. If there had been time . . . But there wasn't.

'Kiss me,' she said.

He couldn't help but smile. That was the second time today a woman had asked . . . no, demanded, he kiss her. It really was extremely flattering.

He bent and pecked her on the lips. 'There.'

'A proper kiss, Andrew,' she pouted.

But he knew himself only too well and what it would lead to. 'No,' he said, rising again. 'That'll have to wait.'

Georgina shivered in anticipation.

'What's wrong with you two?' Sean queried, as he and the rest of the family were having tea.

Kathleen glanced at him. 'I don't know what you mean, son.'

'Oh aye you do, Ma. The atmosphere in this house has been awful for ages. I'm getting sick of it.'

Pat kept his head down and got on with his meal.

'Well, Ma?'

Kathleen was tempted to land Pat in it, well aware of how scared he now was of Sean. 'You're imagining things.'

Alison laid down her knife and fork. 'I don't want any more. I don't like it.'

'Eat up,' Pat growled. 'Food's hard enough to come by as it is without wasting any.'

'What your da says is true,' Kathleen agreed. 'It's a struggle to make ends meet.' She thought of the extra money Sean was giving her and which Pat knew nothing about. That had been, and was, a right Godsend. Even so, it went against the grain to waste food.

'I still don't like it,' Alison complained, a hint of tears coming into her eyes.

'It's great scoff,' Sean declared. Picking up his little sister's plate and giving her a wink, he forked what remained of her meal on to his own plate. 'There, problem solved.'

'You spoil that lassie so you do,' Kathleen said disapprovingly.

'Aye well, what of it?'

Alison beamed at Sean who gave her a second wink.

Pat hated it now when Sean was home, although it was rare enough, mainly confined to mealtimes.

'Are you out tonight?' Kathleen asked Sean.

'It's Saturday isn't it. Of course I'm out. Me and the lads are going for a bevvy.'

Kathleen thought of the Samurai. 'You just take care, that's all. You know Glasgow on a Saturday night.'

Sean grinned wolfishly at her. 'No need to worry about me, Ma. I'll be safe as houses, and that's a promise.'

Pat belched. 'That was terrific,' he declared.

Kathleen thought of how he'd come home smelling of that woman again the previous night. No scent this time, just female smell. Lying there in bed with him snoring his head off it had disgusted her.

'So what about this atmosphere of late?' Sean persisted.

'There isn't any,' Pat replied quietly. 'It's your imagination, Sean.'

'Like hell it is.'

Pat cringed inside.

'So?'

Kathleen couldn't resist it. 'Ask your da.'

'Da?'

Pat picked up his cup of tea and had a swallow before replying. Sean was his mother's boy, always had been. If he found out about . . . It didn't bear thinking about.

'Your ma and I have had a few problems, that's all.'

'What kind of problems?'

Answer that, Kathleen thought.

'Och you know, the sort all married couples have.'

'Oh aye?'

Pat took a deep breath. 'I understand your concern, Sean, but this is strictly between your mother and myself.'

'Not when I've got to come home and put up with it, it isn't.'

'Can I be excused please?' Alison asked.

'Of course, pet,' Kathleen replied.

Alison got down from her chair. 'And can I go out to play?'

'On you go,' Kathleen said. 'Just make sure you put your coat on.'

Alison skipped from the room.

'What's wrong?' Sean demanded belligerently of Pat when Alison had gone.

'I told you.'

'Aye, but what sort of problems?'

Kathleen was enjoying seeing Pat squirm. It was a little bit of revenge.

'It's personal, Sean.'

'Is it indeed, Da. I just hope it isn't causing Ma any unhappiness that's all.'

Kathleen decided to let Pat off the hook. If the truth came out there would be another barney which she didn't want. 'We'll sort it, Sean. Now leave it alone, there's a good lad.'

He nodded. 'All right, Ma. Whatever you say.'

Pat heaved an inward sigh of relief. Thank God and all his angels for that. He rose. 'I'll get on with my paper. Haven't read the half of it yet.'

Sean stared at his mother, unconvinced by all this. If that old swine was giving her grief he swore he'd give Pat a right seeing to. One his father wouldn't forget in a hurry.

'If you're going out you'd better get changed,' Kathleen smiled to Sean.

'I'll be in late. You know what it's like.'

Pat immersed himself in his newspaper.

Pat glanced up from his paper as the outside door snicked shut behind Sean. He'd been worried there for a few minutes. That could easily have become nasty.

Kathleen was piling dishes up at the sink, preparing to wash and dry them. She didn't expect any help from Pat, for a Glasgow man that would have been unthinkable. Nor would she have welcomed his offering – he had his job, she hers.

Pat's gaze slowly traversed the room. How cosy it was, he reflected. And welcoming like. A real home and no mistake.

He thought of Geraldine's house. That was different somehow. He couldn't put his finger on why, it just was. Mind you, it wasn't his home, but there were some places you felt more relaxed in than others.

It was all rather showy there, he further thought, frowning. Not that he didn't like it, he did. And Geraldine was tremendous company, not to mention a damned good hostess, provider of beer and whisky. There was always plenty of that.

He wondered what it would be like living with Geraldine. It was fine and dandy making his Friday night visits, especially what they got up to during them. But could he actually live with her? The day-to-day thing, rubbing along together through thick and thin.

Kathleen began to hum, an old Scottish ballad that was one of her favourites, which made Pat smile. How often had he heard her quietly sing the same ballad? Times without number. He found it a comforting sound, the familiarity of it.

'Would you like another cup of tea?' Kathleen asked over her shoulder.

'No thanks. I've had enough.'

'Suit yourself.'

'But don't let that stop you.'

'It won't, Pat.'

He recalled their courting days. Nothing spectacular, more or less the same as everyone else round there, he imagined. The usual initial shyness, he trying to be the big man, she laughing up her sleeve at him. But still continuing to go out with him nonetheless.

They'd been through a lot together, he mused. Well, you didn't bring up three children and not have problems. Bad times, good times, and he had to admit, earlier on anyway before it had all begun to grind them down a bit, a lot of laughs.

He recalled her getting drunk one night. What a to-do that had been. He helping her stagger home, she apologising profusely with every wobbly step. The hangover in the morning when she'd sworn she'd never touch another drop ever again was something to behold.

And then there was the wedding night. He'd never forget that, it being the first time he'd ever seen a naked woman. There had been experiences before Kathleen mind, oh aye, but nothing really of any consequence. A few fumblings here, a few gropings there. Certainly not the whole hog.

Talk about a blushing bride, Kathleen had been that right enough. It had taken him ages, not that she hadn't been willing enough, to calm her down before he could do anything.

Had it been good? Well, all right, he supposed. But then what did you expect in that situation? He remembered cuddling up to her, holding her, listening to her sleep.

Pat sighed. He was enjoying being in that night, now that Sean had gone, that was. There was a great contentment about it. A rare experience for him of recent years when all he'd really wanted to do was put on his jacket, cap, and go to the pub but couldn't because there wasn't enough money to do so.

He closed his eyes, thinking of him and Geraldine the night before. Wonderful in its own way, and yet . . . There had been something missing. An ordinary something that he both missed and enjoyed.

Kathleen continued to hum, wondering about Bridie and how she was getting on. There hadn't been a letter for a couple of weeks now, but then Bridie, as herself, wasn't much of a letter writer. No doubt there would be one shortly.

Pat yawned. The meal had been a good one even if wee Alison hadn't like it. He felt full and satisfied.

'I might have that cup of tea after all,' he declared.

Kathleen turned to look at him. 'Oh?'

'Aye, if you don't mind.'

She shrugged. 'It's no bother.'

When she eventually came to him with his cup of tea he'd dozed off.

Having been keen to get to The Haven, Andrew was now eager to get away. His conscience was bothering him far more than he'd thought it would. And still there was later to contend with when Georgina might visit him again.

He wanted her to, and at the same time didn't. Why did life always seem to end up so bloody complicated!

'Another ride tomorrow?' Rose asked across the dinner table.

'Why not.'

She flushed slightly, delighted at having got him to agree.

Georgina was smiling at Willie, having devised what she considered to be a sure-fire plan for him to take the drops.

Her stomach knotted at the thought of a second session with Andrew.

Chapter 18

M o Binchy was drunk, which was hardly surprising considering the amount of alcohol he'd consumed. There were four of them out for a bevvy together.

'It's your round, china,' Sean said to Bobby O'Toole, swallowing the remains of his pint.

'Aye, fair enough.' Bobby turned his attention to the bar, waiting to catch the eye of a barman. Being a Saturday night the pub was full to bursting and doing a roaring trade.

'I've been meaning to ask you something,' Mo slurred to Sean.

'What's that?'

'This bint you've been seeing, Muriel. And a lovely lassie she is too. You've taken her back to "the place" often enough, but how come you've never had her in one of the bedrooms?'

Noddy Gallagher laughed. 'That's true enough. How come, Sean?'

Sean, who was far from sober himself, focused on his

companions. 'How do you know I haven't when we've happened to be on our own?'

Mo tapped his nose. 'I can tell.'

'Can you now.'

'Oh aye. Without any disrespect, Sean, I think she'd be a right goer. You should be in there getting your end away.'

Sean didn't like this topic of conversation at all. Why hadn't he taken her into one of the bedrooms? The truth was, though he'd never have admitted it to the others in a million years, he was scared to do so.

'More haufs?' Bobby O'Toole asked over his shoulder. Haufs were whisky.

'Too right,' Jim Gallagher replied, and hiccuped.

Sean was suddenly angry, thinking it a right liberty for Mo to have put him in this position. He tried to act in what he considered to be a nonchalant manner. He could cheerfully have punched Mo.

'That one I had in a bedroom last week was something else,' Noddy declared. 'Talk about squeal, you'd have thought I was slaughtering a pig.'

The others laughed, but not Sean.

'You should have seen the tits on her,' Noddy continued. 'Big as bloody melons they were.'

Sean wished they'd change the conversation.

'That big?' Bobby queried, again over his shoulder.

'Massive. I stuck my face in them and slobbered like a baby.'

'When are you seeing Muriel again?' Jim asked Sean.

'Wednesday night. We're going to the flicks.'

'Why not give her a treat and take her to "the place" instead?'

'I might just do that,' Sean replied in an offhand manner.

'Would you like some FLs?' Mo offered, reaching for his wallet.

'No thanks, I've got my own,' Sean replied in a steely voice.

'Here you are, Sean,' said Bobby, handing him a hauf and a pint.

'Thanks, pal.'

Sean was seething inside. Mo and his big mouth, he could have seen them both far enough. Now he was committed, providing Muriel agreed that was. There again, she might not which would suit him just as well.

He didn't know why he should be so scared of doing what should come naturally after all. There was no reason for him to feel that way. He was perfectly capable.

Right then, he decided. He'd take Muriel to 'the place' and when there give her a right seeing to.

By God and he would.

'Hello, Maid Bridie, your day off again?'

She'd seen him approaching and wondered if he'd talk to her. Her heart was thudding. 'Yes, sir.'

'Oh, what's happened to Sir Ian of Seaton?'

She shrugged.

'Bad mood, eh?'

'Something like that.'

His expression became one of concern. 'Everything going all right in the house? Nobody's giving you aggravation, are they?'

She couldn't help but smile. 'No, nothing like that.'

Bridie thought of the sleepless nights she'd had since falling so hopelessly in love with Ian Seaton. Nights during which her imagination had often run riot. If only he'd been working class like herself instead of who he was. But that could never be. Wealthy and landed gentry he'd been born and that was how he'd stay. The gulf between them was insurmountable.

'Do you mind if I sit with you for a bit?'

That surprised her. 'Not at all.'

He joined her on the bench. 'So what have you been doing today?'

'Nothing much really.'

He raised an eyebrow. 'No more forays into the country-side?'

She knew he was teasing her. 'I didn't want to get lost again. That last time quite frightened me. Who knows what might have happened if you hadn't come along.'

'Who knows indeed,' he mused. 'When we'd eventually found you you'd probably have been stiff as a stone statue.'

What a frightening thought. Scary. To end up like that. She shivered.

'I'm sorry,' he apologised. 'Has that upset you?'

'A little,' she admitted.

'I'm sorry again.'

There was a few seconds' silence between them, then he said, 'I'm going out after foxes tonight. We've been having chickens taken recently due to the blighters.' His face darkened. 'I hate foxes. Destructive beasts.'

'Are there many round here?'

'Oh, quite a few. We try to keep them down as much as possible.'

Bridie wasn't certain about that. Foxes had always seemed rather adorable animals to her.

Ian laughed when she told him that. 'You're a town person, Bridie, not familiar with the ways of the country. Adorable looking or not, foxes are vermin and should be treated as such.'

'I suppose I am a town person,' she said. 'And I'm not learning much about the countryside either. Even though I've been here quite some time now.'

'Well, you hardly get much of a chance to do so.'

'No,' she agreed.

He had a sudden thought. A rather inspirational one at that. 'Would you like to come out with me tonight? After the foxes I mean.'

'Tonight?'

'That's right. I shall leave about ten.' He glanced up at the sky. 'It promises to be blowy later which should be ideal.'

'And why's that?'

'Foxes have acute hearing. Try to get close to them when the weather is still and you haven't a chance. But when it's windy they don't hear nearly as well which gives you a chance.'

Bridie found that rather fascinating.

'Well?'

'I don't know,' she replied slowly. 'I mean, how would I get away?'

'Your time's your own today. Who's to say where you go or get up to?'

Be with Ian alone, just the two of them as they were now. 'How long would we be out for?' she asked.

'A couple of hours.'

Oh, but she'd love that. Not the shooting of foxes, but to be with Ian.

What she didn't know was that he was thinking the same thing about her. He was also excited at the prospect.

'Bridie?'

She emerged from the shadows. 'It's me.'

He laughed softly. 'Any trouble sneaking out?'

273

'None at all.'

'Good.'

He felt different somehow when he was with her. A good feeling, the sort of feeling he might have been searching for all his life. In a way it scared him.

'Have you wrapped up well?'

'Just as you said.'

'It'll be cold out there.'

'I'll be fine, Master Ian. I promise you.'

He hesitated for a second. 'Why don't you just call me Ian. For now anyway.'

'All right,' she whispered, thrilled.

'Then let's go.'

Ian glanced up at the sky. As he'd predicted there was a wind blowing, but there were also the elements of a storm brewing. He wondered whether or not to go on.

'What's wrong?'

He explained to her.

'Oh.'

He could hear the disappointment in her voice and decided they would continue.

'It's so dark,' she breathed.

'There's a moon above.'

'It's still dark.'

He chuckled. 'Townie.'

'I can't help that.'

'No,' he agreed. 'You can't.'

They proceeded over the fields, she at his side.

There was a sharp crack of thunder which brought Ian up short. 'Hell!' he swore.

'Ian?'

He took a deep breath. 'It's all right, Bridie.'

'Are you sure?' Any moment now she expected some

horrible monster to come out of nowhere and attack them. Talk about spooky! Give her a town any day to this.

Thunder cracked again, followed by a brief flash of lightning. Ian knew he should abandon this, but didn't want to lose Bridie's companionship. He produced a squeaker and blew into it.

'What's that for?' she whispered.

'I'm trying to call up a fox.'

He blew into the squeaker again.

What an odd sound, she thought. If she'd been asked to describe it she wouldn't have been able to.

There was an answering bark from what seemed a long way off. Ian blew on the squeaker again.

Another lance of lightning followed by a thunder clap. And then it began to rain. 'Damn,' he muttered.

'Ian?'

'What?'

'I want to go back.'

He immediately broke his gun. It was over anyway. There wouldn't be any foxes that night. Not with this weather. 'All right.'

The moon had vanished, obscured by cloud. And the rain was rapidly increasing in intensity. Moments later it was hammering down.

Bridie thought of how far they'd come, she was going to be soaked through before she got back to The Haven. Even though she was with Ian she wasn't best pleased.

'I didn't think it would rain,' he apologised. 'Honestly I didn't.'

'Well, it is,' she replied almost tartly.

Suddenly the heavens were alight with lightning, flash after flash banging and booming. Bridie wished with all her heart she was in bed with the covers pulled over her head.

'There's a wee hut not far from here,' Ian said. 'We'll take shelter there and hope this passes over.'

'A hut?'

'Rather small I'm afraid. And full of stores. But at least it'll get us out of the rain.'

'You lead then.'

He considered taking her hand, then decided against it. He didn't want her getting the wrong idea. 'Come on then.'

It took them about ten minutes to reach the hut, stumbling through the terrible rain while overhead the lightning continued to flash and the thunder crashed.

'Christ!' Ian swore when they were finally inside. 'If I'd realised it was going to be like this I'd never have come out myself, far less brought you.'

Bridie was trying to catch her breath. 'That was awful.'

'I'm sorry, truly I am.'

'Not your fault, Ian. You weren't to know.'

'Oh, but I should have done. I should have read the signs better.' He propped his gun against a wall and wondered how long the storm would take to abate, if indeed it would before morning.

'You know what I'd love,' Bridie said.

'What?'

'A cup of tea.'

He laughed. He'd have preferred a whisky himself. 'I'm afraid I can't do that for you.'

Bridie was thinking of Glasgow and how different this all was. In a perverse way she was enjoying it.

'What now?' she asked.

'Wait, I suppose. And if it doesn't let up too bad on us.'

Bridie moved, and hit some sacks, almost falling over. There was a smell in the hut she couldn't place, but a nice one. For some reason it reminded her of Christmas.

Bridie suddenly giggled. 'Jeannie Swanson must be wondering where I am. She probably thinks I'm out with a secret . . .' Bridie broke off in confusion.

'A secret what?'

'I can't say, Ian,' she mumbled.

'Of course you can.' It was so dark in the hut he could make out only the merest hint of an outline.

'Lover,' she whispered.

The effect of that statement on Ian was electrifying. 'Lover?' he repeated.

She didn't reply.

'Bridie?'

'Yes?'

'Nothing.'

He cursed himself for being so cowardly. She was only a servant after all. No one to be afraid of. So why should he be afraid?

Because he didn't see her as a servant. He was in love with her, as a woman, that's why. Her station in life had nothing to do with it.

'Tell me about Glasgow,' he requested.

That surprised her. 'Glasgow?'

'Your life there before coming here.'

'What about my life there?'

'I don't know. All of it. Your home for example.'

Bridie had to smile. 'Well, if you can imagine something as different to The Haven as can be then that's it.'

'Was it a slum?'

Bridie was immediately indignant. 'I can't deny we live in a poor part of the city but our house is absolutely immaculate. My ma would be furious if she heard you suggest otherwise.'

He chuckled at her indignation. 'I wasn't meaning to

offend, Bridie, that's the last thing I intended. I was referring to the area you come from. Not your home conditions.'

She relaxed a little. 'Well we don't live in a posh part I have to admit. We're working folk, through and through. But my ma takes great pride in our house. Works her fingers to the bone to keep it neat and tidy so she does.'

'I believe you,' he said softly.

'And Da's a hard grafter. A coalman by trade. Out in all weathers.'

Ian smiled to himself. 'Sounds a bit like me and many others on the estate. We're also out in all weathers. So we have something in common there.'

Bridie hadn't thought of it like that. 'I suppose you do.'

'I don't exactly lead a life of indolence you know. But then you must appreciate that.'

'It's not quite the same, Ian. You're rich with a house that . . . well it's a palace. You don't want for anything whereas we . . .' She trailed off for a moment. 'It was a real problem when I lost my job at the lemonade factory. Not only because my wages weren't coming in any more but the fact that other work was so hard to come by.'

'I understand, Bridie.'

'Do you?' she queried, almost accusingly.

'Oh yes. I might have been born into a well-to-do family but that doesn't mean I'm not aware of what it's like for less fortunate people.'

She wondered what her ma and da would make of Ian Seaton. She hated to think. Especially where her da was concerned.

She was so vulnerable, he thought. So very vulnerable. Which wasn't the case with Moira. Moira had . . . a veneer about her. A class thing? He didn't know. What he did know was he much preferred the vulnerability. It made him feel extremely protective. And more of a man somehow.

'We can't stay here all night,' she said.

'Hardly.'

'And I'm freezing.'

He instantly took off his coat. 'Here, put this round your shoulders.'

'What about you?' she queried in concern.

'I'm made of sterner stuff.'

Bridie shivered, something that had nothing to do with the cold. Her mind was running riot.

'We'll leave it for a little while,' he declared. 'And then if there's no let up we'll simply have to make a dash for it.'

'Yes.'

'Again, I'm sorry I got you into this.'

'That's all right.'

'No it's not. I'm angry with myself. I'm supposed to be the countryman after all. You the novice about these matters.'

How kind he was, and thoughtful. She shivered again.

He listened to the rain rattling against the hut's roof, while outside it sounded like a firework display.

'I can hardly see you,' he said. 'Even though you're standing right there.'

'Nor me you.'

'Perhaps . . . and don't take this the wrong way. If I held you it might warm you up.'

Oh God, she thought. Please.

'Bridie?'

'I am cold.'

'Babes in the wood,' he joked. 'Just like them.'

His arms went round her and she pressed against his chest. He could feel her thudding heart.

'Sir Ian of Seaton,' she murmured.

'Maid Bridie.'

Then, throwing caution to the wind, not giving a damn, he pressed his lips on hers, she eagerly responding.

For the space of a minute or more it seemed that time stood still for the pair of them.

'You know, you're one of the best things that's ever happened to me.'

That shook Georgina, coming as it did so completely out of the blue. 'Willie?'

He beamed at her. 'It's true. When Mary died I thought . . . And then eventually you happened along. You make me very happy. I want you to know that.'

She averted her gaze, guilt and shame strong within her. 'Thank you.'

'I was very lucky. And still am.'

'And so was I,' she mumbled.

He went to her and knelt, something that further disconcerted Georgina. 'We make a good couple you and I, don't you agree?'

All she could think of was Andrew and the pair of them in bed together. What bliss that had been, what sublime ecstasy. And now here was Willie not only proclaiming his love for her but also his devotion. It made her feel so cheap.

'Any regrets?' he asked quietly.

She wished she was anywhere but where she was. How could she answer that? Certainly not with the truth. Willie was a dear sweet man, she couldn't hurt him. Though if he ever found out about Andrew . . . But he wouldn't, she assured herself. He wouldn't. She'd never let the cat out of the bag, and Andrew wasn't likely to.

'Don't be silly,' she smiled.

He took her in his arms and held her close. 'Darling Georgina,' he whispered.

They stayed like that for a few moments and then he released her, rising again to his feet.

'What brought that on?' she queried.

'I don't know. I simply felt like saying it.'

'And I'm glad you did,' she lied. 'Women need to hear such things and so many men don't do it.'

'I appreciate that. Which is perhaps why I did.'

She closed her eyes, remembering Andrew and their lovemaking. While with Willie . . .

'I don't have any regrets either,' she further lied.

'Are you sure?'

'What do you think?'

His smile was one of pure contentment. 'I was thinking, I know we've recently been to Ireland. But how would it be if we had a few days away together? Just the pair of us.'

Her heart sank. 'What about the estate?'

'Ian did such a splendid job I don't have any fears about leaving him in charge again. And it would only be for a few days. A long weekend perhaps.'

'That would be wonderful, Willie.'

'Let's call it a second honeymoon.'

'I'm looking forward to it already.'

'Good.'

She thought once more of Andrew. If only . . . Oh if only . . .

On reaching her room Bridie closed the door and started to strip out of her wet things. She was soaked to the skin.

When naked she vigorously towelled herself then slipped into her nightie and dressing-gown. Sitting on the bed she started combing her hair.

There hadn't been any let up in the storm so in the end they'd had to brave it. Not that she'd cared about the rain by then any more. Ian had kissed her. A dream come true.

He'd apologised afterwards, muttering he didn't know what had come over him. She had replied that it didn't matter. They'd then lapsed into an awkward silence, neither sure what to say next.

Bridie stopped combing and closed her eyes, recalling the kiss. She'd been kissed before but never like that. It was as though . . . She'd felt that kiss right down to the very soles of her feet.

She mustn't be taken advantage of, she thought. She wasn't going to end up at an abortionist's. Look what the outcome of that had been for poor Teresa.

She had to put this out of her mind, she told herself. It was something that had happened on the spur of the moment. Ian was a young man after all, hot blooded as they all were. She didn't mean anything to him, how could she?

Perhaps he'd sensed some of her feelings towards him and the kiss had been his natural reaction. Well, it was possible. Though she'd tried hard not to let those feelings show.

Tried, but possibly failed. She resumed combing, wishing he'd kissed her a second time, and a third, and . . .

'Och stop havering, Bridie Flynn,' she said aloud. It had just been one of those things. Nothing more.

Sean swore and swung his legs out of bed. He felt so bloody humiliated, not to mention embarrassed.

Muriel raised herself on to an elbow and stared at him. 'It doesn't matter,' she said.

'Of course it bloody matters,' he retorted angrily.

'You were just nervous, that's all.'

Nervous! That was a laugh. He'd been terrified.

'Maybe it was my fault,' she said placatingly.

'Aye, that's it. Must have been you.'

Muriel wasn't sure what to do in this situation. She'd never been with a lad who couldn't manage it before. It was a totally new experience for her.

Calm down, Sean counselled himself. And don't raise your voice. He didn't want the others in the next room to hear. He smacked a fist against a palm. 'Shite!' he muttered.

Muriel reached out and touched his back. 'Why don't we try again?'

He wrenched himself away. It would be useless to do so, he just knew it would. 'No,' he growled.

Muriel gazed at Sean, wondering what he might do next in this highly volatile mood. She put a hand to her mouth and worried a nail.

Sean thought of the other lads in the house. He couldn't admit to them what had happened. He'd be a laughing stock, his credibility straight down the pan.

He swung on Muriel. 'You'll keep your mouth shut about this. Understand?'

She nodded.

'Because if you don't I'll mark you.'

Her eyes grew large with fear. 'I won't mention a word, Sean. Believe me.'

'See that you don't.'

She swallowed hard.

Sean glanced down at what dangled between his legs, hating it for failing him. It had been like a dead thing, no reaction whatsoever. He couldn't believe it.

'Get dressed,' he instructed, and proceeded to do the same.

When she was ready he suddenly grabbed her by the throat. 'Mind what I said. If this gets out you're marked.'

When he released her Muriel sagged and sobbed.

'Right then,' Sean declared, pulling himself together. 'Big smiles and you all over me like a rash when we get through there. And let me do the talking.'

'Yes, Sean.'

'It was a big success, savvy? A belter. I'm a real stud.'

He was smiling broadly when they joined the others, Muriel clinging on to his arm.

'Wo-hey!' Mo Binchy called out.

'Wo-hey!' Sean repeated, his smile becoming even broader.

Muriel felt like throwing up.

'What have you done to yourself?' Bridie exclaimed in alarm as Ian came through the front door, a large blood stain on his trousers.

'I got careless and cut myself,' he explained. 'My fault, no one else's.'

Bridie, en route from one task to another, instantly went to him in concern. 'Shall I send for the doctor?'

Ian shook his head. 'No, it's not as bad as it looks. A gash that's all.'

She stared into his face. 'You look in pain.'

He shrugged. 'As I said, a gash that's all.'

Bridie immediately took charge. 'Well, it has to be seen to. We'd better get you to the kitchen and Mrs Coltart's medical box.'

That was what he'd intended and why he'd returned home. The gash certainly needed attention if it wasn't going to turn septic. He smiled when she took his arm. 'Nurse Flynn, is it?' he teased.

Bridie disregarded that, worried about him. This wasn't a time for jocularity. 'If you lean on me I'll help you there.'

He didn't really need help but rather liked the idea of leaning on Bridie. He winced when he started to move again.

'I don't want to get blood on the floor,' he declared.

'Your leg is far more important than that. Blood can always be mopped up.'

There was an authority about her which appealed to Ian. In a way it rather reminded him of his mother. 'This is very good of you,' he said as he hobbled along.

'Nonsense.'

It was one of the few occasions in the day when the kitchen was deserted. 'You sit there,' she instructed, pulling out a chair. She considered trying to locate Mrs Coltart, who might have been anywhere in the house, then decided to deal with the matter herself. She was entirely capable after all.

'Pull up your trouser leg and let me have a look,' she commanded.

He did as he was told. Bridie made a face when she saw the wound, a nasty ragged tear. 'How did you do that?'

'With an axe, would you believe. I'm lucky it wasn't worse.'

She couldn't have agreed more. It was the work of a few moments to pour some hot water and pick up a newly washed cloth.

'You're being very kind, Bridie.'

'Don't talk rot. I'm only doing what any of the others would do.'

He noted how tender her touch was. Firm, yet tender at the same time. Despite the discomfort he was in he was actually enjoying this.

'Maybe it should be stitched,' she murmured.

'It's not bad enough for that. Once bound it'll heal well enough.'

She glanced up at him thinking how brave he was. A real man in her opinion. 'It'll probably leave a scar.'

He shrugged again. 'That doesn't bother me. A small scar is neither here nor there.'

'Hold on a sec,' she said, and went to find a pair of scissors which she used to snip away hair covered in congealed blood.

How lovely she smelt, he reflected. A most enticing smell. He wanted to bend down and touch her but of course didn't.

'There,' she declared at last. 'That's as clean as I can get it.'

'Thank you.'

Rising, she crossed to where Mrs Coltart's medical box was kept, usually used for accidents in the kitchen, and returned with it. From the box she produced a roll of bandage and bottle of iodine.

'This is going to sting,' she said, taking the stopper off the bottle.

He smiled, a smile that quickly turned to a grimace. 'Ouch,' he whispered through gritted teeth.

'I warned you.'

He dragged in a deep breath which he slowly exhaled. She hadn't been exaggerating when she'd said it would hurt. He wanted to jump up and hop around but felt he couldn't do so in front of her.

The iodine applied, Bridie now began to bandage the wound, pulling the bandage tight. There were small brass safety pins in the medical box which she used to fasten the bandage off.

'All done,' she finally announced.

Ian flexed his leg a little. 'You've done an excellent job, thank you.'

'I think you should go and lie down for a while, don't you?'

He considered that a good idea. 'I believe I will.'

She nodded her approval. 'Shall I take you up?'

'I'm sure I can cope.'

'It's no trouble, honest.'

He was tempted, but decided against it. Now the gash had been dealt with he should manage under his own steam. 'I'll be fine, I assure you.'

For a few moments their eyes met and there was something between them, an intimacy.

'What's all this then?'

That sudden intrusion startled the two of them. They turned to discover Mrs Kilbride framed in the doorway. Ian swiftly explained.

'Dear me,' Mrs Kilbride sympathised.

'My own fault,' Ian repeated as Bridie began putting things away again.

He came to his feet. 'Bridie here has been splendid. I couldn't have been better looked after.'

Mrs Kilbride beamed, obviously pleased to hear that.

'Now if you'll excuse me. At Bridie's suggestion I'm going to lie down for a while. The leg is throbbing somewhat.'

'Shall I send you up something, a cup of tea perhaps?'

Ian shook his head. 'I'll have a stiff whisky, that'll do me a lot more good than tea.'

He was at the door when he turned to stare directly at Bridie. 'Thank you again, Bridie. I appreciate what you did.'

She didn't reply, but a faint smile danced on her lips.

Chapter 19

Kathleen woke to find Pat flailing about in bed. 'Pat, what's wrong?'

He didn't reply, his arms and legs continuing to thrash wildly.

'Pat?'

He suddenly sat up, said something she couldn't make out, then fell back again.

Dear God, she thought. When she touched his shoulder it felt red hot.

Kathleen lit a candle, then caught her breath when she saw Pat's face. His eyes were open and staring, sweat streaming down his forehead and cheeks. He looked like a man demented.

'Pat, can you hear me?'

Again there was no reply.

She shook him. 'Wake up. I want to speak to you.'

He turned his head to stare at her, but his eyes were unseeing.

'Holy Mary Mother of God,' she whispered. What was all this? He was in a dreadful state and no mistake.

She had to think, she told herself, forcing herself out of the deep sleep she'd been in. The first thing to do was get Sean. She needed help.

'What . . . what is it?' Sean mumbled a few moments later.

'Your da's been taken ill. Come on through.'

'Ill? Pissed more like.'

'It isn't that. He wasn't out tonight. And he was fine when he went to bed.'

Sean groaned. 'Bloody hell!' Trust the sodding old man. 'Aye, all right, Ma. Just give me a sec to collect myself.'

Kathleen hurried back to Pat who was now dribbling at the mouth. She had a thermometer somewhere, she remembered. Maybe she should take his temperature.

She placed a hand on his forehead, which frightened her. He seemed to be literally burning up.

'I'm here, Ma,' Sean yawned.

'Come and take a look at this.'

Sean crossed to the bed and gazed down at Pat. 'Jesus wept,' he muttered.

'You'll have to run for the doctor, son. This is serious.'

Sean shook his father as Kathleen had done, only more vigorously. 'Da? Da, wake up!' He knew when there was no response that his mother was right. Here was a job for the doctor.

'I'll get round there right away,' Sean declared, and vanished from the room.

Kathleen started to cry, this was awful. What was wrong with him, what was wrong? She wrung her hands praying for the doctor to turn up as quickly as possible.

Pat briefly returned to his senses. Slowly he focused on

Kathleen sitting by his bedside, her expression one of grave anxiety. Christ but he was boiling.

He opened his mouth to speak but nothing came out. No sound at all. And then he was drifting off again. A great black hole beckoned, a hole into which he was falling.

Dr Robertson shook his head, this was beyond him.

'Well, Doctor?' Kathleen demanded, Sean hovering in the background.

'To be honest with you, Mrs Flynn, I don't know what's wrong. So what I'm going to do is go home and read up some books and then come back again in a few hours.'

'Have you no medicine you can give him?' Sean queried.

Robertson considered that. 'Not really. Until I know what the problem is I can't treat it. If I gave him the wrong thing now it might do more harm than good.'

'Some bloody doctor,' Sean muttered ungraciously.

Kathleen rounded on him. 'Sean!' she admonished. 'The doctor's doing his best.'

Robertson shrugged. He was used to this sort of behaviour. It often happened. A natural enough reaction in the circumstances. So many people expected him to turn up, give the patient a pill, and hey presto! Well, sometimes it just wasn't like that.

'In the meantime all I can suggest is you keep him covered. I don't want him catching a chill on top of everything else, and see if he'll take some water.'

Robertson stood up, then regarded Pat quizzically. This really was a poser. He'd never seen anything quite like it. 'As I said, I'll be back later.'

'Thank you for coming at this hour, Doctor. It can't be any fun having to get out of your bed in the middle of the night.'

He wanted to laugh at that. It was an ongoing part of his life he'd never got used to. As for Betty his wife . . . she'd become stoic in the extreme about the telephone ringing in the early hours, or, in this case, a bang on the door.

'I'll be on my way then.'

Kathleen saw him out.

'Would you like a cup of tea, Ma?'

'Oh thanks, son. That would be lovely.'

'I'll put the kettle on.'

Kathleen brought her attention back to Pat. At least the flailing of limbs had stopped. And his eyes had shut. In fact he was now so still he might have been . . .

Kathleen shuddered. What if he died? What then? It didn't bear thinking about.

Pat could hear voices, one of which he recognised as Kathleen's. That gave him enormous peace of mind. He somehow felt safe with her close by.

Kathleen, his wife of so many years. The woman he'd married and who'd borne his children. The woman who was almost an extension of himself.

He knew he'd be all right as long as she was there. Kathleen would take care of him. Wouldn't let him down.

Not as he'd let her down.

The heat had gone out of Pat's body, and now he began to shiver with extreme cold. Kathleen piled the spare quilt on top of the bed, and when that didn't help climbed in beside him and held him close, giving him her own body heat.

It was possible what he had might be contagious, but she wasn't bothered about that. All she wanted was for him to get better again.

'Pat,' she crooned. 'Oh Pat.'

The smallest of smiles crept on to his face.

* * *

'It's hospital for him I'm afraid, Mrs Flynn,' Dr Robertson announced.

'What about those books you went home to read?'

'Didn't shed any light I'm afraid. I'm still stymied. Mr Flynn needs to be seen by a specialist in my opinion.'

'Can I go with him?'

'To hospital?'

'Aye, that's right, Doctor.'

'Of course you can. If you wish.'

'I do.' Then simply, 'He's my man.'

Robertson nodded that he understood.

Half an hour later the ambulance, which Robertson had already ordered, arrived.

Sometime during the journey to the hospital Pat lapsed into a coma.

Ian stopped and sat on a grass-covered tussock. He was on the moor which formed part of the estate. He should be getting on, he thought, there was so much to do. But, as so often of late, all he could think about was Bridie.

He ran a hand through his hair and sighed. It was madness really, he told himself for the umpteenth time. Falling for a servant. Daft beyond belief.

Except he hadn't asked to fall in love. It had simply happened. An event over which he had had no control.

He smiled, recalling the kiss in the hut. How responsive she'd been. And how sweet her mouth. A mouth he yearned to taste again.

Then his mind turned to Moira. That's where his future lay. Or if not with Moira, then some girl like her, of her class and standing. Anything else was a nonsense.

Moira would be a good wife, he thought. And they made a

handsome couple together, everyone said so. There was only one drawback. He didn't love her.

Liked her, yes. Respected her, yes also. And she was certainly beautiful, a real knock out. Far prettier than Bridie.

But it was Bridie he loved, there was no getting away from that. And damnable it was too.

Damnable!

Getting up he continued on his way, trying – and failing – to put Bridie out of his mind.

Kathleen was waiting in a side room while Mr Durie the specialist was with Pat. She glanced again at a wall clock, wondering how long this was going to take. Mr Durie had already been with Pat a good half-hour.

The seconds continued to tick slowly by.

Kathleen stood up the moment Mr Durie, accompanied by Dr Robertson, entered the room. Her expression clearly denoted how worried she was.

'Well, Mrs Flynn.' Durie smiled. 'I've examined the patient and had some tests made. Hopefully we'll know more when we have the results of those tests.'

'So you still can't say what's wrong with him?'

'I'm afraid not, Mrs Flynn. To begin with I suspected meningitis, but that was soon discounted. Then I . . .' He broke off. 'I won't go into all the details, merely that I haven't yet been able to diagnose the problem.'

Disappointment filled Kathleen. She'd been sure Durie would have made a diagnosis by now and they'd know what was what. 'I see,' she murmured.

'Now I suggest you go home and have some rest. You can come again this evening at visiting time.'

Kathleen stuck out her jaw. 'I want to be with him, Doctor. All the time he's here.'

'That isn't possible, Mrs Flynn,' Durie replied sympathetically. 'Hospitals have rules which can't be broken.'

Kathleen's defiance immediately vanished and she crumpled in on herself. 'I'm sorry,' she apologised as she began to weep.

Robertson went to Kathleen and put an arm round her shoulders. 'What I'm sure we can do is let you have a little time with him before you go home. Five or ten minutes say.' He glanced at Durie who hesitated, then nodded.

'So how about that?'

'Thank you, Dr Robertson.'

'There might be a risk involved should you touch him so I'd prefer you didn't. Not for now anyway. Understand?'

Kathleen nodded. 'Anyway, if I'm going to catch anything from Pat I've already done so. I was in bed with him for most of the night don't forget. And I got back in again and cuddled him when he became cold.'

Durie wondered if he should keep Kathleen in for observation 'And how do you feel, Mrs Flynn?'

'Beside myself.'

He smiled. 'I meant physically.'

'Tired. Worried. Nothing else.'

That seemed normal enough. 'I'd like to check you over just in case. Then you can visit, Mr Flynn.'

Kathleen had no objection to that. 'There's one thing I want to ask you, Doctor. And I'd appreciate it if you're frank with me.'

'What's that, Mrs Flynn?'

'Could Pat die from whatever he's got?'

Durie took a deep breath. 'Then frank I'll be. Your guess is as good as mine right now. But I have to admit there is that possibility. He is in a coma after all.'

Kathleen made a choking sound and turned away from the two men so they couldn't see her expression.

Sean was at 'the place' which he had to himself. He was staring at the money belonging to the Samurai. It was kept in a steel box which was now open on his lap. Recently the gang numbers had swollen to thirty-five members but only the originals shared out the cash they brought in every week. Cash that kept growing and growing in quantity as they expanded their operations. Fourteen pubs were now paying them protection plus a great many shops. The gang was rolling in it.

'All thanks to me,' Sean said aloud, and smiled. Yes, the whole thing had been his idea, the gang, the protection, everything. To his way of thinking he was due more than he'd been paying himself.

The others would never know, he reasoned. They got their divvy every week and that was that. What was left over was kept right here in the money box, no one knowing how much there actually was apart from him.

'Fuck it!' he swore softly. It was his right.

He counted out thirty pounds and slipped the notes into his pocket. He then shut and locked the box before returning it to its hiding place.

King of the castle! That was him right enough. He felt no qualms whatsoever about stealing from his friends.

They were all dummies anyway. Not like him.

Mail to the staff was always given out over breakfast. A delighted Bridie accepted the letter from Mrs Coltart and, on recognising her mother's writing, eagerly tore it open and began reading the contents.

She went pale. 'Dear God in Heaven,' she muttered.

Mrs Coltart, who'd just sat down, glanced over at Bridie who was only two places away. 'Something wrong, Bridie?'

Tears sprang into Bridie's eyes. 'It's my da. He's . . . he's . . .' She swallowed hard. 'He's ill and maybe going to die.'

The chatter round the table ceased.

Mrs Coltart regarded Bridie steadily. 'Does the letter say what's wrong with him?'

Bridie shook her head. 'They don't know but he's in a coma.'

She glanced at the letter again, tears spilling on to the pristine white and heavily starched table cloth. 'My ma wants me to go home and see him just . . . just in case.'

'Understandable,' Mrs Coltart murmured.

Bridie gave Mrs Coltart a pleading look. 'Can I?' she whispered.

On brief reflection Mrs Coltart came to the conclusion this was a matter for Mr Seaton to decide. 'Can I have that letter?' she asked.

It was passed to her. 'Wait here and finish your breakfast, Bridie. I shan't be long.'

Finish her breakfast? How could she do that? It was impossible.

Jeannie Swanson, sitting next to Bridie, squeezed her arm while the rest of the table, including Mrs Kilbride, remained silent.

As chance would have it Ian was with his father when Mrs Coltart came in. 'Sorry to bother you, sir, but something's come up.'

Willie and Ian had been deep in conversation about matters regarding the estate, the pair of them in disagreement over one of them. Willie was subsequently in a rather testy mood.

'Yes, what is it, Mrs Coltart?'

She explained the situation.

'Poor lass,' Ian exclaimed in concern.

'Here's the letter, sir,' Mrs Coltart said, handing it to Willie who swiftly scanned it.

'I thought whether or not she was allowed to go should be your decision, sir.'

'You must let her go, Pa, you must,' Ian urged.

'Must I indeed?'

'Well I certainly think you should.'

Ian was right of course, what he would have done anyway. 'I presume she'll want to leave straight away?' Willie said to Mrs Coltart.

'In the circumstances that would make sense, sir.'

'Right then, see to it. She can have as long as she likes, within reason that is.'

'With pay, sir?'

Willie considered that for a moment. 'Yes, with full pay. And I shall also take care of her train fare. See she's given sufficient funds out of petty cash, Mrs Coltart.'

'You're very generous, sir.'

Willie didn't reply to that.

Mrs Coltart was turning to leave when Ian had an idea. 'I think I'll drive her to the station myself.'

Mrs Coltart paused to hear the outcome of this exchange.

'You?' Willie queried in astonishment. 'But you've got work to be getting on with.'

'It won't take that long, Pa. And I'd like to. She's a nice girl, and hard working as I'm sure Mrs Coltart will testify.'

'She is indeed, on both counts,' Mrs Coltart stated quietly.

'So is it all right, Pa?'

Willie shrugged. 'Suit yourself. As long as you make up the time when you return.'

'I will, Pa. I promise. Now I'll go and bring the car round.'

Ian accompanied Mrs Coltart from the room leaving a puzzled Willie staring after his son.

Now why was Ian volunteering to drive a member of staff to the station when there were others who normally did that sort of thing?

'Hmmh,' he mused. Could it be there was something between Ian and Bridie Flynn, something he knew nothing about? It wouldn't be the first time after all that there had been a relationship, purely on a sexual basis of course, between the two classes. Could that possibly be it?

No, he was letting his imagination run away with him. Ian wasn't that sort. It just wasn't part of his nature. At least he didn't think so.

And Ian had Moira, he wouldn't jeopardise that. Surely not! Not for a little dalliance with a maid.

Everyone looked round when Mrs Coltart came back into the kitchen. 'All right, Bridie, go and get packed. You're on the first train home. And you're being driven to the station by Master Ian himself no less. So get a move on, girl.'

Bridie hastily rose. 'Thank you, Mrs Coltart. Thank you.'

'It's Mister Seaton you want to thank. Not only for giving you paid leave but offering to meet the cost of your train fare into the bargain.'

'Ooh!' Bridie breathed, that was a huge bonus.

'Now hop to it. You don't want to keep Master Ian waiting. He's a busy man.'

'Right then,' Bridie said, and, excusing herself, rushed away.

Mrs Coltart caught Mrs Kilbride's eye and they both nodded. This only confirmed yet again what they'd often said to one another. Mr Seaton was a gem of an employer. They didn't come any better. And it looked as though Master Ian was taking after his father in that department.

'Are you close to your dad?' Ian asked Bridie as the car moved away from the house, her case lodged in the boot.

Bridie hesitated for a few seconds. 'I suppose so, sir. Though not as close as I am to my ma.'

'I see. And it's Ian when we're alone.'

'Yes, s . . . Yes, Ian.'

'We don't have to rush by the way. I checked the timetable before leaving and there won't be a train for a while. I'll wait with you at the station to make sure you get safely aboard.'

'There's no need to do that, Ian. I don't want to put you out any more than I have to.'

He grinned. 'I insist. As Jock Gibson the estate manager says, if a job's worth doing then it's worth doing well. And he's right. So put you on the train I shall.'

'You're very kind. Driving me yourself and that.'

'Not particularly kind, Bridie. It's something I want to do.'

She glanced sideways at him, then again at the road stretching ahead. 'About that night in the hut, Ian.'

'Yes?'

'I'll never mention it to anyone.'

'I know that, Bridie.'

There was silence between them, then Bridie said, 'Can I ask you a question?'

'Go right ahead.'

'I've been wondering . . . why did you kiss me?'

299

Tell the truth? He couldn't do that. Not all of it anyway. 'Because I find you very attractive, that's why.'

She tried to digest that. He found her attractive! 'You wouldn't ever . . . try to take advantage of me, would you?'

Ian sighed. How did he answer that one? More than anything else he wanted to take advantage of her, as she put it.

'Because I wouldn't let you. Not you or any other man. Not even if it cost me my position.'

'Don't worry, Bridie, I won't.'

'Thank you, I appreciate that.'

Again silence descended between them. 'Miss Moira's very beautiful,' Bridie said eventually.

If he'd been more worldly wise Ian would have heard the jealousy in her voice. 'I suppose so,' he admitted reluctantly.

There was no supposing about it, Bridie thought. Moira McLaren was gorgeous. The bee's knees. 'Are you . . . going to get married?'

Bridie gulped, what an impertinent question to ask. It was none of her business whether they were or not. But part of her desperately wanted to know.

Now it was Ian's turn to glance sideways at her. 'It's a possibility.'

'Ah!' she breathed.

'Why?'

Bridie shrugged. 'Just curious, that's all.'

'And why should you be curious, Bridie Flynn?'

Oh God, she thought. Because it would break her heart, but she wasn't going to tell him that. 'Women usually are about such things,' she prevaricated.

'Indeed.'

'Oh yes.'

He suddenly felt the almost overwhelming temptation to

pull the car off the road and kiss Bridie. Hold her close. Breathe in her smell.

'And what about you, will you get married one day?' he queried instead.

'I hope so.'

'He'll be a fortunate lad who marries you.'

She flushed slightly. 'Thank you.'

'I mean it.'

She wanted to reply that Moira was fortunate too, more than so. But didn't.

'How is your reading coming along?' Ian enquired, changing the subject.

Much to Bridie's relief.

'There she is,' Ian declared, having spied steam in the distance. The train was right on time.

'How are you getting home from the station?'

'Tram of course. It's too far to walk. Especially with a case to carry.'

'Will you do me a favour?'

Do him a favour! She'd have done anything for Ian Seaton. Well, almost anything. 'If I can.'

Ian pulled out his wallet from which he extracted a five-pound note. 'Take a taxi home on me.'

Bridie stared at the note. 'I can't accept money from you, Ian.'

'Why not?'

'It wouldn't be right. I mean . . .' She broke off in confusion.

He laughed softly. 'It would give me pleasure for you to accept it, Bridie. Honestly. And there aren't any strings attached, I swear.'

'But . . . a whole five pounds!'

'Taxi there and back when you return. Plus a few pounds to spend as you will.'

She regarded him coldly. 'This isn't payment for that kiss I hope?'

He was outraged. 'It most certainly is not. All I was thinking is that in your present state it would be far nicer for you to go by taxi than tram or omnibus.'

Bridie softened. It would be nice. If for no other reason than she'd never ever been in a taxi. Talk about swank! She could just imagine what the neighbours would think when she drew up outside their close. It would be all round the street within minutes.

'Go on,' Ian urged. 'Please.'

'No strings attached?'

'My word of honour.'

She hesitated for only a few seconds longer. 'Now you're being more than kind.'

'Just don't let on to anyone at The Haven that's all.'

'I won't.'

'They might misunderstand. Read into it what isn't there.'

'I understand.'

'Good.'

She slipped the fiver into her coat pocket.

'And, Bridie.'

'Yes?'

'I sincerely hope your father gets better.'

'Thank you, Ian.'

He wanted to touch her, run his fingers down her face. But daren't. There was a hollowness inside him, a sense of loss, at her impending departure.

Bridie stood as the train was now approaching the station. Ian did likewise.

He glanced up and down the platform, they were the only ones there and that's how it seemed it was going to remain.

Bridie wondered how she was going to say goodbye. Shake his hand?

The train tooted just before drawing alongside in great gushes and whooshes of steam. When it eventually stopped Ian led her to a compartment and opened the door.

'In you go then,' he smiled, following her so he could put her case on the overhead rack.

'Thanks again for everything, Ian,' she said rather awkwardly.

'Don't mention it.'

He was about to leave the compartment when, on a sudden impulse, he turned and hastily pecked her on the cheek.

'You take care, Maid Bridie.'

'I will . . . Sir Ian.'

He leapt onto the platform and shut the compartment door. They both stood staring at each other until, with a jolt, the train continued on its way.

'Goodbye, my love,' Ian whispered to himself.

Chapter 20

Bridie let herself in with her key. She laid her case down and went through to the kitchen where she found her mother dozing in a chair.

'Ma?'

Kathleen's eyes blinked open, then delight flooded her face. 'Bridie!'

'I'm back as you asked, Ma.'

Kathleen flew into Bridie's arms and they hugged one another tight. 'Thank the Lord,' Kathleen whispered.

They disentangled themselves. 'How's Da?'

Kathleen shrugged. 'The same I'm afraid. And they still don't know what's wrong with him. A second specialist was called in and he's as mystified as the first.'

Her mother had lost weight, Bridie noted. And there were new lines on her face. Deep lines as though cut with a knife. 'When can I see him?'

'Tonight. We'll go together.'

Bridie nodded, then glanced about her. How good it was

to be home, everything just as she remembered it. 'So how have you been coping?'

'Surprisingly Sean's been very good. Helps me out in all sorts of ways. Mind you, he has the time now that he doesn't work.'

'Doesn't work? Has he been laid off?' This was news to Bridie, Kathleen never having mentioned it in any of her letters.

'Would you like a cup of tea?'

'You sit down, Ma, I'll do it.'

Kathleen sank back into the chair she'd just been dozing in. 'You might as well know, he left Barry's of his own accord. Simply walked out.'

'But why?' Bridie was appalled.

'He doesn't have to work any more. Doesn't need the money. He . . . eh . . .' This was difficult. 'It seems he gets money from that gang of his, the Samurai.'

Bridie frowned as she ran water into the kettle. 'How does he do that?'

'Don't ask, girl. I don't. I've heard stories though. The sort that would make any decent mother weep.'

'That bad, eh?'

'Worse, lass. It appears he's turned into a kind of . . .' She swallowed, finding the word hard to say. 'Gangster.'

'Jesus,' Bridie breathed.

'Him and the others, his chinas, up to all sorts. He's bound to land in jail if he's not careful. But you know Sean, he's not one to be told.'

Bridie knew that only too well. She had a strange relationship with her brother, she reflected. There were many likeable things about him, but even more dislikeable ones. He'd always rather scared her if she was honest. Her da had always been able to control him until that fight which she'd

realised had been a turning point. That night the young
Turk had taken over from the old.

'Does he pay you now? For his lodge I mean.'

'Oh aye, same as before. Only now I get wee extras. And
right handy they come in I can tell you.'

'Where's he now?'

'Search me, Bridie. The pub most like. He spends a lot
more time in there than he used to. Well, he's got more
money now than he had when at Barry's.'

'I'm pleased to hear he's been a help. Now what about
Alison?'

'She's at school as you probably realise. She's been in to
see her da, I thought that best. When she was there I told
her he was sleeping, not that he was in a coma. She doesn't
know how serious it all is.'

Kathleen choked and turned her head away. 'I don't
know what I'll do if he dies, Bridie. Even if it has been
difficult between us for a while.'

'Difficult?'

The kettle now on, Bridie came and sat facing her
mother.

Kathleen's shoulders heaved. 'I shouldn't tell you this,
but . . .' She trailed off.

'Ma?'

Kathleen had to force herself to speak. 'He's been seeing
another woman.'

That rocked Bridie. 'You're joking!'

'I'm not. He confessed when I confronted him with the
evidence.' She didn't mention the terrible beating he'd
given her.

'And what evidence was that, Ma?'

Kathleen told her.

Bridie couldn't believe this. Her father with a fancy

piece, a bit of fluff, on the side. 'Do you know who she is?'

Kathleen shook her head. 'The excuse to visit her was that he was going to a union committee meeting. I was so proud that he was on a committee, only to find out it was all a lie.'

Bridie knelt in front of Kathleen and took her into her arms. 'How awful for you, Ma.'

'You've no idea, lassie. It was as though the world had ended. I've always thought your da and I had a good marriage. Oh it's had its ups and downs right enough, but that's only natural. But for him to go with someone else. That was a bitter pill and no mistake.'

'Oh Ma, I'm so sorry.'

'Not nearly as much as me, lass. I keep thinking I must have failed him in some way. Though how I don't know.'

Bridie released her mother. 'I can't believe you've failed him in any way. You always seemed so . . . happy together.'

'That's what I thought. But it would seem we were both wrong.' Kathleen sighed and closed her eyes. 'I even had Father O'Banion speak to him, but that didn't do any good. He just went on as before.'

'Does anyone else know?'

Kathleen shook her head. 'Just me, you and Father O'Banion. And you musn't say anything, mind. I'd die of shame.'

'I won't, Ma. You can trust me.'

'Aye, Bridie,' Kathleen smiled. 'I can that.'

Kathleen got up. 'I've a few wee biscuits in. Some of them chocolate. Shall we spoil ourselves?'

Bridie laughed. 'Why not.'

Bridie gasped when she saw her father. How old he looked,

and thin. Gone was the roistering Irishman she remembered.

'Dear God,' she whispered.

'Not a murmur out of him since he went into the coma,' Kathleen said.

Pat's face, normally a healthy pink verging on the ruddy, was white and waxen. There were streaks of grey in his hair where there had been none before.

'What do you think?' Kathleen queried in a soft voice.

'He looks terrible.'

'Aye, true enough.'

'And shrunken.'

That too was true, Kathleen thought. If Pat did recover, and please God he did, he'd never be the same man again.

'I usually talk to him,' Kathleen explained. 'I don't suppose it does any good, but I usually talk nonetheless.'

'About what, Ma?'

'Oh, anything and everything. Gossip on the street, remembrances from when we were younger, how Alison's doing at school. That sort of thing. Now you're here why don't you have a go?'

Kathleen sat on the chair by the bedside and Bridie pulled up another. 'Hello, Da, it's me. Back to visit you. What's all this nonsense then?'

Of course there was no reply.

'Would you like to hear about the place where I'm working? It's some house I can tell you. The biggest mansion you could imagine.'

She told him everything about The Haven, with the exception of her falling in love with Ian Seaton.

Geraldine Buchanan stared out of her window at the

coalman below heaving a bag on to his back. Surely that wasn't Pat?

A few minutes later the man was at her door. 'Come away in,' she smiled, and ushered him through. 'You're new.'

'Aye, that's right. On this round anyway.'

'It's usually a Mr Flynn who delivers.'

'Pat, you mean, poor sod's in hospital lying at death's door.'

'Death's door?' Geraldine stammered in reply.

'He's got something terribly wrong with him and they don't know what. He's in a coma.'

'How . . . did that happen?'

The coalman regarded her quizzically. 'A friend of yours, is he?'

'No no, nothing like that. I'm simply concerned, that's all. He's always such a pleasant, cheery chap.'

'They've no idea how it happened. Took him in the middle of the night apparently and en route to hospital he went into a coma. That's all I can tell you.'

'I'll get your money,' a stunned Geraldine said, and hurried off.

When the man had gone Geraldine poured herself a stiff drink. Pat in a coma, at death's door!

As the saying went, you never knew the moment till the moment after.

'What's wrong with your face the night?' Noddy Gallagher enquired good-humouredly of Sean. They were in the pub with Bill O'Connell and Don McGuire.

Sean glared at him. 'Why don't you mind your own fucking business.'

'Sorry,' Noddy hastily apologised. 'Didn't mean to offend annat.'

Sean picked up the whisky in front of him and threw it down his throat. He was in a black anger over what had happened earlier. Or to be precise what hadn't happened.

He'd taken Muriel back into the bedroom and tried again, only to fail a second time. She'd been placatory, but that hadn't washed with him. It had to be the bitch's fault. Had to be. There was nothing wrong with him as he could testify most mornings when he woke. Or on other occasions.

He'd smacked her one, knocking her right off the bed, which had made him feel better. Once outside he'd told her to piss off, he never wanted to see her again. He'd smiled watching her scuttle away like some frightened rabbit.

He'd get another bint and that would make all the difference. That weekend at a dance perhaps. Nor would he have any trouble, they all knew who he was. All he'd have to do was crook a finger at whichever bird took his fancy and she'd come running.

'Oh Christ!' Bill O'Connell swore softly.

'What's wrong?' Don McGuire queried, seeing Bill's expression of extreme apprehension.

'Sean,' Bill hissed.

'Aye, what is it?'

Bill nodded to some young men who'd just come into the pub and sauntered over to the bar. 'Do you know who they are?'

Sean glanced at the newcomers and shook his head. 'Haven't a clue.'

'They're Tong.'

Sean involuntarily sucked in a breath. 'Are you sure?'

'Sure as damnit. I've got an old pal runs with that lot. He introduced me to some of them once. And several of those are there.'

Sean quickly counted them. Eleven in all, while they were only four. Hardly good odds if a ruction started.

'What are we going to do?' Bill asked anxiously.

'Do? Ef all. They're entitled to come in here if they want. They're not causing us any harm.' Sean turned to Noddy. 'It's your shout. You'd better get the round in.'

'Aye, right away, Sean.' Noddy hastily vacated his seat.

'They don't look so tough to me,' Don McGuire declared bravely.

Sean shot him a contemptuous glance. 'Well, they are, if their reputation is anything to go by. Hard men, one and all.'

Sean noted several of the Tong surreptitiously looking in their direction. Shit, he thought. This could well be trouble.

About five minutes later one of the Tong strolled across to stand by their table. He was smiling affably. Though that didn't fool Sean any.

'Which one of youse is Sean Flynn?'

Sean stared into the palest and coldest blue eyes he'd ever seen. 'I am.'

'Oh aye. Well, I'm Big Bill Bremner. Maybe you've heard of me?'

Sean nodded. Big Bill Bremner was the leader of the Tong. He could now see why he was called Big Bill. The man was only slightly over five feet tall, if that. In Glasgow it's well known that the smaller the man the more dangerous he can be. And Big Bill was no exception. He had a reputation for violence and mayhem as long as anyone's arm.

'So you're the Samurai,' Big Bill chuckled.

'A few of us.'

'Doing well I understand, though in a rather unconventional way if I may say so.'

Sean bit back an acid retort. He had no wish to antagonise the bastard.

'All Micks as well.'

Sean had no idea how this was going to turn out. He was just glad he had his razor in his pocket. If he went down it would be fighting.

'That's right.'

Big Bill's gaze swept the foursome. 'The map of Ireland written over all your faces.'

Sean didn't reply to that.

'An awful wee gang I understand. We've got hundreds.'

Again Sean didn't reply.

'I hope you don't mind us coming into your territory like?'

Sean was hating this, feeling humiliated. But he wasn't going to start anything, not when it was eleven against four. He shrugged. 'Suit yourself.'

'Aye, that's right. I usually do.'

A pale-faced Noddy picked up his pint and had a sip. He had trouble swallowing.

'Maybe you'll come up our end of town one day?'

That was clearly a challenge. 'Maybe.'

'I'd like that.'

Sean had no doubt Big Bill would. Should they be so stupid, in their present strength it would be a massacre. 'As you say, Big Bill, one day.'

Big Bill finished his drink and placed the empty glass on the table. 'Interesting meeting you blokes.'

'Likewise,' Sean replied.

'I'm sure.'

The affable smile returned. 'I'll be seeing you.'

Sean nodded.

'Cunt,' he swore quietly when Big Bill was out of earshot. 'Cunt.'

'I thought I might visit my parents for a few days,' Georgina announced to Willie.

'But it's not that time of year!' he protested.

'I know that, but I just fancy going. A change of scenery would do me the world of good.'

An understanding smile came on to his face. 'You mean you want to go round the shops.'

She pretended confusion, as though she'd been found out. 'That will be nice I have to admit.'

Willie disliked it when Georgina went away. He felt lonely, even though there were others in the house. 'If you wish.'

'Just for a few days as I said, not longer.'

That mollified him a little. 'I'll miss you of course.'

She went to him and pecked him on the cheek. 'Good. Then you'll appreciate me even more when I get back.'

'I always appreciate you, Georgina. Never think I don't.'

Guilt stabbed her at what she had planned. Or hoped to plan. 'And I appreciate you, Willie. You're a loving, adoring husband whom I love with all my heart.'

He beamed on hearing that. 'Give me a proper kiss,' he requested as they were alone.

Female Judas, Georgina thought, as their lips met.

Andrew opened the letter and scanned its contents. His eyebrows slowly rose.

'Well well,' he muttered, laying the letter aside. How about that! Whatever else you could accuse Georgina of it wasn't being shy in coming forward.

Go or not? He wasn't sure.

Of course he was, damnit. He bloody well would. Wild horses wouldn't keep him away.

He desperately needed a woman and this one was available.

Jack Riach ran a hand over his forehead, while facing him Hettie waited for him to continue dictating.

'Damn!' he swore.

'What's wrong?'

'I can't . . .' He shook his head. 'I don't know what comes next. It's a blank.'

'Then I suggest that's enough for today, Jack.'

'I suppose so.'

He lapsed into a brooding silence.

'Would you like a cup of tea or coffee?'

'No thank you.'

Hettie stared at him, his face creased with thought. 'Let it go, Jack. Put it out of your mind for now.'

He took off his dark glasses and rubbed his eyeless sockets which, for some reason, were hurting him. 'It's the war, Hettie, the bloody war. Remembering it for the plays was bad enough, but this, being a novel and far longer, is worse. A great deal worse.'

'I think you're doing awfully well so far, Jack.'

'Do you really?'

'Yes. And I wouldn't lie to you. I'd never do that.'

Hettie hesitated, then said, 'The bits about you and me are so true to life, Jack. When you dictate it's as though you were speaking and I was replying.'

'What an idiot I was in those early days,' he mused. 'Young, selfish, full of myself. It took a German grenade to knock all that out of me and see things . . .'

He broke off to laugh mirthlessly. 'To see things as they truly are.'

Emotion welled within Hettie. 'Oh, Jack!'

'Still no regrets? About you and me, that is.'

'Never. And don't ever ask me again. You already know the answer.'

And then he had it. Painful a recollection as it was. 'Pen at the ready, Hettie?'

'Of course.'

'Now what was that last line . . . ?'

'Kathleen.' The voice was hoarse and very faint.

She started, her attention having wandered. 'Pat?'

His eyes were open, recognition there. She quickly grasped his hand and squeezed it.

'What happened?'

'You've been very ill.'

The faintest of smiles played over his mouth. 'I don't know where I was but I often heard you there.'

'I've been with you as much as I've been allowed, Pat.'

'Dreams,' he murmured. 'So many dreams.'

'But now you're back with us, Pat. That's all that matters.' She began to cry.

'Don't, lass. Don't.'

'I can't help it. I'm so happy.'

He closed his eyes for a second, then opened them again. 'Did I also hear Bridie?'

'Aye you did. She came home to be with us.'

'I've been that ill?'

Kathleen nodded.

'What was it?'

'They never found out. They couldn't diagnose you.'

'Difficult as always, eh?'

'That's you, Pat.'

He felt dreadfully weak, and somehow detached, as though he wasn't even part of the real world. 'I love you, Kathleen,' he said.

She stared at him.

'I know I've been rotten to you, but that's over now. I swear it. If I get through this I'll never be unfaithful to you ever again.'

'Oh Pat,' she whispered.

'I don't know what possessed me. But in my dreams I came to realise what I risked losing. And, Kathleen, I don't want to lose that. Not you and me.'

So much emotion was clogging her throat she couldn't speak.

'Will you forgive me. Please?'

Kathleen nodded.

'Jesus, but I don't deserve you. You're one in a million, Kathleen Flynn and I the lucky man who has you.'

She bent over and kissed him on the mouth, a mouth dry as parchment. 'I should call the doctor.'

'Not yet. I want you to myself for a bit. Just the two of us.'

'All right then.'

He gazed at her, drinking her in. Remembering the dreams that had been about the pair of them. Good dreams. Warm dreams. Dreams that had made him realise how stupid he'd been.

He wasn't going to come, Georgina thought in despair, having been dawdling over her meal waiting for Andrew to put in an appearance. Oh well, there had always been the chance he wouldn't be able to make it, or simply didn't want to. He of course hadn't been able to reply to her letter, that would have been far too risky.

She sipped at her wine, a rather nice Mâcon. But the pleasantness of it was lost on her.

'Is madam finding everything satisfactory?'

She smiled at the hovering waiter. 'Yes, thank you. The meal is excellent.'

The waiter bowed and moved away.

For the umpteenth time Georgina glanced round the dining room of the Saltire Hotel where she was booked under an assumed name. There was still no sign of him.

Eventually she finished her main course and ordered a dessert that she didn't want but which would give her an excuse to linger longer.

The dessert was a chocolate concoction with cream on top. Delicious, she thought when she tasted it. And extremely fattening.

And then suddenly he was there, talking to the *maitre d'*.

Andrew glanced up and down the corridor to ensure he wasn't being observed, then discreetly tapped on Georgina's door. He smiled, recalling how she'd let him know which room she was in by dropping her key as she passed him on her way out. He, naturally enough, being a gentleman, had picked it up for her, the only words passing between them being 'thank you, sir'. As Georgina had said in her letter, they had to be most careful. She in particular, as being a native of Perth she was known to many people there.

The door opened and he slipped inside. The door instantly closed again.

'Hello,' he smiled.

'Hello.'

He took in the long free-flowing pink silk negligée she was

wearing over a matching nightdress. She seemed to shimmer in the light.

'I say,' he murmured appreciatively. 'You look absolutely ravishing.'

'It was more *being* ravished that I had in mind,' she retorted, marvelling at her boldness.

He laughed. 'You certainly don't mince your words. I like that in a woman.'

She melted into his arms. 'I was so scared you wouldn't make it, my darling.'

'Well I did and here I am.'

The taut hardness and sheer masculinity of his body sent shivers coursing up and down her spine. While the cologne he was wearing and which she remembered so vividly made her head swim.

'I laid in a bottle of whisky for you should you wish a drink,' she said.

'Later I think.'

'Good.'

He lightly ran a hand through her hair, then down over her shoulders and back, finally letting it come to rest on the swell of her buttocks. Georgina moaned.

'You make me go all liquid inside,' she whispered.

'Do I?'

'Oh yes. A sort of fiery, molten liquid that's quite indescribable.'

He liked that as well.

'And what do I do to you?'

He nudged her with his groin. 'That.'

This time she groaned.

'Why don't I make myself comfortable?' he suggested.

'Here, let me help you.'

Slowly, starting with his tie, she began undressing him.

Andrew watched her in amusement, relishing the power he had over her. A power he'd had over many women. He'd decided during his meal what course their love-making would take. He had a few surprises in store for Georgina Seaton, surprises taught him years previously by a professional.

When he was finally naked she pressed herself against him again and began to rub herself up and down his body.

'Let's get into bed, darling,' she proposed.

'Not yet.'

His hands, which had been motionless while she had undressed him, started to move. Touching, caressing, fondling.

In the end, which was what he'd intended, Georgina was pleading with him to take her.

It was a night to remember.

Chapter 21

M r Durie, the specialist, straightened up from Pat's bed, Pat watching him anxiously. There were two nurses also in attendance.

'You're doing extremely well, Mr Flynn,' Durie pronounced. 'I'm delighted with your progress.' He shook his head. 'I only wish I knew what's been wrong with you but that remains a medical mystery I'm afraid.'

'Will I get it again, Doctor?'

Durie gave a thin smile. 'I simply can't answer that. But my guess, and that's all it is, based on years of professional experience I would point out, is I don't believe so.'

Pat heaved a sigh of relief. 'When can I go home?'

'Ah! A good question. Certainly not this week. I want to keep you in for a while to recuperate and for observation. How do you feel?'

'Weak,' Pat confessed.

'Natural enough. I wouldn't have expected anything else after what you've been through. Any headaches?'

'None, Doctor.'

'And within yourself? Deep down that is.'

Pat considered that. 'The same but different I suppose.'

'Different?'

Pat dropped his gaze to stare at the bedclothes. 'You'll laugh.'

'No I won't, Mr Flynn. I assure you.'

Pat glanced at the two nurses standing po-faced in the background, wishing they weren't there. They made this more difficult somehow.

'It's as though I've had some sort of religious experience. I know that sounds daft but there you have the truth of it.'

Durie smiled. 'Interesting. And something I've heard said before.'

'Really?'

'Yes, Mr Flynn. It's more common than you might imagine.'

Durie pondered for a few moments, then said, 'I'm convinced you're well on the way to recovery. You're a lucky man.'

Pat thought of Kathleen. Yes, he was a lucky man and not just to have survived the illness.

Durie picked up Pat's notes from the bottom of the bed, studied them briefly, then, taking out a pen, added a few additional comments.

'I'll see you again tomorrow, Mr Flynn,' Durie declared, replacing the notes.

'Thank you, Doctor.'

'And don't worry. I'll have you home as soon as possible.'

'Thank you, Doctor.'

'In the meantime try and move your bowels. You haven't so far.'

Pat blanched. The idea of using a bedpan was anathema to him. He intended holding out as long as he could before that humiliation. A bottle was one thing, but a pan!

Bridie was standing at the kitchen window staring out over the back courts and tenements that lay beyond. It was odd, she reflected, this was all she'd known for most of her life and yet now, somehow, she felt a stranger here.

How dirty it all was, and squalid. She watched some wee boys playing 'kick the can', the clatter they were making reverberating round the back courts. One of the boys had a great tear in the rear of his shorts so that his bare bottom was peeping out.

She thought of The Haven and Ian Seaton. Now that her da was on the mend it was high time for her to return there. She'd leave the following day, she decided. There was an early train, she'd catch that.

'Ian,' she murmured wistfully.

'Is there something wrong with you?'

Ian turned to face his sister. 'No, why?'

'You've seemed quite out of sorts recently.'

'Have I?'

'Grumpy to say the least.'

It was because of Bridie, he thought. He couldn't wait to see her again, be in her company. 'You haven't appeared quite yourself either.'

Rose immediately became defensive, the accusation too close to the mark. 'There's nothing wrong with me that I'm aware of,' she lied.

'No?'

'I'd know if there was.'

He saw the beginnings of a blush tinge her cheek and

arrived at completely the wrong conclusion – that it was that time of the month for her.

'Anyway, I've got things to do,' Rose declared, and swept from the room.

If Ian had been out of sorts on account of Bridie then she'd been the same way because of Andrew.

When was she going to see him again? she inwardly raged as she hurried on her way.

'How's Mr Flynn?' Geraldine Buchanan asked the coalman who'd taken over Pat's round.

He shook out the bag he'd tipped into her bin. 'Coming along handsomely from what I hear.'

Relief washed through her. Thank God for that. 'Any news of him coming back to work?'

'He won't be doing that for a while, missus,' the man replied. 'I think I said to you the poor sod was at death's door. You don't recover from that overnight.'

'No, of course not.' Geraldine smiled understandingly.

Again the coalman wondered at her concern for Pat. It seemed odd somehow. More than it should have been. There again, it was none of his business. And certainly not to be remarked on back at the yard.

'Thank you, missus,' he said on giving Geraldine her change.

As she'd done on his previous visit, Geraldine poured herself a large drink when the man had gone.

'Bridie?'

And there he was, at long last. 'Hello.'

'How's your father?' Ian queried anxiously.

'Recovering, I'm happy to say. He's hoping to get home before too long.'

'When did you get in?'

'Late last night.'

'I see.'

He found himself staring deep into her eyes, eyes that were attracting him as though he was a piece of iron being drawn to a magnet.

'I missed you.'

That startled Bridie. 'Did you?'

Ian was suddenly covered in confusion. 'Yes,' he whispered.

And how she'd missed him, dreadfully so. 'How's Miss McLaren?'

'Moira? She's fine. Why do you ask?'

Bridie shrugged. 'I don't know.'

He hadn't heard the jealousy in her voice before, now he did. Could it be . . . could it possibly be?

'I went there on Sunday as usual.'

Bridie's face tightened slightly. 'Did you have a good time?'

He had and he hadn't. It had been pleasant enough, though, if he was truthful, boring. Moira had chattered endlessly on.

Ian shrugged. 'I suppose so.'

Suppose so? What kind of answer was that? 'I must be getting along,' Bridie declared. 'I've a lot to do.'

'Of course. Don't let me keep you.'

Ian wheeled around and walked quickly off, leaving Bridie staring after him.

'More wine?'

Moira McLaren shook her head. 'Not for me, Ian, thank you. I really have had sufficient.'

Ian refilled his glass and then lay back to stare at a

beautiful summer sky. He and Moira were having a picnic by the Coothie Burn which ran through the estate. She was resplendent in a white cotton dress, perfect for the occasion, and large, floppy-brimmed, straw hat.

'Do you remember my cousin Elspeth White?' Moira enquired casually. 'I'm sure you've met her.'

Ian had to think for a moment. 'Oh yes.'

'She got engaged last week.'

'Good for her,' Ian smiled.

'To a veterinary surgeon she only met quite recently. It was love at first sight apparently.'

Ian closed his eyes, enjoying the sun beating down on him. He yawned. 'Excuse me.'

Moira tinkled out a laugh. 'That's all right.'

'It really is the most soporific day. If I'm not careful I'll fall asleep.'

She frowned. 'Not with me here I hope you won't.'

He immediately came on to an elbow. 'Sorry, that must have sounded awful. It's simply that between the combination of heat and wine I find myself wanting to drop off. Nothing to do with you, Moira, I assure you.'

That mollified her a little.

'I must say you look gorgeous today,' he declared.

'Why, thank you, kind sir.'

She did too, he thought. Crackingly so. Any man would be proud to have her as his girl friend. He had another sip of wine and listened to the drone of bees.

Moira studied Ian. 'Elspeth is two years younger than me, you know.'

'Is that a fact?'

'And now she's engaged to be married. I quite envy her really.'

Moira continued to watch Ian's face.

A sudden chill thought came into Ian's mind. This wasn't just making conversation. Moira was hinting that they too should get engaged. He said nothing.

'I understand he's bought her the most beautiful ring.'

Ian continued not to reply.

'The wedding is set for next year in the spring. And he's hinted to her that they'll go abroad for the honeymoon. Imagine!' Moira sighed. 'How romantic.'

'Yes, isn't it,' Ian replied quietly.

'I'd love to go abroad for my honeymoon.'

Ian's heart was sinking fast. What had been a very pleasant afternoon had suddenly gone extremely flat. He sipped more wine.

'It'll be a big wedding of course, hundreds there. I wonder if she'll buy a dress or have one made.'

'You must ask her.'

'Oh I will. I shall certainly have my wedding dress made, and those for the bridesmaids.'

Ian swallowed the remains of his glass and refilled it. 'I sometimes fish in this burn,' he stated, changing the subject. 'I've caught some marvellous trout in it.'

Moira's forehead creased. 'Have you indeed.'

'Oh yes.'

'I've never understood what men see in fishing. It seems quite boring to me.'

'Tranquil more like. For much of the time. And then a lot of excitement when you get a bite, not to mention land your fish.'

'Paris I should think,' Moira declared defiantly.

'Paris?'

'For the honeymoon. You can't get more romantic than that.'

'I don't suppose you can,' Ian replied vaguely.

'I've heard such a lot about Paris. The Left Bank, that sort of thing.'

Ian thought of Bridie, the woman he loved. What a situation to find himself in. A situation he had to do something about if he was to retain his sanity.

Moira's lips thinned. 'Wouldn't you like to go to Paris? I believe the food is out of this world.'

'France has never really attracted me,' Ian replied.

'No? How peculiar.'

He briefly closed his eyes. Decisions were going to have to be made soon. And they weren't going to be easy ones.

'I think we should be getting back,' he said briskly, coming to his feet.

Her disappointment clearly showed. 'So soon?'

'We have been here a good while.'

'But I was enjoying myself.'

As had he, until she'd started on about engagements and marriages. He'd been prepared to stay for several hours more until that had started. Talk about putting a dampener on the day.

'Ian.'

'Yes?'

'Come here.'

Christ, he thought. She wasn't going to let up. 'What for?'

Anger flitted across her face. 'Because I'm asking you to.'

He tried not to show his reluctance as he went to her. 'Now what can I do for you?' he queried, taking her in his arms. Hypocrite, he thought to himself.

'You could kiss me for a start.'

'Now that would be a pleasure.'

'Are you sure?'

He managed a smile. 'Of course. Isn't it always?'

Their lips met and he felt nothing. Nothing at all.

'Hmmh,' he murmured when it was over.

She raised a hand and traced it across his cheek. 'Is something wrong?'

'Why should there be?'

'I'm not sure. You don't seem particularly enthusiastic, that's all.'

'No?'

'Or is it my imagination?'

'Your imagination, Moira. A man can't be at white heat all the time you know. It's not like that.'

'I thought . . .' She trailed off.

'What?'

'We have been seeing each other for some time.'

He laughed softly. 'Hardly that. A little while perhaps.'

'You do like me, don't you?'

'Why would you be here if I didn't? Of course I do.'

'We get on so well together.'

Again he thought of Bridie. That extra something that was there when he was with her. That something which excited him in a way Moira never had.

'Yes,' he murmured.

Her doubts disappeared. 'I'm so fond of you, Ian. Truly I am.'

Fond, now there was a word. There again, he'd never declared feelings stronger than that to her so why should she to him?

'And I of you, Moira.'

He kissed her a second time, then disentangled himself. 'I'll pack up.'

Moira never took her eyes off him while he was doing that. He was acutely aware of her stare.

Sean barged into the pub and beckoned the barman over. 'A pint and a hauf,' he said tightly.

God but he needed a drink, a bucketful of the stuff. He'd had another failure back at 'the place'. A smashing wee lassie called Babs whom he'd picked up a fortnight previously.

He'd got her stripped and into bed, then set to. Except, as with Muriel, nothing had happened. Not a bloody thing.

He stared down at the counter, wondering what was wrong with him. Why? The question raged in his mind. Why! Why! Why!

'There you are, Jimmy,' the barman declared, placing his drinks in front of him.

Sean tossed a pound note on to the counter. Then, in one quick motion, he swallowed his whisky.

She'd had a lovely body too, beautiful tits, even better than Muriel. And she'd been keen, no problem there. He'd thought at one point she was going to devour him. So why hadn't he reacted as he should have done?

An awful thought came into his mind, one that both shocked and alarmed him.

Don't be stupid, he told himself. Nah! There was nothing of the nancy boy about him. He'd never fancied men, the very idea made him want to throw up.

A chap came to stand beside Sean, accidentally nudging him. Sean immediately rounded on the chap with a snarl. 'What's your fucking game, eh?'

Alarm flashed on to the chap's face. 'Sorry, I didn't mean it. Honest. I apologise.'

For a moment Sean considered having a go at the chap, giving him a seeing to, then thought the better of it. The bloke had apologised after all. You couldn't ask fairer than that.

He took a deep breath. 'Think no more about it, pal.'

The chap nodded, his relief obvious, wishing he'd never come into that particular pub or been so clumsy. There was that about Sean which he found extremely menacing. Once he'd paid for his drink he moved away to a table at the far side out of harm's way.

Sean was thinking again about Babs and worrying about himself. Afterwards he'd put the frighteners on her as he had on Muriel. She'd keep her yap shut knowing what would happen to her if she didn't.

Why? he asked himself for the umpteenth time.

Why?

Pat sighed. 'I can't tell you how good it is to be home.'

'Come on, get yourself sat down. Remember the doctor told you you've still got to get plenty of rest.

Pat allowed Kathleen to assist him to his favourite chair and sank gratefully into it. 'I know we came by ambulance and all I had to do was get into it and then climb the stairs when we arrived but it hasn't half taken it out of me,' he declared in a weak voice.

'Well, you've been lying in bed all this while so what do you expect?' Kathleen rubbed her hands together. 'Now how about a nice cup of tea? The sort you can stand a spoon up in.'

'That would be terrific.'

He watched her as she filled the kettle and put it on. Truly it was good to be home, that was no lie. To be home with Kathleen.

The outside door banged shut and Sean came in. 'I thought we'd got shot of you for ever,' he joked.

'No such luck I'm afraid, son.'

Sean studied his father. 'You look like shit.'

'Sean!' Kathleen admonished. 'Language please.'

'Sorry, Ma. But he does.'

Pat ran a hand over his face. He knew exactly what he looked like and Sean was right. But time would deal with that.

'You never once came to see me,' Pat said to Sean.

'Don't like hospitals. They give me the creeps. Ma kept me informed of your progress.'

Pat didn't press the point, he knew better.

'What's for dinner?' Sean queried.

'Lamb chops. A special treat for your da.'

Pat raised an eyebrow. 'They're expensive.'

Kathleen glanced at Sean, then at her husband. 'I did mention Sean's been giving me extra. Well it's been quite a bit extra recently. We can afford them.'

Sean gave a thin, almost wicked, smile. 'That's what comes of being a success in the world, eh?'

Pat refrained from commenting on that, well aware where Sean's money was coming from. He didn't approve, not one little bit.

Pat suddenly felt old. Old as could be.

'Kathleen?'

'What, Pat?'

They'd just gone to bed together.

'I want to say something.'

She didn't reply.

'I really do love you, Kathleen. I told you in the hospital and I meant it. Can we start again?'

'What about her?' Kathleen queried in a tight voice.

'I said, it's over. I'll only see her one more time and

that's to finish it between us.' On returning to work he intended asking for his round to be changed. That would make it easier if he didn't have to deliver Geraldine's coal any more.

Pat put an arm round Kathleen and gently pulled her close. 'I'm not up to . . . well you know what. But can we just cuddle?'

She turned to face him and they embraced.

'It'll be just like it used to be,' he whispered. 'Only better. I swear.'

A warmth of contentment welled through Kathleen. Contentment and peace.

'When I'm up and about properly I want to go and take confession,' Pat said. 'I want to do so very badly.'

'I'm delighted to hear that.'

'And I'll have a special word with Father O'Banion. I want him to know everything's fine between us again and also ask him about those dreams I had while in the coma.'

'Father O'Banion will be pleased.'

'Aye, he will.'

'Now get some sleep, Pat, you need it.'

'It'll be the best night's sleep I've had since it happened. And you know why? Because you'll be beside me.'

Everything had come right again, Kathleen reflected. Surely nothing as bad as Pat's affair and illness would ever blight their lives in the future.

Surely.

'So tell me about your book,' Andrew said to Jack, as they enjoyed their weekly visit to the pub. 'I haven't asked you for a while.'

Jack shrugged. 'As always Hettie thinks it's fine. That's all I can say.'

'Well, I'm sure she's right.'

Andrew gazed about him. The pub was quieter than usual and he wondered why that was. It was a beautiful evening outside, the dying sun ablaze on the horizon.

He turned his attention back to Jack. 'I shall be expecting a free copy when it's published you know.'

Jack smiled. '*If* it is published.'

'I'm sure it will be. You're a natural when it comes to writing, Jack. You've proved that.'

'Plays perhaps, but a novel?'

Jack had a sip from his pint. 'If it is published I'm going to dedicate it to your brother Peter. We were great pals he and I.'

Andrew glanced down at the table. He and Peter had never been the best of friends, in fact they'd quite disliked one another. 'That's nice,' he replied.

'One day I'll visit his grave "over there". I'd like that.'

'You'll pull the novel off if I know you, Jack.'

Jack sighed. 'I wish I had as much faith in myself as you and Hettie have in me. You're pillars of support.'

'And rightly so in my opinion.'

'She's a gem that girl. A real gem,' Jack said in a soft, loving voice.

'She is indeed. As I've said so often in the past, I envy you.'

'And as I've said to you in the past, Andrew, you should get married. You don't want to be rattling around in that big house all by yourself. It's positively unhealthy.'

'That's what Charlotte says. She's always going on at me about the same thing.'

'And she's right. As am I.' Jack paused, then said, 'What about Rose Seaton?'

'What about her?'

'Exactly, what about her?'

'Jack, you know I've been sleeping with her stepmother.'

'Which I heartily disapprove of as you're aware.'

'I disapprove of it myself. But there we are.'

'There's something you're not telling me, Andrew. I can hear it in your voice.'

'Can you indeed.'

'Oh yes. So what is it?'

'Her age, Jack, and the fact she's Willie's daughter puts any relationship out of the question.'

'Scruples, eh? Georgina being Willie's wife didn't stop you there,' Jack commented drily.

Andrew blanched. 'That's below the belt.'

'As no doubt what you two get up to when alone together.'

Andrew had to laugh at that.

'Well?'

Andrew decided to confide in Jack. 'Do you remember the last time I went to The Haven, the Seatons' house?'

'I recall.'

'Well, Rose and I went out riding, just the pair of us, during which she near as damnit proposed to me. Or, to put it another way, tried to get me to propose.'

Now it was Jack's turn to laugh. 'Did she really!'

'She's serious, Jack, believe me.'

'Oh I do, I do. And?'

'And nothing. I wasn't having any.'

'Pity,' Jack mused. 'I have a hunch, and it's only that, she'd be ideal for you.'

'Nonsense. Besides, I don't want people thinking of me as a dirty old man.'

'But you are, Andrew, you are. And always have been. If not old by our standards then certainly dirty.'

Andrew grinned. 'I'll take that as a compliment.'

'Take it any way you like. It's true.'

There was a hiatus between them, then Jack said, 'I think you should reconsider the whole matter of Rose.'

'And Georgina?'

'She's already married. Regardless of what's passed between you, leave it that way.'

'Well, I certainly have no intention of trying to pinch her off Willie.'

'There you are then.'

'I'll get another round in,' Andrew stated, and crossed to the bar.

When he returned the subject of the Seatons was mentioned no more.

Chapter 22

Bridie laid down the book she'd been attempting to read. This was the second book she'd borrowed from Miss Rose that had failed to engage her attention.

Not that there was anything wrong with the books. She simply couldn't get into them and that was that.

She ran a hand over her face and gave a soft sigh. What was wrong with her? This had never happened in the past. Books, any book, had been devoured. Especially those with a romantic flavour as this and the last one had.

She closed her eyes for a brief moment, then opened them again. She knew what the trouble was, of course she did. Fiction didn't grip her any more because of reality. In other words, Ian.

Her shining knight no longer existed on the page but in the very house where she lived. Printer's ink had given way to flesh and blood.

'Sir Ian of Seaton,' she murmured, and shivered. Her own knight in real life.

Well, almost her knight, for there could never be anything between them. But how wonderful to pretend there might.

Jeannie Swanson snorted in her sleep which made Bridie smile. Dear Jeannie, what good friends they'd become. She'd have loved to confide in Jeannie, but that was impossible. Her love for Ian was her secret and would have to remain so.

Strangely, though it had been a hard day, she wasn't tired. Sleep would be a long time in coming.

'Ian,' she said, and shivered again. There would never be another love in her life, she was convinced of that. She was one of those people who fall in love once and once only.

Perhaps she should try for another position, she thought. Already knowing she wouldn't. She'd stay as close to Ian as she possibly could for as long as she could.

Moira McLaren, now there was the lucky one. The lass whom Ian would eventually marry. What she'd have given to be in Moira's shoes. Anything, absolutely anything.

She closed her eyes again, remembering how he'd kissed her, and what she'd felt. Heaven come to earth that had been. Sheer unadulterated bliss.

She laid the book aside and snuffed out the candle flickering by her bedside, plunging the room into darkness.

When she finally did fall asleep it was to dream, as she'd known she would, of Ian Seaton.

Willie was standing at a window watching Rose riding in the distance. The lassie must be mad, he thought. She was riding like one demented. If she wasn't careful she was going to come an awful cropper.

He bit his lip, wondering why it was she'd been so strange of late. And strange she'd certainly been. Moody for a start, and petulant. Taken to abruptly leaving their company for no apparent reason or excuse. It was worrying, extremely so.

He'd speak to her, he decided. It was long overdue. Or should he have Georgina do that? She might be better suited to the task than him.

No, he'd do it. He was her father after all. As such perhaps he could get through to her.

Willie took out his cigarettes and lit up, inhaling deeply. Part of the problem was she didn't have a boyfriend. Though why that should be so he couldn't think. She was pretty enough, and personable. You would have thought she'd have caught some lad's eye.

Of course living on the estate didn't help, though there were always a number of opportunities for her to socialise with her own kind.

Only the previous week she'd received an invitation to a summer ball which, to his amazement and annoyance, she'd turned down saying she wasn't really all that interested. You'd have thought, being young and healthy, she'd have grabbed the chance. But no, not Rose. She'd elected to stay at home that evening.

Was she ill in some way? Could that be it? If she was it certainly didn't show. If anything she was the picture of rude health.

So what was it? For it seemed to him something had to be wrong. Perhaps a holiday might do the trick. Though, on reflection, he could hardly send her on her own. Rose and Georgina together? No, he wouldn't do that. He didn't want Georgina being away for the length of a holiday.

He knew he was being selfish in wanting Georgina to be with him, but that's how it was.

He'd think of something. And in the meantime have a

chat with her, a heart to heart. See if he could find out what was what.

Ian glanced at his alarm clock, and groaned. Ten minutes past two and he still couldn't sleep. All to do with Bridie of course, he simply couldn't get her out of his mind. She was haunting him.

Every time he saw her about the house it was as if his heart stopped. An exaggeration? No, that was exactly what it was like.

Bridie Flynn, housemaid. The girl he'd fallen head over heels for.

'Shit,' he swore.

The thing was, should he do something or not? He was going to look a proper idiot if he made a play for her and she rejected him.

There again, why make a play in the first place? To what end? There wasn't one.

'Damn,' he muttered, and started striding up and down.

It had become a joke between Moira and himself. At least on his part. She was still as keen as ever.

Fond, she'd said. And didn't that just about sum it all up. He was fond of her, and she of him. But what basis was that for a marriage? Not nearly enough in his opinion. Though he knew there were those who would have disagreed with that.

Moira was certainly beautiful, that was beyond dispute. And of a pleasant nature, again beyond dispute. But what chance would they have together when he was in love with another woman? Precious little in his opinion.

There it was then, he was going to have to break it off with Moira. There wasn't anything else he could honourably do.

Pa would be disappointed to say the least. Willie had set his heart on their union. As indeed had Georgina.

But damn it all, it was his life and he had to do what he considered right. And marrying Moira McLaren wasn't. Not by a long chalk.

That decision taken he felt a whole lot better. He'd do what had to be done the following Sunday when he visited the McLarens, then tell Willie and Georgina afterwards.

He felt as though a great weight had been lifted from his shoulders. Atlas without the world bowing him down could not have felt more free.

He wondered what Bridie wore in bed, and how she looked when fast asleep. He also wondered . . .

He pulled his dressing-gown more tightly about him as he continued pacing. Although it was summer the night was chill.

He wondered if there would be a row with his pa when he announced his news. Probably, he decided gloomily. He'd have a couple of swift drams before the encounter.

Willie would try to dissuade him, no doubt about it. But he'd stick to his guns. It was over between him and Moira McLaren, he was determined about that.

And God knows how she'd take it. He could expect tears and probably a tantrum. Not something he was looking forward to. Not in the least.

Andrew stared at the letter, recognising the handwriting. No doubt Georgina was trying to set up another tryst.

He discovered he was correct on reading the two sheets of scented notepaper the envelope contained. Willie was going to London on business and various personal matters for a week. Why didn't he drop by during that time, pretending to be unaware that Willie was absent, and stay the night? Or better still, longer. The tone of the letter was a pleading one.

Andrew laid the notepaper in front of him, then rocked back in his chair.

It would be easy for him to get away sometime during the dates mentioned, and another session, or sessions, with the lovely Georgina certainly appealed.

And then there was Rose.

Bridie was halfway down the stairs carrying a tray, Miss Rose having decided to have breakfast in her room, when it happened.

Somehow she slipped and, uttering a startled cry, went tumbling downstairs, the tray and breakfast things flying everywhere. She landed at the foor of the stairs with a jarring thump, banging her head in the process. For the space of a few moments she lost consciousness.

Ian heard the cry and, not knowing who'd made it or why, dashed to help. 'Christ!' he swore when he saw it was Bridie.

He swiftly knelt beside her as she was coming round. 'Oh, my poor darling,' he said. 'Are you hurt?'

Darling? She hazily wondered at that.

Ian grasped her under the arms and hauled her into a sitting position. 'Can you hear me, Bridie? Have you broken anything?'

'I . . . I . . .' She broke off, confused. Broken anything? She didn't know.

'Oh darling Bridie,' he whispered in concern. 'You must be all right. Please say you are.'

There it was again, darling. What was going on? 'I think . . . I think . . . Dizzy, that's all.'

'Let me check you for broken bones.'

He gently felt first one leg, then the other. 'Nothing amiss there,' he declared when there was no reaction from her.

He did the same thing again with her arms, hastily removing his hand when she suddenly yelped.

Bridie gingerly rubbed the spot. 'It's just bruising. I'm certain of it.'

She flexed the arm. 'See. I must have landed on this one.'

'What happened?'

She grinned sheepishly. 'I wasn't paying attention to where I was going and the next thing I was doing a flying act.'

He smiled back at her. 'Can you stand?'

'I'll try.'

He assisted her upright where she swayed on the spot. 'Everything's going round and round,' she whispered.

'It's bed for you, my girl.'

'But my duties!' Bridie protested.

'Bother those! Someone else can do them. It's up to your bed and then I'll send for the doctor.'

'Oh you can't do that, Ian.'

'But I can, and will. No can't about it. Is everything still going round and round?'

'Yes. Only not as badly as it was.'

'Try to walk. And don't worry, I'll be holding you.'

They gradually made it up the stairs and eventually to her bedroom. 'That gave me ever such a fright,' she stated.

'I'm not surprised. You were fortunate not to have broken anything.'

'I really don't need the doctor, Ian.'

'Yes you do. And I'll have no more argument. Now you

can get yourself into bed. I hardly think it proper I help you with that.'

She felt her face colour. 'No.'

'I'll root out Jeannie Swanson and send her to you. In the meantime you stay here. Right?'

'Right,' she agreed meekly, thinking how masterful he was. She liked that.

'I'll be off then. But back later to see how you are.'

'Thank you, Ian.'

He couldn't help himself, the urge was overwhelming. Bending, he tenderly kissed her on the forehead.

Bridie stared wonderingly after him as he hurried from the room.

'Well?' Ian demanded the moment the doctor emerged.

Dr Duthie was an old man close to retirement, his hair white tinged with yellow, as was his thick moustache. Ian was one of the countless children he'd delivered into the world.

'There's nothing to worry about,' Duthie pronounced. 'She's got a wee bit of concussion that'll give her a headache for a day or two. But apart from that she's right as rain.'

Ian gave an exhalation of relief. Thank God for that! 'Thank you, Doctor. If you'll just send in your bill as usual.'

Duthie's eyes twinkled. 'Oh aye, I'll do that all right, Ian. You can count on it.'

Both men laughed.

'Come in!' Bridie called out some minutes later when there was a tap on her door.

Ian entered. 'The doctor says you've got a headache.'

'It's not too bad. I'll survive.'

He saw now what she wore in bed. A plain night-dress without frills or fripperies of any kind. It became her.

'You've been very kind,' she said, a puzzled frown on her face.

'Think nothing of it.'

'Jeannie came and got me changed as you can see. She was terribly upset.'

Not nearly as much as he'd been, Ian thought. Why, Bridie could have been killed. A broken neck could easily have been on the cards. It didn't bear thinking about.

'I've spoken to Mrs Coltart,' he stated. 'Who was extremely sympathetic. You're to stay off until you feel up to resuming work.'

'Thank you.'

'Don't mention it.'

Unable to hold his gaze, quivering inside, Bridie glanced away.

'Right,' said Ian. 'I'll get on. I've got lots to do today. But I will call back again this evening. Just to see how you are.'

'You mustn't trouble yourself,' she protested.

'It's no trouble, Bridie. None at all.'

The quivering was increasing in intensity. 'Fine then,' she mumbled.

He cleared his throat, desperately wanting to remain but of course that was impossible. 'Goodbye for now,' he said, a slight choke in his throat.

'Goodbye, Ian.'

He hesitated for another moment, then abruptly left.

He could hear them, Sean thought. He could actually hear

them. The bitch was shouting so loudly she might have been an animal being slaughtered.

'Sounds like Mo's giving her a right old slagging,' Bobby O'Toole sniggered.

Dan Smith lit a cigarette then blew a perfect smoke ring at the ceiling. 'I wish it was me in there.'

'Me too,' Bill O'Connell nodded.

Sean closed his eyes. He'd always got on well with Mo Binchy, the pair of them were good chinas. But right then he hated the bastard.

'Are you all right, Sean?'

Sean opened his eyes again and stared at Jim Gallagher. 'Aye, fine. Why?'

'You look a bit odd.'

Sean could just imagine it. Mo on top, the girl squirming beneath, her face contorted with passion. Mo doing to her what he couldn't. A hard core of anger erupted inside him, anger at himself and his inadequacy.

Sean jumped to his feet. 'I fancy a pint. Anyone else coming?'

'You don't have to ask twice,' Dan Smith replied getting out of his chair.

The lassie, Sean hadn't caught her name, gave a great cry of exultation and pleasure.

'Bloody hell!' Bill O'Connell exclaimed, turning to face the wall beyond which was the bedroom where the couple were.

Sean strode quickly from the room and house. He'd had enough. More than enough.

'Hello again,' Ian smiled. He was holding a large bunch of flowers from the garden.

'Are those for me?'

'They are indeed. Like them?'

'Oh yes,' she breathed. No one had ever given her flowers before. She was thrilled to bits.

Ian crossed and gave them to her. 'Jeannie can put them in something when she comes up later.'

Bridie sniffed the flowers. 'They smell gorgeous.'

'I picked them myself.' He looked about him. 'They might help brighten up this room a little. It's somewhat dingy to say the least.'

Bridie laid the flowers on the bed beside her.

'So how are you feeling now?'

'A lot better.'

'And the headache?'

'Not as bad as it was. I shall return to work tomorrow.'

Ian frowned. 'You'll do no such thing. That was a terrible fall you took. You'll stay in bed for another day anyway and no arguing.'

'But . . .' She broke off when he held up a hand.

'Those are orders, Bridie. You'll remain in bed.'

Again she thought how masterful he was. 'If you say so, Ian.'

'I do.'

She glanced down at the bedclothes. 'It's very good of you to come and visit me again. I just hope it doesn't cause the rest of the staff to gossip. You know what it's like.'

Ian hadn't thought of that. Hmmh, he mentally mused.

'Ian?'

'What?'

'Can I ask you something?'

'Of course,' he beamed.

Bridie took a deep breath. This was hard. She only hoped she wasn't about to make a fool of herself. 'Why did you call me darling?'

That both startled and confused him. 'Did I?' He knew damn well he had but was pretending innocence.

'Twice. At the bottom of the stairs.'

He turned away so she couldn't see his expression. A word sprang to mind, the word Moira had used. 'You must know I'm fond of you, Bridie. Very fond indeed.'

She allowed a few seconds to elapse before saying, 'And you kissed me. In here.'

Should he confess, confide in her? He couldn't. He simply couldn't. 'Can you keep a secret, for now anyway?' he queried, noting that his voice was shaking a little.

'If you wish.'

'Until Sunday that is. Then everyone will know.'

'You have my promise, Ian. Whatever you tell me is strictly between the pair of us.'

How adorable she looked, he thought. He wanted to take her in his arms, hold her, breathe in her scent, kiss her.

'I shall be breaking it off with Moira McLaren this Sunday. She and I are finished.'

Bridie's eyes opened wide. 'But why? She's so beautiful, Ian.'

'That's as may be. I certainly can't deny it. But . . . Well she just isn't right for me.'

'I see.'

'Moira and I would be a mistake. For a while I thought differently. But now I know better.'

Bridie was rocked by this news. As everyone else in the house was, she had been convinced Ian and Moira would get married. She didn't know what to think.

'What will your father say?'

Ian gave a wry smile. 'He won't be best pleased. He had his heart set on the union. As indeed did my stepmother.'

'When will you tell them?'

'Sunday evening after dinner.'

'I don't envy you.'

He barked out a short laugh. 'I don't envy myself. All in all it should be quite a day.'

Bridie knew she shouldn't ask, but she couldn't help herself. 'Is there . . . someone else?'

Oh Lord, he thought. He didn't want to lie to Bridie, but how could he possibly tell her the truth? 'Yes,' he admitted, surprising himself with his honesty.

Bridie stared at him. 'Would I know her?'

'Yes,' Ian said very softly.

The quivering she'd experienced earlier returned. Don't be stupid, she told herself. It couldn't be her. Though if only . . .

'You still haven't said why you called me darling,' Bridie mumbled.

Ian took a deep breath, then another. It had been wrong to come here, dreadfully wrong. If he wasn't careful he was going to compromise himself. It would have been different if she hadn't been a housemaid, a working-class lass from Glasgow. And yet, despite all that, the truth remained. He loved her.

'I'd best be going,' he declared abruptly. 'I'm glad you like the flowers.'

'As I said, they're gorgeous.'

'And no work tomorrow,' he said sternly. 'I shall be furious if you even attempt it.'

'I won't, Ian. And your secret's safe with me.'

'Goodnight then, Bridie.'

Their eyes held. 'Goodnight, Ian. I shall be thinking about you on Sunday and hoping it all goes well.'

'Thank you.'

He didn't want to leave. That was the last thing he wanted. What he did want was to stay with Bridie. Not just then, but for ever.

The door snicked shut behind him.

Ian's face was hard as stone when he left the McLarens. What he'd just endured was far worse than he'd imagined.

Moira had been bad enough, but her mother, Delphine! That had been a nightmare. Her verbal abuse was still ringing in his ears.

He desperately needed a drink. No, more than one, several to restore his equilibrium. He'd never forget Moira clinging to him as though that would change his mind. Or the pure venom in Delphine's eyes when she'd been told the news.

He didn't dare glance back in case Moira was at a window which he suspected she might be.

'What!' Willie exclaimed, coming to his feet from the chair he'd just sat in moments before.

They were in Willie's den where he had requested they retire. The den was hardly used by Willie nowadays and hadn't been since he'd married Georgina, Willie much preferring her company to being on his own.

'Broken it off, Pa.'

'But why for God's sake?'

'We weren't right together, Pa. It wouldn't have worked.'

'Stuff and nonsense,' Willie snorted. 'You made a lovely couple.'

Ian sighed. 'Can I help myself to a dram?'

Willie waved a hand. 'Do as you please.'

'You, Pa?'

'May as well.'

Ian crossed to the decanter and glasses sitting atop a bookcase.

He poured out and handed his father a stiff measure. 'There you are.'

'I don't understand. I really don't.'

'Let me put it this way, Pa, how did you feel about Mother when you married?'

Willie studied his son. 'Go on.'

'Were you in love with her?'

Willie's expression softened. 'Very much so.'

'That's how I want to be when I wed. In love with a woman who's equally in love with me.'

Willie's expression softened even further. 'I understand.'

'I don't love Moira, Pa, and never will. Nor does she love me.'

'Did she say that?'

Ian shook his head. 'She didn't have to. I just knew. I was a good match, Pa, and that's a very different thing from love. Oh, we might have rubbed along together but what sort of life is that?'

Willie didn't reply.

'You've been lucky, twice. First with Mother and then with Georgina.'

'Yes,' Willie agreed, nodding slightly. 'I certainly have been.'

Ian saw off his dram and went to pour himself another. He wondered where Bridie was in the house and what she was doing. In the kitchen probably, he decided, with the staff having their meal.

'She's very beautiful, Ian.'

'Indeed she is. But I've learnt a few things along the

way, Pa, and one is that beauty isn't everything. Far from it. Don't you agree?'

Willie regarded his son with new respect. 'I do.'

'Moira's rather shallow which isn't what I want at all. She'd bore the pants off me before long as sure as eggs are eggs.'

Willie smiled. 'Possibly.'

'There's no possibly about it, Pa. Take Georgina for instance, whatever anyone may think of her she's hardly boring. She certainly seems to keep you on your toes and up to scratch.'

'I can't disagree with that,' Willie commented wryly.

'And another thing, they say look at the mother and see how the girl is going to turn out. Well, I saw a side of Delphine McLaren today that I thought most distasteful. You should have heard her, voice hard as iron, almost spitting like a snake.'

Willie laughed. 'Delphine does have a reputation for having a bit of a temper.'

'Bit of one! I'd call it a lot more than that.'

'And getting what she wants. You put a spoke in her wheel which she wouldn't have liked, or appreciated, at all.'

'You can say that again.'

'Georgina will be disappointed,' Willie mused. 'She was as much for this as me.'

'I'm sorry about that. But I won't be changing my mind as far as Moira McLaren is concerned. And that's final.'

'I believe you, son,' Willie replied quietly.

Willie thought of his first wife Mary, and Georgina. Ian was quite right. Marriage without love wasn't worth the candle.

Chapter 23

Sean was doing the rounds collecting protection money, and very nicely the gang was doing too. Every month saw an increase in their take, with that little bit extra, which they were unaware of, to him.

He was coming out of a greengrocer's when Sammy Renton came hurrying up.

'Hey, Sean!'

Sammy's face was flushed and he was gasping for breath when he stopped beside Sean. 'I've been looking for you everywhere. Have you heard?'

Sean frowned. 'Heard what?'

'Wee Pete Murray's fallen foul of the Tong.' Pete was one of the younger members of the Samurai, a lad no more than fifteen.

'How do you mean, fallen foul?'

'A number of them set on him and gave him a hell of a beating. He's been taken to hospital.'

Sean immediately thought of Big Bill Bremner. 'What did Pete do?'

'The stupid bugger was in their territory when they grabbed him for being there. They dragged him into a close and that was that. He didn't have a chance.'

Pete should have known better, Sean thought. 'How bad is he?'

'Pretty bad. They gave him a right kicking.'

'Was he marked?'

Sammy shook his head. 'Nothing like that, just a kicking. What are we going to do?'

'You mean in retaliation?'

'Aye, that's right.'

Sean took a deep breath. This needed thinking about. And seriously. 'Tonight at eight. We'll meet at "the place". Pass the word.'

'I'll do that, Sean.'

'Which hospital?'

'The Southern General.'

'I'll go and see him.'

Sammy beamed. 'He'd appreciate that, Sean. He thinks you're the next thing to God.'

Sean tried not to show the pleasure that statement gave him. Next thing to God! Wasn't that something.

'Eight o'clock,' he repeated.

'Aye, Sean. I'll pass the word.'

'Now off you go. I've got things to do.'

Sean's next port of call was a pub where he sat in a corner ruminating. Was there more to this than appeared on the surface? He wasn't sure.

'We can't let this go,' declared Don McGuire hotly. 'The Tong would think us a bunch of jessies.'

'Aye, we should give one of their lot the same treatment,' said Noddy Gallagher.

353

'I'm not so certain about that,' murmured Jim, Noddy's brother.

Sean focused on Jim. 'Why so?'

'The stupid bastard shouldn't have been where he was. He knows the rules and broke them.'

Sean nodded. 'I agree.'

'They'll still think we're a bunch of jessies,' Don repeated.

Brainpower wasn't exactly one of Don's assets, Sean reflected. Don was a hothead through and through.

'Mo?'

'There's hundreds of them. What could we do except get massacred? It would be four to one if not more.'

Bill O'Connell was in a blue funk about taking on the Tong. He was fervently praying this would come to nothing.

'Pete's got internal injuries,' Sean said quietly. 'There's even the possibility he might die.'

Bill blanched. Holy Mary Mother of God!

'And what if he does?' That was Bobby O'Toole.

'You tell me,' Sean retorted.

Bobby puffed on a cigarette, no keener than most there to go up against the Tong, knowing it would be certain suicide. 'It was his fault,' he mumbled.

'Anyone disagree with that?' Sean queried.

No one did.

Sean closed his eyes. He'd already made up his mind before coming to the meeting that they wouldn't do anything, but it was important everyone had their say.

'Well, Sean?'

His eyes flicked open. 'We let it pass. That's the sensible thing to do. Pete was in the wrong, as Jim says. He's paid the penalty and let's leave it at that.' Sean paused. 'Agreed?'

'Agreed,' was repeated throughout the gathering, with the exception of Don McGuire.

'Don?'

'Agreed,' Don said reluctantly.

'That's settled then. We forget it.'

Pete Murray survived, though he was never quite the same again. A blow to the head had seen to that. For the rest of his life he was referred to as 'daftie'.

Rose was bored, wondering what she could do, when Andrew was ushered into the drawing room. 'Andrew!' she exclaimed in delight.

'Hello, Rose.'

'This is a surprise,' she said, coming to her feet.

'I was more or less passing and thought I'd call in to see how you all were.'

Her eyes were sparkling. 'Pa's away I'm afraid.'

He pretended disappointment. 'Really?'

'In London. Some dreary business or other.'

'Which is why I'm in the area. Business that is.'

How wonderful he looked, she thought. Absolutely scrumptious. 'Will you take tea or coffee?'

'Coffee would be nice.'

She hurried over to the bell pull. 'How are you?'

'In the pink, as they say. And you?'

'The better for your company.'

She hadn't changed, he thought with satisfaction, thinking of the lectures he'd had from Jack Riach. Well, not lectures exactly, more friendly advice.

She'd matured somewhat, he observed. There was a difference to her tone of voice and the way she carried herself. He rather liked it.

Penny, one of the maids, appeared, and Rose ordered coffee and biscuits to be brought.

'Please sit, Andrew,' she smiled after Penny had gone.

'Thank you.'

She sat facing him. 'You're looking terribly well.'

'As are you.'

'I didn't . . . well, let's just say this is a pleasant surprise.'

'I'm sorry Willie's not here.'

'But you'll stay of course. The night, I mean.'

'I'm not so sure now,' he pretended to prevaricate.

'Oh please!'

Alice, there it was again. Not just the way she sat a horse, but Alice.

'Where's Georgina?'

'Oh somewhere about the house or grounds,' Rose replied airily. 'I don't really know.'

'She hasn't gone to London with Willie then.' What a glib liar he was, he thought.

'No.'

'Then I shall have the company of the pair of you.'

Rose fervently wished Georgina had gone to London which would have meant she'd have had Andrew all to herself.

'Will you stay?'

He shrugged. 'I'm not sure that's appropriate with Willie away. It might not seem proper.'

'Oh, stop being a fuddy duddy. Of course it's proper. I shall be furious if you don't.'

He arched an eyebrow. 'Really?'

'Yes,' she stated firmly. 'I shall. So stay the night you will.'

Andrew had to smile at her determination. If only she

knew the real reason for his visit she might not be so insistent.

'So what have you been up to?' he asked.

It was half an hour later when Georgina appeared. 'Andrew! I've just this moment been told you're here.'

He rose and gave her a small bow. 'Rose has been entertaining me. We've had a wonderful chat.'

That annoyed Georgina. 'I'm so pleased.'

'Andrew's staying the night,' Rose enthused.

'That's nice. It'll be lovely having company. Rose has told you that Willie's away, I presume?'

'Yes.'

'He'll be sorry to have missed you.' Georgina's insides were fluttering at the thought of what lay ahead later. She could already imagine herself in Andrew's arms, his strong body thrusting against hers. How she'd dreamed of it, fantasised about it.

'I see you've had coffee.' She smiled.

'Yes we have.'

'So how about something stronger? I could use a sherry myself.'

'How unlike you!' Rose exclaimed. Georgina was usually abstemious where alcohol was concerned.

'A little treat now and again is quite acceptable,' Georgina answered a trifle condescendingly. 'Especially when we have such a nice, unexpected guest.'

'I'm flattered,' Andrew declared. 'Shall I do the honours?'

'Please.'

Rose had been hoping Georgina would have kept away longer, she'd been having such a good time with Andrew alone. She wondered how she could get him on his own again.

Both women had sherry, Andrew whisky, which he was delighted to see was Drummond.

'Now then, Georgina,' he said, resuming his chair. 'What's new?'

Ian was done in. It had been a particularly hard day with a great deal of physical work involved. All he wanted was a bath, some food and then bed.

He came up short when he spotted the Rolls parked in front of the house. 'Damn!' he muttered to himself, recognising the car as Andrew's. He could well have done without this.

He let himself in quietly, pausing momentarily when he heard voices, one being Andrew's. He'd have to suffer the bugger through dinner, he thought. But he would excuse himself as shortly afterwards as was acceptable without being rude. Again he wondered why he didn't like Andrew. There was just something about the man.

Upstairs he stopped when he spied Bridie's rear view going in the opposite direction. His first impulse was to run after and talk to her. An impulse he resisted.

Ian sighed when she disappeared round a corner. What torture it was not being able to pursue her the way he would have liked, to court her as he had Moira. It was absolute agony.

Agony.

Rose woke with the most terrible pain in her stomach. It was quite excruciating.

She'd have to go to the toilet, she decided. This wasn't something for the pot under the bed, it was far more serious than that.

She groaned as she got out of bed. What had brought this

on? She had no idea. It certainly couldn't have been dinner, which had been delicious. Mrs Kilbride was scrupulous about her kitchen hygiene and what she used.

Rose slipped into her dressing-gown and padded to the door. She felt terrible.

She was halfway to the toilet when she heard the sound. A sound which at first mystified her. It was coming from her Pa and Georgina's bedroom.

Suddenly she went beetroot red, recognising it for what it must be. The noise of extreme passion.

Then anger flamed inside her. For who else could be with Georgina than Andrew? 'Bastard!' she hissed through gritted teeth. 'Oh, you rotten bastard!'

And to think she'd never guessed. What a fool she'd been. A blind, stupid fool.

Tears blinked into her eyes as she continued to listen, all sorts of images going through her mind. The kind of images that made her want to vomit in disgust.

How could Georgina betray her father like that? Willie who loved and adored her with every ounce of his being. If there were any vestiges of youth left in Rose they vanished there and then. The harsh realities of life had finally claimed her.

And Andrew, whom she loved, being with Georgina. That hurt. Oh how that hurt. Like a knife plunged straight into the heart, plunged and twisted.

She quietly sobbed, her discomfort temporarily forgotten in the light of this revelation. The plans she'd had disappeared like so many birds released into the sky. Rose rubbed a hand over her forehead, willing herself to continue on to the toilet, and yet somehow unable to do so. And still the sounds went on, all from Georgina.

How long had this been going on? she wondered. Not

that it really mattered. All that did was that it had been. Poor Pa, poor cuckolded Pa. If she was weeping it wasn't only for herself but him.

For a moment she thought of rousing Ian, then decided against it. God alone knew what he would do. She wouldn't have been surprised if he took a gun to Andrew. Took it and used it.

No, this was something she must never speak about. Something she had to keep strictly to herself. If Georgina wanted to play the slut then so be it. Pa would never find out from her. Not in a million years.

As for Andrew, damn him to hell! He was loathsome beyond belief.

Ian had already gone out when Rose joined Georgina and Andrew at breakfast. She felt terrible after an awful night. If she'd slept she hadn't been aware of it. Andrew and Georgina on the other hand were both as perky as could be.

'Good morning, Rose,' Georgina beamed.

She stared at her stepmother, hating her. 'Good morning.'

'Good morning, Rose,' Andrew echoed.

As for him! 'Good morning,' she somehow managed to force in reply.

Georgina frowned. 'Are you all right?'

'Why do you ask?'

'You seem a little peaky.'

'Do I?'

'Pale,' Andrew commented, concern in his voice.

Rose sat and waited to be served. The last thing she'd wanted was to join them for breakfast but thought it would have looked odd if she hadn't. 'Kippers please,' she said to Penny the maid who was in attendance.

'It's a gorgeous day outside. Absolutely wonderful,' Georgina gushed.

'I noticed,' Rose replied, a trace of acid in her voice.

'I think we should go for a long walk,' Andrew proposed.

'I thought you might be in a rush to get back to Dalneil,' Rose answered.

Andrew couldn't have felt better. His session with Georgina had been first class. By God, but she was a quick learner. And enthusiastic with it. Their lovemaking had just gone on and on.

'I'll be happy to do that.' Georgina smiled at Andrew.

Bitch! Rose thought, jealousy tearing at her. After breakfast she intended returning to her room and staying there in the hope that Andrew would have left by lunchtime.

'I wonder how Willie's getting on in London?' Georgina mused. 'I might try and telephone him later at his club.'

But not to tell him what you were up to last night, Rose thought grimly. Oh no, you wouldn't do that, lady. Bitch!

'Did you have any particular plans for today, Rose?'

She glanced dyspeptically at Andrew. How she wished it had been her in that bedroom with him. She he was making love to. She making those sounds of pleasure. Sounds that had been ringing in her ears for most of the night.

'Reading.'

'Reading!' he exclaimed.

'That's right. I enjoy it.'

'I didn't know that.'

She had no appetite whatsoever. She'd have to toy with

the kippers, eat just a few mouthfuls. 'When are you leaving?' she queried abruptly.

Georgina glanced sharply at Rose, not appreciating her tone. 'That's hardly something to ask a guest,' she declared.

Rose didn't reply.

'I thought I might stay another night,' Andrew stated. He was regarding her quizzically, wondering what was wrong. This wasn't the Rose he was used to.

Again she said nothing, but her heart was in her boots. Another night so he and Georgina could be together again. It made her want to spit.

'Should I leave today?' he queried slowly.

Georgina stopped eating to stare at Andrew in dismay. What was this business about leaving today? That had already been agreed between them.

'Suit yourself. Do as you wish,' Rose declared, pretending, or at least trying to, that she didn't care what he did.

'Then I shall stay if you don't mind.'

'I don't.'

What on earth was going on? Georgina wondered. Why this sudden hostility on Rose's part? It was positively oozing out of her. It was as though . . .

Georgina went icy cold inside. Rose couldn't know. How could she possibly? And yet it was as if she did.

Andrew was thinking the same thing, wishing now he'd never come to The Haven. For what if Rose did know and said something to her father! He dreaded to think the outcome of that.

'Is something wrong, Rose?' Andrew asked quietly.

'Wrong? No, why should there be?'

'You seem a trifle . . . upset.'

'Can't imagine why. There isn't a reason.'

Relief washed through Andrew, as it did Georgina who resumed eating.

When Rose's kippers came they tasted like cardboard in her mouth.

After breakfast, as she'd promised herself, she returned to her room where she cried for the rest of that morning.

'I'll leave Willie if you wish.'

Andrew and Georgina were out walking in a meadow with a fading summer sun high overhead. 'Leave Willie?'

'If you wish, Andrew. I want to be with you, not him.'

Andrew thought of Willie, and Ireland where they'd met and been colleagues together. He'd been a rat in his life, he had no illusions about that, but simply couldn't do that to a pal. Though he had to admit it was tempting. A temptation he mustn't succumb to.

'No,' Andrew stated baldly.

Georgina's face fell. 'But we're so good together. A natural couple if ever there was.'

'That's true. But the answer's still no. I won't hurt Willie like that. What I've done, we've done, is bad enough. But for him to find out and then lose you! It would finish him. And you know it would.'

'But what about me?'

Andrew thought of Alice. 'It seems we never get what we truly want in life, that it's all a compromise. If things had been different . . . Except they're not. You have a good marriage, a man who dotes on you. Isn't that enough?'

'No,' she whispered. 'I need more than that.'

Andrew knew then he'd never sleep with Georgina again, that it was all over between them.

'I need you, and what you do to me in bed,' Georgina added, still in a whisper.

'I'm sorry,' Andrew said. 'I truly am.'

She stopped and turned to face him. 'Don't I mean anything to you?'

'Of course you do, Georgina. But there are things which are right and others that are wrong. If you did leave Willie and came to me it wouldn't work.'

'But why?'

'Because Willie would always be between us. A ghost haunting us until the day we die. Believe me, that's how it would be.'

Georgina sucked in a deep breath. 'You're saying good-bye, aren't you?'

'Yes.'

Her body jerked the way a fish does when gaffed. 'Oh please, Andrew, please. I want you so much.'

'We've had a good time together, Georgina, let's just leave it at that. A fond memory.'

'Memory,' she choked.

'That's right.' He took her hand. 'No regrets, eh? Let's never have those.'

She'd never regret Andrew, she thought bitterly. What she would regret was this conversation and his breaking it off between them. If only she hadn't suggested leaving Willie the relationship might have gone on for who knew how long. But suggest it she had and this was the consequence.

'Georgina?'

'I'm fine,' she replied, forcing a smile on to her face.

Should she try and make him change his mind? she wondered as they resumed walking. But she already knew she wouldn't. There had been a finality and determination in Andrew's voice which told her any such effort would be useless.

Never again to experience what she had the previous night, she thought in despair. She simply couldn't believe that to be so. And yet it would be.

Andrew made his excuses and left directly after luncheon.

A puzzled, yet pleased, Rose watched him drive off. Georgina couldn't bear to.

Kathleen glanced over at Pat sitting facing her, reading the evening paper as he usually did at that time of night. Sean was out, Alison playing dollies between them.

'Pat?'

'Aye, what is it?' he answered without looking up.

'It's Friday night. Why don't you take a wee dauner down to the pub? It'll do you good.'

He stared at her in surprise. Kathleen actually proposing he go to the pub! Now there was a turn up for the book. He shook his head.

'Don't worry about money. I'll give you some. Sean was more than generous this week.'

'No, Kathleen. I won't bother.'

She laughed softly. 'Pat Flynn turning down a chance to go to the pub. I don't believe it.'

'Aye, well there you are.'

'I don't understand, Pat.'

He sighed and laid his paper aside. 'An explanation is it, woman?'

'I'm curious.'

Pat closed his eyes for a moment, then opened them again. A smile lit up his face. 'The real reason I don't want to go, Kathleen me darlin', is that I'm perfectly happy to be here with you. I don't need the pub, or the people there any more, or anything like that. Just you and I together in our own wee house is all I ask for.'

Alison had stopped playing to gape at her father.

Kathleen dropped her gaze, touched in a way she'd never been touched before. 'Thank you, Pat,' she whispered.

'No, my angel, thank *you*.'

He picked up his paper again and resumed reading while Kathleen dashed a tear from her eye.

There were times when life truly was worth living, she reflected. They might be few and far between, but there were times.

'It was the waiting that was the worst I think,' Jack Riach said quietly to Hettie. 'The waiting, knowing you were about to be ordered to go over the top and all that entailed.

'The rest was bad enough. The hours, the days, months, you spent thinking, remembering what it had been like before. And what it had now become. And all the time men, chums, disappeared. Killed most of them, wounded the lucky ones. The nightly bombardments that shook the dugout, the whizz bangs and "Jack Johnsons".'

Jack broke off into a brooding silence.

'Would you like a cup of tea?'

He shook his head. 'I sometimes wonder if it isn't worse for me being blind.'

'Why so?'

'Perhaps I remember more than most. Perhaps the images and sounds stay more real in my memory than they do for sighted people. I don't know. But I think I might be right.'

Hettie closed the notebook she'd been writing in and laid it by. 'I would say that's enough for today. You've done your quota.'

'And still I haven't got the end. But it'll come, I know it will.'

'I'm sure, knowing you.'

Jack sighed. 'All those chaps, Peter Drummond amongst them, all gone. Blown to buggery or worse. I still miss Peter like the devil. He was the best friend I ever had, or ever will. Excluding you, of course.'

'There's Andrew.'

Jack smiled wryly. 'Andrew's a friend, but not like his brother Peter. He and I were as close as two men can platonically be.'

'Tommy's at school,' Hettie said.

Jack frowned. 'So?'

'Why don't we go upstairs? I fancy a cuddle.'

The frown was replaced by a smile that curled the corners of his mouth. 'I can't think of anything nicer.'

'Neither can I. And no more talk about the war. Agreed?'

'Agreed.'

He might not talk about it but it was always there, always with him, he thought as, hand in hand, they mounted the stairs.

And that's how it would always be.

Chapter 24

Rose sat listening to her father and Georgina chatting animatedly to one another, Willie having returned from London earlier that day. Ian was dozing in a chair after another hard day's physical work.

She studied Georgina's face which showed no sign whatsoever of her betrayal. All it did show was pleasure at having Willie home again.

If only her father knew what had gone on while he'd been away, he wouldn't be so delighted with Georgina's company then. Quite the contrary.

Georgina reached across and patted Willie's hand as he gazed adoringly at her. Willie couldn't wait till it was time to go to bed and every so often his eyes slid sideways to where a clock was quietly ticking.

Well, Georgina's secret was safe with her, Rose reflected. For a number of reasons, not least the effect it would have on Willie should he find out his wife was an adulteress.

Jezebel, Rose thought. Bitch! And to commit that

adultery with Andrew, the man *she* loved. That was the hardest thing, the cruellest cross to bear.

It was going to be difficult, damnably difficult, but she had to try and forget Andrew Drummond. Though it would break her heart to do so.

How could she possibly retain any aspirations in that direction when he'd . . . She drew in a deep breath. Done that with Georgina.

Willie turned to her. 'You're very quiet tonight, Rose.'

'Am I?'

'You've hardly said a word all evening.'

'Maybe that's because I couldn't get a word in edge-ways.'

He laughed. 'Georgina and I have been rattling on I suppose.'

'Just a bit.'

'Natural after all. I have missed her a great deal and I presume she has me.'

'You know that to be true, Willie.'

Rose had an almost overwhelming urge to leap across the room and slap Georgina's face. Slap it as hard as she possibly could.

'So what have you been up to?' Willie enquired of Rose.

'Nothing much. The usual.'

Willie nodded. 'Have you been riding?'

'Several times. I shall go out again tomorrow morning, providing the weather permits.'

'A pity Andrew hadn't stayed on. He might have gone with you.'

Rose swallowed hard. 'Perhaps.'

'Yes, that is a pity,' Georgina concurred.

Rose couldn't resist it, Georgina not having given any

reason for his sudden departure. 'I thought he *was* going to stay for another day.'

For a brief moment something flickered in Georgina's eyes, then was gone. 'He decided he'd better get home after all. Some matter he'd temporarily forgotten about.'

Suddenly Rose couldn't stand it any longer, the sheer hypocrisy of it all. Her own as well as Georgina's.

She stood up. 'I think I'll go for a walk in the garden.'

'At this time of night!' Willie exclaimed. 'It's pitch black out there.'

'I still want to go.'

'Then you'd better wrap up warm,' Georgina said. 'The nights are drawing in.'

'I'm not a child, Georgina,' Rose snapped in reply. 'I'll wear what I consider appropriate.'

Georgina stared at Rose in consternation. 'I didn't mean to offend. Of course you're not a child. On the contrary, you're quite the young woman.'

And one who hates you, Rose thought. 'I shan't be too long.'

'So you broke it off,' Jack repeated, and sipped his pint.

'That's right. She wanted to leave Willie and I couldn't have that.'

'Well, well,' Jack murmured.

'I take it you approve.'

'Oh yes.'

'The damn thing is she was right when she said we made a good couple, a natural one. That's exactly what we made. And that body! Oh, Jack, you wouldn't believe it.'

'Except she's someone else's wife,' Jack replied drily. 'Wonderful body or not, she's someone else's wife and someone who's a pal.'

'I know,' Andrew said dejectedly. 'That was the swine of it.'

'How did she take the news?'

'She put up a good front, I'll give her that. Though I could tell how hurt she was. I have to admire her self-control as my breaking it off was the last thing she expected.' Andrew paused, then added, 'It was the last thing I expected as well. But what else could I do?'

'You did right,' Jack assured him. 'If you'd strung her along it would only have got worse.'

'And what if she'd told Willie about our affair? That would have been ghastly.'

'You mean, to try and force your hand?' Jack thought about that. 'I suppose it was entirely possible. Mind you, dear boy, have you considered this, she might still.'

'Christ,' Andrew swore. 'I hadn't.'

'Something for you to ponder on.'

'I don't have to. If she leaves Willie thinking she's coming to me then she's mistaken, very much so. That's the least I could do for Willie.'

'Pity he's such a terribly nice chap, isn't it,' Jack commented, again drily.

'Aye, a pity. If he hadn't been . . .' Andrew shrugged. 'Well, who knows.'

'Indeed.'

There were a few moments' silence between them, then Jack said, 'So how about Rose?'

'She was fine. Though a bit testy over breakfast I have to admit. I actually wondered if she'd guessed about Georgina and myself.'

'Could she have done?'

'I don't see how, Jack. She was well tucked up before I went to Georgina's room.'

'Well, perhaps either you or Georgina gave the game away while she was present. It could be she noticed a look or expression and put two and two together.'

Andrew shook his head. 'No, that's hardly likely. I'd lay odds against it. Both Georgina and myself were extremely careful. Even when alone together.'

'Then maybe it was due to frustration.'

'Frustration?' Andrew queried, reaching for his whisky.

'She did lay her cards on the table after all and you haven't done anything about it.'

'I told her it wasn't on because of her age and being Willie's daughter.'

Jack laughed softly. 'But did she believe you? That's the thing. Anyway, women who lay their cards on the table and get rebuffed tend not to take the matter kindly.'

'That's possible,' Andrew mused.

'Will you see her again?'

'Who, Rose?'

'That's who we're now talking about, isn't it?'

'Oh I should imagine so. But not for a while. I shan't be returning to The Haven in a hurry so that Georgina can come to terms with how things now stand.'

'I still think you should marry Rose. I really do. Don't forget I heard her voice and she adores you. You could do a lot worse than that.'

A picture of Alice drifted into Andrew's mind. Dear sweet Alice whom he'd fallen in love with. But she was dead and gone, he'd never see her again in this lifetime.

'I'll get another round in,' Andrew declared, abruptly terminating the conversation.

Ian glanced up and down the corridor. It was a work day but he'd contrived to get back to the house on an excuse.

He took a deep breath. This was ridiculous, utterly ridiculous. But he was going to do it nonetheless.

Unobserved, the staff about their duties elsewhere, this part of the house deserted, he swiftly opened the door and slipped inside, hurriedly closing the door again behind him.

He gazed about, drinking in every last detail of what he considered a rather miserable room. Bridie's room.

There was her bed, neatly made, nightdress folded on top. The same nightdress she'd been wearing when he'd brought her the flowers.

'Bridie,' he whispered.

Was it his imagination or could he actually smell her? He believed he could. Especially when he moved to her bed and stood beside it.

Ian ran a hand over his slightly damp forehead. The woman was driving him insane, every fibre of his being craving for her. He exhaled slowly, balled his fists then released them again.

He thought of Moira McLaren. How she'd become a distant memory in such a short time. It was as though she'd never existed, or at least their relationship. She might be beautiful but she paled into insignificance beside Bridie. Bridie who, for him, shone like a bright star at night. Bridie, who made his pulse race every time he saw her.

'Madness,' he muttered. 'Sheer madness.' How had this happened, how? He didn't know, only that it had and was torture.

Her case was under the bed and he briefly contemplated opening it to see what was inside. No, he decided, that was going too far. A real violation of her privacy. Coming into her room was bad enough, the case would be too much.

He mustn't stay too long, he reminded himself. That

would be folly. How could he possibly explain being in a member of staff's room? He couldn't.

Picking up her nightdress he held it to his nose, the scent of her now strong in his nostrils. He drew it deep into his lungs, savouring it.

Enough, he thought. Enough. Replacing the nightdress, carefully arranging it as it had more or less been, he wheeled about and left the room, striding on his way.

'Bloody idiot,' he muttered to himself. 'That's what you are, a bloody idiot. A complete fool.'

For the rest of the day her scent remained with him.

Mo Binchy, and the girl he'd been sleeping with, Shelagh, Sean now knew her name to be, came off the dancefloor and up to the table where he was sitting. There were ten of them on a Saturday night out at the Trocadero, one of Glasgow's largest dancehalls situated in the centre of the city.

Mo was flushed, partly due to the heat of the place which was stifling, but mostly from the alcohol he'd consumed before getting there.

'I want to speak to you, Sean,' Mo announced, his arm circled round Shelagh's waist.

'Aye, go ahead.'

'In private like.'

There were three other members of the Samurai at the table. 'Can you fellas give us a couple of minutes.'

'Of course, Sean. Anything you say.'

Sean liked that. Anything he said! By God, it was great to have power and respect. The feeling was almost . . . sexual.

Mo and Shelagh sat when the others had moved away. 'We made a decision tonight and I want you to be the first to know,' Mo said.

Sean didn't reply, waiting for Mo to go on.

Mo glanced at Shelagh, who giggled, then back at Sean. 'We've decided to get married.'

That surprised Sean. 'Really?'

'Aye, really. A quick engagement and then the deed itself. What do you think?'

Sean wasn't sure how to answer that. The lassie seemed personable enough, though hardly anything special. But if it suited Mo, then so be it. 'I suppose congratulations are in order.'

Mo beamed. 'I was hoping you'd say that.'

'Thank you,' Shelagh said in a rather reedy voice.

Not his type at all, Sean thought. Far too mousy with a lousy figure. Very little on top that he could make out.

'The thing is,' Mo continued, 'would you be my best man? I'd be honoured . . .' He paused for a moment. 'We'd both be honoured if you'd be that.'

Sean felt expansive. Why the hell not! And it was his right to be asked as the leader of the Samurai after all. 'Of course I will. Consider that a promise.'

Mo reached over and shook Sean by the hand. 'You're a pal, Sean, through and through.'

Sean signalled to the others who'd been at the table that they could return, and soon they too were offering their congratulations.

It was a little later that Bill O'Connell had a word in his ear. 'I've just been dancing with a bird who says she fancies you rotten. Wants to know if she can be introduced.'

'Is that a fact.'

'Good-looking piece too.' He nodded his head. 'That's her over there in the pink dress. You can't miss her, she's ogling you.'

She was pretty too, Sean thought. Quite a cracker.

And with a decent figure, unlike Mo's Shelagh. Should he get her up?

Then he remembered Muriel and Babs and what had happened with them. No, he decided. He daren't risk another humiliation. That would be too much to bear.

He suddenly felt sick inside.

The girl was smiling fit to burst, her eyes an open invitation. He knew she'd do a turn if he wanted it. If not that night then shortly.

He dropped his gaze, breaking eye contact. She'd just have to go on fancying him, that was all. He wasn't going to do anything about it.

'Sean.'

He glanced round at Bobby O'Toole. 'What is it?'

'Look who's here and watching us. Second pillar on the left.'

Sean sought out the named pillar and there standing directly in front of it staring hard at them was Big Bill Bremner, leader of the Tong.

'Shit,' Sean swore softly.

'Do you think he's after a barney?'

'I've no idea, Bob. None at all.'

Sean doubted Big Bill was on his own, that was highly unlikely. The question was, how many of the Tong were with him?

'What shall we do?' Sammy Renton queried.

'I don't know. Hang on tight I suppose and see what happens. One thing's for certain, I'm not leaving with my tail between my legs just because he's here. Apart from anything else it would be a terrible mistake. Believe me. Show weakness and they'll be straight at your throat. For the fun of it if nothing else.'

'Christ,' Sammy muttered.

Sean glanced at Mo who'd gone back on the dancefloor with Shelagh, then at the lassie who'd told Bill O'Connell she'd fancied him. Her expression was one of clear disappointment.

He touched the hardness that was the razor in his inside jacket pocket, and wondered what Big Bill and his people might be carrying. He found he was sweating.

He left it a couple of minutes then looked over again at the pillar. Only now there was no sign of the man.

What did that mean? An ambush when they left the hall? It was a possibility.

A possibility that in the end proved unfounded.

Jeannie Swanson got into bed and pulled the covers up to her chin. 'I'm whacked,' she declared.

Bridie smiled. 'I'm a bit that way myself.'

'The apple tart we had tonight was lovely, don't you think?'

'Hmmh,' Bridie murmured.

'I can't cook much myself. I burn things when I try.'

Bridie laughed softly. 'That must be because you're not paying attention.'

'I find it so boring. That's probably why I'm no good at it. What about you?'

'Oh, I can get by. None of your fancy dishes, mind. Straightforward cooking and baking. My ma taught me.'

Jeannie sighed. 'My ma died when I was wee. There were six of us lived with my da. My older sister Tina used to do the cooking, only she wasn't all that clever at it either. Da was always complaining. Until he took up with my auntie Margaret that was. She'd been married but widowed in the war. She came to live in our house just before I got the job here.'

Jeannie turned on to her elbow to face Bridie.

'There's something I've been meaning to ask you.'

'And what's that, Jeannie?'

'Why don't you read at night any more? It's ages since I last saw you with a book in your hand.'

It was too, Bridie reflected. 'I sort of lost interest,' she replied.

'*You*, Bridie Flynn! I find that hard to believe.'

'Well it's true.'

'But why?'

Bridie shrugged. 'Who knows? These things happen.'

'I must say I'm surprised.'

Bridie wasn't. What fun was there reading about fictional heroes when her own hero was under the selfsame roof? Sir Ian of Seaton, her very own shining knight.

'I'm tired,' Bridie declared. 'Do you mind if I blow out the candle?'

'Go ahead.'

Bridie left her bed, crossed to where the candle was burning brightly, and did just that.

'Goodnight, Bridie.'

'Goodnight, Jeannie.'

'Sweet dreams.'

Bridie smiled in the darkness. That's what it had become, day-dreams as well as those she had in her sleep.

All of Ian Seaton.

Andrew was fed up, another evening by himself with a bottle of Drummond. He really had to do something about it. He was rapidly becoming a melancholic.

Andrew sipped his whisky and wondered if he should stroll down to Jack and Hettie's. They always welcomed him no matter the time and were such good company.

Rose, he thought. What about Rose? It was still too soon to visit The Haven again. He had to give Georgina time.

God, how he hoped Georgina hadn't said anything to Willie. Or didn't in the future. For both their sakes as well as Willie's.

He cursed himself for giving in to the woman in the first place. He should have resisted, refused to play her game.

Some hope, he smiled wryly. Women had always been his great weakness. If it hadn't been one of them, it had been another.

He got up from his chair and started to pace. No, he wouldn't go to Jack's he decided. The pub? No, he wouldn't do that either. It was all right being there with Jack but on his own was rather different. As the owner of Drummond's he didn't want to be seen propping up the bar by himself. That would only lead to talk.

He gazed around the room, memories of happier times flooding his mind. Not that he was unhappy, he wasn't. Just lonely and bored.

Rose, he wondered how she'd fit in here. Probably very well. And he was sure the staff would take to her after the initial surprise in the difference in their ages.

No no no, that simply wasn't on. She was far too young for him. Though ... How had Jack put it? She adored him, Jack had heard it in her voice and where voices were concerned Jack was invariably right. Something he found rather scary.

Not for the first time he thought how he envied Jack the lovely home life he had. What a support and companion Hettie was, and then there was wee Tommy whom they both doted on.

He recalled what it had been like when he, Peter, Charlotte and his younger sister Nell had been young.

The house had reverberated with laughter. And fighting of course, for which brothers and sisters didn't fight?

Laughter and fighting, it brought the place alive. Whereas now, it was like a morgue.

He thought of Ellen Temple with regret. He missed her, and what she'd had to offer. Well, Ellen was now married to that clod of a husband and lost to him. As was the comfort she'd brought.

Jesus, he prayed Georgina didn't blab to Willie. Georgina whom he wished was there with him. It wouldn't have been so dull and dreary with her around.

He stopped pacing by his glass, drained it and crossed to the decanter for a refill. That was something else, he thought. He was drinking far too much nowadays. But drink was company and consolation, both of which he needed.

He knew then what he'd do. Take the Rolls out and go for a drive. It didn't matter where, just a drive.

Pathetic, he thought. That's what you've become, Andrew. Bloody pathetic.

Where was the young blood he'd been in Ireland? Gone for ever. Aged by years and responsibility. But what times those had been. Wonderful times, exhilarating times.

He swallowed his whisky and poured himself yet another.

Ian knew where he'd find Bridie, and sure enough there she was blackleading a grate. He paused in the doorway, she as yet unaware of his presence. Was he doing the right thing? He didn't know, and a large part of him didn't care. He was following the dictates of his heart.

He walked quietly over and halted behind her. 'Hello, Bridie.'

She started. 'Hello, Master Ian.'

She had a smudge on her forehead that he found most appealing. 'How are you this morning?'

'Fine. Just dandy. And you?'

'Not too bad.'

She hesitated, unsure whether to continue with her work or talk. She decided to take her cue from Ian.

'Can you get away for a while this evening?'

That startled her. 'Get away?'

'That's right. For a half-hour or so.'

She thought about that. 'I suppose so. After our meal.'

He nodded. 'Good. Meet me in the stables. I want to speak to you.'

Now she was totally confused. 'About what?'

'Things,' he replied enigmatically.

Bridie stared at him, remembering Teresa. 'I'm not sure,' she stammered.

'Please?'

His pleading look was one she couldn't refuse. 'About nine. I'll make some sort of excuse if I have to and disappear for a bit.'

'I'll be waiting, Bridie.'

She watched him leave the room, completely mysti-fied as to what this was all about. Meet him in the stables?

No matter what she felt for him he'd better not try anything, she thought. He'd just better not. He'd get a right flea in his ear if he did.

Ian was sitting on a bale of hay with a hurricane lamp dimly lighting the stables when she arrived. He immediately rose. 'Thanks for coming, Bridie.'

She didn't reply, nervous in the extreme.

'Why don't you sit down,' he proposed, indicating the bale.

She did, wondering yet again what this was all about. Please God he wasn't going to try and seduce her. She couldn't have borne that, it would have been far too hurtful.

'Was it easy to get away?'

Bridie nodded. 'I said I was off to my room and as Jeannie's busy she won't know that I haven't gone there.'

'Good.'

Ian took a deep breath. This was proving far more difficult than he'd anticipated. 'I took the liberty of bringing along a bottle of wine and a couple of glasses. Would you like some?'

Was he trying to get her drunk, was that it? Her opinion of Ian Seaton, knight in shining armour, plummeted. 'No thank you.'

'Then would you mind if I did?'

'Go ahead.'

Ian poured himself a glass from the already opened bottle, then sat on another bale a little distance away. It was a beautiful atmosphere, he thought. Soft and yellow with shadows dancing on Bridie's face. He felt an enormous sense of peace come over him.

'Well,' he said, and sipped his wine. In fact he'd already had quite a bit of wine that evening in preparation for their tryst.

Bridie dropped her gaze to stare at the floor.

'How's your father?'

That surprised her. 'A great deal better, thank you. He's started work again.'

'No after-effects?'

'Not according to the letters my mother has written.'

'Strange the doctors not being able to diagnose what was wrong with him.'

'He was very ill, Ian. Believe me, I saw him. He was at death's door.'

'I'm sure,' Ian replied hastily. 'I didn't mean to imply anything otherwise.'

She smiled, new confidence coming into her. 'What's this all about, Ian?'

'I wanted to talk to you.'

'Oh?'

He saw her expression and realised what she was thinking. 'Just talk, Bridie. I promise you.'

She believed him and immediately relaxed. 'Go on then.'

Ian was wretched and heady at the same time. Was he doing the right thing or just being a fool? But how could he be a fool feeling as he did?

'The truth is, Bridie, and I won't beat about the bush, I've fallen in love with you.'

She gaped at him, mouth hanging open.

'What do you say to that?'

Chapter 25

Bridie was stunned, completely and utterly. For the moment she couldn't think of anything to reply. Ian in love with her! It couldn't be right, it couldn't be so.

'Well?' Ian queried, now somewhat agitated. He'd made a mistake, he thought. He should never have declared himself. He wished he'd never set up this meeting.

'I . . . I . . .' Bridie trailed off.

'I'm sorry if I've offended you. I just wanted you to know.'

Ian had a large gulp of wine. God this was awful. If he'd been a magician he'd have waved his wand and disappeared.

'In love with *me*?'

'Yes,' he whispered.

'But . . . how?'

'I don't know. It just happened, Bridie.'

It *was* an attempt to seduce her. Had to be. And yet . . .

An Apple From Eden

His tone was anything but insincere. It rang of truth. 'I'm
. . . lost for words.'

'I can understand that. It has come somewhat out of
the blue.'

And then she remembered his kissing her and what that
had been like. 'Don't have me on, Ian, please.'

'I'm not, Bridie. On my oath.' He crossed his heart.
'May the good Lord strike me down if I'm lying.'

Tears welled into her eyes. It was a dream come true.
No, more than that. 'I too have a confession to make.'

There was someone else, he thought. Damn! He should
have known. A chap back in Glasgow probably.

She stared at Ian through eyes shining with tears, her
heart pounding within her chest. 'I love you too,' she
stated.

It was now his turn to be rocked. 'You do?'

She nodded.

'I never guessed.'

'I've done my best to keep it from you. I mean, what
chance had I with you? Our stations in life are so different.
And then there was Moira McLaren whom you were going
out with. I can't . . . couldn't compete with her. Miss
McLaren's beautiful whereas I'm ordinary.'

He slowly smiled. 'You're hardly ordinary, Bridie. At least
not to me. In my book you knock Moira into a cocked hat.'

'I do?'

'Oh yes,' he whispered. He wanted to go to her, take her
into his arms and hold her tight. But guessed correctly, for
the moment, that such a move would be a mistake.

Bridie put her hands together and rubbed a thumb. This
was all so bewildering. It was as though one of the novels
she'd read had come to life. He loved her? Prince Charming
actually loved her. She felt like Cinderella.

'I don't know what to do about it,' Ian said.

'How do you mean?'

'Exactly that. I don't know what to do.'

'Because I'm a servant?'

He flushed slightly. 'Yes.'

'I understand. It's not very practical, is it?'

He shook his head.

'Yet you love me and I love you. There was a day on the staircase when we looked at one another, and that was that. I was head over heels.'

He stared at her in wonderment. 'It was the same for me. The same day on the staircase.'

'Really?'

'It must have been the same day. The French have an expression for it, a *coup de foudre*. The Italians call it "the thunderbolt". Our eyes met and that was that.'

'Yes,' she breathed.

He laid his glass aside, rose and said, 'I'm coming over to you. Is that all right?'

'If you wish.' Again she thought of Teresa. 'No funny business, Ian.'

'There won't be,' he assured her.

He crossed to her bale and kneeled. 'You're crying.'

'With happiness.'

That tore at him. 'I feel like that as well. All sort of . . .' He flushed again. 'Mushy inside.'

She smiled. 'It's the same with me.'

He took her hands in his. 'You and I are meant for one another, Bridie. We were destined.'

She gazed deep into his eyes feeling she could drown in them. 'We're both going to have to think about this, Ian.'

'I agree.'

'There's one thing you must understand.'

'Which is?'

'I won't . . .' She gulped. 'I won't go with you unless we were married. Nor will that change.'

That disappointed yet pleased him at the same time. 'You are attracted to me?'

'Of course, silly. I think you are ever so handsome.'

He lifted her hands to his mouth and tenderly kissed them. He was filled with . . . what? Something he'd never experienced before. Something spiritual, though still very much of the flesh.

'I can't stay very long. I must get back before I'm missed,' Bridie heard herself saying.

'Do you have to?'

'They might wonder where I am.' Nonsense of course, she was supposed to be alone in her room. But enough was enough for the time being.

'Then let them.'

'No, Ian. I have my job to think about. I don't want to lose it.'

'You won't that, Bridie. I promise you.'

'Then my reputation.'

'Or that either.'

'Sir Ian of Seaton,' she murmured.

'Maid Bridie.'

Just being with him was so very special, she thought. Detaching a hand from his she reached up and stroked his cheek. He closed his eyes as she stroked.

'Maybe this isn't a good idea,' she said.

His eyes snapped open.

'I'm still a servant after all. And you're who you are. It's an impossibility, Ian. I hate to say that, but it is.'

'Nothing's impossible, Bridie. My father has often said that to me.'

'I think this is. It's a wonderful dream, Ian, but impossible in the end. You must see that?'

He did, but didn't want to accept the fact. How could he marry a servant, particularly when it was their house she was a servant in?

'Will you meet me again?' he pleaded.

'You mean here?'

'If you will.'

There was nothing she wanted more. 'Yes.'

'When?'

She thought about that. 'Monday would be best.'

'Then Monday it is. Same time?'

She nodded. 'And, Ian, I meant what I said about funny business. None of that.'

'Can I kiss you?'

'If you like.'

He raised her to her feet, then his lips were on hers, his tongue eagerly exploring her mouth.

For the pair of them it was sheer ecstasy.

Pat Flynn was scanning the windows on either side of the road on the lookout for the firm's cards when Geraldine Buchanan suddenly appeared round a corner.

He mentally swore when he spotted her. What in the name of the wee man was she doing in this area? He whooaed Jasper to a halt at her approach.

Geraldine, eyes glittering, stopped beside his cart. 'Hello, Mr Flynn. How are you?'

He touched the peak of his cap. 'Fine now, Mrs Buchanan. I've been ill.'

'I heard.'

'I'm not delivering your coal any more as they changed my round.'

She didn't reply to that, just continued staring at him.

Pat lowered his voice. 'I meant to come and see you when I was better, but couldn't be sure your husband wouldn't be there. And what excuse could I offer for knocking on your door without a bag of coal on my back?'

Liar, she thought. He was lying in his teeth. She was damned if she was going to say how much she'd missed him and their evenings together.

'I understand, Mr Flynn.'

He relaxed a little. 'I'm sorry.'

'That's all right.'

'No I mean it, I truly am.'

She shrugged. 'Fine.'

Geraldine stood her ground waiting for more of an explanation. She considered she was worth that.

'And how are you?' he asked.

'Never better.'

'Who told you I'd been ill?'

'Your replacement mentioned something about it.'

'I nearly died according to the doctors. It was touch and go for a while.'

She raised an imperious eyebrow. 'What exactly was wrong with you?'

'They never did find out. It was something mysterious they couldn't diagnose.'

'I see.'

'I, eh . . . won't be visiting again,' he mumbled, just loud enough for her to hear.

'I guessed that.'

'It's nothing to do with you.'

'No?'

He shook his head. 'Something happened to me in hospital. Something that changed me. It's my wife . . .'

He broke off and sucked in a deep breath. 'I realised how lucky I was and how much she meant to me. That's the long and short of it.'

Geraldine believed him. She could hear it in his voice and read it in his face. In a way she was jealous. It wasn't that Dougal didn't love her, he did. But how could she truly love him if she was prepared to have affairs? Simply sex? Maybe. Or perhaps there was more to it than that. Perhaps she was someone never meant to be faithful.

'Then I'll wish you all the very best, Pat.'

'And I you, Geraldine.'

She hesitated, then said, 'I was worried about you. I really was. I want you to know that.'

'Thank you.'

'I just wish you had found some way of coming round and telling me to my face. You left me feeling such a . . . slut.'

He blanched.

'Goodbye then, Pat.'

'Goodbye, Geraldine.'

Pat drove on, his feelings mixed. But he'd never stray from Kathleen again. Never in a thousand years.

The dreams had seen to that.

'Wake up, girl!'

Bridie started. 'Sorry, Mrs Coltart.'

'You were away with the fairies right enough. Standing there staring into space as though you were having a vision. Were you?'

She had indeed. Herself and Ian together. 'No,' she lied.

Mrs Coltart studied Bridie. 'Your work's fallen away these last couple of days. Is something the matter?'

'No, Mrs Coltart. I'm sorry.'

'Then you'd better give yourself a shake. I won't have slacking in my household. Simply won't have it, hear?'

What was wrong with the lassie? Mrs Coltart wondered as she continued on down the corridor. Slacking was most unlike Bridie.

Ian leapt to his feet the instant Bridie appeared. 'There you are! I was beginning to think you weren't coming.'

'It was difficult to get away, Ian. The meal was delayed and I couldn't exactly leave before it was over. They'd all have thought that extremely strange.'

'Of course.'

Bridie was nervous, though she'd been constantly thinking about this and waiting for it since their last meeting.

'I brought another bottle of wine,' Ian said. 'Can I tempt you?'

Bridie went to a bale and sat. 'I've never drunk wine. Where I come from it's all whisky and beer.'

'In which case you must have some.'

'But only one,' she stated firmly. She wasn't about to get drunk. It wasn't that she didn't trust Ian, but under the influence of alcohol who knew what she might succumb to?

It wasn't a risk she was about to take.

'Here,' Ian smiled, handing her a brimming glass.

'I've often wondered what wine tastes like. Since arriving at The Haven that is.'

'Then have a sip.'

She did. 'It's nice and warming.'

'That's called Châteauneuf du Pape, my favourite. I'm glad you approve.'

Bridie had another sip. It really was nice, and as she'd said warming.

He frowned. 'You look worried.'

'I'm still trying to take on board what's happened. Between you and me that is.'

He nodded. 'Me too.'

'You were being truthful, weren't you?'

'My word of honour, Bridie,' he protested quickly. 'I wouldn't lie to you, or anyone else about something like that.'

She gazed about her. 'What an odd place for us to meet. I know nothing about horses.'

'I do ride myself, though not a great deal. Rose is the one who's keen.'

'Yes, I've seen her out and around on a number of occasions.' Bridie had an alarming thought. 'She's not about to suddenly come in, is she?'

'I doubt it very much. Nor the groom. As far as they're concerned the horses are bedded down for the night.'

How lovely she looked, Ian mused. There was something about her that drew him the way a moth is drawn to light.

Bridie had another sip of wine thinking she could get to like this.

'Can I come and sit beside you?'

She nodded.

He did. 'And hold your hand?'

'Wait till I finish my wine.'

'Of course.'

'I've already told you about my life in Glasgow,' Bridie said. 'So why don't you tell me about yours at The Haven and while you were away studying.'

'It's boring, Bridie. Believe me.'

'I'd still like to hear.'

Ian began to speak and the minutes slipped all too quickly by.

*   *   *

Autumn had finally arrived, Georgina reflected gazing out of her bedroom window. Willie had already dressed and gone about some estate business so she was on her own.

Georgina left the window, crossed to the fire that had been lit earlier and sat in front of it. She'd miss breakfast that morning, having no appetite whatsoever.

There was no doubt about it, she thought. None at all. And, according to the dates and her own instincts, Andrew was the father.

She gently rubbed her stomach, thinking of the life growing inside. Her child. Hers and Andrew's.

Andrew stared at the envelope knowing who the letter was from having recognised the handwriting. He sighed. No doubt a proposal from Georgina suggesting they get together again.

He thought she'd understood when he'd said it was all over between them. Understood and accepted the fact. Apparently not.

He slowly slit open the envelope.

'I wish I could take you to a dance,' Ian declared.

Bridie stared at him in astonishment. 'A dance?'

'Yes, why not. I'd enjoy that.'

She laughed. 'I think I would too.'

'I'd take you in my arms and we'd trip the light fantastic as they say.'

Bridie shivered slightly, imagining it.

'Or a ball, which is just a fancy dance with food. I'd buy you the prettiest gown there was and you'd be the belle of the ball.'

She laughed again. 'Hardly that. Especially if Miss Moira McLaren was present.'

'You'd be the belle of the ball to me, Bridie, which is all that would count. I wouldn't be able to take my eyes off you.'

Nor she hers off him, she thought. How at ease they were together nowadays, and how she looked forward to these meetings in the stables. In a way they'd become her whole life. And Ian, true to his word, had never spoilt them by trying any funny business for which she was immensely grateful.

Ian suddenly frowned. 'Andrew Drummond has written to Pa saying he's paying us a visit. I don't like that man.'

'But why? He's always pleasant, to the staff anyway.'

'I don't know, Bridie, but I neither like nor trust him. He always reminds me of a snake.'

She found that highly amusing. 'Why a snake?'

'Sort of slippery and slimy. At least that's my opinion of him.'

'Well, I can't say he's ever struck me that way. And he always leaves a decent tip. There's certainly nothing mean about Mr Drummond.'

'He's rich you know. Owns a whisky distillery.'

'So I believe.'

'He and Pa were together in Ireland, served in the same regiment. That's where Pa met him.'

'I can't remember if I mentioned but my father fought in the war with the Highland Light Infantry, the HLI. Now there's a famous regiment.'

'They are indeed.'

'Sometimes, when he's in his cups, he'll mention odd things about the war, but not very often. He's always extremely upset after he has.'

'Understandable,' Ian nodded, thinking how lucky he was not to have been caught up in that carnage. Thank God and all his angels he'd been too young.

'What's wrong with Mrs Seaton?' Bridie asked.

'Wrong?'

'She certainly hasn't been herself of late. The staff have been talking about it. Several times she's nearly bitten someone's head off for nothing at all.'

Ian pulled a face. 'There's nothing wrong with her that I'm aware of.'

'Don't repeat this but Mrs Coltart is most concerned. I overheard a conversation between her and Mrs Kilbride in which she said how difficult your stepmother had been recently.'

Ian thought about that. 'Now you mention it she has been a bit tetchy. And off her food. Not that she eats a great deal at the best of times but she's been picking like a sparrow these last couple of weeks. Pa ticked her off only the other night.'

'Maybe she's ill?'

'Or it could be female problems.'

Bridie blushed. 'Ian!'

'Sorry if that offended you. It wasn't meant to.'

'Well . . . it did and didn't. I just don't like that sort of thing being mentioned. Not in mixed company anyway.'

'Then I shan't again.'

'Thank you.'

Perhaps Georgina was ill, Ian mused. For not only was she off her food and tetchy but decidedly pale into the bargain.

'If I learn anything I'll let you know.'

'And it'll be strictly between us,' Bridie promised. 'I'm not one for gossiping and certainly not where my employers are concerned.'

'Good for you, girl.'

She adored it when he called her girl. There was an intimacy about the way he said it that never failed to give her a thrill.

'I've been doing a lot of thinking about you,' Ian stated slowly.

'Oh?'

'Well, *us* really.'

'And?'

'I love you and you love me, right?'

She nodded.

'Well, we can't go on as we are, meeting up in the stables whenever we can.'

She studied him curiously. 'What else can we do? I'm me and you're you. As we've already agreed, considering our different stations in life, an impossible situation.'

'I wonder,' he brooded.

'Ian, you know it is. You'll meet someone else in time, someone suitable and forget all about me.'

He shook his head. 'No matter what happens, Bridie, I'll never forget you. Nor do I think we should dismiss our love so lightly.'

'Lightly! I'm hardly doing that.'

'Well, it seems as though you are.'

She took his hand in hers and squeezed it. 'I assure you, Ian, that isn't so. But as I said, it's an impossible situation.'

'Perhaps not,' he breathed. 'Perhaps not.'

Rose was doing her best not to glare at Andrew sitting across the table from her. She'd hardly said half a dozen words during the entire luncheon, letting Georgina prattle on which she had done most effectively.

Willie sighed and laid aside his napkin. 'You'll have to excuse me, Andrew, but I have a few more hours of work. Things that just have to be done today.'

'I understand, old boy.'

'I'm sure Georgina and Rose will be able to entertain you.'

'You'll have to excuse me as well,' Rose declared, rising as her father had done. 'But I've developed a splitting headache.'

'Poor dear,' Georgina sympathised.

'So if you don't mind I'll go to my room and lie down.'

'Of course,' Georgina nodded, secretly delighted as she'd been wondering how she was going to get Andrew on his own.

Georgina smiled at Andrew when Willie and Rose had gone. 'I thought we might go for a stroll?' she suggested.

'That would be nice.'

'Then shall we get our coats. It's rather nippy out there.'

Andrew came to his feet and helped Georgina from her chair. He guessed this to be a ploy so they could speak together.

'It's a pity you can't stay the night,' Georgina said as they moved away from the table.

'Yes, it is,' he lied. He'd never had any intention of staying the night and had only come to The Haven because of the urgent pleading in Georgina's letter. He was also curious about 'the news' she had for him. Now that sounded rather mysterious.

'So,' he said when they were well out of earshot of the house. 'What's this all about?'

Georgina was suddenly nervous. 'Thank you for coming.'

Andrew didn't reply to that.

'The thing is, Andrew, I'm pregnant. And by you.'

He came up short, stunned. 'Pregnant?'

'That's right.'

'Are you absolutely sure?'

'Absolutely.'

Andrew, without a hat, ran a hand through his hair. 'You've rather caught me by surprise,' he confessed.

'It was always a possibility.'

'I appreciate that ... but ...' He broke off to stare into the distance. 'How do you know it's mine?' he asked softly.

'The dates, Andrew. It has to be you. Please don't ask me to go into the details of why I'm so sure, but I am.'

A baby, Christ Almighty! No wonder she'd been so mysterious about 'the news'.

'How far gone are you?'

'Work it out for yourself. It happened the last time we were together.'

He took a deep breath. 'Let's keep walking. It might look strange if we were seen standing still talking for too long.

'How do you feel about this?' he queried.

'Delighted. I'd given up the hope of ever conceiving. I don't think any woman feels truly fulfilled until she's had a child.'

'Hmmh,' he muttered. 'I presume you haven't told Willie.'

'About you or being pregnant?'

Andrew swallowed hard. 'About being pregnant.'

'No, I wanted to speak to you first.'

He almost didn't want to ask the question. 'Why, Georgina?'

'Because I thought it might alter matters between us.'

'You mean about you leaving Willie and coming to me?'

'Yes.'

They walked a little way in silence before he eventually replied. 'It doesn't, Georgina. I'm sorry, but there you are.'

'I didn't think it would somehow. But I wanted to give you the opportunity. Just in case.'

'It's the same as it was, Georgina. I don't want to hurt Willie.'

'And yet you slept with me.'

'I was wrong to do that, terribly wrong. But the flesh was weak, I'm afraid and you were willing. Or to be truthful, more than willing. Downright eager.'

It might be true but she could have done without hearing that. It was both humiliating and degrading.

'Will you now pass the baby off as Willie's?'

'What else can I do if you won't have me?'

'I won't, Georgina. I want you to believe that and not come up with some crackpot notion that by leaving Willie I'll take pity on you because of the child. I won't, I assure you.'

'You can be a hard bastard, can't you, Andrew Drummond?' she almost hissed.

'When I have to be, Georgina. When I have to be. And this is one of those instances.'

Georgina closed her eyes for a moment, remembering how it had been with Andrew and what it was like with Willie.

'I'll be godfather if you wish?' Andrew smiled.

If they hadn't still been in sight of the house she'd have slapped him.

Chapter 26

They were having aperitifs before dinner and Willie was in an expansive mood. To his irritation Ian found himself in conversation with Andrew. He was pleased Andrew was leaving directly after their meal.

'Excuse me,' Georgina said in a raised voice, rounding on everyone. 'But I have an announcement to make.'

Andrew tensed, guessing what was coming next. Please God, for Willie's sake, she didn't name him as the father.

Georgina hooked an arm round Willie's and gazed deeply into his eyes. She might have been a woman totally in love.

'Yes, my dear?' Willie smiled.

'I had considered telling you this when we were alone, but on second thoughts decided to share it with the family at the same time. And our good friend Andrew of course.'

She paused dramatically. 'I'm expecting a baby.'

Andrew drew in a deep breath and held it, wondering if she was about to drop the second bombshell.

'A baby!' Willie exclaimed.

'That's what I said.'

'By all that's . . .' Willie threw back his head. 'Wonderful!'

'I thought you'd be pleased.'

'Pleased! I'm far more than that. Oh, my darling, my sweet, sweet darling.' He pulled Georgina into an embrace and kissed her.

'Well,' Ian murmured, taken aback. This was a bit of a shock.

Rose flew at Georgina and pecked her on the cheek. 'Congratulations! I'm delighted for the pair of you.'

'And so am I,' Ian added, not quite sure if he was or not. A baby at Willie's age, even Georgina's, seemed a little obscene somehow.

'And congratulations from me,' Andrew beamed. Crossing to Willie he shook him warmly by the hand. 'You old dog, you.'

'This calls for a celebration,' Willie declared, eyes glinting with moisture. 'Jeannie, can you go and fetch some champagne.'

Jeannie Swanson, who'd been handing round canapés, nodded, quickly got rid of the plate she was holding, and rushed from the room. She couldn't wait to tell the rest of the staff.

'How?' Willie queried of Georgina, totally bemused.

Georgina had the grace to blush. 'I think you know how, Willie.'

He was suddenly covered in confusion and glanced guiltily at first Rose then Ian. 'I didn't mean that literally. But . . .'

'It just happened, angel,' Georgina interjected sweetly. 'The way these things do.'

'Of course.'

'Congratulations, Pa,' Ian said, extending a hand.

'Thank you, son.'

'An addition to the family,' Ian mused. 'How about that.'

'How about it,' Willie enthused. He'd said to Georgina they should have a child and now they were going to. It was almost as though God had been listening.

Georgina was steadfastly refusing to meet Andrew's eye, as she'd been doing since they'd met up that evening. Despite her outward show of love and affection to Willie she felt sick inside.

Willie glanced over at Andrew. 'And you must be godfather, Andrew. I insist.'

The look Georgina suddenly shot at Andrew for the briefest of seconds was like an arrow directed straight at his heart.

'I shall be honoured, Willie. Thank you.'

Willie turned again to Georgina. 'When, eh . . . ?'

'We'll discuss the details later, darling. If you don't mind, that is.'

'No no, I fully understand.'

Mrs Coltart appeared carrying a tray on which was the bottle of champagne and appropriate glasses. Now she knew why Georgina had been out of sorts recently.

'May I offer my congratulations, madam,' she said, placing the tray on the sideboard.

'You may, Mrs Coltart. And thank you.'

'And to you, sir.'

'Thank you, Mrs Coltart. Will you see the staff get a drink. I think they should.'

'I shall, sir.'

A baby brother or sister, Rose was thinking. How scrumptious. She absolutely adored babies.

'I'll do the honours,' Willie declared, detaching himself from Georgina and going over to the tray. Seconds later the cork popped and the champagne was flowing.

'A toast,' Andrew proposed when the glasses had been charged and handed round. 'To the newest member of the Seaton family. May his or her life be a long and happy one.'

The wine tasted like gall in Georgina's mouth.

Andrew was deep in thought as he drove back to Drummond House in the Rolls. What a day that had been and no mistake!

Georgina pregnant by him, what a heart stopper. Thank God she'd kept her mouth shut about who the true father was. It would have been a disaster if she hadn't.

The expression on Willie's face when she'd made her announcement was one he'd never forget. He shuddered to think what the expression would have been had Georgina chosen to divulge their secret.

He couldn't have been happier for Willie whom he liked enormously. Willie's joy had truly been a sight to behold.

And he was to be godfather. That both amused and pleased him. He only prayed the child took more after its mother than it did its father. It might be tricky if not.

And what was wrong with Rose? She'd avoided him during the entire day. Something was definitely wrong, but what? All he could put it down to was his not proposing. It could only be that.

Surely.

* * *

'It's for you, Sean,' Kathleen declared, coming into the kitchen followed by Noddy Gallagher.

'Hello, Noddy,' Sean said.

'Aye, hello. I was wondering if I could have a word.'

'Of course you can.'

Noddy glanced over at Pat sitting in his chair and then Alison playing in front of the fire. 'In private like if you don't mind.'

Pat frowned. Gang business no doubt. It was bad enough that Sean was involved without bringing it into his house. He didn't like that one little bit. In fact he downright resented it. Not that he'd say anything mind, at least not to Sean. There was no fear of that.

'Come through to my bedroom, we'll talk there.'

Kathleen's expression was also one of disapproval. It worried her dreadfully that Sean was running with a gang. She'd tried to speak to him about it on several occasions but he'd cut her short declaring he'd do as he bloody well wanted and that was that. On the other hand, she had to admit, though reluctantly, the money he was bringing in was more than helpful. Why, only the previous week, even though Pat was grafting again, he'd upped his lodge once more. Whatever else you said about Sean you couldn't accuse him of not taking care of his family. He was a saint where that was concerned.

'So what is it, Noddy?' Sean queried, closing his bedroom door behind them.

'It's Mo, Sean. The Tong got to him.'

Sean, with Noddy alongside, strode down the ward. How he hated hospitals. He'd never have admitted it but they frightened the hell out of him.

They found Mo at the top of the ward, his face swathed

in bandages. 'You've been in the wars then, Mo,' Sean said, sitting on the single chair provided.

Mo's eyes, filled with pain, fastened on him. His eyes and mouth had been left uncovered. 'Hello, Sean. Good of you to come. You too, Noddy,' he mumbled.

'So what happened?'

Mo swallowed hard. 'Me and Shelagh were in town doing a wee bit of shopping like in Sauchiehall Street. When we'd finished I suggested a drink in the State Bar. You know, that pub in Holland Street?'

'I know it,' Sean confirmed.

'Well, we went downstairs and were having a right old chinwag when it started. As it turned out there were three members of the Tong at the next table.'

'Had they followed you?'

'No, they were there when we arrived. I didn't know they were Tong but they recognised me after a while. They started taunting me, Sean, me and the gang. Said we were all a bunch of fucking poofters.'

That instantly enraged Sean, touching a sore point. His eyes became diamond hard. 'Did they indeed.'

'Aye they did. Poofters, nancy boys and shirt lifters. Said they were surprised to see me out with a lassie.'

Sean fought to control his anger. 'Did they tell you they were Tong?'

'As soon as they recognised me. Though how they did that I don't know. I'd never seen any of them before in my life.'

'What happened then?'

'It all got a bit heated, them threatening and that. Poor Shelagh was terrified out of her wits.'

'I can imagine. Go on.'

'Christ, my face itches,' Mo groaned. 'All I want to do

is scratch but they warned me not to. The doctor that is. Sadistic bastard and no mistake.'

'I said go on, Mo.'

Mo paused, and took a breath. 'I thought there was going to be a barney there and then. I mean, no one calls me a poof and gets away with it.'

Sean winced.

'Then those two big buggers they have at the bottom of the stairs, do you remember them? Huge sods dressed in long black coats, who keep an eye on the place, came over and told the Tong to leave.

'The Tong protested it was all my fault but the coats were having none of it. After a few minutes' argument the Tong were escorted upstairs and shown the door. I, stupidly, thought that was the end of it. I should have known better. Anyway, I eventually got Shelagh calmed down and we had another drink. Then, still very shaken, she said she wanted to go home.'

Noddy was listening to all this in grim silence, thankful it wasn't he who'd gone into the State Bar at that particular time. Three, armed with razors, against one was no joke.

'So up the stairs we went, me carrying the shopping, and out on to Holland Street.'

Mo halted, then swore viciously. 'As I said, I should have known better. They jumped us out of an alleyway. I hadn't a chance against three, Sean. Not with Shelagh there to worry about. I got one good kick in and then I was down and they were at me. Shelagh was screaming her head off as they did their cutting, then they were off like three bullets.'

'Shit,' Sean muttered. 'How bad is it?'

Mo took another deep breath. 'I said the doctor was a sadistic bastard. I doubt his stitching was all that neat and careful. He was sewing me up as though I was a joint in a fucking butcher's shop.'

'How bad, Mo?'

'There are more than twenty marks, Sean, some very deep. I'm going to ... I'm going to ...' Mo's head dropped and he sobbed. 'Look like a monster for the rest of my life.'

Sean's hands clenched, then slowly unclenched. 'I'm sorry, china,' he whispered.

'So am I, Sean. So am I. It means the end of Shelagh and me of course.'

'Maybe not.'

'Don't try and kid me, Sean. What lassie, especially having been through that, would want to be tied up to the nightmare my face is going to be? No no, I've lost her all right.'

'Has she been to see you?'

'Nope. Nor do I expect her to. She's gone, Sean. And I can't say I blame her.'

'Och, maybe that's not the case, Mo.'

Mo almost grinned under his bandages, but it would have been too painful. 'If you were a lassie would you want someone with a face like I'm going to have? I doubt it very much.'

Sean felt for Mo, he truly did. 'How long are you in here for?'

'No idea. Until it heals I suppose. But maybe they'll let me home before then. The doctor says he's worried about infection, though, according to him, they've done all they can to safeguard against that.'

'Can you describe these Tong?' Sean asked quietly.

Mo thought about that. 'Not really. They were just ordinary Glasgow keelies. Nothing that would distinguish any of them. Though I'd know them if I see them again. Oh aye, I'll know them all right.'

Sean had to think about this, digest what he'd been told. 'Shall I have a word with Shelagh?'

'Don't, Sean. Please. Just leave her be.'

'All right then, pal. Now is there anything I can get you?'

'Oh aye, there is indeed. How about a new face?'

'Do you think it was intentional?' Bobby O'Toole asked.

They were at 'the place', Sean and his lieutenants gathered together to discuss what had happened to Mo Binchy. Sean's expression was a dark scowl.

'I don't know,' Sean replied. 'According to Mo it was a chance meeting where one thing led to another.'

'I think they're taking the piss,' Dan Smith said. 'I mean, this is the second time they've had a go. Don't forget Pete Murray.'

'I'm not,' Sean growled.

'They're getting out of order,' Sammy Renton declared.

'And treating us like clowns,' Don McGuire added.

Sean had a gulp from his screwtop. Poofters they'd called the Samurai! Nancy boys and shirt lifters. His stomach knotted with the anger that had been with him since Mo had uttered those words.

He closed his eyes for a few moments, conjuring up a picture of Big Bill Bremner. He'd come to hate that cunt.

'So what do we do?' Jim Gallagher queried.

'What would you do, Jim?'

'I've no idea. Brains aren't exactly my department.'

That raised a laugh, though not from Sean.

'I'm not sure yet,' Sean mused quietly. 'I don't want to rush into anything we might all regret.'

'Why don't we mark one of their blokes in retaliation?' Sammy Renton suggested.

Sean fixed his gaze on Sammy. 'That would lead to more retaliation from them. And so on and so forth until it was all-out war. Is that what you want?'

Sammy paled. 'No.'

'Well, neither do I. Because it's a war we'd lose simply because of numbers. We'd be up against something like four to one, maybe more, which are hardly good odds.'

Sean rubbed his forehead. This was a quandary right enough. He must control his instincts and think clearly. That was what leadership was all about. Or part of it anyway. He mustn't react through anger, though God knew he had enough of that.

Big Bill Bremner, he pictured the man again. There would be a reckoning one day, of that he was determined. But in the meantime . . .

Willie removed his tie and draped it over a chair. 'I've been thinking,' he declared.

Georgina glanced over at him from where she too was undressing. 'That sounds ominous.'

He laughed. 'Not really. It's about you actually.'

'And?'

'Dr Duthie is a grand old chap, bags of experience with pregnant women and childbirth and so on. But perhaps you should go and see a specialist in Edinburgh. Just to be on the safe side.'

Georgina regarded him with amusement. 'We're not being a little over-protective, are we?'

'Certainly not!' Willie blustered. 'But I consider it a good idea.'

'Dr Duthie assures me all's as it should be. So why

bother with a specialist? That would only be a waste of good money.'

'To hell with money where you and the child are concerned. It's unimportant.'

Georgina was touched by that. 'It really isn't necessary, Willie.'

He sat on the edge of the bed and began undoing his shirt. 'As I said, just to be on the safe side.'

'You sound like an old woman,' Georgina teased.

'I do not!'

She wagged a finger at him. 'Oh yes you do!'

'I'm only trying to do what's best, love,' he said in a quiet, contrite voice.

He was suddenly like a little boy, she thought, a warmth springing up inside her. But then weren't most men a lot of the time? Even Andrew on occasion.

'Nothing will go wrong, Willie, I promise you,' she said softly.

'I know but . . . Well this is maybe our last chance to have a child. I want to make sure I've done everything I can. I don't want to be negligent in any way.'

She crossed to the bed and sat beside him. 'You really are a sweetheart you know.'

His face lit up. 'Am I?'

'You certainly are. A lovable, adorable man. I was very lucky to find you.'

She had been too, she reflected. With the state of things after the war she could easily have become an old maid like so many women of her generation. In a way she wished she'd never met Andrew Drummond. Life would have been so much easier without him.

She ran a hand over Willie's hair. 'I'll go to Edinburgh if you wish. Of course I will.'

He turned, put his arms round her and laid a cheek on the valley of her breasts. How at peace he felt there, sublimely so. He drew in a deep breath of the scent of her which he so adored. 'Oh Georgina,' he whispered.

She thought again of Andrew. That was gone for ever. She hadn't reconciled herself to the fact yet, but would. She'd have to. And in the meantime count her blessings.

'Do you think it would be all right?' he whispered.

'Would what be all right?'

'You know.'

She smiled. 'I'm only pregnant, Willie. With quite a way to go yet. Of course it'll be all right.'

'I don't want to hurt you in any way.'

'You won't,' she assured him.

'Or endanger things.'

'You must have made love to Mary when she was pregnant?'

Willie closed his eyes. 'To be honest that was such a long time ago I can't quite remember. But I think I must have done.'

'There you are then.'

Willie sighed with contentment. How wonderful it all was. Georgina, a baby of theirs on the way. What else could he ask for?

'I don't care if it's a boy or girl, as long as it's healthy,' he murmured.

'Then we won't be disappointed.'

'No.'

She started to rock to and fro while he continued to embrace her. After a short while she too felt at peace.

'Come in!' Andrew called out when there was a knock on his office door. It was proving a bugger of a day with all manner of things going wrong. And now he'd just found something else to give him a headache.

'Hello, old chap.'

Andrew looked up and smiled. 'Jack! This is a surprise.'

'I was bored and thought I might take a turn up here to find out how you are. Are you busy?'

'Nothing that can't wait. Come and sit down. There's a chair in front of my desk.'

The woman who'd escorted Jack up to Andrew's office closed the door and returned to her duties. Although Jack knew the way to the office it was a difficult route and someone always accompanied him in case there proved to be a problem.

Jack found the chair and sat. 'Any free whisky going today?' he asked hopefully.

Andrew laughed. 'For you there's always some. I'll get it.'

'I hope you're joining me. I hate drinking on my own.'

'You're damned right I'll join you. I could just use a dram.'

Jack sniffed. 'You know this office has always smelt the same as long as I've known it. The same as when your father was here.'

'Really? I can't say I've noticed.'

'Well, you wouldn't when you're here so often. It takes an outsider to recognise these things.'

Andrew poured two large drams and placed one in Jack's hand. 'That'll stiffen your backbone,' he joked, returning to his own chair.

'I wasn't aware it needed stiffening.'

'You know what I mean.'

Jack smiled. 'Your arse in parsley, old boy.'

Andrew smiled also. '*Slainte.*'

'*Slainte.*'

They both drank.

'I confess,' Jack said. 'The real reason for me calling is that I couldn't wait till Friday night to hear what happened at the Seatons. Damned curiosity got the better of me.'

Andrew leant back in his chair. 'What Georgina had to say was something of a shock, Jack. She's pregnant, by me.'

'Aahhh!' Jack breathed.

'She wanted to give me one last chance to change my mind. Which I didn't.'

'And Willie?'

'Is ecstatic, believes the baby's his. He was happy as a dog with two tails when I left.'

'Well, well,' Jack mused.

'Georgina made her announcement that night at dinner after we'd spoken earlier. Carried it off rather well I thought.'

'No regrets then?'

'None, Jack. None at all.'

'That's good, old boy. Now what about Rose?'

'Gave me the cold shoulder all the time I was there. Simply didn't want to know.'

'Give her time. It's hurt pride, that's all.'

'I'm rather coming round to your way of thinking you know. Though Heaven knows how Georgina would react.'

Jack laughed. 'That could be a problem.'

'But that's a bridge we'll cross when we come to it. *If* we come to it.'

Jack drained his glass. 'Dashed fine whisky that.'

Andrew smiled. 'I'll get you another.'

*   *   *

413

'I've decided, I'm going to marry you,' Ian stated.

Bridie stared at him in astonishment.

'I'm going to marry you,' he repeated. 'I've thought long and hard and that's what I'm going to do.'

Bridie shook her head. 'You're havering, Ian. I said to you before that's an impossibility. Our stations in life, the fact I work for your father . . .'

His expression became grim. 'Bugger the class system, it's a load of old nonsense anyway. Archaic in the extreme. You're as good as me, the only difference between us is that I come from money while you don't.'

'And that money makes a huge difference, Ian. You're well educated, live in a mansion and own untold acres whereas I hail from the humblest of Glasgow tenements and used to work in a lemonade factory. My accent is as broad as they come while yours is refined, the voice of a born gentleman. And think what people would say. They'd be horrified, accusing you of letting the side down and all that.'

'Gentlemen have married beneath them before,' he argued.

'But not a servant from their own house. One day down on my hunkers cleaning a grate and the next swanning around like Lady Muck, ordering about the self same servants I've been working alongside.'

Ian had to grin at the picture that conjured up. He could just imagine Mrs Coltart's reaction. Not to mention Mrs Kilbride's.

Bridie's tone softened. 'You would shame your father, Ian. And surely you wouldn't do that.'

'Georgina never came from a grand or moneyed family.'

'I know, I've heard. But it is a professional background. And she didn't know anyone in the area when she arrived as your da's bride. She was acceptable, Ian. I would never be.'

He jutted out his chin defiantly. 'I'm still going to speak to my father.'

Her eyes moistened. 'Then you're a fool, but I love you all the more for it.'

'There must be a way, Bridie. There must.'

'No, Ian, I don't believe there is. We're never to be. At least not in this life.'

'I'm still going to speak to Father. And I'll do so tomorrow while he's still in such a good mood over this baby.'

'There'll be a row.'

'Let there. But he'll hear me out.'

'And what if you get me the sack?'

Ian hadn't thought of that. 'I'll ensure you don't. You have my word on that.'

'I still wish you wouldn't. Even though it breaks my heart to say it.'

'I love you, Bridie Flynn, and won't be denied. So there.'

The next evening, he thought. That's when he'd request to see Willie alone.

'Come here,' she said. 'My prince, my hero.'

'You sound very melodramatic when you talk like that.'

'Do I?'

'Very.'

'But you are my prince and hero. Something no one can ever take away from me.'

Chapter 27

Mo Binchy laid Shelagh's letter aside. She might have at least called on him, he thought bitterly, but no, she'd taken the easy way out and written.

It was as he'd known it would be. She didn't want to see him again, she said, because of the violence he was caught up in. But he knew better. Oh, aye, so he did. The real reason was his face and the monster he'd been turned into.

Reaching out for the letter he slowly crumpled it into a ball which he laid on his bedside table.

Tears appeared in his eyes that were soaked up by the swathe of bandages.

'This is a joke I presume?' Willie said, staring in disbelief at an extremely nervous Ian.

Ian shook his head. 'No, Pa. I've never been more serious in my life.'

'Bridie Flynn,' Willie muttered. By all that was Holy.

'I love her, Pa, and she loves me. That's the long and short of it.'

'Is it indeed,' Willie replied sarcastically.

'Yes, Pa.'

He mustn't lose his temper, Willie told himself. That wouldn't do any good at all. 'And how long has this been going on?'

'Long enough for us both to know our own minds.'

'I see.'

Willie rose from the chair in his study and crossed to the whisky decanter from which he poured himself a hefty one. He didn't offer one to Ian. He took a substantial gulp, shuddered slightly, then topped up his glass again after which he returned to his chair. From there he studied Ian thoughtfully.

'The whole idea is preposterous, you must realise that?'

'Unusual perhaps, difficult even, but hardly preposterous.'

'Of course it is!' Willie snapped back. 'She's a servant, for God's sake. A maid.'

'That's right.'

'And you want to marry her?'

'I intend to, Pa.'

Willie took a deep breath, then had another gulp of whisky. 'We'd be a laughing stock, son. Doesn't that bother you?'

'Of course it does.'

'Well then?'

'It'll blow over in time. People will forget.'

Willie barked out a short laugh. 'I doubt that very much. Country folk have long memories as you should well know. And what about the social aspect? You'd never be invited anywhere decent again, and if you were they'd be sniggering at you, and her, behind your backs. Not a very pleasant prospect.'

'No,' Ian agreed in a low voice.

'So let's forget this nonsense and pretend this conversation never took place.'

'I'm sorry, Pa. I can't do that.'

Willie sighed. 'What about the family name, does that mean nothing to you? You'd be dragging it down into the dirt.'

'There's nothing wrong with Bridie,' Ian retorted hotly.

'Except that she's working class.'

'That is precisely what's wrong with her. She probably holds a knife and fork the way a navvy would a pick and shovel.'

'Those niceties can be taught.'

'And her voice? Every time she speaks it's like walking down Sauchiehall Street. Fine for a servant lassie but hardly for the wife of my son.'

Ian couldn't help himself. 'I didn't know you were such a snob, Father.'

Willie's eyes flashed, momentarily betraying his anger. 'But I am, Ian. I most certainly am. Though I would hardly describe it as snobbishness.'

'But it is, you must see that.'

'I don't agree,' Willie said emphatically. 'We have our place and they theirs. That's how things are and always will be.'

'You make me ashamed of you.'

'You ashamed of *me*!' Willie finally exploded. 'Don't be impertinent, boy. It's me who at the moment is ashamed of you. Why, you're beginning to sound like one of those bloody socialists, scum of the earth.'

Willie brought himself back under control.

'And what about the rest of us? Myself and Georgina? Not to mention Rose. Why should we have to live under such a stigma, for it would affect us as well you know. We'd be pariahs.'

'We could get married and go away for a while, Pa. Then return later.'

Willie shook his head. 'That would only be putting off the evil day. No, such a marriage is completely out of the question. I forbid it.'

'And what if I go ahead and marry her anyway?'

Ian was quite capable of doing that, Willie thought. There was a strength in the lad he'd seen growing over recent years. 'Then you'd pay the price.'

'Which is?'

Willie stared his son straight in the eye. 'I'd throw you both off the estate then disinherit you.'

That shocked Ian to the core. 'You wouldn't!'

'But I would, son, and you'd better believe it. At the moment you're my son and heir. Marry that girl and you cease being the latter.'

This was the last thing Ian had expected. Thrown off the estate, leave The Haven. He couldn't even begin to comprehend such a thing. It was unimaginable.

'Isn't that rather drastic, Pa?' he choked.

'Yes, I'd say so. It merely reflects how strongly I feel about all this. Don't forget I've got Georgina and Rose to think about as well. I'm not having our lives ruined because of you and a housemaid.'

Ian swallowed hard. 'Can I have some of that whisky?'

'Help yourself.'

Willie watched Ian's back as he crossed to the decanter. That had certainly put a spoke in the lad's wheel. He knew how much Ian loved The Haven. Well his choice was simple, between two loves. The Haven and Bridie Flynn.

Besides, he wasn't at all convinced Ian did love the lassie. It could well be an infatuation which he didn't realise being young and inexperienced with members of the opposite sex.

Ian noted his hand was shaking as he raised the glass to his lips. To say he was stunned would be a complete understatement. Lose The Haven! It made him feel sick just to think about it.

Willie lit a cigarette and blew smoke in Ian's direction. 'Well?' he demanded harshly.

'I've got to consider this, Pa. It's not a decision I should make on the spot.'

'I'm glad to hear it.'

'And there's no . . . alternative?'

'None.'

The fiery liquid burnt its way down Ian's throat into a knotted stomach.

'You'll get over her in time, I promise you,' Willie said softly.

'I won't, Pa. This is the real thing.'

'I got over losing your mother, though it was hard. Damn hard. Then I met Georgina and look how happy we are. You'll meet someone else, I can guarantee it.'

'It's just not fair,' Ian whispered.

'Life isn't, son. That's a lesson you'll have to learn and which I thought you would have by now. It isn't fair at all.'

Ian replaced his glass, a vision of Bridie swimming before his eyes. He had to talk to her as soon as possible.

'Thanks for your time, Pa,' he said in a cracked, slightly sarcastic, voice.

Willie didn't reply.

Ian turned on his heel and left the study.

Sean and a few others were playing pontoon at 'the place' when Dan Smith burst into the room. Sean was in a good mood as he was winning.

'What's your hurry?' Sean demanded, glancing up. He then took in Dan's expression. 'You look like you've seen a ghost.'

Dan winced while Sean went back to studying the cards.

'It's Mo,' Dan gulped.

'Aye, what about him?'

'He's dead.'

Sean paused for a moment, then laughed. 'Go on, pull the other one. It's no' April Fool's you know.'

'He's dead I tell you.'

Those grouped round the table turned to stare at Dan, disbelief on all their faces.

'Dead,' Sean repeated slowly.

Dan nodded.

'How?'

'I went to see him, take him a few things like. Give him a wee bit of company. But when I got there his bed had someone else in it.'

Dan paused. He couldn't believe this either.

'Go on.'

'I spoke to the Sister to ask where he was. Apparently he died this afternoon.'

'Holy fuck,' Sean swore viciously.

'Of what?' Noddy Gallagher queried.

'Septi . . . septi . . . I can't remember the word she used. But blood poisoning.'

Sean closed his eyes for a brief moment, then opened them again. 'And how did he get that?'

'From being marked of course. The Sister explained they'd done all they could but apparently it wasn't enough. The blood poisoning hit right out of the blue and Mo was gone before they knew it. She was awfully sympathetic.'

Dan slumped into a chair and ran a hand over his face. 'Is there any bevvy in the house?'

Sean reached into a pocket and pulled out a crisp white fiver. 'There's none so go and get some. I think we all need a drink after this.'

Mo dead!

'The fucking Tong. May they all roast in Hell,' Jim Gallagher hissed.

'Aye,' his brother Noddy agreed.

Sean's right hand clasped and then unclasped again. The Tong would pay for this. By God and all His angels they would.

Ian jumped to his feet the moment Bridie appeared in the stables. Going to her he took her into his arms and held her tight.

'What's all this about, Ian? You were in a right old state when you spoke to me earlier.'

'How long have you got?'

'No more than half an hour, then I'll have to be back.'

Ian led her to a bale and sat her down. 'I talked to my father about us.'

She stared into an anguished face. 'I take it he wasn't best pleased.'

'He says if I marry you, or insist on marrying you, he'll throw us both off the estate and disinherit me.'

Bridie was appalled. 'Disinherit you! Oh, Ian.'

'He meant it too, believe me. I expected a row, all manner of reactions, but to disinherit me . . .' He trailed off.

'Well, that's it then.'

'No it isn't!' Ian retorted angrily. 'I'm not going to be beaten so easily. I'm not going to just cave in.'

'The Haven is your whole life, Ian, you told me that once.'

'It was. But now you both are. I can't give up either of you.'

'You're going to have to, Ian. And it's going to be me. I can't have you losing The Haven on my conscience. That would be too great a burden to bear.'

Ian wrung his hands.

'I said it was an impossible situation, Ian, and this just proves me right.'

'There must be a solution. There must be,' Ian croaked in despair.

'You say your father meant it.'

Ian nodded.

'Then there isn't.' But there was, she thought. Though it wasn't the solution Ian was after. There was nothing else for it, she was going to have to hand in her notice and return to Glasgow. What else could she do? If she remained it would just tear them both apart.

Ian put his arms round her. 'I won't give you up, Bridie. Now I've found you I'll never let you go.'

'And The Haven?'

'I won't let that go either.'

'Dear Ian,' she said, and kissed him on the cheek.

He drew the scent of her deep into his lungs. How he wanted Bridie, so much so at times it was a physical ache. But he wouldn't even try and break his promise to her.

She'd only sleep with him if they got married and that's how it would have to be.

They fell silent, each lost in their own thoughts.

Willie stared across the room at Georgina who was reading a magazine. Rose was tinkling on the piano. Despite innumerable lessons when younger she played atrociously.

He'd been thinking about Ian and the conversation he'd had with his son. So far he hadn't mentioned it to Georgina and the question he was mulling over was, should he?

It was rare for him to keep something from his wife, especially something of such importance. And it was the same with her, she told him everything.

He could just imagine what Georgina's reaction would be if he did confide in her. Fury on the one hand, possible hysterics on the other. She would no doubt have it out with Ian which wouldn't help matters one little bit.

No, he decided, it was best he kept this to himself. Best for all concerned.

He smiled, imagining the look of horror on Georgina's face at the idea of being related to a housemaid, especially one who'd been in their service. She'd be mortified to say the least. If he was a snob, which Ian had accused him of being, then Georgina was a far bigger one.

But then, he reflected, that was often the case with the middle classes, from which Georgina had come.

Sean watched stony-faced as the coffin was lowered into the grave. The pallbearers were all relatives of Mo's.

The Samurai were there in force to pay their last respects to a fellow gangmember and friend. They were standing in a group to one side of the official mourners.

The Binchys hadn't been at all pleased when they'd

turned up, but nothing had been said, though Mr Binchy had given them the most contemptuous of looks.

Sean glanced over at Mrs Binchy sobbing loudly and in a state of near collapse. It was only her husband holding her upright that stopped her tumbling to the ground.

'Ashes to ashes, dust to dust . . .' the priest intoned.

Sean fingered his black tie, remembering Mo and the laughs they'd had together, hating the Tong bastards who'd killed him. The heavy marking had been bad enough. But death, that was something else entirely. He hadn't failed to note that the ex-fiancée Shelagh hadn't put in an appearance. Probably too ashamed to do so, he guessed.

He gazed at Mrs Binchy's normally handsome face now ravaged with grief. The woman seemed to have aged ten years overnight if not more.

'I'm glad that's over,' Sammy Renton declared as Sean and his lieutenants sat down in the nearest pub.

'It's the first funeral I've ever been to,' Bill O'Connell confessed.

'Me too,' Noddy added.

'You, Sean?' That from Jim Gallagher.

'Aye, I've been to them before. Though never to one that was a pal and of my own age group.'

'At least the rain held off,' said Don McGuire. 'There were times when I thought it was going to bucket down.'

'Let's have a kitty,' Sean suggested. 'And I don't know about youse lot but I'm going to get pissed as a fart. Deid mockit beyond belief. Mo would have approved of that.'

Several others nodded their heads in agreement.

'So what now, Sean?' Sammy asked.

'How do you mean?'

'About Mo. I know you said we can't take them on because they outnumber us, or mark one of them in return as that would just lead to it all getting out of hand. But surely there's something?'

Sean sighed. If there was he wished he could think of it. He tossed a couple of pound notes on to the table in front of him. 'Bill, you get them in. Whiskies and chasers.'

'Aye right,' Bill replied, rising. He added his contribution to the pile on the table before taking some out and heading for the bar.

An old man shuffled over to their table. He was wearing a dirty shirt without a collar over which was an ancient greasy coat. Grey bristles surrounded a thin, vicious mouth filled with cracked yellow and black stumps. On his head was a cap as greasy as, if not greasier than, his coat. The smell of him was appalling.

'Can I have a word, son,' he said to Sean, doffing his cap.

'Aye, what is it, Tally Jack?'

'I want to say how sorry I was to hear about Mo. I knew him since he used to run the streets as a wee shaver. He was a good lad.'

Sean nodded. 'One of the best.'

Tally glanced about him, then back at Sean. 'There's something I want to tell you.'

He eyed the money on the table. 'No' for cash like. I usually charge, but not this time. This is for Mo.'

'Let's hear it, Tally.'

'I get around a lot, here there and everywhere. All over the city doing a wee bit business now and again. Well, I was in a Tong pub the other night, The Thistle, do you know it?'

Sean shook his head.

'It's their main pub, at one time the landlord was one of them. Anyway, Big Bill Bremner and some of his cronies were there when a newcomer arrived with the news of Mo's death.' Tally Jack paused dramatically. 'Do you know what Big Bill did?'

'What, Tally?'

Tally's eyes opened wide in indignation. 'The swine laughed, so he did. Thought it helluva funny.'

Sean went icy cold inside. 'He laughed?'

'That's right. He even bought a round to celebrate.'

Sean's eyes had become diamond hard. Laughed and bought a round to celebrate!

'Cunt,' Noddy whispered venomously.

'Aye, you're right there, son,' Tally nodded. 'I was disgusted so I was. Fair disgusted. In fact I was so upset I left beer in my glass and just walked out. That's how disgusted I was.'

Disgust wasn't what Sean felt, it was total and utter outrage. Had Bremner no respect whatever!

Sean reached over and extracted a ten-shilling note from the pile on the table. 'Here you are, Tally. Take that.'

Tally shook his head. At that moment, down to his last tanner and with a terrible thirst on him, ten shillings was a fortune. 'I said I wouldn't take cash, son, and I won't. That wasn't why I told you.'

Sean smiled. 'Take it and have a drink on Mo. I insist.'

Tally Jack sniffed, his willpower crumbling. 'Well, if you insist. If you put it like that.'

'I do.'

A filthy claw of a hand accepted the note. 'God bless you, son.'

'And you, Tally Jack.'

The old man shuffled away, heading for a spot further down the bar.

'Cunt,' Noddy repeated.

Sean, a deep frown creasing his forehead, remained silent. When he finally did speak again it had nothing to do with Mo or Big Bill Bremner.

Sean was drifting off to sleep when it came to him. His eyes snapped open and he sat up in bed.

'Of course,' he muttered. 'Of course.'

If Big Bill Bremner would agree.

Wrapped up warm against the bitter cold, Ian was standing outside watching dawn break. Gradually light flooded the landscape, a truly beautiful, magical sight.

A lump came into Ian's throat. How could he give all this up? He couldn't. He belonged here and would die here. He was as much a part and parcel of the estate as any of the trees, fields and all the other living, growing things.

As part and parcel of the estate as he wanted his son to be in time. This was his inheritance and the inheritance he would eventually pass down. An inheritance that had been in the family for hundreds of years.

He sighed, torn inside. There had to be an answer to his dilemma. Some way to make his father accept Bridie as a daughter-in-law.

There just had to be.

'Ah, Bridie,' Willie said, without the customary smile on greeting staff. 'Close the door behind you.'

She did, then crossed to stand in front of his desk. 'Thank you for seeing me, sir.'

He laid down his pen and leant back in his chair. He

stared at Bridie through uncompromising eyes. 'So what can I do for you?'

'Ian spoke about us, I understand.'

Willie nodded. What was she going to do, put forward some sort of argument in favour of the union? He waited.

'Can this be confidential, sir? Just between the pair of us. I don't want Ian finding out.'

'If you wish.'

Bridie clasped her hands in front of her. 'I want to give you notice, sir. If it's all right I'll leave at the end of the month.'

That startled Willie, being so completely unexpected.

'It's best if I simply slip away quietly, sir, without anyone, least of all Ian, knowing. That's why I want it to be just between the pair of us. I appreciate how inconvenient it'll be for you but I'm sure you'll soon find a replacement.'

Willie took out his cigarettes and lit up. 'You must love Ian a great deal,' he said softly.

'I do, sir. With all my heart. That's why I must go.'

He studied her, thinking what a remarkable girl Bridie Flynn was. She'd have made Ian a worthy wife, if only her background had been different.

'This is a big sacrifice you're making, Bridie.'

'I can't stay, sir, that's out of the question feeling as I do about Ian, and he me. Nor will I let him lose The Haven. I told Ian I couldn't bear that on my conscience. Besides, it would be between us for the rest of our lives together. I don't want Ian choosing me and secretly regretting what he's lost.'

Willie nodded. 'You're very wise, Bridie.'

She flushed. 'Not really, Mr Seaton. It's only common sense.'

'There's many wouldn't see it that way, but there you are.'

'So are we agreed, sir?'

'We are indeed, Bridie. We are indeed.'

'And you won't tell anyone. Not even Mrs Coltart. If anyone else knew it would be bound to get out and perhaps back to Ian.'

'Strictly between the pair of us, Bridie. My word of honour.'

'Thank you, sir.'

'End of the month, eh? Pay day.'

'Yes, sir.'

'Then I suggest you leave in the middle of the morning when Ian is out at work.' He made a mental note to instruct Jock Gibson to send Ian to a far part of the estate.

'I'll do that, sir.'

Willie frowned at a sudden thought. 'Does Ian know where you live in Glasgow? He'll try and follow you if he does, I shouldn't wonder.'

'No, sir, I've never mentioned my address. Or even the area I come from. We have chatted about Glasgow on several occasions but I've never been specific.'

That was a relief, Willie thought. Trying to find a single lassie in Glasgow without even knowing her general whereabouts would be like trying to locate the proverbial needle in a haystack.

He then remembered he had Bridie's home address on file. He'd remove that when she'd gone back about her duties and destroy it.

Willie cleared his throat, momentarily embarrassed. 'I must say I admire you for this, Bridie. Very much so.'

She didn't reply to that.

'I shall see, and don't take this the wrong way, that you're amply rewarded for your understanding.'

'Oh no, sir! That's not necessary.'

'You'll need to tide yourself over until you get another position. Making that easier for you is the least I can do. Please accept the gesture as one from a grateful father.'

Bridie bit her lip. It would come in useful after all.

'Well?'

'It seems like a bribe, sir.'

'Nothing of the sort. Don't forget you came to me, I didn't approach you. So how can it possibly be a bribe?'

She was still uncertain. Taking money in the circumstances seemed so cheap somehow.

'Please, Bridie. And even if you say no it'll be in your pay packet anyway.'

She relented. 'Very well, sir.'

'And furthermore, I shall drive you to the station personally and see you safely aboard your train.' And out of our lives, he thought.

'That would be kind of you, sir.'

A great pity, he reflected after she'd gone. He approved of Bridie Flynn. But not her background.

At least not where Ian was concerned.

Chapter 28

A nervous Shelagh was ushered into the room where Sean was waiting for her. He eyed her coldly. There were four others present, including Noddy who'd fetched Shelagh, Jim Gallagher, Bobby O'Toole and Sammy Renton. They had no idea why Sean wanted to see Shelagh.

Shelagh's hands were twitching and there was fear in her eyes as she halted before Sean.

'I hope this isn't an inconvenience,' Sean said sarcastically.

'No.'

'You weren't at Mo's funeral,' he accused.

She hung her head.

'Felt guilty, did we?'

She gave a small nod.

'I thought as much.'

Sean took a deep breath, and slowly exhaled, enjoying her discomfiture. For some reason he found himself thinking of her and Mo in the bedroom next door and the cries of passion he'd overheard. That put an edge to his voice when he next spoke.

'I want you to do something for us.'

'Anything,' she croaked.

'Good.'

His lips thinned outwards in an evil smile. 'Ever heard of Big Bill Bremner, leader of the Tong?'

'Mo mentioned him once or twice.'

'Well, I want you to carry a message to him.'

Her head jerked up and her eyes flew open. 'Me!'

'Aye, you.'

'But why me?'

'Because you're a lassie and, as such, presumably safe. It's too risky sending one of us.'

Shelagh gulped.

'There's a pub called The Thistle that he uses a lot. I believe he goes there every Saturday night, sometimes staying till last orders. Other times he and some of his chinas go on elsewhere. Another pub or the dancing probably. The point is that he's there on a Saturday night around seven o'clock.'

She hadn't noticed it before but she did now, a black-handled razor on the arm of Sean's chair. She almost wet herself.

'What's the message?' she choked.

'One to one?' Peter O'Toole said to Sean when Shelagh had gone.

'Aye, just the pair of us, face to face, with assurances there'll be no repercussions from the side that loses. This way numbers don't count, you see. It'll be just Big Bill and me.'

Noddy shook his head. 'You're taking a helluva risk,

433

Sean. If Big Bill is even half as good as his reputation he'll do for you.'

'Oh I don't think so,' Sean replied confidently.

The others, wary now, stared at him. 'What have you got up your sleeve?' Noddy asked.

'Not up my sleeve, Noddy. But in my hand.'

Noddy frowned. 'What does that mean?'

'It'll be a razor, won't it?' queried Sammy.

'It doesn't have to be, does it?'

'They're traditional. That's what I'd have thought you'd use.'

'As, hopefully, will Big Bill. And you'd both be wrong.'

Sean rose and crossed to the mantelpiece. Reaching up he unhooked the Samurai sword hanging there.

'Holy fuck!' Noddy exclaimed.

'I wonder if Big Bill will laugh when he sees this,' Sean said mildly.

Ian ran a hand over his fevered brow as he prowled the corridors of the house as he'd been doing for the past hour.

He was having terrible trouble sleeping of late. He'd go to bed whacked out, then next thing he knew it was two or three in the morning and he was wide awake again. Tired still, but wide awake. Experience had taught him that once that happened he wouldn't drop off again. If he stayed in bed he just tossed and turned, all the while thinking of Bridie.

Bridie . . . Bridie . . . Bridie . . .

Time after time he found himself creeping past her door, imagining her inside. Desperately wishing he was there with her.

Bridie who now haunted him through every waking

434

moment. Bridie whom he loved. Bridie whom he had to give up The Haven to have.

Ian groaned and again ran a hand over his forehead. Although it was cold he was raging hot inside. If he hadn't known better he'd have thought he was coming down with something. But it was Bridie doing this to him.

There had been occasions recently when he'd thought he was going mad, completely losing his mind. And maybe he was.

Ian Seaton, mad man. He smiled at that. Funny really, if it wasn't so serious.

Despite the earliness of the hour he'd go downstairs and have a drink, he decided. That might calm him down a little. And if one didn't do the job then he'd have two.

Or perhaps even three.

It was shortly before breakfast that Bridie spotted Ian at the far end of the corridor she'd just turned into. She immediately stopped and shrank against the wall.

Had he seen her? How could he when his back was to her?

Dear God in Heaven, she thought. How could she possibly endure this? There wasn't a day passed that they didn't bump into each other somewhere. And now he wanted to meet her in the stables the following night.

Well, she wasn't going to go. She'd say afterwards that she hadn't been able to get away, that Mrs Coltart had set her some extra duties.

Another fortnight before she left, a whole two weeks. Every moment would be torture.

And what would it be like when the time did arrive to leave? Could she just walk away?

She had to, she reminded herself. She simply had to. No matter the pain and anguish it caused her.

Leave and never see Ian Seaton again. For both their sakes.

'How are you today, Georgina?'

Georgina smiled at Rose across the table. 'Fine, thank you. Tip top as Willie might say.'

Willie beamed at his wife. 'You look positively radiant, my dear. Pregnancy certainly suits you.'

'But doesn't help my waistline. I'm fast becoming quite swollen.'

'You mustn't fret about that. Your waist will soon come back after the baby's born. You'll see.'

'It will if I have anything to do with it. That I promise you.'

'But nothing too hasty, darling. Gently does it shall be the order of the day.'

Georgina didn't reply to that. Instead she glanced over at Rose, her expression clearly indicating to Rose that her stepmother wasn't going to pay any heed to that advice.

'Well?' Willie demanded.

'Of course, Willie. Of course. Whatever you say.'

He nodded his pleasure and got stuck back into his plate of bacon and eggs.

'Did you speak to him?' Sean asked the moment Shelagh was brought into the room.

'I did.'

'And?'

'He's agreed. Tomorrow morning, eight o'clock on Glasgow Green. You're to bring two others with you, no more, and he'll do the same.'

'And no repercussions afterwards.'

'He agreed to that as well. Seemed to find it all rather funny if you don't mind me saying.'

'Big Bill seems to find a lot of things funny.' Well the bastard would be laughing on the other side of his face come morning. He was determined about that.

'Can I go now?'

'Aye, beat it.'

There was no word of thanks, nor did Shelagh expect any. She scurried from the room and out of the house. In the street she heaved a huge sigh of relief, thankful beyond belief that was all over.

'So it's on,' Jim Gallagher said softly to Sean when Shelagh was gone.

'Aye.'

'Who do you want to go along with you?'

Sean glanced round the assembled group. 'You and Noddy. That all right?'

'Fine by me,' Noddy replied.

'And me,' said his brother.

Sean picked up the sword that was lying by his chair and placed it on his lap. There the light caught it causing it to gleam and flash.

He took out a clean handkerchief and began polishing it, though it hardly needed that. 'Tomorrow, the morn's morn,' Sean whispered, and smiled.

Andrew threw down his newspaper and stared into the roaring fire. Saturday night and here he was home alone again. Just like the previous Saturday and Saturday before that.

Truth was, he was bored witless and had been for ages. Day in, day out it was the same old routine. Get up, go to work, come home again and that was that with the exception of a Friday night with Jack.

He should get away for a few days, he thought. If only he had a business trip coming up, that would break the monotony, but he didn't have one planned for several months yet.

Call on Charlotte and John? That was a possibility. Then he remembered John wrote his sermon on a Saturday night so that ruled that out.

He tried to think of something to do, and failed to come up with anything.

Jack and Charlotte were right about his getting married. At least then he'd have someone to come home to and share things with. And it was high time he provided himself with an heir. That was another thing.

Which brought him to thinking about Rose. It really was a bit soon to return to The Haven. He'd meant to leave it a while yet.

There again, a weekend away would do him the world of good. And he'd have Willie for company which would be enjoyable.

'Damn it,' he muttered. He would go the following weekend, if Willie agreed that was.

He needed some distraction.

Sean emerged from 'the place' to find Noddy and Jim had arrived while he'd been inside. He was carrying the Samurai sword wrapped in a length of old canvas.

'Christ, it's freezing,' Noddy complained, slapping his hands together.

'Aye, well you won't be when we get there. It's a good walk,' Sean retorted. He was feeling buoyant in the extreme. Almost euphoric.

*   *   *

'They're already there,' Noddy observed when they got to Glasgow Green, a large expanse of parkland situated on the north bank of the river Clyde.

Three of them as agreed, Sean noted. That was fine then. 'Must be keen,' he muttered sarcastically.

Jim shivered, a tremor that had nothing to do with the cold. He didn't like this one little bit, though he hadn't said so to Sean. His brother Noddy shared his foreboding.

They marched over the grass until they came to the Tong, Big Bill flanked on either side by his companions.

'You're late,' Big Bill said. 'We were beginning to think you'd had second thoughts, Flynn.'

'Not me. And we're not late. You're early.'

'Is that a fact.'

'That's a fact . . . Bremner.'

Big Bill eyed the canvas length Sean was carrying. 'What's that?'

'Something to wipe that stupid smile off your face. Or should I say smirk.'

'Let's get on with it,' Big Bill snarled. 'You talk more than a bloody lassie.'

Big Bill removed his jacket, extracted a razor from an inside pocket, then handed the jacket to the man on his right. He flicked the razor open.

'Let's see if you can fight as well as you can rabbit.'

Sean gave Jim the canvas length to hold while he too took off his jacket which went to Noddy. Accepting the canvas length back again he slowly unrolled it.

'Holy shite!' one of Bill's seconds exclaimed when the sword was revealed.

Big Bill's eyes had narrowed. 'What's your game, Flynn?'

'This is my weapon.'

'But it's a fucking sword.'

Now it was Sean's turn to smile. 'Full marks for being observant. A sword it is. Or to be more specific, a Samurai sword. The sword of an ancient Japanese warrior.'

Sean hefted the blade. 'Ready when you are, Bremner.'

'I'm not fighting against that.'

Sean chuckled. 'Scared, are we? Where's the fearless Big Bill Bremner I've heard so much about? The man who'd go up against anyone or anything.'

He hefted the sword again. 'Well run along then . . .' He paused, then added, 'Poofter. Shirt lifter. Bender. Queer.'

Big Bill's face went puce. 'You cunt!'

'Let it go, Bill,' one of the other Tong pleaded. 'No one will blame you or think less of you if you walk away.'

'Maybe not to his face but they sure as hell will behind his back. He'll be a laughing stock,' Sean mocked.

That was too much for Big Bill who launched himself at Sean, his razor whirling in an arc.

Sean danced to one side and the razor whistled harmlessly past. He was enjoying this, his intention being to thoroughly humiliate Bill. And hurt him before he was finished.

Big Bill was incredibly fast. A swift change of direction and he was again coming at Sean, razor upraised, ready to strike.

Noddy and Jim watched anxiously, both praying this wasn't going to get out of hand and that Sean knew what he was doing.

Sean dodged a second blow, then whacked Big Bill across the seat of his trousers using the flat of his blade. 'You should never have laughed over Mo's death, that was a mistake,' he spat.

Big Bill halted to catch his breath and try to think of what to do next. Like a suddenly released spring he galvanised into action.

This time the razor was so close it actually nicked Sean's ear. Sean's reply was a swipe at Big Bill's belly.

The cutting edge made contact, slicing open the front of Big Bill's shirt. Big Bill himself was unharmed.

Big Bill moved forward, then hastily retreated again as the sword carved through the air. Before Sean could reverse his swing Big Bill was on him.

Fear leapt in Sean as, with a roar of triumph, Big Bill went for his throat.

Sean managed to grab Big Bill's wrist, warding off the blow. Using his free hand Big Bill punched Sean again and again.

Sean pushed Big Bill away and thrust with his sword, only instead of cutting Big Bill as he intended, he misjudged the whole thing and the blade of the sword sank deep into Bill's chest.

'Oh my God,' Noddy breathed.

Big Bill looked down at the blade impaling him, his vision already starting to blur. 'You done me,' he croaked.

Sean pulled the sword free, blood gushing and spurting from the wound. Within the space of several seconds Big Bill's front was stained completely red.

It was a miracle Big Bill remained upright as long as he did. He swayed on the spot for several seconds, then tumbled to the ground where he lay still.

The others, including Sean, stood watching in horror. Realising he was still holding the sword Sean dropped it.

One of the Tong hurried to Big Bill and knelt beside him, quickly establishing that he had stopped breathing.

He looked up at Sean with undisguised hatred in his eyes. 'You've killed him.'

Sean took an involuntary step backwards, his eyes riveted on Big Bill's body. He found he was having trouble breathing. He simply couldn't believe this.

There was the blast of a whistle in the distance. Noddy whipped round to gaze in the direction it had come from. What he saw were two policemen racing towards them.

'Come on,' he said urgently, grabbing Sean by the arm. 'We've got to get the fuck out of here.'

'What?' A dazed Sean frowned.

'The polis. We've got to get the fuck out of here!'

Noddy, Jim and Sean began running in one direction away from the police, the remaining Tongs in another.

Noddy slammed the front door of 'the place' behind them and they staggered through to the sitting room where Sean collapsed into a chair.

'Jesus Christ,' said Jim, running a trembling hand through his hair. This was disastrous.

'They'll never work out it was me,' Sean declared hopefully.

'Of course they fucking well will. The entire Tong must know Big Bill was fighting you this morning. With Big Bill dead one of them's bound to squeal to the police for revenge.'

'There weren't to be any repercussions. It was agreed.'

'That was before you killed him. That alters matters.'

'It would be their word against mine.'

'You left the sword behind, Sean. Your fingerprints will be all over it. That'll be enough to . . .' He trailed off and swallowed hard. He'd been about to say 'hang you'.

This was a nightmare, Sean thought dully. How had it all gone so terribly wrong?

'I think you should get out of Glasgow, Sean,' Jim Gallagher advised.

'Out of Glasgow?'

'That would be best. If the police do get your name, and I believe they will, they'll be searching for you everywhere. Murder is murder after all. Not to mention you're a gang member and they all loathe the gangs.'

That was true enough, Sean thought.

'Hold on,' said Noddy, and broke away.

'I could use a drink,' Sean muttered.

Jim glanced about, spying an unopened bottle of beer from the night before. He fetched that and handed it to Sean. 'There's nothing stronger in. I finished the last of the whisky myself.'

Sean undid the screwtop and had a long swallow. Closing his eyes he conjured up a picture of Big Bill's body, its front bright red with blood. He shuddered at the memory.

'There's not much left in the kitty,' Noddy announced. 'On account we had the divvy up Friday. But there's enough to keep you for a while.'

Noddy laid the money on the table, then took out his wallet and counted the contents. 'I can add four quid to it. Jim?'

'I've got a fiver on me. Sean can have that as well.'

'Thanks, lads,' Sean mumbled, and had another mouthful of beer.

'So what are you going to do?' Noddy queried.

'As Jim suggests and get out of Glasgow. I don't like it but it makes sense. I'll go home first . . .'

'No no,' Noddy interjected. 'You don't want to involve

your folks in this. And what are you going to say to them anyway? That you're off on a wee holiday. They'd hardly believe that.'

'But I'll need clothes.'

'Buy some more when you get the time. You won't need much. But I'd keep away from your house if I was you. If for no other reason than should the police discover you've taken clothes then they would realise you'd scarpered the city. Leave things as they are and they'll spend more time searching for you here.'

Sean nodded. That too made sense.

'Better still,' Jim said. 'You and I are roughly the same height and weight. I'll go home and get some of my clobber for you. How's that?'

'Good idea,' Noddy enthused.

'I won't be long,' Jim declared, and hurriedly left the room.

Noddy sat facing Sean whose face was white and drawn. 'What a cock up, eh?'

'I never meant to kill him, Noddy.'

'I know that.'

'Mark him, yes. Do him damage, yes. But not kill him.'

'I believe you, but the police won't see it that way. All they'll know, and the jury, is that a man's dead and you did it.'

Sean had another long swallow, thinking his world had just collapsed around him. He knew this was a day that would haunt him for the rest of his life.

Sean stared out the carriage window as Glasgow vanished into the distance. How long before he saw it again? That was anyone's guess. Like the true son of the city that he was he'd miss it terribly.

*   *   *

'Rose, we have to speak.'

Andrew had managed to corner her at last in the library. On entering the room he'd closed the door firmly behind him.

'We have nothing to talk about.'

'Oh yes, we have. This can't go on, Rose. If I've offended you I apologise.'

'Offended me!' she exclaimed. 'Oh, you've certainly done that. You . . . rotter.'

'And why am I a rotter? You have the advantage of me.'

She gazed balefully at him, wanting to slap his face, tear at him with her nails. 'How could you, Andrew Drummond? How could you!'

'How could I what?' he asked patiently. At last it seemed he was about to get to the bottom of Rose's hostility.

Rose turned away from him and crossed to the window. Should she tell him what she knew, or not?

'Rose? I'm waiting.'

'You've been sleeping with my stepmother.' There, it was said.

Andrew went cold all over. 'Why do you say that?'

'Because it's a fact. I heard the pair of you together. It was disgusting.'

'Heard us?'

'I had to go to the bathroom one night and passed Georgina's door. It was the time that Pa was away. There was no mistaking what I heard. The pair of you . . .' She trailed off.

'I take it you haven't spoken about this to Willie.'

She whirled on him, eyes blazing. 'Of course I haven't. Nor will I ever.'

Relief welled through Andrew. Thank God for that.

'The worst thing for me was making such a fool of myself over you. And all the while you were . . . consorting with Georgina.'

'It's over between us, Rose. I swear.'

'Huh!'

'It is, Rose. You have my sacred word on that.' He had a sudden thought. 'Is Georgina aware you know?'

'No. I've kept it strictly to myself until now.'

Andrew nodded, again relieved. 'I'm sorry you found out, Rose. I truly am.'

She glared at him.

'And you didn't make a fool of yourself. I assure you.'

'Why, Andrew? Why?'

He shrugged. 'It was madness of course, sheer folly, on both our parts. I suppose I can only say the flesh was weak. That's not an excuse, merely an explanation.'

'But she's your friend's wife.'

'You're right. I think rotter probably sums me up rather well. I wouldn't hurt Willie for the world . . .'

'And yet you did that to him,' she interjected hotly.

'Yes,' he admitted, shamefaced. 'I did. Though give me some credit for ending the relationship. The guilt just became too much.'

'Have you any idea the effect it would have on Pa if he ever found out?'

'I do,' Andrew replied softly. 'That was why it had to finish.'

'It should never have started in the first place,' she retorted fiercely.

'No, it shouldn't. But life isn't black and white, Rose. It consists of many shades of grey as you'll find out. And we're all only human after all. There are very few saints about in my experience.'

'But to betray a friendship in such a way is despicable.'

'Indeed it is. I totally agree. If I could undo what happened, please believe me, I would. Not only madness but insanity.'

Rose snorted. 'You're pathetic, Andrew.'

'Maybe.'

'Do you love her?'

He smiled. 'That emotion never came into it, Rose. At least not on my part. It was purely physical.'

Rose blushed, marvelling that she was still attracted to him. If only this had never happened.

'I hope in time you'll come to forgive me, Rose.'

She didn't reply.

A heavy-hearted Andrew withdrew, leaving her alone with her thoughts.

Chapter 29

'Bridie, I know you've been avoiding me,' Ian stated, glancing round to make sure they weren't being seen or overheard.

'That's not true,' she lied. 'Honestly, I've been terribly busy.' Only a few more days to go, she thought, and then she'd be gone. Part of her couldn't wait for her departure, another part was dreading it in the extreme.

'How about tomorrow night? We'll meet up in the stables as usual.'

She'd go, she decided. A final rendezvous, a last remembrance.

'Can you manage that?'

'Yes.'

Ian uttered a huge sigh of relief.

'Although it really is silly, Ian. We've no future together.'

'I'll think of something,' he replied desperately. 'There must be a way. There just has to be.'

'Not without you losing The Haven.'

He groaned, wanting to sweep her into his arms, cover her with kisses. Be one with her.

'The usual time,' he said. 'All right?'

'Give or take ten or fifteen minutes. I'm not the free agent you are.'

He smiled. 'I appreciate that.'

Ian couldn't resist it. Reaching up he touched her cheek. 'Till then, Bridie.'

He swiftly snatched his hand away when Andrew Drummond suddenly appeared. Drat the man.

'Right then, you understand,' he said to Bridie, now brisk and businesslike.

'Yes, Mr Seaton.'

'That's fine then.'

Ian turned and walked away in the opposite direction to Andrew.

Bridie gave Andrew a small curtsey before hurrying by.

Sean came up short when The Haven came into view and his mouth dropped open. By all that was Holy! He'd known it was a big house, but not that *big*! It was vast.

He stood for a few moments admiring it, a wry smile dancing on his lips. He couldn't help but compare it with their home in Glasgow. Compare! There wasn't any comparison. Nor with the dirty streets he normally inhabited compared to these lush and rolling surroundings.

He didn't really know why he'd come here, never having been particularly close to Bridie. Yet she was family, and that was what he needed now. Perhaps he could get a job at The Haven. It was at least worth a try. And who would think to look for him there?

He thought of the article in the previous day's paper

saying that the police were wishing to interview Sean Flynn in connection with the death of William Archibald Bremner. He'd laughed at the Archibald bit, but the article itself wasn't funny.

As Jim had predicted someone had given the police his name, and now all they had to do, should they apprehend him, was match his fingerprints with those on the sword.

Well, he was a long way from being apprehended yet. And that's how he intended it would stay.

The future would take care of itself. For the moment only the present mattered.

'Come in!' Willie called out when there was a rap on his study door. He didn't normally work on a Saturday but these accounts were pressing and required dealing with.

Mrs Coltart entered. 'Sorry to disturb you, sir, but there's a young man come to the kitchen door inquiring if there's any work available. He mentioned you by name.'

'Did he indeed,' Willie replied. 'Do I know him?'

'I doubt it, sir. He's from Glasgow. Somewhat rough spoken but pleasant enough.'

Willie frowned. Normally Jock Gibson would have dealt with this but Jock was off ill, bad with arthritis.

'Well, you'd better show him in,' Willie declared, not appreciating this interruption. He was anxious to get finished and join up with Andrew for a couple of drams and whatever.

The young chap Mrs Coltart ushered in minutes later had black hair and black eyes. Willie judged him to be in his early twenties.

'Mr McDougall,' Mrs Coltart announced, and left them.

'Thank you for seeing me, sir. I appreciate it,' Sean said affably. He'd decided to use a false name as he could hardly use his own. He'd chosen a Protestant one thinking that would give him more chance of a job.

There was a spare seat in the study but Willie didn't indicate that Sean should sit. 'So how can I help you, Mr McDougall?'

'I'm after a job, sir, and am hoping you might be able to give me a start.'

Willie grunted. 'You're a Glaswegian, aren't you?'

'That's right, sir.'

'So what are you doing out here so far away from home?'

Sean had his story prepared. 'I got laid off from the iron foundry where I'd been since a lad. I tried and tried but there's just nothing doing in Glasgow at present. It's chronic so it is. I did consider going to Edinburgh or one of the other big cities but from what I hear unemployment's as bad there.

'Then I had the idea of trying my luck in the country where I thought things might be different. And so here I am.'

Willie was curious. 'Why this area?'

'No reason, sir. I got on a train and then got off again when it took my fancy. And that happened to be here.'

Willie laughed softly. What a bizarre way of going about things. 'How did you get my name?'

'I'm staying at a pub called The Clachan, sir, which I'm sure you know. I was speaking to the landlord last night, chaffing like, and he said you're one of the biggest employers around and I should come and see you.'

There was something shifty about McDougall, Willie decided. He couldn't quite put his finger on it, but definitely something shifty. There again, it might simply be because McDougall was a townie.

'Well I'm sorry, Mr McDougall, but I have absolutely nothing going at all. Nor do I foresee anything coming up in the near future.'

'I understand, sir.'

'Besides, agricultural work is hardly what you're used to.'

'I learn quickly, sir. I can graft and labour with the best of them. I'm sure it wouldn't take me long to learn the ropes.'

Willie believed that. Though why he couldn't say. But he'd decided against this McDougall and that was that. 'I'm sorry,' he repeated.

Sean touched his forelock. 'Thank you for your time anyway, sir. I can see you're busy.'

'Goodbye then, Mr McDougall.'

'Goodbye, Mr Seaton.'

Sean found Mrs Coltart waiting for him out in the corridor. She personally escorted him to the kitchen door where he'd entered the house.

When he was a fair distance away from The Haven Sean stopped and stared back at it. Well he hadn't got the job, but no matter. A place like that must be crammed full of valuables, a number of which he intended would soon be his.

He smiled. Bridie hadn't seen him which meant she wouldn't be implicated in the burglary he now intended. No one would make the connection between McDougall and Bridie Flynn. Why should they? Apart from the fact they were both Glaswegian there was nothing whatsoever to link them.

He'd never done a burglary before, but it shouldn't be too difficult. The idea had come to him as he'd been escorted out by Mrs Coltart.

It should be a nice little haul to keep him going for a time. With a bit of luck he might also be able to find some cash, certain that a man in Seaton's position must have some stashed somewhere.

Humming jauntily he continued on his way.

Sean lay on his bed, having bid goodnight to the landlord of the pub and others half an hour previously. Shortly he would open his window and shimmy down the drainpipe situated a little to the right of the window. That was how he'd go and that's how he'd return.

In the morning he'd pay his bill and be off with no one the wiser about what he'd been up to.

Thankfully it was a moonlit night, Sean reflected, as he padded across the terrace at the rear of the house. In his hand he was holding a screwdriver he'd acquired earlier.

The house itself was in total darkness, hardly surprising considering the hour. So far everything was going hunky dory. All he had to do now was get inside.

A pair of french windows presented themselves. These shouldn't be too difficult, he thought, and set to with the screwdriver. Even though this was the first time he'd attempted such a thing he had the doors open in under a minute.

Like taking sweeties from a baby, he smiled to himself.

Ian drifted out of sleep, the memory of his dream about Bridie still clear in his mind. Such a lovely dream it had been too. The pair of them married, happy as could be.

He sighed as he came fully awake, knowing this was going to be another night of tossing and turning unless he did something about it. Something that was becoming all too regular an occurrence.

He wondered what time it was. Two or three in the morning no doubt, that was when he usually woke.

He swore softly as he swung his legs out of bed and reached for his dressing-gown. Standing, he belted it round him. Then he slipped his feet into soft leather slippers.

Sitting on the bed he yawned. God he was tired, but there was no point in trying to drop off again without a few drams inside him.

He'd be seeing Bridie that night in the stables, he thought, which bucked him immeasurably. A short while only, no doubt, but precious, precious time alone together.

He would never have believed a person could be so much in love – aching, agonising love that lifted you to Heaven one moment, then dumped you into Hell the next.

'Bridie,' he whispered. What pleasure saying that name gave him. But not nearly as much pleasure as being in her company.

He came to his feet and headed for the door.

Ian stopped and frowned. Now why were the lights in the drawing room on? How unlike Mrs Coltart who meticulously did her rounds after the family and staff had retired. He'd never known her leave lights on before.

And then he heard a sound, a rustle of movement. Someone was inside. But who? Someone who, like himself, couldn't sleep?

He moved silently forward to investigate what was going on.

Sean couldn't believe it. No money yet, but lots of small knick knacks, all, to his eye anyway, worth a great deal. He picked up a silver and enamel cigarette box which would be easily disposed of and dropped it into the sack he was carrying, making a mental note not to forget the study where he'd been interviewed. If there was cash on the premises that's where it would be. He just hoped it wasn't in a safe.

'What the hell do you think you're doing?'

For a brief moment the two men's eyes locked, Sean frozen to the spot at having been discovered.

'It's the police for you whoever you are,' Ian declared, and strode forward.

Sean remembered the french windows were still open, dropped the sack, and hared towards them.

'Oh no you don't!' Ian exclaimed, and rushed to head Sean off.

Sean cried out as he was taken in a rugby tackle, the pair of them crashing to the floor.

'Bastard,' Ian hissed as he grappled with the smaller man.

Sean, thoroughly frightened now, knowing that if the police got hold of him they'd find out who he was, squirmed and punched at the same time. He managed to land a solid smack on Ian's throat.

But Ian was far stronger than Sean, and far fitter, thanks to his work on the estate. Although dazed and choking he pulled Sean to his feet and hit him hard, Sean flying back across the room to fall in front of the fireplace.

Ian glared as he advanced on him. 'Bloody thief!' he accused in a strangulated voice.

Sean jumped upright, wishing to hell he had his razor on him. He'd soon make short shrift of this bloke if he had. But in the confusion and panic of fleeing Glasgow, it had somehow got left behind.

As Ian closed, Sean threw a lucky punch which connected

full on Ian's chin. Ian staggered backwards, but didn't go down.

Sean tried to dash past but Ian was able to catch him by the jacket and next moment the pair of them were back on the floor again rolling round and round as they fought.

Sean gasped for air, he couldn't take much more of this. His chest was on fire, his breathing agony.

Ian took hold of Sean's arm and tried to force it into a half nelson, a manoeuvre Sean wriggled free from. He aimed a kick at Ian's crotch which missed, though it caught Ian heavily on the thigh.

Again Sean attempted to make a dash for it and again Ian got hold of him and yanked him to the floor.

As they flailed about Sean's hand came into contact with something metal. A sideways flick of his eyes told him it was a poker.

There was a sickening thud as the brass handle of the poker smacked into the back of Ian's head.

Bridie and Jeannie Swanson were chatting between themselves, en route to the kitchen for the customary cup of tea before starting work, when a terrible scream rang out from downstairs.

They both halted in their tracks. 'Holy Mary Mother of God, what was that!' Bridie whispered.

They looked at one another, then, simultaneously, set off at a run.

They reached the drawing room at the same time as Mrs Coltart. An hysterical Meg Somerville, another of the maids, was hanging on to the door post.

'What is it, lass?' Mrs Coltart demanded, grasping Meg by the shoulder.

Meg was wild eyed, her face the colour of putty. 'It's . . . it's . . .' She broke off and gulped.

'It's what, Meg?' Mrs Coltart prompted, in a kinder, more sympathetic tone.

'It's Master Ian. He's been murdered.'

That one word was like a red-hot steel spike plunged into Bridie's brain.

Mrs Coltart left Meg and hurried into the drawing room.

Bridie forced herself to follow. It couldn't be true. There was some sort of mistake.

Mrs Coltart was kneeling beside Ian's body. Around his head was a great deal of congealed blood.

Bridie knew from just looking at Ian that he was dead. Uttering a low, stricken moan she slumped to the floor.

Willie, sitting on a sofa with Georgina alongside, was a man demented. He kept clasping and unclasping his hands, unable to take his gaze away from the bloody stain by the fireplace. Ian's body had been removed a few minutes previously.

Andrew and Rose were also present, they too sitting side by side. Rose was in an obvious state of shock.

Detective Inspector Ralston and Sergeant Murray returned to the room having accompanied the body out to the waiting ambulance. The Sergeant produced a notebook and pencil.

Ralston went over to stand in front of Willie who continued to stare at the blood stain.

'I'm sorry to have to do this, sir, but I must ask some questions,' he said quietly.

Willie didn't reply.

Ralston glanced at Andrew. 'Perhaps a drink?'

Andrew rose. 'I'll get him one.'

'Sir, can you hear me?'

Willie slowly nodded.

'Good. Now as I say, I'm sorry I have to do this. But the questions have to be asked.'

'Can't you just leave us alone,' Georgina snapped. 'Can't you see the state he's in. The state we're all in.'

'That's all right, Georgina,' Willie whispered. 'The chap's only doing his job.'

'Thank you, sir.' Ralston took a deep breath. 'Now, first of all, did your son have any enemies?'

Willie, still staring at the blood stain, frowned. 'Not that I'm aware of. He was well liked by everyone.'

'I see. According to your housekeeper Mrs Coltart a number of items are missing which could mean your son disturbed a burglar and that his death was the outcome.'

'Here you are, Willie, get that down you,' Andrew said, handing Willie a large glass of Scotch.

'Georgina?'

She shook her head.

'Rose?'

'No thank you. I'd be sick if I drank alcohol.'

Andrew returned to the decanter to pour himself a stiff one. He too was in a state of shock, though not nearly as badly affected as the others. Poor Willie, he kept thinking. Poor old chap. What a blow.

'There haven't been any burglaries in the area for quite a while, sir, and we caught that blighter, a gypsy who was passing through. Have there been any strangers around here of late?'

'No,' Willie croaked, and had a gulp of whisky. In his mind he kept envisaging Ian's body and the horror of his first sight of it.

'Are you certain, sir?'

'Quite.' Willie hesitated, frowned, then glanced up at the Detective Inspector. 'That's not true. There was a man here yesterday looking for work. Name of McDougall. There was something about him I didn't like, a sort of shiftiness, so I told him there was nothing available and sent him on his way.'

'McDougall, eh?'

'From Glasgow,' Willie added. He then repeated the story Sean had given him about being laid off and having come to the country to find work.

'Glasgow,' Ralston mused. That was interesting. 'I don't suppose he mentioned where he's staying?' Ralston asked, thinking the man was probably sleeping rough.

'As a matter of fact he did. The Clachan pub. He's staying there.'

'Is he indeed,' Ralston smiled. 'Can I use your telephone again, sir?'

'Help yourself.'

Willie went back to staring at the blood stain.

Sean was about to go down and pay his bill, then leave, when the door to his bedroom opened and two men strode in.

Rozzers, they had it stamped all over them.

His shoulders slumped. The game was up.

'Bridie, can I come in?'

A tear-stained Bridie let Mrs Coltart into her room.

'Are you all right?'

All right? She'd never be all right again. 'I'm sorry, Mrs Coltart, truly I am.'

Fresh tears appeared, to go coursing down her face.

Mrs Coltart was puzzled. They were all upset, dreadfully

so, but why was Bridie taking it so badly? It was clear how distraught the girl was.

'Why don't you take the rest of the day off, Bridie.'

'Thank you, Mrs Coltart.'

Mrs Coltart took Bridie by the arm and guided her to the rumpled bed where they both sat. 'Is there anything you want to tell me?'

'No, Mrs Coltart,' Bridie choked.

'It won't go any further. I promise you. Sometimes it's better to talk.'

And talk Bridie desperately wanted to do. 'Oh, Mrs Coltart,' she whispered, gazing at the housekeeper through eyes filled with pain. 'I loved him you see. And he me.'

That jolted Mrs Coltart who'd never guessed. Not even had an inkling.

Bridie poured out her heart.

Willie lifted the phone which he'd been called to answer. 'Yes, Detective Inspector?' He re-entered the drawing room where the others were still gathered after taking a call from the Inspector. He went straight to the decanter.

'Well, darling?' Georgina queried.

He poured himself a drink then turned to face them. There was a lump in his throat which felt the size of an egg.

'They apprehended McDougall at the pub just as he was about to leave and catch a train. The Detective Inspector said we were fortunate it's a Sunday with a diminished service otherwise he would have already been away.'

Willie paused, then went on, 'They found a number of items in McDougall's luggage, one a silver and enamelled cigarette box which tallies with the description of the one Mary gave me years ago. I've been asked to go to the station and identify McDougall and the items.'

Andrew immediately rose. 'I'll drive you.'

Willie nodded his appreciation, then downed his whisky in a single gulp.

'I can't help it,' he said. 'I simply can't.' And with that he began to cry.

Georgina was swiftly by his side to enfold him in her arms.

'Ian, oh Ian,' Willie sobbed.

Andrew came across Rose halfway down the stairs sitting on a large windowsill gazing out.

'Hello,' he said.

She glanced at him, her expression grim as could be. It was now Monday morning. Nobody except Andrew had appeared for breakfast.

'Have you seen Pa?' she asked.

Andrew shook his head.

'He must still be in his room then.'

'I suppose so.'

She returned to gazing out the window. 'I wish I'd been nicer to Ian,' she said wistfully.

'Nicer?'

'We were always jibing at one another. But there were times when I was downright cruel to him. How I regret that now.'

'You were brother and sister, that sort of thing is common between siblings. We were forever at each other's throats. But it didn't really mean anything. And it certainly didn't reflect how we felt about one another. I admit I really never got on with my brother Peter, but that was a clash of personalities more than anything else. We were so very different you see.'

Rose didn't reply to that.

'Quite normal. Honestly, you've nothing to reproach yourself about.'

'I still wish it had been different. And now he's gone it's left such a big hole in all our lives. I don't think Pa will ever get over what's happened.'

'Maybe not get over, Rose, but he will come to terms with it. Time is a great healer after all.'

She smiled. 'You're very sweet, Andrew. And it's kind of you to offer to stay on for a bit and help.'

'It was the least I could do. Willie needs a friend right now and that's what we are. He'd do the same for me.'

'I'd like to think he would.'

'I know he would.'

Andrew reached out and touched Rose gently on the face. In a strange way Ian's death had brought things totally into perspective. Where there had been doubt before none now remained. It was as though . . . a calmness had descended on him.

'Perhaps this isn't the time or place, but please, and I beg you, forgive me for Georgina. I'm only a mortal man after all, with all the weaknesses men have. Perhaps more weaknesses than many. I desperately want your forgiveness, truly I do. And hope things might go back to how they were between us. I need your trust again, a trust I give you my solemn oath I'll never again betray.'

She gazed up at Andrew, in her heart of hearts wanting to believe him.

He knew he'd said enough for the present. 'I'll leave you to your reflections, Rose.'

Andrew withdrew his hand and strode off down the stairs, Rose staring at his retreating back.

She continued to stare in that direction long after he'd disappeared.

Chapter 30

Willie sat staring vacantly ahead. He was unshaven, his hair rumpled and, despite the fact it was almost noon, still in his pyjamas and dressing-gown. His mind was numb with grief.

Georgina let herself quietly into the bedroom having been about household duties. She gazed in concern at her husband – her heart going out to him.

'Willie?'

He blinked, then focused on her. 'I was just thinking about the war,' he said.

'The war?'

'I remember wondering at the time what it was like for those thousands and thousands of families who received the dreaded telegram. Now I know.'

'Oh Willie,' she whispered. Crossing the room, she knelt beside him.

'The years it takes you to bring up a child. To teach them this and that, go through all the pains they experience while growing up, the emotional expenditure. And then, right at the beginning of manhood, with everything before them, to have them taken from you. I could accept it more easily if it had been due to illness. That, though unfair, you can somehow understand. But to lose them due to an act of sheer wanton violence . . .' He broke off and swallowed hard.

'I know,' she said softly.

'At least in the war when your boy went off you knew it could happen. But we had no warning whatsoever. One day Ian was alive, the next dead. And for what? That's the galling thing, for what? Nothing, when you come down to it.'

'Would you like a cup of tea, Willie?'

He shook his head.

'Anything else?'

'No, Georgina.'

A wave of great tenderness swept over her. She felt bad enough, but how must he feel? The reflection of that was all too obvious in his face.

'Why don't you go back to bed and sleep for a while? You had hardly any last night.'

'I still wouldn't sleep. All I can think of is Ian. In my mind I keep going over conversations we had, times spent together. He was a good lad, Georgina, and I was extremely proud of him.'

He took a deep breath. 'How am I going to face the funeral? It'll be a nightmare. A complete nightmare that doesn't bear thinking about.'

'You'll get through it, Willie, you'll see. And I'll be there to support you. And Andrew. Don't forget we'll be amongst friends. They'll all understand and be with you, my darling.'

There was silence between them for a few seconds, then Willie said, 'We must play "Onward Christian Soldiers". That was Ian's favourite hymn. I remember him mentioning it once.'

'Then we shall.'

'"Onward Christian Soldiers",' Willie repeated, and slowly shook his head.

'How's Rose?' he asked.

'I spoke to her a little while ago and she's bearing up.'

'Good. That's good.'

'Now why don't I take you through to the bathroom and shave you. I haven't done that for years.'

He smiled in memory.

She took his hand and tugged him to his feet. 'Come on. And after the shave you shall have a nice long bath. A proper soak, you'll enjoy that.'

'Yes,' he whispered. Halfway to the bathroom he stopped. 'I keep thinking it's all a bad dream and that any moment I'll wake up and find Ian's still alive. Only it isn't a dream, is it?'

'No,' she said.

The instant Bridie thought of it a sense of tranquillity descended on her, driving out the demons that had been tearing at her since hearing that awful word, murdered, and finding it to be true.

She sighed. Yes, that was what she would do. Had to do.

She slipped out of the house in the dead of night. Underneath her coat she was wearing only a nightdress.

She shivered. It was cold, but not as cold as it had been earlier at the funeral. What a turn out it had been, the church packed, with many people having to stand.

Mrs Coltart had insisted she sit beside her, the only person other than Mr Seaton to know her secret. He hadn't spoken to her since Ian's death. Perhaps he'd temporarily forgotten how it had been between them. *Was* between them, she corrected herself.

She glanced up at the sky which was heavily overcast. It might snow, she thought. The night had that feel about it.

A little way from The Haven she turned and looked back. Her stay there had been a happy one, she reflected. She had no regrets.

She walked to the cemetery and through it to Ian's grave adorned with the many wreaths and flowers that had been placed on it.

She removed some of the flowers to make a space for herself. Then, taking off her coat which she placed aside, she lay down on the freshly dug earth.

'Oh, Ian, my darling, my true love,' she whispered. 'We couldn't be together in this life but we can in the next. It's all been solved, you see. Now we shall be as one for evermore.'

She'd been right about the snow. Large flakes of it suddenly appearing to come spiralling down. Soon the flakes had increased in intensity until there were myriads of them dancing and weaving their way from Heaven.

Bridie closed her eyes and conjured up a picture of Ian in her mind. Sir Ian of Seaton, her knight in shining armour, her prince, her lover for all time.

She began to feel drowsy as the cold seeped into her. Not the unpleasant experience she'd imagined, quite comforting really.

'Ian,' she murmured.

And then he was there beside her, smiling, holding out his hand for her.

'Awful,' Andrew said quietly. 'Just awful.' He'd found Rose on her own. The pair of them were now alone together.

'She loved Ian apparently. None of us knew that.'

Andrew shook his head. 'It makes you think, doesn't it?'

'Yes it does.'

They were silent for a few moments, Andrew thinking how lovely Rose looked. He could just imagine her at Drummond, the lady of the house.

'Do you mind if I sit down?'

She gestured to a chair. 'Please do.'

'Life's a funny thing,' he mused once he was seated. 'As my father Murdo used to say, you never know the minute till the minute after.'

'True enough,' Rose agreed.

'"Father forgive them for they know not what they do."'

Rose blinked at him. 'I beg your pardon?'

'I was quoting scripture. Or as best as I can remember that is. Whatever, the sentiment is right.'

'I don't understand.'

'I was talking about me and how stupid I've been.' He took a deep breath. 'Have I lost you, Rose?'

She glanced away and didn't reply.

'Forgiveness is a great thing, Rose. Do you have that quality in you?'

Again she said nothing.

'I swore to you that I'd never betray you again and I won't. You have my word on that.'

'Do I?' she queried softly.

'Yes.'

She turned and stared into his eyes, looking for the truth. This was far too big a decision to make a mistake. In his eyes she saw the real Andrew, that of a child. But there again, weren't most men precisely that?

'What are you asking?' she demanded.

'Let's give it a bit of time, to get over all this for a start. And then maybe . . . if you'll have me . . .' He broke off in sudden confusion and embarrassment. The latter most unlike him.

'I love you,' he whispered. 'God knows I've fought against it because of our ages. But I do.'

His eyes were pleading, desperate almost as she continued to gaze into them. She melted inside, her feelings rushing to the surface. 'We do need that time you spoke about, most certainly.' Then, huskily, 'I love you too.'

And so it was sealed. There was an understanding between them.

'Dear me,' Jack Riach declared. 'She froze to death.'

'Covered from head to toe in snow when they found her.'

It was the first Friday night since Andrew's return from The Haven and, as usual, he and Jack were in the pub.

Jack knew this was the ending he'd been searching for for his novel. He'd have to re-jig it a bit of course but apart from that it was perfect.

'It only came out afterwards that she and Ian had been in love,' Andrew went on. 'A truly tragic affair.'

'Indeed.'

'A pleasant lass too.'

Jack groped for his pint and had a sip. There was part

of him felt ghoulish, grasping, as Andrew had called it, a tragic affair, but it suited his purposes and he hadn't known either of them. And, after all, hadn't it been worse with his plays about the war? He had been friends, fought and almost died, with many of those people.

'There's something else.'

'Oh?'

'I've decided to marry Rose. We have an understanding. But it'll take time, Jack. It'll take time.'

Jack's scarred face creased with delight. 'That's wonderful.'

'If it does come off I hope you'll be my best man.'

'I'd be honoured, old boy. Honoured.'

'In the meantime keep this strictly to yourself and Hettie.'

Jack tapped his nose. 'Mum's the word. You can count on it.'

Andrew leant back in his chair and sighed, visualising Rose in his mind and wishing she was there. Wanting her company.

Wanting it with every ounce of his being.

Andrew picked up his pen and stared at the sheet of paper in front of him. 'Dear Willie,' he began.

He went on to say he hoped Willie was starting to come to terms with Ian's death and then suggested he might visit again shortly, if that was agreeable.

Andrew smiled to himself. Of course he continued being concerned for his friend but there was quite another reason for the proposed visit.

The letter was the first of many and the start of his courtship of Miss Rose Seaton.

Epilogue

A ndrew and Rose emerged from the gloom of the church into brilliant sunshine which made them both blink. Overhead the bells began to peal.

Willie, directly behind the couple, couldn't help but glance across the graveyard to where Ian was buried, and close by Bridie Flynn. He had mixed emotions about Bridie, whose brother it had been who'd murdered Ian. Not only Ian but another chap in Glasgow which made him a double murderer. Murders for which Sean Flynn had now paid the ultimate price. He wouldn't be killing anyone else.

At least the girl hadn't known it was her brother who'd killed Ian, that was something she'd thankfully been spared.

Georgina moved up beside Willie. 'It was a beautiful ceremony,' she said. 'It couldn't have gone better.'

Willie hadn't been too sure about the wedding when Andrew had first brought it up, but Rose had put his worries to rest and so he'd consented to the marriage and given them his blessing. Andrew as a son-in-law, he reflected not for the first time. What a bizarre thought.

'Wasn't James good?' Georgina crooned, and kissed the baby she was holding.

Willie beamed at his new son and heir. As healthy and lusty a boy as you could imagine. He was certain James was the spitting image of Ian. There again, it might only be his imagination.

He thought of how close he and Georgina had become since Ian's death.

As for Georgina, she had no regrets about Andrew. Her feelings for him had vanished. The only man she wanted now was Willie, good in bed or not.

His failings simply didn't matter to her any more.

Jack Riach took Hettie by the hand. 'Don't let me fall down the steps,' he whispered.

'I won't.'

'I'd look awfully silly sprawled on my backside. They'd all think I was drunk.'

'Which you will be later,' she teased.

'Damn right. And you will be too I hope.'

'We'll see.' She smiled.

Jack sighed with pleasure. His novel had been submitted to the publishers some months previously and they were very excited about it. They were certain it was going to be both a critical and financial success. He'd promised himself to start another before the year was out.

Andrew turned to Rose and stared into her eyes. 'Happy?'

'You have to ask?'

'No, Rose. I don't suppose I do. I know I certainly am.'

A cheer and applause went up from the onlookers as the bride and groom kissed.

Passionately.

THIS SIDE
OF HEAVEN

PART ONE

Dragonholme
1911–12

1

Sheila hummed to herself as she trudged along the tow path that would shortly join up with the narrow dirt road leading down to Dragonholme. She was on her way back from Bogside Farm, where she'd been buying eggs, a journey she made once a fortnight.

It was early July, and so far the summer of 1911 had been a glorious one. A glance at the fat sun hanging heavily overhead told her it was getting on for teatime. She started walking faster, as some of the eggs she was carrying were wanted for the evening meal.

A few minutes later she came in sight of the sea. What she saw on the horizon caused her to come up short and catch her breath. Could it be? Was it them?

Twenty-eight dots: twenty-eight boats. The number couldn't be coincidental; it had to be the fleet coming home! Excitement gripped her, her da and brothers were coming home, and Eric – beautiful, adorable Eric whom she loved to distraction, he was coming home as well.

There was a strong northerly blowing which meant that the fleet would be tying up before long. She calculated that if the wind didn't change they'd be entering harbour in less than an hour.

From her clifftop vantage, she must be the first of the village to spy the fleet. She must hurry down to Dragonholme and cry the news so that all would be ready in time for when the catch was landed, the first catch to come into Dragonholme that season.

The sound of a horse snorting behind her made Sheila jump. Whirling round, she found herself looking at a middle-aged man on a hunter.

'Who are you?' he asked, in a voice that expected answers. His eyes never left her face.

A toff – one of the gentry, Sheila thought, instinctively straightening her shoulders and raising her chin.

'Sheila Beattie,' she replied politely.

'From Dragonholme?'

She nodded.

'You'll be Davey Beattie's daughter then?'

That surprised her. How would her da know a toff like this?

'I am,' she nodded, almost making it sound like a challenge.

'A fine skipper, one of the best along this coast; and that's saying something,' the gentleman replied with a thin smile.

Sheila turned and pointed out to sea. 'That's the fleet coming home. I just spotted them a minute ago.'

The black hunter, a vicious-looking beast, pawed the ground while the man shaded his eye to gaze in the direction she was pointing.

'Aye, so it is. And no doubt that'll be the *Bluebell* leading the way.'

Bluebell was the name of her father's boat. It was a new drifter, a Zulu, launched only the previous year. Davey had invested every penny the family possessed on its purchase.

'As admiral of our fleet it's his place to be out front,' Sheila informed him proudly.

The man's eyes twinkled, amused by her immediate and fierce show of pride. 'How old are you, lass?' he asked suddenly, his eyes no longer on the fleet.

That's none of your business, Sheila thought. 'Sixteen, sir,' she answered grudgingly. Her mother would die if she thought she'd been rude to a gentleman.

Suddenly Sheila knew who this stranger was, who he had to be. He must be the new laird who'd bought Dragonholme Hall after the death of the old laird, Mr Magnussen. Dragonholme Hall was in the valley about half a mile away. The original Hall had been built a thousand years ago by Einar Hairybreeks, the leader of the vikings who'd founded the village. Vikings who'd

8

come, and stayed, and after a while had intermarried with the local Scots.

'You must be Mr Campbell,' she dared, really looking at him for the first time.

'Aye, that's me,' James Campbell smiled.

Sheila immediately curtsied as she'd been taught, as she'd always done when coming into the presence of the old laird, a right kindly man if ever there was one. She looked up at James Campbell, but there was no kindness in those eyes.

'Excuse me, sir, but I'll have to be going,' she said, suddenly anxious to be gone. 'I must away down to the village and cry the news about the fleet.'

James Campbell pursed his lips, his hand thin and white against the neck of his monstrous horse. He was disappointed she was leaving him so soon. He'd taken to the tawny-haired girl. She was pleasant company.

'Till the next time then,' he answered slowly, patting Satan's gleaming skin.

'Good-bye,' Sheila mumbled, and without waiting for a reply started running along the road, her basket of eggs clutched securely to her side.

At the point where the road fell away in its descent to the village she turned to gaze behind her, and he was still there, exactly as she'd left him; facing out to sea, his eyes fixed on the home-bound fleet. For no reason she could think of and despite the heat of the day, an ice-cold shiver ran through her. Then, shaking herself, she hurried on her way.

Mrs Johnstone, whose husband crewed the *Fear Not*, was the first person Sheila saw to shout the news to. Within minutes all of Dragonholme knew that the men had returned from the northern fishing grounds, and that the same number of boats were coming back as had left at the beginning of May when the fleet had set sail for Lerwick in the Shetlands.

Peg Beattie, Sheila's mother, was already looking out the gutting knives when Sheila burst into the house, flushed and breathless. In her mid-forties, Peg was stout but still handsome, her face marked as much by kindness as by hard work and care. Sheila was the youngest of her children, and the only girl. Her sons were all aboard the *Bluebell* with Davey.

Peg paused in what she was doing, her brows drawn, her eyes clouded.

'Ten days earlier than last year. The fishing must have been poor for them to be so far down the coast this early in the month,' she said.

'I hadn't thought of that.' In her excitement Sheila had completely forgotten that the fleet weren't expected till the end of next week.

At that moment Rhona and Maggie came flying in through the door. Rhona was married to Jack, Peg's oldest son, and Maggie to Dougal. Both of them lived close by. Peg's youngest son, Bob, still lived at home and shared the back room of the two-roomed house with Sheila.

Sheila got on great guns with Rhona, but not with Maggie, who was considered a pain in the bumbeleerie. The trouble with Maggie was that she was domineering and overbearing, and though it didn't bother Rhona or Peg, who knew how to handle her, Sheila was too young and fiery herself to bother about diplomacy.

'You and Rhona get the table and I'll help Ma with the packing boxes,' Maggie said to Sheila.

Sheila put her hands on her hips. 'Since when did you start giving orders in our house?' she demanded.

Maggie made a gesture of impatience. 'I'm not giving orders. I'm merely getting things organized.'

'It sounded very much like orders to me.' Sheila glared at her sister-in-law defiantly.

'This isn't the time for bickering. Sheila, do as Maggie has suggested,' Peg said firmly.

'Come on then,' Sheila said to Rhona, and led the way out of the house round to the partially covered lean-to at the rear where the gutting table was kept out of season, wrapped in an old tarpaulin.

'Where are the weans?' Sheila asked as they walked to the back.

'They're already away down to the harbour,' Rhona smiled. 'They were too excited about seeing their father to wait for me.'

They uncovered the heavy table with its hinged legs.

'You shouldn't let Maggie rile you,' Rhona advised.

'It's that manner of hers. It aye puts my back up.' Sheila grunted as she and Rhona lifted the table up into a carrying position.

But even Maggie's faults went from Sheila's mind as she and Rhona staggered down to the harbour where they set the table up in what was traditionally the Beattie spot. Minutes later Peg and Maggie joined them, their arms filled with packing boxes.

'There are more boxes still to come,' Peg said, laying the gutting knives out on the table.

Maggie was already shrugging into one of the heavy leather aprons that had been inside the topmost box she had been carrying. When she saw Sheila glowering at her she said, 'I'll get them if you like.'

'You can both get them,' said Peg, nipping that in the bud. Even though Maggie had volunteered herself for the task there could still have been a fight.

Sheila and Maggie returned to the house leaving Rhona to sort out the boxes that had already been brought down, and Peg to hone the knives to razor sharpness on a whetstone that had been in the Beattie family time out of mind.

Just outside the harbour entrance Davey gave the signal for the lug rig to be dropped. Creaking and flapping, the sails, tanned black from successive dippings in cutch, sank on to the deck where Uncle Matt was waiting ready to square them away.

Sheila watched in admiration as the *Bluebell*'s black painted hull, her name picked out in gold leaf, swung towards that part of the quayside where she was to be tied up. Oh, but she was bonny right enough; with her white wheelhouse and mastheads, blue gunwhales, and dark azure blue coamings and hatches. Sheila thought she had never seen a finer boat.

With a resounding bump the *Bluebell* kissed the quayside, causing its sixty-foot masts to quiver high overhead. It was Bob who sprang on to the quayside to secure her fore and aft. A second later, he was in his mother's arms, hugging Peg tightly and saying how grand it was to be back again in Dragonholme.

One after the other the fleet entered the harbour: the *Muirneag*, the *Star of Hope*, the *Foamcrest*, and the *Gypsy Queen*.

And there was Eric, her darling man, bobbing up and down as he tried to wave to her and attend to his duties at the same time. Like a young tree he was, strong and straight and just a bit wild. His eyes were the palest blue, his blond cropped hair so bleached from the sea as to be almost white. Sheila's heart hammered within her at the sight of him, and she gave up a silent prayer of gratitude to the Good Lord for having seen fit to bring him home safe and sound.

Dougal had his son, wee Dougal, cradled in one arm, and his daughter, Violet, in the other, Maggie beside him, staring up into her husband's face with unconcealed joy.

Rhona and Jack were embracing, while Ian stood by his da's side, one finger in his mouth, the other hand clutching hold of Jack's sweater as though to ensure that Jack wasn't going to suddenly disappear again. A queer, quiet lad was Ian, fairy-touched, said some, but lucky with it, somehow.

There was no wife there to greet Uncle Matt. No wife and no daughters or sons. Auntie Lily had died six years ago, and they'd been a childless couple. Uncle Matt was Davey's older brother, but had never owned a boat of his own or even been the skipper of one. Uncle Matt was a man who liked to take orders, not give them. It was a wise man who knew his own level, Davey had once said, and although the conversation hadn't been about his brother, it was Uncle Matt that Davey had had in mind.

The *Gypsy Queen*, Eric's father's boat, was tied off now, and Eric himself was hurrying towards her. He stopped just short of her, his body trembling, embarrassed to hug her in public.

'You look well,' she said, clasping her hands behind her. What an awful trite thing to come out with, she silently scolded herself. But, like him, she felt constrained by being surrounded by so many folk.

He couldn't seem to hold still.

'Aye, and so do you.'

Eye into eye they stared at one another. All she wanted to know passed between them that way. He still loved her, she was his special lass, his one and only.

'Later then?' he finally whispered, his eyes darting nervously around.

'When?'

'As soon as you can get away. After you've eaten. I'll be waiting.'

'The usual place?'

Eric nodded. 'And I'll bring a wee something to keep out the cold.'

'You daft haddie, it isn't cold at night at this time of year,' she laughed.

The corners of his sparkling eyes crinkled with his laugh. 'I'll bring it anyway, just to be on the safe side.'

She reached out and touched his hard, calloused hand, so filled with emotion that she thought her heart must surely explode.

'All right you lot, can we get back to work now!' Davey called from the deck of the *Bluebell*. As always he was puffing on his old clay pipe which, like nearly all the fishermen he knew, he smoked turned upside down.

The Beattie brothers jumped back aboard the *Bluebell* to begin the business of hand winching the catch on to the quayside. From there it would go to where the women

13

had set up. Eric gave her one last smile and returned to the *Gypsy Queen* to help his da and brothers do the same.

Soon their knives were flashing. Sheila, Peg, Rhona and Maggie expertly gutted cran after cran of herrings, taking it in turn to break from this chore to pack the gutted fish into boxes, covering them with salt to keep them fresh.

The herring scales got everywhere – over their faces, up their arms, even under their clothing and headscarves – but none of the women minded. There was no point in complaining, even if they did. Fish were money. In fact, fish were their whole survival. What was a little physical inconvenience weighed against that?

At long last their boxes were full, but still the gutting continued, for part of the catch was to be taken home and smoked.

McPherson, the carter, put in an appearance, he and his son stacking the Beattie boxes alongside the others he'd already collected. He kept careful tally in his fish book. McPherson would be taking the Dragonholme catch through to Portnessie where the buyers and railhead were. Portnessie was a small fishing port ten miles further up the coast, and the buying and selling centre for all the villages thereabouts. From Portnessie some of the fish would go to the markets in Edinburgh and Glasgow, while another portion would eventually find its way to Poland, Latvia, Germany and other European countries.

Finally, with the sun just about to go down, the gutting was finished for the day. Sheila, Rhona and Maggie started humping the fish to be smoked to the smoke-house behind the Beattie home. While the younger women were doing this, Peg washed down and tidied up the area where they'd been working.

As was the custom on the first day back in the home port, once the catch was unloaded the men had all gone to the pub. Seeing that the gutting was finished and the packed fish on its way to Portnessie, the men would now begin to make their way home for the evening meal.

After that, many of them would return to the pub again to carry on where they'd left off.

When the fish to be smoked were all put away Rhona and Maggie returned to their own homes, and Sheila to hers, making straight for the hand pump in the kitchen where she gave her hands, face and hair a thorough wash.

A pot of lentil soup that Peg had begun that morning was now bubbling invitingly on the cast-iron range, alongside which a dozen herrings were being cooked on the brander.

Peg cut the best part of a loaf into thick slices, then started buttering each slice. Back from the pub, Davey sat in his usual chair by the side of the range gazing deep into the glowing coals. Bob was in another chair, having a quick snooze before the meal was dished up.

'You're home gey early this time round?' Peg prompted quietly, her eyes darting from her buttering to Davey. He had never been a talkative man, but she knew him so well that words weren't needed.

Davey roused himself from his reverie. 'The fishing wasn't so good further north, but picked up a wee bit once we got down to Peterhead. Apart from that, the shoals are coming south more quickly this year.' He paused for a moment, staring past her. 'But don't ask me why, it's just one of those things.'

'We'll do all right out the season though, won't we?' Peg asked softly, a hint of worry tinging her voice.

Davey sniffed and knocked some dottle from his pipe. 'What we brought in today was far and away our best catch to date. Let's just say that from here on in we'd better do an awful lot better than we have up to now.'

Peg bit her lip. Despite her own suspicions, this wasn't what she'd been hoping to hear. Fear clutched at her insides. The fishing had been marvellous for the past thirty-odd years, but that didn't mean it would continue to be so. She remembered only too well the hungry times of her youth when the fishing had been diabolical and poverty had covered the east coast like a shroud.

Sensing Peg's worry, Davey gave her a reassuring smile. 'Wait till we get to the Silver Pits, they've never let us down yet,' he said. The Silver Pits were particularly rich grounds that the Dragonholme fleet fished working out of either Hull or Grimsby.

'Aye, the Silver Pits,' echoed Peg, cheering considerably. Davey had always been lucky there.

A few minutes later Peg told Sheila to rouse Bob, and started to serve out the soup. The eggs that had originally been planned were now forgotten; fish and the sort of soup that sticks to your ribs were what were needed for men who'd been on the sea.

'Ah,' said Davey, as she passed out the dishes. 'Now that's a fair treat for an old sailor.' He quickly finished his soup, holding out his bowl for seconds. As Peg laid the second bowlful before him, she saw that a frown had darkened his face. 'Is something bothering you?' she asked.

Davey broke a slice of bread in half, then into quarters. 'I was just thinking about steam trawlers. There are more than ever fishing this year, including six new ones out of Portnessie.'

'Owned by James Campbell, him that's bought Dragonholme Hall,' chimed in Bob, suddenly remembering that he could use his mouth to talk as well as eat.

'Aye, that's a fact. Campbell's added them to the fleet of sail trawlers he owns. It must have cost him a pretty penny to buy six of them at one go.' Davey was visibly impressed by this show of affluence and success. As a drifterman, Davey disliked sail trawlers and loathed the new steam variety. He believed that the steam trawlers ripped up the beds below the fishing grounds, destroying the feed.

'He's a self-made man, you know,' Davey went on, unusually talkative. 'He's not one of those who comes into this world with a silver spoon in his mouth.'

'I met him the day,' Sheila joined in. 'He said you were one of the best skippers along this coast.'

16

Davey blinked. 'Met who, girl?'

She had everyone's attention now. 'The new laird. I was coming home from the farm when he came up behind me on a great black horse. I had just spied the fleet at the time.'

'And he talked to you?' Peg prompted, always curious about lives so different from her own.

Davey interpreted Peg's question in his own way. 'And why shouldn't he speak to her?' he wanted to know. 'Sheila's just as good as him who was born in a house in Portnessie exactly the same as this one.' As far as Davey was concerned, being free and Scots were all the qualifications a body needed in life.

'He might have been born in a house like ours, but he speaks right posh now. A proper gentleman and no mistake,' Sheila went on enthusiastically.

Davey tugged at his beard, his sudden indignation already on the wane.

'Aye, well Campbell spends a lot of time in Glasgow and Edinburgh. London even, I'm told. He'll have picked up his new speech and manners there no doubt. But don't be misled by his outward appearance or the way he sounds now. Underneath it all James Campbell is *still* fisher folk, and a damn fine skipper in his own right.' Davey paused, then went on in a tone that was almost coy. 'And he said I was one of the best skippers along the coast, eh?'

Sheila nodded.

A smile teased at the corners of Davey's mouth. He was well pleased by the compliment.

'So what's his wife like?' Peg asked eagerly.

Davey helped himself to another slice of bread. 'I've never seen her, but I've heard she's genuine Edinburgh Morningside.'

'What does that mean?' asked Bob, his face screwed up in puzzlement and his spoon in mid-air.

'Ach, don't you know anything?' scoffed Sheila. 'Morningside is where the Edinburgh toffs live; them

17

that never do a stroke of work and ride around in fancy carriages all day long.'

'And the women wear beautiful gowns and have hands that are like velvet to touch,' Peg added, her eyes taking on a faraway look as she tried to imagine herself with such luxuries. She'd never owned a gown in her life; her hands were as hard and workworn as any man's.

'All I know,' said Davey, 'is that there's a family; two boys. Both of whom go away to school in the English fashion. You know, a school where they actually live.'

Peg shook her head in maternal condemnation. 'I've always thought that a gey uncivilized way of doing things, sending wee mites off on their own like that. But there you are, the English are an uncivilized race if ever there was one.' There was a general murmur of agreement.

'The Campbells can only have moved into the Hall during the past day or two,' mused Peg. 'I know for certain that the decorators were still there at the end of last week.' How long would it be, she wondered, before she clapped eyes on Mrs Campbell? Almost every woman in the village was dying to get a look at her. Wait till they heard that the laird's wife was Edinburgh Morningside!

Sheila cleared away the soup bowls and placed the herrings on the table. After slicing the first one open Davey asked for the white stuff to be passed. The word salt was never uttered by him – every fisherman knew it was unlucky.

'What I don't understand,' said Sheila, 'is why Mr Campbell would want to buy Dragonholme Hall. Why come here where he's a stranger? If he wanted a bigger or grander house why not buy one in Portnessie? Or Glasgow, or Edinburgh?'

Davey chuckled. 'It might well be he fancies being called the laird, as is his entitlement now that he owns the Hall. It's been said before now that there's a streak of vanity in the man.'

18

Having finished all that he wanted to eat, and not one for sitting around chatting, Bob excused himself. 'I'm away back to The Haven,' he said, giving Peg a peck on the cheek. 'Good food always makes me thirsty.'

'Collecting Thomasina McLean on the way no doubt?' Sheila teased.

'Listen to the pot calling the kettle black,' Bob jibed back. 'As if you won't be seeing Eric Gifford later.'

'I might just go for a walk with him,' Sheila replied airily.

'We all know about your walks,' Bob said, giving his mother and father a meaningful wink.

Sheila blushed and looked away. Bob grinned with his success in embarrassing his sister. It was a rare day when he got the better of her.

Davey cleared his throat and stared into his cup of strong tea. He knew damn well what the young ones got up to, hadn't he and Peg been young themselves once? But it was wrong of Bob to hint at such goings-on in front of his parents, particularly his mother: it showed a certain lack of respect. 'I think you'd better run along before you say any more,' Davey advised quietly.

Realizing that he'd overstepped the mark, Bob muttered his good-byes and strode off into the night.

'I'll clear up,' Sheila said, starting to collect the dirty plates together.

Peg stared at Sheila, remembering what she herself had been like at that age. She and Davey had been courting then, just as Sheila and Eric were now. Davey had been working on a Skaffie called *Buttercup*. Peg brought her gaze on to Davey and a mellow warmth filled her. He was a man in a million, her Davey. She wouldn't trade him for all the tea in China. 'Never mind the dishes. Go off and see your lad,' Peg said to Sheila, shooing her away.

'Are you sure, Ma?'

'Aye, of course I am. Away and enjoy yourself. Just don't come in at all hours. Remember tomorrow's a working day.'

Davey lit his pipe, thinking it was going to be strange when their last two were gone from the house. He was going to miss Sheila in particular. As his only girl he'd always had a special soft spot for her. 'Well,' he said, reaching his hand out to Peg. 'It's good to be home.'

Once outside, Sheila paused to stare over Dragon-holme. There was a vibrancy in the very air that had been missing these past few months. It was the men being back; they added something when they were there, and took it away with them when they went.

She turned left at the harbour to head for the Gifford hut which was high above the tide line a little ways along the beach. There were a number of huts on this stretch of beach, used by the families who owned them for storage purposes.

The Gifford hut, as they all were, was an old undecked boat that had been cut in half breadthwise, one half, keel uppermost, embedded firmly into the sand, and planking added to make a wall of the open end into which a door had been set.

The door swung open to her touch and she peered into the darkness, knowing instantly that Eric was already inside, as he'd promised he'd be. She could feel his presence.

An arm encircled her shoulders and he drew her gently to him. She gave a soft moan as his lips found hers.

A few seconds later, he let her go while he knelt at the bottom of the door, stuffing a strip of old sacking into the chink so that the lamp he was about to light wouldn't be seen by passers-by. A Lucifer match flared, and the hut suddenly shone with a soft yellow glow.

He would have taken her in his arms again immediately, but she held him back, wanting to look at him, at every inch of him, leaner and darker than she had remembered. 'It seemed like an eternity,' she whispered, her hands holding his.

'I know,' he breathed. 'I felt the same.'

'I thought about you every day, and dreamt about you

20

every night,' she said, turning her eyes away from his in shyness.

He touched the top of her head with his lips. 'I forced myself not to think about you during the days. That would have been just asking for an accident. But I did dream about you during the nights,' he whispered, his mouth against her skin.

Suddenly she felt weak. All the months of loneliness and missing him rushing in on her. All the hours spent in dreams. She closed her eyes for a few moments, opening them again to find that she was back in his arms, her breasts hard against his chest, her happy tears trickling down her cheeks.

Gently, almost delicately, he undid her blouse, his roughened hands more pleasing than silk against her skin.

She helped him remove her clothes until at last she stood before him. She watched him as he removed his clothing. If they had been in the best hotel in Edinburgh, she couldn't have been happier. There wasn't a gentleman in the world worth half of Eric. There was no other man whose touch could so excite her, to whom she would offer herself and her love.

There was no finesse about his lovemaking: he was a rough-hewn man making rough-hewn love, but he brought her to heights of ecstasy, made her heart and body soar. Caught in a whirlpool of sensation, every nerve in her body tingling from his touch, she called out his name again and again. At last the world returned to what it had been, and there was Eric. Eric, her lover, her darling man, grinning down at her, his face damp with sweat, his eyes filled with love.

Later, he moved away from her to reach for the bottle of whisky he'd laid on the floor before she'd arrived. Eric swallowed a mouthful of whisky then extended the bottle to her.

'To keep out the cold?' she teased.

'Aye, that's right,' he nodded, giving her a fly,

conspiratorial wink which made her laugh. He often made her laugh. Laughter and love, what more could she want?

She took a sip of spirit, then another. 'That's grand,' she said. She was used to taking a dram, now and then, but enjoyed it more when he was with her. 'Marika will be telling Duncy round about now,' Sheila said, passing back the bottle. Marika Sigurdson was her great friend. The pair of them had been close pals since they were wee. Duncy Laidlaw was Marika's boyfriend.

Eric frowned. 'Telling Duncy what?'

'That he's bairned her. She found out just after he sailed.'

'So it's a wedding then,' Eric smiled, one arm around her.

'And soon. She'll have him at the altar before the fleet moves on.'

It never occurred to either of them that Duncy might not agree to the marriage. Duncy had made Marika pregnant, and when that happened the man married the woman concerned, that was one of the many unwritten rules by which the community lived.

'I'm to be best maid,' said Sheila, thinking of the new dress she'd made for the occasion, and in which, Peg had assured her, she looked a right treat. It was on the tip of her tongue to say that she thought it was high time they were wed also, or was it his intention to wait until she, too, was bairned?

She could just picture her and Eric in *their* own wee house, *their* curtains hanging on the windows, *their* braw wooden press, the status symbol every wife in the village set such store by, in the corner of the kitchen. Coming to the hut was all right at first, but now they'd outgrown it. She was sixteen and he eighteen; how much longer did he plan to wait for goodness sake? They were both more than ready for marriage and settling down.

She decided not to chisel him about it, though, not on his first night back. Soon, however, soon it would have

22

to be settled. Certainly before the fleet sailed south. She'd wait until the perfect opportunity presented itself.

'The fishing's been dreadful,' Eric said, taking another swallow of whisky.

'So my da told us.'

'I've never known a year like it,' he muttered, back at sea in his mind, thinking how few decent catches they'd had so far, and how many bad ones. Hopefully the home grounds would be luckier for them, hopefully. . . .

She ran one hand over his body, down the hardness of his chest and the smoothness of his belly. The male body held no mysteries or embarrassment for Sheila, not when she'd been brought up sharing a bedroom with three brothers, her only privacy a sheet hung up so that it screened her bed from theirs.

'What does your da say?' she asked quietly, her hand stroking his long muscular leg. She wanted a really stunning press, varnished inside as well as out, with elaborate fancy work on the corners; thistles say, or acorns, and intricate scrollwork along the beading.

'He doesn't know what to think,' answered Eric, his voice coming from far away.

January, she decided, that would be the best month for them to be kirked, for the boats would be laid up then, undergoing their yearly overhaul, and he'd be ashore.

True, the season had been a bad one so far, but all that would change when her da took the fleet to the Silver Pits, she was sure of it. Eric would finish the season with a good share, enough for them, on top of everything else, to afford a few days' honeymoon in Edinburgh where the fabled Princes Street was.

There were many fine shops in Princes Street, the best in all Scotland it was said, one of which was bound to have the press of her dreams, a press to outshine all others in Dragonholme.

'Oh, Sheila,' Eric groaned, 'I have missed you so.'

2

Dawn was a distant glimmer on the horizon as the Dragonholme fleet began slipping from the harbour on the high tide.

Sheila stood on the quayside along with the rest of the womenfolk. It was their custom to come down to see their men off. There was a stiff breeze, she noted. The fleet would make good time to the home grounds.

She felt marvellous this morning, overjoyed to be young and alive and so in love. She'd seen Eric and briefly held hands with him before he'd gone aboard the *Gypsy Queen*.

Finally the *Bluebell* pulled away from the quayside. First in, she was last out, but once beyond the harbour she would quickly take her place at the head of the fleet.

There was a clack of clogs behind Sheila, and then Marika was beside her. Marika's eyes shone brightly in the dark. 'A week this Saturday,' Marika said excitedly, the words coming out in a rush.

Sheila swept her friend into her arms and hugged her. 'Who's to be the best man?' she asked when they pulled apart.

'Tarry Dunbar,' Marika replied, pulling a face. Tarry's Christian name was John, but everyone called him by his Tee name, or nickname.

Sheila didn't like Tarry. He was a loud-mouth, a braggart and a bully, who had far too big a tip for himself. She'd never understood how Duncy, one of the nicest lads you could ever hope to meet, could be so pally with him.

'He was Duncy's firm choice,' apologized Marika. Not only did she know of Sheila's aversion to Tarry, she wasn't madly keen on him herself.

24

'That's all right,' laughed Sheila. 'I can put up with him for the day. I half expected it to be him, anyway, so it's no real shock.'

'We'll get him drunk after the meal and maybe he'll pass out early on,' suggested Marika with a giggle.

'Good idea. Once he's said his speech and done his business I'll make sure his glass is aye brimming,' laughed Sheila enthusiastically. A flat-on-his-back-for-most-of-the-evening Tarry Dunbar would suit her just fine.

Marika hiccuped. 'Indigestion,' she explained. 'It's been terrible these past few days.'

The women had started to move back to the village now, having their own work to be getting on with. Sheila and Marika, who was talking non-stop about her wedding plans, fell in behind Peg, Rhona and Maggie.

As Marika chattered on Sheila couldn't help but feel a wee bit jealous. January wasn't all that far away, she consoled herself. The time would soon fly by, and then it would be Sheila Beattie walking down the aisle to have a gold band put on her finger.

At her front door, Sheila said good-bye to Marika, then hurried round to the smokehouse where she found Rhona and Maggie already hard at it, filling up barrels with brine water into which the fish would be put to soak. Leaving them to get on with that she started getting down the tenters, the long poles on which the fish would be threaded so that they could then be hung on the hooks high overhead.

Peg wasn't there, she was round the back of the smokehouse loading up a wheelbarrow with fuel for the fire. This fuel was oak chips and sawdust, which gave the finished kipper its distinctive and nutty flavour.

Maggie and Rhona had been talking, but now Maggie addressed herself to Sheila. 'You've got a glow to your cheeks that I haven't seen there for some time,' she said lightly, her lips curled into what Sheila interpreted as a smirk.

Sheila paused to tuck a stray wisp of hair back under her headscarf. 'What's that supposed to mean?' she snapped back, knowing only too well what Maggie was insinuating.

Maggie's smile got even broader. 'You must have had a good night, I'm thinking, that's all.'

'And what's that to you?'

'There's no need to get so het up Sheila, I'm only passing the time of day,' Maggie replied, assuming an innocent expression.

Oh, how her sister-in-law annoyed her! If Rhona had said that to her they would have had a good laugh together, but not so with Maggie. Maggie was always trying to take the rise out of her, and largely succeeding.

'If I've got a glow on my cheeks this morning then that's more than I can say for you. You look bloody haggard.'

'Don't be cheeky!' Maggie screeched.

'I'll stop being cheeky if you'll stop trying to stick your knife into me!' Sheila snapped back.

'I was doing no such thing!'

'Liar!'

'What in the name of the Wee Man is going on here?' Peg exclaimed, standing in the doorway, hands on hips.

Sheila jerked a thumb at Maggie. 'She started it.'

'And you're too over-sensitive by far,' hissed Maggie.

'So what sparked this off then?' Peg asked.

A sudden silence fell inside the smokehouse. Sheila had no intention of telling her mother what Maggie had said to her, nor had Maggie.

'Am I going to have to do this all by myself?' Rhona grumbled, up-ending a box out of which a cascade of herrings tumbled into one of the barrels of brine.

Maggie grabbed the opportunity. 'I'm right with you, Rhona,' she said, and hurried over to lend a hand.

Sheila took a deep breath. 'The tenters are all laid out ready. What shall I do now, Ma?'

Well, whatever had happened, it seemed the incident

was now closed, Peg thought. Still, best to separate these two for a while, she told herself, and knew the chore she'd send Sheila on. 'Your da's told me he wants the spare net brought down from the loft as there's a lot of repair work needing doing on the one he's using. The change-over will be made the night after they've docked, and we'll start the repairs tomorrow afternoon. We're going to need some new mending needles, so I want you to run up to Taggart's and get them for me.'

At the door of the smokehouse Sheila noticed that Maggie, behind Peg's back, was giving her a filthy look. In reply she stuck out her tongue at Maggie, then put a thumb to her nose and waggled her fingers. Feeling much the better for that she set off on her errand, whistling as she went.

Tom Taggart was a man her da's age who stumped around on a wooden pin. He'd lost the lower part of his left leg in an onboard accident over twenty years before.

Having purchased the needles and had a bit of a crack with Tom, Sheila was about to make her way back to the smokehouse when her gaze fell on a cottage a wee bit up the road. The idea came to her like a bolt from the blue. Why hadn't she thought of it before! The cottage had been lying empty since the previous winter when its former occupant, old Granny Mutch, had passed on at the grand age of eighty-six.

Leaving Tom Taggart with a hasty 'good-bye', she abruptly left the shop.

Going to the cottage, Sheila opened the door and went inside. All Granny's possessions had long since been taken away by McPherson the carter who'd transported them to Lufften, where Granny's only surviving relative lived. The place was manky, but then what could you expect? The walls and floor were filthy, and the range was caked with grease, but aside from that, there was nothing wrong with the kitchen or the second room ben that a good dose of elbow grease wouldn't put right. Nothing wrong with the cottage that some curtains and

27

sunshine wouldn't fix. It would be perfect for Eric and her.

As far as Sheila was concerned, the biggest attraction about the cottage was that it was rented accommodation, and as such ideal for a couple just getting started who'd be needing to watch their silver for quite some time to come. She knew the cottage to be part of the Dragonholme estate, as were about a quarter of the houses in the village. The rest, like her da's, were privately owned. The Dragonholme estate, of which the Hall itself was the centre, comprised much land, several woods, a small trout loch, some houses in Dragonholme, and the entire clachan of Knockhammie, situated roughly mid-way between Bogside Farm and the Hall.

For several minutes, she wandered from one room to the other, seeing it as it would be. Then she realized how time was getting on. She'd better get right back or Peg would be giving her what for. Slamming the door behind her she ran down the hill, the lee wind blowing in off the sea making her cheeks burn and her hair, freed of her headscarf, stream out behind her.

'Now there goes a bonny sight,' said Tom Taggart to Handy Dandy McKechnie, a retired fisherman and former crewmate of Tom's.

Handy Dandy was just quick enough to glimpse Sheila's flying figure as it flashed by the window. 'Oh, aye, oh aye indeed,' he replied, and he and Tom exchanged smiles, each remembering other bonny young lassies long ago, and the good times he'd had with them.

Sheila couldn't sleep. She was hot and sticky, and the bedclothes seemed a ton weight on top of her. Bob had gone off ages back and was now snoring fitfully beyond the curtain.

Throwing the bedclothes aside, she rose and shrugged into a dressing gown, then lit the lamp on her bedside table. Crossing to the far side of the room she laid the lamp on a wooden chair that stood beside a large metal-banded kist, or chest, in which, during the past few years, she'd been accumulating many of the things a bride was expected to provide for her new home.

Kneeling in front of the kist she opened it, staring down at its contents, the items of which she could have reeled off in a list without missing a one.

At the very bottom of the kist were four pillows and two bolsters, each filled with feathers and down which she had gathered herself. On top of these were four fluffy blankets and two baby-blue ones, then came a half a dozen sheets made of Egyptian cotton, one dozen Turkish towels of various sizes and colours, a hard-wearing tablecloth for weekdays, a damask one for Sundays, a complete set of crockery, and finally, a number of kitchen utensils.

It was a well-filled kist; everything the best money could buy. Eric would have no cause for complaint there she assured herself. In her mind she could see the contents of her kist in use in Granny Mutch's cottage, her dream press presiding in the corner, Eric relaxing by one side of the range, she at the other getting on with some knitting or a wee bit of mending, the pair of them talking over the day's events just like her ma and da did when Davey was at home.

That range was gey past it mind, the brander was broken and she'd noticed several cracks along. . . .

'Will you put that light out and let a body get his sleep?' Bob grouched, pulling himself up on one elbow and glaring biliously at her.

'Sorry,' she mumbled contritely, silently closing the kist. Swiftly, she re-crossed the room, turned out the lamp and got back into bed.

Semple, the factor, would be in Dragonholme this coming Friday, as he was every Friday to collect the estate rents. She'd seek him out during her dinnertime and chisel him about the cottage.

Her last conscious thought was that it had turned awful humid and close, quite unlike the weather they normally had at this time of year.

On the Friday she waylaid Semple who listened sympathetically to her request. 'As there's no one else after the place I don't see why it shouldn't be yours,' he said with a smile.

Filled with elation Sheila thrashed the terms out there and then. When that was concluded she asked the factor not to mention this to any of the other villagers for the moment. 'We've not quite made the announcement yet,' she confided sweetly. 'You know what people are like.'

As she'd expected, Semple had told her that in order to guarantee tenancy she'd have to start paying rent straight away, which she agreed to. Oh well, she thought philosophically, that would give her plenty of time to get the cottage ready for when she and Eric eventually moved in.

That night Eric took her to The Halibut's Tail for a drink. She was bursting to tell him about the cottage. In fact, she had been intending to tell him, using it as a catalyst to get him to propose to her that very night, but had decided against it when she'd seen the mood he was in, which was morose to say the least.

All the way to the pub he'd gone on non-stop about how bad the fishing in the home grounds was turning out to be. 'Disastrous,' he kept saying. 'Bloody disastrous.' What the *Gypsy Queen* had taken so far hardly added up to one full hold. Where were the great shoals? It was the question everyone was asking, but not even Davey had come up with an answer.

No, she decided, watching him leaning against the bar waiting for their refills, it was definitely not the time to winkle a proposal out of him. Although he smiled when he caught her eye, his expression was still grim.

While Eric was at the bar, Tarry Dunbar and several

members of his crew entered the pub. Although only in his early twenties, Tarry owned and skippered the *Locarno*, a small Skaffie that had passed on to him when his da bought a bigger boat. Tarry stopped briefly to chat boisterously with a group of drinkers he was friendly with, then swaggered over to stand beside Eric, where he demanded loudly to be served some pints of heavy, and could Charlie Renton, who was serving, be quick about it.

Eric came back to Sheila. 'He's well guttered,' Eric said, nodding in Tarry's direction.

'They all are. Pissed as newts,' Sheila agreed.

'Ach well, it's a Friday night. If you can't let off a bit of steam then, when can you?' grinned Eric.

'I don't mind folk letting off steam. It's when they get obnoxious with it that I object.'

They sipped their drinks in silence for a few minutes.

'Your da's thinking of moving the fleet on to the Silver Pits the week after next if the fishing doesn't improve,' Eric said at last.

Sheila blinked. That was news to her. Davey hadn't mentioned a word at home about taking the fleet south so soon, at least not in front of her. She said nothing, but the look in her eyes was a question.

'Aye, it really is that bad,' Eric said, shaking his head.

'Now, don't you worry, you'll make up the season's pay when you get to the Silver Pits, I'd stake my life on that,' Sheila smiled, convinced she was right. As Davey had said, the Silver Pits had never let him down yet. No, the fleet would make up its money all right, but if they went south so early it meant she wouldn't have her darling Eric with her for as long as she'd thought. She would have to move quickly. And then a new idea struck her: he was bound to be in a mellow mood the night of Marika and Duncy's wedding. That was when she should get him to commit himself. The night of the wedding it would be, she decided.

They finished their drinks and decided to go for a stroll

along the beach. Once outside Sheila commented on the queer weather, saying she found it unusually oppressive.

'Even out at sea it's muggy.' Nor would this strange weather make it any easier for them to locate the missing big shoals. It was a known fact that weather conditions affected upper level fish and the way they ran.

Sheila clutched Eric's arm when there was a sudden commotion round the side of the pub, then the night air was punctuated by a shrill cry of pain.

'What the hell's that all about?' Eric exclaimed, moving swiftly to the corner of the pub to see what was going on.

I might have known, Sheila thought, when she saw that Tarry and his friends were there. But the figure struggling in their midst, who was that?

The figure cried out again, a pathetic sound that tore at her heartstrings.

'It's wee George Jorgesson, I recognize him now,' said Eric grimly. Removing Sheila's hand from his arm he told her to stay where she was, but she was having none of that and hurried after him.

George's face was tear streaked, his eyes starting with terror. His trousers and pants had been pulled down to his ankles, the lower part of his body smeared in hot sticky tar.

Tarry looked up at Eric and Sheila's approach, the tar dripping from the brush in his hand. 'It's my new deck boy's brothering. I'm taking him to sea for the first time on Monday,' Tarry explained.

Wee George averted his head, mortally ashamed that a lassie should see him like this.

Tarry waved the dripping tar brush in front of him. 'It's how I got my Tee name, it was done to me at my brothering.'

Brothering was a tradition on the east coast, a rite of passage performed by a lad's future crew mates before his first expedition. When the brothering was over and done, the boy was acknowledged to be grown-up, a man among men.

32

Eric had nothing against brothering, ruefully remembering his own, but it was plainly obvious that George had had more than enough.

'And where did you get that tar?' asked Sheila. 'Did that just happen to be on hand?'

Tarry grinned. 'You could say that it was around.'

These were a right bunch of animals, Sheila thought, shooting Eric a look of disgust.

'Not done yet though, eh wee George?' crooned Tarry, and dipped the brush back into the can.

Wee George moaned and started to cry again. In a sudden explosion of energy he tried to struggle free, but the two men holding him fast merely tightened their grip.

'I think it should stop now,' Eric said quietly.

Tarry paused in what he was doing to glance over his shoulder at Eric. 'Why don't you and that bird of yours just fuck off,' he replied with a smile.

The *Locarno* crew members all grinned. Obviously they thought this was great sport.

Eric knotted his fists, knowing that if it came to a fight he was on a hiding to nothing against so many. But he couldn't walk away and leave George to this lot.

Sheila was well aware of how things were developing and knew it was up to her to get George off the hook. For no matter what the provocation, Tarry daren't strike a woman who wasn't his wife.

Going to Tarry she put her hand on the brush handle next to his.

'I think you've proved what a big brave man you are,' she said sweetly.

Tarry coloured, but didn't let go when she tried to pull the brush from his grasp.

'Give it to me, Tarry, or so help me the way I'll tell this story round the village will make you a laughing stock for months to come,' she promised.

Tarry wasn't scared of any man in Dragonholme, or the Lothians come to that, but public ridicule did scare him as Sheila had known only too well it would. Slowly, reluctantly, he relinquished his grasp on the brush handle.

'Why don't you chaps go back to the pub and get yourselves another drink?' Sheila suggested.

There was a hiatus lasting a few seconds while Tarry fought back his anger and frustration. 'Aw to hell with it, I was done anyway! Let's get to The Haven where the next round's on me,' he declared loudly.

Tarry stamped off past Eric, shooting Eric a filthy look as he went by, his crew members hurrying along after him.

Sheila heaved a sigh of relief when they vanished round the corner then turned to George who was sobbing silently now that his ordeal was over.

Wisely she held back and let Eric be the one to help George.

'Come on, stop greeting, you'll live,' Eric said gruffly.

Sheila, Peg, Rhona and Maggie were out front mending the nets that had been used in the northern grounds when a horse and carriage drew up before them, and a short stocky man with a pug face and a blue bonnet got down from the driving seat.

This was Wally Simpson, the laird's ghillie.

'Good-day to you, Mrs Beattie,' said Simpson to Peg, who acknowledged the ghillie with a nod of her head, thinking to herself, now what does he want?

Simpson cleared his throat. 'It's your daughter I'm after having a word with,' he stated simply.

'Which of them did you have in mind?' asked Peg, her mending needle slipping through the net quick as a darting minnow.

Simpson screwed up his right eye, then cocked his head to one side. 'I thought you only had the one daughter and that the others were daughters-in-law?'

Peg had never liked Wally Simpson. He was a sly,

34

sleekit man. 'Are you being impertinent, Mr Simpson?' she snapped in reply, putting her hands on her hips.

Simpson stared at her. Peg standing like that reminded him of a picture he'd seen recently in the newspaper portraying a newly launched Dreadnought.

'Not in the least, only getting my facts straight,' he lied, in the slow, lazy drawl that he knew irritated people. He enjoyed irritating people – probably his only natural talent – and walking all over them given half the chance.

'Well, there's Sheila at the end. State your business to her,' Peg said coldly.

Simpson walked down the line of nets till he was facing Sheila, and insolently eyed her up and down.

'I suppose looking is about all you can manage at your age,' Sheila said, causing Rhona and Maggie to giggle.

'I've never heard the like!' spluttered Simpson.

'Ach, you hear all sorts round here, just as you meet all sorts,' Sheila smiled.

Simpson drew himself up to his full height, which wasn't considerable, and puffing out his chest, said in what he considered to be a crushing tone. 'I'll have you know you're addressing an Elder of the Knockhammie kirk.'

What a pompous wee pipsqueak, Sheila thought. 'Is that a fact?' she retorted, still smiling. 'Dearie me, they must've been right hard up!'

Rhona put a hand over her mouth to smother her laughter.

'So what can I do for you, Mr Sampson?' Sheila asked sweetly.

'Simpson,' he corrected crossly.

'Are you here as an Elder or as the laird's *servant*?'

Simpson went puce, at an uncustomary loss for words. Then, swallowing hard and wishing he'd never started this, he went on, 'Mr Campbell has sent me to fetch you to the Hall. He wants to speak to you.' An expression on his face clearly said that the eccentricities of James Campbell were no concern of his.

Peg's eyes opened wide, while Rhona and Maggie turned to stare both quizzically and speculatively at Sheila.

'What does he want to see her about?' Peg asked.

'I've really no idea,' Simpson answered truthfully.

It had to be about Granny Mutch's cottage, Sheila was thinking, and her heart sank within her. Something had gone wrong with the arrangement she had made with the factor, she just knew it! Hell and damnation, she swore inwardly, that cottage had been perfect.

'Sheila?' Peg prompted.

Sheila was about to explain to her ma about the surprise she'd been planning to spring on Eric, but changed her mind when she saw Simpson gazing quietly into the distance, listening intently to every word.

'I'll tell you the story when I return,' she said, and ran into the house where she put on her best shawl, the Chinese one that Eric had bought for her in Lowestoft the previous year.

Simpson, brandishing a whip and making noises that were supposed to convey his impatience, was back in the driving seat when she returned outside. 'I shouldn't be too long, ma,' Sheila assured Peg, giving her mother a quick peck on the cheek. Rhona held the carriage door open for her as she climbed inside.

'I'll be dying to hear what the inside of the Hall is like now they've had it completely done out,' Rhona whispered through the open window.

Sheila's reply was a conspiratorial wink. Then, in a loud voice, she cried out, 'You can drive on now, Simpson!'

Simpson snorted, his mouth pinched into an expression of distaste. Just who did she think she was, giving *him* orders? Wisely, though, he didn't climb down to dispute the matter with her; he had no wish to be at the receiving end of any more of her jibes. He cracked his whip and muttered darkly to himself.

It was the first time Sheila had ever been in a carriage,

and the experience was certainly a pleasant one. I feel just like Lady Muck, she thought. On spying Mrs Johnstone, she stuck her head out of the window and waved, laughing delightedly at Mrs Johnstone's look of stunned incredulity. She settled back into the plush seat, knowing that word of her being in the laird's carriage would be round Dragonholme like wildfire. Mrs Johnstone would see to that.

On arriving at the Hall they didn't draw up at the main entrance, but round to the side where the staff came and went and general deliveries were made. Simpson jumped down and strode through the door, leaving Sheila to make her own way after him.

Once through the door, she went along a hallway to another door that was ajar, following the sound of Simpson's voice, in conversation beyond. Passing through this door she found herself in a large kitchen where Simpson was talking to a woman who was obviously the cook.

Simpson turned to Sheila. 'Wait here,' he said, more rude than officious, and went marching off, his bandy legs making him sway from side to side as he walked.

'I'm Mrs Tripp,' the cook said, coming to Sheila and smiling.

'And I'm Sheila Beattie. I'm here to see the laird.'

Mrs Tripp's smile was kindly. 'So Simpson was saying. He's gone to tell the laird that you've arrived. While you're waiting, would you like a cup of tea? There's one freshly mashed.'

An Englishwoman, Sheila thought, automatically on the defensive. Tea was masked north of the border, not mashed. 'That's very kind of you. I'd love some tea,' she answered politely, suddenly feeling uneasy and out of her depth.

The girl's reply had been stilted, her manner distant, and Annie Tripp knew why. It was nearly always the same when she opened her mouth to a stranger since coming to Scotland to take up this post. 'Are you

37

surprised that I haven't got horns? I'm told that many of you Scots think we English do,' she asked, but not unkindly.

Sheila had met a number of English men before, but never an English woman. Of course she knew the English didn't *actually* have horns, that was just an old wives' tale. Just as she knew that their woman didn't eat newborn Scots babies, as some inland people still believed, in the more remote areas where they never had any truck with the Sassenach.

Sheila gratefully accepted the cup that was offered her. The woman was doing her best to be friendly. It would be rude of her not to be the same. 'I've never believed the English are as bad as they're painted. Nobody could be *that* bad,' she replied gravely.

Annie Tripp stared at Sheila, then, realizing it had been a joke, burst out laughing. Sheila joined in. When Simpson returned to say that the laird would see Sheila now, he found the pair of them having a good crack together, as though life-long friends.

Sheila thanked Annie for the tea, and followed Simpson out of the kitchen into another hallway which eventually led them into a large reception area. Avidly she glanced about her, taking everything in, the furniture and decorations, the very smell of the place, for she'd be expected to describe what she'd seen down to the last detail when she got home.

They ascended a sweeping staircase that brought them on to the Hall's second level. Here the walls were wood panelled and there was a thick, burgundy-coloured carpet underfoot.

They passed several suits of armour, then plunged into a small tunnel-like hall at the end of which was an oak door. Simpson rapped loudly.

'Come in!' called out a deep, masculine voice.

Simpson opened the door, gestured to Sheila to enter, and closed it behind her once she was inside. James Campbell was seated at a huge desk, a mass of papers spread out before him, his back to the window and the world outside.

38

This room, clearly the laird's private study, was plain in comparison to what she'd seen of the rest of the Hall. The floorboards were bare but highly polished, the walls and ceiling a clotted-cream colour. Apart from the desk, there were only two items of furniture in the room; one a bookcase crammed to overflowing, the other a small table by the window on which stood a replica of a steam trawler of the latest design.

'I'll be with you in a moment,' Campbell muttered without looking up, as though barely aware that she was there.

An instrument on a corner of his desk caught her attention. She recognized it to be a sextant from the description Davey had once given her. Davey didn't own one himself, scorning such aids to navigation. Davey and his like navigated by the stars and an intimate knowledge of the sea and sea-bed, being able to locate with pin-point accuracy and shoot their nets on any spot they wished.

'Paperwork, the bane of my life,' said James Campbell, and with a sigh threw down the pen with which he'd been writing. And then he raised his eyes to look at her. My God, he thought, she's prettier than I remembered. Pretty and oddly disarming. This was going to be harder than he had thought.

'I usually take a glass of sherry about this time. Would you care to join me?' he asked.

But Sheila was too anxious to perform the rituals of politeness. 'It's about Granny Mutch's cottage, isn't it, sir?' she blurted out.

He dropped his gaze, going on as though he hadn't heard her, opened a drawer in his desk and took out decanter and two glasses.

'Not for me, sir, I've just had some tea,' Sheila said and bit her lip.

James Campbell slowly poured himself some sherry, staring at the rich colour of the liquid as it filled the glass, realizing that she'd brought the smell of fish in with her. It was a smell he could remember as far back as he had memory, and one he had never tired of. The smell of fish was the smell of the sea, and as far as he was concerned the smell of the sea was the very breath of life itself.

He coughed, acutely aware of her presence, of the roughness of her clothes and the wildness in her bearing. How real she was compared to his wife Fiona, that lady of light and air, whose delicateness always seemed so brittle, as though she might break if handled too much, like a Dresden figurine would if grasped too tightly. Who was so much a lady that she didn't seem a woman.

'I'm afraid it is about the cottage. The fault's entirely mine. I neglected to tell the factor I had plans for it,' he explained, in a tone that wasn't at all like the firm but sympathetic one he'd intended using.

Instantly the image she'd had of the cottage, of her and Eric's home, vanished, bursting like a bubble. She'd known that's what it was, what it had to be! Disappointment welled within her at this verification of her worst fears.

'I wanted to tell you face to face that the fault was mine, and that no blame can be attached to Semple for what's occurred,' he went on. He tried to look her straight in the eye, but what he saw there caused him to glance away. It's not at all like you to be so bloody soft, he berated himself.

Despite the depth of her disappointment and hurt, Sheila knew there was no use arguing. The cottage was the laird's property, his to dispose with as he pleased.

'Thank you sir,' she whispered, and turned to go, determined not to let him see her cry.

'Wait!' he called out, not wanting her to leave, not like this. 'Semple said something about you getting married?' He held his glass in his right hand, nervously moving it between his fingers.

She'd asked Semple not to mention that round the village, but the laird was hardly the village. 'It's not settled yet,' she replied quietly, wishing he would let her flee.

40

He sipped his sherry, studying her over the rim of his glass. A silence as loud as an explosion stood between them. What a magnificent young woman, he thought. There was a wildness and a warmth about her, an air of straightforward determination that he hadn't encountered in years. She was precisely the sort of lassie he would have wanted to marry if he hadn't been so intent on success and status. 'But you are *planning* to get wed?' he prompted at last.

'Oh yes, sir. January, probably. It's just – well, we haven't got round to telling our families yet,' she lied. It was too personal a matter to explain to the likes of him.

He wondered at the pang of jealousy that stabbed through him. After all Sheila Beattie was nothing to James Campbell. 'May I inquire who the lucky man is?'

'Eric Gifford, sir. His da owns the *Gypsy Queen*, of the Dragonholme fleet.'

'Well, I'm sure your Eric is a fine upstanding lad,' he replied with a smile.

'He is,' Sheila whispered in reply, and then suddenly, without warning, tears were rolling down her cheeks. Turning away she hastily dabbed at them with the corner of her shawl.

For the first time in years, James Campbell found himself in a situation he couldn't control. This was awful. There was no place for sentiment in business, he reminded himself, but there was no conviction in his heart. Rising, he crossed to her and handed her his hanky. 'Use that,' he commanded.

She wiped her face, and blew her nose. 'I'm ever so sorry,' she muttered, furious with herself for having broken down.

'I think you should have that sherry,' he said and filled a second glass, which she accepted without protest.

When she was once more in control of herself, although still a little shaky inside, she said, because she could think of nothing else to say, 'My da told us that

41

you're a self-made man, and that you were born in a Portnessie house that's just like ours.'

Campbell nodded, memories of the old times, the hard grafting times, flooding back. 'I started with a Coble that I got for next to nothing because they're not popular on this part of the coast, and went from there.'

'You must be extremely clever.'

Flattery, he asked himself? But no, she was not a girl like that. She would say only what she meant. 'The business side of the fishing industry has always fascinated me as much as the fishing itself. I've worked very hard at each, and been lucky with both.'

'How many boats have you got now?' she asked, feeling better now that they were talking about things she understood.

'Seventy-two.'

She pursed her lips and whistled, forgetting the embarrassment such a gesture would cause her ma. She'd known he owned a lot, but seventy-two! Why he owned nearly three times as many boats as there were in the entire Dragonholme fleet! 'You must be rich as Croesus.'

Campbell laughed. 'Let's just say it's been a long time since I've had to worry where my next crust of bread is coming from. And of course I have interests other than the boats, they're only part of my empire.'

Empire! The word jarred with her, and she remembered her da saying there was a streak of vanity in James Campbell. A rather large streak, she'd say, to use a word like that. Vanity and ego.

'Do you still own the Coble?' She asked impulsively. The answer she got was an insight into James Campbell that she hadn't expected. A strange look came into his eyes so they almost seemed to gleam metallically. 'I do,' he replied softly. 'Once something's mine it stays mine forever.'

Sheila found his words chilling, so that, involuntarily she pulled her shawl close. Here was a man capable of great ruthlessness, even cruelty. A man who thought differently from anyone else she'd ever known. 'I really must be getting along,' she said, and finishing what was left in her glass she laid it beside the sextant.

But still he didn't want her to leave, and wracked his brains for a topic that would prolong the conversation. 'How have the Dragonholme fleet been doing?' he asked, though he was far from ignorant of the bad luck they'd been having.

Sheila shook her head. 'It's bringing back hardly anything at all.'

'It's the same with my fleet. At the moment I'm not even covering costs, let alone making a profit.'

'Have you any idea why the shoals came south early this year?' she asked, as intrigued as all the villagers of Dragonholme were by that mystery. It was the question none of the fishermen could answer.

Campbell barked out a harsh laugh. 'Shoals! It's a bit of an exaggeration to call what's come south shoals. Small schools, I would term them.' Crossing to his desk he shoved various papers aside to reveal an Admiralty map. 'Ever heard of the Royal Society?' he demanded, smoothing the map out flat.

'No,' said Sheila, wondering what he was up to now.

'Well, they're a very august body of gentlemen who have a great thirst for knowledge, and it was several of their members who reported that there have been severe underwater upheavals in the Norwegian Sea just south of the Arctic Circle.'

Sheila stared down at the spot on the map where he was pointing, and there was the Arctic Circle clearly marked. To the north was Jan Mayen Island, with Svalbad, Spitsbergen and a large chunk of the Greenland mainland further north still.

Campbell's finger moved over to come to rest again in Western Russia, just below the Kara Sea. 'And around here, in what was very likely part of the same disturbance, there have been a number of earthquakes and eruptions.'

'Are you saying all this has something to do with the herring?'

'As this all took place in late April, it could very well be so,' he said slowly. 'Thinking about that, after reading the Royal Society's report, I wondered if the great shoals had come south even earlier than we'd imagined.'

Sheila's eyes widened. 'You mean the great shoals might be continually ahead of our fishermen this season and that all they're catching are the stragglers?'

Her own personal scent, mingled with the heady aroma of the sea that she'd brought in with her were making his senses reel, throwing him back to days he'd forgotten he remembered. And that tawny hair, thick and lustrous, the thought of it spread out against his hand, the thought of himself enveloped by the smell of her. . . .

'To discover if that was the case, I sent a couple of trawlers ahead of my fleet, having them fish well in advance of where we would normally be at this time of year.'

'And?' Sheila demanded expectantly.

Campbell shook his head. 'I was wrong. My boats never made contact. Wherever the herring are, it isn't further south.'

Sheila frowned in thought, trying to piece together all the terrible clues. 'You said the underwater upheavals were severe. What if they were so severe they killed the great shoals?'

James Campbell stared at her as though she'd slapped him. 'My God,' he whispered. Could it be true?

'Is it possible?' Sheila asked in a cracked voice.

It was several seconds before Campbell could reply, and when he did it was reluctantly, as though afraid of his own imaginings. 'I suppose it is. Mother Nature has wiped out entire races of people before now, so why not the great shoals of herring?'

Both knew that if she was right not only that season would be affected, but many more to come. It could take a score of years for the herring to breed themselves back to anything like the numbers they'd been. What Sheila was suggesting was the virtual annihilation of the herring industry as it now existed. Whole villages in Scotland and England would go bankrupt at the end of either this season or the next.

The thoughtful silence that had fallen between them was broken by Sheila. 'This mugginess is becoming unbearable,' she complained, suddenly awares that her entire body was sticky with sweat.

Campbell smiled, dabbing at the sweat on his own brow with a hanky.

'It's a direct result of those volcanic eruptions in Western Russia. The ash the eruptions have spewed into the atmosphere has created a sort of hot blanket. Up until now, it's been felt mostly at sea. This section of the east coast and a belt round Stavanger in Norway are the first land areas to be hit.'

Despite his vanity and arrogance, his knowledge and intelligence impressed her. He wasn't bad looking, either, for such an old man.

It was a rare occurrence for James Campbell to change his mind after he'd committed himself, but he did so now. He'd become so taken with Sheila during the past few minutes he didn't want her to think ill of him. On the contrary, he wanted quite the reverse. 'I've decided to let you have the cottage after all,' he said abruptly. 'I had intended building on to the property, but we'll forget about that for the time being. As for the rent as it stands, I won't expect you to start paying that until you actually move in. You can consider that my wedding present to you and your young man.' He set his glass on the desk with finality.

Sheila was completely taken aback. The last thing she'd expected was a total turn around on his part. 'Thank you, sir, thank you,' she stammered, her face glowing with renewed excitement.

'The pleasure is entirely mine, Sheila Beattie,' James Campbell smiled.

*   *   *

45

She was halfway home when it started to rain. At first there were only a few light drops, but these quickly intensified until it was pouring down. The light paled to murky grey, and then grew darker still. In the driving seat, Simpson fought to control the horse which was snorting and rolling its eyes in fright.

When Sheila alighted in front of her house the rain was actually bouncing a foot back off the ground. I hope the fleet's all right, she worried, as she hurried inside.

She awoke as the sound of the crash reverberated round the room. 'What the. . . !'

'Don't fash yourself, it's only thunder,' Bob said from beyond the curtain.

'Are you up?'

'Aye, I'm over at the window watching the gale. It's quite a spectacle.'

As she got out of bed there was another crack of thunder. It might have been her imagination, but it seemed to her that the walls shook from it.

'The thunder started about half an hour ago,' Bob said when she joined him at the window. 'I'm surprised it hasn't wakened you before now.'

A jagged streak of lightning split the sky, followed by another and another. Off in the distance Sheila could hear the roar of surf pounding the beach.

'God help all fishermen who're on the sea this night,' Bob said with feeling, thankful he wasn't one of them.

'Look!' said Sheila, pointing to where a blue glow had suddenly appeared in the north-west.

Bob was well acquainted with the Northern Lights, but he'd never seen anything like this before, nor heard of anything like it.

'Probably something else caused by the ash spewed into the atmosphere by the Russian volcanoes that erupted a few months back,' Sheila said, airing her newly acquired information.

Bob looked down at her, both amused and amazed. There were times when his sister came out with the damnedest things.

'The laird told me about the volcanoes when I was at the Hall,' she explained, and went on to tell him about the Royal Society and the underwater upheavals in the Norwegian Sea.

'My God!' breathed Bob, echoing James Campbell, when she told him it could be a possibility that the great shoals had all been destroyed.

The loudest crack of thunder yet exploded above the house. This time she was certain: the walls *did* shake.

Davey stood on the quayside and stared out to sea, a sea that was a seething green and white cauldron. The thunder and lightning had stopped, but that eerie blue glow was still to be seen in the north-west.

The wind tore fiercely at his oilskins; a warm wind with enormous power and fury behind it. In the harbour the boats bobbed and dipped, yawed and juddered; the heaving water alternately sucking at, then crashing against their hulls.

'Well, Davey, what's the verdict?' Rab Gifford asked.

The men of the Dragonholme fleet had formed themselves into a semi-circle behind Davey, awaiting his pronouncement.

Davey removed the battered clay from his mouth. 'I say we stay in harbour. My feeling is that, bad as this blow is, it's going to get an awful lot worse as the day goes on,' he said slowly.

Several of the men swore in their disappointment at losing a day's fishing. Tarry Dunbar was one of them.

Eric glanced across to where Sheila and the other women were waiting. He gave her the thumb's down sign, then gestured that he wanted a word with her.

As the men started to disperse Eric hurried over to Sheila, pulling her to one side so that their conversation wouldn't be overheard. 'I'll arrange to be doing some work on our gash floats and corks in the hut this afternoon,' he whispered. 'Can you make it?'

'I could well be busy,' she replied vaguely.

His face dropped. 'I don't often get a weekday free this time of year.'

'Ach, don't panic,' she interjected with a playful smile. 'I'll be there.'

'Right then. I'll be expecting you.' She often teased him, and he often misunderstood.

Walking back to the house, Sheila was joined by Davey. Everyone else in the family had gone ahead.

'Now what's this you've been telling Bob about underwater upheavals in the Norwegian Sea?' he demanded.

By that afternoon, as Davey had predicted, the gale had worsened considerably. By the time Sheila arrived down on the beach, mountainous rollers were crashing ashore, filling the air with the hiss and howl of the angry sea.

As she opened the door of the hut a gust of wind caught it, wrenching it from her hand to send it banging inwards. Eric looked up from where he was sitting on top of a coil of new warp line and grinned, thinking how magnificent she looked with her hair whipping to one side and her cheeks burning fiercely from the driving spume that had been lashing her since nearing the beach.

Sheila made no effort to reshut the door, wanting it to remain open so that the dramatic exit she had planned would be unhindered. Planting her hands on her hips, exactly the way she'd seen Peg do countless times, she glanced around her in dismay.

Eric's grin changed to a frown. 'What's wrong?' he asked, rising and tossing aside the knife he'd been using.

'This place. It's been so long since I've seen it in the daylight that I'd forgotten how filthy it is.' An expression of disgust clouded her pretty face.

48

Eric looked about him in bewilderment. 'All the huts are like this. Our's is no worse.'

'Glue, paint, manky tackle of all sorts,' she sniffed. 'Some love nest!'

'Oh, now Sheila – ' he began in alarm, going to her and trying to take her in his arms, only to be pushed away.

'Not here, not any more. I do have some pride!' she snapped, eyes blazing with anger.

Eric was at a complete loss. What had suddenly got into the girl? 'You don't mean that,' he said, trying again to take her into his arms, only to be repulsed a second time.

'Oh yes I do!'

'But you've never complained about the hut before.'

'Well, I'm complaining now. A man expecting a woman to make love in conditions and surroundings like these has no respect for her, no respect at all.' And with that she wheeled around and strode back the way she'd come, leaving a shattered Eric gawping after her.

But as soon as her back was turned on him, her fierce expression instantly changed into a broad smile. Not a bad performance of outraged indignation, even if she did say so herself! That had knocked some of the complacency out of him. It was high time he learned she wasn't to be taken for granted.

She was just rounding a small dune when she saw something that made her come up short. Sitting on its rear, about a dozen feet away, staring at her, was a large hare. Sheila went cold all over. It was an omen of the worst sort to meet a hare. In the old days it had been said that witches turned themselves into hares and in that disguise wrought great evil.

I shall go intill a hare,
With sorrow and sych and meikle care;
And I shall go in the Devil's name,
Ay while I come home again.

Sheila clearly recalled the lines that Peg had told her one dark winter's night when the men had been out and

49

they'd sat huddled round the fire. Peg had got the lines from a travelling spaewife who'd sworn it was the incantation that Isobel Gowdie, the most infamous of Scottish witches, had used when she'd wanted to transform herself into a hare.

The hare's liquid brown eyes gazed into Sheila's, then slowly it lifted its front right paw and jerked it in her direction.

'Oh!' She exclaimed, taking a step backwards.

'Sheila! Sheila, wait up will you!' Eric shouted behind her. She turned as he came puffing to a halt by her side. 'You don't half move quickly when you've got your dander up,' he gasped.

She grabbed hold of his arm, squeezing it so hard in her anxiety that it caused him to wince.

'What is it?'

She swung round to point out the hare, only to find that it had gone, vanished without trace.

Eric's approach must have sent it scuttling away, she told herself. It was well known that hares were naturally shy and timid creatures, although that particular hare had seemed neither shy nor timid. On the contrary, it had been bold in the extreme. The way it had jerked its paw at her! She shuddered at the memory.

As she didn't go on to explain about the hare, Eric mistook her upset, thinking it had to do with him. 'Don't fall out with me, Sheila. It never occurred to me that the hut might be offensive to you. It's just always been such a safe meeting place,' he pleaded.

She took a deep breath, then smiled inwardly. He was netted, but she wouldn't land him yet. That was planned for Saturday night during the wedding reception. 'I haven't fallen out with you, it's just . . . well, I suppose I expected more of you,' she replied, disappointment and sadness in her voice. She resumed walking and he strode beside her.

'In what way did you expect more of me?' he demanded.

She answered obliquely, then a little further on switched the conversation to children, saying what a delight her nephews and nieces were, and how it must be grand to have children of your own, particularly boys to carry on the family name and tradition.

By the time they reached her house she had Eric visualizing himself as a grizzled skipper whose stalwart sons not only idolized him but crewed for him as well. And she had completely forgotten about the hare.

Tarry just wouldn't pass out. Sheila had managed to see he was fed drink after drink – all extremely large ones – but still he kept on his feet, yelling and wheeching like a demented Kelpie.

Sheila and Eric had thought they might have trouble with Tarry after the incident with wee George, but although they'd both been aware of him occasionally glowering darkly at them nothing had actually been said.

'Take your partners for the Gay Gordons please!' cried Murdo Sigurdson, Marika's da, from the raised dais on which the two accordion players were seated.

The reception was being held in the Community Hall, and including the children who were continually running up and down and getting under everyone's feet, there were just under fifty people present.

Sheila and Eric got up for the dance, finding themselves behind the sparkling Marika and the flushed Duncy. The ceremony earlier had gone off without a hitch. Marika had looked so absolutely radiant as she'd walked down the aisle on her da's arm that Sheila hadn't been able to stop herself from crying when Marika said, 'I do'. Despite Eric whispering to her several times to stop 'greeting like some big bairn', she had continued from that point right through to the end of the ceremony.

Sheila brought her attention back to the immediate present as the dance got under way, laughing to see fat Mrs Arbuthnot shaking her enormous backside at the man behind, not unlike the way the Clydesdales on Bogside Farm shook their bottoms when the summer flies and midges were bothering them.

Out of the corner of her eye she saw McPherson, the carter, arrive to take Marika and Duncy on their honeymoon which was to be spent in Pittlody, a picturesque clachan some seven and a bit miles inland.

She couldn't help thinking of the honeymoon she planned for Eric and herself. Going to Pittlody was all right, but to Edinburgh and Princes Street where she'd find that braw dream press she was after, now that's what she called a honeymoon – one to remember for the rest of her life! She gave Eric such an exuberant smile that he nearly tripped.

It had been a smashing week for her with Eric ashore, a week when all her dreams seemed so within her reach that the world was filled with only happiness and song. Even Eric's restlessness over the fleet's forced inactivity couldn't mar her mood for long.

Sheila glanced across to where Tarry and a few of Duncy's pals were sneaking out of a side door. They'd be off to 'fix' the cart on which Marika and Duncy would be travelling through to Pittlody, she guessed.

At the end of the dance Marika signalled to Sheila and the two of them took themselves off to the cludgie, or ladies' toilet.

'I feel so nervous,' Marika giggled. 'You'd think we'd never done it before.'

'Ach, don't be daft, there's nothing to be nervous about,' laughed Sheila. 'Anyway, Duncy's put away so much of the cratur I'll be surprised if you get more than a peck on the cheek out of him later.'

Marika giggled again. Sheila didn't know her Duncy: drink never affected him in that department.

There was a tap on the door which Sheila answered. Murdo Sigurdson handed in Marika's going away clothes and announced that the newlyweds' cases had been loaded aboard the cart.

When Marika was ready she turned to Sheila. 'How do I look then?'

'Pretty as a picture, *Mrs Laidlaw*,' Sheila smiled.

'You're the first to call me that,' Marika whispered, having been waiting all night for the thrill of being addressed by her new name.

Sheila took her plump friend into her arms and hugged her tightly. 'I'm so pleased for you,' she choked. 'I can't tell you how much.'

On leaving the cludgie they found all the guests lined up waiting for them, a sheepish Duncy standing at their head with his arm crooked for Marika to take.

While the accordionist played 'I Love a Lassie', everyone followed the happy couple outside to cheer them on their way. Old boots, several ancient corsets, and the largest pair of drawers Sheila had ever seen (donated by Mrs Arbuthnot) hung and dangled from the rear of the cart. The *pièce de resistance*, however, was in the centre of the cart where a giant mock carrot with a round white pudding impaled upon it had been stuck.

A cascade of rice fell over Marika and Duncy as they climbed on to the cart. Duncy raised a roar of ribald laughter, catcalls and jeers when, pretending to notice the carrot for the first time, he remarked in a loud aside to Marika that he couldn't for the life of him think what it was supposed to mean.

'Right then, all set for the off?' McPherson asked from the front of the cart, flicking his whip over the horse when Duncy gave him the nod.

Marika's bouquet flew through the air, straight into Sheila's waiting hands.

'You next then, lass,' said Mrs McDuff, who was standing beside Sheila and Eric.

Sheila gave Eric a sideways look to ensure he'd heard that, then turned back to watch the cart roll off into the darkness with Tarry and some other rice throwers pursuing it.

Sheila nudged Eric and whispered that she wanted to

show him something. Then, with him following, she forced her way to the rear of the throng and took his arm.

'It's a lovely bouquet, don't you think?' she asked coyly, and held it up for him to smell.

'Oh, aye, real nice.'

'I've never caught one before, did you know that?'

He shook his head, a little confused by all the celebrating he'd been doing. 'Well, it's a fact,' she said softly, and leaned her head against his shoulder.

Arm-in-arm, they started up the street, Eric, roused by the night air, noticing that the wind had fallen again. The clouds were still low, though, and swirling frenetically as if being stirred by some unseen, heavenly spoon. 'Where are we going?' he asked.

'I told you, I want to show you something.'

'But what?'

'Wait and see,' she teased.

He let out a sigh. Women! How exasperating they could be at times. Still, he had to admit that he couldn't do without them, especially Sheila. He couldn't imagine life without Sheila.

She stopped in front of Granny Mutch's cottage. 'What do you think?' she asked.

He stared about, not sure what he was supposed to be looking at. 'Think of what?'

'Follow me,' she said mysteriously, and led him inside.

Just to the right of the door were two candles and a box of Lucifer matches that she'd put there that morning. A match flared, then a candle spluttered alight. 'Hold that,' she instructed, handing him the candle.

Eric was bewildered. What in the name of the Wee Man was she playing at? Why bring him here?

She faced him squarely, a look in her eye of which he might have been more wary were he more sober.

'I've decided there's to be no more lovemaking between us,' she said baldly.

'What!' The candle in his hand shook, throwing crazy shadows on the wall.

'No more lovemaking,' she repeated, her expression one of immoveable resolution.

He stared at her aghast. 'I thought it was only the hut you objected to?'

'So you then went on to think maybe the woods or the dunes or somewhere like that would be all right?'

'Well, where else is there?'

'You're my own darling man, Eric, but you have one tiny fault. You have no imagination.'

That was a relief. He was still her darling man. He couldn't be getting the elbow. 'If the hut, the woods, the dunes, in other words all the usual places that courting couples use are out, then where do you suggest?' he asked slowly.

'I'm sick to death of old tarpaulin and such, and the worry that someone might walk in on us. I want privacy, Eric. Assured privacy.'

'But the only way to get that in a small village like ours is to – ' He trailed off as the penny dropped. So that was it – that was what all this was about! Now he knew why her behaviour had been so odd and erratic since he'd come back to Dragonholme. Marika being bairned must've sparked this off. Aye, that would be it. 'I suppose this cottage is for rent?' he asked quietly.

'I believe it is,' she answered casually, as though he'd been the instigator all along and not she.

'Perhaps someone else has already spoken up for it?' he speculated, unable to repress a smile.

'I happened to have a conversation with the factor just the other day, and if I remember correctly he mentioned in passing that it was still available,' she said with a shrug, and proceeded to light the second candle.

Happened to have a conversation. Mentioned in passing. Eric laughed inwardly. His Sheila was something, that was certain.

Sheila went over to the box cavity bed and peered into the recess. 'With sheets and blankets it must be right comfy, and *private* in there,' she said appraisingly.

He'd been thinking to give it another year before getting wed; at the end of next season, when there might be a bit more money to hand. But maybe Sheila was right and it was foolish to delay what would happen anyway. He certainly had no intention of losing her. 'It would make a fine family home, there's no denying that,' he conceded.

'Needs a few things doing to it. The range, for example, should be replaced, but apart from that there isn't much that some elbow grease wouldn't put right,' Sheila enthused.

He had enough money saved; not quite as much as he would have liked, but enough. The trouble was that some of that was going to be eroded if this damned awful season didn't pick up. 'I suppose a grand wee but and ben like this won't stand empty long,' he mused.

'I shouldn't think it will.'

He tapped at the floor with the toe of his shoe. 'No doubt the fleet will be moving on to the Silver Pits directly this gale is over,' he said.

'Aye, but you'll be back again at the end of December, then it's straight into January. January's always been one of my favourite months.'

So it was a January wedding she planned.

'No lovemaking unless privacy is assured?' he repeated, raising an eyebrow.

'Not a bit.'

He crossed to the window and stared out. She wasn't the only one who could play games, he decided. He'd indulge in a little teasing of his own. 'That Rosie McCullough has fairly grown up I was thinking the night. How old is she now?'

'Fourteen,' Sheila replied, her lips pursing.

'As a wee lassie she was always keen on me, did I ever tell you that?'

'Often,' Sheila answered through gritted teeth.

'I could be mistaken but I thought she was giving me the come hither when we were up doing The Grand Old Duke of York,' Eric said.

56

'Was she indeed?'

'Some figure, eh? Who would have thought such a skinny runt of a child would grow up to be such a *big* girl.'

Sheila began to seethe. If he thought he was going to give her over for that Rosie McCullough, then he had another thing coming! If he so much as laid a hand on Rosie she'd scratch the eyes out of his head.

Suddenly, Eric laughed, loudly and uncontrollably, unable to keep it up any longer. He was delighted with himself for getting his own back. From now on, Sheila wasn't going to get things quite so much her own way as she had. 'I'll make a bargain with you,' he said, when he'd finally stopped laughing enough to speak.

'What's that?'

'You compromise on the lovemaking and I'll compromise on the wedding.'

She stared at him for a second. Then she, too, started to laugh. He'd had her going that time. This was a new side to Eric, and one she liked.

'It's a bargain.'

He came to her and took her into his arms, his mouth eagerly seeking hers. As they kissed his hand began to caress her breast.

She broke off kissing, her hand on his wrist. 'Haven't you got something to say first?' she whispered.

'You mean *the* actual question?'

'*The* actual question.'

He took a deep breath to steady himself. After all, it wasn't every day a man proposed. He opened his mouth, but before he could utter a word the church bell started to clang loudly and stridently.

'Oh, hell!' Sheila swore, then was instantly filled with remorse. When the church bell rang outwith a Sunday something calamitous had happened.

Eric had gone rigid with the first clang, but now he galvanized into action. 'Come on!' he exclaimed, and blew out the two candles. Grabbing her wrist he pulled her towards the door.

Out in the street they joined a stream of people heading for the church, where a large crowd had already assembled.

Sheila spied her da, with her three brothers at his back, pushing his way to the front. 'What's happened?' Davey shouted, but no one had an answer; nor did anyone know who was ringing the bell.

The minister appeared from the manse. He had no idea either why the bell was being rung.

And then, quite abruptly, the clanging ceased. A few minutes later a red-faced Tarry appeared, breathless from having run down the stairs from the bell tower. With Tarry was Ian McPherson, the carter's son.

'What is it, Tarry?' Davey demanded. 'Why are you ringing the bell?'

Tarry thrust Ian in front of Davey. 'You repeat to the admiral what you told me at the reception,' Tarry commanded.

'My da sent me through to Portnessie with a load this morning and I'm only back ten minutes since,' Ian explained nervously.

'Get on with it!' urged Tarry.

Ian took a deep breath, unused to being the centre of so much attention. 'The Portnessie fleet went out last night and has found a big shoal at the Broken Crags. When their cutter came back at midday it was fair brimming over with fish,' he said. The Broken Crags was located in the most northerly section of the home grounds.

The Portnessie fleet was made of trawlers. Trawlers operated in a different way to drifters, staying at sea for some time and sending their catches back by cutter. Drifters, on the other hand, came in and out of port, usually on a twenty-four-hour basis.

'We must set sail right away to catch the ebb tide,' Tarry commanded.

'Aye, the morning could be too late,' piped up Mr Johnstone. 'The Portnessie men might have scooped the entire shoal by then.'

· 'Now wait – just wait a minute!' ordered Davey. Rubbing a hand over a stubbled chin, he glanced up at the sky as Eric had earlier, to note that the wind had fallen away.

'What do you say, Davey?' Tarry urged with pleading in his voice. 'Do we put to sea?'

'Let's away down to quayside and have a look first,' Davey replied, and instantly the crowd surged in the direction of the harbour.

On the quayside, Davey consulted a barometer, and found it ominously low. The sea itself was choppy, but nothing like the broil it had been.

'We're wasting time,' Tarry said in exasperation, the crew of the *Locarno* ringed about him.

'A big shoal. We need those fish,' Dougal whispered to Davey, and Jack, hard by Dougal's side, nodded his agreement.

Conditions had improved, Davey could hardly deny that. They were certainly far better than the previous night when the Portnessie fleet had gone out. And yet . . . and yet. . . . It wasn't the low barometer that was holding him back, but something intangible, an instinct honed by years of experience, that warned him to stay ashore.

'What's the verdict?' asked Robin McDuff who crewed *The Willie*.

'I say we stay tied up,' replied Davey sternly, his eyes serious with responsibility.

Tarry gave an exclamation of anger, smashing his fist against his thigh.

He's drunk, Sheila thought, then remembered that he should be, considering the amount of whisky he'd consumed that day.

'You can say what you like, Davey, but the *Locarno*'s going after those fish,' Tarry growled defiantly, thrusting out his lower jaw.

'If Tarry's going, then I'm going,' spoke up Olaf Johnstone, skipper of the *Fear Not*.

'You should do as the admiral recommends, that's the way it's always been with us,' Eric said to Olaf.

'There speaks a right coward, a man who hides behind his lassie's skirts,' taunted Tarry.

Eric flushed bright red. 'I'm no coward,' he replied in a low voice.

'Are you not?' leered Tarry. Turning to his crew, he winked lewdly, causing them to laugh and snigger.

'Mind yourself, Tarry Dunbar!' warned Rab Gifford. No one called a son of his a coward.

'So how about you, then, Mr Gifford? Will you put out with me?' Tarry jibed.

Rab looked to Davey, then back to Tarry. 'I do as the admiral says,' he replied reluctantly. 'I'm staying in harbour.'

Tarry hooted. 'I can see where Eric gets it from now,' he howled. 'A real chip off the old block.'

In unison the Gifford lads stepped forward. This sort of insult wasn't to be borne. Just who in hell did Tarry Dunbar think he was!

Pinchie Murray, skipper of the *Happy Return*, decided he could turn this to his own advantage. 'I've done really badly this season, so I'm going with Tarry,' he said to Eric. 'If you'll entertain the idea, then you're welcome to take Duncy's place. I'm a crewman short with him off on his honeymoon.'

'If my da says not to go out, then you shouldn't,' Sheila warned, tugging at Eric's arm.

'Your lassie's speaking,' smiled Tarry. 'Time for you to jump.'

Eric was churning inside. Tarry had put him in such a position that he had to go, there was nothing else for it. If he didn't he'd never live it down. Not to himself at any rate.

Sheila was furious. Tarry's accusation was complete nonsense. No fisherman who went on the boats was a coward. If anything they were all, including Tarry, the complete opposite, the bravest of the brave. Tarry was mixing up cowardice with caution, bravery with foolhardiness.

'I'll sail with you, Pinchie,' replied Eric, the colour having drained from his face.

'No!' bellowed Rab. 'When my boys go to sea it's in the *Gypsy Queen*. We'll sail for the Broken Crags as well,' he declared.

The *Locarno*, the *Fear Not*, the *Happy Return* and the *Gypsy Queen*: four boats out of twenty-eight were now committed against their admiral's advice. Every eye present came to rest on Davey.

If they went on their own, Davey's days as admiral would be over. But that was not what bothered him. It was a fine thing being admiral, but it wasn't the be all and end all. What worried him was making the right decision for everyone. Although his instincts told him to stay ashore, there were times when instincts had to be over-ridden, when a gamble had to be made against the odds. Was this one of those times? If Sheila was right and the great shoals had been destroyed in the Norwegian Sea then this might be the last substantial amount of herring they would take this season. Was his caution foolhardy?

The circumstances were extraordinary, and extra-ordinary circumstances called for extraordinary deci-sions. Not only might this be the last decent catch of the season, it was also clear that the men wanted to go. Four boats were already committed, and many other skippers and crews were straining at the leash: he could read it in their faces.

Davey took a deep breath. 'If you are determined to go, then we'll all go,' he announced. 'We'll take a chance on the weather.'

A collective sigh ran through the crowd. Some of the men smiled, others laughed and jostled each other hap-pily; but there were only tight, drawn faces among the womenfolk. They'd do their smiling and laughing when the trip was over and their men were safely home again.

Tarry looked straight at Sheila and gave her a mocking

61

wink. He'd got his own way, and that never failed to make him happy.

Sheila glared back. She would never forgive Tarry Dunbar for challenging her father's authority and insulting Eric the way he had.

All around Sheila men were hurrying off to get changed into their sea gear. By her reckoning, they had less than half an hour to get the fleet away.

She told Eric she'd wait for him beside the *Gypsy Queen*, then stared after his broad back as he ran to catch up with his father and brothers. It was an image she would never forget: Eric hurrying away, his fair hair flying, his movements urgent with excitement, her darling man, her blond viking.

Jack was the first back to the *Bluebell* to give Rhona a squeeze and a cuddle, and Ian a kiss on the forehead. The so-called fairy-touched lad stared at his father with huge worried eyes, and his lower lip trembled.

'There, there, my wee man, I'll be back before you know it,' Jack smiled, and tousled the boy's hair before setting him down again.

Then came Dougal to say good-bye to his family, Davey and Bob shortly behind him.

'Now don't fash yourself woman, it'll be all right,' Davey said to Peg, abruptly turning away from her to shout out an order to Uncle Matt, who'd just jumped aboard.

At the *Gypsy Queen*, Sheila rejoined Eric. 'Old Granny Mutch's place is a grand cottage, you did well to think of it,' he said, taking one of her hands in his. She looked at his large, strong fingers encircling hers.

'I'll be standing right here when you get back,' she said solemnly. 'You can ask me that question then.'

'What question's that?' he asked innocently.

'You know fine well which question I mean,' she retorted, and stuck a finger into his ribs.

They both laughed. 'Ach, to hell with it, I don't care who sees!' he said, and taking her into his arms, kissed her right there in front of everyone.

On the deck of the *Gypsy Queen*, Alastair Gifford wolf-whistled.

'Would you take a look at that!' he exclaimed, nudging his brother Don.

'Come on Eric, there'll be plenty of time later for the winching!' Rab cried, having just cast off the aft line.

At the harbour entrance the *Muirneag* was already passing out to sea, while behind her came the *True Vine*, *Nonsuch* and *Locarno*.

'See you tomorrow,' Eric whispered to Sheila. Roughly breaking their embrace, he leapt from the quayside on to the bow of the *Gypsy Queen* and loosed the for'ard line.

The last boat to leave the harbour was the *Foamcrest*, and as she did the wind freshened, immediately causing the fleet to pick up speed.

'Good luck to all the bonny men!' cried Mrs Henderson as the *Foamcrest* cleared the harbour entrance, as she did every time the last boat cleared the harbour entrance when the fleet put to sea.

Sheila suddenly felt completely limp, drained of all energy and vitality. It had been a very long day. She wondered how the men, most of them a wee bit drunk from the celebrations, could find the strength to face the sea.

'Let's all go back and have a nice cup of tea,' Peg suggested, forcing her eyes away from the departing fleet. 'I think that's what we all need. A nice cup of tea.'

Halfway home, it began to rain.

Despite the rain, the heat returned and all during the night the temperature mounted steadily. Sheila woke out of a fitful sleep just before three to find she was wet with sweat. In the thick, oppressive darkness, she lay listening to the night sounds, the hammer of rain on the roof, the whistle of wind that was making the chimney pots rattle, the rustle of leaves and the creak of trees.

She could hear Peg snoring in the front room, and thought about the *Bluebell*, the *Gypsy Queen* and the rest, wondering how they were getting on at the Broken Crags.

In her dream, Eric had been making love to her in the bed at Granny Mutch's. So vivid had the dream been that she could still feel his body on hers. But thinking of the fleet reminded her of other things. What if she was right? What if the great shoals had been destroyed in the Norwegian Sea? That would mean terrible hard years lay ahead for them, years with the sort of constant, hopeless hardship that Peg had known in her youth.

If that was to be, had she and Eric a right to get married? Alone in her small bed, she could feel the warmth of his kiss on her lips. If hard times did lie ahead, she'd rather face them as Eric's wife. Anyway, and she gave a rueful grin, two could starve just as easily together as they could apart. It would be a January wedding, then, no matter how the season turned out.

Still feeling restless, Sheila rose and crossed to the window where she frowned. The rest of the village slept peacefully, but there in the north-west that strange blue glow had reappeared. Sheila stared at it with troubled eyes, only certain there would be no more sleep for her that night.

Some with shawls covering their heads and shoulders, others with their hair blowing free, the women of Dragonholme lined the quayside, waiting for the dawn to come up. Off in the north-west the blue glow had grown to twice the size it had been earlier that morning when Sheila had first noticed it.

The sea itself was fierce. Wave after angry wave crashed against the quayside throwing spume high into the air. The rain had stopped. But the wind had worsened, howling and moaning like a demented spirit.

The dawn came weakly over the horizon, frail shafts of pale light struggling to illuminate the thick grey sky.

'Do you see anything yet, Sheila?' Peg asked anxiously.

Sheila strained her eyes, willing the black sails to suddenly appear; but there was nothing to see but the sea and the sky and the dawn coming up. 'No sign yet,' she answered, trying to keep her own voice cheery.

Behind the women, the gutting tables were all laid out ready, the gutting knives upon them. Off to one side stood McPherson, the carter, with his son, and beside them were Handy Dandy, Tom Taggart, and the other old and disabled men of the village.

Handy Dandy started to sing 'Rock of Ages', his strong baritone disturbing some gulls close by, sending them wheeling high into the air, cawing and crying their protests.

Tom was the first to take up his friend's song. But soon everyone there in the strange dawn light joined in, taking comfort and solace from the hymn. 'Rock of Ages' was followed by 'There is a Green Hill Far Away' and that by 'Jerusalem'.

An hour passed, then another and another. The tide began to turn and still there was no sign of the fleet.

Of course, they all agreed, they hadn't expected the fleet home with the morning tide, they'd only been there just in case.

The wag-at-the-wa' clock ticked away the seconds as Sheila busied herself with the day's housework, or pretended to busy herself. For some reason she wasn't really accomplishing very much. Nor was Peg, despite the fact that she was bustling frantically around the house, doing this, that and a dozen other things at once.

'This heat!' complained Sheila pausing to wipe a sheen of sweat from her brow.

'Aye, it's more like I imagine Africa to be than the east coast of Scotland,' Peg replied, dusting an ornament she'd dusted not half an hour since.

Both women looked up as the clock struck the hour and the cuckoo popped out. Another ten or fifteen minutes and the tide would be turning again.

'Shall we get down there then?' Peg asked, abandoning her dusting to reach for her shawl, unable to conceal the concern in her eyes.

They called by for Rhona and Maggie, and with the children trailing along beside them, made their way down to the quayside where a small knot of women had already gathered.

Jack and Rhona's son, Ian, had the saddest expression Sheila had ever seen on a child. He stared disconsolately out to sea, as though he saw things the other watchers didn't.

The strange blue glow in the north-west was larger than ever, spreading across the sky like ink slowly spreading over blotting paper.

She glanced again to the north-west, to find that the colour of the glow had deepened to violet, and in its centre streaks of lightning were flashing one after the other.

She had thought it would be cooler down here by the quayside, but in fact the flying spume and spray which spattered her face might have come from a kettle halfway to being boiled.

'It must be a good catch, don't you think?' asked Peg suddenly. 'They'd be back by now if there was nothing there.'

'I'm sure you're right, ma,' agreed Sheila. And thought to herself of course she's right, the catch must have been even better than they hoped it would be.

It was well over an hour later when Lena Murray gave a sudden cry of joy and threw up her arms. 'There they are!' she shouted. 'Look! There they are! I'm sure it's them.'

Sheila cupped her hands around her eyes. Were those sails or low flying clouds? At this distance it was almost. . . . And then she too let out a shout. Yes, they *were* sails, the fleet was coming in.

66

Soon afterwards, Sheila was able to count the dots; twenty-eight of them, just as there should be. Peg put her arms around Sheila's shoulders and hugged her close, her smile broad, her eyes shining with relief.

Nearer came the fleet, every boat sitting low in the water, heavy with fish.

It began to rain, lightly, almost gently, but the wind blew harder than ever. Even as they stood there they had to hold on to one another to stop themselves from being blown over, or away.

Thunder shook the heavens. Jagged, powerful bolts of lightning lit up the almost purple sky.

Aboard the *Bluebell* Davey was crouched over the wheel. It worried him that the boat was so sluggish, and he considered lightening his load to regain some buoyancy. Eventually he decided against it; every fish was precious when this might be the last decent catch of the season.

Below deck in the *Gypsy Queen* Eric paused to sniff the air which had suddenly become charged and tainted with a metallic smell which stung his nostrils and made him want to cough.

Tarry Dunbar was grinning broadly as he steered the *Locarno* in the wake of the *Bluebell*. He'd known he was right to go to the Broken Crags, and what a haul it had been! The Portnessie fleet was still there, but wouldn't be able to do much fishing in weather as foul as this. He'd land his catch, and then turn right round again as soon as the weather cleared and get himself another capacity haul out of what remained of the big shoal.

Sheila was eyeing with trepidation the black clouds that were quickly piling up in the south-west, looking like nothing so much as thick, black smoke from a furnace. The clouds stood out eerily against the violet glow surrounding them.

And then, without any warning, the wind dropped completely away, leaving the boats bobbing on a churning sea.

Davey glanced at his aneroid to discover that it was rising at an alarming rate.

Even Tarry's smile had vanished. God damn it! he raged silently. There would be no second haul for him if this lack of wind went on for any length of time.

But the wind stayed down and the sea rose even higher, rushing and leaping in mad fury, tossing the boats about as though they were mere toys.

'Water!' yelled Uncle Matt, and seconds later a huge mountain of water broke over the *Bluebell*. Uncle Matt's legs became entangled in a line and he was smashed against the deck.

Jack and Dougal fought their way for'ard to help him but just as they reached him a second mountain of water, even larger than the first, descended on them from nowhere. Jack and Dougal were swept off their feet and carried overboard. Instantly they vanished beneath the surface of the angry sea.

Davey stared at the spot where his two sons had gone over, his face so immobile it might have been carved from stone. Despair and the most profound grief he'd ever experienced welled through him. His hands gripped the wheel as though not even the ferocity of the wind could dislodge him. Beyond feeling, beyond despair, he stared into the broiling water as though what had happened might be undone. Then something in him snapped.

'Take the wheel,' he ordered an ashen Bob.

From no wind at all to a raging hurricane took less than a minute, and during that brief space the *Fear Not*, and the *Martha Somerville* were both swamped. Chaos ruled the waters. There was not a man aboard the boats who was not stunned by what was taking place.

'Merciful Jesus!' gasped Peg, while a few feet away Mrs Johnstone, whose man crewed the *Fear Not*, gave a great animal cry, and, sinking to her knees, buried her head in her hands.

It was hell on earth. Sheila, battered by the furious

winds, clung to her mother, her eyes fixed on the nightmare before them, while overhead the sky itself seemed
about to be torn apart. It was impossible to believe that
what was happening was real.

She watched in fascinated horror as the *Muirneag*
turned over, then sank almost immediately. Beside her,
she could feel Peg shaking.

A giant wave towered over the *Locarno*, drawing the
vessel broadside-on and right underneath it, heeling over
towards it. And then the wave fell.

The *Orion*, the *Star of Hope* and the *True Vine* all broke
apart, while the *Happy Return*, Pinchie Murray's boat,
dipped into a trough and just didn't reappear.

On the *Bluebell*, Bob's voice rose against the sounds of
death, 'Our Father, which art in Heaven. . . .'

On the quayside Sheila too began to pray. Softly,
automatically, 'Dear God in Heaven, please help us. Dear
God, please. . . .'

'Sheila!' Eric screamed, the last word he ever spoke,
and then the broil closed over him.

Sheila heard that scream, though not through the raging elements, or the roar of death, but in her mind where
it rang out clear as a note from a cleanly struck bell. 'Eric!'
she wailed, clutching on to her mother's hand. 'Eric!'

Peg had begun to weep. Beside her Rhona and Maggie
were frozen with shock. As the *Gypsy Queen* had gone
down, so too had the *Bluebell*.

3

Early on the day of the funeral fishermen from up and
down that part of the coast started to arrive in
Dragonholme to honour and pay their last respects to the
dead.

The men of Eyemouth came, followed by those of

Burnmouth, Cove, Coldingham, Portnessie and the Forth ports of Musselburgh and Newhaven.

Grim-faced men in blue serge, they gathered by the kirk where they spoke in soft voices and occasionally, unobtrusively, handed the bottle round.

When it was time to call the congregation the kirk bell tolled, a sad mournful sound that tugged at the heart and caused more than one grim face to turn away and shed a quiet tear.

Sheila knew it to be only her imagination, but it seemed to her that with each toll of the bell the name of a boat that had gone down rang out.

The *Bluebell*, the *Gypsy Queen*, the *Pilgrim*, the *True Vine*, the *Harmony*, the *Muirneag*, the *Locarno* – God damn Tarry Dunbar and may he roast in Hell for evermore! – the *Star of Hope*, and on and on, the names of nineteen boats out of the twenty-eight that had put out to sea. A hundred and five men drowned, and only seven bodies recovered, washed up on the beach during the few days following the disaster.

A few minutes, that's all it had taken for her whole world to be turned inside out. Her da, her brothers, the man she loved, all taken, all gone. At first there had been hysteria; then a still coldness. Now she felt only a numbing emptiness; a week ago she wouldn't have believed that the human body could be so cold and vastly empty.

Peg appeared strong and controlled as they made their way to the kirk, but Sheila knew it to be no more than a brave act. Inside, she knew, her mother was completely destroyed.

The sun shone brightly high overhead in a duck-egg-blue sky, through which a few wisps of cloud floated. It had been like this since the morning after the boats had gone down, that last terrible maelstrom marking the passing of the freak weather.

Women in black were converging on the church from all sides. So many widows, thought Sheila, so many widows, and fatherless children holding their mother's hands or clutching on to their skirts, their eyes wide with fear. There were three fatherless bairns in their own family now: wee Dougal, Violet and Ian. It was some comfort, at least, to know that they'd be financially secure for some time to come. The *Bluebell*, like all the other boats, had been insured. Peg would divide the money equally between herself, Maggie and Rhona, the way Davey would have wanted, and considered just.

A man stepped out of the Cove contingent and raised his cap to Peg. His name was Ramsay McLaren. He was a trawlerman through and through and he and Davey had been old adversaries. All that antipathy was forgotten now, though, for he'd greatly admired Davey as a person, and as a fisherman.

'Thank you for coming here this day, Mr McLaren,' Peg said.

McLaren nodded. He'd come, he was there. He didn't have to tell Peg what that meant. She knew.

Music was playing as they entered the kirk: 'Abide with Me'. The minister's wife was doing her best at the organ which was usually played by Alex Coburn who'd gone down on the *Harmony*.

The Gifford women were already there, as were the Johnstones, Sigurdsons and many others. Marika and Duncy were with her ma, Marika clinging on to Duncy, both only too aware, and profoundly grateful, that he owed his life to their honeymoon. Otherwise he would have been aboard the *Happy Return*, Pinchie Murray's boat, and one of those lost.

When all the mourning relatives were gathered inside, the other members of the village filed in, led by James Campbell and his wife Fiona. When they had been accommodated, the visiting fishermen took those seats remaining.

A throng of fishermen was left crowding at the back, with even more beyond them. The minister ordered all exterior doors to be opened so that the service could be heard outside as well as in. These fishermen then arranged themselves into several large groups round the open doors.

The minister held up his hand. 'Dearly beloved, let us pray,' he said.

Sheila bowed her head, but instead of concentrating on the minister's words, her mind was filled with pictures of Eric during their last short time together. Remorse stabbed at her as she remembered how she'd denied him her body and her love. Days that they could have spent making love had instead been spent holding him at arm's length, playing silly games just to make him propose.

But how was she to know what was going to happen, her heart cried out? How could she possibly have foreseen the dreadful fate in store for him, and so many other fine men?

Oh, Eric! she wailed to herself. Never to see him again or to hold him close, or hear his laugh, or see him smile. It was a sin, she knew that, but she wished she was dead too, her body alongside her darling man's down there in sight of Dragonholme where the *Gypsy Queen* lay.

James Campbell's gaze was fixed on the back of Sheila's head. She'd been in his thoughts night and day since the day in his study when he'd said she could have Granny Mutch's cottage after all.

She haunted him: that tawny hair, those sparkling eyes, that fierce determination, the look of gratitude she'd given him when he'd told her she could have the cottage that had made him go weak at the knees.

When he tried to study his accounts he saw her image staring back at him; when he gazed out to the sea her face appeared before him, calling him on. He was being stupid. He was behaving like a fool. He'd told himself that a hundred times over, but it had done no good. He'd told himself a hundred times that she was young enough to be his daughter, and in love with another man, but even that didn't stop his obsession.

Then the disaster had occurred, and the Gifford lad had gone down with the others. There would be no marriage now; the young man she loved was dead and gone. Did that mean he stood a chance?

James Campbell ground his knuckles into his thighs. A butterfly drawn irresistibly to nectar, that was how he felt every time he saw her now. A moth winging frantically towards the flame. Oh, he told himself, he was being ridiculous; succumbing to middle-age fantasies, searching for his youth in the arms of a girl. But nothing could deter his heart.

With a snort, he raised his eyes determinedly to the pulpit, and tried to concentrate on what was being said. Within seconds, however, his willpower was completely overridden and his gaze was once more on the back of Sheila's head.

James Campbell awoke with a start. He was trembling all over, and filled with a terrible fear. He'd been thinking in his sleep about Sheila Beattie.

With nearly all the young eligible Dragonholme men dead, her own family's source of livelihood gone, and no work in the village, what was to keep her there?

There was the mother of course, but was that enough? He doubted it. Not for a beautiful spirited girl like Sheila.

The mother would have the insurance money from the *Bluebell* to fall back on, of course, so there was no immediate hardship for her or her family. But that in itself worked against keeping Sheila in Dragonholme, for it freed her to go elsewhere to find work – to eventually find herself a new man.

The thought of never seeing Sheila again filled him with panic and a dull sense of loss. In the dark, quiet, lonely room James Campbell made a vow to himself. He vowed that Sheila Beattie would stay in Dragonholme, no matter what.

He knew he wanted her for himself. And what he wanted, he always got. One way or the other.

*　　*　　*

73

Some days later, Sheila and Peg were sitting on either side of the range, each preoccupied with her own thoughts. The house hadn't been cleaned or even tidied since the disaster. Neither of them had the will or the energy to do anything more than get from one day to the next.

Sheila looked up when there was a rap on the door. 'I'll get it,' she muttered, thinking it was one of the neighbours. But it wasn't a neighbour. It was a tall, thin man wearing grey pin-striped trousers, a black jacket and a homburg. In his right hand he carried an attaché case.

'Miss Beattie?' the man asked, doffing his hat.

'Sheila Beattie, that's right.'

'I'm Mr Dunwoodie from Eyemouth. I handled your father's marine insurance.'

'You mean the *Bluebell*?'

'Exactly,' replied Dunwoodie, smiling evenly and politely to hide his nervousness. This was going to be absolutely awful, but it had to be done.

Peg rose and smoothed down the front of her crumpled dress. It was indicative of her state of mind that it didn't bother her that the house was in a mess. She'd been sleeping badly, and it showed in the tightness and pallor of her face.

'Come away in, Mr Dunwoodie. Davey mentioned you to me,' she called out.

Dunwoodie went to Peg, and shook hands with her, then spoke in sombre tones the little speech of condolence he'd prepared.

Sheila offered to make a cup of tea, which he refused. Peg gestured him to a seat, and having sat, he busied himself removing various sheets of paper from his case.

'I've been expecting you, Mr Dunwoodie,' Peg said, giving him a wan smile.

Dunwoodie shuffled his papers, paused, coughed, then shuffled his papers again. This was turning out to be even more difficult than he'd anticipated. For a brief second he considered reneging on the deal he'd made

74

with James Campbell, then told himself not to be a bloody fool. Sentiment had no place in business. It was the chance of a lifetime, and if he didn't grasp it firmly with both hands he would regret it for as long as he lived.

Only five years old, Dunwoodie's was a tiny agency compared with the two giants in this field – Grant and Lisle of Aberdeen and John Kerrigan of Peterhead – who between them handled about seventy-five per cent of the Scottish boats. But that would change when he landed the entire Portnessie fleet, as Campbell had promised. With them on his books his agency would have a chance at the really big time. Besides, he reassured himself, Campbell had assured him that everything would be all right; no one would be hurt by their little deception. All he had to do was adjust the company's records and tell one small lie to Mrs Beattie. What could be simpler?

'I'm afraid I've got some bad news for you,' Dunwoodie said, finally turning his attention to Peg.

Peg glanced in surprise to Sheila, then back again to Dunwoodie. 'What does that mean?'

Dunwoodie, his expression one of sympathy and concern, glibly spoke his lie. 'Mr Beattie's monthly renewal payment fell due the week before the tragedy. The money never arrived in at my office. Consequently, and it pains me to say so, the *Bluebell* wasn't covered when she went down.'

'Oh my God!' whispered Sheila.

Peg shook her head. This just wasn't like Davey, he'd always been so meticulous about such matters.

Dunwoodie brought out the reasons he'd known would make sense. 'I believe your husband invested all his capital in the *Bluebell*.'

Peg stared at him, numb with disbelief, able only to give the smallest of nods.

'As it's been such an appalling season to date, I can only think that he became acutely short of cash and neglected to make his payment on time. It is regrettable and unfortunate that this non-payment coincided with the loss of the boat.' Dunwoodie gave a little cough.

'Had he ever faulted on a payment before?' asked Sheila.

'That was the first time since I started handling his business, and I believe the first time ever.' His eyes showed nothing but concern.

'Then surely the insurance company can make an allowance for one lapse?' Sheila's voice was shrill with desperation.

Peg said nothing.

'I'm sorry,' Dunwoodie said softly.

'You mean you won't even speak to them about it?'

'I mean I already have, and the answer was no.' Dunwoodie turned to Peg for support, but she seemed barely aware that he was still there.

Sheila felt as if the world was crumbling around her. They'd been counting on the insurance money. Without it, things would be bad enough for her and Peg, but what was it going to be like for Rhona and Maggie? They had bairns to clothe and feed.

Peg passed a weary hand across her brow. She felt she'd aged a dozen years since watching the *Bluebell* sink; she felt she'd just aged that again.

Dunwoodie didn't even bother to ask if Davey and his sons carried life assurance, knowing the answer would almost certainly be no. He'd never met a fisherman who didn't believe that it was unlucky and tempting fate.

Dunwoodie slipped his papers, props in this charade, into his attaché case, then rose. Having done what he'd come to do, he couldn't wait to get out of the house. 'And now I'll have to go, I have many other calls to make today,' he said apologetically.

'Yes, of course,' whispered Peg.

'Were any of the other boats behind in their payments?' Sheila asked.

The daughter was certainly a beauty, Dunwoodie

76

thought as he shook his head sadly, unaware that Sheila was the cause of Campbell's scheme.

Peg and Sheila saw him to the door, and he told them again how sorry he was to be the bearer of such bad tidings. When he was gone, Peg, in a tremulous voice, instructed Sheila to wait a minute to let him get clear, then to run and tell Rhona and Maggie to come over. There was no point in putting off bad news.

Peg poured out some drams, whisky of Davey's that had been lying in the press. When Rhona, Maggie and the weans were assembled, Peg broke the news as gently as she could, in a voice that was barely more than a whisper, then passed around the drams.

Rhona looked down at Ian and started to cry, the tears running down her cheeks, her sobs soaking her otherwise motionless body. Maggie, however, went completely still. She might have been poleaxed.

'What about my house?' Rhona choked through her tears. 'You know it's only partly paid for, Ma. I was counting on my share of the insurance money to pay off the rest.'

'So was I,' Maggie whispered, drinking off her dram in a single gulp.

Rhona rested her head in her hands. 'I have fifteen pounds to my name,' she said softly. 'Fifteen pounds.'

'And I've got seven pounds twelve and six,' said Maggie.

Neither amount was going to get them very far.

Peg alone was calm, as though beyond her own hurt and fear. They'd have to talk this through, she said. It was no time for self-pity. Rhona wiped away her tears, and, clutching Ian to her bosom, brought herself under control. Violet and wee Dougal took themselves off in a corner where they began playing with an old tin tray that Davey had brought back years before as a souvenir of Cromer.

The women talked for hours, their voices strained but unemotional. They might have been discussing anything

– a special occasion, or a daily event – might have been any four women just passing the time of day. In the end, Rhona decided that she couldn't keep her house. She would go to work if she could, but there was no work in Dragonholme not connected with the fishing. No – as far as she could see there was only one path left open to her and that was to try and sell the house and move back in with her parents. She and Ian would be all right there. They'd manage somehow.

But Maggie had no parents to return to. They had died within months of one another after she and Dougal were married. She had a sister in Coldingham, but Lizzie would hardly welcome her with open arms. Lizzie lived in a two room but and and ben with eight bairns and had enough problems of her own.

'Then you must move in here,' Peg said to Maggie after they had been through all the possibilities.

Sheila's heart sank. As sorry and sympathetic as she felt for Maggie, the last thing she wanted was to live under the same roof as her sister-in-law. The pair of them would just never get on together, no matter how great the tragedy that united them.

'There's nothing else for it. She was my son's wife and they are Dougal's children,' Peg said to Sheila later when they were alone again.

'Nothing else we could do,' Sheila agreed. 'Nothing else at all.'

On the same day that Maggie, wee Dougal and Violet came to live with Peg and Sheila, word arrived in Dragonholme that the great shoals had reappeared in the southern North Sea. In Upper Scruff, Clay Deep, Tea Kettle Hole and the Silver Pits they were to be found teeming in unbelievable numbers.

In a world that seemed to have lost all its hope, all reason of existence, the reappearance of the great shoals gave the entire village a new surge of life and the promise of normality. The sense of gloom that had descended on all of Dragonholme with the tragedy shifted. Once again there was activity and an undercurrent of excitement. Once again the village began to bustle and smile.

What remained of the Dragonholme fleet – nine boats out of the original twenty-eight – elected a new admiral and put to sea for the first time since the disaster, heading south. The entire village turned out to wish them luck. Not a soul left the quayside until the last sail had been waved out of sight.

Living together it didn't take long before Sheila and Maggie were squabbling night and day. As Peg said, the only time there was any peace was when both of them were asleep. For her mother's sake, Sheila tried to hold her temper, but on several occasions it got so bad between her and Maggie that she had to run out of the house, not wanting Maggie to see her greet, and had ended up in Old Granny Mutch's place where she cried until she could cry no more, thinking of how things would have been if Eric had lived; if she still had dreams.

One afternoon when they were all sitting outside the house doing various tasks, the weans playing tumble-your-wilkies, there was the clip clop of horse's hooves and the laird, mounted on his black hunter, appeared at the top of the rise.

Peg was preparing to give James Campbell a cordial nod as he passed by, but he surprised all three women by reining in and dismounting. The children, eyes wide, left off their game, following his every movement as he tied off Satan and strolled over to Peg. Only after he had formally introduced himself and engaged her in several minutes' polite conversation did he get around to the real purpose of his visit. 'I've heard about the trouble you had over the *Bluebell*,' he said sympathetically. 'It's a sad business indeed.'

Peg nodded, even more awed by him than the children

79

were. 'Aye, it was that,' she said softly, embarrassed by his knowledge.

James looked away towards the treacherous sea. 'Aye, a sad business.' Then, turning back to her suddenly, he said, 'I think there's a way I can help you.'

Peg drew herself up to her full height, her shyness gone. It was kind of him to offer and she appreciated his kindness, but things hadn't come to such a pass with them yet that they had to accept charity. They had always got by and they would still.

'You misconstrue my meaning, Mrs Beattie,' Campbell said gently, making it clear that he was one of them, after all. He wouldn't insult the wife of Davey Beattie by making such a gesture. No, what he had in mind was the position of maid that had suddenly fallen vacant at the Hall. 'I thought that perhaps your daughter Sheila would be interested in the post,' he concluded.

The wage he proposed was so handsome that even Peg's natural reservations were weakened. Her eyes moved from Campbell to Sheila and back again. It would certainly solve some problems.

'Would I be living in?' asked Sheila.

'Yes indeed, with all found.'

'It does sound like a good opportunity,' ventured Peg.

'I had to sack the girl we had,' Campbell continued. 'She was lazy and I won't tolerate that at any price. I thought of your Sheila because she struck me as a concientious and industrious worker. I'll warrant I'm not wrong?'

'I'd recommend her to anybody, even the King himself,' Peg replied proudly.

The poor lassie James Campbell had given the sack had indeed had a lazy streak in her, but not nearly enough for her to merit being discharged. She'd gone because it suited James Campbell's purposes. And James Campbell's purposes had become the only important thing in the world. Although he was now standing quite calmly and normally in the bright light of the sun, for all the

80

world like a man who needs a servant, his obsession with Sheila had become the strongest passion in his life.

'Well, Sheila, what's your answer then?' Campbell asked with a smile.

'I think, sir,' said Peg, 'that we'd better have some time to think about it.'

'I accept,' interrupted Sheila. 'There's nothing to think about. When would you like me to start?'

'Shall we say you come up to the Hall on Sunday evening, and begin Monday morning?'

'I'll be there, sir.'

'Excellent, that's settled then!' Campbell beamed, and giving Peg a small salute by touching his riding crop to his hat he walked smartly over to Satan, untied his horse, and swung himself into the saddle.

Satan snorted and pawed the ground, then he and Campbell were clattering away up the street, Satan's hooves striking sparks from the cobbles.

'Now there's a stroke of luck!' cried a still-shocked Peg as they watched man and horse thunder away.

'What a nice man,' said Maggie.

Yes, Peg and Sheila agreed. Imagine him going out of his way to help them because the *Bluebell* hadn't been insured. Yes, he was a nice man, she said, a really nice man.

On Sunday evening after tea, Sheila duly presented herself at the Hall as had been arranged, going to the same side entrance that the ghillie Simpson had taken her to the day he'd brought her to see the laird.

Annie Tripp, the cook she'd made friends with on that visit, was there to greet her, pumping her by the hand and saying how marvellous it was they were going to be working together, and would Sheila like a cup of tea and a slice of cake?

Sheila was halfway through her second slice of cream sponge when a maid called Agnes Robertson joined them, back from her day off. A middle-aged woman, originally from Glasgow, Agnes had been in service all her life. Sheila took a shine to Agnes, who obviously reciprocated the feeling, and soon the three of them, Sheila, Annie and Agnes, were chattering away like old friends.

There was another maid, Agnes said, called Pat Dyer, but her job was to attend to Herself, as Mrs Campbell was known below stairs by the staff. Her ladyship was very grand, Agnes explained with relish. Right out of the top drawer and hoity toity with it as well. Not like his lordship at all.

'Do they get on, then?' asked Sheila, overwhelmed with curiosity.

Agnes shrugged, rolling her eyes at Annie. 'After a fashion,' she said.

There was a warm, friendly atmosphere in the kitchen. Sheila couldn't believe that it didn't extend throughout the house. Laughing at Agnes's impersonation of Herself, she still thought life here was going to be pleasurable, even fun.

Annie was clearing away their dishes when Hay, the butler, appeared. Sheila could tell instantly that what Agnes had said about Hay was right. He was a lovely old man. How could she be anything but happy here?

Hay added his welcome to Annie and Agnes's, then informed Sheila that after she'd settled into her room Mrs Campbell would like a word in the library. The working day started at six, he went on, and she was expected to start promptly. Breakfast for the staff was laid out at five-thirty, and removed again at five minutes to six.

All the introductions out of the way, Agnes then took Sheila along to her room.

'Toilet, my room, Pat's, and this one along at the very end is your,' said Agnes, and on arriving at the last door on the landing, she opened it with a flourish and ushered Sheila inside.

The fragile evening light still filled the tiny room.

'Hardly the Ritz, but it beats some I've had to put up with in my time,' Agnes sniffed. 'I'll let you freshen up and then I'll come back to show you to the library. Herself doesn't like to be kept waiting.'

After Agnes had left, Sheila stared round her new quarters. The room was small but fairly well furnished. There was an iron sprung bed, and a mattress with clean sheets and blankets folded neatly at one end, a wash-stand with a bowl and jug, a free-standing, ornately decorated wardrobe, and a solitary wooden chair. Inside the wardrobe were two clean uniforms hanging on the rail.

She unpacked her few belongings, hanging her clothes alongside the uniforms and then put the few treasured knick-knacks round the room. Perhaps it was just homesickness, but suddenly she felt the tears come to her eyes. Suddenly, more than anything, she wished she had a photograph of Eric to put out. A photograph of him so handsome and happy – her Eric – but he had never had one taken.

The room wasn't exactly cosy as it was now, she thought, but with a wee bit of effort she'd soon have it a proper home from home. Fussing in her pocket, she pulled out a handkerchief to dry her eyes. Yes, soon she'd have it a proper wee home.

'Come in!' called out an extremely well-spoken female voice when Agnes knocked on the library door. Sheila's heart gave a little leap. Agnes, with Sheila behind her, entered and curtsied.

'Sheila Beattie, the new maid, ma'am,' announced Agnes, giving Sheila a little nudge so that she would curtsey too.

Fiona and James were playing backgammon, he with a glass of claret and half empty decanter on his side of the table, she with a look of determined concentration.

Fiona beckoned Sheila over, and Agnes didn't so much

leave as vanish. Suddenly Sheila felt shy and awkward, a lump of a girl compared to the stunningly graceful and elegant woman before her. Perhaps this was all a mistake and the day-dreams she'd been having since the afternoon of the laird's visit – the fantasies of a new, exciting world free from sadness – were only the foolish dreams of a child.

James Campbell looked up suddenly from the board and smiled at her – almost as though he'd read her mind.

'I'm pleased to meet you Sheila,' pronounced Fiona Campbell, with all the warmth of a December morning. 'I believe you're the girl who lost her father and three brothers in that terrible disaster,' she said, throwing her dice.

Fiona had been deeply moved by the funeral service. As she told everyone who would listen, there had been so great a sense of suffering and loss inside the church that just being a part of the assembly had left her drained and weakened for days afterwards. 'A terrible happening – a terrible happening indeed,' she fretted, knocking her husband's counter from the board.

'It's the price of fish, ma'am,' Sheila replied in a whisper.

Fiona stared at her blankly. 'The price of fish? Whatever do you mean?'

Sheila gave a thin smile. 'Men's lives, ma'am. That's the real price of fish.'

Once more James Campbell raised his gaze to Sheila, a look of open admiration in his smile.

'I think, my dear,' he said, 'that it's your move.'

Sheila was the first to join Annie Tripp in the kitchen next morning. She had had some trouble getting off to sleep the night before, lying nervously awake long after the rest of the house was asleep, dozing fitfully now and then, only to be awoken by her mother's voice or a dream of Eric's face. This morning, though, she was feeling

quite cheerful. As the staff gathered around the enormous kitchen table, talking and laughing as they ate the
plentiful breakfast, even Sheila's feelings of loneliness
began to fade. Last night she had felt frightened and
alone, but this morning she felt among friends.

They were all laughing at Agnes's story of Herself
taking to her bed for three days when they ran out of her
favourite imported mustard, when a shadow fell across
the table.

There stood Simpson, the ghillie.

'What's this the cat dragged in?' he demanded, glowering at Sheila.

'This is Sheila Beattie,' Agnes explained. 'She's taken
over from Min.'

'Mr Simpson and I have already met,' said Sheila,
meeting his eyes.

'The new maid?' Simpson mused, and gave a dry
humourless chuckle.

Sheila stared at him boldly, but the others averted their
eyes, beginning to talk again, though softly, among
themselves.

Simpson sat at the other end of the table, facing Hay.
'I'll be having the porage, then,' he announced.

'None on the day I'm afraid,' replied Annie.

'Why the hell not?'

Sheila glanced at Hay, who was steadfastly addressing
his attention to the plate in front of him. For some reason,
Hay was scared of Simpson, Sheila guessed. Why else did
Hay allow him such liberties in the butler's domain?

'Because we've run out. I can't give you what I haven't
got, Mr Simpson, now can I?'

'Bloody bad management if you ask me,' Simpson
grumbled. 'Let me have some of the scrambled egg then.
I hope it's better than the last lot you made.'

Annie banged a plate on to the table in front of him.
Looking across at Sheila, she raised her eyes to heaven.

Agnes excused herself and fled the kitchen.

They're all scared of him, Sheila thought. Did he

behave like that all the time, or was it laid on especially for her?

'I'll have a cup of tea then,' Simpson called to Annie, spraying crumbs of egg and bread all round him.

'I thought it was Dragonholme Hall I'd come to, not the piggery on Bogside Farm,' Sheila said suddenly to no one in particular. Simpson's head rose immediately, his eyes dark with fury.

'I'll have no lip out of you, girl. Mind your place.'

Without another word Sheila rose from her place, took her dirty dishes to the sink, then headed for the door. Just before it closed behind her, she popped her head back in.

'Oink!' she said. 'Oink! Oink!'

It was just after midnight as James Campbell reached for the whisky and poured himself yet another dram, well on the way to being drunker than he had been in many a month.

He was sitting at the desk in his study, a pile of important-looking papers spread before him. He'd come here directly after dinner, ostensibly to get on with some pressing paperwork, but had, in fact, been unable to concentrate on clauses and data, unable to drag his thoughts away from waking dreams of a young girl with tawny hair and an impish grin. Sheila had been with them for ten days now, and he could no longer remember what it had been like without her – without the sound of her laughter bubbling in the hallways, without her smile lighting the dour and gloomy, the lonely rooms of Dragonholme Hall. Every day his fascination with her intensified, his need to hear her voice or catch a glimpse of her bustling through her chores became more obsessive. Had it been so long since anything other than work – than his own determination to succeed, to prove himself – had given him any pleasure? So long since he had been able to smile, to feel joy touch his heart like a warming sun?

Now, however, he had to be away from Dragonholme for some time. He had to go down to Grimsby to sort out a problem with the fleet, and from there he had to go to Germany for at least a week. No matter how well things went, it would mean his being away for at least three or four weeks. Three or four weeks away from Sheila.

Getting up from his desk he crossed to the window, staring out over the sea. All his energy, all his passion and all his dreams had been spent on the accumulation of power and of money. And that, he realized, his mind constructing images from the darkness of the night, was all he had. Power and money – not happiness; not love.

Confused by the whisky and by the turmoil in his own heart, James Campbell leaned his head against the glass. There had been several women in his life – many before Fiona, and one or two after – but not one of them had ever touched his soul or roused in him these feelings of longing and hope.

'I love her,' he whispered into the night. 'I love her.' And he was filled with amazement and wonder.

Outside the walls of his mansion, the wind whispered back his words. I love her. I love her.

But would she ever be his? He might hope to have her body – he was not, after all, either an unimportant or an unattractive man – but it was not her body alone which he craved. He wanted her: her friendship and her lips against his own; her sympathy and trust; her passion and her concern. As much as he wanted to make love to her, he wanted her affection even more.

Swaying slightly, he returned to his desk and helped himself to another drink. Perhaps, when he came back from Germany, he would be able to make some changes in his life. If he could convince Fiona to stay in Edinburgh (and surely that would be no difficult task; there was nothing she hated more than being stuck in the middle of nowhere, as she put it), he might be able to approach Sheila as himself, get to know her – let her get to know him.

Perhaps, he thought, losing himself once more in alcoholic fantasies, perhaps there was hope for him yet.

But James Campbell wasn't the only one who was obsessed with Sheila that night. Wally Simpson, lying abed in his cottage a quarter of a mile from the Hall, was thinking about her as well. It was not love, however, that kept him awake.

That Beattie bitch, he thought to himself. She was undermining his authority, making him look a fool in front of the others. More than that, she was turning them against him. It wouldn't be long before they were all laughing at him, right to his face. She needed taking down a peg or two, and he was just the man to do it. To do it and enjoy doing it. Oh, aye, he'd enjoy doing it, all right, he'd certainly do that.

If only he could think of how.

'So tell me about the family,' Sheila said to Agnes. 'I know they have two boys at fancy schools in England, but that's all.'

The pair of them were sitting at the kitchen table, polishing the silver while Hay had a sleep on one of the chairs by the fireplace. Pat Dyer had gone off to Edinburgh with the Campbells when they'd left an hour previously, and Annie was down in the cellar stock-taking her supplies.

'There are just the two boys, Drew and Robert. Drew is the oldest, but he's left school now, although I couldn't say where he is or what he's doing. He's a bit of a strange fish is Drew.'

'And why wasn't Robert home for the school holidays? Don't either of them come to visit their parents?'

'He went to France with friends or something like that,' said Agnes. 'Pat says he'll be back at Christmas.'

'And will Drew be visiting the Hall then do you think?'

'Your guess is as good as mine. He could come. Then again, he might not. You'll meet him eventually, though. Neither of the boys is a patch on their father,' concluded Agnes with a wink.

Their chatter ceased immediately as Simpson came into the kitchen from outside, smirking as though enjoying a private joke.

'Are they away then?' Simpson asked, knowing full well that they were. He'd been standing on a nearby hillside, watching the carriage drive off.

'Aye, they're away,' Agnes answered, without looking at him and vigorously rubbing a soup spoon.

Still smirking, Simpson looked directly at Sheila, who was doing her best to ignore him, and then sauntered over to the sleeping butler.

'Been at the sherry again, Hay?' he bellowed suddenly.

A startled and frightened Hay came instantly awake. 'Eh! Eh!' he exclaimed. 'What?'

Simpson's smirk widened into a leer. 'I said, have you been at the sherry again, old man?'

Hay sat up, straightened his clothes, then smoothed back his hair, playing for time until he'd pulled himself together.

'What are you saying?' he asked at last in a mild voice.

Simpson squatted so that he was on eye level with Hay. 'I know you've got a taste for the laird's sherry, old man, and that not content with helping yourself during the day you pinch bottles of the stuff when you think no-one's looking.'

Hay went white as a sheet. His gaze darted first to Agnes, then to Sheila. Both of them pretended to be so thoroughly engrossed in what they were doing that they seemed unaware that there was anyone else in the room. In reality, though, they were all ears.

Now what's all this in aid of, wondered Sheila as she buffed a gravy boat.

Simpson shook his head and tut tutted. 'Here's the

laird hardly gone, and already you're drunk on duty. Drunk to the extent of passing out,' he accused.

'I am not drunk, and I have never passed out!' replied Hay indignantly. 'I was only enjoying a wee nap, that's all.'

'There's only one type of person the laird hates more than an idler, and that's a thief,' Simpson said evenly.

Hay stared at him in horror. What a totally odious man. If it weren't for Simpson, this would be the most perfect post. And how on earth had Simpson found out about the sherry anyway? He'd thought he'd been so careful, but obviously he hadn't been careful enough.

'The sack with no second chances and no reference, that's what the laird would give you if he found out,' continued Simpson. 'And at your age it wouldn't be so easy for you to get more work.'

Hay stared into Simpson's mean and greedy eyes. 'Why are you telling me all this?' he asked at last in almost a whisper.

Simpson rose and stretched, teasing out the time before replying. He'd blackmailed Hay once before, but what he was holding over Hay now was far more serious. The first time had been only a test. A test that Hay had passed.

At last he spoke. 'With the laird and Herself away for some weeks, you won't be needing the same amount of work done indoors I'm thinking,' he said. 'As I have more than I can cope with, I thought it would be a friendly act on your part to lend me one of the maids as a help.'

Sheila paused in mid buff. So that was it. It wasn't Hay he was after at all. It was her.

Simpson squatted down so that he was face to face with Hay. 'Well?'

Hay licked lips that were dry. What could he do other than comply? He was trapped, snared by Simpson, who only had to pull the snare tight to do for him. Being a ghillie Simpson was a dab hand with snares. Hay

90

couldn't help feeling a certain kinship and sympathy with the many rabbits Simpson had brought back for the pot.

'I'm sure that'll be all right,' he mumbled feebly.

Simpson gave a triumphant smile which he directed straight at Sheila. 'I think I'll have little miss smart mouth there,' he said.

Sheila wanted nothing more than to tell him to take a running jump. How could she though? If she refused to co-operate Simpson would report Hay, and Hay would almost surely be fired. She couldn't let that happen to the old man. He'd been kindness itself to her since her arrival at the Hall. And Simpson, of course, had said all this in front of her so that she would know what a refusal on her part would mean. 'I'll be delighted to help you,' she said pleasantly.

Hay breathed a sigh of relief, and threw Sheila a grateful look. My God, he thought, I've never needed a sherry more than I do right now.

Simpson nodded curtly. Oh, this was going to be rare! 'Tomorrow then. Be ready,' he said, and strode from the kitchen.

'You were right,' Agnes said vehemently after Simpson had gone. 'He is a pig.'

With as much dignity as he could muster Hay thanked Sheila, then hurried off to his room.

There was an autumn nip in the air, Sheila thought, as she followed Simpson along the track through a small wood of firs. They'd come about three miles so far, she judged.

On leaving the wood they skirted a loch, coming eventually to some bogland from which several long strips of peat had already been taken. 'Have you ever dug peat before?' asked Simpson.

Sheila shook her head, understanding now what the unusual-shaped spade he'd brought along was for.

'I'll show you how it's done then,' he said. 'Pay attention.'

He cut the brick of peat expertly, having done it countless times before; then he cut another and placed it beside the first.

Sheila caught the spade when he threw it at her. 'Let's see you do that,' he ordered.

It wasn't nearly as easy as it appeared, but then she hadn't expected it to be. Her initial efforts were disastrous, but gradually she began to get the hang of it.

'Hard graft, wouldn't you say?' Simpson smiled.

'I'm used to grafting,' she answered in an unconcerned tone. 'I was brought up to it.'

For a second anger flashed in his eyes. She had an answer for everything, this one. 'I'll be back when it's time for you to knock off. And no slacking, mind, or I'll be having that word with the laird about Hay after all.' And with that he strode away.

Sheila started to hum, as if she were enjoying what she was doing, sure that that would annoy him. 'Oink!' she said to his retreating back. 'Oink! Oink!'

She woke next morning feeling as though she'd been through the heavy mangle Peg used at home for wringing out the washing. She'd never been so stiff, every muscle in her body aching excruciatingly.

It took her three times longer than usual to get dressed, and when she came to walk she found that she was hobbling.

Outside the kitchen she took a deep breath, willing her body to function and behave as it did normally. 'Morning!' she called out cheerily as she breezed in through the door.

Agnes paled on seeing Sheila's hands. Her palms were covered in blisters and were red raw in patches. 'That's terrible,' she muttered, pointing at them. 'Whatever have you been up to?'

Simpson slurped his tea. Hay seemed to be having trouble with his breathing.

Annie dished out a pair of kippers for Sheila, watching in concern as Sheila had difficulty in holding her knife and fork.

'I'll put something on those hands after you've had your breakfast,' she said.

'There won't be time for that,' Simpson snapped, gesturing at the clock on the wall. There was only a minute left before the staff were expected to start work.

It was Sheila's own fault that her hands hadn't been attended to the night before, but she'd been so totally exhausted when she'd arrived back at the Hall that she'd bypassed the kitchen, and gone straight up to her bed where she'd fallen instantly asleep. Her intention had been to come down later and get a bite of supper and have her hands attended to then, but she'd slept right through till morning.

'Time to get going,' shouted Simpson, getting to his feet. 'It's peat cutting again today. We wouldn't want to get a late start, would we?'

'Oh good! I enjoy the fresh air and exercise,' smiled Sheila forcing herself on to her feet. At least she had the satisfaction of seeing a scowl come to his face.

The sea gently lapped the beach, a playful puppy dog compared to the terrible monster it had been the day it had swallowed her future and her past.

She could see Eric everywhere: here was a large tuft of marram grass on which they'd once sat; there the black rock he'd chased her round on her fourteenth birthday. But most poignant of all was the Gifford hut where they'd spent so many hours making love, and which she was now staring at, dreading entering, yet being drawn there as iron to a magnet.

It was her day off and she'd just been to see Peg. She hadn't intended visiting the beach, or the hut, but somehow, as though they had a separate will of their own, her feet had brought her here.

A lump came into her throat as she entered. Of all places, this was the one she most identified with Eric. It was here she'd given him her virginity and her love.

She remembered the last time – *the last time!* she thought, and moaned softly, still not able to truly believe she'd never see him again, that he was gone forever.

Hot tears burst from her eyes and slowly she sank to her knees. 'Oh Eric! Eric!' she wailed. But only the sound of the sea answered her call of grief.

'You look dreadful,' said Annie Tripp, handing Sheila a cup of tea.

Sheila knew she looked dreadful. She couldn't have expected to look otherwise after the amount of crying she'd done in the Gifford hut. Inside her, though, there was a new feeling of peace.

'It's my ma,' said Sheila slowly, telling at least part of the truth. 'I'm worried about her. She's having a hard time of it right now.'

'Is the money you're giving her not enough?' There was genuine concern in Annie's voice.

'No, it's not that. My sister-in-law is living with her now . . . and – '

'And they're not getting along?'

'No,' sighed Sheila. 'It's just awful. They're not getting along at all.'

'Aye, two grown women sharing a kitchen is always a problem,' agreed Annie.

'I'm really worried about my ma, though,' Sheila went on. 'She used to be so outgoing. She always kept everything going. Now she just wanders around like a ghost. It's as though she died with Da and the boys.'

'And how's her health?'

'She's lost weight. But she doesn't seem to have any energy any more. She acts as if everything is an effort.'

'Ah well,' said Annie gently. 'She's bound to be feeling bad, isn't she. I'm sure she'll get over it in time. It's you I'm worried about right now. You're half dead on your feet.'

For the first time all day, Sheila smiled. 'You are kind to me,' she said. 'I'll be all right. I'm just a bit tired.'

'That's right,' said Annie, nearly helping Sheila to her feet. 'You go upstairs and get some sleep. You'll feel better in the morning. You'll see.'

'Yes,' said Sheila. 'I'll feel better in the morning.'

Simpson stood watching Sheila cut and stack the peat bricks. That's a strong bitch, that one, he thought to himself, his eyes moving along her firm young body, along the muscles of her arms and the swell of her breasts. A strong bitch, that one. Strong and spirited.

His plan that the task would break her wasn't working. By now he had expected her to be begging for his kindness. Please, Mr Simpson, I'll do anything you ask. Please, Mr Simpson, I'll never laugh at you again. Please, sir, isn't there something I can get you that you want?

And suddenly, standing there watching her body strain against her clothing as she worked, Simpson realized what he wanted. And an expression of unholy joy suffused his face.

James Campbell swung himself up on to Satan in such a way that anyone watching him would have thought, now there's a happy man! My, but it was grand being back at Dragonholme. James Campbell exalted to himself. And a full fortnight before he'd thought possible. How thoughtful of Max Abelman to die and make the trip to Germany impossible for several months! How kind of Fiona to insist on staying in Edinburgh! 'I'm not going back to that mausoleum till I'm ready,' she'd screamed at him. 'It may be your idea of living, cooped up in that monstrosity, but it's not mine. I want to be with people who don't smell of fish. I want to be surrounded by beauty, not by a bunch of fishermen and their ugly wives.' Thinking of Fiona, he smiled. With a bit of luck she'd stay in Edinburgh till Christmas.

He couldn't wait to see Sheila. Why she should be out helping Simpson and not working in the house baffled him. And what on earth was wrong with Hay? He'd thought the man was going to faint when he'd shown up unexpectedly.

Satan trembled beneath him, eager for a good run. Once clear of the stables, James touched the black horse on the flanks and Satan immediately broke into a trot and seconds later into a full gallop.

The directions Hay had given him to locate Simpson and Sheila hadn't been at all clear; but he'd find them. Even if it took him the rest of the afternoon he'd find them.

She had been working alone for what seemed like hours, cutting the bricks and then stacking them, cutting them and stacking them for what seemed like days, waiting for Simpson to come along with the cart. Every muscle, every bone in her body ached and her throat was parched – Simpson had forgotten to give her any ration of water. She had just stopped for a moment, squinting up at the sky to try to judge the time, when Simpson and the cart appeared over a hill. She had been so happy to see another person, even Simpson, and so eager for a drink, that she hadn't noticed the peculiar way he watched her as she hurried towards the cart.

'Did you bring me some water?' she panted as she reached him.

'It's in the cart,' he said, nodding his head, his eyes not moving from her. And even when, kneeling on the floor of the cart, she had turned back to say that she couldn't find the water, it must be up front with him – and had seen him there, suddenly standing right behind her with his belt in his hands – even then she hadn't understood.

'I'm going to give you something that's even better than water,' cooed Simpson, squatting down beside her, one hand already clasped around her wrist, the other reaching out to touch her breast through the thin cloth of her blouse. 'Much much better than water.'

And then she screamed. She screamed, summing all the strength her broken body could muster, and shoved him off balance, scrabbling over the side of the cart and on to the ground. He caught her easily, wrestling her back to the ground, his hands tearing at her clothes, his weight pinning her down, the belt slapping her across the face.

'You little bitch,' he screamed over and over. 'I'll show you who's boss around here. I'll show you – '

Simpson felt the new presence first. Sheila was still fighting and screaming, when he suddenly looked up – up and straight into the eyes of James Campbell. The next thing Simpson knew, he was being jerked into the air.

'It's not my fault,' pleaded the ghillie. 'She was asking for it. I had to teach her a lesson.'

'And now I'm going to teach you one.'

Only when she heard James Campbell's voice did Sheila stop screaming. Streaked with dirt and blood, her clothes in tatters, her body still shaking with sobs, she watched as the riding crop was raised for the first time.

After that, she must have fainted. When she came around, she was back at the hall, in a strange bed, and sitting beside her, lightly dozing, was Annie Tripp. Sheila closed her eyes and tried to remember what had happened. Slowly, it all came back to her: the cart and Simpson, the animal fury of his attack, the terror that had shaken her very soul – and something else. The riding crop, Simpson's gibbering screams – and then a quiet, gentle voice saying 'It's all right, Sheila, it's all over now. You're safe again. It's all right, Sheila', and the strong arms around her, lifting her against his chest and the beating of his heart.

*　　*　　*

By the time Sheila was feeling well enough to leave the guest room James Campbell had insisted she be put in when he brought her home on that dreadful afternoon, Simpson had been sent packing. The incident in the field had become common knowledge in Dragonholme, although the laird had forbidden its discussion, and Simpson had slunk off in disgrace.

It was also common knowledge, of course, that the laird had Mrs Beattie brought to the Hall on the following day to see her daughter. Peg told everyone not only about the wonders of the Hall itself and the hospitality and kindness of James Campbell, but of his almost fatherly concern for Sheila; how he apologized over and over for letting any harm come to her while she was under his roof.

'Her own da wouldn't have been more upset,' she later commented to Maggie. 'It makes me feel much easier, knowing she's in such good hands.'

While she was confined to her bed, the laird came to visit her several times a day, bringing her presents (a book or two he thought she might enjoy reading, a bunch of flowers, a new dress to replace her damaged clothes) and sitting for hours, teaching her to play backgammon and cards, telling her stories about the world outside Dragonholme. Although he had wanted to immediately dismiss Hay when he first heard the details of her ordeal with Simpson, Campbell eventually gave in to Sheila's pleas for leniency towards the old man.

'I can't keep him around, not after all that's gone on,' he reasoned with her, 'but I can give him a good reference to be going on with. I don't think I can be fairer than that.'

No, thought Sheila, he probably couldn't, not a man like James Campbell with all his private rules and principles, his strict standards of right and wrong. She knew him well enough now to know that though he was, at heart, a kind and giving man, he was so afraid of seeming weak or malleable that he rarely showed any sign of softness or common compassion. His business associates knew him as a hard and remorseless man, and so, too, did his employees, his family and the few people who might consider themselves his friends. Fair, most people would have said of him, James Campbell's a fair man, but no more than fair.

A week after James Campbell rescued her from Simpson, Sheila was ready to start work again, but the laird refused to hear of it. 'You'll take another week off,' he ordered. 'I'll have no arguments.'

On the Tuesday she was summoned to the kitchen, where Annie handed her a picnic basket. 'He gave me instructions last night to make it up and have you carry it down to Kettil's Cut for mid-day,' she explained, shaking her head in perplexity. 'I don't know what's got into him lately. He's not been himself for weeks.'

It was a fine, clear morning, and Sheila enjoyed the walk to Kettil's Cut which was reached through Kettil's Cave. Kettil had been one of the Vikings who'd come over with Einar Hairybreeks, but just why the inlet and the cave were named after him was open to speculation and some wild imagining by some.

Sheila carefully made her way through the hollow-sounding cave, coming out where it opened on to the Cut. To her surprise James Campbell was alone, and near him, tied up at the water's edge, was a boat she'd never seen before, only heard about: a Coble.

He had been sitting on a rock, waiting for her, and rose quickly at her approach. 'Well,' he said, grinning like a boy. 'What do you think of my first boat?'

Sheila put down the picnic basket, then walked up and down the Coble's length. It was well maintained, painted not long since by the looks of her. But she seemed very small compared to the Zulus, Fifies and Skaffies Sheila was used to. The name on the battle-axe bow was *Enterprise*. 'They don't do well running before the wind,' she remarked.

Campbell laughed. She was right. That was the craft's weakest point. 'They're inclined to go too fast then, and when they do that they can easily lose steerage and broach,' he agreed.

'But she's a bonny craft all the same,' said Sheila, fascinated by the way the deep forefoot flattened out and the keel disappeared. She knew from what Davey had told her about Cobles that underneath the flat-bottomed rear section of the boat were fixed twin keels, the aft ends curved like the runners of a sledge. It was rare to see this particular type of English boat, for none were built in Scotland.

'I keep her in the Portnessie repair yard usually,' he explained, 'but suddenly I had the desire to see her in the water again.'

Herring gulls screamed raucously overhead, and Sheila shielded her eyes against the sun to watch them wheel and dive. She'd been taught as a child that gulls were the incarnations of dead fishermen. Listening to their calls, it was not impossible to believe.

'Have you ever been on the sea?' Campbell asked, interrupting her reverie.

'Don't you know it's unlucky to have a woman aboard a fishing vessel?' she laughed. 'My da would've skinned me if I'd so much as stepped on to the *Bluebell*!'

'Fishermen worry too much about luck,' he said sharply. 'A man makes his own luck, and that's an end of it.'

Sheila stared at him in unmasked shock. No other man she'd ever known – not her da, nor her brothers, nor her Eric would ever have said such a thing.

'A man should rule his destiny, not be ruled by it. That's what I believe,' said James Campbell, as though challenging the universe.

Sheila took a deep breath, studying him closely. She could see now how James Campbell was different to other men; and why he'd succeeded where others would never have tried. A man who believed as he did was either a fool or a force to be reckoned with. She watched him as he stared towards the horizon. He was not a fool.

'How about having a trip out with me?' he asked suddenly.

'You mean now?'

'Of course! That's why I had you bring the picnic basket. I thought we could sail out a bit and have lunch together.'

But she was a servant! Servants didn't lunch with the employers; it was unheard of. 'I don't think that would be right, sir,' she stammered.

'I say what's right and wrong. And I want to take you out on the *Enterprise*. But not against your will, mind. I won't do that.'

She glanced out to sea. How often she'd wanted to go out there – knowing that, like the rest of the women in Dragonholme, she never would. Well, here was her chance. Perhaps it was not only men who could rule their own destinies.

She took a deep breath. 'Could you take me out to where the fleet went down?'

Campbell frowned. 'Are you certain you want to go there?' he asked gently.

She nodded, surprised to see the concern in his eyes.

They made the short trip in silence. When they reached the area where the fleet had gone down, he dipped the sail and dropped anchor. Sheila stared into the grey-green depths, in her mind's eye seeing the *Bluebell*, *Gypsy Queen* and all the other boats, for ever imprisoned beneath the surface of the sea. 'Oh Eric,' she whispered, her heart filled with pain and longing; her head with memories. Minutes went by like seconds as she gazed, transfixed, into the secret depths. Hypnotized by her own unspoken grief, by the hurt she'd been denying for so long, Sheila rose slowly to her feet, her eyes fixed on a vision at the bottom of the sea. 'Oh, Eric,' she cried. 'Oh, Eric – '

James moved quickly, grabbing her just as she was about to fling herself overboard. She screamed and tried to fight him off. With an oath, he pulled her back and forced her down on to the floor of the boat.

When finally she was still, the face that looked up into his was terrible in its agony. Wordlessly, he clutched her to his bosom while she sobbed and sobbed.

Later, after her tears had ceased and a tranquil silence had grown around them, he suggested that they have lunch.

'If we don't eat after Annie's gone to all this trouble, she'll get back at me by overcooking dinner,' he joked, pulling the cork out of the wine bottle with a pop.

Sheila smiled. It was obvious that he would not speak about the incident unless she wanted – not even to her.

'Thank you,' she whispered as he handed her a glass.

'Have a sandwich. They're delicious.'

She accepted the sandwich, a hard-boiled egg, a piece of chicken – each new bit of food being pushed on her with the admonition that Annie would be upset if the lunch came back barely tasted.

'No, really,' she began again. 'I must thank you. I don't know what came over me.'

He tilted his head back and drained off the wine in his glass. 'Don't thank me now,' he grinned. 'I haven't done anything yet.'

Out there, in the old boat, far from the wealth and power of his life, he seemed like a different man. She guessed that he talked to entertain her, to divert her, but she soon found herself caught up in his jokes and stories, his anecdotes about the awful gaffes he had made on his first expedition into society.

In a quiet tone he then spoke about Edinburgh and Morningside, and how he'd once been dazzled and impressed by the grand folk who lived there: folk with lineage, sophistication and fine fine manners. Not for him his own kind. He'd make money out of them all right, he'd decided, but he would no longer be part of the common herd. He would be somebody. He would get to the top – and he would stay there.

Fiona had been beautiful, and well connected. Her family was not only descended from the Royal House of Stewart, but they were also wealthy. She had birth and breeding and charm. And he had thought that he could want nothing more.

But as time had passed he'd come to realize that what had so attracted him was without substance and, ultimately, boring.

'Are you saying you don't love your wife?' Sheila asked in a whisper, afraid to look at him.

The sun blazed above them, the sea flowed beneath them. They were all alone in the world.

'I loved the idea of her,' he replied at last. 'I still do, in a way.'

'And does she love you?'

He gave a wry smile. 'I was different. A rough diamond. I brought a sense of danger into her life, something she'd never had before. Her parents were against the marriage, of course, which only made me more desirable. She knew they would never forbid the marriage. Fiona can twist them round her little finger – so she enjoyed becoming my wife. I was scandalous.'

'It's a long chalk from the sort of world I'm used to.'

His smile became broader. 'Yes,' he said, toasting her with his glass. It is that.'

'Why did you invite me out in your boat today?' she asked eventually.

'I was wondering if you'd be interested in a new job,' he smiled.

'A what?' she asked, taken completely by surprise. 'What sort of job? Aren't you satisfied with my work?' she queried cautiously.

'Oh, I'm satisfied with you, right enough.'

'Then what's wrong?'

103

'Nothing's wrong. I just thought that a girl of your obvious intelligence might like to do more than dusting and cleaning. How would you like to be my clerk at the Hall?'

'A clerk!' she exclaimed in astonishment.

'More my personal assistant, really. I would train you to deal with correspondence and many of the minor details that take up so much of my time.'

'But I've never had any training. What if I make mistakes?'

'Of course you'll make mistakes. That's what life's all about. Besides, there would be another pound a week.'

'It sounds absolutely marvellous!' she breathed, barely able to believe this was really happening. Wait till she told Peg!

'Is it agreed then?' he asked, extending his hand.

'Agreed,' she replied enthusiastically, and took his hand in hers and shook it.

Efficiency, she decided, that was a major key to James Campbell's success. His businesses ran like well-oiled machines.

He'd once described his businesses to her as his empire, and that's exactly what they were. The profits they made were quite staggering. Besides the estate and Portnessie fleet there was the Portnessie repair yard, thirty-six houses in the town, ten shops that supplied most of the domestic needs of his fishermen and their families, another repair yard in Dunbar, a canning factory in Dunbar, extensive property in Glasgow, Edinburgh and Dumfries, and a part share of the Yellow Funnel Shipping Line worth two-and-a-half-million pounds.

Of all his businesses the one that fascinated Sheila most was the Portnessie fleet, and even in the three weeks she'd been James Campbell's clerk she'd picked up an enormous knowledge about it and how it was run so successfully. At the end of this current season, now doing well after the initial terrible start, he intended placing orders for three new steam trawlers, bringing the total owned by him to nine trawlers, and seventy-five boats.

One of the new trawlers was to be called the *Sheila B*. She'd blushed when he'd told her, not knowing where to put herself when he'd laughed at her embarrassment. The *Sheila B*! Every time she thought about it a thrill ran through her.

Her desk was in the study, facing his – not to keep an eye on her he'd explained, but so they could pass letters, invoices and the like to one another without the trouble of having to get up. A typical example of his efficiency that, she thought.

She glanced round when the door banged open and Campbell came striding in. Immediately she knew from his expression that something was wrong. 'What is it?' she asked.

'Ian McPherson, the carter's son, is downstairs. Your sister-in-law has sent him to fetch you. It seems your mother has had some sort of attack.'

Instantly Sheila was on her feet, her face ashen, her mind electric with fear.

Less than ten minutes later, she and Ian were careering towards Dragonholme, the horse pulling the carriage going flat out.

'A lot of fuss and bother about nothing,' Peg said when she saw Sheila framed in the doorway.

Sheila kept quiet till the doctor had finished his examination. 'How is she?' she asked at last.

'Tough as an old guttie boot,' Dr Eckemyr replied.

'Thanks for the compliment,' joked Peg. 'I'm an old boot now, am I?'

Eckemyr ran his fingers through the little hair he had left, then stared down at Peg. 'There really isn't all that much wrong with you – not physically, anyway. My guess is you've been brooding too much,' he said kindly.

Peg's eyes clouded over, and the despair and desolation she'd come to know so well swept through her like a cold, heartless wind. 'My man and three sons. Wouldn't you brood?'

Eckemyr had no answer to that. 'All I can suggest is that you keep yourself as active as possible. There's no medicine I can prescribe to cure what's wrong with you.'

Sheila took her mother's thin and suddenly aged hand. 'You must try and take better care of yourself. What would I do if anything happened to you?' she said gently. 'You must eat more, for a start.'

'I can't eat when I've no appetite, and I haven't had that since . . . since – ' A choke came into her voice and she turned her head away.

'I know. I know,' whispered Sheila, squeezing Peg's hand, a hand that seemed frail and lifeless in hers. And she did know. But she had reached her nadir that day aboard the *Enterprise* with James Campbell, and now was on the road back. But what could help Peg find her way back from all that pain and grief?

Sheila stayed the night and left again for the Hall after breakfast. Peg seemed a great deal chirpier, and even attempted to have a little toast.

As Sheila made her way to the Hall she thought about Ian McPherson and Maggie, and the looks the pair of them had been exchanging when they'd thought no-one was watching. Those looks had told her why Ian had been at the house when Peg had had the attack, and she presumed Ian was now a regular visitor there.

Yes, James Campbell was right in what he'd said to her as they turned the *Enterprise* back towards Dragonholme that afternoon that seemed so long ago: life did go on.

The Portnessie fleet had returned home from the south the previous day and, as was Campbell's custom, he was giving a dinner for the skippers and their wives, followed by a party for all crew members. He'd asked Sheila to accompany him through to Portnessie as his business

106

associate, saying it would be a good thing for her to meet his people and they her.

They were staying at the Buccleugh Hotel, the larger of the two hotels that Portnessie boasted.

Sheila stood before the full-length mirror smoothing down the front of the new dress the laird had insisted on buying for her that afternoon. It was a braw dress right enough, by far and away the brawest she'd ever owned. It was not the one she'd gone into the shop to buy – which had been far simpler and cheaper – but it was the one James Campbell had chosen for her.

She wasn't at all nervous about the dinner due to start in half an hour, she told herself. After all, she'd been brought up among fishing skippers and their wives: wasn't she herself the daughter of an admiral? But if she was being truthful, she was a wee bit uneasy about going as James Campbell's partner. Working alongside him was one thing, socializing with him quite another.

She thought suddenly of Fiona Campbell, so effort-lessly elegant and confident, and felt common. She prayed she wouldn't do anything that would make James Campbell think she'd let him down.

You're being bloody daft, she told herself. How could she do anything among her own kind that would let him down? They'd all be fish out of the same barrel – even James Campbell, despite the fact that he was boss and owner and now spoke with the accent of the gentry. She knew she would have been petrified if she'd been asked to accompany him into a social group other than her own, but there was, of course, no danger of him ever doing that.

For a few moments she gave way to day-dreaming, imagining herself at some posh do, all dolled up in silks and satins, gliding about gracefully the way Fiona Campbell did and speaking with the same Morningside plum in her mouth.

The image conjured up in her mind was too much. Her face creased into a smile and she began to giggle; but there was part of her that had been thrilled by what she'd visualized, no matter how ludicrous it might seem, and yearned for it.

Some minutes later there was a knock on the door and James Campbell entered, carrying a chilled bottle of champagne and two glasses.

He'd prepared a funny little speech, but that was now forgotten as he stared at Sheila. Had she asked him he could have told her she didn't need silks, satins or a posh accent; she was simply quite stunning as she was.

'You're beautiful,' he said, the words out of his mouth before he knew it.

Sheila blushed and turned away. 'It's kind of you to be gallant.'

'No, no. I mean it. You are.'

She glanced at him out of the corner of her eye, very much aware of the strange fluttering inside her that his words had caused. 'Thank you,' she murmured.

'I thought we'd have a glass together before going down. Just to get the evening started on the right note,' he said.

When he popped the cork he made a hash of it, spilling champagne over the carpet and nearby wall. He'd made a hash of opening the bottle because he hadn't been watching what he'd been doing. He'd been watching Sheila Beattie instead.

Wheeches and cries rent the air; the party was well under way – and a rather grand and exciting party it was, too.

Sheila was thoroughly enjoying herself. Her cheeks were flushed from a combination of alcohol, excitement and the noisy heat of so many people having a good time.

At dinner, Sheila had noted the curious looks from the women present, and had known too well the question in their minds. She should have expected it, of course. A powerful and charismatic man such as James Campbell escorting a young and attractive woman, whether or not she was his assistant, was bound to cause comment, if not gossip. Besides, she thought, rather chuffed, if those looks had been curious they had also been envious.

She glanced over to where James was deep in conversation with a skipper called Innes whom she'd been introduced to over dinner. There was a tap on her shoulder and she turned to find Tod McAlpine smiling at her. Tod was a handsome young man her own age whom she'd already been up on the floor with a number of times, and who was obviously much taken with her.

'Would you care for another birl? It's a reel,' Tod said.

'Aye, I'd like that tine,' she replied. Taking his hand, she walked out on to the floor with him to join the other dancing couples.

'You're the belle of the ball here tonight,' he whispered, and gave her a cheeky wink.

Then the music started up and away they went, Sheila wheeching with the best of them. As she whirled round she caught sight of James Campbell looking darkly in her direction, but then he glanced away, pretending he hadn't been staring her. Jealousy, she thought. That look had been one of unabashed jealousy. She liked the idea that that was how he felt about her.

When the dance was over she thanked Tod and joined the energetic group of onlookers around the edge of the room. Could it be true that James Campbell was jealous? Could it be true that a man who might have any woman he chose would choose her?

'It's getting like a bakehouse in here,' said James Campbell's voice beside her. She'd been scanning the room for him, but somehow he'd managed to sneak up on her.

'You gave me a start,' she laughed.

'How about a breath of fresh air?'

'Is it all right for you to slip away?'

'You mean because I'm mein host? If I'm paying for this ceilidh, I'm entitled to do as I like,' he said, more sternly than he'd intended.

109

Did he ever relax his authority? She stiffened. 'Does that mean it's an order?'

He grinned at her like a boy. 'It would give me great pleasure, Sheila, if you'd step outside with me,' he said with mock solemnity, then winked. 'Besides, there's something I'd like to show you.'

'Show me what?' she asked, not sure of whether he was teasing or not.

'Come and see,' he said, already leading her towards the doors.

Outside an icy wind blew off the sea and against their faces. Away from the frenzy and uproar of the party, the night was entirely theirs. Not a soul seemed to be stirring. As they walked, he talked about these Portnessie streets in which he'd grown up, pointing out the places of his childhood almost as though he were a child again.

Even though Dragonholme was only ten miles away, Sheila had only visited Portnessie twice before for an hour or two.

Just as she was wondering where they were headed, they turned into a narrow cul-de-sac, at the end of which was the wreck of what had once been a stone but and ben house. The roof had long since gone, and what remained was falling apart.

James Campbell gestured to the ruined house. 'Where I was born,' he announced.

There was a sad, forlorn atmosphere surrounding the house that tore at Sheila's heartstrings. 'Do you still own it?'

He went to the house and laid his hand against it. He might have been delicately touching another person. 'Aye, I never sold,' he replied softly.

'Then why have you let it get to this state? It's a criminal waste, so it is,' Sheila flared. It angered her to see what could be a respectable dwelling allowed to rot away.

James smiled at her anger, understanding it. 'I don't want to live here, nor do I want anyone else to. Then

110

again, I also don't want to pull it down. This house is very important to me: it's where my ambition was lit. I want to be able to return here from time to time and remember how it was. See and hear the past, if you like,' he explained, his voice thin and strained.

He looked lost standing there, she thought. Lost and lonely – not at all the confident and iron-willed James Campbell she was used to. She was pleased she'd seen him like this. It made him more human. 'Did you have it hard as a wee boy, then?'

He was a while in answering, his mind in the past, recalling, remembering. Finally he spoke. 'My da was a drunk, and a mean bastard with it. Just after my third birthday he came home at the end of the season to announce he'd never go fishing again, which, a man of his word, he never did. Nor did he ever work again, not a hand's turn. So it was left to my ma to provide for the family which she somehow did by bait gathering, net mending, and anything else that would turn a copper coin.

'There were two older than me: a sister and brother. Maggs died when she was six, Kenny when he was ten; both of consumption. Money my ma earned that should have gone on food for them went down da's throat instead. I can remember Kenny's funeral as if it were yesterday. Mum cried her eyes out, but I never shed a tear. "You're a hard wee bugger, son," Da said to me after we'd buried Kenny. And I replied, "When you finally go to Hell I hope the Devil puts you in the fieriest furnace he's got."

'I expected a good clout round the lug for that, but he didn't hit me, or even reply. Instead he took himself off to the pub and drank himself into a blind stupor on rum bought him by sympathetic fishermen who knew he'd just come from burying his eldest boy.'

Campbell paused to pull out a packet of cigarettes and light one for himself. Then he went on. 'I ran around for years with no shoes and my bare arse hanging out of my breeks; a figure of fun to some, a figure of pity to others.'

111

He blew a perfect smoke ring which the wind caught and whipped away. Leaning against the front of his house he said, 'As soon as I was old enough I signed on as crew for a chap called McLaren. I started as galley boy, saved every farthing I could, and worked like three slaves.

'I had the incentive to work that hard, you see, for I'd sworn a great oath that I was going to be a somebody one day. That I would rise above the poverty and squalor by hard graft and using the brain the good Lord had given me. I'd show everybody.'

He paused to draw on his cigarette, face hidden in shadows and smoke. 'From a tiny spark, that ambition grew inside me till it became like some huge, hungry beast needing to be forever fed, never satisfied no matter how much it was given.' He paused, as though undecided about continuing, then took an audible breath. 'To achieve the ends I'd set myself I became ruthless in the extreme. I did a few things I'm still ashamed of, but I couldn't stop. I had to win.

'The *Enterprise* was the first rung on my ladder to success. Two years after buying her, I bought my first decked trawler: and, the year following that, one became two, and then two became four, and four eight, until, finally, I was the man you now know, the success I'd always dreamed.'

He was no longer lost and lonely as he'd been a few minutes before. He was now potent; yes, that was the word: potent – and in this mood reminded her of his black hunter, Satan.

'What happened to your ma and da?' she asked quietly.

'I hadn't long joined McLaren when Ma passed away, worn clean out. Without her to take care of him, Da died less than six months later.'

'Why did your da refuse to work any more?'

James gave a bitter smile. 'Ma used to make excuses for him, talking about bad arthritis, bronchitis – itis this and itis that – but the real truth was that he was just plain lazy.'

112

'Your ma would have been proud to know what you'd achieved.'

His bitter smile became a sneer. 'She might have been proud of me, but I never had anything but contempt for her.'

Sheila looked at him in shock. 'Why? You admit your ma worked her fingers to the bone for you!'

'Maybe so, but this house aye belonged to her, so there was never any need for her to keep my da on like she did. When he stopped working she should have thrown the sod out on his ear. Maggs and Kenny might still be alive if she'd done that. I blame her as much for their deaths as I do the old man.'

'Perhaps she wasn't as strong as you are. Perhaps, for all his faults, she always loved your da?' Sheila suggested softly.

But his expression became grim and thunderous. 'What about Maggs and Kenny? Didn't she love them, too?'

'You make it sound so black and white. Even I know things in life are just never like that.' She searched his face in puzzlement, looking for some kindness. 'You're a very unforgiving man,' she said at last.

'I am that,' he fairly shouted. 'I always have been and and I always will be.' He threw what was left of his cigarette down on to the ground and ground it beneath his heel.

'This wind is starting to cut through me,' she said, shivering. 'I think we should go back.'

But he just stood there, looking past her, his face locked by some powerful emotion. 'James,' she said gently. 'James, I think we should go.'

It was done before he'd realized it. He caught her to him and pressed his lips on hers. She stiffened, her mouth unyielding, but then the sheer force of him overcame her and her lips parted.

Had she forgotten what it was like to be lost in a kiss, to forget everything within the power of an embrace? Or

113

had she never known before such a hungry passion, such an overwhelming longing? When at last they pulled apart, he held her at arm's length, his expression both serious and concerned. 'As we've been talking about love,' he said thickly, 'I think you should know that I've fallen in love with you.'

Love! But he couldn't love her! It had rather excited her to think that he fancied her – just as it had always pleased her to flirt a little with an attractive man. But love? A man like him, and she little more than a girl – a fisherman's daughter who knew little of the world beyond their harbour – was he lying to her to seduce her? 'I think we'd better get back now,' she said quickly, turning away. 'They'll be missing you.'

He caught her chin and pulled her head to face him. 'I know exactly what I'm saying, Sheila. I've thought about nothing else for months and months now. I love you, Sheila. I need you.'

She jerked her head and turned her back on him – but did not shrug herself free when his arms encircled her from behind. 'Did you bring me here just to tell me this?'

'No. I just wanted you to see where I was born. And then . . . and then I couldn't bottle up my feelings any longer.' He moved his hands to her shoulders and turned her around. 'Have I made a complete fool of myself then?'

'No,' she answered quickly, reaching out to touch his cheek. 'No, never a fool.'

They stood staring at one another in silence, for minutes that might have been hours; for hours that might have been minutes. 'I think we *had* better return,' he said eventually, and, tentatively taking her arm, led her back up the cul-de-sac.

Sheila lay in bed, knowing he was going to come to her. Ever since bidding him good-night and coming upstairs, leaving him behind to have a dram with a skipper who

114

wanted a private word, she'd been waiting nervously for his rap on the door, unsure of what she should do – listen to her heart or her head.

She knew what Peg would say. How would she feel about being the mistress of a married man? But he was not just a married man: he was James Campbell, and his kiss had awakened in her yearnings she'd never known before and a feeling of joy that made her want to run shouting through the village, he loves me! *He* loves *me*! Peg would say she was a silly girl. Silly and wrong. Wrong to take up with a man who already had a wife. But Sheila had learned something in the past months. She had learned that happiness is fleeting. She had learned to take the moments as they came – to use them and enjoy them, for they might never come again.

But Eric had been dead such a short time. Would it be a betrayal to his memory, to what they'd had together, to give herself to someone else?

There was no rap. The door opened, and he was standing before her.

'I knew you'd come.'

He closed the door behind him. 'I knew you knew. I want you Sheila,' he said simply. 'I need you.'

The time for bereavement was over. Yesterday was gone, but not forgotten. This moment signalled a new beginning. 'And I need you,' she whispered back, her eyes warm with tears.

The days flew past. Winter gave way to spring, and spring to summer, the world all new and dancing with colour. James Campbell was like a man reborn. If it had been love for Sheila that he had felt before, all those long and lonely nights of his wanting her, of imagining what it would be like to lose himself in her arms, then there were no words to describe what he was feeling now. For years his only thought had been of winning, of getting everything he wanted no matter what the price. Mad with his obsession, he had forgotten the things that now seemed all that mattered: he had forgotten how to love, how to give, how to laugh.

If anyone noticed the change in him – if Fiona, for instance, wondered what had lifted the severity and gloom from his manner, or wondered where he was going when he passed her door in the late hours of the night – they were wise enough not to let him know.

Sheila had, in fact, had a complex conversation with Fiona – a conversation about flowers that, beneath its surface talk of blooms, and seasons and the art of arrangement, had held a clear message: I don't mind about the *affaire* as long as you are both discreet. But she had kept it from James because she was unsure of what the message might mean. That Fiona had enough to occupy her time and was glad to be relieved of some of her more distasteful wifely duties? Or that Fiona was used to his flirtations and was not going to bother herself over her husband's going to bed with a servant? When he was with her, she was sure that he loved her, and felt her own love growing day by day as Eric's memory began to fade away. The guilt and confusion she had felt at first had been replaced with affection and trust. But on those nights when she lay by herself, wondering if he might still come that night, no matter how late the hour, she found herself questioning not only Fiona's passive complicity, but James's motives as well; and she was a girl once more, wishing she were home with Peg where things were safe and she knew what was what. In the morning, however, she would forget her fears with his first smile or his brusque 'Good morning'.

The pleasure she took in being with him was matched by the joy she took in working with him. He often said that it was a stroke of genius that he had thought of making her his assistant. She had a natural head for figures and a natural aptitude for business. Not only was she able to instantly grasp the most complex problems, but she had an intellect that he knew rivalled his own.

116

'You are the perfect partner for my life,' he repeatedly told her. 'Without you I am halved.'

Sheila ran out of the house around the corner to where the smokehouse stood. With a hand against one of its walls to steady herself, she threw up, again and again, until finally she was retching on an empty stomach.

Peg, her ma, was gone. 'Don't worry about me, lass,' Peg had whispered. 'I'm going to join your da and brothers. I'll be a lot happier there than I am here. But it grieves me sore to leave you behind.'

'Don't die, Ma!' she'd wailed, but Peg's mind had been made up long since, and no tears could change the course she chosen.

Peg had smiled softly, and the lines and years had seemed to drop away with the cares of her life. The breath had whistled from her and her chest had stilled.

'Is she . . . ?' Maggie had asked in a quavering voice.

Sheila had nodded and Maggie had stumbled backwards, collapsing into a chair and bursting into tears.

At least the end had come quickly. There hadn't been more than a few minutes between Peg collapsing and her dying; not even long enough for the doctor to get there, though Ian McPherson had gone running for Doctor Eckemyr moments after the collapse.

Sheila was grateful she'd been there when it had happened. That had been some consolation. It was Sheila's day off and they'd had the entire day together. She couldn't help but wonder if Peg had somehow controlled events to fall out as they had, dying on a day of her own choosing when her last remaining child was by her side.

Sheila straightened, then went to a free-standing water tap by the side of the smokehouse where she rinsed out her foul-tasting mouth.

Feeling better, she returned to the house to find that Dr Eckemyr had arrived and was in the process, assisted by Ian, of lifting the body into the cavity bed. When the

117

body was laid out, Eckemyr covered it with a sheet. 'I am sorry,' he said to Sheila.

'There didn't seem to be any pain.'

'Heart failure, I think,' Eckemyr said, and Sheila gave him a grateful smile. So he also thought that Peg had died of a broken heart.

Being the weekend Ian had brought over a bottle of whisky with him so he poured out drams for them all. Shortly afterwards Eckemyr took his leave, saying he'd be back in the morning to make out the death certificate.

After the doctor left, Sheila went to sit beside the cavity bed, where, lost in a dream, she recalled many scenes from her childhood. Aye, it had been a rare house to be born and brought up in. What fine people her ma and da had been. So many memories, so many happy times: a vibrant family, full of life, which was now, with the exception of herself, all gone.

As the hour was getting late, she decided to return to the hall for some things and to explain that she would be returning home that night to sit with Maggie.

On arriving at the Hall she let herself in by the front door, not wanting to face anyone else just yet, and made her way upstairs to seek out James. She desperately wanted James's arms about her, to lay her head against his chest, to cry and have him comfort her.

'And neither the girl nor the rest of the family ever suspected?' a male voice was saying.

Sheila stopped and frowned. James was with someone, and it was a voice she knew; but whose?

'Everything's fine, Dunwoodie,' James said shortly.

Dunwoodie! Of course, the insurance agent.

'It nearly broke my heart to lie to them like that,' whined Dunwoodie.

'But you forced yourself, eh?' said James with a humourless laugh.

118

'Aye, I did that, Mr Campbell. We all have our price in this none too savoury world we inhabit, and you certainly knew mine.'

Both men had been hard at the bottle, she could tell that from their slurred speech. But what did Dunwoodie mean by saying that he had lied? And what was fine?

'At the time I didn't realize it was the lassie you were after. It wasn't till I heard she'd come to work for you that I put two and two together. I can't say I blame you for wanting to get her in your power,' Dunwoodie chuckled. 'I remember thinking at the time what a handsome piece she was. A real cracker!'

'Aye, you have as fine an eye for the lassies, Mr Dunwoodie, as for an extra few bob.'

Dunwoodie chortled. 'It was all so easy. I didn't even have to change my books. The *Bluebell* payment hadn't been put through yet.'

Sheila went cold all over. Had that man just said that the *Bluebell* had been covered after all? She was suddenly overcome with nausea. When she was once more sufficiently in control of herself to listen to what they were saying it was only to discover that they'd changed the subject and were now talking about London where, it seemed, Dunwoodie had recently had occasion to visit for the first time.

Quietly as a mouse Sheila stole away to her bedroom where she sat in the darkness, lost in thought.

. . . *The lassie you were after* . . . *wanting to get her in your power* . . . *didn't even have to change my books* . . .

These words reverberated round and round inside Sheila's head as she tried to make sense of what she'd overheard.

To begin with, she knew James had switched agencies handling the insurance of his fleet from John Kerrigan of Peterhead to Dunwoodie, but when exactly had that been? Then she recalled the date: *after* the disaster.

So what was James's part of this arrangement? And Dunwoodie's part?

. . . It broke my heart to lie to them . . . I didn't even have to change my books . . . the Bluebell payment hadn't been put through . . .

Dunwoodie's involvement, on James's instructions, was clearly to make it appear that Davey hadn't paid that last premium. But why should James Campbell not want what remained of the Beattie family to get their due?

. . . The lassie you were after . . . it wasn't till I heard she was working for you that I put two and two together . . . .

Oh, my God. All this was because of her. Because James Campbell always got what he wanted, no matter what the price.

'You bastard. You devious, callous, conniving bastard!' she whispered into the empty room.

She'd known from the beginning that he was ruthless, but to capitalize on the Dragonholme disaster and upset so many lives for a whim – that was beyond forgiveness.

She began to weep; soft, warm tears which trickled down her cheeks. 'Oh, Eric!' she whispered, and the trickle became a torrent. 'Oh, Eric! What have I done? Oh, Ma!'

She was still weeping when she decided she'd have to leave the place. She couldn't continue on at the Hall after what she'd learned.

She could go home, except Maggie was ensconced there, and she couldn't bear the idea of living with her sister-in-law. Anyway, if she went home James would soon seek her out and she never wanted to see or speak to him ever again.

Let Maggie and Ian McPherson have the house. It would be her wedding present to them, for they'd soon be getting married, no doubt about that.

As for the funeral arrangements, Maggie would have to take care of those. Peg would understand why she didn't attend the service and burying after, why she had to away that very night.

She had some money; not a great deal but certainly

enough to pay a train fare and keep her going for a few days. Then there were several items of jewellery James had given her: nothing excessively valuable, but what they would realize from a pop shop should keep her going till she found another job.

With the room still in darkness she packed a small case, keeping what she would be taking to a minimum, as she was going to have to walk to Portnessie, all ten long miles of it. And from there to where? That was a question for which as yet she had no answer.

When she was ready she sat down again. She would wait until James and all the servants were fast asleep before leaving the Hall.

Midnight was chiming when she heard him stagger up the stairs, the last to go to bed. She waited a further hour to be completely on the safe side before slipping from her room.

On the clifftops overlooking Dragonholme, she paused to stare down at the village where she'd been born.

'Wish me luck Ma,' she whispered, and, turning abruptly she strode off towards Portnessie, heel and toe, never looking back.

PART TWO

The Harvest Red
Christmas 1913–17

'You have sown for the Day, you have grown for the
    Day;
Yours is the Harvest red.
Can you hear the groans and the awful cries?
Can you see the heap of slain that lies,
And sightless turned to the flame-lit skies
The glassy eyes of the dead?'

From 'The Day', author unknown
Daily Express, 1914

4

John Kelly, one of the fly men, had a reputation for being obnoxious when drunk, which he was certainly being right then. 'Come on, give us a kiss,' he said to Sheila, having trapped her against some flats stacked in the passageway waiting to be taken to the paintdock and turned into a part of the house William Wallace once owned in Elderslie.

Sheila liked John well enough – he could be a good laugh at times – but she had no intention of kissing him, even in Christmas fun.

'Let me pass, John,' she pleaded.

'Not until I get a big smacker,' he persisted, grabbing her round the waist and attempting to pull her closer. She did her best to resist.

'Think about your wife!' Sheila hissed.

'Bugger her, what she doesn't see she'll no' be worried about.'

She pushed and strained. He might be small, but by God he was strong. Of course, heaving the flying scenery up and down night after night was bound to develop his arms.

'Are you all right, Miss Beattie?' a cultured voice inquired.

John Kelly whirled, pressing Sheila into the flats with his back, to glare at the speaker. It was Mr Lack, the actor playing the pirate king in the pantomime. 'Piss off, Englishman!' John ordered angrily.

Mr Lack looked from John back to Sheila who pulled a pleading face. 'Perhaps you'd like to accompany me downstairs, Miss Beattie?' Lack suggested, taking a step forward.

The knife appeared in John's hand as though by magic,

its blade viciously hooked and encrusted with rust. 'On your way,' he spat.

It was the first time anyone had ever pulled a knife on Lack and he was quite stunned by it. He managed to keep cool, however, appearing as unconcerned as though John were threatening him with no more than a strand of wet spaghetti.

Sheila knew John: he was a hard wee nut and that knife was no empty threat. Having pulled it he'd use it. Better a kiss than a stabbing. 'I'll manage Mr Lack, thank you very much,' she said in a tight voice.

'You heard the bint, now fuck off!' snarled John, his knife hand weaving a figure of eight pattern in front of him.

Lack was blond and slim, almost boyish in looks and build, but he wasn't as soft or the pushover that he looked – as opponents on many a rugger field had found out. When circumstances called for it, as he deemed these did, he could be quick-witted and articulate as well as packing a punch.

Lack stared at the knife, then up again at John. 'Just a nick from that rusty thing would be enough I think. A couple of days and I'd be a mortuary case as a result of septicaemia,' he said.

John blinked. 'Septi what?'

'Septicaemia. Blood poisoning. In other words what I'm saying is that the chances are exceptionally high that even a nick from that knife would kill me.'

'It would serve you fucking right for sticking your neb in where it's no' wanted,' retorted John.

Lack gave a lazy smile. 'It would be first-degree murder, and the penalty for that is the hangman's noose,' he said evenly, and clenching his fist made a pulling gesture at the side of his neck.

John recoiled a fraction, and blinked again. The actor's mime had been extremely explicit; he could almost feel the hemp round his throat.

'Now I'm escorting Miss Beattie downstairs, so will you please stand aside,' Lack said in an inoffensive tone, but still with command and authority in his voice, and coming forward laid his hand on Sheila's arm.

For several moments John hesitated. Then his nerve broke and he lurched away, thereby releasing Sheila. It was only a kiss he'd wanted, he told himself. How in the Hell had they got on to the hangman's bloody nooses!

Sheila would have hurried off down the passageway, but Lack held her back, forcing her to walk at a normal pace. Neither spoke until they were downstairs and backstage when Sheila said, 'Would that really be first-degree murder?'

Lack smiled, his eyes twinkling. 'I've absolutely no idea; but our friend from the flys believed it would be,' he laughed, 'and that's all that matters.'

Sheila laughed as well. He had some nerve to him, this Mr Lack, with his youthful good looks and his polished good manners.

'Well, I'd like to thank you for putting the fear of God into him.'

'I am at your service,' he said with a mock bow. 'Obnoxious drunks my speciality.'

They began to chat about the success of the show, and the success of the party, when suddenly a high voice interrupted them.

'Oh, there you are. I've been looking everywhere for you. Are you ready then?' Trisha Alexander asked Lack, breathlessly appearing from nowhere. Trisha was the female juvenile lead playing Princess Ismela in the season's production of *Sinbad*.

So that's how the land lies, Shiela thought, with an unexpected twinge of disappointment.

'You know Miss Beattie, of course,' said Lack.

'I should think so. She fitted me for some of my costumes,' Trisha replied, and gave a tinkling laugh.

'I didn't have that pleasure. It was the other wardrobe lady who fitted me for my solitary costume,' smiled Lack. The Queen's Theatre boasted two wardrobe mistresses: Pat McLuskey was one, Sheila the other.

127

They chatted for a few minutes, then Lack and Trisha said good-night and left Sheila to make her way on to the stage where, despite the lateness of the hour, the theatre's 1913 Christmas party was still in full swing. She was searching for Pat, with whom she shared digs, finally finding her in the auditorium getting well acquainted with a bottle of malt whisky. 'Pished as a newt,' said Pat, and hiccuped.

'You're not the only one,' grinned Sheila.

He wasn't a bad actor at all. She'd certainly seen a lot worse, Sheila decided from her vantage point in the wings where she'd been watching Lack in his biggest scene, his dual with Sinbad, at the conclusion of which he and the other dastardly pirates were thoroughly routed.

It was the day after the party and the first house. Hangovers and their cures were the main topics of conversation around the theatre.

Thrust, cut, parry by Sinbad, then a whack with the flat of the sword on Lack's bottom, the sound of the whack coming from a pair of clapper sticks operated off stage. Clutching his bottom dramatically Lack leapt up and down, the audience roaring, shouting, 'ooh! ooh! ooh!' then ran from the stage followed by his band of cut-throats.

'So may all pirates be vanquished!' Sinbad boomed to the audience, flourishing his scimitar above his head, and was rewarded with an enthusiastic round of applause.

Sheila hadn't realized she was standing where Lack made his exit. She was right in his way when he came off, which flustered her as she hadn't wanted him to know she'd been watching him. Once he was masked from the audience by the return, he stopped to smile at her. 'How are you today?' he whispered.

'Not too bad, considering,' she replied, pretending to be engrossed by Sinbad.

'It was a good party, I enjoyed it.'

'I did too,' she replied, flashing him a brief smile.

He was about to ask her if she'd like to come to the green room with him for some tea when she excused herself, saying she had to get on, and walked away. He stared after her thoughtfully.

'Miss Beattie?'

Sheila turned to find Lack hurrying along the corridor to catch up with her. 'Hello again,' she smiled. It was four days since he'd caught her watching him from the wings and they hadn't spoken since.

Lack had been making discreet enquiries about Sheila and had been relieved to discover that she didn't have a boyfriend, not so far, at any rate, as anyone could tell.

New Year's Eve was only a couple of nights away. Nearly everyone else in the theatre came from Glasgow and was planning to celebrate it at home with their families. Lack, however, like Sheila, had no family around and couldn't go home as there was a show on New Year's day.

'I was wondering if you'd be interested in going to a dance after the second show on New Year's?' he asked nervously.

She looked at him quizzically. 'What about Trisha?' she asked before she could stop herself.

'What about her?'

'Aren't you and she . . .' wondering if his blank expression was sincere, '. . . friends?'

His laughter was infectious. 'Goodness, no. Well, yes of course we're friends, but . . . you didn't think that . . .'

She felt herself blush scarlet, at a complete loss for words. It was a long time since she'd felt herself attracted to a man.

'So how about Hogmanay then?' he asked eagerly, pretending not to notice her embarrassment.

'I'm afraid I've already promised to go to a small "do" with Pat McLuskey,' she said with undisguised disappointment. 'I'm sorry.'

His handsome face clouded. 'That's rotten luck for me.'

At that moment he seemed so young and vulnerable that her instinct was to sweep him into her arms and cuddle him like a child. But he wasn't a child, she reminded herself. He was a fully grown man who'd coolly stood up to John Kelly's knife. Suddenly she had the suspicion that this young and vulnerable reaction to her refusal was an act. He was an actor, after all. How many unsuspecting females had he twisted around his little finger with this pose, she wondered, but with no trace of anger.

'Can't I persuade you to change your mind?' he cajoled.

'I've given my promise to go, and I never break my promise,' she replied firmly.

'Oh, well. Integrity is a good quality. Some other time, perhaps,' he said, shrugging.

'Perhaps.'

'There's no need to worry about me. I can aye go to the McKillops on my own,' Pat McLuskey said when Sheila told her about Lack's Hogmanay invitation.

'You'll do no such thing,' snapped Sheila. 'Anyway, I've already agreed to go to the McKillops, and I've no intention of letting either you or them down.'

It was late that night. Sheila had just arrived back from work to the room they shared to find Pat in the process of painting her toenails blood red. During the week they both worked days, including Saturdays, and alternate evenings. In the daytime they made and maintained costumes; in the evenings they had to be on hand for emergency repairs.

Sheila found it a fairly exacting job, due to the long hours more than anything else, but one she enjoyed. Her life was now as different to what it had been at Dragonholme as chalk to cheese. She often thought about the village and her family, but tried not to remember her time at the Hall or James Campbell. When she did allow herself to think about him, the warring emotions of loathing and betrayal, disgust and disillusionment brought so much pain and confusion that it nearly tore her apart.

'Has Mr Lack nowhere to go then?' Pat asked, glancing up from her task.

'So it would seem.'

'Ach, we can't leave the poor man all alone on Neer'day, that just wouldn't be right at all! And him a Sassenach, too. What will he think of Scottish hospitality?' Pat had been in the theatrical profession for over twenty years and had spent too many lonely nights on her own not to want to help someone in the same situation.

'He's bound to find some party or other he can go to,' argued Sheila. 'There are always stacks of them on New Year's Eve.'

'Do you like him?'

Sheila tilted her head, apparently absorbed in consideration of Pat's painted toenails. 'I hardly know him,' she answered offhandedly.

'That's not what I asked you, hen. Do you like him?' Pat persisted.

For some reason, Sheila found it hard to meet Pat's eyes. 'Well, I certainly don't dislike him,' she replied.

'Then why don't we have a wee word with the McKillops and see if they'll extend their invitation to include Mr Lack? I'm sure they'll be agreeable.'

'I know he has a car, so that would mean a ride to Maxwell Park and back again,' Sheila said.

Pat bent again to her toenails. Sheila might pretend the car was an important item of consideration, but she wasn't pulling any wool over Pat's eyes. Sheila was keen, which made Mr Lack the first man she'd ever shown any real interest in since coming to work at the Queen's Theatre sixteen months before.

*   *   *

Sheila and Pat, the pair of them dressed to the nines, arrived outside Lack's dressing room. 'You knock,' Sheila whispered to Pat, suddenly as nervous as a girl.

The door was opened almost immediately by Lack still in his dressing gown, a towel draped round his neck. 'Come in, come in,' he greeted them. 'I'm sorry I'm running a little behind.'

The dressing room was tiny and rather smelly. Sheila noticed that the ceiling was not only badly cracked, but was actually coming away in bits.

Lack saw her staring round. 'Hardly the Ritz, I'm afraid, but then one doesn't exactly expect luxury in the theatre.'

'This dressing room *is* the Ritz beside some I've seen,' laughed Pat. 'I could tell you stories that would curl your hair.'

'I'm sure you could,' he smiled.

There was an opened bottle of wine on his dressing table and three glasses. With a mock bow, he filled the glasses and handed one to Sheila and one to Pat. 'To get the evening started,' he toasted, raising his own glass.

'Wine!' laughed Pat. 'I don't think I've ever had wine on New Year's Eve before.'

Lack dived under his dressing table, re-emerging with two bottles of Glenfiddich. 'I wouldn't want to break any old Scottish traditions,' he winked. 'So I bought these to bring along.'

Pat's eyes shone. 'With a couple of bottles of that there's not a house in Scotland you wouldn't be welcome in,' she said, winking back.

Sheila sipped her wine. It was excellent. Judging from his taste in drink and clothes, Mr Lack was used to the very best. 'Nice claret,' she said appreciatively. 'It's a long while since I had any.'

Lack stared at her in astonishment. An ordinary person in Glasgow knowing about wine was about as rare as finding gold nuggets down a coalmine. 'You're a connoisseur?' he queried.

'Hardly! But I can tell the difference between a beaujolais and burgundy, or a hock and sauterne.' There were still some things she had to thank James Campbell for, she thought ruefully.

'It's all either red or white to me,' laughed Pat.

'Do you drink Scottish wine yourself?' Sheila asked Lack, a mischievous twinkle in her eye.

'Scottish wine? Surely there's no such thing?'

'Oh, there is indeed. And it's world famous, isn't that so Pat?'

Pat nodded her agreement.

'Scottish wine? But grapes don't grow in this climate.'

'Who mentioned grapes?' teased Sheila.

He knew then that his leg was being pulled, but decided to go along with the gag anyway. 'So where do I try this famous Scottish wine?' he asked.

'Well you certainly won't get it from the same place you get Scottish champagne.'

'Scottish champagne now? I suppose that's world famous as well?'

She pretended to give that much thought. Having difficulty in keeping the laughter that was bubbling inside her out of her voice, she answered, 'It's famous all right, but not quite as famous as the wine. What's your opinion Pat,'

Pat shook her head. 'I agree. Not *quite* as famous.'

'Would you like to try some Scottish champagne?' Sheila asked.

'You mean you have some here?'

'Oh yes!' she grinned.

What on earth was she going to come up with, he wondered, thoroughly enjoying this little game. 'Then I'd love to.'

Sheila laid down her glass and went to the sink in the corner. Filling a teacup that was on the soap ledge, she took the cup to Lack and presented it to him.

'Water!' he exclaimed.

'Also known as Scottish champagne.'

133

'And Scottish wine?'

Sheila pointed to the bottles of Glenfiddich. 'What the posh sometimes call whisky,' unable to contain her laughter any more.

'A good one,' he acknowledged, and removed his dressing gown to reveal he was fully dressed with the exception of his jacket and tie.

Sheila watched him intently as he knotted his tie. His concentration on what he was doing had produced a deep furrow at the top of his nose, and, for some inexplicable reason, she found it fascinating.

When he was finally ready, he opened an old cake tin standing on one side of his dressing table and took out a single red rose and a box of chocolates. The rose he handed to Sheila, the chocolates to Pat.

'A rose in December! How on earth did you manage that?' Sheila asked in amazement.

He gave her a knowing wink, but didn't reply.

'You appear to be extremely resourceful,' she said.

'Aren't all actors?' he joked, but he was obviously pleased by her appreciation.

'I'll go and get the car,' Lack said as they came on to the street. 'I park it behind the hotel.'

A few minutes later the car purred into view. Sheila gaped in disbelief and Pat's mouth dropped open as she whispered, 'What a stunner!'

It was a Rolls-Royce Silver Ghost. The woodwork was yellow, including the toolbox on the right-hand running board; the running boards, mudguards and general bodywork matt black; the hood and headlights gleaming white.

'Climb aboard!' a grinning Lack said, and opened the passenger door for them.

Pat went into the back expecting Sheila to sit with Lack, but Sheila climbed in with Pat instead. Glancing at Lack she caught the look of disappointment in his expression.

A Silver Ghost, Sheila thought in some awe. How did

a struggling young actor come to own a car like this? 'This is yours?' she asked.

'It is, indeed. It was a present for my twenty-first,' he replied, as though it was the sort of present everyone got for their twenty-first.

'Somebody must like you a great deal,' Pat said, running her hand over the dimpled black leather on which she was sitting.

It was his mother, actually, who'd given it to him, Lack explained, adding, a little shamefacedly, that his mother had always been in the habit of spoiling him. And having been made a gift of a Silver Ghost he certainly wasn't going to refuse to accept it, now was he?

Pat hastily agreed, saying he would have to have been ninepence in the shilling to refuse something as beautiful as this. She'd be happy to accept a Silver Ghost any day of the week, she laughed.

Sheila asked Lack if he knew the way to Maxwell Park, and he replied that he thought he did, but perhaps she should come up front to be on hand to guide him in case he went wrong. Somewhat primly she retorted she could guide him just as well from the back of the car, thank you very much.

Pat turned her face away from the pair of them, and smiled.

Maxwell Park was on the south side, and it took them just over twenty minutes to get there. The tenement where the McKillops lived was at the end of a quiet cul-de-sac tucked away from the main thoroughfares so Lack had no qualms about leaving his car there.

They mounted stairs that were well-kept and had recently been whitewashed at their ends; the landing windows they passed gleamed. As Glasgow tenements went, this quite clearly was one of the better examples.

Jack welcomed them warmly with a kiss each for Sheila and Pat, and shaking Lack's hand vigorously, stated he was delighted Mr Lack could join them for Hogmanay. Lack then passed over his two bottles of Glenfiddich, and Sheila

135

the bottle of blend she and Pat had brought along as their contribution, and away in they went.

Sheila counted fourteen people already in the front room, Maureen McKillop immediately coming over to the newly arrived party to express her delight that they'd come. Maureen then took them round and introduced them to the others who were, without exception, neighbours from up that close or from closes nearby.

There was a friendly atmosphere in the house which made Sheila feel right at home. Turning to comment on this to Lack, she discovered he was already chatting to, or being chatted up by, a good-looking (although, in Sheila's estimation, blowsy) young woman called Christine Templeton.

Dancing was in progress, the music coming from a phonograph that had been installed on top of the sideboard. The carpet in the room had been rolled up and the furniture pulled back, and everyone had the look about them of people out to enjoy themselves.

Sheila watched Lack dance with Christine, miffed that he hadn't got up with her first; but then if Christine had asked him he could hardly have refused her, she told herself, could he?

A man called Rog asked Pat on to the floor, saying that as his wife had gone to the toilet he was free to enjoy himself for five minutes. Clutching Pat to him he went straight into an old Glasgow dancehall favourite called the Palais Glide, or, alternatively, in the rougher establishments Ra Moonie.

'Sorry about that, I was abducted,' Lack grinned at Sheila on his return from the makeshift dance floor. To which she replied, a little more frostily than she'd intended, that as abductions went he'd given the definite impression of suffering no pain.

Sheila puzzled Lack. At times she seemed to like him, quite a bit he thought, while at other time he might have been something decidedly nasty the cat had dragged in and presented to her.

136

'You've got a sharp tongue in your head. Has anyone ever told you that before?' he asked.

Instead of answering his jibe she handed him her empty glass, obviously wanting it refilled. Instead, he set it down on a handy surface and gave her a razored smile.

'Why don't you two show us what you can do?' suggested Pat, dancing past cheek to cheek with Rog, whose wife was glowering from across the other side of the room.

'I don't really feel like dancing just now,' said Sheila.

'That's all right,' said Lack. 'I fully understand if you're not very good at it. Lots of people are unco-ordinated.'

Sheila flushed. Unco-ordinated! What a bally cheek! She retorted hotly that she was not unco-ordinated; in fact she was a damn good dancer, so there Mr High Faluting Englishman!

The slow grin that tugged the corners of his mouth upwards told her she'd fallen for that one hook, line and sinker. Without further comment she followed him to the centre of the floor when he took her hand and led the way.

They danced in silence, each staring over the other's shoulder and wondering what his or her partner was thinking.

The dance finished and they clapped politely. Sheila was about to move off the floor when he grabbed her arm and pulled her back to him. They exchanged a glance, but nothing more.

The next record was a waltz. Snugly they came together and their bodies moved as one. 'Why did you become an actor?' she asked, genuinely curious, for although she was now well used to actors after sixteen months in the theatre it still seemed to her a strange profession for a man to follow.

He explained that when he was at school it had been his intention to go into business, then halfway through his fifth year he'd been approached to take part in a play,

137

which he'd only eventually reluctantly agreed to, thinking he would be bound to hate it. But it hadn't turned out that way at all. On the contrary, he'd found being in front of an audience thrilling and exciting in the extreme. When the play was finally over he'd known, beyond the shadow of a doubt, that being on stage was what he wanted to do with his life.

'But don't you find it boring repeating the same performance over and over?'

He laughed warmly. No two performances were the same, he explained. Each was different, depending upon the mood of the actors and, of course, on the reaction of the audience. Certainly no two audiences were ever identical.

It was during the first performance of that school play that he'd discovered what it was like to be truly alive, for every nerve end in the body to be jumping with excitement, even terror. Once experienced, it became a drug that had to be repeatedly administered till at last one was a hopeless addict.

The thought of ever having to give up the stage was just too awful to contemplate, deprived of the liveliness and exhilaration he felt when treading the boards would be tantamount to being dead.

As Lack spoke his voice assumed a vibrancy that was almost contagious. She had rarely met a man so completely caught up in and committed to his chosen profession.

They were in the middle of their sixth dance when the record was stopped and Jack McKillop told everyone to listen for the bells that would herald midnight and the dawning of the New Year.

While the gathering waited expectantly Maureen McKillop hastily passed round drams. Sheila was holding hers and straining her ears like all present when she became aware that Lack's arm was around her waist.

She looked at him and smiled, and as she did the bells started to ring.

'Wait for it!' whispered Jack McKillop urgently, for it was unlucky to toast the New Year until after the last peel had sounded. 'A happy 1914 to one and all. May it be the best and most prosperous year of our lives!' Jack cried as soon as the bells had died away.

'A happy New Year to you, Mr Lack,' Sheila murmured, mesmerized by his pale blue eyes which appeared to be getting larger and larger the longer she stared into them.

'I think it's time you called me Andrew,' he replied.

'A happy New Year, Andrew'.

'A happy New Year, Sheila,' he said, linking his arm with hers. Arms entwined they toasted the New Year.

Then amid the shouts and laughter welcoming the new year, he kissed her.

'Come in!' Sheila called out when there was a knock on the Wardrobe door. It was Andrew whom she'd been expecting for a fitting.

The play following the pantomime was called William Wallace, and was about the legendary Scottish hero's struggle against the English prior to his execution at the London site of Smithfield, where he'd been hanged, drawn and quartered. Andrew was cast as an English major.

It was six days since Hogmanay, during which time Andrew had thought a great deal about Sheila, and she about him. Yet since the night of the party they'd only said hello to one another in passing.

Sheila had wanted to stop and chat on several occasions, but her pride hadn't let her. He was the man, after all! It was his place to stop her. If he didn't want to go out with her again, that was his misfortune.

Brusquely she told him his costume was the one on top of that hamper over there, indicating the hamper with a nod of her head. 'You'll have to try it on,' she snapped.

Pat suddenly announced she'd make some tea, and left

the room to fill the kettle as there wasn't a tap in Wardrobe.

There was a screen which Andrew went behind. 'I really enjoyed myself at the McKillops,' he called over the top. 'That was a New Year party I won't forget in a hurry.' There was no reply. He thanked Sheila again for taking him along.

'Your coming along was Pat's idea,' she replied tartly, the words no sooner out of her mouth than she regretted them, for as true as they were, they were hardly the full truth.

Andrew winced. Jesus, she had a tongue on her! Despite that, he liked her. The question was, did she like him? For the past six days he had thought of little else; but she blew so hot and cold that it was impossible to tell.

Take the party, for example. She'd been great fun in the dressing room beforehand, then distant in the car during the drive. Once at the party she'd finally thawed, but on the drive back she'd again sat in the back seat like some tailor's dummy, only speaking, and then curtly, when spoken to. What was a man to make of such behaviour? He was damned if he knew.

He struggled into his britches, which were far too tight. He could only do up half his buttons. He emerged from behind the screen just as Pat returned, saying that tea would be up in a jiffy, and did he like Abernethy biscuits? 'I may never be able to eat again,' he winked, holding his britches together.

'Let's have a look at you then,' Sheila said, laying down the costume she'd been working on and coming to stand in front of him.

The coat more of less fitted, she thought. Well enough anyway to get away with. But the britches were another matter entirely.

Andrew squirmed, then made himself stand stock still when he saw Pat's look of amusement. He wasn't a person easily embarrassed, but the sight of Sheila fiddling around with his trousers might just do it.

140

Sheila told him to take the britches off again, which he did, but not before returning behind the screen first. He obviously had no intention of allowing Sheila to see him in his undershorts. This wasn't lost on Sheila who, having retrieved the britches from where he'd slung them over the top of the screen, grinned at Pat. Pat mouthed back, 'Maybe he's got sparrow legs?', causing Sheila to snicker and Andrew to stick his head round the side of the screen to see what was going on.

After the fitting and after tea and Abernethies, Andre lighted himself a cigarette, chatting happily away.

Sheila paid him scant attention, pretending to be engrossed in her sewing. With Sheila silent, Pat did most of the talking, yammering away like some demented budgie. She didn't fail to notice, however, that although Andrew was listening to her, replying enthusiastically, every so often his eyes strayed towards Sheila.

Finally and reluctantly, Andrew said he had to be going. He stubbed out the remains of his cigarette. 'Will you need me for another fitting, then?' he asked Sheila. Without looking up, she replied that she would, and that she'd leave a message for him on the notice board when he was to come again.

Andrew had presented himself in Wardrobe still undecided whether to ask Sheila out or not, but he now made up his mind he would do, half expecting to be turned down.

Clearing his throat, he said he intended driving out into the country this coming Sunday for a breath of fresh air, so much needed after being cooped up in the theatre day after day, and he was wondering if Sheila would like to go with him. He'd thought they might stop at a hotel for lunch, or at a nice pub if they could find one.

Sheila paused in her sewing, for just a heartbeat. So he *did* want to see her again! Why then had there been six whole days of what amounted to his snubbing her? She would refuse him, she thought, then told herself not to be so stupid, say no now and that could well be the end of it

141

between them. On the other hand, she didn't want to appear too available.

'Pat and I – ' she started to say.

'Pat's to come also, that was what I meant the three of us going for a spin together,' he quickly interjected.

Liar! she thought, and gave Pat a look that told Pat she was to accept the invitation.

'I'd love to go,' Pat smiled.

'Agreed then,' said Andrew, and swiftly arranged a time to call and pick them up.

After he'd gone Sheila glanced over at Pat, and they both burst out giggling.

'You're not making it easy for the poor fellow,' Pat said when their giggling, which had come close on hysterical, had finally subsided.

Sheila's reply was that anything easily got wasn't respected, she had no intentions of being a piece of theatrical fluff to be picked up and laid down whenever he felt like it, and the sooner he learned that the better.

She returned to her sewing, and within seconds was humming happily to herself, planning what she would wear.

Pat listened to the humming, wondering how she could side-step the Sunday spin without it being obvious that that was what she was doing.

He was an excellent driver, Sheila thought, the Silver Ghost responding to his every touch as though it were an extension of himself.

Her thoughts drifted to Pat whom they'd left back at the digs suffering from bad monthly pains. She hoped Pat was all right and felt guilty about leaving her, but Pat had been insistent she and Andrew go ahead without her.

It was a bitter January day, the wind swirling and gusting round the Rolls as they drove through the bleak but attractive countryside. Off to the left were white-tipped hills, while over to the right, just out of sight, was the Firth of Clyde.

'Do you think we could stop for a few minutes?' asked Sheila. 'I'd like to walk over and see the Firth.'

Andrew immediately checked his mirror, then drew the car into the side of the road, thinking he wouldn't mind a stretch of the legs at all.

Getting out of the Rolls, they made for the Firth – together, yet apart. There had been a barrier between them since Andrew had picked her up, and both were painfully aware of it.

He'd made a mistake in asking her out again, he was thinking, she didn't like him, was only tolerating him for reasons of her own.

They topped a rise and Sheila came up short, sucking in her breath at seeing the blue-grey waters of the Firth spread before her.

'I've missed the sea so much since being in Glasgow, but I suppose that's only natural having been born and bred beside it,' she said wistfully.

'So where is it you come from?' he inquired.

'A wee fishing village I'm sure you've never heard of. It's called Dragonholme, and is over on the east coast not far from St Abb's Head,' she replied, her voice filled with love and longing.

'A fishing village. Does that mean your people are fisherfolk?' he asked, intrigued.

In halting tones she told him about the disaster, and how she'd lost her da, three brothers and an uncle and her fiancé in one fell swoop; and how her ma, broken-hearted by what had occurred, had lost the will to live.

Andrew listened, appalled. What a terrible thing to have happened! How awful it must have been for her. 'I'm sorry, truly I am,' he whispered.

She tried to put on a brave smile, but it came over more as a grimace than a smile.

Andrew picked up a stone and threw it at the Firth, but

they were still too far away for the stone to hit the water. It bounced off a small tussock instead.

'Is it because you're still in love with your dead boyfriend that you're so prickly with me?' he asked quietly.

'Prickly?' Sheila echoed.

Not wanting to look into her face right then he picked up another stone and threw that. 'You blow hot and cold with me. I never know what's going on.'

But she countered his question with one of her own. 'Why did you wait six days before asking me out again?'

'I couldn't make up my mind whether or not you liked me, and it seemed up until just now you didn't. But having learned of Eric I can't help but wonder if it's not that you dislike me but can't forget how much you loved him?'

Sheila took a deep breath. What a muddle – and it would seem the blame for that was hers. 'I like you fine,' she said slowly. 'Very much so, in fact; but I'm a bit chary of your motives.'

'What do you mean by that?' Andrew demanded in undisguised amazement. She told him actors came and went and she had no intention, no matter how much she liked him, of being someone's Glasgow conquest. For what else would it be, especially with the difference in class between them. She was working class, there was no hiding that. Just as there was no hiding his real background. Extremely rich middle-class men didn't have serious relationships with working-class girls. Affairs, yes, but not serious relationships. 'Do you think I'm so simple that I don't know that?' she asked at last.

'I see,' Andrew murmured. By God, she'd thought this through far more than he had. It was a huge relief to know she did like him. Perhaps as much as he liked her.

In reply he said that her argument about their difference in class was correct, but only as far as it went. His background might be middle class, but he was no longer that, for as an actor he was officially, by law, classed as a rogue and a vagabond, and as such she was his better.

144

Sheila laughed in spite of herself. 'You're making it up,' she accused.

'Not so!' he protested. Actors *were* officially classed as rogues and vagabonds, alongside beggars, sundry villains and the like, and had been since the Middle Ages. 'Of course, he continued. 'If you look at it another way, in reality we are classless, mingling as we do with the very highest and lowest, the proud and the humble.'

'You've a way with words all right,' she smiled. 'I'll have to give you that.' She then went on to say that he might be a classless rogue and vagabond, but what about his family – they surely weren't?

'I am my own man,' he said, bowing theatrically but with his eyes serious. 'I don't need anyone's approval to take up with someone, or for anything else I might want to do.'

Well, thought Sheila, I guess that's pretty clear. There was no question that he was telling the truth.

She then asked him what his plans were for when he left the Queen's Theatre at the end of the season, and he replied he wasn't sure yet. He could ask to stay on for another season (and he considered the chances high that the management would agree to this), or he could try to get into one of the other two repertories that the grey city boasted.

'But eventually?' Sheila prompted.

Eventually it was the West End for him. That had always been his dream. He needed a few more years' experience, of course, but then it was Shaftesbury Avenue. He wouldn't be satisfied until his name was in lights; top of the bill.

He would make it, too, Sheila thought. He had the talent, he had the looks, and he certainly had the drive. 'By then Glasgow and the people you met there will be only a distant memory,' she teased.

'And who do you mean by that?' he asked, only partially joking.

Sheila looked away.

145

He went on. Who was to say, he wanted to know, what would be the case? He certainly had no way of seeing into the future. It seemed to him she was trying to run, gallop even, before she could walk. They'd only just established they liked one another, for goodness sake, and already she had him forgetting her. Why not take things a step at a time and see how they developed?

Was she being over cautious, she asked herself, or just over-reacting against the hurt of losing Eric – and that other hurt, her betrayal by Campbell? Or was she merely using her common sense? Perhaps it was a combination of both, she decided. She did have a fear of being hurt again, of having love snatched away – but there was nothing foolish in that. How else was she to protect herself?

She suddenly realized that the barrier which had been between them was gone. Glancing over at his handsome profile, she felt completely at ease in his company. At ease and happy to be with him. It had been a long time since she'd felt so whole and so good.

They sat and watched the ever-moving sea. Sheila could have watched all day without ever being bored. Some seagulls passed overhead and Andrew remarked that it must be a marvellous sensation to fly, to be able to wheel, dive and soar as those gulls were doing. He said, dreamily, that he'd give his eye teeth to be a bird for just ten minutes.

Later Andrew turned to her and asked her how a fishergirl from the untamed coast had come to be working in the Glasgow theatre. She didn't want to tell him about James Campbell, so she told him that her mother's death had been the last straw, she'd just had to get away from Dràgonholme because of the many painful memories the place held for her. 'I just got on a train,' she said softly. 'And when it ended its journey in Glasgow, I stayed.'

As for getting a job in the theatre, the answer to that was simple. Pat McLuskey had already been staying at the house she'd taken digs in, and through her she'd got the job at the Queen's Theatre. The theatre needed a second wardrobe mistress; she'd therefore applied for the position, and landed it. Shortly after this, because they got on so well together, she and Pat had decided to share a room to cut down their expenses.

Andrew said he admired her for taking on and making a success of a job she'd had no previous experience with, to which she replied that wasn't true. She'd been brought up mending, patching, altering and re-making the family clothes. She could turn a shirt collar, put in a buttonhole, or even cut out with or without a pattern if called upon to do so; the position of wardrobe mistress had held no mysteries or terrors for her; what she had to do was only what she'd already been doing all her life, only with fancy costumes rather than ordinary clothes.

They talked at length till finally both were freezing from the cold. He raced her back to the Silver Ghost, and allowed her to win.

They had lunch in a wee pub called The Clansman's Arms and then drove further up the road and parked in a spot overlooking the Firth.

They talked and talked, delighting – even revelling – in one another's company.

When they finally parted late that evening it was with the utmost reluctance, each hating the thought of being away from the other.

It was a click, as the Glasgow expression went.

That Tuesday Andrew asked Sheila if she'd care to come back to his rooms after the second show for a bite to eat. He was a dab hand with the frying pan he assured her, and promised he'd turn out something tasty.

Sheila retorted she wasn't going to have a man cook for her; she'd never be able to take him seriously again. Andrew bowed his head, pretending to be chastised. She could cook, and he would open the wine – but would she come?

147

'No funny business?'
'No funny business.'
Then she would come.

Crown Crescent had once been very grand; the homes of wealthy tea importers and successful merchants; but now it was tatty at the edges, a geriatric giving way to age and mounting neglect.

Andrew's rented rooms consisted of a bedroom, reception room, kitchen and toilet, and were on the ground floor. 'Well what do you think?' he asked anxiously when they were inside.

Her impression was of genteel shabbiness; like the building, the contents of the rooms had seen better days. The carpet was threadbare in places, the two armchairs had bits of stuffing hanging out, and the pot containing the aspidistra was badly cracked. 'It seems very comfortable,' she proclaimed.

Andrew breathed a sigh of relief that the place had found favour. He showed Sheila where everything was in the kitchen, then returned to the reception room where he lit the fire he'd laid before going to the theatre. When he was certain the fire had taken hold he opened a bottle of claret and took a glassful through to Sheila, who said it was just what the doctor ordered.

She made scrambled eggs, which they decided to eat sitting on the floor in front of the now blazing fire. As he poured more wine she asked him to tell her about his career to date.

He'd started at the Theatre Royal, Brighton, he told her, where he'd spent five seasons in all before moving on to the New at Nottingham. After the New he'd gone to the Grand at Swansea, from there to Canterbury, and then to Glasgow.

Soon the eggs were gone and more wine had to be opened. Andrew talked non-stop as he described the many plays he'd been in, and the parts he'd taken.

Sheila was completely relaxed, her initial nervousness at coming to his rooms having disappeared within a few minutes of actually entering them. She closed her eyes and let the heat from the fire wash over her. This was bliss!

It was past three a.m. when the Silver Ghost pulled up in front of her digs. 'I enjoyed that tremendously,' said Andrew turning to her in the darkness.

'So did I.'

'I feel I've known you all my life instead of only a short while.'

She moved towards him ever so slightly in the dark.

He kissed her, and she experienced the same overpowering sensation she'd felt when he'd kissed her at the McKillops' Hogmanay party.

She whispered good-night. He came round to her side to help her from the car, and kissed her again, standing watching as though entranced as she hurried off into the shadowy, gas-lit close to swiftly disappear up the stairs.

It was hours later before she finally got to sleep because of thinking about him. Andrew had exactly the same problem.

Weeks flew by, turning into months, and Andrew asked the management if he could stay on for another season. The management informed him that the Queen's Theatre would be delighted to have him continue in its employ.

Summer officially arrived to find Andrew playing in *Trelawny of the Wells* by A. W. Pinero, taking the part of the flamboyant Ferdy Gadd (for which he'd received excellent notices) and rehearsing Shakespeare's *Julius Caesar* during the day.

One night during the Trelawny run, 28 June to be exact, Andrew, having given the matter a great deal of thought, brought Sheila home to his rooms after the show with the intention of springing a surprise on her.

Sheila dropped into a chair as soon as she entered the flat. 'Lord, am I whacked,' she sighed. *Julius Caesar*, due to open the following week, was proving a particularly heavy play from the wardrobe point of view because so many costumes were needed, a lot of which Sheila and Pat were having to make themselves.

Andrew poured two hefty whiskies and gave her one. 'You take a drink of that,' he instructed. 'Then close your eyes and hold out your left hand.'

When her eyes were firmly closed he groped in his pocket for the small box he'd acquired at the jeweller's earlier that day during his lunch break, and placed it in the palm of her hand. As he stepped back her eyes immediately snapped open again.

Sheila stared at the box for a few seconds, then placed her drink carefully on the floor. Slowly, with trembling fingers, she opened the box. In the middle of the pale blue satin interior was a diamond ring.

All she could hear was the hammering of her heart. 'What's this?' she whispered.

'A surprise.'

'A surprise? But what does it mean?'

He knelt beside her. 'It means that I'm asking you to marry me.'

She looked up at him, then brought her gaze back to the ring. 'Why?' she demanded softly.

He knew what she wanted him to say, so he said it, and it was the truth. 'I love you,' he whispered. 'I love you more than I ever thought possible.'

Tears came into her eyes which she quickly wiped away.

'It'll mean moving around a bit until we eventually get settled in London. Will you mind that?' he asked.

She shook her head. As long as they were together, that was the main thing; she'd have gone to Timbuctoo if he'd wanted.

'I love *you*, Andrew,' she admitted. It was the first time she'd ever told him.

He took her hands in his and said that he could no more imagine life without her now than he could imagine being anything other than an actor; as far as he was concerned the match was perfect. Sheila's eyes were filled with tears as she whispered that she couldn't imagine life without him either.

He watched eagerly while she tried on the ring which, completely against the odds, was a perfect fit.

It was a gorgeous ring. Sheila held it up to the light, causing its stones to shoot off bluish rays. It must have cost a great deal, but that didn't matter at all. If it had been made of tin she would have been just as proud to wear it.

Throwing her arms round him she pulled him close and kissed him. 'Oh my darling,' she whispered, holding him tightly. 'I have never been so happy in my life. I never dreamed it was possible.'

Andrew looked down, as though studying the carpet. 'As we're now engaged,' he said hesitantly, 'I was wondering if . . . how about you staying the night?'

'Do you take back the ring if I don't?' she teased.

Smiling, he shook his head.

She wanted to stay with him – very much so. But one thing had to aired between them. It was a subject she'd skirted clear of before because it belonged to the past and had nothing to do with him. But now that he'd asked her to be his wife it was only right and proper that he knew. 'I'm not a virgin,' she said bluntly, suddenly, her voice and body tense.

He'd been almost certain that she wasn't, despite her steadfast refusal to sleep with him, and had asked himself if that mattered to him, to which the answer had been an unqualified no. She'd loved Eric and given herself to Eric – how could he hold that against her when he was asking her to do the same? She would have married Eric if he had lived; now she would marry him, which was his good fortune.

'Well I'm not a virgin either, so neither of us can complain,' he replied.

She laughed. It was an honest answer, like the man himself. Then she was in his arms again, kissing him, touching him, being kissed and touched in return.

Breaking away, she disappeared into the bathroom. She took her time, finally slipping into one of his clean shirts. She looked at herself in the mirror, then combed her hair again. She wanted to be just right for him.

He was sitting up in bed reading the paper with a frown on his face when she returned. 'What is it?' she asked.

Immediately he tossed the paper aside. 'Some Austrian Archduke has been assassinated at a place called Sarajevo.'

'Is that important?'

'Only to the Austrians I should think,' he said, and held out his arms for her.

Sheila was trying to get a stain out of a white toga and Pat was hemming a skirt when the door to the Wardrobe banged open and Andrew burst in, standing rigidly in the doorway staring at them.

'We've just declared war on Germany,' he announced in a tight, dazed voice. The date was 4 August.

'Oh my God!' exclaimed Pat, sinking back on to the cutting table.

Sheila was stunned. Like many she'd convinced herself it would never come to this, that sanity would prevail.

'Listen!' said Pat, and crossing to the closest window, opened it wide. The sound of cheering and singing invaded the Wardrobe, a little way off at present but coming closer with every second.

A few minutes later an excited procession passed along the street below, some men waving their caps as they marched, others their fists. A few women were dancing with their skirts pulled up almost to their knees while others were holding poles from which union jacks and lion rampants fluttered. Children of all ages were dashing in and out of the adults. The atmosphere was of a carnival.

'War,' whispered Sheila, the reality sinking home, and glanced at Andrew in sudden fright.

'It'll all be over by Christmas, bound to be,' Pat murmured.

The three of them stood at the window watching the procession till it finally tailed off, then vanished from sight.

'All over by Christmas, bound to be,' Pat repeated, this time with more conviction in her voice.

Sheila stood watching in the wings while Andrew and the rest of the cast formed themselves into a line to take their bows. It was the final performance of the first week of *Julius Caesar*.

The house was only a quarter full, disappointing for a Saturday night, even if it was Shakespeare; but with the country newly at war people were bound to have things on their minds other than entertainment.

The performance had been a splendid one, but nonetheless the applause was thin, starting to die away after only the second bow. The Deputy Stage Manager running the Prompt Corner gave the cue and a stage hand started to run down the curtain.

And then it happened; a solitary female voice, reedy but filled with emotion, began singing 'God Save the King'.

The man on the curtain paused, uncertain whether to carry on or not. He looked over to the bewildered DSM who didn't know what to do either.

A second voice joined the first, then another and another, till the national anthem was ringing throughout the auditorium.

The actors, caught with the rag still above their heads, came to attention and joined in.

Sheila could feel her skin prickling with the sentiment

of the moment, with the unity of everyone there. Here was a reflection of the national will, of defiance and stubbornness, of loyalty to, and support for the Crown. The message was clear and unequivocal; it wasn't only God Save the King; it was also sod the Kaiser.

There are moments in the theatre, often unscripted, which are electrifying, and this was one of them.

The conclusion of the anthem was followed by a few seconds' hiatus, then simultaneously, as though cued, everyone began to clap. And this time the clapping, despite the small numbers involved, threatened to raise the roof.

Sheila noticed that when Andrew and the other men came off stage after the rag had finally been lowered their chins were jutting out and they were walking with more pride than she'd ever previously seen. Already they were like soldiers, soldiers marching into battle.

She felt a wave of fear and nausea come over her.

Later that night, after they had made love and were lying together, his arms still around her, her head against his shoulder, he began talking about what he called the 'grand finale'. Everyone had been full of it backstage, and the management were so impressed they were going to have the national anthem sung after every show, the cast and other employees taking the lead.

And talking about rumours, he went on, unaware of the look of worry that had come into her eyes, had she heard that German soldiers were cutting the breasts off captured Belgian nurses?

But she had a rumour of her own to tell him; a great battle had been fought in the North Sea and the German navy was now at the bottom.

Andrew laughed. The way he'd heard the story it was the British dreadnoughts which had been sunk.

'Norrie Brunton, the man they call Caveman, has joined up. He expects to be going away sometime next week,' said Sheila in a low voice.

Andrew said that men were joining up in tens of

thousands, the response, apparently, to Kitchener's poster 'Your Country Needs You!' That poster with its pointing finger seemed to be everywhere. And every man who saw the poster knew the finger was pointing directly at him.

She reached out just to touch him, to remind herself of his solidity, of his aliveness, of the exquisite beauty of their love. Had it been such a short time ago that she had believed she would never again be happy? Never again know love?

She comforted herself with the thought that the recruiting offices were accepting single men but not married ones yet. Like everyone else, Sheila believed that the conflict would be over sooner rather than later – long before they got round to taking married men. It was up to her, therefore, to save Andrew from his own impetuousness.

'Why don't we get married right away?' she asked, suddenly cuddling against him.

'There's no rush is there?' he asked smoothly, knowing damn well that she believed there was.

'Well,' she said softly, almost shyly, kissing his chest. 'I could get pregnant any day . . . I wouldn't want that without being married.'

Andrew smiled to himself, kissing the top of her head. She thought she was being clever, but she wasn't pulling any wool over his eyes. He knew precisely what was going on in that pretty head of hers, and if it was possible he loved her all the more because of it.

The theatre was going dark for three weeks after *Julius Caesar*, he reminded her. For the first blank week he had to be away from Glasgow on business, unavoidable business, but they'd be married the moment he got back. 'How's that?' he asked, his lips seeking out hers.

'You promise?' moving her mouth just out of reach. 'You won't change your mind?'

'I swear it.'

'And what's this urgent business?'

'Just something I've got to see to in England.'

'But you'll be back in a week?'

His hand moved along her body in a way that was both startling and familiar. 'In a week,' he whispered. 'In just one week.'

Sheila glanced yet again at her watch. It was six minutes to eleven and they were booked to be married on the hour. Where oh where was he?

'Are you sure he knows the address?' asked Pat.

'Of course he does,' snapped Sheila. She'd told him no less than four times when they'd spoken on the telephone the night before last. He couldn't have got it wrong.

Perhaps his train was late? Or perhaps he'd missed the damn thing altogether! She'd strangle him if he had, she promised herself.

She'd wanted to meet him at the station, but he'd been insistent that they meet in front of the Register Office, although for the life of her she couldn't think why.

Martha Street Register Office she'd told him. She could hear the words as she'd said them into the telephone echoing in her mind. A sudden terrible thought struck her. Was there more than one Martha Street? Could he be even now standing in some other part of Glasgow, cursing her the way she was cursing him?

Control yourself, girl, she told herself. If there was another Martha Street the chances of it also having a Register Office must be . . . what? A million to one? Something like that.

'The train might have got stuck at Beattock – that's always happening,' Pat suggested.

He should have come back yesterday, then. He should have given himself some time in hand, Sheila thought.

'How do I look?' she asked Pat for the hundredth time.

'Absolutely smashing,' Pat replied, unable to resist a smile. In fact, Sheila looked exceptionally beautiful today, despite her nerves.

Sheila smoothed down the sides of her skirt. She was wearing a grey, two-piece costume she'd bought in Arnott Simpson, considering it elegant and just the thing for a wartime register wedding. Only now she wasn't so sure. 'Is it too severe, do you think?' she wondered out loud.

'It's just perfect,' Pat assured her, trying to hide her own jitters as best she could. Where was the bloody man! Typical actor, thought Pat, a rotten timekeeper.

Perhaps he'd got cold feet and was standing her up? As soon as the thought occurred to Sheila she started to tremble all over. He wouldn't do that to her – not her Andrew, surely! Tears started to stream down her face.

Suddenly Pat clutched Sheila's arm. 'Chalky White,' she said, pointing to a familiar figure hurrying towards them. Chalky was an actor in the company, and a great friend of Andrew's.

Sheila realized then that Chalky wasn't alone; that he was with the figure in uniform striding alongside him. A look into the face above the uniform caused her to give a small cry of anguish, for the face was Andrew's, the uniform that of the Royal Flying Corps.

Andrew, grinning sheepishly, immediately began to apologize for being late. En route from the station, he and Chalky had stopped off for a quick drink and somehow they'd spent longer at the bar than they'd intended. Chalky was to be the Best Man, he explained.

It was plain to Pat that Sheila wanted to be alone with Andrew. 'Come on, Chalky,' she said, grabbing him by the arm. 'Let's go inside to find out what room we're meant to go to.' There was no doubt it was an order. Meekly, he followed her up the steps and in through the glass-panelled doors.

Sheila stared at the uniform and the face smiling at her above it. He was handsome in it, right enough, there was no denying that. Then, the tears still streaming down her face, she laid into him. Why hadn't he told her what he planned to do? Why had he gone sneaking off behind her back to join up?

157

His defence was that he'd known she would have made it as difficult for him as she was able, if she'd known. Could she deny that? Of course she couldn't. And as for being sneaky, what did she think she'd been in trying to get him to the altar as quickly as possible just to save him from entering the Forces?

Sheila dabbed at her eyes, trying to save her make-up from any further destruction. 'What about the theatre?' she nearly whispered.

'It's all taken care of,' he assured her.

'How long before you have to return to England?'

'Three days,' he replied, not looking into her eyes.

'I remember that day we went down to the coast, you said you'd love to be able to fly. It seems you're about to achieve your ambition.'

'That's why I chose the RFC,' he replied quietly.

'I could hit you!' she choked.

'I'd prefer it if you kissed me,' he smiled.

'I would understand if you didn't want to marry me now until all this is over,' he whispered, not disentangling himself from her embrace.

She wished her tears would stop. 'If we've only got three days then we'd better make the most of them,' she said at last.

Hand-in-hand, they climbed the steps and went into the Register Office.

5

It was early November. Sheila was sitting in Wardrobe, staring at the latest death and casualty lists issued from the great and terrible battle being fought at the Ypres salient in Flanders, a battle that was now raging into its fourth week.

Day by day, Sheila had been following the seemingly

158

endless lists in the newspapers, growing more and more appalled at the carnage being wrought, all the young men dying so far from home.

She thanked God her Andrew was still in England. At least she thought he was. He certainly had been up until a few days ago according to his latest letter which had arrived that morning. It was encouraging to know casualties amongst the RFC and their naval equivalent, the RNAS had so far been light. She could only pray they continued that way.

Sheila gratefully accepted the cup of tea Pat handed her. 'How frustrating it is to be doing such silly work in times like these,' she sighed to Pat. 'I should be doing something for the war effort. Making some contribution.'

Pat mumbled her agreement, peering over Sheila's shoulder at the printed lists. Pat had lost a cousin the previous week at a place called Messines Ridge.

Pat thought about her cousin who'd come from down in the borders where his family had farmed since the days long ago, when the area had been known as The Debatable Lands, debatable between Scotland and England that is.

He'd been a carrot top with a wandering left eye she recalled; small, but wiry, and surprising in strength for his size. He'd been a lot younger than she, by twenty years or more, and the last time she'd seen him he was only a wee lad, mad keen on collecting birds' eggs. Now he was dead at a place called Messines Ridge, and the thought brought a lump to her throat. In her jewellery box back at the digs she still had a blown blackbird's egg he'd given her.

'Ever heard of the VADs?' Pat asked.

Sheila had. There had been several references to them in the newspapers recently. 'Aren't they nurses?'

'Voluntary Aid Detachments,' explained Pat. 'They're women volunteers who assist the nurses,' going on to say that she knew there was a branch of the organization not far from the theatre. I heard about it in the McKillops' cafe,' she added.

Helping the sick and wounded appealed to Sheila. Not only would it be a contribution to the war effort, it would also be a constructive one.

'I'd be willing to join – what about you?' she asked Pat.

'I'll find out what I can, shall I?' offered Pat. 'And I'll fix an appointment for the two of us as soon as possible.'

For the first time since Andrew had gone back to England, Sheila felt bright and cheered within herself.

Commandant McNair of the St Andrew's Ambulance Association, one of the number of societies affiliated to the British Red Cross Society, was a fierce-looking woman who gave the impression she could've dealt singlehandedly with the entire German Army, and probably the Austro-Hungarian Army as well.

'So you want to be VADs,' she growled, prowling round Sheila and Pat, eyeing them from head to toe.

'If you'll accept us,' Sheila answered politely.

Commandant McNair stuck her face close to Sheila's and said it wasn't all forehead bathing and hand holding you know. Many of the things a VAD was expected to do were dirty, disgusting, and anything but romantic. How would she feel about washing a soldier's shitty backside for example?

Sheila replied coolly that she'd had three brothers, so having to wash a man's backside, shitty or otherwise, wasn't going to offend her any.

Commandant McNair grunted; this one was a definite possible she thought. Transferring her gaze to Pat she asked Pat what her reaction was to what she'd just said.

Pat answered she'd spent nearly her entire working life in the theatre, which was just like that – apparent gloss on the outside, an awful lot of shit underneath. She'd cope.

'You'll have to study before going on the wards.

You'll need a first-aid certificate and another in home nursing first,' Commandant McNair explained.

'How long will that take?' asked Sheila. McNair replied that that depended on what the person doing the studying had between her ears.

'And how many hours would we be expected to work in a week?' asked Pat, bravely.

The Commandant replied simply, 'As many as you are needed. Some of our women are putting in a hundred hours plus on the wards.' Why did they think more volunteers were so desperately needed?

Pat was taken aback. She'd thought this was a part-time organization. If the women were putting in so many hours, were they being paid? Commandant McNair explained tartly that their ladies did not expect a pecuniary reward for what they did. The society was strictly a voluntary one.

'Well, I'm sorry for taking up your time,' said Pat, blushing. 'But I'm a working woman and I need to earn my living.'

'And what about you, Mrs Lack?' Commandant McNair queried, turning on Sheila.

With Sheila things were different. Prior to leaving, Andrew had told her he had a monthly allowance paid into his bank account, an account he had instructed the bank to make into a joint one. While away he would have his RFC pay to take care of his needs. His allowance was therefore available to Sheila to either save or use as she saw fit. Because of this, unlike Pat, she didn't have to continue to earn her own living.

Going behind her desk, the Commandant wrote Sheila's name and address in a black book. That done, she informed Sheila that she was accepted to start studying. When could she begin attending the daily classes?

'I'll have to give proper notice at the theatre first. As soon as that's served, I'll be free to start the classes.'

Leaving the Commandant's office they made their way back to Wardrobe. 'I'm going to miss you like hell, you know,' said Pat glumly once the door had shut behind them.

'We'll keep in touch,' promised Sheila.

Pat pulled out a bottle of sherry she'd secreted away. 'Sod these poxy costumes – let's get drunk,' she said, trying to sound cheerful.

Sheila put her arms around Pat, hugging her warmly. 'I'll get some glasses,' she half laughed, half cried.

Sheila rubbed her eyes which were sore from staring at the textbook in front of her. Time for a break she decided, and yawning, rose and crossed to the window.

Since their wedding she had been living in what used to be Andrew's rooms, and was now well settled in. She had rearranged things to suit herself, including getting rid of that dreadful aspidistra and replacing it with several attractive potted plants she'd bought from the local florist. She'd been brought up to believe that aspidistras were unlucky; no fisherman would give one house room.

The street outside looked eerie. The streetlamps, dimmed since September, combined with the light fog to make the city streets look both foreign and unreal.

Staring into the soft yellow and grey gloom, Sheila thought of Andrew who'd been over in France for some weeks now. He had gone to join the No. 5 Squadron, flying a plane called a Henry Farman which he described as a sort of box kite with wings.

According to Andrew, his main job was that of reconnaissance; flying over enemy positions and then reporting back what he'd seen. He'd been at pains to tell her that none of the planes on either side were armed, if you discounted pistols and rifles, that is. The greatest danger, apart from the wind carrying you so far behind enemy lines that you couldn't get home again (the wind, he said, always favoured the enemy in this respect) was ground fire. The trick was to stay above that. He, of course, always made sure that he did.

Andrew had become friendly with a man called McCudden, of whom he thought particularly highly, and another named Strange who'd made a reputation for himself by going aloft with a machine gun strapped to the nacelle of his Farman. But the CO, a Major Higgins, had promptly commanded him to dismantle it on his return to the ground.

In Andrew's estimation, the men of the RFC were an odd bunch: nearly all individualists, many of whom had been private flyers before the war; others roped in from various cavalry regiments in the belief that a keen eye and good sense of balance were essential in flying aeroplanes.

They may have been an odd bunch, but they were also a terrific bunch. Andrew thought each and every one of them deserving of respect and affection.

It was the poor bloody infantry he felt sorry for. Dug into their trenches, they were taking a terrible pasting. He was glad he'd joined the RFC. Unwittingly, it had been the wisest of moves on his part.

As for the flying itself, he absolutely adored it, and they all spoke well of his ability, even McCudden, who was far and away the best flyer in the Squadron.

With a wrench, Sheila brought her thoughts back from Andrew and France. It was time to return to her studying. There was a lot for her to get through yet before being able to finally call it a night.

She returned to sit again at the table, and within seconds was once more immersed in her textbook.

Cowcaddens General Hospital was a Gothic edifice of dirty grey stone and towering spires, looking to Sheila like the evil magician's castle of fairy tales.

Once through the doors the smell hit her immediately; a combination of antiseptic, anaesthetic, and . . . And what? It was something she couldn't put a name to. Later she did. The hard-to-define ingredients were very obvious really; they were called fear and pain.

The highly polished floor squeaked beneath her duty shoes as she followed the signs directing her to the administration section.

There were nine girls already assembled in the sparsely furnished room into which she was eventually shown. All of them turned to stare at her as she came in. Automatically she smiled, but not all of them smiled back.

She made a beeline for an empty chair in a corner and sat. A dark-haired girl close by nodded to her, and she nodded in return; but the girl didn't make any attempt to start a conversation, so neither did she.

An eleventh girl arrived, went through the process of being scrutinized, and joined several girls standing together whom she evidently knew.

Sheila was the only one from the St Andrew's Ambulance Association. The rest were from either the Red Cross or the St John Ambulance Association, obvious from the colour of their uniforms: blue for the Red Cross, grey for St John, with the Red Cross or St John emblem on their apron bibs.

'So I told her, she didn't have to worry about that as she'd probably seen more cocks than many a chicken farmer,' a tall girl with sandy-coloured hair and a beaky nose said loudly in a frightfully Kelvinside accent. Her companions burst into laughter, while most of the others in the room smiled, some nervously.

'You *didn't* say that Georgina!' one of the tall girl's companions exclaimed in an equally plummy voice.

'I most certainly did,' Georgina replied, and she and her companions burst out laughing again.

Georgina and company were unmistakably upper-class girls, as were a number of the others, she judged. The remainder, after careful scrutiny, Sheila guessed to be middle class. Which meant that she, the only working-class woman there, was the odd one out.

Sheila stared at the braying Georgina. That's a right bitch, that one, she thought.

A final girl arrived, completing the group, and directly

behind her a nurse who introduced herself as Matron Carswell. There was a brief speech of welcome, then Matron Carswell read out a list of names: the VAD and the ward she was assigned to. Sheila's ward was called McLaggan.

On reaching the end of the list, Matron Carswell snapped her notebook shut and told them to find their own way to their assigned wards; it would be good practice for learning the layout of the hospital, she said, and swept from the room.

Girls assigned to the same ward were teaming up to find their way together, but Sheila had to go on her own as she'd been the only one assigned to McLaggan. She finally found it, on the fifth floor, but as she entered through its green swing doors an agonized scream rang out from within.

'Who are you?' a voice demanded.

The speaker was in the uniform of a Ward Sister and looked desperately tired, the sort of tired that comes from a combination of strain, overwork, and a great deal of lost sleep.

Sheila gave her name, and the information she'd been assigned to McLaggan by Matron Carswell.

'Bed six on the left, assist the nurse there,' Sister snapped, hurrying past Sheila and out of the ward.

Bed six had screens around it. Sheila went quietly behind them, there to discover a rather horsey-faced nurse removing the covering from a dressing trolley. The patient was a young man in his late teens whose left arm was heavily bandaged.

'Excuse me,' Sheila whispered hesitantly. 'Sister sent me to assist.' Barely looking at her, the nurse told her to remove the bandage. The young man watched fearfully as she started to do so.

The bandage came away, and the dressing with it, losing such a terrible stench that Sheila thought she might be ill.

The nurse then handed Sheila a metal bowl and told her

165

to stand a little to the side while she attended to the wound which went clean to the bone and was suppurating badly.

The bowl contained strong antiseptic into which the nurse dipped a wad of cotton wool. She then applied the sodden wad directly to the wound.

Sheila blanched and the young man whimpered. 'Sorry, Tim, but it has to be done,' the nurse said shortly. Disposing of the first wad, she then applied a second.

The nurse re-bandaged Tim's arm herself, doing so briskly and efficiently, yet with care and tenderness. When Tim had been attended to, the nurse instructed Sheila to bring the screens down to bed eleven where another dressing had to be changed, then wheeled away the dressings trolley leaving Sheila to get on with it.

As Sheila manipulated the first of the three screens down the ward, she saw that Sister was standing at the top of the ward watching her. She also counted two nurses other than horsey face moving amongst the beds, and one other VAD.

The man in bed eleven only had one leg, bandaged from mid calf downwards, and was unconscious. When the screens were in place round the bed, the same nurse reappeared with the trolly, from behind another set of screens, and told Sheila to remove the bandage, then disappeared again leaving the trolley behind.

Slowly, Sheila unwrapped the bandage, revealing a foot that was completely black. She stared in horror when one of the toes suddenly fell off.

Trembling all over, she bent down and picked it up. It was dry to the touch, and black inside as well as out. There was no blood.

For a wild moment she had the insane idea that she could somehow stick the toe back on. What with? Glue? she asked herself and gave a short, hysterical laugh.

A hand appeared to take the toe from her grasp. Glancing up she saw it was Sister. 'It wasn't my fault. It just dropped of its own accord,' she stuttered.

'First day on the wards?'

Sheila nodded.

It was best for them to be thrown in at the deep end, that way time was saved on weeding out the ones who were temperamentally unsuitable and time was of the essence, Sister thought.

'Can you continue?' she asked.

Sheila took a deep breath. She was going to see an awful lot worse than a toe falling off, she told herself. 'I'm all right now,' she answered gamely.

Sister personally put a new dressing and bandage on the black foot, telling Sheila in a soft whisper as she worked that it was doubtful the patient would last the day. He was a captain in the Seaforth Highlanders called Haliburton who was being kept heavily sedated with morphine, receiving an injection every two hours.

When Captain Haliburton had been attended to, Sister told Sheila to go away up to her room which was just inside the ward doors and clearly marked. The kettle was kept there, and Sheila was to take it into the sterilizing room opposite and brew up. 'You'll find everything you need in the cupboard underneath the poisons cabinet,' she added cheerfully as Sheila walked away.

By the end of Sheila's first shift, which lasted twelve hours, she had swollen feet and numbed senses.

She had also wheeled Captain Haliburton's body down to the mortuary.

As the days passed Sheila's life became a continual round of cleaning, bed making, blanket baths and temperatures.

More wounded arrived, some by sea, others by rail, a great many still verminous and filthy from weeks in the trenches, the ones who'd come by rail often exhausted by extended weeks of travel.

Each man was supposed to be labelled with his name, number, regiment, type of wound and whether or not an anti-tetanus injection had been given, but sometimes the label read GOK: God Only Knows.

Wounds often went septic and the pus had to be drained out through tubes which it was Sheila's duty to clean. This tube cleaning was constant, as were changing the dressings and the application of hot fomentations.

Ether and chloroform were notoriously difficult to administer and tended to have an adverse reaction on the patients; pain killers were distributed so sparingly that they might have consisted of a hundred per cent gold dust.

Gradually Sheila got used to the stink of suppurating and septic wounds till finally the smell ceased to bother her, even the noxious stench of gangrene.

Then, in March, news started to filter back of a great new battle being fought at a place called Neuve Chapelle, and soon after that the casualties began to arrive in torrents, packing every ward to capacity. When ward saturation was reached, patients spilled out into the corridors which soon became lined with beds.

It was then that the decision was made that the VADs would take up residence in the hospital, only leaving on their days off. This was a decision regrettably arrived at, Sister assured them, but necessary due to the ever mounting pressure on the hospital. She hoped they all understood. The only space available for a dormitory for the VADs was in the bowels of the hospital, directly behind the mortuary.

Two days after the announcement, Sheila, clutching a suitcase containing personal belongings, presented herself at the dormitory where she was assigned a bed.

The first night confusion reigned. 'It's like being back at bloody school!' Georgina Murchison-Stewart announced. She was the same Georgina who'd been part of Sheila's intake, and over the next few days she set herself up as self-appointed leader of the VADs.

'What about you, Lack, where do you come from?' Georgina called out to Sheila one evening, addressing her loudly from across the dormitory.

Sheila was sipping a cup of cocoa. 'The name's either Sheila or Mrs Lack,' she replied levelly, heartily disliking Georgina and the way Georgina had about her.

Georgina's eyes narrowed. Up until now, she had more or less dismissed Sheila as beneath her contempt, but something in Sheila's tone warned her that here was another very strong personality – perhaps even one to rival her own.

Georgina's cronies were all staring curiously at Sheila. From her speech she was plainly working class, yet there was nothing subservient or deferential about her. If she knew she was inferior to them she certainly didn't show it.

Sheila continued sipping her cocoa, knowing Georgina's eyes were riveted on her.

'Where do you come from *Mrs* Lack?' Georgina asked eventually, smirking to her friends over the cleverness of her own mockery.

The dormitory had gone quiet. Georgina and her cronies weren't the only ones curious about Sheila. Though there had been a few other working-class VADs at this hospital, she was currently the only one, and it was obvious that if the others accepted her at all it was only because there was a war on.

'I come from the east coast of Scotland,' she said evenly. 'From a village called Dragonholme.'

'And what do people do in Dragonholme?' asked Georgina archly.

Sheila smiled her sweetest smile, 'They fish.'

'A fishergirl!' Georgina exclaimed in her most patrician tones.

Elspeth Crichton, one of Georgina's pals, sniggered behind her hand.

'Is your husband a fisherman then?' asked Georgina. She might have been interviewing a potential scullery maid.

'He's at the Front.'

'Ah, a Tommy!' winking at the audience. It was clear what she thought of Tommies.

'And do you have a man at the Front?' Sheila asked with a smile. She already knew the answer from a conversation she'd overheard in the canteen.

Georgina scowled, but made no reply.

'Do you?' Sheila persisted.

'I have many men, if you must know,' Georgina snapped.

'Of course,' Sheila agreed sweetly, and, turning her back on Georgina, effectively dismissed her.

Georgina's face flushed bright pink with anger. She had no boyfriend, at the Front or anywhere else, a situation that did nothing to improve her disposition. She glanced around edgily. Some of the girls were grinning, others denied their poker faces by the expression of amusement in their eyes.

I'll get you for that you little peasant, she thought, glaring at Sheila.

The following night, after what had been a particularly arduous day (they'd lost four men on the ward and two from the corridor outside the ward), Sheila came down to the dormitory from the canteen where the food had been of its usual low standard.

She sat on her bed to take off her shoes, and right away the niff hit her. When she saw the bump under the bedclothes she thought, Christ! they've stuck an amputated limb in my bed!

But it wasn't a limb, as she discovered on peeling back the bedclothes; it was a dead tunny roughly three feet long.

She stared at the fish, thinking how incongruous it looked in these surroundings. Across the dormitory Georgina and her cronies were giggling, obviously considering this a great jape, to use one of their own words.

170

A girl in one of the beds next to Sheila, saw the tunny and screamed, which caused the giggling to erupt into full-blown laughter.

Grasping hold of the tunny's tail with both hands Sheila lifted it up so that the entire dormitory could see it. 'Has anyone lost a sardine?' she inquired straight-faced, which produced hoots from all round.

She had a sudden inspiration then of how to turn this to her advantage. Walking down to the one table that served the entire dormitory for letter writing and the like she heaved the tunny up on to it. She'd be back in a tick, she said, and hurried off to the kitchens where she succeeded in borrowing a boning knife.

Returning to the dormitory she flourished the knife aloft, declaring that as a person or persons unknown had been kind enough to donate the fish, the very least she could do was give the dormitory a professional demonstration on how to dress it. All those interested gather round, she instructed, and every single girl did, even Georgina and her chums, albeit bitterly disappointed that this wasn't turning out at all the way they'd hoped.

Sheila hadn't lost the knack of her old skills, gutting and boning the tunny in a few seconds. When she finished with a flourish the watching girls applauded.

'Now, who would like something decent to eat after that rotten food we had in the canteen?'

Sheila took the tunny to the kitchens, where she persuaded the staff to allow her to use one of the ovens. When it was cooked to a recipe of Peg's she took it back to the dormitory where everyone (with the exception of Georgina and her group) had a good tuck in.

'Some bright idea,' muttered a piqued Georgina, glowering at Elspeth whose idea it had been.

'It looks delicious. I wish I had some,' Elspeth murmured wistfully in reply.

Sheila's bed reeked of tunny when she got into it, but that didn't bother her in the least. One up for us fisher-girls she thought jubilantly, starting to drift off to sleep.

For the first time in a long time she dreamt about the Dragonholme disaster, seeing again the *Bluebell*, the *Gypsy Queen* and all those other bonny boats disappearing into the sea. Vividly, she saw the *Gypsy Queen* beneath the water and Eric, struggling frantically, floating off to be swallowed in a single gulp by a monstrous tunny the size of a whale.

She awoke just before dawn covered in cold sweat and filled with fright.

Nor did she get back to sleep before it was time to get up and start the long hard day ahead of her.

On 18 April Sheila was called into Sister's office. 'It seems your husband has connections in high places. He's back in Glasgow and you're to be given seven days off. He'll pick you up at the front entrance at four-thirty,' she said shortly.

Sheila stood staring at Sister, trying to make sense of her words. Andrew was home. Andrew was in Glasgow. Giving a cry of delight, she leapt in the air.

'I take it,' said Sister, 'that this is good news.'

'Oh, yes, the very best,' Sheila replied excitedly.

Seven days' holiday to spend with Andrew, just like that, completely out of the blue. It was unbelievable!

'He's timed things well as we're comparatively quiet at the moment,' Sister continued, her mouth unsmiling, but her voice almost humorous.

Sheila glanced at the clock on the wall behind Sister's desk. There were thirty-five minutes before his arrival. She was restless with impatience for those minutes to tick away.

'Well,' said Sister drily, 'I can see I'll get no more work out of you today. Why don't you go off duty now and get yourself ready?'

'Oh, thank you, Sister,' Sheila effused, so excited that she reached out to shake the older woman's hand. 'Thank you so much.'

As the door closed behind her Sister called out, 'Remember, Mrs Lack, no running in the corridors!'

At twenty-five past the hour, Sheila was standing outside the front entrance, smiling expectantly. She had butterflies in her tum and kept hopping from foot to foot, causing more than one person entering the hospital to give her a sideways glance.

Dead on time, the Silver Ghost, retrieved from the garage which had been storing it, came into view. Then the car was parked and Andrew was whirling her round and round, the pair of them laughing joyously, unable to stop themselves from kissing. A passing doctor gave them a wolf whistle, but neither paid any attention.

She had so many questions to ask – thousands it seemed – but for the moment it was enough to have him there beside her, with his arms around her and his lips on hers.

'Oh, Andrew,' she said over and over, her heart so full that she could barely speak. 'Oh, Andrew, I've missed you so.'

'Not half as much as I've missed you, love,' he laughed. 'This is one of the first times in my life that I felt justified in using my connections to get special privileges.'

'So how *did* you manage to pull this off?' she wanted to know, so happy to be sitting beside him, so far away from the nightmare of the war.

Just for an instant the smile left his face. 'I'll explain about that later,' he said, brightening again. 'Later,' giving her meaningful wink.

'Oh, you'll have forgotten by then,' she laughed.

It was only later, while she lay on the bed, watching him across the room as he poured them each a whisky, that she remembered how close they really were to the guns and the deaths.

She noticed then how much older he looked. Of course, all the men who came back from the Front had aged but with Andrew it was something more.

Something about his manner; about the way he moved and did things. The expression in his eyes. It was not just his body which had been changed by the war: it was his heart and mind as well.

'How did you get your leave?' she asked again.

He came to the bed and sat beside her. 'It's a compassionate leave,' he said slowly. 'The old girl's dying. I just got word a few days ago. That's why everything was so rushed.'

'Your mother?' Gently, she took his hand. 'But what happened?'

'The doctors say it's cancer. They don't give her more than a few months to live.'

He would be driving home in the morning to spend some time with his mother before she went, and he'd be taking Sheila with him.

'If you . . . if you'd rather go by yourself – ' she began.

'No,' he said, taking her once more into his arms. 'I wouldn't.'

They set off early the next morning, and arrived in Manchester late that afternoon. It was Sheila's first trip south of the border. Her excitement delighted him.

The Lack house was situated in the suburb of Withington, just off the Wilbraham Road. Set in its own grounds it was the largest house she'd ever been in, with the exception of Dragonholme Hall. It was constructed of what had once been red bricks, which were now black with soot and grime. 'That house is a hundred and twenty-seven years old,' Andrew informed her as he parked the Silver Ghost in the driveway. 'And was probably only its original colour for twenty-seven of them.'

Of course, she had known all along that Andrew's family was rich – his father had been a successful industrialist – but she had not quite realized just how rich. Not even the Rolls had prepared her for this.

174

'Don't be nervous. Mother will adore you, I know she will,' he assured her as he helped her from the car.

But Sheila was nervous, and even Andrew couldn't calm her. She prayed that Mrs Lack wasn't going to be some grand lady who despised her on sight. She didn't want Andrew to be caught between them, his mother and his wife.

Ollerenshaw, the butler, answered their ring. 'Mr Andrew,' the old man cried in delight. 'It is absolutely marvellous to have you home.' And then added, the perfect English butler again, 'I am very sorry about your mother.'

Andrew introduced Ollerenshaw to Sheila. 'It is an honour and pleasure to meet the young master's wife,' he said solemnly. 'All of us are looking forward to having you here.'

Taking them inside the house, Ollerenshaw showed them the room that had been specially prepared for their coming. Andrew left Sheila there to get washed and changed while he went to see his mother.

On the writing bureau near the window was a picture which caught her attention. It was old and sepia tinted, the photograph of an earnest young man and a bonny young woman, clearly his wife. Sheila recognized them immediately as Andrew's parents – the resemblance was unmistakable.

In the past, Andrew had often spoken to her about his father, for whom he'd had great admiration. Oliver Lack had inherited a small ball-bearing factory which he'd soon turned into a large ball-bearing factory. One by one, he'd bought other small factories after that, and done the same to them. At the time of his death he'd owned seven booming factories in all.

Oliver Lack had always planned that Andrew, his only child, would succeed him in business. He'd been bitterly disappointed when Andrew had announced his intention to become an actor.

Oliver and Sarah Lack had done their utmost to

persuade Andrew to change his mind, but to no avail. Finally, though reluctantly, they'd accepted that Andrew would follow his chosen profession, the theatre.

It was to their eternal credit that once they'd accepted this there had been no recriminations, and the pair of them had come to see Andrew the first time he'd gone on stage, even though the part had been a dismally small one.

When Oliver Lack died, his factories had been sold, and the realized capital invested. When Sarah Lack followed her husband, everything would go to Andrew.

She was just finishing making herself presentable when Andrew reappeared. 'My mother would like to meet you now,' he said, looking at her with pride.

'How do I look?' Sheila asked. She'd chosen to wear a simple but attractive dress that she'd run up for herself when working at the Queen's Theatre.

'Absolutely fine,' Andrew answered, giving her a kiss.

'You're certain it's all right?'

'Couldn't be more so.'

'How is she?' she asked at last, as casually as she could.

Andrew's eyes clouded over. 'Skin and bone. I nearly cried at the sight of her.' He was silent for a moment, staring out through the window behind her. 'But she can't wait to meet you.'

Andrew led her along the corridor, and up a flight of carpeted stairs. Pausing before an oak door he gave Sheila's arm a reassuring squeeze. Then, taking an audible breath he rapped on the door.

A reedy voice called 'Come in.'

Inside the bedroom, the curtains had been drawn, the one source of illumination a bright bedside lamp. Mrs Lack, white-haired and terribly frail-looking, sat propped up against a bolster and pillows. She wore a shawl round her painfully thin shoulders.

Death was already in the room. Sheila could smell it. It was a smell she'd become well acquainted with at the hospital.

'It's good to meet you at last, my dear,' Mrs Lack smiled, her voice little more than a whisper.

Sheila came forward and took the dry, skeletal hand in her own. 'It's good to meet you, also,' she said sincerely, and, on a sudden impulse, bent down and kissed the old woman on the cheek.

Her eyes shone as they moved up and down her daughter-in-law. 'Bring Sheila a chair over so she can sit beside me. She and I must get acquainted,' she ordered Andrew with unexpected vigour. He immediately brought the chair and placed it where his mother instructed.

Sheila's nervousness evaporated completely as she and Mrs Lack, who insisted she call her Sarah, began to chat.

They spoke about Sheila's job as a VAD and her previous employment at the Queen's Theatre where she'd met Andrew. Then she talked about Dragonholme as she hadn't talked about it in years.

Minutes ticked past to become half an hour, then an hour. Finally Sarah announced that she was tired, and had to sleep. But would Sheila and Andrew come to her again after their supper? Sheila spoke for both of them. 'Of course we will,' she said. 'You just rest.'

Sarah glanced up at her son. A soft, knowing smile twisted the corners of her mouth. 'You picked a good woman, Andrew. I heartily approve and so would your father.'

'I knew you'd like her,' beamed Andrew.

'If only this war hadn't . . .' Sarah trailed off in despair. She'd have given every penny she possessed for the war not to have happened, and Andrew not to have gone into uniform.

But it had, and he had, and there was nothing she could do about it.

As Andrew closed the door behind himself and Sheila, they could hear his mother weeping.

*   *   *

Two nights later Sarah Lack died in her sleep, not making it to the end of the month after all.

He'd got home just in time, Andrew said to Sheila, then broke down into floods of tears. He'd loved his mother dearly, and they'd been very close, despite the disappointments he might have caused her.

Sheila took her distraught husband into her arms and rocked him back and forth as though he were a child.

6

It was 15 July 1916, and the Battle of the Somme had been raging for a fortnight. Already the casualties were enormous, stretching even further the already thinly stretched medical facilities and personnel. Several days after the start of the battle, word had arrived back in Britain that more doctors, nurses and VADs were desperately needed. Sheila, who'd volunteered some time previously, was one of those now told they were going to France.

The night before, she'd left Portsmouth in a destroyer. Only halfway across the Channel she'd become aware of the far off sound of the guns. Since then it was a sound to which she had become accustomed, getting steadily louder the nearer they got to the Front.

She was tired, irritable, hungry and extremely thirsty. There was no food on the train, or water, except what individuals had brought along with them, and no one seemed to have any idea of when they were likely to arrive at their destination.

Rising, she made her way to the toilet, only to discover, as she had the previous seven times she'd tried, that it was engaged. 'Damn!' she muttered, and fought her way through the crowded corridor and back to her . seat.

She thought of Andrew safe in Egypt, where he'd been posted directly after his leave. At least that was one less fear to contend with. The intense heat and boredom were his principle complaints, with bedbugs and flies coming a close second. According to him the most popular form of entertainment was a game they all played of seeing who could get most bugs skewered on a pin.

She smiled to herself. As far as she was concerned he could stay in Egypt till the war ended. Far better bored and sticking bugs than hazarding his life at the Front.

The others from Cowcaddens General with whom she'd come over had left her at Boulogne. From there they were proceeding to St Omer. Her own orders were to report to a Casualty Clearing Station, a CCS at Maricourt, which was apparently just to the rear of what, until the first of the month when the Somme offensive had started, had been the most forward British positions.

Tired of thinking and worrying and wondering, she finally closed her eyes and fell into a restless sleep.

It was in the early hours of the next morning that the train shuddered to yet another of the many halts that had taken place during the journey. This halt, however, was different. Word spread rapidly from carriage to carriage that all medical personnel were wanted outside on the platform.

After the heat and fug of the train the outside air was cold and sharp. Sheila stamped her feet, rubbed her hands briskly together, and wondered what this was all about. She soon found out.

A hospital train emerged from the dark to stop at the other side of the platform. Less than a minute later the first fleet of ambulances started drawing up outside the station, ambulances packed to overflowing with wounded.

The hospital train had been carrying its own special complement who'd begun unloading equipment the moment the train stopped. Many of these now broke away to make for the queuing ambulances.

Lights were strung overhead and fires lit to boil water. A stretcher was dumped in front of Sheila, and a doctor in attendance brusquely told her to do what she could for the patient. Somebody called out a name and the doctor hurried off.

Sheila bent to her patient instantly. He'd been shot in the side of the head and through the chest. A grip as strong as a vice grabbed her and pulled her down.

'Trones Wood. We all went in and only I came out again,' the man choked, blood running down the side of his chin.

She stared into the man's eyes, unable, somehow to turn away. The eyes flickered, then closed for the last time.

Gently, Sheila disengaged the hand still gripping hers.

Seven hours later the hospital train finally pulled out leaving the dead behind for burial and a platform stained bright with blood.

Welcome to France, she thought as she climbed back aboard her own train and returned to her seat. Welcome to bloody France.

It took Sheila three days to get to Maricourt. She finally managed the final stage of her journey by hitching a lift with an ammunition lorry going up to the Front.

The CCS consisted of a group of large tents clumped together, surrounded by an assortment of smaller ones.

The first thing Sheila did was seek out and report to Matron Fenwick whose name was on the orders, who said she was pleased to have Sheila with them. As Sheila was Scots she'd billet her in with the only other Scots VAD they had.

Fifteen minutes later the other Scots VAD finally showed up at the spot where Sheila had been told to wait. Sheila was astounded to see who it was. Just my luck, she thought with a sigh.

Georgina Murchison-Stewart stared at Sheila out of a

face haggard from strain and fatigue. She'd come to France just a little over eight months earlier.

Without uttering a word of greeting or even acknowledgement, Georgina instructed Sheila to follow her, taking her to the Quartermaster's Store where Sheila was issued with three army blankets and a large canvas bag in which, she was assured, she would find everything needed for comfort.

She was rather sceptical about that claim – *everything* she would need for comfort in one canvas bag – but later found this to be absolutely correct.

On opening this Pandora's box, she discovered a folding cot, a cork mattress, a washstand, a small table, a canvas pail in which to carry water, a lantern, an enamelled plate, a drinking cup, knife, fork and teaspoon. The claim hadn't been exaggerated after all.

On leaving the Quartermaster's Store, they went to a two-man tent, which, Georgina informed her, would be their temporary home.

Oh, Lord, thought Sheila, who'd been hoping against hope that it would be a larger tent, housing a number of women.

And then, like dawn rising out of a bleak night a smile came on to Georgina's face. 'I can't even begin to tell you how marvellous it is to have someone here from Glasgow, particularly someone I know!' she said, and fell upon Sheila to hug her tightly.

'Do you remember that tunny?' Georgina laughed, when at last she'd released Sheila.

Sheila nodded. 'How could I ever forget that blessed thing?' laughing as well. It was going to be all right between them; Georgina had changed since coming to France.

The days that followed were a nightmare as the Battle of the Somme continued and thousands of wounded passed through the Maricourt CCS.

Trones Wood, which she'd first heard of from the lips of a dying soldier in an unknown railway station, became engraved on her heart as a place of terrible human suffering and destruction. So also did Bernafax Wood, Caterpillar Wood, Bazentin-Le-Petit Wood and Contalmaison.

In yet another wood called Delville, the South Africans went in and were annihilated, fighting gallantly and gloriously to the bitter end. As the South Africans were making what would turn out to be their supreme sacrifice of the war, their British comrades of the 3rd, 7th, 9th and 21st Divisions, fighting on either flank, were also suffering horrendous losses.

Then the Anzac Corps came into that part of the Line, only to be mown down along the narrow front from Guillement to Bazentin-Le-Petit.

Sheila overheard an Australian Lieutenant describe, bitterly and with awe, where he and his men had fought as 'a place so terrible a raving lunatic could never imagine the horror of it'.

After the Anzacs came the tanks, few in number, but, when working, effective in the extreme, striking terror into the German infantry as they crawled along the tops of the German trenches enfilading them with continuous machine-gun fire, closely followed by small parties of Tommies throwing hand grenades on the survivors.

Sheila woke with a start, wondering what had wakened her. Then she heard a rustle in the darkness and knew Georgina was also awake.

'Would it disturb you if I put my lantern on?' she asked softly.

'Not at all,' Georgina answered immediately. 'The only reason I haven't put on mine is because I didn't want to wake you.'

Sheila's lantern filled the tent with a soft, yellow, glow. Sitting on the ground in front of her cot with a drinking cup in one hand and a half empty bottle of gin in the other, was Georgina. Swallowing the contents of her cup, she grimaced as though taking medicine. 'Want some?' she asked, holding up the bottle.

Sheila hesitated for a second. It was against station rules to drink, even off duty, but something in Georgina's expression caused her to pass her own cup across with a sleepy smile. 'What are we celebrating?' she asked, as Georgina poured her out a large measure.

'Nothing,' Georgina said, lifting her own cup in the air in a mock toast. 'This is called medicine to help you get to sleep.' With that, she tossed back her drink and immediately poured herself another.

'Do you often have trouble sleeping?' Sheila asked, trying to sound as causal as possible as she watched the other woman take another greedy swallow of gin.

'Oh, no,' Georgina laughed without any humour. 'Not often. Sometimes I'm so exhausted I could sleep standing up.' She stared down into the clear liquid in her cup. 'Sometimes. But other times I close my eyes and all I see is an endless line of dead and dying soldiers.' She lifted her eyes to Sheila's, almost defiantly. 'Just like the line I see when my eyes are open.'

It took no imagination for Sheila to see it too. Scots lads, English boys, Welsh and Irish, Canadians and Indians, South Africans, Frenchmen and even Germans, all marching by, waving, cheering, grinning like kids on an outing, and disappearing down a long road at the end of which they would be blown away like so many leaves in a high wind.

Outside, it began to rain, the drops hitting against the canvas making a disconsolate sound which seemed to echo the mood within the tent.

'How long have you been seeing this procession?' Sheila asked quietly, her eyes not moving from the other woman's pale, strained face.

'Since the middle of my fifth month,' Georgina answered, her voice flat. 'It was right after this boy I used to

183

know, this boy from Kelvinside, died in my arms of gas
gangrene.' A tremor ran through her that was noticeable
even in the poor light. 'He'd always been such a lovely
lad. When we were young, I'd been pretty sweet on him,
I suppose. You know, the way kids are.' Tears filled her
voice and her eyes. 'He was one of the funniest people
I've ever known. He made everybody laugh.' Silent sobs
shook her body.

At that moment, an 'Archie', as the German flak was
called, cracked directly above the tent. Both women
jumped. A few seconds later, another cracked not far
away in the direction of Mametz.

Georgina, a wry smile on her lips, poured them both
more gin. 'I buy this from one of the ambulance drivers.
You can bet he does a brisk trade.' Against the background of the rain, Georgina's voice sounded like a cry
for help. 'Lots of people have trouble sleeping.'

Thinking of what had to be faced daily at Maricourt,
Sheila wondered how long it would be before she, too,
was doing business with the ambulance driver.

Sheila stared up at the place in the sky where a hapless,
dark FE was desperately twisting and turning, trying to
evade a German Albatross D1 which was hot on its tail.

Because of Andrew, she had taken an interest in the air
war, and had learned to identify most of the machines by
sight.

Of late the tide had turned against the RFC and RNAS,
both of which were taking an exceptionally hard
hammering.

Thanks to the technical advance of aeroplanes and
related equipment the air war had changed dramatically
since Andrew had been at the Front. It was a long time
now since pilots had been limited to taking pot shots at
one another with pistols and rifles. Now the war in the
sky was just as deadly as on the ground, perhaps even
more so.

Of the German aces Oswald Boelcke was the most feared, replacing the now dead Max Immelman, killed in June, as the German Number One: while on the British side the violin-playing Albert Ball was without question the highest rated.

Sheila had no way of knowing it, but the pilot of the Albatross she was watching, just returned from the Russian Front where he'd been flying bombers, was a young Prussian aristocrat who would shortly become the greatest ace of them all, Baron Manfred Von Richthofen.

As she continued to watch, the FE began wheeling all over. Obviously the plane was being flown by an experienced pilot who knew he mustn't let the Albatross get in the blind spot behind him.

Then more planes appeared, and suddenly the sky was full of them.

The original FE flattened out, having apparently lost sight of the Albatross for the moment. The much faster Albatross surged up beneath the FE so close that Sheila held her breath for a collision seemed imminent, and at that point-blank range Richthofen fired.

The FE's propeller slowed, jerked, then stopped; and the British machine went down, swinging and jerking with the observer's head no longer visible in the front cockpit.

The FE turned over and next moment two bodies fell from it, one still as it plummeted to the ground below, the other futilely grabbing at empty air as though in the hope the air might somehow suddenly turn into something solid on to which he could grasp.

Sickened Sheila averted her head as the living airman smashed into the earth a little beyond the station. Then she ran towards him, knowing the impact must have been fatal, but going to him anyway. Just in case.

High overhead, the Red Baron saluted his fallen foes.

*　　*　　*

It was a Friday afternoon and the Battle of the Somme was now into its third month. The weather had been atrocious all day, which had stopped planes going aloft. It didn't, however, stop the infantry, who were now not only fighting the Germans but also the infamous Somme mud, many of them not certain which they hated most.

Sheila had become so used to fatigue that she couldn't remember what it was like not to be dropping from exhaustion. That afternoon marked thirty-six hours since she'd last been to bed.

She hardly noticed when it began to rain again, rain that beat against her face and made her already wet clothes even wetter.

She plunged a hypodermic into the arm of a Tommy who, as part of Gough's Army, had helped take Thiepvel, and smiling told the man he was one of the lucky ones; it was Blighty for him.

The soldier, with three fingers and a foot missing, agreed that yes, he was lucky; then the injection started to take effect and he began to drift off to sleep.

Sheila gazed about her, wondering which section to go to next.

'Hello, Sheila,' said a sudden voice behind her.

She turned and blinked. 'Yes?' She had a vague sense that she knew this airman who was staring at her so intently, but so great was her tiredness that she couldn't understand why he seemed so familiar.

He could see how worn out she was by the dark rings under her eyes and the gauntness of her cheeks. 'Oh, my darling!' Andrew cried and swept her into his arms for a kiss.

'Andrew!' she gasped when the kiss was finally over. She held him at arm's length and gazed at him in total wonder. How grand he looked. The tan and moustache suited him, no wonder she hadn't recognized him right off. 'Oh, Andrew! Is it really you?'

He lifted her off the ground in an ecstatic hug. 'Of course it's me, you silly,' he laughed. 'Of course it's me.'

When at last he released her, he asked, hopefully. 'I've got three days; can you get away?'

But Sheila shook her head. That was impossible, with the battle still in progress. 'But how did you get here?' she wanted to know, suddenly afraid that his presence must mean that he'd been posted to the Front.

'No fear, my love,' he said, unable to stop touching her. 'I've been posted to England.' He shook his head, 'Surely there's some place we can talk that's out of the rain?'

'There's the mess.'

Georgina, who'd come over to see what was going on and had been listening to the conversation suddenly intervened. 'Bugger the Mess,' she shouted. 'There's the tent with a bottle of gin in it. You two go there, I'll cover for Sheila for a couple of hours.'

'Are you mad, Georgina?' asked Sheila her hand held tightly in Andrew's. 'I can't take that amount of time off. Besides, we'll be for it if we're caught with a man in our tent.'

'There are occasions,' said Georgina in her old voice, 'when rules should be broken. And this is most certainly one of them.'

'It would appear to be our only chance of being alone together,' Andrew said quietly but with insistence.

'Well . . .' Sheila looked from one to the other. 'Well, what the hell.'

Once inside the tent, she rooted out Georgina's gin, pouring Andrew a fair-sized measure and herself a smaller one.

He took a sip of his drink, but almost immediately laid it aside. 'Come here to me,' he commanded softly. 'Come here.'

She had thought about this moment for so long – through all these nights and days of hell. To touch him again; to lie in his arms. She'd planned to look beautiful for him. Instead she looked like something the cat hadn't even bothered to drag in, but had turned up its nose at disdainfully.

187

'I don't give a damn how dirty you are, or how louse ridden,' he whispered, removing her clothes. 'You're my Sheila, the woman I love. That's all that matters.'

Later, when it was over, they began to catch up on one another.

'I've been trying to get posted back to France for ages,' he said, ignoring the flicker of fear in her eyes. 'But I got nowhere. Then six weeks ago, new orders came through for me out of the blue.'

She was suddenly cold all over, her happiness already dissolving in reality. Sheila shivered. 'Not to the Front?' she whispered.

He turned to give her a level, serious gaze, but couldn't hold it, for he could see how desperately anxious she was. A smile twitched at his lips.

'Not to the Front, worse luck. I've been posted as an instructor at London Colney.'

Relief rushed through her. 'How long do you expect to be there?' she asked as calmly as she could.

He shrugged. 'Your guess is as good as mine. What I can say is I would be very surprised if it was for less than six months. I've never heard of anyone being posted as an instructor for less than that.'

Six months – possibly longer. With a bit of luck, he might even ride out the rest of the war in that posting. She thought of Kaiser Bill, and raged inwardly at him for starting this terrible business. If he was made to roast in Hell for all eternity for what he'd done, it wouldn't be punishment enough.

She glanced sideways at Andrew, and prayed for the umpteenth time since he'd gone into uniform that he'd come out of the war in one piece. Please, God, she said silently. Please.

And when it was all over, as some day it must be, it would be back on the boards for him, and with her to help him he'd carve out a name for himself, a name that would blaze out in lights on Shaftesbury Avenue.

Her rage gave way to a warm tingling of pleasure, for

in her mind she could see those lights, and Andrew the world-famous actor.

There was only one thing more to make her dream complete; his child, his children.

She ran a hand down his arm, on to his chest, then across the tightness of his belly to hold him again. Six months more of safety. It was more than most people got – but not nearly as much as she wanted.

'Oh, Sheila,' he sighed. 'I do love you.'

After Andrew had gone, promising to come back next day, she returned to her duties. About twenty minutes later a nurse stopped by where Sheila was changing a soldier's bandages to inform her that Matron wanted her right away.

Matron Fenwick glanced up at Sheila's approach, her mouth forming into a thin, disapproving line. She was terribly disappointed, she said, having hitherto thought very highly of Sheila who, it now seemed, had let her down. In curt tones she informed Sheila that a man had been seen leaving her tent. 'What do you have to say for yourself?'

Jesus, Sheila thought, and they'd been so careful, too. It just went to show you, there were unseen eyes everywhere in a place like this. Wearily she nodded, and said it was true, but it wasn't the way it looked.

'How was it then?' Matron Fenwick snapped.

'The man wasn't just any man. He was my husband, Lieutenant Andrew Lack of the RFC. He's just come over from England to try and spend a few days of his leave with me. Of course, I had to tell him that was impossible.'

The hard lines of Matron Fenwick's face immediately softened. 'And how long has it been since you last saw him?'

'Over a year. He's been in Egypt.'

Matron Fenwick picked up a pencil and fiddled with it. The matter had been officially reported, so an official reason, in other words an acceptable excuse, would have to be recorded. 'You wished to discuss certain important domestic matters in private, and there was no private space available?' Matron Fenwick suggested.

Stunned it took Sheila a few seconds before nodding her head in agreement. It was certainly as near the truth as dammit. Bless you, Matron, she thought. You're a real smasher!

'How long's his leave?' Matron asked quietly.

'He can stay round here for three days, then he's got to return to England. He's to be a flying instructor at London Colney.'

Suddenly overwhelmed by everything, Sheila swayed grabbing hold of Matron's table to stop from tumbling over. Hastily she apologized.

'When did you last sleep?' demanded Matron.

'Over forty hours ago now,' Sheila replied, giving a small grin.

Matron Fenwick went back to fiddling with her pencil. She was completely whacked herself, having been on the go just as long as Sheila, but she hadn't had the shock of suddenly being reunited with her husband. Nor would she ever be reunited with Charlie; he'd died of gas poisoning at Ypres.

In a gruff voice Matron Fenwick told Sheila to go and get her head down. In her present state she'd probably kill off more Tommies than she'd help. 'And has your husband arranged to see you again?'

'Yes, Ma'am. He's returning to Maricourt tomorrow. But I'll send him packing straight away.'

'You'll do no such thing!' Matron Fenwick rapped out in reply. There might be a war on, but that didn't mean it had to be all pain and suffering; there was room for a little joy and happiness as well. 'Where is he staying?'

'With No. 11 Squadron. Andrew has friends in the squadron.'

Matron Fenwick's features lit up with interest. No. 11 Squadron was Albert Ball's wasn't it?

Albert Ball was a great hero, held in highest esteem by the British Forces and public alike. During this Battle of the Somme his reputation had become one of almost Godlike proportions.

'I want you to take twenty-four hours' leave, starting from the moment your husband gets here tomorrow,' said Matron Fenwick.

Sheila was astonished. 'But I can't possibly!' she protested, though only half-heartedly. 'Not while the battle is still in progress.'

Matron Fenwick told Sheila to let her worry about such things. Besides there were five new VADs due in later that day, so Sheila's absence wouldn't be that noticeable. 'I only wish I could send everyone off for twenty-four hours. Heaven knows they need and deserve it. But, of course, that's quite out of the question,' Matron Fenwick sighed.

Returning to her tent Sheila discovered that Andrew's personal smell had remained behind him. Closing her eyes she savoured it, then with a smile began to undress.

When Georgina found her later she was still smiling, only half undressed, and curled in her cot sound asleep.

He'd said he'd come at the same time as yesterday, and almost exactly to the minute, he arrived. Sheila was ready and waiting for him when he showed up in a staff car driven by a Sergeant Roper, a blunt Yorkshireman from the Dales.

Andrew let out a whoop on hearing that Sheila had twenty-four hours' leave, immediately bundling her into the back of the car and instructing Roper to get them out of there before the good Matron Fenwick had a change of heart.

As the car roared off, he kissed her. She wriggled out from under him, 'We'll be seen,' she laughed.

'I don't give a fig who sees us,' holding her tightly. 'Right now I'd snap my fingers at old "Boom"

Trenchard himself.' Trenchard was the head of the RFC in France.

Just beyond Maricourt, they came upon an infantry battalion waiting to go into the line. The men were sitting quietly, many with cigarettes dangling from their lips, all with packs hanging heavily from their shoulders. None were talking; every one of them resigned to his fate.

As the staff car passed the battalion their colonel glanced at his watch, and they all rose to their feet and adjusted their equipment. Then they went marching down the road to meet whatever lay in store for them.

A grim-faced Sheila watched them go, wondering how many would end up in Maricourt before the day was over, and how many would die out there in the terrible grey mud.

Andrew tried to break the sudden gloom that had sprung up between them by saying cheerfully that with only twenty-four hours at their disposal he didn't think it worth their while trying to get out of the battle zone, and he was certain there wouldn't be an inn or hotel in the area that hadn't long since been taken over by the various Services and Armies; which left Château Roisselle, 11 Squadron's current, and temporary HQ. How would she feel about them spending her leave there?

'I'd be happy to spend the entire twenty-four hours in a trench, as long as you're with me,' she smiled.

The Château Roisselle had seen better days. Two of its four spires had been blown off, and there was a boarded-up hole in a side wall where it had taken a direct hit from a British gun when in German hands.

There were several large, fairly level fields on the right of the château which were used as an airfield. Repair and overhaul facilities had been set up, and mechanics could be seen busily working on aircraft as they drew up. The squadron itself was in the air, away on a mission.

Andrew took Sheila into the château where arrangements were quickly made. Sergeant Dummit, a fierce-

192

looking fellow with the black patch of a pirate over one eye, said a bath would immediately be drawn for Mrs Lack, and in the meanwhile refreshments would be sent up to Andrew's room. It seemed that there were no inflexible rules any more in this terrible war. Life would only concede so much to death.

The château had at one time been opulently furnished, but that had been before the war. The rich colours that had been everywhere were now faded, the rugs and carpets in ruin. There were pinpricks of light in the roof where it had only recently been strafed by a German aeroplane.

On entering their bedroom, Andrew closed the door behind him, then pulled Sheila into his arms. They were still kissing five minutes later when there was a discreet knock which turned out to be Dummit with an ice-cold bottle of champagne and the news that Sheila's bath was ready.

Once Dummit had left them, Andrew opened the bottle with a bang, and poured champagne straight from the bottle into Sheila's mouth, then into his own. He swallowed some, put his hand behind her head, brought her lips to his and kissed her again then forced what remained of the champagne in his mouth into her's.

Sheila shrieked and jerked away, champagne running down her chin. 'What sort of trick was that?' she laughed.

'A most deliciously insanitary one,' he replied.

The last thing she did before leaving the bedroom to meet the returned squadron was to put a dab of precious perfume (the only bottle she possessed had only a few drops left in it) behind both ears, and wished again that she had a civilian dress to wear instead of her VAD uniform.

The chatter of conversation ceased the moment she appeared. 'Oh, I say. Isn't she an absolute corker!' a voice exclaimed, followed by another angrily telling the first to mind his manners.

Sheila smiled as she descended the stairway. Andrew, eyes shining with pride, hurried forward to greet her with a soft hello.

Andrew started his introductions with James McCudden, a handsome man with an aquiline nose. 'My oldest friend in the RFC!' Andrew declared as McCudden shook her hand and welcomed her to the 11th.

Round the gathering they proceeded, Sheila's hand pumped again and again, and even kissed by a chap called Rodders who proclaimed loudly that the Frenchies weren't the only ones who could be gallant.

'And this is Albert Ball,' Andrew said.

Albert Ball was young, slim, and clearly of a highly strung, nervous disposition. His eyes had a brooding, intense quality and were strangely unblinking, which she found unsettling, yet attractive at the same time. There had been a Siamese cat in Dragonholme once. Albert Ball reminded her of that cat.

Ball shyly shook hands with Sheila, muttering that Andrew was indeed a lucky fellow, and he would be honoured if the pair of them sat next to him at dinner.

'The honour would be ours,' she replied.

More champagne appeared, and Rodders confided to Sheila that the cellar was full of the stuff. 'The Hun made such a quick exit that the champagne got left behind,' he laughed. 'For which 11 Squadron is extremely grateful.'

They had no sooner sat down to dinner, Sheila on one side of Ball, Andrew on the other, than a glass was rapped with a fork and Lieutenant Walters asked them to drink a toast to their new comrade, Lieutenant Arthur Pyle, who'd joined the squadron two days previously and made his first kill that afternoon by shooting down a Roland.

'Lieutenant Pyle!' rang round the room.

'Speech! Speech!' someone cried out, followed by the table being thumped repeatedly by a battery of fists.

Blushing furiously Pyle came to his feet. He cleared his throat, drank some . champagne, then cleared

194

his throat again. 'This is even worse than facing the Hun,' he admitted, which earned him clapping, cheers and a piercing whistle from Rodders.

'Tell us the story of what happened,' Lieutenant Lewis prompted. It was a tradition in the squadron for pilots to recount their first hit.

He'd got the Roland more by luck than skill, Pyle told them in an embarrassed voice. He and Sam Moxby had been flying at seven thousand feet above Baupaume when they spotted a Roland and LVG, but not the balloons which they'd been expecting.

He and Moxby had attacked simultaneously with their Le Prieur rockets, he the Roland, Moxby the LVG. Streaming flames the LVG fell away, but although his rockets streaked round the Roland they didn't hit it.

The Roland then dived, he went after it firing his Lewis, and the Roland, silly sod of a pilot, instead of pulling away from the bullets, turned straight into them. Raked from front to tail the Roland went into a spin from which it never recovered.

'And that was how it was,' Pyle said in conclusion.

Albert Ball led the applause which consisted of thumping the table with both hands and singing, 'For He's A Jolly Good Fellow'.

Pyle, relieved that was over, sat down and beamed around him. Someone then presented him with a large tankard of champagne that he was obliged to see off in one go.

When Pyle had accomplished this the applause became even more thunderous. Lieutenant Morgan-Jones jumped up on to the table, where he thumped his feet instead of his hands.

Just as well it's an extremely strong table, thought Sheila, as knives, forks, glassware and dishes went flying.

The meal itself turned out to be superb, by far the best she'd had since coming to France. The pudding was a lemon sorbet that literally melted in the mouth.

Unfortunately not many of the pilots ate theirs, pelting one another with it instead.

The champagne continued to flow in a never-ending river. Bottles of whisky, brandy and port were brought in as alternatives. Sheila noticed that Albert Ball was one of the few who drank sparingly.

During an ebb in the hilarity, Rodders asked Andrew what machine Andrew would be teaching the new boys to fly on at London Colney. 'The BEs,' he replied.

Hearing him, Ball looked up suddenly and, in an angry voice, declared that the BE was a bloody awful plane. 'It's too stable by half,' he continued. 'Flying one in France is tantamount to suicide, if you ask me.'

Silence fell around the table. Every eye was trained on Ball. 'The BE can't climb to the height required in the time required to outmanoeuvre the German machines,' he went on. 'They're no match at all for the German planes, if you want the simple truth.'

Suicide! 'Do you mean they're unsafe?' asked Sheila, thoroughly alarmed.

Ball chuckled dryly. 'Quite the contrary,' he said. 'They're safe as houses. They're ideal for training, but they're lethal in action.' Ball's expression became sour and morose. 'No 11 Squadron's fortunate because we're equipped with French Nieuports,' he explained to Sheila. 'But many of the other British squadrons are still flying the BE and FEs and even antiquated Farmans against Fokkers and Albatrosses that can dance rings round them.'

As for the newer planes the Royal Aicraft Factory were coming up with most of them were worse than useless.

The trouble was that the scientists and engineers at the Factory refused to accept the facts. According to them, and their slide rule calculations, the new British machines were unbeatable, a theory the Germans disproved daily by shooting them wholesale out of the sky.

Ball's eyes flashed with fury. If the situation was bad before, it was even worse now that the Germans had taken to flying in formations they called Jagdstaffels, or

196

hunting squadrons, equipped with fast intercept fighters flown by pilots of picked and proven quality.

'Jagdstaffels,' Sheila repeated. The very word tasted of terror and death.

'Staffels for short,' Lieutenant Walters said quietly.

Ball opened his fist, then closed it again. The RFC had to have a plane of comparable standard to the German fighters, he said, swinging round on Andrew, and they had to have it in *quantity*. If they didn't, and he shrugged, then there wouldn't be an RFC left before long. And without the Flying Corps, Haig and the Army might just as well pack their kitbags and go home, for the war would be lost.

Ball fixed Andrew with his gaze and said that as an instructor at London Colney Andrew would undoubtedly have occasion to speak with the scientists and engineers working at the Factory. Somehow Andrew must impress on them the dire necessity for a new fighter that performed *in the air* as well as it did on their damn silly pieces of paper. Such a new fighter must come soon, or it would be too late.

Sheila stared in awe at Albert Ball. The power and the passion coming from him at that moment was so strong it was almost tangible. Ball, she realized, wasn't merely a derring-do fighter, but a man of intellect and imagination as well.

Albert Ball uncurled his fist like a flower greeting the morning Sheila thought, and held it out to Andrew. 'Will you do your best on behalf of all pilots and observers in the Corps to talk some sense into those thick heads over there?' he asked quietly.

Andrew accepted the hand, shaking it with strength and resolution. 'I'll make it a personal crusade, you have my word on that,' he replied.

Ball nodded, then suddenly smiled. The spell was broken.

Shortly after that, Albert Ball excused himself, saying he was off to bed.

Sheila watched Andrew watch Ball go, Andrew's expression one of candid admiration.

All these bonny men are heroes, Sheila thought. Every last one of them.

Sheila woke to the sound of throbbing engines. Beside her, Andrew stirred, then also awoke.

Her mouth was dry and she felt washed out. Too much of that champagne last night, she told herself, thinking that it might have been too much, but it had been lovely.

She listened to a plane take off, followed by a second and a third.

'The dawn patrol, they go out every morning at this time to try and catch the German bombers,' Andrew said, giving her a kiss.

After the squadron had gone they lay in each other's arms in silence; he wishing he was flying with No 11, she thankful he wasn't.

Outside the window the many lamps and torches that had been used to illuminate the take-off area were now extinguished, and gradually the room darkened.

Suddenly, Sheila felt frightened. She snuggled up closer to Andrew, putting both arms around him and holding him tightly.

Somewhere a bird started to sing. She remembered a wounded Tommy at Maricourt telling her that he'd heard one singing in the middle of No Man's Land, only seconds after the guns stopped.

Soon she would have to return to the horrors of Maricourt, to the stream of wounded that arrived daily from the Front, to blood and pain and that awful despair.

But not yet, not quite yet. For the moment she had the song of a bird, and she had Andrew. She couldn't have asked for anything more.

'Make love to me darling,' she whispered.

Slowly and tenderly he obeyed her, as though trying to make it last forever.

Later, when the squadron returned, they went down to breakfast. Sheila was halfway through her egg when she remembered there was something she wanted to ask Rodders.

She looked around for him, but he wasn't at the table. There was another empty chair which she realized should have seated Lieutenant Pyle.

She turned to McCudden whose grim expression told her what she wanted to know. Rodders and Pyle hadn't come back from the dawn patrol.

It was the afternoon of 6 April 1917, and the newspaper Sheila was reading cried the news that America had, at long last, declared war on Germany.

Like the rest of the country, Sheila was filled with elation – and profound relief. This *had* to be the beginning of the end for the Germans.

Laying the paper aside, she ran a hand across her brow. It had been a long, wearying journey from Maricourt.

Her leave was for a month, but she wouldn't be returning to Maricourt at the end of it. When she'd left Maricourt was in the process of being dismantled and moved to a more forward position.

What had been the Maricourt CCS was to be set up again at Rancourt where fresh personnel would be taking over. All the Maricourt personnel had been given long overdue leave, and would be going to new postings on their return to France.

Sheila had said good-bye to Georgina several hours before at Euston station. Georgina was taking the train from there to Glasgow, while Sheila'd travelled across town to catch a train for London Colney just south of St Albans.

She'd considered telegramming Andrew from London that she was coming, but had decided against it. The distance was so short, she'd probably arrive before the telegram.

Nor had she written to him from France to tell him she was coming. They'd only been notified three days before their departure so there'd been no time for anything but packing up. It was going to be quite a surprise for Andrew when she turned up out of the blue. She could hardly wait to see his face, or have him in her arms again.

How marvellous it is to be home again, she thought as the train puffed on. Even if home for the moment was England rather than Scotland. If Andrew could get some leave of his own, perhaps they could go up to Glasgow. She'd missed the grey city far more than she'd ever imagined she would.

They would stay in their rooms in Crown Crescent, which had been kept on all this while, and she would see darling Pat again. She'd had a number of letters from Pat in France. She was still working at the Queen's Theatre, where the programme was now, according to Pat, a constant diet of patriotic plays and shows.

Thinking of the theatre filled her with warmth – that daft world whose inmates took it all so seriously, where magic really did exist, and where happiness of unbelievable intensity could be caused by a full house and good review.

Strangely, she hadn't missed Dragonholme at all. It was as if that part of her life had receded so far back in time that she'd only dreamt it.

She dozed for a little while, dreaming that she was back working with Pat, and that Andrew was again playing the pirate chief in Sinbad the Sailor. She smiled in her sleep to see Andrew being whacked on the bottom by Sinbad, and he, clutching himself, leaping up and down shouting 'ooh! ooh! ooh!'

Finally arriving at London Colney, she got a taxi to take her to an inn close to the aerodrome.

As soon as she'd registered, she explained the situation to the landlord's wife, who gave her permission to ring the aerodrome on the pub telephone. On getting through she asked for Andrew, but was told that he wasn't avail-

200

able. She left a message telling him of her arrival, and where she was to be found.

There was still no sign of Andrew when dinner time came around, so she asked for a tray in her room.

She was in the middle of her meal when the door suddenly burst open, and there was Andrew, dishevelled and out of breath. 'I only got your message ten minutes ago,' he gasped. Then they were hugging and kissing as though neither had believed they would even meet again.

'How on earth did you get here?' he demanded at last.

Quickly she told him about the CCS at Maricourt being closed down, and moved to Rancourt, and how she, and everyone else there, had got leave as a result.

'Just think, we've got an entire month together now. Isn't that wonderful!' she exclaimed, nearly breathless herself with excitement. But then she noticed a worried look in his eyes. 'What's wrong?' she asked quickly.

'Nothing,' he assured her, the look gone. 'You just look very thin.'

'Oh,' she said lightly. 'I had a bout of dysentery a little while ago. But I'm all right now.' She couldn't look at him without smiling. 'I've never felt better in my life.'

'You should have written and told me you were ill,' he admonished.

She laid a palm against his cheek. 'You're so gorgeous,' she said softly, staring at him as though she would never see enough.

'Oh, no,' he whispered, beginning to undo her blouse. 'You're the one who's gorgeous.' The blouse slipped to the floor. 'Even thin as a rail, you're the most beautiful woman I've ever known.'

'You'll never leave me, will you Andrew?' she breathed, wanting to hold him so close that they could never be parted.

'Nothing could make me leave you,' his lips on her face, her neck, her breasts. 'Nothing in the world.'

And so lost was she in the passion of their lovemaking

201

that she forgot about the fear which shadowed her every moment, forgot about the world in which they lived, where happiness was a moment with no past and no future.

'Nothing at all,' he repeated.

And so joyous was she at his touch, that she believed that what he said was true.

But even as he entered her, a voice in the back of Andrew's mind was saying, tomorrow, tell her tomorrow.

The next morning, he insisted on taking her first thing to the aerodrome.

'But why?' she asked, laughing as he pulled her from the bed. 'At least give me time to get dressed.'

'I told you, woman,' he said, scooping her into his arms. 'I've got something I want to show you. Now, either you get dressed right now, or I'll carry you there just as you are.'

There were several aircraft dotted about, but Andrew led Sheila to a model she had never seen before. 'Well, what do you think?' he asked, running a hand lovingly over the plane's fuselage.

'I can tell she's a fighter and a beauty,' agreed Sheila. 'Is it new?'

Did she recall the mission Albert Ball had charged him with at Chateau Roisselle?

'Oh,' said Sheila. 'Now I understand.' She should have realized from the excitement in his eyes.

'Well, this is the machine Ball says we need. It's called the SE5. Isn't she something?'

'You've flown it then?'

His smile grew even broader. 'I've done a lot more than that,' he grinned. 'I'm her test pilot. Many of the modifications we've made on her have been the result of my flights.'

Test pilot! Angrily, she turned on him, close to tears.

'You never told me you were doing anything so dangerous!'

'For God's sake, Sheila. There's nothing in this war that isn't dangerous.'

'No,' she sighed at last. 'I suppose there isn't.'

'There's something else,' he said slowly.

'Something else?'

And then he told her that a new squadron, No. 56, was being formed at London Colney. 'It'll be the first to fly the SE5s in combat,' he announced, unable to contain his excitement. As though in a trance, she listened while he talked about the new squadron's mission in France, where it would be commanded by Ball, and would, as Andrew put it, give Baron Von Richthofen hell.

'When does the squadron leave?' Sheila asked, when finally he was through.

'We leave tomorrow at dawn,' Andrew answered quietly.

For several moments she just looked at him, unable to accept what he was saying – what she had known for a long time he was going to say. 'What do you mean, *we*?'

'James McCudden's taking over from me as instructor,' he said flatly. 'I've requested to join the 56th and I've been accepted.'

If she had found him with another woman she couldn't have felt more betrayed. 'You requested to go?'

'We're to be based at Vert Galland.'

Vert Galland? There were two CCSs near there. She would somehow have to manipulate it so that she was posted to one of them. If she and Andrew were both going to be in France then she was going to do everything in her power to ensure they were close to each other. Tears sprang to her eyes, sobs shaking her body. To hell with her month's leave, she thought. She didn't want that now. All she wanted was to get back over there, as soon as possible.

'Things could have been worse, you know,' he said,

taking her into his arms. 'We could have passed one another en route.'

Crying even harder, she clung to him as though nothing would ever pull her from him.

'You have to understand, love,' he said gently. 'I can't train these young lads, then send them over to fight a battle I'm protected from. I couldn't live like that.'

She didn't sleep a wink all night, although, for his sake, she pretended to.

They'd agreed not to say good-bye. 'Well,' she'd said, as jauntily as possible, 'it's hardly worth the breath. I'll be seeing you at Vert Galland before you're even settled in.'

She lay still, her eyes closed while he rose from their bed to dress. Barely breathing, she listened to him grope about in the dark.

When he was dressed he came around to her side of the bed where he stood staring down at her for several minutes. Reaching down he lightly touched her hair, then tip-toed from the room.

After he'd gone she sat up, leaning against the headboard, and wept. Once she was composed again she got dressed and went downstairs. Letting herself out into the pub's rear courtyard, she stood shivering in the morning chill, her gaze focused on the distance.

Dawn was breaking when the first flight of 56 Squadron took off, five brown birds winging their way heavenward, the front bird flown by Andrew.

'Good luck my darling, see you soon,' she whispered, blowing a kiss in the direction of the vanishing plane. From the aerodrome, a second flight took to the air.

She waited till the last plane of the third, and final, flight had vanished from view, then hurried back indoors to pack her things.

Her key to returning prematurely to France lay in Glasgow with the St Andrew's Ambulance Association and/or the Cowcaddens General Hospital.

The sooner she was in Glasgow the sooner she'd have the new orders and the posting she had to have.

Sheila stumbled through to the toilet, her hand clasped over her mouth. This was the third morning in a row that she'd been nauseous. She put it down to the upset stomach that had been bothering her off and on for the past week.

It was a few days over a fortnight now since she'd arrived back in Glasgow. Despite all her efforts, she still hadn't succeeded in cutting short her leave. The powers that be had decreed she was to have a month off, and the powers that be seemed determined that a month off was what she was going to have, whether she wanted it or not.

Pat McLuskey arrived just after midday with a bottle of milk and six fresh eggs, intending to make an omelette for their lunch.

When she suggested this, and that perhaps they could put some onions in the omelette if Sheila had some, Sheila went a pale shade of green and sank into a chair.

'What in the name of the Wee Man's the matter with you?' asked Pat, her face serious with concern.

Sheila ran a hand across her face. 'I'm feeling hot and cold at the same time,' she explained. 'And I ache all over. I've been sick three times this morning, as well.' She smiled wanly. 'It's been like this for days and days. Do you think I'm coming down with the flu.'

'And it's only in the morning you're being sick?' asked Pat.

When Pat had established that Sheila had also been off her food it seemed to Pat she might have the answer. It certainly wasn't flu. 'You could be pregnant, you know,' suggested Pat.

Pregnant! Sheila made a rapid calculation, then shook

her head. 'Sixteen days is far too soon for me to be showing any signs,' she said firmly.

'That's just where you're wrong,' countered Pat. 'The body is quite capable of showing signs this early on.'

Could she be pregnant? Sheila wondered.

'You'll be delaying your departure now,' Pat said.

But Sheila looked shocked. 'I'll be doing no such thing!'

'But if you are pregnant, you owe it to yourself and the baby not to go back to France,' argued Pat.

'What if I'm not, though? What if it's only a bug I've picked up?'

Pat knew only too well how headstrong and stubborn Sheila could be, whether wrong or right. She would have argued further if she'd thought it would have done any good, but knew it wouldn't. On the contrary, it would only make Sheila more determined.

It was 8 May, the day Sheila had anxiously been awaiting, for it was the day she was to start back to France – and Andrew.

Commandant McNair, of the St Andrew's Ambulance Association, had finally arranged for her to be posted to Larache, the closest of the two CCSs near to Vert Galland.

Pat had come around to see Sheila and Georgina off. Georgina, at this moment fetching a taxi, would be travelling to France with Sheila, though her destination was a general hospital in Hazebrouck.

'Look out the window to see if there is any sign of Georgina,' Sheila said impatiently.

Pat leaned out into the street. 'There's a taxi turning into the far side of the Crescent,' she called back.

'That'll be her,' Sheila shouted excitedly, and hurried through to the bedroom to put on her cloak.

In the bedroom, she paused to glance around her. Three or four months and I'll be back here, she thought.

206

She was now certain that she was carrying a child: his child, their child – hers and Andrew's.

She had decided to keep her secret for as long as she was able so she could spend as much time near Andrew as possible.

Her reverie was interrupted by voices in the reception room. Georgina was here, the taxi was waiting, it was time to go. As excited as a child herself, she gathered up her things and charged into the other room. But the moment she saw Georgina's face she knew something was wrong. 'What is it?' she whispered, her eyes darting from one friend to the other.

In reply, Georgina handed her the copy of the Glasgow Herald she was holding, but Sheila wouldn't touch it, recoiling from the newspaper as though it were alive.

Georgina knew then she was going to have to break the news verbally, to have to actually speak the awful words. 'Albert Ball and five other members of his squadron were shot down and killed yesterday,' she recited as though the paper's words had been burned into her brain. 'I'm afraid . . . I'm afraid that Andrew was one of them.'

A voice, which Sheila recognized as her own, spoke from what seemed a long way off. 'They're quite certain Andrew's dead? There couldn't be some sort of mistake, a mix-up perhaps?' asked the voice.

'There's no mistake,' Georgina said softly.

In her mind's eye, Sheila saw again the FE she'd watched shot down over Maricourt, and the still alive pilot falling . . . falling . . . falling. . . .

Pat sprung forward to catch her just before she hit the floor.

PART THREE

The Steering Star
1923–24

'I must go down to the seas again, to the lonely sea and
the sky,
And all I ask is a tall ship and a star to steer her by. . .'

From *Sea-Fever*, by John Masefield

7

Sheila laid down the Fair Isle she was knitting for wee David with a sigh. How boring life had become since her son started school when he turned five in January, she thought. Before that she was always busy just taking care of him, even though the money she had come into on Andrew's death had made it unnecessary for her to ever work again. Ever work or ever worry. Though she had known the Lacks were well-off, she hadn't quite realized just how well-off. She now had money beyond her wildest dreams. Money enough to send her son to the finest school in Glasgow, money enough to have anything she desired, money enough to never have to worry again about anything in the future.

Directly after Andrew's death – while the war dragged on and the estate had yet to be settled – she moved back to Crown Crescent with Pat. Without Pat's support and companionship, she doubted that she would have made it through those awful months, her heart and spirit broken, Andrew's child growing within her despite her terrible grief. If there had been no Pat to buck her up and keep her going, no Pat to help her to the hospital that bitter winter's morning, the snow feet deep on the road and a razor-sharp wind blowing off the Clyde on the day that David was born, Sheila doubted that she would be here at all, snug in her posh house in Kelvinside with her best friend and darling son.

Sheila's reverie was interrupted by Pat's return from shopping. Pat no longer worked in the theatre, but as Sheila's companion and housekeeper, an arrangement with which they were both extremely happy. Sheila enjoyed having a friend around the house to chat to, and Pat, who lost her job when the Queen's Theatre closed late in 1919, was relieved to have a secure position as well as a long-term friend.

Pat could have found a position elsewhere as a wardrobe mistress, but she preferred working for Sheila, or, to be more precise, she preferred helping Sheila with David, whom she loved as her own.

Pat was talking about her trip into the town. While Sheila listened, she noticed for the first time how peaked Pat was looking. It had been a long, grey winter for them all. Perhaps she should take Pat and David for a drive in the country now that spring was here.

'How about a cup of tea now?' asked Sheila once Pat's tale was over of the wifey in the tram who'd been so fat she'd got stuck in her seat. 'You look like you could use a pick-me-up.'

'I'll make it,' said Pat, already on her way to the kitchen.

That evening, as she was tucking David up in bed, he suddenly asked Sheila to tell him about Dragonholme. 'What's brought this on?' she laughed. Although she'd often told him about the village, he'd never before expressed any special interest in it.

It was then that she had the idea. 'I'll do better than that,' she promised, kissing him soundly. 'What if you and Pat and I all take a drive to Dragonholme next weekend?'

Immediately David sat up. 'Will I be able to go out on a fishing boat?' he asked excitedly.

'I couldn't promise you that,' she laughed. 'But if there's a boat in the harbour I'll see what I can do about getting you taken aboard and shown around. How's that?'

'Oh,' cooed the little boy. 'That would be marvellous. I can hardly wait. You won't go and change your mind, will you?'

'Of course not,' she assured him. 'I want to go as much as you do. We'll leave directly after breakfast on Saturday and stop for a picnic lunch on the way. How's that?'

Sheila's heart was pounding as she left David's bedroom. She hadn't had any contact with Dragonholme since running away from James Campbell all those long years ago.

After Andrew's death she hadn't been able to bear the thought of returning to Dragonholme, the scene of the other great losses in her life. It had taken all her strength to cope with Andrew's death without having to face those other ghosts as well.

Now it seemed enough healing had taken place within her for her to be able to return. And with that decision all the love she'd always had for her home returned as well. For the first time in a long while she felt really excited about something – excited and, yes, thrilled.

Sheila stopped the Silver Ghost at the top of the descent into Dragonholme, staring down at the place where she'd been born and raised.

She gazed over the cluster of houses, remembering each individual one, and the families who lived in them, as though she'd been away only a day or two.

Finally, she turned her eyes out to sea, out to the spot where the disaster had occurred, where her childhood had vanished into the depths of the sea.

Tears glistened in the corners of her eyes as she saw again that violet glow and angry black clouds; heard again the crashing thunder and remorseless wind.

'Are you all right Mummy?' asked David, his hand reaching out to take hold of hers on the steering wheel.

'I'm fine, darling,' she replied in a voice trembling with emotion. 'There's nothing for you to worry about. I'm just very happy to be home in Dragonholme after all this time.'

Pat stared worriedly at Sheila guessing the real reason for her tears.

From there they drove to the family house. Sheila

remained sitting in the car, staring at the house for several minutes, before going in.

'It's awfully small,' said David, impatient to get out of the car. 'I want to see inside.'

Some of the furniture and bits and pieces had gone, otherwise it was exactly as she remembered. Glancing round she visualized the family as it had been: Davey with his battered old clay dangling upside down from his mouth; Peg kneading dough on the table; Bob in his chair day-dreaming about Thomasina McLean; Dougal and Jack, having just popped in, sitting by the range arguing about something or other while Davey looked on.

Sheila went ben to the room she used to share with Bob, crying out with delight to find her kist still where she'd left it.

Eagerly she opened it, staring down at the once-treasured items she'd gathered together for her marriage to Eric. She explained to Pat about the contents of the kist as she rifled through them; the four pillows and two bolsters, the four fluffy white blankets and two baby blue ones, the half-dozen sheets made of Egyptian cotton, the twelve Turkish towels.

She would take the kist with her when they returned to Glasgow, she told herself. It would occupy a place of honour in the Kelvinside house.

'Oh, but it's grand to be back!' she exclaimed, closing the lid of the kist again.

She took David and Pat to the smokehouse, showing them round it, pointing out things she thought might be of interest. This was another place laden with memories for her, and filled with ghosts.

Then she led the way to the house loft where, in bad weather, the nets had been hung up to dry, and the spare ones stored; the tarry smell of them lingering though the nets were so long gone.

'Can we go to the harbour now?' David asked, having been as patient as a small boy could be while his mother rooted around what he saw as a musty old cottage.

214

'Right,' she cried, grabbing his hand. 'We'll start for the harbour this instant. Come on Pat, we'll leave the car here.'

Tom Taggart's chandler shop had closed down, that was her first surprise. The second came as they neared The Haven, her da's favourite pub, which stood dark and cheerless in the afternoon sun. 'I don't understand it,' she said turning to Pat with a bewildered expression. 'Everything seems to be shut down.'

And so many houses were empty, just as her own home was. Some were boarded up, but most were simply empty, their doors snicked shut, their occupants vanished.

This wasn't the Dragonholme Sheila knew; the one whose memory had comforted her when she felt most frightened and alone.

What had happened to the busy little village filled with life and laughter that had once been her whole world. Now it was little more than a ghost town; little more than a shell.

There were four boats tied up in the harbour. 'Look, David,' Sheila cried excitedly, her heart fairly leaping at the sight of them. Coming closer, she saw they were the *Foamcrest*, the *Nonsuch*, the *Silvery Dart* and the *Rising Sun*, three Zulus and a Scaffie, all survivors of the disaster that now seemed to her to have happened a lifetime ago.

The closest was the *Foamcrest*. They strolled along the quayside to it, Sheila enthusing as they walked. 'It was aye a bonny boat,' she smiled. 'I can remember when old man Olafson bought it to replace the *Jean*. He was right proud of it. You would have thought it was the finest boat in the land.'

A man came on deck and bent to pick up some gash tackle. He was heavier than when she'd last seen him, and the beard was new, but she recognized him instantly.

'Hello, Duncy!' she called out, smiling.

He paused to glance over at her, frowning in puzzlement for a few moments. Then a smile of recognition lit his face. 'Sheila Beattie!' he shouted, and jumping down beside her, vigorously pumped her hand.

'How's Marika and the family?' she asked.

'Marika's fatter than ever. And there are three weans now; another boy and girl to add to the first girl we had,' Duncy replied with a grin.

Sheila introduced Pat, then David. Solemnly Duncy shook hands with David, saying that it was a great pleasure to meet a son of Sheila Beattie's. 'You ma's an old friend of ours. Why, I can remember when she was no bigger than you are now.'

'Here, less of the old,' chided Sheila gaily. 'And it's Sheila Lack, not Beattie.'

Sheila explained that David was desperate to have a look over a boat. 'Are you now?' he asked, turning to David. 'Then you've come to the right place.'

Duncy helped David clamber on board the *Foamcrest*. Leaning over the side, David called to Sheila, 'Aren't you and Pat coming too?'

'Women aren't allowed on the boats. It's bad luck. Pat and I will wait for you here. By the way, Duncy,' she asked, as they were about to go below. 'When did you start crewing for the Olafsons?'

Duncy, suddenly sombre, turned back to the side. 'Ronnie Olafson was washed overboard during the war,' he said quietly. 'Since then I've taken his place.'

'Sheila! Sheila!' shouted a voice behind her as David and Duncy disappeared into the *Foamcrest*.

Sheila turned on hearing her name shouted, and there was Rhona flying towards her with outstretched arms.

They embraced, kissed, and embraced again. 'Mrs Johnstone cried the news to me that you'd been spied coming down here. I came running right away,' said Rhona breathlessly.

Trust Mrs Johnstone, Sheila thought. At least some things hadn't changed.

'What happened to you? Why did you disappear like

you did?' demanded Rhona, oblivious to Pat's curious stare.

'My ma's death rather threw me – after everything else that happened,' she said quickly. If no gossip had been spread after her flight she wasn't going to start it now.

'Aye,' said Rhona, suddenly subdued. 'I thought that was what it was.'

'My son's on board the *Foamcrest*. Duncy's showing him round,' Sheila went on, changing the subject.

Rhona's mouth opened wide in surprise. 'A son! When did you get married? Where's your man?'

'It was a long war,' Sheila smiled ruefully. 'I'll tell you about it later.'

'Oh, lass,' whispered Rhona.

'And this,' said Sheila, pulling her forward, 'is Pat McLuskey. My dearest friend.'

Rhona immediately asked them to come up to tea. 'That would be lovely,' agreed Sheila. 'We'll be along just as soon as David is finished aboard the *Foamcrest*.'

'Wonderful,' beamed Rhona. 'I'll get away back and put the kettle on. We'll have a proper chat, just like the old days.'

David was full of the *Foamcrest* when he eventually, and reluctantly, rejoined his mother. Did she know what a warp was? He did, Duncy had explained that to him along with so many other things that he could barely get all the words out of his mouth fast enough.

'Marika will never forgive me if you leave without calling in,' said Duncy.

'I'll pop in some time this evening. I couldn't go without seeing Marika.'

'Right, then,' said Duncy. 'We'll be expecting you. And what about your husband? Is he with you too?'

Sheila took hold of David's hand. 'My husband died in France,' she said shortly.

Duncy muttered that he was sorry, and ruffled the lad's hair. 'My father was a famous pilot who flew with Albert Ball!' announced David. Duncy gave a wan smile. Sud-

217

denly Sheila asked the question that had been troubling her since coming in sight of the harbour. Where were the other boats?

Duncy turned his face out to the sea. 'This is all that's left,' he said, as though from far away. 'The other five boats that survived the disaster were sunk in the war with all their crews. Three of them on the Dover Patrol, two in the Adriatic.'

'That's all?' she whispered, her voice like an echo. Only four boats left from the Dragonholme fleet. Four boats and a handful of men. If the disaster had crippled the village, the war had substantially destroyed it entirely.

'Are we going to have tea now?' David interrupted her reverie, disturbed by the look on his mother's face.

'Aye, love,' she smiled. 'We're going to have tea.'

Rhona welcomed them at her door, Ian standing beside her. Ian had grown into a fine young man with a serious air about him.

To begin with, David was shy of his much older cousin, but Ian put him at his ease with his quiet, gentle way. Before long they were playing together in a corner of the kitchen. At least, David played while Ian looked on.

'I'm sorry I never got in touch,' Sheila apologized, once they were settled down over their tea. 'I always meant to, but somehow I just never did. I hope I didn't cause you any worry.'

'Oh, no,' smiled Rhona. 'I know that bad news travels the fastest.'

As the afternoon dwindled, Sheila told Rhona about France – and about Andrew. Once it had seemed that it was happiness that bound people together; but now, she thought, noticing the sympathy in Rhona's eyes, that it was loss.

'With the village in such decline, how on earth are you managing to get by?' she asked at last.

Rhona gave a wry grin. 'I gather shells from the

218

seashore and make them into ornaments which I sell, in Edinburgh,' she explained. She went to a cupboard and came back with a box of tiny figures made of shells.

'What a clever idea!' exclaimed Pat.

'How did you ever think of it?' asked Sheila.

Rhona confessed that she hadn't. Ian had brought home a book from school about Iceland. Leafing through it, she'd come across a large picture of seashell ornaments.

'I thought they were very appealing, so I decided to have a go at making my own. After all, what did I have to lose except a little effort and a pot of glue?'

It had taken her a while to get the hang of it. Then she'd made a round hundred and, using up her tiny savings, had taken them to Edinburgh in the hope of selling them to one of the big Princes Street shops.

'And it worked!' she laughed. 'That shop took a thousand a year, while another in the old part of the city had a standing order for seven hundred and fifty. I'm still in my parents' house, but it's been mine since they died, so it's not the lap of luxury we're living in,' she went on. 'But it keeps the roof over our heads and the wolf from the door.'

'Well I certainly have to hand it to you,' said Sheila. 'You've got more spirit than most people. By the way, what happened to Maggie?'

'Oh, Maggie and Ian flitted through to Portnessie soon after you left. But what about yourself?' asked Rhona. 'What are you doing now?'

Rhona was delighted to hear that despite all the tragedies she'd withstood, Sheila at least had no worries about money. As she said to herself, if your husband was destined to die young far better he left you wealthy than poor.

But what of Ian, for whom she'd aye had a soft spot – how was he getting on?

'Well,' said Rhona proudly. 'Miss Dalziel, his teacher, says he's very brainy and could go far, given the chance.'

219

She did not have to add that it was unlikely that chance would be given. 'One thing's certain, though,' she said sharply. 'He'll not be going to sea.'

It was clear to both Sheila and Pat that Rhona was more worried about her boy than she would admit. He was due to leave school fairly soon, but then what? There were only two choices: either he helped Rhona with her small business, hardly a job for a lad with his brains; or they upped sticks and flitted through to Edinburgh in the hope that he'd find a suitable position there.

'And what about all the folk who've left Dragonholme?' asked Pat. 'Where have they gone?'

Rhona sighed. 'Dragonholme was largely a village of widows and weans after the disaster,' she said slowly. 'After the war there were more widows and little chance for any more weans.'

Some of the old folk, like Handy Dandy and Tom Taggart, had passed on and were buried in the village cemetery. A number of the wives, the younger ones that is, had eventually moved away to bide with relatives elsewhere, or to look for new husbands, or both.

As for those who'd been children at the time of the disaster, most of those were grown up now, the lads leaving first to try and find a berth somewhere, inevitably putting down roots in the port that adopted them, and the lassies following. For them there was no point in staying on in a village with no young men.

Rhona sighed again. With no work and no men and no babies being born, or precious few anyway, it was only a matter of time, and a short one at that, before Dragonholme ceased to exist altogether.

'But why hasn't the laird done something to help?' asked Sheila. After all, he was supposed to be the protector of the people.

Rhona rolled her eyes. 'It's years since James Campbell even set foot in Dragonholme,' she informed them. 'Of course he knew the state the village was in. How could he possibly not when he lived in Dragonholme Hall? But it's as though he's lost all interest in the village,' she went on. 'It's almost as though he's turned against us.'

'That doesn't sound like the James Campbell I remember,' said Sheila.

'Aye, well he's had his share of misfortune, too,' said Rhona, not unsympathetically. 'First Robert was killed in the war, then Drew. When Mrs Campbell got the second telegram it was too much for her. She had a heart attack and died herself there and then.'

'Oh, the poor man,' said Pat, momentarily forgetting the things the poor man himself had done.

'Poor Mrs Campbell,' whispered Sheila. Her money certainly hadn't brought her happiness.

It wasn't until later that she wondered if James's abandoning of Dragonholme had been because of her; because it was her village, forever associated with her in his mind.

'We won't get out of touch again,' she assured Rhona as they parted. 'You can be sure of that.'

Sheila paused to listen to the fair-sized sea that was running, whitecaps rolling off it to pound against the shoreline. She'd just come from Marika and Duncy's where she'd spent a good hour talking over old times and renewing her friendship with them.

Before Marika and Duncy she'd been to see Miss Dalziel, the schoolmistress, who'd given her much to think about concerning Ian.

As there was a cold bite to the air she didn't stand listening to the sea for long, but hurried on her way, her feet clattering on the cobbles as she walked.

Coming up to The Halibut's Tail, Sheila saw it was still open and, on the spur of the moment, decided to take herself in for a dram.

The pub was empty except for Mr Meekie the landlord who insisted on buying her the drink, although it was obvious trade was so poor he could ill afford the gesture.

221

The paint was flaking from the walls, and all joy had gone out of the place. She sat on a chair by the miserable peat fire and stared into her whisky, thinking about what Miss Dalziel had told her.

Ian was a brilliant scholar, quite gifted, according to the schoolmistress, and most certainly had what it took to go to university. The big stumbling-block were the entrance exams. Quite simply Ian needed better tuition than it was Miss Dalziel's ability to provide. Without that tuition there was little chance he'd pass the exams.

It seemed to Sheila, as she sipped her drink, that the answer to the problem was Kelvinside Academy. Of course that would necessitate Ian moving through to Glasgow, or even he and Rhona together, should Rhona not want to be parted from him.

Money would be no problem of course. She could set them up in a wee house of their own if that was what they wanted. Then again, they could stay in her house in Kelvinside: it was certainly big enough, God knew.

If Rhona elected to go with Ian, though, that would be one more family gone: another nail in the coffin.

Finally Sheila decided to talk the matter over with Mr Lumsden, the Academy's headmaster, before mentioning it to Rhona and Ian.

She glanced up as a second customer entered the pub, a young man whose face was vaguely familiar.

The young man ordered two half pints at the bar, and stood talking for a few minutes with Mr Meekie. Then he ordered two more drams of whisky, picked them up and strolled over to where Sheila was sitting.

'Will you allow me to buy you a dram? A sort of thank you for the bit of help you once gave me,' he asked, smiling.

By his speech and manner he was clearly from the village, but she couldn't put a name to the face.

Noticing her puzzlement, he gave an amused laugh. 'I know I've changed but surely you recognize me?' he said.

'Give me a clue. Remind me about this bit of help I once gave you.'

He sat down and placed the fresh dram in front of her. He had warm brown eyes that were twinkling mischievously, and enormous broad shoulders, muscular even by fishermen's standards.

The young man gestured about him. 'Do you remember a night just before the disaster, when you and Eric Gifford, on your way home from here, rescued a lad who was having a rather nasty brothering?' he smiled.

It all came flooding back then: Tarry Dunbar and the crew off the *Locarno*, the boy with the trousers round his ankles while Tarry painted his crotch and backside with tar.

'You're wee George Jorgesson!' she exclaimed.

George nodded, joining in her laughter. 'That's who I am, right enough.'

'Not so wee anymore,' Sheila murmured, indicating his massive shoulders, and they both laughed more.

'I owe my life to that brothering, and Tarry's cruelty,' he reminded Sheila, for as a result of the brothering he'd been in bed for a month, and consequently he'd missed sailing aboard the *Locarno* when the fleet went out after the big shoal.

They reminisced for a while, then Sheila asked George if he was crewing one of the four remaining boats left to Dragonholme.

'No I'm not,' he said. 'I left Dragonholme before the war, and settled in Eyemouth. I've been crewing there for a real nice man named McFadyen. Or I was anyway. Unfortunately McFadyen's decided to retire because of his age. He's got the arthritis bad.'

'So what will you do now?' asked Sheila.

George sipped his dram, becoming almost morose. 'It's on account of his decision to retire that I'm here in Dragonholme.'

McFadyen's sons all had boats of their own, so the old man's would be up for sale. 'He's given me first refusal, because he knows I'm mad keen for a boat of my own.'

George had some money of his own put aside, but not nearly enough for the boat's asking price. He'd gone to Edinburgh in the hope of raising capital there, but to no avail. The Edinburgh bankers had turned him down flat because he didn't have any collateral, as had the Glasgow bankers when he'd tried them.

As a last resort he'd returned to Dragonholme to ask James Campbell to lend him what he needed, but Campbell's reaction had been the same as the bankers: no collateral, no loan.

'You took a risk in going to Campbell,' commented Sheila. 'It would be just like him to buy McFadyen's boat for himself, to add to his Portnessie fleet.'

George shook his head. 'I knew I was safe on that score. McFadyen bought his boat, the *Sheila B.*, from the laird in the first place. It's the only boat James Campbell's ever been known to sell. He wouldn't want it back.'

The *Sheila B*! Sheila dropped her gaze so George wouldn't see her smile. So James had got rid of the boat he'd named after her. My God, she thought, he must have been angrier than I thought.

It was clear that George was unaware that the boat had been called for her; he wouldn't have mentioned its name quite so casually if he had.

Sheila could picture the trawler as she'd last seen it, a sweet craft right enough. And for the first time in all these years felt a pang of almost affection for the man who had named it.

'What do you intend doing now?' she asked.

'There's nothing I can do. It's lost to me. I'll stay the night with my ma, then go back to Eyemouth in the morning and tell McFadyen to put the *Sheila B.* up for sale.'

As though it was only a matter of curiosity, she asked him about the state of the industry since the war. George brightened. 'It's never been better. The great shoals are now greater than they've been within living memory.'

George's eyes sparkled. 'If only I could get hold of a boat I could easily pay its costs off within a few years.'

224

'And what price is McFadyen asking?' The amount he named was reasonable enough.

It was on the tip of her tongue to tell George she would lend him the money, but it was always her policy to sleep on any important decision if she could, and that was what she would do now.

Going up to the bar she ordered two more drams.

Sheila woke with a start having been restlessly tossing and turning since going to bed several hours before. She and David were in what had been her ma and da's bed, Pat through in the other room in her old one.

She turned to look at the snoring David. How she loved that wee boy. He had become her whole world.

The *Sheila B*, that's what was running around and around in her head. That's what had woken her.

Something was bothering her about lending George the money to buy the boat, but what? It certainly wasn't the amount involved. Even if she lost the lot, which she'd ensure couldn't happen, it was money she would never miss. So what was niggling her?

And then the answer came to her. How blind could she be? Rather than helping George buy the boat she should be buying it for herself. It was named for her after all – and it would be a damn fine investment. And, she thought with a tingle of excitement that she hadn't felt for years, it would really anger James Campbell.

Her own boat, a thrill ran through her just to think about it. And she could . . . oh, the things she could do.

She sat up, her mind racing as she made plans. Without her realizing a part of her that had been empty for a long time had begun to be filled again.

At breakfast next morning Sheila announced to Pat and David, somewhat mysteriously, that she was going off

225

for a few hours on a matter of business, and she thought it best they remain behind.

'Oh, fine,' Pat replied, 'I'll take David down to the shore to play.'

Shortly afterwards, George was astonished when Sheila knocked on his mother's door to say she'd give him a run down the coast to Eyemouth, if he wanted, an offer he readily accepted.

He stared in wonder at the Silver Ghost, giving Sheila a strange sideways glance before getting inside.

It didn't take long for them to reach Eyemouth where the Eyemouth fleet lay in the harbour. It would be another couple of months yet before it set off for the Shetlands and the northern fishing grounds.

The fleet was a bonny sight, she thought. One which stirred memories long forgotten and brought her heart into her mouth. And there was the *Sheila B.* tied alongside the other eight steam trawlers of the fleet.

Sheila stopped the Rolls by the quayside, then got out and strolled over to look at the boat.

The *Sheila B.* had been so well-cared for that it might have been newly launched instead of thirteen years old. Nor was she worried about the state of its engine; an owner who cared for the outside of the boat cared for the inside as well.

So that was it. Her mind was made up – if indeed it wasn't before. 'Will you introduce me to your Captain McFadyen?' she asked George, standing by her side.

George nodded, wondering what the hell she was up to. They climbed back into the Rolls and he gave her directions to the McFadyen house.

Lang Jake McFadyen was as tall as his tee name suggested, and well into his seventies. Because of arthritis his back was permanently bent, his hands hooked into claws, and when he walked it was with a shuffle. She couldn't understand why he hadn't decided to retire earlier.

Mrs McFadyen showed Sheila into the best chair,

226

then hurried off to put the kettle on. Lang Jake and George sat over the table facing Sheila.

Sheila came straight to the point. She told Lang Jake she was interested in buying his boat and as George hadn't had any luck in coming up with the money would he consider selling to her instead.

'Is that right? You can't raise the asking price?' George nodded reluctantly.

Jesus, but she was quick off the mark, George thought. And not a word about what she intended all the way down here. She might have said! Rising, his face flushed, he stalked from the room.

Sheila stared after him, thinking what a fool she was not to have said something to him. Of course he'd think she'd been using him. With difficulty she brought her attention back to Lang Jake who was regarding her with an amused and patronizing expression.

'Ach, you can't possibly be serious, Mrs Lack. It's unheard of for a woman to own a working boat,' Lang Jake chuckled.

'It may be unheard of, but there's no law against it,' she replied sweetly.

Lang Jake knocked dottle from his clay, then began cleaning out the bowl with a stained pipe cleaner. He could hardly wait to get out and tell his mates about this.

'I want that boat,' Sheila stated quietly, steel in her voice.

Lang Jake laughed. 'You're havering, woman. What can you possibly know about herring boats and the like?'

Sheila fixed him with a cold stare. 'My father was Davey Beattie, the last admiral of the Dragonholme fleet. If you'll recall, he went down with my three brothers in the disaster.'

That wiped the smile off Lang Jake's face. 'I myself worked for James Campbell as his personal assistant. He taught me a great deal about the fishing industry.'

It was now plain to Lang Jake that this was no ordinary lassie, this one knew how to stand up for herself in a man's world, and probably win gey often as not. He'd be wrong to dismiss her lightly.

'So your maiden name would've been Sheila Beattie,' he mused.

She knew what he was getting at. 'If you're asking is the boat named for me, it is.'

'Well, well,' murmured Lang Jake, tamping down his new fill.

Mrs McFadyen bustled back in carrying several plates stacked high with potato scones, crumpets and tea cakes which she laid on a pouffe beside Sheila.

Lang Jake was remembering Davey Beattie whom he'd met on a number of occasions, the last time in Southwold when they'd had a good bucket together. He'd liked and respected the man.

Sheila was now absolutely determined to have the boat. Not conscious of the gesture, she stuck her jaw out defiantly.

'You've no mad notions about actually sailing aboard the boat yourself have you?' he asked at last. 'There's not a crew in Scotland or England would entertain such a thing.'

'I have no intention of going to sea myself,' she said shortly. 'I'm only too well aware of what fishermen think about women aboard boats. No, I just want to be the owner.'

Sheila mentioned the price that George had been asked. 'Aye,' said Jake. 'That's a special price for George, whom I'm very fond of. The price to anyone else would be higher than that.'

Sheila pretended to consider this. 'And what do you think about George as a potential skipper?' she asked.

'George is a natural seaman,' a new look coming into his eyes. 'Young as he is, he'd make a fine skipper.'

That was what she had wanted to hear. 'I'll tell you what,' she now said. 'If you sell it to me at the price you'd expect from anyone else, I'll make George skipper.'

This was a big chance for George, and well Lang Jake

knew it. Sure, George would get another berth easily enough, but being made skipper! Without a boat of his own he could wait a dozen years or more for that to come about.

Lang Jake grinned inwardly. He liked this woman's style. She certainly had a shrewd head on her shoulders. How could he possibly turn down his price *and* such an opportunity for George? He couldn't – as she'd been counting on. He named a fair market sum and, with no dickering, she agreed.

'You'll be making history,' Lang Jake said, extending his hand.

History. She hadn't thought of it like that, but it was true enough. She spat in her hand before slapping it into his.

Lang Jake roared with laughter.

George was standing outside staring glumly down at the harbour and the boat that was meant to be his.

He looked up at her approach. He didn't have to inquire what the outcome of her meeting with Lang Jake had been, the answer was written on her face.

'Congratulations,' he muttered, averting his eyes.

She thanked him for that, then gently reminded him that the *Sheila B.* had already been lost to him. If she hadn't got it someone else would have.

'There used to be a small repair yard in Eyemouth,' she went on. 'Is it still in operation? Do you have any idea how busy it might be right now?'

'Oh, aye,' he said slowly. 'It's still going strong. Last I heard it wasn't turning down any new orders, if that's what you mean.'

That was lucky, Sheila thought. It saved her contacting Tom McIndoe up in Aberdeen to find out if he could fit in what she wanted done.

'How would you like to skipper the *Sheila B.* for me?' she asked suddenly.

George turned to her in amazement. This was the last thing he'd expected.

Sheila went on. 'There are two conditions, though. First is that the *Sheila B.* is converted into a drifter, for I'll not run a trawler. Second is that its home port becomes Dragonholme. Now what do you say?'

'Can I choose my own crew?'

'Skipper's privilege,' she smiled

He looked down at the *Sheila B.* which he'd thought had gone out of his life forever, then back at the woman beside him. 'Done.'

If Glasgow had a Bohemian quarter then this small enclave of mean grey streets just off the Byres Road was it. In these ramshackle tenements students from the Art School congregated along with theatrical people and down-at-heel intellectuals. It was an area frowned on by the good folk of Glasgow who are inclined to view any artistic aspiration or endeavour as the pursuit of the shirker.

The close Sheila turned into had grey slate underfoot and was lined halfway up its walls with cracked and chipped tiles, the rest covered with ancient whitewash.

She found the name she was seeking on the third flight up; G. Hurley the name plate proclaimed. She knocked and waited.

She'd written to Graeme Hurley the previous week suggesting she call round at this time and speak with him, but had received no reply. Despite this, partly because she was the persistent type, but more because Graeme Hurley had come so heavily recommended, she'd decided to call anyway.

After a minute, with no response from within, she knocked again. Mr Lumsden, the headmaster at Kelvinside Academy, had warned her Hurley could be strange in his ways, and had explained why.

She knocked a third time, and was rewarded by hearing the faint tread of a footstep.

The door slowly opened and a pale face poked round. 'Yes, what is it?' the face asked.

Sheila stated, in her most officious voice, who she was, and that she'd written him for an appointment.

Graeme Hurley coughed, a barking cough that quickly splintered into a series of hacking smaller ones. Disappearing behind the door he spluttered into the handkerchief he was never without.

When the coughing attack was finally finished he told her she'd better come in, then led the way along a dark and dingy hallway.

The parlour he ushered her into was light and airy, which were about the only good things that could be said for it. The ceiling, particularly its fancy plasterwork, was encrusted with dirt, the wallpaper might have been up a hundred years or more.

Seeing Sheila glancing around, Hurley muttered apologetically that he was a bachelor and housework wasn't exactly his strong suit. When he asked if she'd care for a cup of tea she hastily declined.

Sheila began to wonder if she'd made a mistake, then reminded herself it was as a tutor she was interested in Hurley, not for his housekeeping abilities.

He was somewhere in his mid-thirties she judged, and not such a bad-looking chap either, now that she had a chance to study him properly. His skin was striking, being extremely sallow, almost translucent in places, while his eyes were the saddest she'd ever seen. The eyes of a poet she thought, a description that fitted them perfectly.

Hurley ran a hand through his deep auburn hair, then coughed again, turning away quickly when he did. Sheila sat on a none too clean armchair and waited for the coughing to subside.

'Sorry about that,' he mumbled when it was over.

'That's all right. I understand.'

231

There were many he would have challenged for making such a statement, but he didn't Sheila. Reaching into his inside jacket pocket he pulled out her letter and waved it at her as though it was a flag. He said he was surprised old Lummie had recommended him after giving him the sack. 'You did know I had the sack didn't you?' he asked aggressively.

Sheila cleared her throat. 'Mr Lumsden told me he'd regrettably had to let you go because of your health.' A teacher who had to take as much time off as Hurley did, Lumsden had explained, was unfortunately no use to him, no matter how excellent that teacher was.

Hurley tossed the letter aside and said perhaps Sheila could explain the situation to him herself.

Sheila started at the beginning, with her idea to send her nephew Ian to university, should he be capable. She then related the conversation she'd had with Miss Dalziel.

Her next step had been to see Mr Lumsden, to ask if Ian could be taken on at Kelvinside Academy. Very politely, Mr Lumsden had turned Ian down.

If Ian had been younger, Mr Lumsden said, he would have been delighted to accept the lad, but not now when Ian was deficient in so many pertinent studies for the university entrance exams, and would need so much personal attention.

'Mr Lumsden didn't think it would be fair to Ian to take him on at this late stage,' she went on. 'Psychologically. If he was as bright as Miss Dalziel said he was, it could damage him to be so behind the other boys.' She smiled wanly. 'He seemed to think that Ian would completely upset the balance of the class.'

Graeme Hurley broke in to say that he totally agreed with Mr Lumsden. No good school would take Ian on at this late stage. 'Some of the not so good ones might,' he added. 'But the chances they could get him through the exams at this stage are slim.

'Tell me more about Ian's background,' he prompted.

She told him of Dragonholme, of the disaster in which Ian's father, Jack, had been drowned, and of how Rhona now earned a living making ornaments out of sea shells. When she was done, she asked if Hurley had any tutoring engagements at the moment. Hurley shook his head. He told Sheila he had a small private income which took care of his needs; he didn't have to work. He didn't have to add that since leaving the Academy, he hadn't.

'Mr Lumsden said you were one of the best all-round teachers he'd ever come across. That if anyone could help Ian you were the person.'

Hurley opened his mouth to reply, but before he could do so a fresh bout of coughing hit him, far more severe than the other two.

Sheila watched in pity as the coughing wracked his body. Finally she rose and went through to the kitchen where she ran a glass of water and brought this back to him. He grabbed the glass and greedily drank its contents.

'Where were you gassed?' she asked when he had recovered enough to answer.

He gave her a baleful look. 'The Somme.'

There had been a number of mustard gas attacks by the enemy during the battle, all of them towards the end. 'You were lucky to survive the gas,' she said kindly. 'Not many did.'

This time his look was one of irritation. 'What would you know about it?' he snapped.

'I know because I was there,' she replied evenly.

He blinked in astonishment. 'You were?'

'I was a VAD with the Casualty Clearing Station at Maricourt. I was there for nine months.'

His breathing was a lot easier now, the searing agony that had seized his lungs had subsided. But he knew it wouldn't last for long. He had at least a dozen major attacks every day, and innumerable minor ones.

He excused himself and left the room to fetch a clean hanky. When he returned, he told her he'd come through

Maricourt in mid-October, having been gassed at Le Transloy. 'I can recall the action,' she said, 'but not you.'

He gave her a wry smile. 'I'd be surprised if you did. The CCS was bursting at the seams with casualties when I was there. Even if you'd tended me yourself, why should you remember me?' The look in his eyes was almost a challenge. 'Or I you, come to that?'

A very bitter man, Sheila thought, watching him closely.

Returning to the subject of Ian, Hurley said he'd like to help, he genuinely would, but unfortunately he was going to have to decline. 'To put it bluntly,' he said defensively, 'I don't think I have the strength for a task like this.' It was clear she was being dismissed.

With a flash of insight, Sheila realized that Hurley's health was only part of his problem. He'd also lost confidence in himself. What a waste, she thought, what a terrible terrible waste.

Rising, she said she was sorry to have bothered him. He replied that he'd enjoyed the company as he didn't have all that much.

He led the way back down that dark and dingy hallway to the door which he opened for her. There she paused, reluctant to be defeated.

She was going down to Dragonholme in a couple of weeks, she told Hurley. Why didn't he come with her and meet Ian? There could be no harm in that. She'd be interested to hear what he had to say about the lad. When Hurley didn't answer right away she added, 'Some sea air would be good for your lungs.'

Hurley glanced away. 'I'm sorry,' he mumbled.

Sheila moved towards the stairs, then suddenly wheeled around again. In a voice ringing with scorn she said, 'I'm sure there were many who fell at Le Transloy who, if it was possible to ask them now, would gladly trade places with you. Rotten lungs and all. And becoming you they wouldn't funk the rest of your life, they'd make the best of it, thanking God they were alive to do

234

so.' And with that she marched off down the stairs. When she got home she thought what an awful thing that had been to say to the man. Nonetheless, it was what she'd felt and, harsh as her words had been, she couldn't regret them.

Two days later the telephone rang in the Kelvinside house. It was Graeme Hurley to ask Sheila if the invitation was still open for him to accompany her to Dragonholme.

She told him to bring pyjamas, they'd be staying overnight.

It had been a quiet drive down, David in the back with Pat and asleep for most of the time, Hurley up front beside Sheila. He only spoke when spoken to, and spent most of the ride staring out at the passing scenery with those sad and suffering eyes of his. She didn't know what he was seeing, but it certainly wasn't the view.

Between Hurley's agreement to come to Dragonholme and the visit itself, Sheila had corresponded with Rhona, asking Rhona's permission to bring Hurley to see Ian, and explaining what she hoped it might lead to. She also asked Rhona to help her by making temporary accommodation arrangements for the crew of the *Sheila B*. They would make their own permanent ones in due course.

Rhona had been enthusiastic about Hurley – she and Ian were looking forward to meeting him.

Immediately after the introductions, Rhona put out the lunch, a large fish pie that gave off clouds of steam when she cut into it.

David tucked into his plateful, declaring it scrumptious. Pat said it was so delicious she was certain to have some more. But Hurley only picked at what he had in front of him, finally leaving most of it with the excuse to Rhona that he never had much of an appetite.

Rhona was dishing up the rhubarb tart and custard

235

when Hurley got a major attack, jumping up from the table so quickly he knocked over his chair he fled the house.

Rhona, her face filled with concern, watched his blundering exit, then turned to Sheila who explained to her and Ian about Hurley having been gassed in the war.

'Poor man,' said Rhona, shaking her head in sympathy.

After about five minutes Hurley returned and tried to apologize, but Rhona shushed him, saying apologies were completely unnecessary.

'Does it hurt when you cough like that?' Ian asked.

'Like the Dickens,' Hurley replied, almost smiling.

It had been a simple enough exchange, but Sheila, watching the look that passed between them, felt some sort of bond had been established between the pair of them. A good sign, she thought.

After lunch Sheila suggested that Hurley and Ian be left together for a while. Before departing for Glasgow, Hurley had told her he intended giving Ian a series of short tests.

Sheila went outside, glancing at her watch. It was nearing time for the arrival she was so eagerly looking forward to. 'Come on, David,' she called. 'I'm taking you down to the harbour. There's a surprise there for you.'

David was instantly excited. A surprise! What sort of surprise? Laughing, Sheila replied that if she told him it would cease to be a surprise, so he'd just have to wait his horses.

On reaching the quayside, Sheila glanced back the way they'd come to see the villagers coming down to join them. Within a few minutes almost the entire village of Dragonholme had gathered.

'There it is!' cried Lena Murray a little later, pointing.

Sheila's heart swelled within her when she picked out the *Sheila B.* in the distance. She'd spoken by telephone to George the previous day and he'd assured her the

236

conversion was a first-class job; the Eyemouth yard had done the boat proud.

'I can't see,' complained David. She picked him up and pointed to the boat. 'That's ours, David. Yours and mine. We own it,' she said proudly, her eyes shining.

David squealed with delight, giving his mother a big wet kiss on her cheek. He wanted to know if he could go out on their boat, and was disappointed when she replied not yet. 'When you're a little older I'll ask George to take you out for an hour or two,' she promised.

David wasn't pleased. 'I want to go today,' he insisted but Sheila was adamant. Not until he was older. He would have to settle for that.

As the *Sheila B.* sailed into the harbour, George sounded its horn again and again. The onlookers clapped and cheered.

She had instructed that the name *Dragonholme* be emblazoned on the boat's stern, denoting Dragonholme to be its home port. More than one of those present had tears in their eyes.

George skilfully manoeuvred the *Sheila B.* into the old *Bluebell* spot, then a member of the crew jumped ashore and demanded to know which of the ladies was Mrs Lack. When Sheila said she was Mrs Lack he handed her the for'rard line and said George had thought she'd like to tie off the *Sheila B.* for its first time in its new home port.

It was a gesture she appreciated. Calling David to her side she told him they'd do it together. There was a rousing cheer from the crowd.

When the boat was secure, George came on to the quayside and introduced his crew to Sheila and the villagers.

There were five crew, plus George, three of them married, the other three bachelors. She shook each of the five by the hand and welcomed them to Dragonholme.

'When will your families be arriving?' she asked.

'They'll be getting into Dragonholme in two days time,' a crewman named Shet Perlie informed her.

Sheila replied that that was excellent, and that

237

appropriate accommodation had been arranged for all concerned, but before they were shown that accommodation would they care for a drink?

The crew of the *Sheila B*. greeted that with broad grins and a nodding of heads. She then said to the other fishermen present that she hoped they'd join them at The Halibut's Tail so the men could all get acquainted. 'The drinks are all on me,' she laughed.

'This is the happiest day Dragonholme has known in a long time lass,' gossipy Mrs Johnstone said to Sheila as the men made their way to the pub. In that instant the germ of an idea was born in Sheila's mind.

At The Halibut's Tail Mr Meekie welcomed them with open arms.

That night, after David was asleep Sheila, Hurley, Rhona and Pat sat down with a bottle of whisky. Hurley said he agreed with Miss Dalziel, Ian was university material, no doubt about it. But Ian did need considerable coaching, both in new subjects and in those he was already studying, if he was to pass the entrance exams.

'So will you take him on?' Sheila asked bluntly.

Hurley rubbed his jaw, his eyes all the while studying her. 'It would be an honour,' he said at last. 'I'd enjoy teaching a boy with so much intelligence and potential.'

Rhona was smiling, but it was a strained smile. 'Well,' she said, 'I'll wind up the ornament business and we'll move through to Glasgow as soon as possible.'

'That's that then,' said Sheila, topping up their drams.

Hurley announced he wanted to make a toast. Raising his glass he said: 'To Ian getting into Glasgow University! And may he turn out to be an even better novelist than Sir Walter Scott.'

Rhona's glass stopped halfway to her mouth. 'What do you mean "novelist"?'

'Hasn't Ian told you? That's what he wants to be,' Hurley grinned.

238

Rhona gave a tiny laugh. 'This is the first I've heard of it.'

'He can certainly tell a marvellous story when he wants to,' said Pat. During her previous visit, Ian had regaled her with several tales he'd made up.

Fairy-touched, Sheila thought. That was how Ian had always been described since a wee boy. Aye, he'd make a fine novelist. What more ideal calling for a person the fairies had touched than that of a writer?

She woke next morning to the clamour of gulls screeching on the roof. Beside her was David, and beyond him Pat. The three of them had had to share the front bed while Graeme Hurley took the back room.

David would sleep for a while yet, Sheila thought, and Pat was still well out for the count. She decided to get dressed and go outside to have a look down at the *Sheila B.* for the sheer pleasure it would give her to see it there.

Slipping out the front door, she was surprised to find Hurley standing gazing out to sea. 'You're up early,' she said.

He gave her a smile. 'I've already been for a long walk along the seashore,' he said enthusiastically. 'Now I'm absolutely ravenous. I can't wait for breakfast.'

Sheila stared at him in amazement. 'That's certainly a change of tune from yesterday when you told Rhona you never had much of an appetite,' she remarked.

Hurley grinned. 'It's years since I've felt this hungry. Maybe you were right about the sea air. In fact, I actually got a decent night's sleep for the first time in years.'

'That's marvellous!' she said, looking at him more closely. He did look better: there was even a hint of colour in those sallow cheeks of his.

Hurley ran a hand through his hair, then gazed back out to sea, in the same way he had in the car during the drive down; staring at one thing, but seeing quite another.

Beside him, Sheila followed his gaze and sighed, thinking about the idea Mrs Johnstone had given her yesterday afternoon. My God, what an achievement that would be. That would be something to be really proud of! Could she pull it off, though? She watched the colour of the water change beneath the sunlight. Why not? At least she could give it a damn good try.

She glanced at Hurley's face, and was shocked to see it had become contorted in agony, twin rivers of tears streaming from his eyes.

'What is it?' she asked hesitantly.

He'd forgotten she was there. He groped for his hanky, embarrassed that she'd seen him crying.

He'd never spoken about this to another soul, but felt he could with her. She'd been there, after all; she'd know what he was talking about.

In a voice that seemed to come from far away, he talked of the Somme and the horrors he had seen there.

He told Sheila of his friend Brian Robertson, drowned before his very eyes in a huge shell crater filled with mud that Brian had stumbled into.

They'd done their best to get Brian out, but the mud had defeated them, dragging the screaming and pleading Brian down to his death with a final obscene plop.

'That terrible mud,' he said quietly. 'We all had nightmares about it. That vast ocean of mud, rippling when the wind blew, filled with traps for the unwary, traps that claimed victims with horrible regularity.

'I'm haunted by Brian's screams,' he said. 'His and the screams of the others.'

Sheila shivered in the warm morning air. She had heard other accounts of the mud related to her while at Maricourt, often by men she'd later learned had gone back to the mud, to be claimed by it in turn.

Hurley talked on, describing the action at Le Transloy when he'd been gassed, saying how he'd fumbled for his mask, while all around him men were writhing as their lungs burned out. 'It felt like my lungs were on fire,' he

240

said. Holding his breath, he'd slipped the mask on, then beat as hasty a retreat as he could.

He'd passed Sarge Copland running round in circles like a chicken with its head cut off, and John Mitchell whose eyes had been bulging so much they'd made him giggle hysterically inside his mask, and Lance Corporal Timms, quite dead, kneeling as though praying, and all the while the gas swirled around, not that much deeper in colour than many yellow fogs he'd experienced in the depths of a Glasgow winter when every fireplace in the city was going full blast.

Sheila suddenly realized she had a pain in her right hand. Glancing down, she found blood between her clenched fingers. She'd made so tight a fist she'd broken her flesh with one of her nails.

When Hurley was finally finished, he hung his head for a few moments, then turned his gaze back to the sea.

They stood for a little while in silence, the world waking up around them, each remembering.

Eventually, Sheila broke the silence.

'If you'd like that breakfast now I'll cook it for you.'

He faced her with a smile. 'That would be lovely.'

After breakfast they discussed the return to Glasgow. It was agreed that they'd start directly after lunch.

Sheila wanted some time on her own to think, so she arranged for Pat to take David off to play. When they'd gone, she went down to the quayside where she sat on a coiled rope staring at the *Sheila B.*, in her mind going over and over the idea she'd had the previous afternoon. It could work; she was certain it could.

When Sheila spied George she waved him over and they sat together for a good hour while she fired questions at him. If he thought she was behaving peculiarly, he didn't show it.

When lunchtime came Sheila went to Rhona's. Hurley was sitting in front of the fire with his shoes off and a cup of tea in his hand. 'I've come to a decision,' he said when Sheila came in. 'I've been waiting for you to announce it.'

Immediately, she was alarmed. Had he decided against tutoring Ian, after all? Was he going to give up already?

Clearing his throat, Hurley said he couldn't remember when he'd last felt so well. 'Since this morning, I've been like a man reborn,' he beamed. 'I would never have thought it possible. It seems to me,' he went on, 'that I could stay that way if I remain in Dragonholme. It's the air,' he laughed. 'You told me the air would do me good.'

Hurley glanced over at Rhona, then back to Sheila. 'It also seems a great shame to me that Rhona would lose her small business by coming through to Glasgow. She needn't do that if I stay here.'

This was something Sheila hadn't even dare hope for. She looked over at Rhona. It was clear how relieved she was at the thought of not having to leave her home.

Hurley went on to say there was little left for him in that dirty city anyway. Here he not only had some of his health back, but had found the beginnings of a sense of peace as well.

Hurley stared at Sheila. She knew he was now talking again of the Somme. What had passed between them that morning had been some sort of exorcism for him, or at least the start of one. Dragonholme wasn't only good for his physical health.

Hurley said he would return to Glasgow with them that day as planned, for he had to put his affairs there in order. Then he'd come back to Dragonholme with all speed, and begin the task of getting Ian ready for his exams.

Sheila told him he could use her house here as long as he liked, for which he thanked her. He would take her up on that offer until he could make other arrangements.

With a sniff Rhona turned again to her cooking. She'd been dreading going to Glasgow. Her stay there would have been purgatory – she who was used to village life and the fresh smell of the sea forever in her nostrils. She would have suffocated in the city, stifled by its claustrophobia. Aye, that would have been the way of it, sure as eggs were eggs, and herring herring. She offered up a silent prayer to God, thanking him for her reprieve.

When she dished out the lunch, Graeme Hurley got twice the plateful anyone else did, and he ate every last morsel of it.

The great day arrived for the boats – they could hardly be called a fleet anymore, although Sheila intended altering that – to sail north. She motored down to see them off.

George, starting his first season as skipper, was the proverbial cat with two tails, and one who'd fallen into a bucket of cream at that.

Sheila met the wives and weans who'd moved through from Eyemouth, already knowing from Rhona that they were well settled into their new homes.

Houses had been easy to find for these families, thanks to so many in the village lying empty. George, of course, had been staying with his ma, the other two members of the crew having gone into digs which they'd return to when the *Sheila B*. fished the home waters and again at the end of the season.

As was traditional, everyone in the village came down to the quayside to wish the boats and the men who sailed them good luck.

Graeme Hurley stood with Rhona and Ian. Only the week before he'd moved out of Sheila's house and into a small cottage he was renting from the Dragonholme Estate.

Sheila looked from the *Sheila B*. to the other boats. The age of sail was definitely past, she thought; steam was the thing now, and the thing into which she'd be putting her money. But you had to hand it to the sailing craft, they had style and romance.

She grinned to herself. She could just hear Davey, her da, telling her not to be so soft; there was nothing in the

243

least romantic about fishing boats, sail or otherwise. But he'd have been wrong; there was.

The Rising Sun, the smallest of the boats, was first away, then the *Foamcrest*, *Silvery Dart* and *Nonsuch* in that order. Last of all, and as far as she was concerned best of all, was the *Sheila B.*, George blowing its horn as the villagers cheered and waved, no-one cheering louder or waving harder than Sheila herself.

They waited on the quayside until the last boat had vanished over the horizon, then reluctantly turned for home.

Sheila had only taken a few steps when she happened to glance up at the cliffs towering over Dragonholme. Automatically, she held her breath.

There, looking down on her, a figure on horseback was silhouetted against the bright sky: a figure she recognized instantly.

James Campbell had also come to see the boats away.

8

Sheila thought the *Friend's Good Will*, squat and truncated in appearance, an ugly vessel. It certainly had nothing like the graceful lines of the *Sheila B*. But the *Friend's Good Will* was up for sale. It was the first steam drifter to come on to the market that season, and Sheila was determined to buy it.

She'd driven up to Buckie two days before, in order to have a comprehensive report made on the boat. The report had been favourable. Despite being sixteen years old, the *Friend's Good Will* was still structurally and mechanically sound and had a long working life yet remaining to it.

The reason the boat was on the market was that its owner and skipper had suffered a serious accident off

Lerwick. His hip had been severely crushed, and as a result of that he'd never walk again, far less go to sea.

The sale of the *Friend's Good Will* was to be by public auction on the quayside beside the boat. When Sheila arrived there was already a small knot of people there.

She was well aware of the curious glances cast in her direction. A good-looking and expensively dressed woman all on her own wasn't exactly a common occurrence at such an occasion.

After a while a man came over, raised his cap, and asked her if she wasn't the Miss Beattie who'd worked at one time for Mr Campbell? She nodded that she was.

The man introduced himself, and Sheila recalled doing business with him years ago. They shook hands, then chatted for a few moments, after which he melted back into what had become a sizeable throng.

She wasn't worried about the ever-growing numbers, though. Most of those present would be spectators come to watch the bidding.

Dead on noon, the advertised time, the auctioneer jumped on to a small platform, banged his gavel, and announced the start of the sale.

A number of people looked at Sheila in surprise when she made her first bid. None of them had ever known a woman to bid before. The auctioneer paused, momentarily thrown. 'Are *you* actually bidding?' he asked Sheila in a pedantic schoolmasterish tone.

Biting off a blistering reply, she said in a loud, clear voice, 'Yes, that's correct.'

The auctioneer looked around, presumably for advice. When none was forthcoming, he shrugged and continued with the business in hand.

One by one the bidders dropped out, until the only ones left where Sheila and someone on the far side of the assembly, hidden from her view.

Sheila raised her bid again and again, and still the other bidder continued to top her. She chewed her lip when what she'd set herself as a maximum price was reached, then bid once more.

There was no hesitation from the other bidder in topping her yet again. Telling herself that this was absolutely her last bid, she went up a double amount.

The auctioneer had hardly recognized this last bid of hers when she was topped a final time. The auctioneer looked at her inquiringly, and waited.

Having set her heart on owning that boat it took all her self-control to shake her head, knowing the price the *Friend's Good Will* was already fetching to be well in excess of its actual value.

The auctioneer offered the *Friend's Good Will* one last time, then banged his gavel. 'Sold to Mr James Campbell!' he announced with finality.

Sheila flushed with rage. James Campbell! She should have known! Who else could be so determined?

As the crowd began to disperse she noticed that several of the men were smirking at her, obviously pleased to see her lose out after having had the audacity to intrude on what they considered a male province. Silly sods, she thought. They hadn't heard the last of her yet.

She was about to move off when suddenly James Campbell was there in front of her, his face so hard and expressionless it might have been carved from granite.

'Hello, Sheila,' he said.

He'd aged considerably since the last time they'd met. His hair was grey, his body now so thin that his clothes just seemed to hang on him.

'You did that for spite didn't you?' she snapped back instantly. 'You've no need for a drifter. You know damn well you only have trawlers in your fleet.'

The very sight of her was driving him wild. Though his face showed no emotion, he wanted to sweep her into his arms, to kiss her, to hold her to him, and never let her go.

But all he could say was, 'Is that any way to greet an old friend?'

'You mean that stealing my boat from me *is*?' she countered.

If she could convert a trawler into a drifter, then why shouldn't he do the reverse? he teased, smiling thinly. He'd known she'd be stumped for an answer to that one.

James Campbell's penetrating gaze made her want to squirm. He seemed to be staring into the very depths of her being. She had forgotton how powerful a man he was.

Disarmingly he then confessed that the reason he'd attended the auction in person was so that he could speak to her.

It surprised and disturbed her to realize that her heart was pounding.

As for his buying the *Friend's Good Will*, he genuinely had intended converting the boat and adding it to his fleet (which was a lie, his intention all along having been to do as he was about to do). But as Sheila had accused him of spite, and because she obviously wanted it so much, then she would have it, a present from him to her. And with that he handed her the boat's purchase papers and other documents.

She stared in astonishment at the papers in her hand.

'Now, can we go somewhere where we can talk?' He knew a pub that was rather nice where they could have a drink together.

'Talk about what?' she demanded, finally finding her voice.

'About something very much to your advantage,' he replied mysteriously, all his old charm still with him.

Perplexed, she just stared. The last thing she wanted was a drink and a chat with James Campbell. But still she could not find it in her to say no.

'Let's go then,' she replied stiffly, avoiding his eyes.

She flinched when he took her arm, but didn't object or remove it from his grasp.

In the pub he settled them into a quiet corner. When he returned with their drinks he asked her why she'd been after the *Friend's Good Will*. 'I can understand why you bought the *Sheila B.*,' he smiled. 'She was named for you, after all. But why the *Friend's Good Will*?' He'd obviously been puzzling over that.

There was no reason why she shouldn't tell him, she thought. He'd find out soon enough.

She couldn't help the anger that crept into her voice. 'I'm only doing what you, as laird of Dragonholme, should have done,' she said. 'And that's to breathe life back into the devastated village.'.

She explained that it was her plan to buy as many boats as she was able, boats that would be based at Dragonholme, and whose crews and families would live there.

Men and work, those were the keys to revitalizing Dragonholme. By bringing in both she'd restore the village to the thriving community it had once been.

All the while she spoke, he said nothing. He could feel his own blood moving as though it had been sleeping for years.

She was right about the village, of course. He had not so much neglected it, as abandoned it. As though by watching it shrivel he was getting back at her. Oh, the fire of her, he thought, as she went on excitedly about her plans. Had he ever known anyone else with so much spirit?

At one point he'd considered selling the Hall, taking himself away from the places forever associated with her in his mind. But in the end he hadn't been able to sell. No matter how much it hurt, he couldn't bring himself to sever the tie with the place where he'd spent the happiest days of his life.

'So the rumour's true that you've come into a fortune?' he asked at last.

She nodded.

'Your husband was killed in the war I heard?'

'Aye.'

'I lost my two lads then. And Fiona of the shock.' He

248

stared at his hands against the top of the table, then raised his face to hers with something of a smile. 'But I expect the gossips have told you all about that.'

'I'm sorry,' she whispered, almost speaking his name.

'Fiona opened that second telegram, read its contents, screamed, and fell down dead. Just like that. I'll never forget that sound till my own dying day.'

She took a sip of her drink. Since the disaster it just seemed to have been death, death and death again.

'You said you wanted to talk about something that was very much to my advantage?' she prompted.

'I really did think I'd got over you,' he began slowly, his voice barely audible. 'That I'd pushed you into the background once and for all. Then you returned to Dragonholme, and all the old feeling erupted. And I realized that I'm still as much in love with you as I always was.'

'I don't love you,' she said, her voice as hard as rock. 'I will never forgive you for what you did to my family. For what you did to me.'

Breath hissed from him. 'So that was the reason you ran away. You found out.'

'I overheard you and Dunwoodie talking that night you were both drunk.'

His hand grabbed hers across the table. 'I know I was wrong, but that doesn't make my love wrong.'

She jerked her hand free. 'I don't want to hear any more.'

'You've more than yourself to think about, you know. You've a son, you must consider what's best for him. It's not good for a boy to be brought up without a father.' He leaned towards her so that she could almost feel his breath. 'Marry me and I'll be that father to him,' he pleaded.

She couldn't believe what she was hearing. 'Are you mad? Marry you? After what you did?'

'You're not thinking my proposal through,' he argued.

My God, she thought, he is mad! 'What is there to think through? My mother would have lived longer, and certainly in far easier circumstances, if it hadn't been for what you and that pig Dunwoodie did. And what about the hardship you caused my sisters-in-law and their children?'

'But I loved you. I only did what I did because I loved you.'

She didn't know whether to laugh or to cry. 'Love? Is that what you call love? Do you know, I think you must be the most selfish bastard I've ever known.'

'I don't know what else I can say to convince you.'

She moved as though to stand up. 'There's nothing you can say.'

His face had lost all its colour. She had to accept his proposal, she had to. In all the fantasies he'd had since learning of her return – in all the fantasies he'd had when it seemed he would never see her again – she always forgave him in the end.

'I don't want you to ever speak of this again. It's a ridiculous suggestion,' Sheila said, suddenly on her feet and pushing in her chair.

There was no trace of his usual composure as he staggered to his feet. 'There's nothing ridiculous about it,' he said in a choked voice.

She stared at him levelly, all the old anger burning once more. 'You disgust me,' she said. 'You fill me with disgust.'

But, in his mind's eye, he could see her as he'd often dreamed of her, her body naked and her arms reaching out for him, her smile warming him, his own self dissolving in the ecstasies of love.

With a sudden movement he grabbed her wrist, squeezing it so hard she gasped with pain. 'You don't mean that,' he whispered.

She tried to pull herself free, but he wouldn't let go. She had no wish to make a scene.

'If you won't be my wife at least consent to be my mistress again. It can't have meant nothing to you. You loved me once. You'll love me again. Just give me a chance.'

'You've had your chance, James Campbell,' she said with all the dignity she had.

Then the volcano of his emotions erupted, so that he lost all control over himself.

Regardless of where they were, he threw himself on her, pressing his lips against her unwilling ones in a kiss.

Sheila struggled against his assault. With her free hand she struck at his face, raking her nails the length of his cheek.

With a cry of pain, he pulled away from her. The side of his face was marked with four thin lines of blood.

'Try to force yourself on me ever again and so help me God I'll kill you,' she spat out in fury.

His passion spent, he felt only humiliation and shame. He'd made a complete fool of himself, and how that hurt – far more than a damaged cheek.

'Get away from me,' she ordered.

Another customer walked the length of the bar for the water jug, turned and glimpsed James's face, looked startled, then scuttled back the way he'd come.

James groped for his handkerchief, holding it to his bleeding cheek. He wanted to lash out, hit someone, and the someone he wanted to hit most of all was himself.

As he rose to go his gaze lit on the purchase paper and other documents for the *Friend's Good Will*, lying beside Sheila's drink. His hand swooped down to snatch them. In a voice that shook he told her he was damned if she was going to have that boat after all.

It was such a pathetic gesture, that all she could do was laugh.

To James Campbell, that laugh was as sharp as a knife, and far more lethal. He strode from the pub, banging the door behind him. Outside, he would have sworn that he could still hear her laughing.

'Campbell was right about one thing,' Pat was saying. 'David does need a father. It's not good for a boy to be

251

brought up with only women.' Sheila had just related to her what had happened in the Buckie pub.

Sheila was tired after the drive down from the north, but, despite the lateness of the hour, it would be a good while yet before she'd be able to sleep. There were too many things running around inside her head for that.

'Are you saying I'm spoiling David, or mummying him?' she asked slowly.

Pat shook her head. 'No, of course not. All I'm saying is that any child lacking one of its parents will grow up sort of lopsided, if you know what I mean.'

Sheila had never thought of it like that. She pictured David upstairs in his bed, and her heart went out to him. But she had herself to consider also, or was that selfishness on her part?

'It's been six years since your Andrew died, and you're still a very attractive woman.' Pat paused. 'How old are you?'

Sheila had to think for a moment. 'Twenty-eight. Twenty-eight, my God. Until recently she'd felt more like fifty.

Pat shrugged. 'You've a whole life still ahead of you. I'm sure Andrew wouldn't have wanted you to go on playing the widow forever. He'd want you to find someone else, just as you found him after you lost Eric.'

Pat was right, of course. And Andrew would have agreed with her. But not yet, she wasn't ready for another man yet. She needed more time to heal the wound of grief still open within her. Only since she'd repaired her ties with Dragonholme had the ache begun to diminish.

She changed the subject, then after a while went up to her bedroom, taking a large whisky with her.

Damn James Campbell for buying the *Friend's Good Will* out from under her, she thought angrily. If it hadn't been for his interference the *Friend's Good Will* would now be hers. How long till another stream drifter was put up for sale? God alone knew, it could be weeks, or months, and in the meantime she was seething with impatience. How long could she wait?

Well, she decided at last, exhausted by her own busy brain, she would continue going after boats as they came on the market, but she could also help matters along herself. It was so simple a solution that she wondered that she hadn't thought of it before: she would have more boats built for her.

And she knew exactly who she wanted to build them.

Tom McIndoe was a right old man now, his hair snow white, his shoulders stooped, his face tramlined with age. But he still owned McIndoe's Shipyard, and still ran it with a rod of iron. He also still built some of the bonniest boats to be seen in any herring fleet. When Sheila had been James Campbell's assistant she'd often dealt with Tom, and the pair of them had been great pals.

He greeted Sheila warmly, ushering her to a hard-backed chair.

Sheila liked Tom McIndoe's office. It was a real man's place, smelling strongly of tobacco smoke and male bodies. There were plans and drawings everywhere; on top of his desk and strewn all round it.

She came straight to the point. She wanted him to build four drifters, similar in line to the *Sheila B.*, but completely up-to-date.

Tom nodded. 'Aye,' he said in a deep, rough voice, 'I can do that, no bother. Mind you, they'd cost a fair bit.' He judged her with his open blue eyes. 'I presume the person on whose behalf you are acting is aware of that?' He knew she hadn't worked for James Campbell in years, but she had explained very little in her letter.

'I'm not acting for anyone. I want those boats for myself.'

Tom sat back in his chair with an astounded expression on his aged face. A woman owning fishing boats! He'd never heard the like.

'I take it you've no objection about building for a woman?' Sheila asked drily.

Tom stared up at the ceiling while he considered whether he did or not. Just because he hadn't done it before didn't mean to say he shouldn't, but it was novel, oh, aye, it was certainly that!

'As far as I'm concerned a woman's money is the same colour as a man's,' he replied at last, with a broad smile.

'There speaks a true Aberdonian,' Sheila grinned back. 'Now what about delivery, when can I have them?'

Tom rose from behind his desk and told her to come with him to the window. There he pointed to the yard below which was bustling with activity, and where a number of new hulls could be seen in various stages of construction.

With proud satisfaction in his voice, he informed her that the yard was working flat out, with orders stacked up waiting their turn. It would be two years before he could deliver the four drifters.

Sheila's dismay and disappointment were evident. Two years was an absolute eternity.

'I can't deliver before then,' Tom assured her.

She stared down at the yard, her gaze moving from hull to hull, the majority of which were going to be trawlers. She watched a gang of riveters, admiring the dexterity and expertise with which they drove home each individual rivet.

Two years? That wasn't satisfactory at all. Turning to Tom she said so, and added, sadly, she'd have to take her business elsewhere.

'But we're the best,' he said reasonably.

'*One* of the best,' she corrected him.

He repeated it would have to be a two-year delivery date. She repeated that that was unacceptable and she'd have to take her business elsewhere. Her mind was already considering the alternatives.

It went totally against the grain for Tom to let an order slip away like this. There had been too many lean times in the past when the yard had been empty and he'd have given an arm and leg for one drifter, far less four. Frantically he began mentally rejigging schedules, trying to find some way in which to accommodate this determined young woman.

A silence hung heavily between them for a full minute, then, with a sigh, Sheila thanked him for seeing her and said she'd be getting along.

Her hand was actually grasping the door knob when Tom said softly that with an awful lot of switching about he could deliver two of her boats in six months, the other two a year after that.

Sheila knew once an initial compromise had been made the way was open for others to follow. Without turning round she said two in six months, the remaining two six months after that.

Tom stuck a finger in a hairy ear and waggled it up and down. He replied somewhat grudgingly, that if she recalled he always sealed a new order over a dram. She answered she took water with hers.

They had three whiskies each, by the end of which Sheila had bargained the price down considerably.

She was happy, jubilant, and slightly drunk when she finally returned to her hotel.

Six weeks later, Sheila was back in Aberdeen to attend the sale by public auction of the pipe stalkie, the *Rowland*. Steam drifters were often called pipe stalkies by Scottish crews because of the tall, thin, funnel sprouting behind the wheelhouse.

The weather, despite it being July, was wet and blustery as she strolled on to the fish wharf where the auction was to take place. Some minutes later the auctioneer climbed on to the makeshift platform that had been erected for him and announced the start of the sale. As he spoke Sheila became aware of an all too familiar figure staring at her coldly, and her heart sank.

255

James Campbell, graven-faced, thought to himself that he was going to enjoy this. He was newly determined that if he was to be denied, then so also would she be. He'd made up his mind to destroy her dream of revitalizing Dragonholme, and in the process be revenged for the rejection and humiliation he'd suffered that day in Buckie – that he'd been suffering since the day she left him.

Her worst fears became justified as the bidding progressed. Eventually, she too dropped out knowing that even if she'd bid every last penny she possessed James Campbell would still have topped her.

She felt sick when the *Rowland* fell to him. You bastard, she thought, but refused to let her frustration and anger show.

James Campbell shot a smile of triumph in her direction, then, in a gesture of dismissal, turned his back on her.

'It would've looked grand tied off in Dragonholme harbour,' a voice said beside Sheila.

The speaker was a woman Sheila recognized, but couldn't quite put a name to. Realizing this the woman smiled and said, 'Aye, it's been a long time, right enough. I'm Mrs Burnside now, but you knew me when I was cried Rosie McCullough.'

Rosie was one of the many lassies who'd finally been forced to leave Dragonholme because of the shortage of men. She now told Sheila she'd come to Aberdeen where she'd married a fine, handsome man by the name of Hector Burnside. Prior to the sale, Burnside had been skipper of the *Rowland*.

Rosie went on to say she and her husband had heard how Sheila had bought the *Sheila B.*, and when they'd seen her there that day they'd rightly assumed she was after the *Rowland*, 'We'd been sore hoping you'd get it,' she finished.

Sheila was puzzled, and asked why Rosie and her husband should want that. Rosie replied wistfully that she had a great hankering to go back and live in Dragonholme. If Sheila had got the *Rowland* her Hector had been going to ask if he could keep his job as skipper. If Sheila had agreed, that would have meant they could have set up home in Dragonholme rather than Aberdeen.

Sheila asked where Hector was now. 'He's gone to ask James Campbell about staying on as skipper. But we don't hold out much hope of success. Campbell has a habit of promoting skippers from within the Portnessie fleet.'

Rosie was exactly the sort of person Sheila wished to bring back to Dragonholme. She would gladly have reinstated Hector as skipper, providing his previous employer gave him a good reference that was.

They talked about the past for a few minutes, and as they chatted it came to Sheila that perhaps she could bring Rosie back to Dragonholme after all, for wouldn't she be looking for a couple of skippers in three-and-a-half months' time?

She knew Hector Burnside would almost certainly still be unemployed then, for with the season under way skippering jobs wouldn't exactly be thick on the ground.

Sheila told Rosie that. 'If your Hector doesn't get the job with Campbell,' she said, 'then I'd like a word with him. I'll be in my hotel room all evening if you care to call for a drink. If you don't I'll know he's got the job.'

Rosie's eyes lit up, and she was effusive in her thanks.

Sheila left the wharf feeling a little better and in a fighting mood.

At the back of seven, Sheila had just finished putting a telephone call through to David and Pat when there was a knock on her door. Rosie and Hector, she thought, crossing to it; but she was wrong, for when she opened the door Tom McIndoe, clutching his bowler, stood revealed.

Tom, looking quite wretched, apologized for disturbing her, and asked if he could come in.

She took his hat and light coat, which she put to one side, then offered him a dram. 'You'd better pour yourself a glass as well, lassie,' he advised. 'For I'm the bearer of bad news.'

Sheila glanced at him sharply. This must be some sort of ploy on his part to postpone the delivery dates he'd agreed to. Aye, he's had second thoughts, and is now trying to pull a crafty one on me, she told herself, handing him his whisky. But she was wrong.

Tom swallowed his hefty dram in a single gulp, shuddering as it went down. He glanced hopefully across to where the bottle stood, and Sheila told him if he wanted another to help himself.

Tom was hating every moment of this. It ranked high amongst the worst things he'd had to do in his entire life. 'I was going to write,' he said to Sheila. 'But I heard you were in town for the auction of the *Rowland*, so I thought I'd come by and see you instead.'

He shifted uncomfortably where he stood, his ears a bright pink from embarrassment.

Alarm suddenly locked her body. There was something wrong here, something far worse than she'd at first imagined. 'What is it Tom?' she asked quietly.

Tom drank more whisky, after which he asked her if she had a family. 'Yes,' she said in surprise. 'I have a wee boy called David. He's just over five years old.'

Tom nodded. With a lad of her own she might understand. 'I have three sons,' he said. 'They're all grown up now, of course. They're working in the yard. They're good sons. Grant, the eldest, he'll become head of the firm when I die.'

Tom rubbed his forehead, finished what remained of his dram, and poured himself a third without even bothering to ask. Rounding on Sheila, eyes wide and vulnerable, he told her he was hellishly sorry but he had to cancel her order; he couldn't build the four drifters for her after all.

She stared at him as though he'd suddenly started speaking in a foreign language. 'What?'

Tom took a deep breath, then began to explain. James

258

Campbell had been to the yard several days previously. Campbell had come to ask if it was true he was building boats for her, and he'd told him the truth.

Campbell had then threatened him. If he went ahead with the order, Campbell would ensure no further orders were ever placed with the yard. And furthermore, the existing ones, with exception of hers, would all be cancelled.

Tom said he was in no doubt whatever that Campbell was capable of carrying out such a threat, for in recent years he had become undisputed leader amongst the fleet owners. King Campbell the man was even cried by some. If Campbell put the word out that his yard was to be banned, then banned it would be.

Tom went on to say he had his three sons to think about. If it had only been him he'd have told Campbell to take a running jump and damn the consequences, but the yard was bread, butter and the future for his lads. Matter of principle or not, it wasn't in him to take that away from them.

Having got that off his chest Tom sat and slumped over his again empty glass.

She couldn't blame Tom. The poor old man had been put in an impossible position. And Tom was right in considering James's threat not to be an idle one; James Campbell didn't make threats he wasn't prepared to carry out.

Crossing to Tom, she knelt by his chair and put her arm round him, telling him not to worry, she'd get her boats somehow, and she was only sorry he'd had to go through what he had.

She added she could well appreciate what it had been like for him to have to come and tell her this.

'What on earth did you do to him lassie?' Tom asked thickly.

'It's not what I've done to him that counts,' she smiled. 'It's what I'm going to do.'

*   *   *

It was four days since the Dragonholme boats had arrived back to fish the home grounds, and marvellous hauls they were having; a continuation of the superb catches they'd been taking in the northern waters. As seasons went, this was proving to be a bumper one for them.

Sheila was extremely pleased with George Jorgesson, who'd turned out a first–class skipper, just as Lang Jake McFadyen had said he would, with a nose that could·sniff out herring the way a dog can aniseed.

George and the *Sheila B.* were out at sea that morning, while Sheila herself was in Portnessie to attend yet another auction of a pipe stalkie. She had high hopes of getting the boat in question, having indulged in what Pat McLuskey described as 'a wee bit of stage management'.

The auctioneer was the one who'd been at Buckie. A dozen or so feet to Sheila's left stood James Campbell, over on her right Hector Burnside.

She and Burnside hadn't even looked at each other, far less acknowledged one another. Nor would they.

The *Lorella* had been built in Berwick in 1910, and was a good, solid, reliable boat. It had been recently painted; black, French blue, and grey, which enhanced its appearance.

The bidding got off to a brisk start, nearly all eyes coming to rest on James Campbell when he made his first offer. It was now well known that he'd bought the last two drifters to come on the market and had converted them to trawlers in his own Portnessie repair yard.

Hector Burnside, appearing anxious and concerned, joined in the bidding, giving the man who'd topped him a glowering, sideways, glance.

One by one the bidders dropped away till at last there was only Sheila, James Campbell and Hector Burnside left. Finally Sheila shook her head when the auctioneer looked to her for fresh bid, and turning, swept through the crowd and off the quayside.

The next ten minutes were agonizing ones. Then Hector Burnside came bursting into the hotel lounge where she'd arranged to meet him, his face wreathed in smiles.

Sheila wanted to let out a whoop, but managed to restrain herself.

'He fell for it, just as you thought he would. He made no more bids after you'd gone,' Hector told Sheila, handing her the *Lorella*'s purchase paper and other documents, which she accepted with a trembling hand.

Two boats she now owned. Two out of the twenty she meant to have. Putting the purchase paper and other documents to her lips she kissed them.

'Pick a crew, but don't be hasty. Take your time. I want the best of those still looking for berths. And when they and the *Lorella* are ready, join up with George Jorgesson and the other Dragonholme boats,' Sheila ordered.

'I will Mrs Lack,' Hector replied respectfully.

'You've taken quite a chance in what you've done, you know. It won't take James Campbell long to find out we've put a fly one over on him, and he isn't a forgiving man.'

'I have what I want in being a skipper again, and Rosie has what she wants by being able to go back and live in Dragonholme. Sure, I've stuck my neck out, but as far as I'm concerned it's worth it. Anyway, I've every faith that you'll see I never get into the situation where Mr Campbell is able to carry out a reprisal against me,' Hector replied honestly.

She was touched by his declaration: and it served to remind her she was now responsible for people other than David and Pat.

'I'll do my best never to let you down, Hector. You have my oath on that.'

Sheila laughed with delight as she completed the second box of herrings she'd gutted since the boats had come in a short while before.

261

She'd come down to the shoreline to watch their arrival, and a braw sight it had been, too, with the *Sheila B.* leading them in.

It was Shet Perlie's wife who'd asked if she'd like to lend a hand, and she'd immediately answered that she'd be only too happy to.

When the last box had been filled and loaded she went down to the water's edge where she washed the knife she'd been loaned by Agnes Perlie.

As she did this she thought of how much she was enjoying living again in Dragonholme where she, David and Pat were settled into the family house for the summer. If it weren't for David's schooling, she'd sell the house in Glasgow and move back on a permanent basis.

She spied Rhona further down the shore, and waved. Rhona was holding a bag, which told Sheila that Rhona was out collecting seashells.

Sheila made a gesture that indicated drinking tea, and Rhona shook her head and pointed to the bag. The message was clear: Rhona had a lot more shells to collect before the tide, already well turned, came in.

Marika strolled over. 'Just like old times, eh Sheila?' she said happily.

'Almost,' Sheila replied, thinking it would be like old times indeed when there was a full Dragonholme fleet again, and the men living in the village to crew such a fleet.

'Mrs Johnstone isn't feeling too well and has taken to her bed. I dropped by earlier for a wee chaff,' said Marika.

'Is she bad?'

'Nothing that a few days in bed won't cure. That and a dram or two.'

Sheila smiled. Mrs Johnstone was well known to like her dram, although that was something the biddy could little afford nowadays.

'I'll drop by later with a half bottle,' Sheila said.

Sheila returned the knife to Agnes Perlie, saying she'd

fair enjoyed that. Then she went back to the house where she found Pat knitting and David playing with some tin soldiers behind a chair.

'There's a letter come for you – I put it over there beside the bread bin,' Pat said.

Sheila read the letter through, swearing under her breath. 'It's from the Renvoize Yard in Cornwall. They've turned me down as well,' she said angrily.

Pat's mouth tightened with concern. 'They were the last were they not?'

'The last in a long list from Lerwick to Falmouth. Every British yard that builds fishing boats has now turned down my order.'

She screwed the letter into a ball, and threw it from her. King Campbell was what Tom McIndoe had said James was cried, and by Christ that was right enough.

'Is there nowhere else you can try?' asked Pat.

'Perhaps Holland or Brittany, but I would have imagined he would have thought of that. He has strong connections over there as well. I've no doubt he can cut me off there just as he can here,' Sheila answered, her voice leaden with despair.

David glanced round from behind the chair where he was playing, saw his mummy's expression, and burst out crying.

Sheila immediately went to him and scooped him into her arms. She rocked him back and forth in an effort to console him.

'You look so unhappy,' he wailed, and hugged her tight.

Tears sprang into her own eyes then. He was such a dear wee lad, and aye concerned for her, just as his father had always been.

She took him over to where there was a bottle of lemonade – lemmy loo he called it – and poured him a glass. That stopped his crying, and brought a smile of pleasure to his face.

'Didn't you once tell me that Georgina pal of yours

from the war belonged to a family that owned a big Glasgow shipbuilding yard, a yard that's built several of the P&O and Cunard ships?' Pat said suddenly.

It was something that had come to Pat just as she was going off to sleep the night before, and which she'd forgotten about again until the last few moments.

'Yes I did,' Sheila answered, recalling the conversation. The yard in question was the MS Yard in Yoker, a large concern and the fount of the Murchison–Stewart money.

'Well maybe they can help somehow. If nothing else it's at least worth a try,' Pat suggested.

'But they build ocean liners!' Sheila protested.

Pat shrugged. 'It seems to me it wouldn't do any harm to have a word with them. They can only say no like everyone else after all.'

Pat was quite right; they could only say no, Sheila thought. She had everything to gain, and nothing to lose.

The big problem was that she hadn't been in touch with Georgina for ages. They had seen one another, and frequently corresponded, after the war. Then Georgina had married a stockbroker chap called Donald Galloway, and their relationship had petered out.

'Well?'

Sheila refilled David's glass, and gave him a quick kiss on the tip of his nose.

'I'll write this evening,' she replied.

Georgina lived in the Newlands Manor House, a splendid example of the very best of Scottish architecture. Newlands was an area in Glasgow's south side where the toffiest of the toffs lived, and the Galloways were the toffiest of the lot.

Sheila exclaimed on seeing that Georgina was pregnant, with only seven weeks to go.

Georgina, the picture of blooming motherhood, told Sheila this would be her third: there being Katie, whom

Sheila had met, and Kirsty, whom Sheila hadn't yet met.

Sheila handed over the mindings she'd brought, and said she'd have to send something for Kirsty. Georgina told her the girls were upstairs; they'd be down shortly.

Georgina commented on how well Sheila was looking, and expressed disappointment that she hadn't brought David with her. Sheila explained there'd been a long-standing arrangement for Pat to take him to Calderpark Zoo that day. He was mad keen on snakes, and this was to be a special treat before he returned to school at the conclusion of the summer holidays.

'Oh but it's grand to see you again!' Georgina breathed, and coming to Sheila swept her into her arms, hugging her hard.

They talked of Maricourt. Sheila told Georgina about Graeme Hurley who'd passed through there near the end of the Somme, and how Graeme was tutoring her nephew in Dragonholme, and doing a grand job of it too.

'And how about you, have you found anyone else yet?' Georgina asked.

Sheila gave a small smile, and shook her head.

Georgina returned Sheila's smile, but her eyes showed her concern. It was a long time since Andrew's death, and if Sheila hadn't been counting the years, she had.

Over coffee, Sheila got down to the real reason for her visit. 'This isn't purely a social visit, Georgina. What I wanted to know was if your family still owned the MS Yard.'

Georgina gazed at her over her cup, one eyebrow raised in surprise. 'Yes, we do. My brother Johnnie's in charge since father retired and took mother off to live in the south of France.' Georgina sat her cup down on its saucer, waiting for some explanation. 'Well?' she said at last. 'Are you going to tell me what is going on?'

Sheila slowly stirred her coffee. 'I'd like to meet your brother. I'm looking for a man who knows about boats.' And with that, she launched into her story.

*   *   *

Georgina brought Johnnie down to Dragonholme the following Sunday. She'd persuaded him that he'd been working too hard and needed a break; and that a day trip to her friend Sheila's on the coast was just what the doctor ordered.

Georgina and Sheila had already decided that Georgina wouldn't tell Johnnie that Sheila particularly wanted to speak to him. That fact would emerge in Dragonholme.

Johnnie Murchison-Stewart was short and stocky with a broad, flat face. Physically, he and Georgina were as different as chalk and cheese. All they had in common was their sandy-coloured hair, and the fact that neither of them would have won a prize in any beauty competition.

Georgina and Johnnie arrived in Dragonholme at lunchtime to find the cold buffet that Sheila and Pat had prepared already on the table.

Sheila took to Johnnie right off. There was a bluff, no nonsense quality about him that reminded her of Davey, her da.

'I hope the drive here wasn't too much for you,' Sheila said to Georgina as they sat down to eat. 'It's a pretty long ride.'

'Not at all,' Georgina assured her happily, helping herself to the ham. 'If anything, I feel elated by it.'

'Georgina's been telling me about the little tent you had to share at Maricourt,' Johnnie said conversationally. 'It's just as well you got on together.'

'We didn't always. Not when we were at Cowcaddens General Hospital,' Sheila admitted with a smile.

Georgina blushed.

'Oh?' prompted Johnnie, looking from his sister to her friend.

'When I first met her she considered me a right little peasant,' Sheila grinned.

'I wish I could deny it,' said Georgina ruefully. 'But, unfortunately, it's true. I was a proper stuck up prig in those days.'

Johnnie helped himself to bread. 'If the war did

266

nothing else it helped change a lot of out-of-date attitudes, and a damn good thing too.'

There followed a conversation about how the class structures had begun to change during the war, and were continuing to change. The old barriers between the classes were now not nearly as rigid as they once had been.

'I'm glad something decent came out of all that awfulness,' Sheila said quietly but not without bitterness.

Pat and Georgina exchanged an anxious look. Neither of them had any doubt as to what – or whom – she referred.

An awkward silence settled on the company for a few seconds, finally broken by Sheila herself when she asked, 'What did you do during the war, Johnnie?'

Normally he glossed over his years in service, but now he felt it necessary to go into some of the details. 'I was a junior officer in the Navy, for most of the conflict. Aboard the *Galatea*, a light cruiser.'

'I know that name,' Sheila said thoughtfully.

'The *Galatea* had the dubious honour of being the first British ship to make contact with the German fleet at the Battle of Jutland. She was talked about in the newspapers a lot for a while.' Even in the homely warmth of Sheila's cottage, he could vividly recall that long ago afternoon of 31 May, 1916. He gave a wry smile. 'I was very lucky. Just before Jutland I was nearly transferred to the battle cruiser *Queen Mary*, which was blown up and sunk with her entire crew.'

Again, a heavy silence settled over the table while everyone thought about the twists of fate by which men lived and died.

Johnnie's talking about the sinking of the *Queen Mary* gave Sheila the opening she needed. 'As someone who's been close to being sunk yourself, you'd be interested in the Dragonholme disaster,' she said.

Johnnie raised one sandy eyebrow. 'What disaster was that?'

267

'Why don't you and I walk down to the beach after lunch and I'll tell you all about it,' she smiled.

Across the table, Georgina gave her a small nod of approval.

As Sheila and Johnnie strolled through the village after lunch, she chatted on about Dragonholme, and her childhood there. She spoke of Davey, her ma, her brothers, and Eric. She could speak of them now without pain, but not without sadness. Then she spoke about the Dragonholme fleet.

'They were such bonny boats, she sighed, her eyes far away. 'All twenty-eight of them. And I tell you this, Johnnie, when they came sailing into harbour laden down with fish, and the wives and the sweethearts and the friends were all there waving and calling to them, and the seagulls were circling and shrieking above, and . . .' She trailed off, tears falling down her cheeks. 'There wasn't a better or more inspiring sight this side of Heaven,' she finished. in a whisper.

Her words touched Johnnie deeply. His eyes rarely left her as they continued down to the beach.

They stopped a few feet up from the furthest reaches of the water, and there Sheila told Johnnie how the disaster had happened, and how it was now her dream to rebuild the lost Dragonholme fleet and save the village from extinction. He listened to her entire story without saying a word.

Sheila laid Johnnie's letter down, feeling sick with disappointment. When Pat and David arrived back at the house almost twenty minutes later they found her sitting staring blankly into space.

'What's wrong with you?' Pat demanded.

Sheila took a deep breath, and brought herself out of her dream. 'I've finally heard from Johnnie Murchison-Stewart at MS,' she said.

'He received Mr McIndoe's plans safely then?' Pat asked excitedly.

'Yes, he did.'

Walking back from the beach the day he and Georgina had visited Dragonholme, Johnnie had quizzed her about drifters, the building of which he'd admitted he knew nothing about.

He'd wondered if Tom McIndoe up in Aberdeen would let him have the plans for the boats that Tom had intended building. She had said she would write to Tom and ask him to send Johnnie the plans, pretty certain that Tom would comply for friendship's sake.

'Well, when do you get your boats?' Pat prompted.

Sheila smiled hollowly. 'I don't.'

'What? But I thought he'd committed himself.'

'I was taking a lot for granted, apparently. He said he would like to build them for me, and I suppose in my enthusiasm I took that to mean he would.'

Pat took the letter Sheila handed her. 'So why won't he?'

'Not won't, *can't*. He'd hoped to be able to manipulate the orders his yard has on its books so that he could fit in my tiddlers. Apparently he's tried, and it's impossible. Every square inch of the yard is booked solid for years to come. So far in advance he can't even give me a date when he could start work on my order.'

'Oh, lass!' Pat whispered. This was a cruel blow indeed.

'It seems James Campbell has beaten me after all,' Sheila said. But her tone was more angry than resigned.

Sheila's eyes opened suddenly, and she wondered what had wakened her. It wasn't David, who was sleeping peacefully by her side.

She was about to turn over again, when she heard a scraping sound right outside the front door, followed seconds later by a muffled cough.

Sheila froze. As was the custom in Dragonholme, the door wasn't locked. Whoever was out there only had to turn the handle to walk right in.

There it was again, more scraping; as if the person was running something over the door. What could be going on?

Moonlight shone through the window. With that to guide her, she slid noiselessly from the bed, tip-toed over to the range, and picked up the old brass-handled poker standing there.

Her heart was racing, the blood pounding in her ears, as she stealthily crossed over to the door, stopping, breath held to listen. All she heard was the rustle of a breeze, nothing else.

Lifting the poker high, she grasped the door handle and jerked the door open suddenly. But whoever had been there was gone.

Something flashed down the road, black on white. Putting a hand on the door she started to lean forward to try and get a better view, then pulled her hand away with a cry. The door was covered with something which from the smell and texture could only be one thing.

In the still moonlight her eyes scanned the sleeping houses and shadowy landscapes, but there was nothing to be seen. What sort of person, she wondered, would do such a filthy thing? And why to her? With one last look around, she went back inside, this time bolting the door behind her.

After washing her fouled hand, she sat herself down on one of the kitchen chairs. She was too awake now to go back to sleep, her mind spinning with turbulent thoughts. In all of Dragonholme, there was no one she could think of capable of such a disgusting act. There was no one who wasn't her friend. Was it some sort of joke she wasn't seeing because it was in such bad taste? No, that couldn't be it. If it wasn't some crazy outsider, it must be someone with a grudge against her.

And then she thought of James. As crazy as it sounded, there was no one else it could be. He was the only person in Dragonholme with any reason to hate her or to wish to frighten her.

Well, she was damned if she was going to let him get away with it. She'd confront him, face to face, and tell him what she thought of this sort of childish, revolting behaviour.

Her first impulse was to get dressed right then and march into the Hall, waking them all up if necessary, especially his lordship.

On second thoughts, though, she decided to wait till morning, when she would be in total control of herself when she saw him. She knew James Campbell well enough to know that he regarded female emotion as weakness. If she went to him now she would only end up in tears of rage and hurt.

She would shed no more tears for James Campbell, she decided grimly. Not one.

The next morning, having got up early to clean off the door before David could see it and upset himself, she told Pat what had happened during the night. Directly after breakfast she climbed into the Silver Ghost and pointed it in the direction of the Hall.

It was her first visit there since she'd run away to Glasgow. Seeing it up close again brought a sudden rush of memories and feelings that made her heart skip a beat.

Annie Tripp had left James's employ shortly after Fiona's death, as had Agnes and Pat Dyer. Annie, she'd been told, was living in London, working for a family in Bloomsbury. She had no knowledge of where either Agnes or Pat might be.

She'd heard that a lot of the Hall had been closed down, and even from the outside she could see that this was true. It didn't take an expert eye to see that exterior maintenance had been badly neglected. The roof and large areas of the walls needed attending to.

She remembered the roof of another grand house, then. One which when she'd seen it had been recently strafed by the guns of a German aeroplane. In the peaceful morning she shuddered at the memory. All those dear dead boys, including her own Andrew, blown away like so much chaff in the wind.

She thought of Lieutenant Lewis who'd been among those sitting down to dinner that night in the chateau. It had been a relief to discover he'd survived; she'd read recently he was making something of a name for himself as a writer.

James McCudden, Andrew's friend had been among those killed, though in his case, ironically, as the result of a simple flying accident towards the end of the war when he'd stalled on take-off and crashed into a wood.

She wondered if Château Roisselle had been restored to its former glory after hostilities ended, hoping it had. As for Dragonholme Hall, she considered it criminal that James Campbell was allowing it to rot around him. In its own austere way, it was every bit as imposing as that French château.

The butler who answered her knock was new to her. 'Good morning,' she said in her most formal manner. 'I would like to see Mr Campbell. Tell him Mrs Lack is here.'

The butler eyed her coldly, making no move to show her into the house. 'I'm afraid the master is not up yet,' he informed her archly. It was obvious he didn't consider Sheila a good enough reason for disturbing the laird.

'Oh no?' said Sheila, her temper boiling again. 'Well it's about time he bloody well got up,' and with that she brushed past the astonished man and into the small reception room. It had a musty smell about it, and was crying out for a good airing. She ran her hand along the top of a picture, and the rim of a vase, wiping the dirt from her fingers with a grimace.

272

Some minutes later James appeared in the doorway, a dressing gown hastily thrown over his pyjamas. His hair was dishevelled, his eyes puffy, and his cheeks flushed. It took no special talent to guess that he'd been drinking heavily the night before.

'Why have you come bursting into my home like this?' he demanded, though it was clear he was more astonished than angry to see her.

'Shit.'

James blinked, visibly taken aback.

'Shit, or if you prefer, shite,' she repeated, her colour high with anger and her eyes ablaze.

He had the uneasy thought that were she a man she would hit him.

'I've no idea what you're raving about,' he snapped back. 'It's a little early in the morning for visiting.'

'Did you do the smearing yourself, or did one of your toadies go sneaking down to my cottage last night and do it for you?' she yelled, stepping towards him with a hand raised.

James cleared his throat, suddenly realizing that she was serious. 'I think you'd better sit down and explain to me what this is all about,' he said calmly. 'Just what are you accusing me of?'

God he was good, she thought. She'd expected some show of guilt or embarrassment, but there was no hint of either. In a voice rigid with frost, she described the events of the previous night, and how her reasoning had inevitably brought her to him. 'After all,' she concluded, 'you're the only person around who has ever tried to hurt me or mine.'

When she was done, he turned on her angrily. 'What sort of man do you think I am?' he shouted. 'Do you think I run around in the middle of the night, playing practical jokes?'

'I know exactly what kind of man you are, James Campbell,' she replied, looking at him as though she could see right through him. 'That's why I'm here.'

He offered her a seat, but she refused to sit down. 'Well, this time, Mrs Lack,' he said smoothly, 'you are very wrong. You might ask yourself what you think I have to gain by such a trick.'

She drew herself up to her full height, eyeing him coldly. 'A man who wouldn't stop at depriving a poor widow of her rightful monies, wouldn't stop at smearing a little shit on a door. A man who would destroy an entire village just because of his own stubborn pride is capable of anything. I don't think that what you do or do not have to gain has anything to do with it.'

Speechless, he stared at her for some seconds. For the first time since she ran out on him he understood not only that she didn't love him, but that she felt nothing but contempt for him. All these years he had kept within him the secret thought that she loved him still, that the joy with which she had filled his life and his dreams had touched her too. Even now, even after his humiliation in the pub, he had refused to believe that there was nothing left, that he had destroyed her feelings for him so completely that nothing could redeem them.

'I didn't do it,' he said softly, incapable of fighting. 'I swear it.'

Her expression didn't change, but a sudden look of uncertainty flashed through her eyes. 'If you didn't do it, or arrange to have it done, then who did?' she asked challengingly.

But it was there, just a shadow of fear, just enough to make his heart ache. If only he didn't still love her. If only he weren't even now prepared to do anything she asked, to make any sacrifice, anything at all, if only she would be his. 'I'm afraid,' he said, his tone one of dismissal, 'that I can't help you there. Perhaps you have more enemies in Dragonholme than you thought.'

'But you still maintain it's not you?'

'Not this time,' he smiled. If she would give him a sign, if she would ask for his help, then he would give it.

She picked up her purse from the table on which she'd

laid it. 'You're not only contemptible,' she said hotly, her colour rising with her voice. 'You're despicable as well.'

'You don't need the butler to see you out, do you? You know the way well enough, I'm sure.'

The outside door banged behind her. Sheila stood on the steps for a minute, collecting her wits, wondering what to believe. From behind the heavy door of Dragonholme Hall, she thought she could hear the faint sound of James Campbell's laughter.

Sheila was chaffing with Betsy Thomson, wife of one of the *Lorella*'s crew, when she saw a familiar car appear in Brae Street. It was the car in which Johnnie Murchison-Stewart had brought his sister Georgina to Dragonholme the Sunday they'd come down together.

Hastily, Sheila took her leave of Betsy and hurried after the car which was now headed in the direction of her house.

'Johnnie!' she cried in greeting as he climbed out of the driver's seat. She could see now that he was alone.

Glancing round he caught sight of her, and gave her an acknowledging wave.

'Well this is a pleasant surprise,' she said to him on reaching his side.

'I was going to write, then decided to come down instead,' he smiled.

A tightness in his voice told her something was wrong. 'Come away in and we'll have a cup of coffee, or a dram if you prefer?'

'I'll have both if you don't mind,' he laughed as they went inside.

Pat was there with David and Ian. Sheila poured Johnnie a stiff whisky, then made coffee for the three adults. When Johnnie kept to polite conversation, she realized he wanted to talk to her privately, and suggested they go back outside, which he readily agreed to.

'Now what's this all about, Johnnie?' she asked, perching herself on a front mudguard of the Silver Ghost.

Johnnie's eyes clouded with the shadow of anger. 'I had a visit at the yard from your Mr James Campbell,' he said heavily.

'Oh, aye?'

'I've no idea how he found out, but he knew that you'd approached me to build four drifters for you.'

'And?'

'What he didn't know was that I'd already turned you down. He thought I'd be going ahead with the order.'

Sheila stared at Johnnie attentively. 'So what happened?' she prompted.

'He threatened me!' he exploded, his expression still showing his astonishment. 'The man had the gall, the bare-faced cheek, to threaten me!' It was obvious that no one had ever threatened him before.

Sheila had to restrain a tiny smile. 'Then you explained to him you'd turned me down and that was that?'

Johnnie's chin rose aggressively, proudly. 'I did nothing of the sort. I told him my affairs were none of his business, and for him to get the hell out of my office!'

Now she did smile, her laughter easy and warm. 'Good for you. And did he?'

'He did indeed. But not before saying I would never get another order from the Yellow Funnel Line, in which, apparently, he has a great many shares – and a great deal of influence. And that their current order with us would be cancelled.'

'What size of ship is that to be?'

'An eighteen-thousand-ton cargo vessel for the Far East run.'

Sheila blanched. 'You mustn't lose an order that size on account of me, Johnnie. If you won't tell him, then I'll see he finds out that you're not building my drifters.'

'Oh, but I am!' Johnnie winked. 'I couldn't very well not do them now.'

276

Sheila's heart leapt. 'But you've no space at the yard. You said so in your letter.'

'I have space now that I won't be building for Yellow Funnel. I intend building your four drifters in the space their ship would have needed.'

'But it'll cost you financially. My four drifters will come nowhere near compensating you for what you'll lose on the other order.'

A hard, determined expression came into Johnnie's eyes. 'I will not be blackmailed, Sheila. Not by Campbell or anyone else. All his interference will achieve is to allow me to do what I would have preferred all along. To build your boats. The loss of a little income is neither here nor there.'

'He has so much influence . . .'

'Not in my world he doesn't. About all he can do is cancel the Yellow Funnel order and that's it. Frankly, Sheila,' winked Johnnie, 'if I'd understood from the beginning what a pompous tyrant the man was I would have said yes if it meant building them in the road.'

'Oh James Campbell, you had me beaten and didn't know it. Now you've inadvertently given me, and Dragonholme, a reprieve! Sheila could contain her excitement no more. On sudden impulse she jumped to her feet and threw her arms around Johnnie.

'You won't be sorry,' she laughed.

It was the week before Christmas, 1923. Sheila, David and Pat were at the MS Yard for the handing-over ceremony. The four drifters had been launched a fortnight previously; since then the finishing touches had been made, and they'd been fitted out.

Sheila was ecstatic about the boats; even Tom McIndoe with his vast experience of building fishing craft couldn't have come up with better. Johnnie, and the MS Yard, had done her proud.

David clutched Sheila's hand and stared at the drifters

riding in a line. The foremost was called the *Andrew*, after his father, the one behind the *Davey B.*, after his grandpa, the third the *Peg B.*, after his granny, and the fourth the *Dougal B.*, after the oldest of his uncles who'd been killed in the Dragonholme disaster. He liked the *Andrew* best, although it was no different from the others.

He looked round for George Jorgesson, who was somewhere about. He wanted George to take him on board the *Andrew* so he could go behind the wheel and pretend to steer. George was good at games and pretending with him. George was fun.

Johnnie was standing beside Sheila ticking items off a list. He was triple checking to ensure everything was just as it should be. He intended the handover to be as smooth as silk.

The crews of the four drifters were present, all men hand-picked by George and Sheila. They would be sailing the boats down the Clyde, round the top of Scotland, then southwards to Dragonholme where the boats would remain till the start of the season.

Of the twenty-four men who'd be working the boats, twenty-three were new to Dragonholme, sixteen of them bringing families with them when they'd arrived to take up residence. The population of the village had now doubled since Sheila bought the *Sheila B.*

David spied George and waved to him, wriggling his hand free from his mother's when George beckoned him over. Sheila let David go, then turned to Duncy Laidlaw with a smile as he came up to her. She'd made Duncy skipper of the *Peg B.*

'I thought this the appropriate moment to thank you for the chance you've given me, Sheila. Neither Marika nor I will ever forget it,' Duncy said shyly.

'I know you could have been a skipper before now if you'd chosen to leave Dragonholme, so it's no favour I'm doing you: only giving you what's long past your due,' Sheila said lightly.

'No one will work harder for you, I promise you that.'

278

'I know,' she answered softly, giving his hand a squeeze.

She watched Duncy walk away, lurching from side to side in a typical fisherman's gait. The boat cried for her Ma would be well safe in his hands. Peg would have been pleased he was to be the skipper – she'd always had a soft spot for Duncy Laidlaw.

Johnnie made his final tick. All was now ready; the handing-over could take place. He signalled to the two apprentices waiting close by, who immediately ran off to his office. Then, in a loud voice, he called everyone to gather round, raising his hands for quiet. When he had it he made a short speech about the drifters and how pleased the yard had been to build them. With that, he presented the papers of ownership to Sheila. It was now her turn to make a speech.

There were tears in her eyes which she couldn't hide. 'I just want you all to know how proud I am – for myself and for my son – to be the owner of these very special boats. I wish all who sail in them well, and that every trip will be a successful and prosperous one.' She smiled through her tears as the crews raised a cheer. Her voice trembling, she went on to thank the yard workers who'd built the boats, saying what a grand and expert job they'd done. Putting her hands together she applauded their effort and the fishermen joined in.

At the conclusion of her speech the two apprentices pushed their way through the crowd, each carrying a crate of whisky and a box of glasses.

Drinks were quickly poured and the new drifters toasted by name.

When that was over, George started getting the fishermen aboard. He himself was sailing on the *Dougal B.* as an extra crew member. Sheila had wanted him to be with the boats on their passage round the top of Scotland, for he was now admiral of her six boats, if not yet admiral of the other Dragonholme four as well.

'Without you this day would never have been possible. I'm forever in your debt,' Sheila said to Johnnie.

Johnnie blushed, glancing down at his shoes.

'Johnnie?'

He looked up again.

Taking hold of his lapels she kissed him squarely on the lips. 'Thank you,' she whispered.

George, standing to one side waiting for a word with Sheila before he too got on board, watched the gentleness of the kiss she gave to Johnnie. Of course, he should have known there was more between those two than a contract. For the first time, he really looked at Johnnie Murchison-Stewart – at his appealing face and expensive clothes; at his obvious poise and self-assurance.

Ach it was a daft notion anyway, he told himself, to think a man like he had a chance with a woman like Sheila. Daft beyond belief to even think that she would ever let his rough hands touch her, would ever touch his lips with hers.

As the four drifters steamed off down the Clyde Sheila gave a special wave to George, who was staring straight at her, and wondered why he didn't wave in return.

9

Sheila swallowed some beer, glad to wet her throat. It was absolutely boiling in the Community Hall where Rhona and Graeme Hurley's wedding reception was being held. She took another swig, and sighed with happy weariness. She'd just come off the dance floor and was feeling exhausted but merry.

Sheila stared across to where Rhona was chatting with Mrs Jorgesson, George's mother. How radiant Rhona looked; how radiant and how happy. Aye, ecstatically happy. It was a long time now since those nightmare days after Jack's death – those lonely, empty years.

It was just over a month ago that Rhona had come to

the house one night in a fit of giggles, to tell Sheila she was getting wed to Graeme. She was carrying his child.

As for Graeme himself, the man was hardly recognizable as the whey-faced cougher Sheila had brought to Dragonholme only one year before. The good sea air and Rhona's cooking (for, though he had his own wee house he'd eaten most of his meals with Rhona and Ian) had worked wonders. There was now permanent colour in his cheeks, sparkle in his eyes, and a new excitement in his heart – though that was more down to love than diet, Sheila thought.

The reception had been deliberately timed for the night before the Dragonholme boats sailed to the northern fishing grounds. That way, there were two celebrations instead of just one. For days before, Sheila had been driving everyone mad with her plans for the party, and indeed, the whole village seemed to have been involved in them. And now the whole village was here laughing and dancing, talking and smiling – almost as though the past had never happened.

She glanced over to where Rhona's Ian was shyly talking to a lass belonging to one of the new families, a bonny lass who was hanging on his every word.

They were all pleased with Ian's progress. Graeme Hurley was doing as marvellous a job with the boy as with himself.

Sheila gazed contentedly around the hall. It had been a long time since she'd felt so excited and so alive – so full of purpose. Could it have been only a year ago that the thought of David's going to school had filled her with such dread and a sense of futility? Only a year ago that she had felt so tired and so old? Then the only joy in her life had been her son – now it was her life itself that offered joy.

Sheila was just wondering if she was up to another whirl around the dance floor, when she spied her other sister-in-law, Maggie, and her husband, Ian McPherson. She had seen them once or twice during the past year, but had never had the opportunity or the desire for a serious conversation. Seeing them both across the room, obviously enjoying themselves, she decided that the time might be right for the word she'd been wanting to have with McPherson. By all accounts, he was prospering in Portnessie and had a finger in a number of lucrative pies.

Even as she approached them, a smile on her lips, Sheila was thinking to herself that the years hadn't changed Maggie at all. She was still the same bitch she used to be, a little older and leaner now, a little less hungry and less frightened, but still petty and obsessed with her own interests.

'Well, Sheila,' exclaimed Maggie as she came up to them. 'How nice to see you. And what a smashing party this is. It must have cost a fortune.'

Sheila gave the other woman an unenthusiastic hug and shook Ian's large, rough hand. 'You're looking well, the two of you,' she said sweetly. 'I hope you've had enough to drink and all.'

They stood chatting for a while, Maggie seeming to confine her comments to how the other women looked or danced or how drunk their men were, until finally Sheila could take no more and turned to McPherson with a different look in her eye and a different tone in her voice. 'I think,' she said, 'that I might have an idea you'd be interested in.' Instantly, he was all ears. Sheila Beattie's reputation as a shrewd and astute businesswoman had not escaped his notice.

Sheila told him about her plans for revitalizing the village. 'My original aim was to own twenty boats by the end of five years,' she explained. 'But lately I've been thinking of increasing that figure. If the six boats we're sending out this year make the same sort of profit as the two we had last season, nothing, in fact, will stand in my way.'

The problem, she continued, was that with the village beginning to get back on its feet there was a new need for the shops and businesses that had previously closed down to open again. The chandler's was a prime example of what she was talking about. Already it was so desperately needed that it couldn't fail to start to show a handsome return within a couple of years for whoever had re-opened it.

Then again there was Ian's father, who was somewhere in the hall. He wasn't getting any younger. How would the Dragonholme fish get to Portnessie when the old man died. Wouldn't it be worth Ian's while to consider going into partnership with his da? Once the partnership was formed they could modernize, get rid of the old horses and carts and replace them with lorries which were far more efficient, and less expensive to run.

Ian's initial response was no less than she'd expected. 'Why don't you invest in all this yourself?' he asked.

'I might be well off,' laughed Sheila, 'but I'm not Carnegie. The bulk of my capital is tied up in my boats. I don't have anything extra.'

Maggie chipped in then. 'If these shops and all are such excellent investments why hasn't the laird been tempted? Isn't James Campbell known as a man always out to further line his pockets whenever possible?'

Sheila had to laugh. 'James Campbell has lost all interest in Dragonholme,' she explained. 'He never comes near the village any more. He'd be the last person to invest, profit or no.'

Ian stroked his chin. 'Well,' he said at last. 'You've certainly given me a lot to think about. It'll all need looking into, of course. But, aye, I'm interested, right enough.'

They left it at that. After a few minutes, Sheila excused herself to go and check on David, who was careering about the hall with several of the other children present.

He had a dirty face from crawling underneath chairs, and a skinned knee, but he was obviously thoroughly enjoying himself, so Sheila left him to get on with it.

Hector and Rosie Burnside danced by, Rosie

wheeching and kicking the air as they went past. Sheila looked for George, thinking she'd like to have a dance with him, but he was nowhere in sight.

She was a wee bit concerned about George. It was nothing she could quite put her finger on, but over the past months it seemed to her that he'd been more and more formal with her rather than less. Even though they had had to work so closely and she had come to rely not only on his skill and expertise but on his quiet support and understanding, she sensed that they were less friends now than on the day she re-met him in the pub.

She had a birl with Shet Perlie instead, then was collared by Miss Dalziel who asked if she might have a word.

Miss Dalziel said she wanted to speak to Sheila about Graeme Hurley because Hurley was employed by Sheila. Now the thing was this; she'd been soldiering on as schoolteacher past normal retirement age because, with the state the village had been in, she'd known no one would replace her, and what would have happened to the small amount of children left to Dragonholme then?

But it wasn't a small amount anymore, thanks to the new families Sheila was bringing in; and the truth of the matter was that with the increased numbers she just couldn't cope. She wanted to stand down and spend the days left to her at home and in her garden.

The obvious choice to replace her was Hurley, a far, far, superior teacher to what she'd ever been. With him at the school it wouldn't only be Ian Beattie who could pass university entrance exams.

But as Sheila was Hurley's employer she felt it only right and proper to get Sheila's permission before talking to Hurley himself. If he agreed to apply for the job there would be no question about him being appointed, she could vouch for that.

Sheila said of course Miss Dalziel had her permission to speak to Hurley. She didn't see why he couldn't be schoolteacher and also tutor Ian.

The newlyweds weren't going away on honeymoon, so Miss Dalziel said she'd have a chat with Hurley sometime during the next week.

This was excellent news, Sheila thought after Miss Dalziel had left her, and felt as pleased as if she'd arranged it herself. A teacher of Graeme Hurley's ability would do no end of good for the youth of Dragonholme, and give Hurley a fine secure post into the bargain.

She glanced round to see Ian McPherson staring at her thoughtfully. Waving, he then turned his attention back to Maggie who was deep in conversation with Lena Murray.

She had lied to Ian. It was well within her financial ability to open up some of the shops and other businesses she'd spoken to him about, but she didn't want to. She felt that it was important that Dragonholme belonged to all its people, not to one person alone.

About an hour-and-a-half later, she found David fast asleep behind the casks of beer that made up a large section of the bar, and decided it was time to go home. She told Pat to stay, but Pat insisted on going home as well. They agreed to take it in turns to carry the sleeping boy back.

Having made their good-byes they went out into the cool, starry night. 'He's becoming a ton weight,' sighed Sheila as they made their way along the time-worn path. 'Soon he'll be too heavy for the two of us combined.'

They were just passing the graveyard, walking slowly and companionably beneath the familar sky, when a figure suddenly leapt out from behind a headstone and struck Pat a blow on the temple which knocked her senseless to the ground.

It all happened so quickly that Sheila could only stand and gape, her arms automatically tightening around her sleeping child. Then the short, stocky figure whirled on her.

Sheila broke into a run, but had only got a few yards when the assailant caught up with her. An arm encircled her throat, and at the same time she was punched in the back so hard that she dropped David.

She tried to scream, but couldn't find the air. She heard David start to cry, then she was propelled into the graveyard itself where she was flung to the grass between two stones.

Her only thought was of David. It didn't matter what happened to her as long as he was all right. 'Run, son! Run!' she gasped as hands frantically tore at her dress. All she could see was a hideously distorted face looming over her.

She tried to scream as he tugged and tore at her underdrawers but had barely the strength to whimper. With one last effort she started to sit up, only to be hit savagely in the mouth and knocked prostrate again.

Her underdrawers ripped and fell apart. She moaned in revulsion as a hand grabbed and squeezed her viciously. Then she heard him fumbling with his own clothes.

'Mummy!' David called out from close by. He hadn't run as she'd told him to.

The man laughed, a sound with no humanity in it, and threw himself on top of her.

But he never entered her. Just as he was about to, he suddenly flew sideways, rolling over and over in the sloping grass.

Quickly George bent to Sheila. As he did, the attacker leapt to his feet and went racing off through the graveyard.

When Sheila saw George's anxious features peering down at her she let out a cry of relief. Then David, tears streaming from his eyes, was in her embrace, she instantly calming, and soothing him, telling him it was all over now, George had come to their rescue and frightened away the nasty man.

George hurried over to Pat who was groaning as she started to come round. The temple where she'd been hit had already swollen into a sizeable lump.

He decided to leave Pat for the moment, and ran in the

direction the would-be rapist had taken, Sheila shouting after him to be careful.

Still consoling the extremely distraught David, Sheila tugged her dress down to cover the lower half of her body which had been completely exposed. Her now useless underdrawers lay to one side, having been ripped right down the middle. She shuddered to think what had so nearly happened to her.

Sheila and David made their way to Pat who was sitting up and nursing her head. 'It feels as if it has been used as a football,' she moaned.

They were all standing holding on to one another when George returned. 'I'm afraid the bastard's got clean away,' he said angrily. 'Did you recognize him by any chance?' he asked Sheila.

'No,' she sighed. 'He must have been wearing a mask – his face was all distorted.'

George stared out across the silent stones. 'All I saw was what he was doing to you,' he said thickly.

'About to do,' she whispered gently. 'You stopped him before he did.'

'Thank God for that,' he said, thinking that wouldn't make any difference if he could yet get hold of the man; he'd still beat the bastard to a bloody pulp.

He'd escorted them to their house before returning to the reception to warn those there of what had happened. His intention was to roust out a number of the men still sober enough to be of any use and make a search of the village and seafront. 'It was lucky I decided to go home right after you,' he said to Sheila as they walked, 'or there's no knowing how things might have turned out.'

On reaching the house, he ushered them inside, then waited till Sheila had locked the door. They watched him run as fast as he was able back to the Community Hall.

Sheila got David stripped and into bed where he lay noisily sucking his thumb. She then attended to Pat's bump, putting a hot bread poultice on it to bring down the swelling. Sheila didn't have to tell Pat how lucky she'd been; a blow such as she'd had could quite easily have been fatal.

When the hot poultice had been bandaged into position, Sheila took off her clothes and went to the sink where she gave herself a good all-over wash. In the middle of this she started to shake, her body convulsed with sobs. Pat came over to her and the pair of them clung to one another. 'I could murder a drink,' Sheila said at last. While she put on her dressing gown, Pat poured them both large drams.

Sheila sat with David until he finally drifted off in a troubled sleep. Then she joined Pat sitting by the range where they talked in low tones, speculating about how George and the others were getting on in their search.

A little under an hour later George returned to tell them their attacker hadn't been found. The men had scoured the village from top to bottom, but to no avail.

With no hesitation, he accepted a dram from Sheila. 'Every man in Dragonholme's been accounted for,' he told her. 'So your attacker was most definitely an outsider.' He took a grateful drink, 'Everyone's pretty relieved about that, I can tell you.'

George added that Ian McPherson, who'd aided in the search, would be reporting the matter to the police in Portnessie.

George finished his whisky, and Sheila promptly poured him another. He watched her as she set the bottle back down. She was pale, her features drawn; he thought she looked absolutely marvellous.

He asked her if, in the light of what had happened, she wanted her boats to delay sailing northwards for several days, but she said she didn't see any advantage in that – in her opinion it was best things went ahead as planned.

'You're no doubt right' he agreed. 'The boats will have to go sooner or later. I just hate the idea of the women being left alone when there's a maniac on the loose.' But did not add that it was she who particularly concerned him.

'Aye,' laughed Sheila. 'We fisherwomen are a tough breed, God help us. Besides, we won't be completely alone. Graeme Hurley, Mr Meekie from The Halibut's Tail, and a few others will still be here.'

George sat with them a few minutes longer, then left, and Sheila set about changing Pat's bread poultice which had gone cold.

'A helluva nice man that,' Pat said.

Sheila agreed; George was a helluva nice man. It was on the tip of her tongue to tell Pat the story of George's brothering when she and Eric had rescued him from Tarry Dunbar and the crew of the *Locarno*, but decided against it. For some reason, she didn't want anyone laughing at George, not even in Pat's good-humoured fashion.

Later, when Pat was asleep, Sheila sat in front of the grate with a dram in her hand, her face serious with thought. James Campbell, had he been behind that night's attack? If he had been then this was a frightening dimension to his vendetta against her. Fouling her door was one thing; tonight's incident quite another. Though she could believe him capable of anything – some part of her refused to accept this.

She was certain of one thing: the man himself hadn't been James. He'd been the wrong shape, and even if he'd somehow disguised his shape, she'd still have known if it had been him. A dozen different things would have given that away.

On the other hand, of course, it was entirely possible that her attacker was completely unconnected to James, a violent lunatic simply passing through the district.

Sheila sipped her whisky, then worried a nail. So what should she tell the Portnessie police when they arrived to take a statement from her? Did she tell them about the trouble she'd been having with James? Or not? Did she explain the reason for their rivalry? Make the private past public knowledge and cause for gossip and speculation? Would that help either of them?

But then if he was involved, might not even scandal be preferable to a successful repeat of tonight's attempt? Who was to say it would have stopped at rape? Might not murder have been the end result?

Sheila wiped clammy sweat from her forehead, and drank more whisky.

Only after hours of agonizing, did she decide to give James the benefit of the doubt. She would not mention her suspicions to the police when they came. Sheila sighed as she prepared for bed. In her heart of hearts she just couldn't believe that James Campbell was responsible for the night's events.

Pray God that she wasn't wrong.

Sheila stared up at the partially completed hulls of the three new drifters Johnnie was building for her. They were going to be real beauties, just like the other four from the MS Yard. These were to be called the *Jack B.*, *Bob B.*, and *Albert B.* The first two after her brothers, the last after Albert Ball.

She was in Glasgow to finalize the sale of her house in Kelvinside. She, David and Pat had moved, lock stock and barrel back to Dragonholme three weeks before.

The only thing that had stopped her moving earlier was David's education, but with Graeme Hurley now ensconced as Dragonholme's teacher she had been able to take David away from Kelvinside Academy secure in the knowledge that he would continue to be taught to the same high standard.

And oh how marvellous it was to be back living permanently in Dragonholme! All three of them were loving it.

She glanced over to where Johnnie was deep in conversation with one of his gaffers. Dear sweet Johnnie; he'd become a good friend to her. And she hoped she'd become the same to him.

No, friendship wasn't the right word, she told herself.

290

It was more than that. He was something of a cross between a father and a brother to her.

'Mrs Lack! Mrs Lack!'

Sheila looked round to see Sandra Urquhart, Johnnie's personal secretary, running towards her.

'You're wanted urgently on the telephone by Miss McLuskey,' Sandra gasped, her face flushed and her eyes worried.

Fear gripped Sheila. Something must have happened to David! Pat would be ringing from the village's one telephone box, the only telephone in Dragonholme. It could only be an emergency.

Side-by-side Sheila and Sandra hared for Johnnie's office. Sheila snatched up the telephone as soon as they were in the room. 'What is it Pat?' she demanded, trying to prepare herself for the worst.

Something had happened all right. George Jorgesson was in hospital in Peterhead. All Pat could tell Sheila was the name of the hospital and that George was in a bad way. She had no other details.

'I'll have to go to him,' Sheila shouted into the receiver, not waiting for Pat's reply. 'I'll leave immediately.'

She drove away so quickly her tyres actually smoked. She barely said good-bye to Johnnie.

What in God's name had happened?

The all-pervading smell of the Royal Victoria Hospital, Peterhead, brought back a host of memories – buried memories of Cowcaddens General and Maricourt.

She found out which ward George was in, made her way there and asked to see Sister. Sister McKechnie couldn't have been anything other than a nurse. Everything about her from the tone of her voice to her air of efficiency epitomized the species.

Sheila introduced herself, explained she was George's employer, then asked the extent of his injuries and present condition.

291

George hadn't been in an accident at sea, as she'd decided must have been the case, but a fight ashore. Until a few hours ago the doctors had thought him to have internal injuries, but it had now been established that he didn't.

What he did have was severe bruising. So severely beaten was he, in fact, that he would be off work for the next several weeks. The doctors were adamant about that; he was to have as much rest as possible until the bruising had disappeared, otherwise there could be long-term damaging effects.

'Of course,' replied Sheila. 'That's only reasonable.'

'To you, maybe, but not to Mr Jorgesson,' said Sister McKechnie. He seemed intent on getting back aboard his boat as soon as possible. Sister was obviously determined that this wouldn't happen. 'I'll keep him where he is now until I think he's recovered sufficiently to be discharged,' she concluded.

Sheila said that sounded just like George, who must be fretting in the extreme of being laid up. She appreciated it wasn't visiting hours but could she still see George? 'I've driven all the way from Glasgow to see him,' she pleaded.

Sister McKechnie pursed her mouth. 'That would be highly irregular,' she said shortly.

Sheila replied that she was only too well aware of how big a favour she was asking; rules were rules after all, that's what had been drummed into her when she'd been trained.

'You were a nurse?' Sister McKechnie asked, her look softening fractionally.

'VAD. I served in France.'

'I also served in France.'

Within a few minutes they discovered several people they knew in common.

'Wait here,' Sister told Sheila at the end of their conversation, and disappeared out of her office to order screens put round George's bed.

'Follow me,' she instructed when she returned, and led Sheila down the ward to George's bed where the screens were already in place.

Sheila whispered a thank-you to Sister McKechnie, then turned to the heavily bandaged George. 'I should have thought to bring you some grapes,' she smiled.

'I'm glad you didn't. I hate grapes,' George said, trying to match her smile, but ending in a wince of pain. 'I feel as though I've been run over by a road roller.'

'You look it,' Sheila winked.

George started to chuckle, and winced again.

Sheila ignored the chair provided, and sat on the edge of the bed. 'Tell me about it.'

'I finally met up with the skipper of the *Zodiac*, a huge brute of a Highlandman called Red McGregor,' George explained.

Sheila sighed. All the way here she'd been wondering if this might be to do with the *Zodiac*, one of the Portnessie fleet that had been giving her boats a lot of trouble recently, and costing her a considerable amount of money.

The *Zodiac* had been using its propeller to slice through the warps which held and controlled each individual net, as well as smashing the buoys keeping the net afloat so that the net sank to the bottom and was lost.

Five of Sheila's nets had been lost this way during the past two-and-a-half weeks, and now her admiral had been hospitalized.

George went on to say that the morning before, the *Sheila B.* had been peacefully fishing when the *Zodiac* was spied bearing down on it; and it was obvious what the Portnessie boat's intentions were.

He had already briefed the crew what to do in such an event. They immediately winched the warps aboard and brought lengths of heavy chain on deck. These chains were then attached to the warps at the points where the warps were normally just under the water, and the warps let out again, the chains disappearing into the sea; and the

Sheila B. had pretended to go on fishing. It had been George's ruse, and a good one.

As he'd expected, the *Zodiac* had borne down on the *Sheila B.*'s warps, and just as its propeller was about to make contact with them he had winched the warps in several feet.

His plan had worked as he'd hoped. The warps had been sliced through all right, but at the same time the lengths of chain had wound themselves round the *Zodiac*'s propeller, causing one of the blades to shear away.

The *Zodiac* had wallowed helplessly while the *Sheila B.* retrieved its net, then the *Sheila B.* had steamed away leaving the *Zodiac* to its own devices.

'It was a damn ingenious plan,' Sheila said. 'What happened next?'

After unloading their catch last evening, they'd all gone to Mother Mary's Bar for a celebration on having got their own back on the *Zodiac*. Unknown to them, the *Zodiac* had been taken in tow by another Portnessie trawler and later that evening was brought into Peterhead where it would be laid up until its propeller had been replaced.

At this point of the story George stopped, embarrassed. Continuing, he said it had been about half past eight when the lads had moved on elsewhere, leaving him at Mother Mary's on his own.

Misunderstanding his embarrassment, she asked where the others had gone.

He told her didn't know where they'd gone on to.

'George Jorgesson, you're fibbing,' she teased. 'Tell me where they went.'

There was no getting away from telling Sheila, it was clear she wouldn't give up. 'You promise you won't tell anyone? Some of the men are married,' he stammered.

Sheila grinned. She was pretty certain she knew now what was coming next. 'I promise.'

In a small voice George said his crew had gone to a

brothel much frequented by fishermen, a place where the prices were reasonable and the lassies clean.

'But not you?' Sheila teased.

George blushed, and glanced away. He hadn't gone with the lads because there was only one woman who interested him nowadays; the one sitting on his bed.

But Sheila didn't notice his discomfort. 'Go on George,' she urged.

He told her it had been shortly after the lads had left him that Red McGregor and the crew of the *Zodiac* had appeared in Mother Mary's, having been scouring Peterhead for him and the crew of the *Sheila B*.

McGregor had introduced himself, then said he intended revenging what the *Sheila B*. had done earlier to the *Zodiac*.

He had replied it was McGregor's fault. It was the *Zodiac* which had started it all by cutting warps. But the fiery McGregor wouldn't accept his action had been justified. Like all natural bullies McGregor loved dishing it out, but couldn't take it in return.

'Did you find out if McGregor's warp cutting was on James Campbell's instructions?' Sheila asked.

'Aye,' said George. 'That much came out in my brief conversation with McGregor.'

McGregor had gone for him and, although he'd done his best, it had been no contest. The last thing he remembered prior to waking in Accident and Emergency was Red McGregor lifting him high into the air, then throwing him through an opened trap in the bar floor into the cellar beneath.

Having explained to Sheila what had happened, George then said he just had to get out of the hospital and back aboard the *Sheila B*. Tied up in Peterhead harbour the boat was losing money, and the men not earning.

'Don't you worry about the boat,' she assured him. 'I'll sort everything out.' She then asked him to recommend a member of the crew to take over as skipper, and while he was ashore she'd have Hector Burnside act as admiral.

She assured George he wouldn't lose financially because of this. He would still get his full share. She would also come to a personal arrangement with the man taking over as skipper.

George insisted he was well enough to return to sea that very day. Sure he'd be stiff and sore for some time, but he'd manage.

Sheila could see how stubborn George was going to be, and knew him quite capable of running away from the hospital the moment he was mobile. 'You'll stay ashore until I say otherwise,' she ordered, 'or I'll sack you.'

George was in no doubt Sheila would carry out her threat. She wasn't the type of person to make one unless she meant it. Reluctantly he agreed to stay where he was: he'd have agreed to anything rather than lose captaincy of the *Sheila B.*

It was then that Sheila had an idea. Excusing herself from George she found Sister McKechnie in the linen cupboard, and there explained what she had in mind. Sister was uncertain till Sheila gave her word as an ex-VAD that George would be properly cared for.

'Well,' said Sister slowly. 'I could certainly use the bed.'

Sheila shook her hand before she could change her mind.

Rejoining George, Sheila told him he'd be leaving the hospital next morning after breakfast. 'I'll drive you to Dragonholme to do your recuperating there,' she explained. 'When you're fully fit I'll drive you to wherever the *Sheila B.* is offloading. How's that?'

'Thanks,' George said, briefly but gratefully.

'I'll be telling your ma exactly what you can and can't do, and you'll obey her to the letter, or suffer the consequences,' Sheila warned.

'I understand.'

'Good,' said Sheila. 'Then we've got a deal.'

A few minutes later Sheila was heading for the harbour. As she walked, she was thinking about James Campbell and Red McGregor.

When Sheila arrived back at the hospital next morning she found George ready and waiting for her in Accident and Emergency. He was still on the trolley used to wheel him down from the ward.

Two porters took the trolley out to where the Silver Ghost was parked, then manhandled George into the front passenger seat.

'Tell me all you know about this Red McGregor?' Sheila asked George once they'd left Peterhead behind.

'As I said to you yesterday, he's a Highlandman. Comes from a fishing village called Findochty over in Banffshire. He's got a well-deserved reputation for being vicious and cruel. Because of that he's had trouble in the past keeping steady employment. I heard he left the fishing boats for a while and joined the Merchant Navy, then suddenly a month ago, he reappeared as skipper of the *Zodiac*.'

'Does he still live in Findochty?'

'I've no idea. I would have thought myself he'd be based in Portnessie now he's with the Portnessie fleet. What I can tell you is his crew must be the dregs. No decent fisherman would sail under the likes of that scum.'

Sheila pressed for further information, but that was all George knew about Red McGregor. She lapsed into silence, sunk in thought.

A dozen or so miles down the road George broke into her reverie by asking what had happened about the man who'd attacked her the night before the boats had sailed north. She'd never said another word about it since.

'The police investigated the matter, but no arrest was ever made. There didn't seem to be any clues.'

'Yon bastard will never know just how lucky he was I didn't get hold of him,' George said quietly.

297

There was a depth and intensity in George's tone that startled Sheila so much that she glanced sideways at him. What she saw was written clearly on his face caused her to catch her breath. It was if a door had suddenly been opened through which she could see for the first time what lay beyond. Now she knew why he'd been acting so strangely of late. It was nothing whatever to do with his position of admiral as she'd thought, but because he was in love with her.

They hardly spoke for the rest of the way.

'So how is he?' Pat asked, handing Sheila a glass of wine. It was night and Sheila had just arrived in; David was upstairs fast asleep.

Plonking herself into a chair, she told Pat about George's fight with Red McGregor, and why it had occurred.

'It's a bad business, right enough. We can only be thankful he wasn't injured worse than he was,' Pat agreed grimly.

'James Campbell ordered the *Zodiac* to cut my warps. McGregor admitted that to George,' Sheila continued.

'So what are you going to do about it?'

Sheila ran a hand across her face. She was so tired she could hardly think straight.

'Why don't you have a word with Johnnie? There must be some awful hard men working in that yard of his. Perhaps one of them could sort out this Red McGregor,' Pat suggested.

'No, I won't meet violence with violence. Knowing James Campbell, that's a game I'd end up losing in the long run.'

'What will you do then?'

'I haven't the foggiest yet. But I'm going to have to think of something.'

Sheila drained her glass, and Pat said she'd pour her a refill.

When Pat returned to Sheila's chair with the wine it was to find Sheila fast asleep, and gently snoring.

As she seemed comfortable enough Pat covered her with a travelling rug, and left her there.

Sheila carefully unwrapped the bandages round George's torso, and was encouraged by what she saw. He was healing fast.

'I think you can have the bandages off for good next weekend,' she said, starting to bind new ones on in place of those she'd just removed.

'I can hardly wait. He does nothing but moan about the itching,' Mrs Jorgesson sniffed.

'Well they do, like mad!' George complained.

'He's just a big wean,' Mrs Jorgesson said to Sheila, knowing that would infuriate George, which it did.

'Don't make them so tight this time, you constrict my breathing,' George said to Sheila.

Her response to that was to pull the bandages even tighter. He yelped, and glared at her.

'The tighter the better,' she smiled sadistically.

'Will I get the lad's present you made for him?' Mrs Jorgesson asked George.

David was instantly all ears and attention. 'What present? What is it?' he demanded eagerly.

'Just a wee something,' George replied.

Mrs Jorgesson left the room. David literally vibrated with impatience till she returned with a fishing line which she handed to him. The line was wound on a beautifully carved wooden frame that had been varnished a dark oak colour. It wasn't just a fishing device, it was a work of art.

Somewhat embarrassed, George shrugged and said it was only a minding he'd knocked together from some old bits and pieces that had been lying around. The line itself, complete with hook and lead weight, had been cut from a long line used to catch white fish out of the herring season.

It was clear to Sheila how much love and care George had put into the gift, and she was touched by it.

'Thank you, George, it's really smashing,' David breathed, clutching the gift to his chest.

George gave a soft laugh. It pleased him greatly that David was so thrilled. Reaching out, he ruffled the boy's hair. 'When your Ma says it's all right for me to leave the house I'll take you down to the harbour and show you how to use it properly,' he promised.

'How about tomorrow, Mummy? Can George take me to the harbour then?' David pleaded.

'Well,' said Sheila thoughtfully. 'I don't suppose a little light activity would do George any harm. All right. Tomorrow it is.'

David gave a whoop of delight. Good old Mum!

'Thank God. It'll be like being let out of prison after a spell inside,' sighed George.

Sheila finished her bandaging and stood up.

'Have you time for a cup of tea?' asked Mrs Jorgesson.

'No thanks. I'm due to call in at the chandler's shop for a chat with Ian McPherson. I'll have tea there. Have you heard that the shop is doing so well Ian is going to open a new general store soon?'

Mrs Jorgesson's eyes gleamed. 'Aye, I did hear. It's right good news so it is. It makes you feel the village is well and truly coming alive again.'

'It's rare news indeed,' agreed George.

It was all beginning to come together – just as she'd hoped and planned – Sheila thought. Then she remembered the *Zodiac* and Red McGregor.

'I received a letter from Hector Burnside this morning to say the *Zodiac* cut the *Peg B.*'s warps day before yesterday, and its net was lost,' she told George.

George's face clouded with anger, and frustration. 'The *Zodiac* has got to be stopped, or you might not only end up losing money, but become a laughing stock into the bargain.'

It was later, when she got Brodie's report, that Sheila

300

remembered what George had said about being made a laughing stock; and decided, in light of the information Brodie had given her, that that was the weapon to employ against McGregor.

Mr Brodie was a small, rotund man who wore rimless spectacles perched on the end of his nose. He reminded Sheila of a mole.

It was Johnnie who'd helped Sheila find Mr Brodie, whose offices were above a pawnshop in Glasgow's Trongate. The faded gold lettering on Mr Brodie's door proclaimed him to be a Private Investigator.

Mr Brodie came well recommended. A man to be trusted, and a most diligent worker, Sheila and Johnnie had been told.

Mr Brodie had shown Sheila to a chair, then had sat facing her. 'Now what can I do for you, Mrs Lack?' he had asked.

He'd listened intently, occasionally making a note on the pad in front of him, as Sheila spoke.

'Being the sort of person McGregor is he must have something to hide – something the police might be interested in, for example,' Sheila had concluded.

Brodie nodded; his brief was explicit. 'And for how long do you wish me to go on digging?'

'As long as it takes,' Sheila had replied, convinced there had to be a 'something' in McGregor's background.

After Sheila had gone Brodie had got out his map of Scotland and looked up Findochty. He'd never heard of the place.

That's where he would start.

James Campbell had been knighted to become Sir James Campbell of Dragonholme. To celebrate the event he was throwing a hoolie for the men of his fleet who were now fishing the home waters.

Sheila sat in the Silver Ghost outside the hotel where the hoolie was being held, the palms of her hands damp with sweat, telling herself to get on with it. She turned to the pretty lassie sitting beside her. 'Will you be embarrassed?' she asked.

'For what you're paying me, I'll walk in there starkers,' Chrissie McGowan replied in her distinctive working-class Glasgow accent.

Sheila grinned. 'That won't be necessary.'

'I just hope this doesn't backfire on you,' Chrissie said.

'So do I,' Sheila said drily, and got out of the car where she waited for Chrissie to come round and join her.

It was the beginning of September, and so far that season Sheila's boats had lost nearly two dozen nets, thanks to Red McGregor, the *Zodiac* and James Campbell. Tonight, she hoped, was going to be the end of it.

As they entered the Buccleugh Hotel, Sheila recalled staying there all those years ago when she'd worked for James. It seemed like more than a lifetime ago. Where had that girl gone, she wondered, as they passed through the lobby.

The hoolie was at the rear of the hotel where Sir James had taken over the grandly styled ballroom. A sit-down meal had been served earlier, after which the tables and chairs had been removed, and the musicians brought on. An adjoining cloakroom had been turned into a bar where drinks were being dispensed in a never-ending flow.

Sheila stopped dead centre of the main ballroom entrance and stared around. By sheer willpower she demanded her presence be noticed, and was gratified to see that it was. Shock waves began to ripple through the room as she made straight for a face she recognized from the past.

She had chosen her outfit carefully. In a simple black dress with matching shoes, she looked stunning as she scythed through the crowd to Tod McAlpine, who used to be a friend of her brothers. A plumpish female, clearly

302

Mrs McAlpine, stood at Tod's shoulder, and beside Mrs McAlpine a man Sheila was certain had been at her da's funeral.

As she walked, voices whispered all around her. Out of the corner of her eye she saw a woman nudge the husband in the ribs.

On reaching Tod she said hello. Then, without waiting for an introduction to Mrs McAlpine, she asked Tod which of those present was Red McGregor, skipper of the *Zodiac*.

The atmosphere was electric. Many of the dancers had stopped to stare in her direction – as more and more people in the room were doing.

Tod glanced about, then pointed to where a group of men stood drinking. 'McGregor's among that lot, he's the chap with the red beard,' Tod said quietly to Sheila.

Sir James, deep in conversation, was almost the last to become aware that something untoward was happening. Frowning he looked around to see what was going on. It was then that he saw Sheila, making for McGregor, and momentarily lost his composure.

Long before Sheila reached McGregor's group she was the focus of everyone's attention. Even the musicians had stopped playing, several of them climbing on to their chairs to get a better view.

Sheila heard her name whispered over and over, Mrs Lack who owns the new Dragonholme pipe stalkies, aye, her that was Davey Beattie's lass.

She stopped about three feet away from the man with the red beard. McGregor had small mean eyes in a fleshy face; he also had the most massive chest she had ever seen. His arms were thick with muscles. Poor George never had a chance, she thought.

She froze inside for a moment, not at all sure she could pull it off after all. Then she saw amusement in those dark, vicious eyes and something else – contempt? Yes, that was it. He was contemptuous of her.

303

Her resolve instantly hardened again. She would go through with what she'd come to do. As she could gut a herring with a knife, so she'd now gut this bastard with words.

'I wanted to see the scum who's been cutting my warps,' she said in a loud, ringing voice.

Sir James started to force his way through the crowd, then halted, not at all sure how to handle the situation.

McGregor looked Sheila up and down, the way a farmer might a cow at an auction. If he'd been hoping to phase her by this action he was disappointed. 'How's that boy you call your admiral?' he asked, sneering.

McGregor's question gave Sheila the perfect opening, and saved her having to use the one she'd already worked out in advance.

'The boy, as you call him, is twice the man you are McGregor,' she replied.

McGregor gave a roar of laugher. 'How can Jorgesson be twice the man when I beat the shite out of him!'

Sheila smiled. 'I was talking about being a man where it counts,' she said. Around her, the room was so quiet you could have heard a feather fall.

The dangerous eyes became hard as flint. 'What are you talking about?'

A laughing stock was the phrase George had used to her, and that was what she intended making of McGregor. Individual pride and prowess; fishermen held these virtues above all else, and consequently were particularly vulnerable on either count.

'Maybe George Jorgesson can't beat you in a fight, but there's other things he can get up besides his fists.'

McGregor went white, throwing the myriad freckles dotting his face into sharp relief.

Sheila stared at McGregor, waiting for the denial she knew would come.

'You're a fucking liar!' McGregor snarled, knotting his hands into fists, wishing she were a man and could be beaten into silence there and then.

304

'Why did you never marry, McGregor?' she asked sweetly despite the trembling in her legs.

'That's none of your business!' he blustered in reply.

Close by a young woman sniggered which enraged McGregor even further.

'I don't talk to fools or women,' he shouted, making to push her aside.

Sheila held her arm out straight in front of her, the hand flopping. 'I've got a new Tee name for you McGregor. Forget being called Red, from now on you're Droopy McGregor.'

McGregor seemed to shrink where he stood, his face contorted as though her laughter was causing him physical pain.

'I say it's a lie, and it's your word against mine,' he countered when her laughter finished.

Sheila crooked a finger, and instantly Chrissie McGowan was by her side. She could see the panic in McGregor's eyes and guessed correctly he was desperately trying to remember if Chrissie had been some woman he'd failed with in the past, in the days before he'd finally given up trying.

Sheila stared at McGregor, knowing his impotence had been the result of a fight he'd been involved in many years previously. Mr Brodie's report had been most thorough.

'Do you still maintain I'm lying?'

'Yes,' he hissed in reply.

'Then I'd like you to meet Chrissie McGowan, the best looking prostitute in Glasgow's Blythswood Square. All you have to do to prove me a liar, and that you are the man you claim, is take Chrissie upstairs to a room I'll pay for, after which Chrissie can come back and give us the verdict.'

One of McGregor's group guffawed, a bad mistake on his part. McGregor's fist lashed out and the man fell to the floor with a bloodied mouth.

'That's enough. This has gone far enough,' Sir James said, having finally decided to intervene.

Sheila swivelled to confront her main adversary. 'McGregor didn't cut my warps of his own accord, but on your strict instructions. Well no matter how many of my warps are cut, or nets sunk, my boats will continue to fish and try to restore life to a village that has suffered the greatest disaster the east coast has ever known.

'I can only say this; if the positions had been reversed my da and the men of Dragonholme would have done everything in their power to help Portnessie revive, not try to hinder it by despicable means.

'By doing what you are doing you demean the men who work for you, and the good name of fisherfolk in general,' Sheila said.

A growl of approval filled the room. They all knew about the warp cutting, but few had agreed with it. The Dragonholme boats posed no threat to their living, so why should this action be taken against such close neighbours? It was a question nearly all the Portnessie fishermen had asked themselves, and not one had come up with an acceptable answer.

Sir James could feel the mood had swung against him. Sheila had won this particular battle, no doubt about it. To continue warp cutting after what she'd just said would be to lose the men's goodwill; and that he wasn't prepared to do.

Sheila read her victory in James's face. Now was the time to go, she told herself, and turned on McGregor.

'Goodnight Droopy,' she smiled, winking.

Laughter errupted throughout the room.

Sheila and Chrissie McGowan swept from the ballroom, the laughter buoying them on their way.

'Oh but that was rare!' said Chrissie, wiping tears from her eyes once they were outside.

Sheila ran behind the Rolls to be sick.

10

It was early Saturday evening and, as had become her custom since taking up permanent residence again in Dragonholme, Sheila had gone to the Fairy Dell to gather wild flowers for the next day's church services.

She did the gathering, and delivered them to the church. Later Mrs Mitchell would come along and do the arranging. Mrs Mitchell had been arranging the church flowers for over twenty years.

Mr Mitchell was dead. He'd been one of those to survive the disaster, only to lose his life on the Dover Patrol during the war.

The Mitchells had two sons. The oldest had come back to the village with his family when George had offered him a berth aboard the *Albert B*. The other son was currently working on a boat of the Dunbar fleet, but also would return to the village when a place could be found for him aboard one of Sheila's boats.

David always accompanied Sheila on her trips to the Fairy Dell, carrying her basket there and back again. He thoroughly enjoyed the church flower picking, as Sheila called it.

The Fairy Dell was sheltered on three sides by the tall firs of Loki's Wood, and all manner of wild flowers and herbs grew there in profusion. It was by far and away the best spot for flowers and herbs for miles around.

Sheila hummed to herself as she picked the best out of a clump of bluebells. She'd just had a letter from Johnnie that morning confirming her order for two new drifters. In his reply Johnnie had said he hoped to have them built and ready for the start of the next herring season.

She had nine pipe stalkies at sea now; two more would bring her total to eleven, and the Dragonholme contingent to fifteen in all. Just a little over half of what the original fleet had been before the disaster.

She paused in her musings when a shadow fell across her's, a shadow that had a long protrusion in front of it.

She straightened and turned, putting a smile on her face as she did. The protrusion was a shotgun.

The man was short, stocky and white-haired. He had a thick beard, and full moustaches, and was a stranger to her.

Or was he? There did seem to be something oddly familiar about him. Something about his hard, empty eyes. Involuntarily she shivered.

David didn't like those eyes either. Coming to his mother he took hold of her skirt and pressed himself against her.

'Can I help you?' Sheila asked.

The twin barrels of the shotgun slowly rose till they were level with her midriff. The finger curled round the right-hand side trigger tightened.

'Oh have I dreamt of this moment, bitch,' the man whispered in a voice that made Sheila's flesh creep, and David press himself even harder against her.

And then she knew. She realized just who the stranger was. No stranger at all, but Wally Simpson, who'd once been James Campbell's ghillie, and who'd so mistreated her.

'You!' she gasped.

Simpson laughed evilly. 'I've been watching you a long time now bitch, waiting to pay you and his High and Mightiness back for what you did to me all those years ago; and this is it.'

'Don't be so ridiculous,' she said bravely, and grabbing David's arm made to move off.

She heard the shot as though it had happened somewhere else. With a cry of pain she tumbled to the ground. The hand she put to her cheek came away again bright red with blood.

'You leave my Mummy alone!' David yelled, and launched himself at Simpson.

'David!' Sheila shrieked, quickly crawling after him.

Simpson whirled the boy around, and put his free arm under David's chin, exerting just enough pressure not to choke the lad, but hold him still.

Sheila froze, and stared up into those cruel eyes that she now recalled so well.

'Let the boy go' she ordered.

Simpson brought the shotgun up, and rested its barrels on David's right shoulder. He then slid the barrels backwards till their ends were pointed directly at David's ear and about an inch away from it.

She couldn't believe this was happening. One minute she and David had been having such a lovely time together, the next . . . this nightmare brought on by a monster out of the past.

'Bang!' laughed Simpson.

Sheila gasped.

'I'll do anything, anything at all. Just let the boy run home,' she pleaded.

'It was a grave situation when I last had you on the ground,' Simpson said, and chuckled.

Grave situation? What was he babbling about? 'I don't understand.'

'Thinking about it afterwards I was pleased that your friend intervened, for now I've come up with something far far better. A plan that's going to kill my two birds with the one stone.'

David began to cry.

'I still don't understand.'

'I was wearing a mask. Does that help?'

Sheila gazed at him in horror. 'That night after the Hurleys' wedding! It was you!'

'In the dead centre of Dragonholme. Get it? *Dead centre*. A joke,' Simpson explained and chuckled again.

So the attempt hadn't been engineered by James. Her instincts had been right after all.

She remembered other things. 'And the fouling on my door. Was that you as well?'

'An indication of what I think of you,' Simpson leered.

'Mu . . . mmeee,' whispered David.

'Don't worry, darling. Everything's going to be all right,' she soothed, trying to put assurance and conviction into her voice.

Part of her mind was numb; another part was whirling madly around and around.

Madly. *Mad.* The world leapt out of her. Mad. Of course, the man was out of his mind.

She looked again into those eyes – and saw something there she hadn't seen before. Something that caused her stomach to contract into a tight knot of fear and the blood turn to ice in her veins. 'Let the boy go, please. He never hurt you,' she pleaded.

Simpson released David, who immediately ran to Sheila to be enveloped in her arms.

'Get up bitch,' Simpson commanded, gesturing with the gun.

'We're going for a walk now, down to the shore,' Simpson said.

She put her hand to her damaged cheek. At least the bleeding had stopped.

David clutched on to her as she stumbled in the direction Simpson indicated. Perhaps somewhere along the way they could make a break for it, she thought.

'Try anything funny and the lad gets it first, understand?' Simpson said, as though reading her thoughts.

Soon the Fairy Dell was lost to view behind them, while ahead the blue glint of the sea could now be seen.

'What did you mean, kill two birds with one stone?' Sheila asked as they trudged along.

'*My* two birds I said. You being one, his High and Mightiness the other.'

There it was, he planned to kill her. But it wasn't herself she was concerned for, it was David. It was inconceivable to her that her son would also die at the hands of this maniac.

'You'll hang, you know. You can't get away with it.'

'Oh, but I can. I only plan to attend to you. The lovely part is that Campbell will get the blame and he'll be the one to swing for your murder.'

'Why should the police think he killed me?'

'Because when your corpse is found this shotgun I'm holding will be lying alongside it, and the gun belongs to Campbell.'

'Campbell will deny it,' she said, her heart filled with despair.

'That won't do him any good. It's common knowledge he's been your enemy this long while. The law will put two and two together, and come up with five.'

Sheila thought of George Jorgesson. If only he'd been there to intervene as he'd done that night in the graveyard. But George was hundreds of miles away in the southern fishing grounds.

'It wasn't easy getting into the Hall for this gun. It's taken me ages to work out my plan so I wasn't caught or spotted. And it had to be a Saturday, the day you'd be going to the Fairy Dell. I didn't want his High and Mightiness finding out about the theft and reporting it, did I?' Simpson laughed.

They struggled down a slope, and along a path that brought them to the entrance of Kettil's Cave.

'In you go,' Simpson instructed.

Sheila recalled that day long ago when she'd brought a picnic down to James Campbell who'd been with his Coble in the Cut beyond.

As if reading her thoughts Simpson said, 'It's also common knowledge that this is a favourite haunt of Campbell's and that he brings that wee boat of his in here a lot. The fact you're discovered here will damn him even more.'

David sobbed, a sound that threatened to tear Sheila's heart apart. There had to be a way out of this for him, there just had to be!

They emerged from the rear of the cave into Kettil's Cut. As she'd known it would be, the tide was going out.

The water was choppy and full of swirls and eddies.

There was only one thing she could do to give David even the semblance of a chance: she must jump Simpson and keep him occupied as long as she could while David ran for his life.

But that wasn't going to be easy. So far Simpson had maintained a distance between them which made that impossible. The answer was to keep him talking, caught up in what he was saying, while she inched towards him.

'What I must ask you is why? So the laird fired you, and thrashed you into the bargain for what you'd done to me, but that's no reason for murder. Not after so many years.'

Simpson's eyes narrowed, and his mouth thinned to a slash. 'I had everything when I worked for Campbell: power, position, security. Then you came along and tried to undermine my authority. You, a chit of a lassie, putting yourself up against *me!*'

'Your so-called authority wasn't based on respect but fear and bullying. You hated me because I was the only one with the guts to stand up against you,' she snapped back, slowly moving herself and David closer to Simpson.

'Do you know what I was reduced to after the laird threw me off the Dragonholme Estate? Seasonal work, picking potatoes and the like. And when that wasn't available I starved, and had to sleep rough without even a roof over my head.'

'Why didn't you get another job as a ghillie?'

'Why don't you ask James Campbell. He saw to it that no one would give me a decent job again.'

'In other words, what you threatened Hay with happened to you. I'd call that justice,' she declared.

She'd succeeded in making him so furious that he didn't notice her getting closer and closer. Another foot should do it, she judged.

And, please God, when I shout to David to run, make sure that he does. Like the wind.

312

'I walked the streets of Edinburgh for a while, begging for a crust. Can you imagine the humiliation of that?'

'I wouldn't say it was nearly as humiliating as being nearly raped,' she mumbled.

'You deserved what happened to you!' he roared.

'And so did you, Simpson. Every humiliating second of it.'

She let David go, and tensed her body in preparation. One more step, that's all she needed, one more step.

Then the unexpected happened. There was a creak of wood, and snap of sail, and James Campbell's Coble shot into the Cut with James just about to lower canvas.

James saw Sheila, and paused in what he was doing to frown.

Simpson stared out over the Cut at the Coble and James in astonishment. This was the last thing he'd expected.

Sheila took her chance and threw herself on to the shotgun. 'Run, David! Run!' she screamed.

But despite the tears David was his father's son. He had no intention of running away and leaving his mother fighting with this nasty, scary man. He began pummelling Simpson with his tiny fists.

James stared at them in stunned bewilderment. What was going on?

Sheila knew she couldn't keep it up for long. Physically, she was no match for the powerfully built Simpson who still retained a great deal of the strength he'd had when younger.

A barrel of the shotgun went off, the blast deafening to Sheila whose head was less than a handspan away from the stock. Shot ricocheted off the rockface beneath them, all of it whistling harmlessly away, most of it peppering the sea like suddenly falling hail.

Uttering an oath, Simpson swiped David aside, sending him rolling to the edge of the rockface where it fell almost perpendicularly into the water below.

Sheila, her head still ringing from the blast, twisted

313

round to see what had become of David, momentarily relaxing her grip on the shotgun. It was enough for Simpson, who tore the gun from her grasp, then hit her with it, thwacking both barrels hard against her belly.

Sheila went down, gasping for air. Why oh why hadn't David run as she'd told him to?

James snatched up a barbed steel gaffe and drew it back to throw it as a spear. He was about to launch the gaffe at Simpson when Simpson fired the second barrel.

James dropped the gaffe as he was lifted right off his feet, and thrown backwards. The next thing he knew he was in the sea, and sinking fast.

Simpson was enraged. This ruined everything, the lovely beautiful plan he'd hatched to kill the Beattie bitch and send his High and Mightiness to the gallows. Those hard, cruel eyes came to rest on David at the edge of the rockface.

Sheila read Simpson's intention in his face. 'Nooo!' she shrieked.

Simpson's right boot lashed out to thump into David's chest. Uttering a thin, keening cry David vanished over the rock edge to be swallowed by the broil beneath.

Simpson snapped the shotgun open, and fumbled for cartridges. But before he could reload Sheila was upon him. Wailing, she clawed ribbons of flesh from his cheeks with her nails.

The water round James was streamered in pink as he fought his way back to the surface. He wondered where the colour was coming from, then realized that it had to be from him. He glanced down to see that blood was covering his chest.

David had been lucky. He'd gone under, and come up again. His flailing hands had banged against a spur of rock a little above the waterline, and this he was now grimly hanging on to.

The undertow tugged at his small body, seeking to drag him out of the Cut into the open sea. His teeth chattered with fright as he doggedly clung to the rockspur. Directly above him he could hear his Mum and the crazy man fighting.

James gratefully gulped in air when he finally broke surface. He was facing out of the Cut, so the first thing he saw was his Coble drifting back the way it had just come in.

Sheila fought like one possessed. Knowing David could barely swim, and what the water was like in the Cut, she believed him dead or drowning.

James's only thought was to get to Sheila. His strokes were feeble and when he coughed blood flooded from his mouth. But he made himself go on. He must save her: nothing else mattered.

Sheila managed to knee Simpson with all her strength.

Screeching in agony, Simpson whirled around, away from Sheila, and by doing so went right over the edge of the rockface. He was still screaming when he hit the water.

'The boy! The boy's underneath you!' James shouted, having spied David himself.

'Mummee, I'm here,' David cried plaintively.

The mists of rage that had taken possession of Sheila vanished, throwing herself flat she looked over the edge of the rockface. Sure enough there was David clinging on for dear life.

She pulled herself over the edge as far as she dared, and stretched down her right arm, the stronger one. 'Grab hold and I'll pull you up,' she commanded.

Simpson's hands shot out of the water behind David, followed instantly by Simpson's head and shoulders.

Simpson glared malevolently up at Sheila, then brought his gaze on to David struggling to catch hold of his mother's straining fingers.

Simpson reached out and caught hold of the same rockspur that David was hanging on to. Then he put a palm on David's head, and forced it underwater.

Sheila scrambled to her feet again and was about to jump on top of Simpson, but James reached the ex-ghillie

315

first. James's arm went round Simpson's throat and squeezed.

Simpson let go of David as he fought for air and freedom, but James would allow him neither.

James took a large breath and forced himself back down into the depths, taking the struggling Simpson with him.

David was again clinging to the rockspur, coughing, spluttering and crying.

Sheila was about to try and reach him a second time with an outstretched arm when suddenly she had the idea of using the shotgun to give her extra reach. She snapped the gun shut before poking it and herself over the rock edge.

'Grab on to it David,' she yelled.

David grasped the end of the barrels with one hand, then the other.

Slowly he climbed upwards slipping once, but swiftly recovering.

When David had a secure grip of her arm Sheila let the shotgun go, its usefulness over. She hauled David up the rest of the way till at last he tumbled over the edge to collapse in a sodden heap beside her.

'Oh!' she choked, and began crying tears of relief.

'Mummeee!' David wailed, and buried his face in her bosom.

'It's all right, it's all over now,' she told him, stroking his dripping hair. Then she remembered James, who'd just saved her boy's life.

Crawling back to the rockface edge, she gazed over. There was no sign of either James or Simpson.

Part of the water had darkened in colour. Moments later, Simpson bobbed to the surface floating face down. He was obviously dead.

When James resurfaced Sheila thought he too was gone, but after a couple of seconds his eyes blinked open. He was dreadfully weak.

'Over here,' Sheila called out. It was plain that he was disorientated.

He didn't have it in him to swim properly, so he paddled towards her as best he could.

Sheila glanced over to where she'd last seen the Coble, but it was gone. Simpson's corpse, floating spreadeagled downwards, was rapidly following suit. Soon it too would be out on the open sea.

James was lightheaded, his senses reeling. He eventually reached the spur of rock and crooked an arm over it, gasping for breath. Each breath was a sheet of searing flame.

Sheila reached down and he was able to grab hold of her extended hand.

'Wait a minute yet,' he said, staring at the stained water around him. He could only just see her, staring down at him with a look of tenderness and compassion that he'd never thought he'd see again. 'Is the boy all right?' he whispered.

'Yes, he's fine. But we must get you out of that water.'

James grimaced as the swell banged him against the rock wall. The pain was building quickly now, he was ablaze inside with it. 'All right,' he said, nodding.

Sheila strained, and he made what effort he could.

It wasn't all that far, the length of her arm, he thought. It might have been a million miles.

He made a second attempt, and this time didn't even manage the few inches upwards he had before. Releasing her hand he grasped hold again of the rockspur.

Sheila stared at him. She'd been able to haul David all the way up. But David was a wee boy. A full-grown man, and one as badly wounded as James, was a different proposition entirely.

'Try once more,' she urged. Miracles had been known to happen after all.

'It's no use, Sheila, it can't be done. You know that as well as I do,' he gasped.

She read in his expression that he was resigned to his fate. 'I'm sorry,' she whispered, fresh tears streaming down her face.

317

'So am I, Sheila, but not for this. For all the horrible and misguided things I've done to you.' His voice faltered. 'Everything I did was prompted by love, Sheila. You must believe that.'

'I know,' she sobbed. 'Oh, James I do believe you.'

'Can you possibly forgive me?'

'Yes,' she choked out. 'Yes, I can.'

Neither of them thought to suggest she run for help. They both knew there wasn't time for that.

'One last touch?' he pleaded, and held up a straining hand.

Their fingers pressed together, then his moved away. She saw that he'd let go of the rockspur and was being taken by the tide.

'Away home now,' he said evenly.

At the spot where the rear of Kettil's Cave opened out on to the Cut she paused. A wind sighed in off the open sea, and somewhere a herring gull screeched raucously.

She turned to give James a farewell wave. But there was no-one there to wave to.

Postscript

Sheila and David were on the cliffs overlooking Dragonholme. They'd just come from Dragonholme Hall where they'd left Johnnie Murchison-Stewart and Helen Drummond, the woman Johnnie would shortly be marrying.

Johnnie's and Helen's had been a whirlwind romance, and in Sheila's opinion they were a couple ideally suited to one another. She couldn't have been more happy for Johnnie, and had already promised to be godmother to the first wean when it arrived.

After James's death, Dragonholme Hall and the attendant estate had been put up for sale, and Sheila had

318

seriously considered buying them. In the end it had come down to a straight choice, the Hall and estate, or Dragonholme fleet restored to what it had been before the disaster. Her capital wouldn't stretch to both. Her decision had been to continue rebuilding the fleet.

All this had coincided with Johnnie's romance, and when she'd confided to him that she'd have to give up the idea of owning the Hall, he'd surprised her by asking if she'd mind if he went ahead and tried to purchase it, confessing he was another who'd fallen under the spell of the village and its environs.

Mind? She'd been delighted. And that was how the new laird of Dragonholme Hall had come to be Johnnie Murchison-Stewart.

Johnnie and Helen intended honeymooning abroad, then returning to the Hall. As Johnnie still had to run the MS Yard in Yoker he'd be keeping on his Glasgow residence, but he and Helen would be down at the Hall at every possible opportunity.

'Look!' shouted David excitedly, and pointed southwards, out to sea.

Sheila raised her eyes. There were tiny black dots on the southern horizon. Hastily she began counting them.

'Is it George, Mummy? Is it the boats coming home for the winter?' David demanded.

She remembered a far off day when she'd stood almost on this exact spot and watched the old fleet come in from the north. The day she'd first met James Campbell.

So much had happened since then; so very much. In a way, well . . . it was as if the wheel had come full circle.

'It must be, the number's right,' she replied with a laugh.

David let out a whoop. George was coming back to Dragonholme. George who was a man, and his pal, and so much more fun to be with than women.

'You've missed him, haven't you?' she smiled.

David nodded.

She'd missed him too, and had thought about him a

319

great deal. Thoughts that had nothing to do with him being a good sailor.

'Let's go down and meet him,' she said.

Hand in hand Sheila and David made for the road that would take them down into Dragonholme, and George.